EUCALYPTUS GOTH

Also by Brian Craddock

Short Fiction
The Red Heart
The Angel of Isisford
Plato's Cave
The Black Shuck
The Blue Frog Falls
Ismail's Expulsion
The Watchman
The Divinity of Akobi
The Cemetery Children
Hivuninga Island
Punk's Not Dead
Ikiryō
Masala Nightmares

Essays
Defining the Body Horror Concept Within Clive
Barker's Nighbreed (The Body Horror Book)

EUCALYPTUS GOTH

BRIAN CRADDOCK

BROKEN PUPPET BOOKS
An imprint of Oscillate Wildly Press

Typeset in Meridien-Medium

ISBN-13: 978 0 6481128 0 8
Printed in Australia

Visit us online at: www.oscillatewildlypress.com

IN MEMORY OF ROGER

'One must still have chaos in oneself to be able to give birth to a dancing star.'

Friedrich Nietzsche

'Soon we will be at the stage where he will be offering us a free set of steak knives.'

Paul Keating on John Howard's
1996 election campaign.

CONTENTS

PART FOUR

PROLOGUE: THE BEST CURE IS PREVENTION, NOT THE BAND

We didn't know the jumper, but we knew he was a goth because there were a few people on the scene who said they knew him. The news on the idiot box and the Courier Mail next day just reported him as a suicide: young Caucasian male.

It's a thirty metre drop from where he jumped, somewhere near the middle of the Story Bridge, after midnight on a Friday. Did anyone see him, a skinny boy with buck teeth and long black hair in his ratty clothes the colour of the night? Probably not. It's doubtful he would have been too visible dressed entirely in black, fresh out of one of the clubs in the Valley.

There's no safety barriers along the length of the bridge, unlike the Gateway further out. That bridge used to get its fair share of jumpers, too. Nine alone when it opened ten years ago in 1986, but they put three-metre high anti-jump barriers on it a few years ago and according to the Queensland Suicide Register there was initially nearly a ninety percent reduction in suicides out there, although that number has since been sullied by several successful attempts. I've been out that way, the Murarrie area, and there're plenty of reasons to kill yourself. Fucking depressing place.

His friends were out clubbing a few nights later, trying to score free drinks and all the attention they could get. But we're a fucking cruel lot, sometimes, and not all the attention they got was particularly nice. That's what you get, I guess, for trying to capitalise on tragedy.

Up until six years ago, there had been in total forty-two suicides on the Story Bridge since the mid-Eighties, but in the six years since then there've been sixty-one suicides. We calculated that at about eight deaths a year. One every six weeks. The odds aren't looking favourable for everyone's favourite river-city!

Thank fuck the papers didn't pick up on the fact he was a goth. Could you imagine the shit we'd have flung at us then? Talk of depression and mental illness and how wearing all-black leads to suicide. They'd get it all wrong and vilify us as Devil worshippers with a death-wish. There'd be sage shakings of heads and little kindergoths dragged into family discussions to try and avert their errant trajectories toward a damaged lifestyle.

Oh wait, we cop all that already, and there's the rub.

PART ONE

UNCLE KEV

I fucking hate Brisbane sometimes. Especially on Sundays.

It can feel like life just grinds to a halt here, especially after five on a weekday when the city practically shuts down and you're hard-pressed getting a coffee let alone a decent one. It'd be easier to skip out to the airport and catch a plane to Melbourne and snatch a coffee from an all-nighter and jump a plane back to Brissie again before the dawn sun breaks the horizon. Not that I drink coffee, mind.

People have started calling it 'Brisvegas' to take the piss out of just how uneventful it can be. They got the name from a CD that was released a couple of years ago, and it sums up our feelings perfectly. There's no way you could mistake the scorn from a moniker like that.

My Uncle Kev used to say it was a nice place to live but you wouldn't want to visit here. He travelled around a lot, hitch-hiking up and down the east coast of Oz mostly, moving from pub to pub and boozing away his dole checks. He'd been abused by my grandfather when he was a kid, so he's got a few memories he'd like to try and drown out.

At the moment he's holed up in a room at the Terminus, the backpacker place just next to the train overpass on Melbourne Street in South Brisbane. I passed him on the Victoria Bridge the other day, and he was carrying a case of Fosters back to the hotel with him. I tried a joke on about how he was having one for the road, on account of he was taking it for a walk along the bridge, but he got stroppy, grumbling about how the Terminus only sells on tap.

But I got him to agree to a catch-up, at least. At the backpacker pub he's holed up at, naturally. Alcoholics don't like to venture far from their nest.

The Terminus hasn't changed a bit. Like Uncle Kev.

I stayed here once, in 1994. I was homeless at the time, and it was August so there was still a bite to the winter air, and I'd wandered into the Terminus one night unchallenged, this scruffy goth boy mingling with all the foreign travellers. I'd gone up onto the roof and found a banana lounge to sleep on, wrapping my cape around me. Cape's were still kinda fashionable on the scene, then. A little less so now, especially for guys. During the night I'd been woken by some long-haired cunt standing next to me, blabbing some shit about it being as cold as a nun's cunt, but I'd been too tired to stay lucid and had fallen asleep again with him still standing there. When I'd woken at daybreak I wasn't happy with myself that I'd been so reckless about the potential danger I'd been in, and have since then managed to sleep safer when I'm living homeless.

The stairs of the Terminus haven't changed much, either: still dark and creaky with worn and musty carpet on them. On the way up I pass a couple of tanned girls and a hairy cunt coming down, making room for the girls to pass but then deliberately forcing the guy to grumble and slide against the wall while I lumber my way to the top. Kev's room is down the end of the corridor on the third floor where the single rooms are. The rest are share with bunk-beds in them.

When he opens the door, he's holding an opened can of Fosters. The pong of Imperial Leather soap hits me like a wave, his preferred soap as far back as when I was a kid.

'Getting stuck into the Holy Communion already, I see,' arching my eyebrows in the direction of his can.

'Nah, no church for me,' he goes, missing the joke. 'Just shift those papers,' he instructs, waving his hand at a pile of newspapers on a rickety chair by the window. The dates on them go back two weeks.

'You been here a while, then?'

'Nah, not long at all, I gotta admit,' he lies. 'Got in just after the New Year, in fact.'

'I'm staying over in Spring Hill at the moment,' I offer. 'Not too far away.'

Uncle Kev just nods. He's not that much interested in the world outside of a bottle, to be honest.

'How's ya dad?'

'He's not bad,' I say, aware he hasn't seen his brother for a couple of years at least. 'Mum, too. I haven't seen them in a while, myself.'

He grimaces, the best at a smile he can offer. He gets really awkward in company other than his own. Or maybe it's just me. My Nan drank heavily when Uncle Kevin was still in the womb, and as a result he was born with ocular hypertelorism, a condition whereby his eyes are further apart than they should be. More like gravitating toward the side of his head rather than staying central to his face. And they sorta bulge, like they're being forced from their sockets from behind. When we were kids my brother Rory and I nicknamed him The Mongaloid and he once overheard us. He never snitched to our folks, though. Just clammed his emotions up and walked away, something he does very well and has been doing all his life.

A train rumbles past, so close I reckon I could almost lean out the window and touch it. We stare out at the people staring back in, then the train is gone and the view of the museum and the city return, shimmering under the summer heat.

'Head downstairs for a pint?' he goes.

The beer can sits unfinished on the side-table, but for the seasoned alcoholic any opportunity for a top-up is not to be sniffed at. Luck's on his side because I'm feeling like a tipple.

'Sure, but it'll be wine for me. Something local. The French can get fucked if they think I'm touching their stuff while they bomb the shit out of those atolls in Polynesia, the cunts.'

He doesn't react to this, outwardly, but I can see that subtle shift of nuance in his eyes like he thinks I'm a know-it-all fucker. He's always felt that way about me. I'm probably only having a wine just to stick it up him and come off as a snotty cultured drinker. Family has that effect on me.

The bar staff are more than familiar with him, addressing him by name and pouring his choice of poison without even asking. Another give away that he's been here longer than after the New Year. I order a glass of red, and they rummage around for a while until they finally find a cask and squeeze some out.

'Farking hot, ay?' says this guy along the bar.

'Yep,' nods Kev without looking at him, eyes only for the liquid amber that sits before him.

'Pushin into the thirties today,' the guy remarks, leaning on both his elbows but still managing to raise his glass to his lips.

'It's the humidity,' I chime in. 'From that cyclone up north. That's making the heat worse.'

'The humidity, eh?' the guy goes, closing one eye and boggling the other at me while he leans back like he's about to fall off his perch.

'Yep,' I go, unable to resist mimicking Uncle Kev.

And it's true: January is proving to be especially warm this year and the humidity is starting to kill us all, no thanks to Cyclone Bazza ripping across the Cape York Peninsula, or *Waypundun* as my Murri mate Alan calls it. It seems unfair to have the humidity but not the rainfall, given we've had a drought going on for about five years now. It's getting rough wearing black coats in this smothering heat. If we're truly lucky, it'll flood. Not some pissant one, either, but one of Biblical proportions, wiping out entire continents.

Kev's feeling peckish so he asks the barwench for some peanuts, and she tosses him one of those thick-foil packets with the peanut in a top-hat wearing a monocle and carrying a cane.

'Is there anything more capitalist,' I ask the room, raising my glass of wine as if in toast, 'than a fucking peanut with a monocle selling other peanuts to eat?'

The barwench has a wry smirk but otherwise it's a tough crowd.

'This is the nephew,' goes Kev to the barwench, as if to explain an anomaly.

'Funny sort,' laughs this old cunt in the corner that they've been calling Snowy, ogling me with reserved menace.

'Yep,' says Kev, lifting his beer.

Fuck. What a sad place.

'You should hitch a ride out west, Kev, and go see Dad. I reckon he'd be keen to see ya. Mum, too.'

'Maybe,' he muses. 'I'm in town for a bit. Dole mob want to assess me again.'

'What for? I thought you were already on the disability pension?'

'Am,' he grumbles. 'This is for me eyes, but.'

That explains why he doesn't make much eye-contact. Old fucker's going blind!

'Alright, so long as you're around for a bit, I might see you again.'

I scull the rest of my wine, pulling a face at the taste. It's fucking awful.

'Another one?' he quickly says, nodding at my empty glass.

'Nah, gotta be off anyway,' I reply. 'Don't wanna drink the place dry on you.'

'Be doin me a favour, I admit,' Kev goes, patting his pot-belly, finally cracking a joke. 'You keep drinking like a fish, it'll happen to you, too.'

'Nah, not me,' I go. 'It'll make me lean.'

He snorts in derision.

'I'm serious,' I insist. 'Lean on walls, on tables, on my friends.'

My joke elicits nothing from him at all. Not even the hint of a smile. What a fucking dour cunt my uncle's become.

I bid him a cheerio and get the fuck out of there, using a catch-up with my mate Twix as an excuse to leave, though I've no intention of catching up with any ol Joe Blo today. The heat might be stifling but I'm just glad to be airing off the stagnant ammonia smell of the old bar. I associate the smell with dead dreams and wasted lives.

I check my watch and see that I spent less than an hour with my uncle, and yet it feels like an interminable length of time. Some people are like that, they just drain your energy like they've tapped your soul direct and keep coming back for refills.

Coming across the Victoria Bridge in only a pair of old shorts is good old Ledrud, his long grey beard waving in the wind as his grotesque feet slap the tarmac. He's got the longest and dirtiest toe-nails I've ever seen on man or woman, and his skin is leathery and brown from where he sunbakes on the riverbank outside the Art Gallery.

Ledrud nods to me as we pass each other, me up on the footpath and him on the road. I've never seen him walk on the footpath, not even when the buses go past him with inches to spare. They honk their horns, of course, but it's no use: he won't step up onto the footpath for no cunt. He's adamant that the world must bend to him.

Some cunts romanticise the homeless, like we're living vessels of arcane knowledge just because we've lived it rough, because we've seen life through the other end of the toy kaleidoscope, expecting us to drop pearls of wisdom like we're Sufi's on safari. During England's Georgian era, it was fashionable for rich cunts to have depressed old men like Ledrud living in one's garden. Ornamental hermitage, they called it. It's where today's common garden gnome comes from.

You know the last thing I ever heard Ledrud say before he apparently took up his vow of silence (we only assume it's a vow of silence because he's never actually told anyone it is)?

In his fractured Slavic accent he said to me: 'Dante, I can feel the lice starting to build their homes just on the inside of my butt hole.'

THE SÉANCE

Raven parks the car in front of two impressive pillars with Celtic crosses on them, on a triangular patch of lawn at the top of Spook Hill, and we all pile out. Shame, cause ol Twixxie here had this cute lil kindergoth chickadee calling herself Ursula sitting on his lap the whole way here in order to fit all six of us in Raven's bomb. I'd insisted, of course. A true gentleman would. It was all I could do not to crack a fat, though. I'll continue my flirting with the little doll as the evening goes on and have her by midnight, I reckon.

'Make sure the handbrake's on,' jibes Jess, who like me and Raven is tonight using her scene name – which is Xanthe – because it impresses the young ones, the three kindergoths Raven's brought along. 'We don't need the sisters dragging the car away.'

'Fuck, don't say that,' replies Raven with a shiver.

We make our way back around to the junction of Twelfth and Thirteenth Avenues, though in reality it's actually the junction of Eleventh and Twelfth Avenues but no-one can tell because some joker keeps yanking the sign down. I know it's Eleventh Avenue cause I've met the acting assistant sexton a few times and he told me Thirteenth Avenue's actually down the hill a bit more near Eighth Avenue, pointing out that the streets inside Toowong Cemetery don't look like they run numerically because of the way they wind around the hills.

Raven reckons at the junction of Twelfth and what is actually Eleventh we can raise the mega-spirit itself, the Angel of Death.

'Back down there is The Grove that we passed,' I tell the others, referring to an area devoid of tombstones where the council dumps old tree branches and landscaping supplies. 'It's so haunted that even during the day the hairs on your neck will stand up.'

'Cool,' says one of the two boys, Jeremy. 'I wanna go down *there*.'

'No you fucking don't,' I warn. 'Seriously, lads, you do not wanna go down there. Especially on your own.'

'Why not?' one of them challenges.

Sod it.

'Bad shit will happen, that's why,' I tell them in a way that says *don't ask any more questions.*

'What kind of shit?'

'Don't worry about that now,' I say, getting annoyed. Don't these kids give up?

Jess holds up the book: the Necronomicon. It gets everyone's attention and stops the hundred and one sodding questions.

It's the Avon Books version, a small paperback with an impressive cover and little information as to its true origins. This is the Peter Levenda version that he made anonymously for the occult shop The Magickal Childe in New York when people kept pestering the owner to track down Lovecraft's fictional book. I know all this, of course, but I'm not telling any of the others this, not even Jess or Raven. Not when everyone thinks I can use the book to summon a spirit with, even if it is only myself that says I can. Malik got me this copy from a New Agey shop in the same building he studies in, but I've seen them in Archives on Charlotte Street all the time for only five bucks. He reckons his brother could get me something way more serious, but this one's suitable enough for my needs.

One of the lads wants to have a look at the book, so I hold them back as if from a disaster.

'No-one can touch the book except me or Xanthe.'

'Or me,' adds Raven, a bit peeved.

'Me, Xanthe and Raven,' I amend.

'What for?' asks Ursula.

'If you're lucky, I'll let you touch it later,' I wink at her, but she just frowns at me. She's gonna need more buttering up or I'll be resorting to rubbing one out later while I imagine her spread-eagled and starkers.

We've got capes for most of us because Jess brought spares thank fuck, and those that don't have one we make stand back further from the chalk inscriptions drawn on the road. The tarmac is old and cracked, not very smooth, and the chalk gets destroyed quickly in our administrations. Raven keeps swearing as it snaps and crumbles, and at one point she accidently drags her knuckles across the bitumen and tells me to 'fucking well do it myself' after she catches me laughing.

Finally we get the seal drawn, a mandal of twenty one squares with various symbols in most of the squares.

'Do not step near or on this mandal,' I warn everybody in a dire tone, holding my hands out as if to stay them.

Ursula looks well impressed at last, to my satisfaction.

'The dagger of Inanna, if you will, Xanthe,' I intone, glancing to Jess.

We needed a copper dagger but couldn't find one, so we've substituted it with a steel one from Jess's kitchen and along the blade we've drawn the word INANNA with a Nikko pen.

She places the blade in the centre of our *Work* while Raven places four candles at each extremity and lights them with her Bic.

'We will now call upon the Angel of Death,' I declare solemnly.

'Wait,' goes one of the lads with a sense of urgency in his voice.

We all freeze and strain our ears for the sounds of Normals, ready to run. All of us, that is, except for the lad.

'What is it, Craig?' whispers Raven.

'What do *we* do?' he says, glancing at the other kindergoths.

'For fuck's sake,' I blurt, as we all relax again.

Raven pretends to strangle him. 'You bloody dork; you scared the shit out of us.'

'Sorry,' he says softly. 'But I've never done this before. What are we three supposed to do?'

'Just stand there and be collateral if all goes wrong,' I snap.

'Twix,' Jess says in a parental tone.

'You just witness,' says Raven to the kindergoths.

Fuck, I like that! *Witness.*

'Yep,' I go, regaining my composure. 'That's why you guys are here. The Witness is an important role. Stay silent, and watch!'

'Okay,' goes Craig.

'Silence!'

He glances at the other joker and Ursula as they all share a stifled snigger, like they're in a highschool classroom still.

'Let's get on with it,' pushes Jess, so we resume our places and begin the incantation anew.

I'm no further into it than the first time around when the trees across from us light up, shadows streaking across their canopies. They plunge back into darkness and then the gravestones to their left are illuminated.

'The Angel of Death is here!' shrieks Ursula.

'Shut the fuck up,' hisses Raven.

'Run!' I yell, realising it's a car and making a bee-line straight for a wide tombstone behind me only several paces away, barrel-rolling behind it, the fucking cape getting tangled around my ankles and tripping me over before I can make cover.

Raven and Jess have scattered in different directions, but the other three are stumbling around like fucking drunks with one of them even trying to collect up the candles and nearly setting himself on fire because the stupid poonce didn't blow them out first.

'GET THE FUCK DOWN!' I shout at them, finally crawling behind a tombstone myself.

They run and duck behind some marble monoliths on the other side of the road, getting caught in the beam of headlights as they do so. The car grumbles around the bend and squashes one of the candles that the lad dropped. It rolls to a stop in front of our seal, the headlights illuminating just how poorly drawn it is. Then as it guns away again along Eleventh Avenue, a window rolls down and this burly bloke's voice calls out: 'Go home, you fucking freaks!' Boof-headed laughter comes from the car as it disappears around the hill.

'I don't want to stay here,' quivers Craig like a pansy.

'Yeah, we should probably move,' says Raven.

'What for?' I ask. 'Because of them? They're not gonna come back.'

'Let's go further that way,' Raven suggests, pointing beyond another crossroads where a gazebo sits. 'There's more trees over the hill. More cover.'

'Fine,' I sigh, and we pack up our stuff into Raven's car. 'Who wants to walk over?'

'Me,' Ursula pipes up, embracing my arm.

'Right, me and Ursula will meet you guys over there,' I go before anyone else gets a chance to volunteer for the walk.

I lead her away and smirk as one of the lads, not Craig but the other one, Jeremy, watches us with big sad puppy-dog eyes.

'I've been writing a lot of poetry lately,' I go, cause chicks love poetry. They think it makes a bloke seem more sensitive and shit.

'Poems are stupid,' she goes, the rude little wench.

'Not mine,' I retort. 'But that's alright, I won't bore you with one.'

'Thanks,' she goes, but I was hoping my reverse-psychology would've meant she begged to hear it. 'Why do they call you Twix?'

'Glad you asked.' I hold a thumb and a pinkie up. 'One for the pink and one for the stink. Can't tell you which is for which. You just have to pick a side and find out.'

She stares at me then cracks into a cute laugh.

'That's stupid,' she goes, and I force myself to smile as if I don't care what this little minx thinks. It's just as well she's got a nice pair of chesticles.

'Well, they thought it was alright in Melbourne,' I sniff.

'You've been to Melbourne?' she gasps, just as expected.

Finally, something that impresses the little chickadee!

'Course. Loads of times,' I say, even though the recent trip was my first time. 'Way better clubs, although the Brisbane scene's a lot stronger, strangely enough.'

'I'm so jealous,' she gushes.

'Maybe I'll take you one day,' I say, imagining us in our own hotel room away from the distractions of her mates. 'I might even move down there one day.'

Raven speeds past and Craig hangs out the window barking like a dog as they shoot down Third Avenue.

'Bugger me, shut the fuck up!' I call out to em.

Raven knows better than to be driving like a maniac through here, especially in that old rust-bucket. There's enough dings all over it already, and the sodding wheels could fall off and crash into some graves. Then we'd be up shit creek.

I lead Ursula as we cut across between the graves and the trees and wait on the far avenue for the others to finally make their way around. When they get here we find a decent spot, far more secluded, and decide this time to set up our séance on the flat concrete of a gravesite where at least the chalk will yield better results. Jess unpacks the candles, the book and the chalk.

Raven's not too keen on the idea, though, calling it sacrilegious. So while we debate the wrongs and rights of it, we don't even notice this guy coming up the road in the dark until he's about thirty feet away. Raven sees him first and nearly screams, making us all spin toward the figure in a mad panic.

'Fuck, it's just some bloke,' I whisper hoarsely to the others.

'Maybe he's a serial killer,' Ursula whispers back, and we make fun of her but secretly I'm hoping she's not right. I get goosebumps thinking about the possibility.

He comes up, introducing himself as the onsite sexton, and like a complete poonce I drop that I know the assistant sexton, omitting that it's barely a passing acquaintance.

'Then you of all people know you're not meant to be mucking around in here,' the sexton says touchily. 'Least of all at night.'

'Oh yeah, we know that,' I reply. 'We're just hanging out, is all.'

'We've had some graves vandalised,' he says matter-of-factly, like an accusation.

I flip open my wallet and flash him my security licence. 'No worries, mate,' I go with a wink. 'I'll keep this lot in line.'

He just sniffs and looks at Raven when she goes: 'We'd never do that. We love cemeteries and respect them too much.'

The sexton gives her a puzzled look, glancing down at our séance paraphernalia on the gravesite and the spray-painted pentagram's and stuff all over her car that she and Malik did just before Christmas as a drunken laugh.

'Yeah, can see that,' he says strangely and tells us that we need to be out by ten o'clock, then trudges back down the hill again.

'That was creepy,' murmurs Ursula quietly, as though the sexton might still hear her even from a great distance.

'Nah, it's all good,' I say cheerily.

'Let's not do the séance,' says Jess suddenly.

'What? Why not?'

'You know,' she shrugs. 'Just too busy, and the sexton's probably keeping an eye on us now.'

'I agree with Xanthe,' says Raven.

Judging by the looks on the lads' faces they do, too.

'Fine,' I sigh.

I was hoping to make out with Ursula on a grave, maybe even fuck her brains out if I can get us alone long enough without Raven or Jess poking their noses where they're not wanted. Dante's been crashing at my place for a while now and I don't need him getting in the way of a good time, unless he's decided to stay the night with his uncle.

I'd heard so often from chicks about how lads only have one thing on the brain that I'd grown up under the assumption they're not interested in casual sex. This meant I was oblivious to their advances when all I wanted to do was root like a rabbit. Realising this simple error took so long that I've spent my early twenties trying to cram in as much fucking as possible, erasing the years of celibacy as though they never existed. This little cupcake would make a fine addition, if I can just get the chance.

'What're we going to do now?' asks Craig.

As it is, I happen to know just the perfect thing, and it might still get me laid.

'Crypts,' I announce with an evil grin.

'We're not digging anything up, Twix,' admonishes Raven. 'We're leaving.'

'Not here,' I respond, 'in the Valley.'

'Where in the Valley?' goes Jess.

'You know that vacant block of land across from All Hallows' School? There.'

'Junkies hang out there, Twix, you dork,' says Raven, rolling her eyes.

'There's crypts in the Valley?' asks Ursula, incredulously.

'You bet,' I go, hugging her tight to me. 'I'll take you.'

'Okay,' she yelps excitedly. That's my girl.

'I'll drop you off, then,' says Raven. 'Because I'm going home.'

'Party-pooper,' teases Jess.

We get the car packed again, and Jess comes over to me and says quietly: 'What's goin on with you and Ursula?'

'Not much,' I lie.

'Bullshit,' she disputes. 'I've seen you all night grooming her.'

'Fuck off, Jess,' I go. 'I can do whatever I want.'

'What about Karen?'

'What about her? We broke up, remember?'

Jess shakes her head. 'Jesus, Trav. You're not even trying to get Karen back.'

'We're having a break,' I explain, which is mostly true. In fact, truth is Karen dumped me last month. Kind of like an early Christmas pressie.

'Yeah, fair enough,' she hisses, 'but that doesn't mean you go around fucking every underage girl in the meantime.'

She storms off around the other side of the car, parking her arse in the passenger side seat. Raven raises an eyebrow at me and tilts her head as if to ask *what's up with her?*

The trip back to the Valley is awkward, so Raven blasts some music. Her tape-player is busted so she tunes the radio to 4ZZZ and some black metal blasts from her crappy speakers. Jess reaches out and turns the volume up exceedingly loud, and to my relief the deafening music actually eases the tension in the car somewhat. The lads even start headbanging along.

To be expected, Jess doesn't want to join us catacomb hunting so only me, Ursula, Craig and Jeremy get dropped off in the Valley. Who cares anyway? I've heard that Jess has genital warts and has passed it on to others.

'Where are they?' says Craig.

'The warts?'

He looks puzzled. 'What warts?'

'You mean the catacombs?' I correct myself.

'Yeah,' he says, his mouth open like a fish.

'What warts?' persists Ursula, her brow crinkled with worry.

'I meant catacombs,' I say, then add: 'They're right there.' I point at the concrete wasteland in front of us that's bordered by Wickam, Ann, Gotha and Gipps streets.

'There's nothing there,' whines Jeremy.

'Duh, it's a crypt, so it's underground, *au naturel*,' I enlighten the dumb fuck, pleased as punch to be able put into practice the second language I've been learning. '*Au naturel* is French for *of course*.'

Ursula and Craig climb up onto the concrete flats and start walking off, so I scramble after them, careful not to trip over because the slabs of concrete are uneven.

'Where's these crypts, or catacombs, then?' asks Craig, skimming a shard of smashed glass across the concrete.

'Here somewhere,' I boast, running ahead to have a look around. 'The church were going to build a cathedral called the Holy Name here but they went bust and eventually sold the land in the 80s.'

'How do you know all this?' goes Craig.

'I've been around,' I say proudly. 'Seen things come and go.' I'd actually heard about the crypts from T-Rex Tony, who used to come here as a teenager back in the mid-80s.

'You're so fuckin old, man,' laughs Craig, kinda contemptuously, and Ursula laughs too.

While I won't respond to their taunts, it hurts a bit, I'll admit.

We spend a while searching for the entrance, but come up empty-handed. We do, however, find the alcoves and a length of wall with decorative balustrades along Ann Street at least. Craig starts kicking at one of the balustrades to try and make it fall down onto the street.

'Oi, stop it, ya motherfucker,' I growl. 'These were heritage-listed a few years ago.'

'So?'

'So I'll break your face open if you wreck em,' I threaten, unable to resist checking to see if Ursula's awed by how I stand up to Craig. I think she is.

'Did you find them?' Jeremy yells from the middle of the concrete wasteland.

'Nah, they don't exist,' Craig yells back, wandering over to him.

'They do,' I insist to Ursula.

'Maybe they got filled in,' she says sadly.

'Maybe,' I muse. 'Stop vandals, or grave-robbers.'

'What's to rob from a grave anyway,' she says. 'Just dead bodies.'

'Never underestimate the sexual desires of some people,' I grin. 'Necrophiliacs would love it down there.'

'What's necrophiliacs?' she goes, legitimately in the dark as to it's meaning. 'Is that something to do with warts?'

'Necrophilia is the sudden urge to crack open a cold one!' I laugh, but Ursula still looks confused, so I add: 'Sex with dead people.'

'Oooh,' she goes, and either still doesn't get the joke or is still trying to work out how sex with corpses works, because she remains unamused.

The lads have wandered down near Wickham Street, and Ursula is walking ahead of me to join them.

'Wait up, babe,' I go, but she obviously doesn't hear me because she starts walking a bit faster.

By the time I catch up they've gathered together under the sign for Gotha Street and are talking about how to tear it down for their bedroom wall. Ursula seems keen to have it, and before I can volunteer to get it for her Jeremy is shimming up the pole and tugging at it, complaining that it won't come down without force.

'I'll go grab a brick or something,' says Craig excitedly, running across the road to scrounge around an old shop front.

The much taller Telecom – or Telstra as it's now called – building next door dwarfs the shop and there's a drunk bloke passed out on the front steps. Craig kicks the bloke awake and runs back across to us, cackling like the fucking cretin he is. But Ursula is amused by his antics, cracking up and falling on the ground, barely able to contain herself.

Jeremy starts whooping up on his perch.

I don't know what the hell I'm doing here. I should have just gone back with Jess and Raven.

I walk off without bidding them adieu, and when I glance back I notice the three kindergoth haven't even realised I've left.

It's not until I'm down the street that I remember I should've given Ursula my card so she can keep in contact. I got them made up at a vending machine in the Transit Centre when I went down to Melbourne. Twenty for five bucks. Didn't get to hand that many out. Maybe putting STUD under TWIX was a mistake. It's sort of meant as a joke, but the girls in Melbourne just laughed for some reason.

I reckon Ursula wouldn't have laughed.

PIXIE FLIPS BURGERS

In a fucked up attempt to make us normal, and get us away from dressin in black all the time and hangin out with me friends (who Mum calls 'losers'), Mum and Dad have joined forces and are makin us work at Dad's sucky burger franchise while the school holidays are on. It's pretty fucked that two people can hate each other so much that they normally devote all their energy into literally fuckin each other's lives up, but then together they gang up on me who hasn't done a single fuckin thing to them.

To make things worse, last night Dad brought over one of his poxy fucking uniforms that he makes everyone dress in and cheerfully went: 'My daughter's first job and first uniform.'

I just went back: 'Looks like a prison uniform.'

They made us try it on to see if it fits.

'It's uncomfortable,' I'd complained, to deaf ears, but.

'Let me get a photo, Prue,' Mum had gushed proudly, rummaging around for the camera while I just stood there like a fuckin mong.

The bus ride here was a fuckin nightmare. I was totally fuckin paranoid that I'd get recognised in this stupid fuckin uniform. I could never live that down. I still had me Pantera hoodie over it, and tried to hide the collar by hugging the neck of the hoodie tighter, but ya could still see the stupid thing pokin out. And if Dad thinks I'm wearin those god-awful pants, in bottle-green no fuckin less, he can go jump off a cliff! They're still at home on the floor where I chucked em in disgust last night. He'll have to be happy with torn stockings and cherry-red Doc's.

The bus stops half way along Main Street in the middle of Kangaroo Point and I have to walk all the way back to Dad's shop.

The dread I feel walkin up to the doors of this place is worse than any hangover, but. I can feel myself literally shrinking smaller as I get closer. For all these years the sweet smell of burgers and fries comin from these places has always made a stoked feelin in us, like if we're driving past and I smell it all cookin, I gotta beg Mum to turn round and do the drive-through. Now I'm afraid that I'm gonna start connectin the smell with this shitty fuckin sensation of dread.

Inside is just as worse. Again, what used to feel like a welcoming, now feels like I'm literally facin the executioner. All these cunts with their fakeness that I used to make fun of are now going to start showin us how to be just like them. It's killin me inside. Dad sees us from out back and comes out and hurries me past the counters out back to where they make the burgers.

'Goddamit, Prudence, where the hell are the slacks?'

Slacks. Fuck I hate that word, as much as I hate my name. I hate seeing his lips form the word and spit it out at us. He's rubbin his forehead like I've given him a headache already.

'They're stupid,' I tell him, and feign boredom, crossing me arms defiantly. 'And don't call me Prudence.'

'It's part of the uniform,' he snaps. 'This isn't hanging-around-with-your-loser-friends time, Prue. This is work. You need to take it seriously. Get that ridiculous jumper off.'

He calls over to this liddle blonde girlie as I pull me hoodie off, and asks if she can get him a spare pair of 'slacks' from the storeroom.

'Now listen to me,' he says sternly, raisin his finger for emphasis. 'This is a test, if you like. I need you to buckle down and learn the ropes. You're not getting any younger, Prudence.'

'I'm fifteen,' I remind him.

'You're on a slippery slope, is what you are,' he says snootily, then thanks blondie for passin him the pants. She gives him a *want-ya-cock-sucked-sir?* smile and toddles back to her job, lookin us up and down and literally havin a liddle laugh behind her hand at the front counter with the other bitch there. I'm about to ask the fuckin slut what she thinks is so funny when Dad reaches for me tit and starts gropin us.

'Fuck off, ya perve,' I snap, slappin at his sausage-fingered hands. The fuck?

'Your name badge, Prue,' he goes, and looks at us like *I'm* the weird one, but he's blushin bright red coz I called him a perve. Those sluts at front laugh and gape open-mouthed at one another, like they can't believe I did that. Dad stammers: 'I asked if you wanted me to put it on. You didn't say anything.'

'I didn't hear ya,' I go, takin the badge out of his fidgety hands, eyein him warily just to make him feel even more uneasy. If he thinks it'll be a breeze forcin us to work here, he can think again.

The badge has my full name across it. PRUDENCE. Above it reads: IN TRAINING. How fuckin embarrassing is this?

'I can't wear this,' I go.

Dad sighs dramatically. 'What's wrong now?'

'Me name's Pixie.'

'I should know your name because I gave it to you right after you came out of your mother.'

'For fuck's sake!' I spit, disgusted by the mental image of Mum's twat pushin us out, except liddle baby version of me. Fucking gross!

But my cunt ova father stands there literally glarin at us until the name badge's on, then he takes us over and pairs us up with that fuckin blonde bitch, who he introduces as Olivia. Of course that's her stupid name. Like she's fuckin *all that.*

Olivia 'shows me the ropes', as the old tosser keeps puttin it. She explains everythin like she's talkin to a two year old. She's wastin her breath, but, coz I'm literally not listenin to a word she's sayin. Instead, I'm hummin *The Beautiful People* coz she's exactly the kind of cunt I think Manson wrote the song about.

I notice Dad's got his fuckin poxy plastic Jesus on a cross up on the wall above the deep fryer. The screw holding it up looks pretty loose. It's only a matter of time before the Son of God gets another baptism, I reckon. When Olivia shows us how we squeeze the paper cup so that less fries can fit into it, I notice she sneaks a liddle peek at Jesus up there. It figures that she's the religious type.

Once we're at the end of the liddle tour, she literally leaves us on me own at a register. When there's no-one linin up she's chattin to the other girl, who doesn't bother introducin herself, thank fuck. A couple of people try and line up in front of us, but I just hang back and play with the chipped polish on me nails instead. They get the hint pretty quickly and change to Olivia's line, who gets shitty about havin to do all the work.

'It'd be great if you could just do your job,' she says to us with a smarmy smile, literally noddin her head repetitively.

'Have ya got Parkinson's disease,' I ask in a deadpan voice. 'Doin that thing with ya head makes it seem like ya do.'

She stops noddin and keeps servin, but when her queue's finished she heads back through the burger prep area and snitches on us to Dad, who comes chargin up with a stupid scowl on his face. The sight of him puffin his chest out, swingin his arms like he was somethin ova fuckin big shot cracks us up somethin shockin. I'm sure the other two girls are impressed by his performance, but.

'Okay, Prue, I'm starting you on drinks,' he goes.

'Look, I already agreed to help out in ya shop, didn't I? So quit orderin me around all the time.'

'Prudence, I'm telling you, not asking.'

'You're not the boss of me!' I snap back.

'In every sense of the word, I am,' he goes, tryin to use his clever word play to trick us. He grabs us by the arm and pulls us over to the drinks machine.

'You're hurtin my arm,' I complain, even though he isn't, but he ignores us. Seems I'm not the only one learnin here.

He gives us a run-down on how the drink machine works, his voice shaky with anger. There's three buttons that read *S*, *M* and *L*.

'Customer wants a drink, you take the corresponding cup, fill it with ice.' He demonstrates as though to a retard, fillin the cup with ice-cubes that tumble and rattle down noisily. This bit I actually like. I could literally just do the ice all day.

'Then you place it under the dispenser, like so. S for small, M for medium, and L for large.'

'Who'd have guessed?' I joke.

He pushes the button and dramatically places his fist on hip, like he's posin for a fashion magazine. This cunt takes the job way too seriously. It's ice and Coke, for fuck's sake. The black fluid gushes down over the ice cubes, meltin them a bit. They sink inside the cup a bit, and the machine stops automatically.

'See how it goes down?' He tips the cup so I can see that the drink only reaches three-quarters the way up. 'The machine is designed to only fill part of the way. It won't fill or overfill a cup designated for its function. Next, you top it up with some more ice so that the drink reaches the lip of the cup. Pop a top on it, pass it to the girls at front. Simple.'

When he says *pop a top on it*, there's a hint of the theatrical in his voice. I imagine he would normally ponce like a fuckin fag if he was talkin to the mong liddle tarts that work for him, makin them giggle sweetly. Cunt knew I'd just take the piss and tried to downplay it, but.

'Can you guess what we do if they don't want ice?' He literally pauses, probly actually convinced that I'm gonna warm to this fuckin game. He blinks, as if recoverin his memory of who he's talkin to, then clears his throat. 'Of course not. Why would you care? Anyhoo, we just add the small and medium buttons together and that'll fill a large cup with no ice in it. There,' he goes, pushin the cup into me hands, 'now you try it.'

He stands back to watch us, doesn't bother explainin what to do if someone wants a small or a medium drink with no ice in it. I go through the motions, which are fucking easy as, and at the end he claps his hands together once and declares all is good, spins on his heel and disappears back round to the burger prep area. He's pretty annoyed by now. Whatever.

I keep me back to those two bitches on the registers, and just do the drinks. A piece of my soul disappears into every cup I pour, and I start to fantasise that if I keep this up long enough, eventually I can smuggle my entire soul outside, literally digested in the bodies of hundreds of people, spreadin like a virus through the world. I'd fuck everyone up from the inside, and there'd be fuck all anyone could do to stop me. Antibiotics wouldn't work, coz I wouldn't actually be a virus, which is an organism. They'd look, they'd get scientists and world fuckin leadin doctors to check everyone, but no-one would be looking for me soul, especially not pieces of my soul. I could pass into any one of those doctor cunts who checked out all the other cunts. I would be invincible.

'How many times do I have to say it?' Olivia's voice jars us from me daydreamin. She's right next to us, literally pullin a mightier-than-thou look, the stupid cunt.

'What the fuck do ya want?'

She puts her hands on her hips and sighs, but there's a nervous twitch in her eyes, like she's a liddle bit scared of us. 'Two large Cokes and small lemonade,' she says, still talkin to us like I'm a child.

'Righto, keep ya cotton panties on,' I say over me shoulder for the benefit of the customers.

She stalks back to the counter and apologises to the family on the other side, then her and the other slut scoff and throw bitchy looks at us.

The guys workin on makin the burgers chuckle and rib each other, one noddin in my direction to the other. I death stare the cunts but they just snigger louder and put their heads down, continuing to flop the lettuce and pickles onto the buns.

It feels like high school all over again. I fuckin hate it here so much.

When Dad comes round and tells us it's lunch break, he hands us some cash and says I can get something in-store if I want. I snatch a burger off the warming tray and Olivia gets uppity, loudly declaring that I can't just take food out of the kitchen area and that I need to line up like everyone else, but me father puts out a hand to shush her. I storm out of the place pullin me Pantera hoodie down over this fuckin clown costume.

Gettin outside literally feels like freedom. It feels like every day when the last bell rang at school and ya jumped the fence and got the fuck as far away as possible from the place. I put as much distance as I can between meself and my newfound hell, and the sound of the traffic roaring past a few feet away becomes an immense comfort. I'm miserable, I suddenly realise. Really, really miserable.

I can't go back, and I don't need to. Straight up Main Road is the Story Bridge, so I head in that direction. I'll spend the rest of the day in the Valley. That should cheer us up. I might see if Dee Dee is around and score something, just a liddle choof should do it.

Thanks to working for me Dad, the burger tastes like a fuckin disappointment now. Great, just fuckin great. I toss the fuckin thing into the traffic and see it splatter across some cunt's windshield, but the traffic is too bumper to bumper for him to suddenly stop, so he's just gonna have to accept that it's a shitty day.

You and me both, cunt.

RUNNING TOWN

I've been in Brisbane for a total of two weeks and I'm already flyer dropping with Megan, who's basically my new friend, running around the city and putting flyers up on noticeboards for the new club she's running at the Land's Office next Friday night. I love this city! We're hitting the usual spots, apparently: Rocking Horse, Skinny's, Record Market *and* Record Exchange, the Metro cinema down on Edward past Kent Records, and of course Velvet Web and Underworld Realm which are the goth shops.

She's showing me the traps because, like, I only recently moved up from Melbourne and I'm still pretty unfamiliar with a lot of the shops here. I'm used to, like, Peril 305, Missing Link, Morticia's, Atrocity, Space Age Books and Heartland Records. I still pine for them, even though a change of scene has been great. Basically, I was feeling stifled in Victoria, by the old crowd, and not least of all by my ex. I needed a fresh start, period.

Brisbane's quite small compared to Melbourne. The buildings don't quite reach as high and there's, like, a lot more sunlight reaching street-level. I get why people refer to this as a big country town: I can walk from one end of the city to the other without breaking a sweat. Just jokes. It's actually really bloody hot up here so I'm sweating like a pig! It's crazy. Gotta laugh, though, right?

The other thing I like about up here is that accommodation is so easy to find. I stayed with my sister Lisa and her husband in Toombul for the first week, expecting to be there at least a month before I found my own place, right, but all I did was turn up to the real estate agent's, grab a key and check some places out, and then pick one. Application approved next day, and I had my own flat on Gillingham Street in Buranda before the week was out! Absolutely no-one else was even vying for the property unlike in Melbourne where it feels like a competition to try and outbid other would-be tenants.

Lisa tried to talk me out of renting Southside, though. Apparently there's this thing about South of the river versus North of the river here, and the rivalry gets crazy serious.

'Go the tits on those two,' this utter yobbo bloke says to his friend as they ogle us.

Megan rolls her eyes. 'Pfft,' she sniffs. 'Boys will be boys.'

But they don't have to be, do they? I just smile back at Megan, because, like, what can we even do about it?

I already knew of Megan through a mutual friend, Twix, who I met at Die Graft club at The Chamber in South Melbourne. He came down for New Year's Eve, citing a desperate need for a change of scenery after he split up with his girlfriend; totally understandable. He wasn't popular down there, though, because he came off as a bit arrogant. All froth and no beer, everyone thought. But I, like, gave him a chance anyway and swapped addys with him since I was already coming up here to live. I thought it'd be good to know someone in my new city besides my sis. So we hung out a bit before he left and became good friends, and he regaled me with stories about his friends here in Brisbane – including Megan – so I trust his judgement. Besides, Megan's turned out pretty cool. Twix introduced me to her when he took me clubbing at the Normanby as soon as I got here. She was one of the few people I actually got to meet, because it kinda felt like he was keeping me to himself. Like, maybe he's got a soft spot for me?

There's a bunch of goths hanging in the middle of the terracotta mall that basically runs several blocks through the heart of the city, as they say. The Queen Street Mall, they call it, though it doesn't look so regal.

Megan's like: 'That's Malik,' nodding towards the tallest of the throng, a guy almost six foot tall wearing a long black coat and, like, teashade glasses. The ones John Lennon used to sport. 'The blonde girl next to him is Xanthe and I'm not sure who the other two are. Only seen em around.'

'Hey Eggy-Meggie,' grins Malik, and hugs her until she squeals.

Then she hits him on the arm. 'You know I hate that name.'

'Have a flyer,' I pipe up nervously, thrusting one at him.

'Okay, if you insist,' Malik says charmingly. He reads aloud: '*The Hanging Garden*. Like the Cure song? Aw, yes! You did it, Megs!'

'*Creatures kiiissing in the rain...*' sings Xanthe, swaying on the spot and looking into space, like she's lost in memory.

Megan beams and she's like: 'Yep! My first club. You coming?'

Malik's like: 'Fuck yeah! With bells on!'

'Or spikes,' laughs Xanthe, referring to the copious amounts of spikes and studs on Malik's leather dog-collar and wristbands that, like, gets disapproving looks from the clueless yuppies giving us a wide berth as they do their window shopping.

'Great,' smiles Megs, then adds: 'Won't be any Marilyn Manson played, though. Fair warning.'

Malik pouts at this news, turning faux-sad eyes to me for moral support.

Megan formally introduces me to Malik and Xanthe, telling them that I know Twix.

'Ah yeah,' nods Xanthe with a knowing smile, 'just don't take him up on any offers to chase after the Angel of Death.'

'Okay, I'll keep that in mind,' I chuckle, not sure what she actually means by it.

One of the strangers, a heavy-set girl like myself with naturally dark rings around her eyes, shakes my hand. 'Hi Alex, I'm Abi and this is Erina. Welcome to Brisbane.'

'Merry meet,' I chime, and Xanthe says it's cool to meet another pagan, even though there's heaps of people on the goth scene that identify as such.

Erina just smiles at me while Abi introduces herself to Megan – since they don't actually know each other, either – but I notice that neither Erina nor Megan acknowledge one another at all, almost like they're deliberately trying to avoid each other even though, like, Megan said she doesn't know her.

Everyone fusses over the flyers even though they're, like, just photocopies. Goth clubs don't make a lot of money, if any at all, and everything about the scene is so DIY as a result. When something new pops up there's a level of interest in it that outweighs the production values. Everything goths do scene-wise in Australia basically comes from our own pockets, so we make-do.

'Where have you been since moving up?' asks Abi.

'Only here, in the city,' I admit. 'And, like, Buranda, of course. That's where my flat is. On Gillingham Street?'

She's like: 'You should check out the Valley markets on Saturday morning, then. It's the ant's pants. We could catch up.'

'That'd be great. But I won't be able to buy anything. I'm basically dead broke after the move.'

I haven't got the phone connected yet, either, as that's just another cost, so we arrange to meet outside the Valley McDonald's come Saturday morning. She seems pretty nice.

Megan and I keep going with the flyer dropping, leaving the others to their thing. I've noticed the heat's, like, picking up a bit now that we're getting closer to midday. Megan steers us into the Myer Centre to cool down for a bit, where we get a bottle of juice each.

'Finances are pretty tight, huh?' says Megan, picking up on my comment to Abi about the markets.

'Yeah, the dole only pays so much,' I admit, taking a swig on the juice. 'Damn, I needed that.'

'If you need to put down places you've looked for work,' offers Megan, 'you can put down mine. It's in the Valley, the pawn store in McWhirter's.'

I raise my eyebrows in delight. 'I've always wondered what it's like to work in one of those.'

'You know I mean P-A-W-N, right?'

'Oh,' I say and we both start giggling at my stupidity. Talk about laugh!

'I hope you freaks didn't steal that,' this guy's voice suddenly says.

He's standing behind the palm fronds and staring at us, pointing at our juices. He looks like a homeless bum who was recently employed in, like, an office or something, because he's got a business suit on. There's basically something a bit off about it, though. And his hair's scruffily hoiked into two short pigtails.

Megan asks what he's gonna do about it if we didn't pay for the juice, and the guy, like, stalks around and says he's gonna go dob on us, then sits down with a smile. He's obviously unhinged.

'I'm surprised we haven't bumped into you already,' says Megan, and introduces him as Dante, one of her friends. If I remember rightly, Twix's best friend is called Dante. This must be him.

Dante's dropped the psycho act now and waves across the table at me.

I didn't realise it but my heart's been pounding fast, because I thought he was going to go all psycho on us. 'Shit, sorry. Merry meet. I thought you were some crazy homeless bloke.'

'I am,' he grins.

'Yeaaah, Dante sleeps on the streets a lot,' Megan smirks playfully. He pinches her on the leg so she kicks him. 'Cheeky!'

'What's this then?' he says, grabbing one of the flyers off the table. '*The Hanging Garden*?'

'Yeah, my club,' says Megan. 'Remember I told you I was going to do one. Ta-dah!'

'Aw, nice one, Megs!'

She tells him how we've been walking all over town putting them up.

'You girls are doing it all wrong,' he crows. 'You wanna jump on the City Loop bus. It's totally free. Zip you girls around in no time.'

'Cool beans. Thanks for the tip,' I say.

Getting a gander at the redness on my arms, he's like: 'Keeps you outta the sun, too.'

'I'm not used to so much sun,' I admit. 'I'm actually, like, surprised at how big the goth scene is up here, actually.'

Megs rolls her eyes. 'You've opened Pandora's Box,' she moans.

Dante leans in like we're gathered around a camp-fire for a story. 'You know why it's so big up here? Precisely because of the sun!'

'Should be the other way around, right?' I say, remembering that this guy's crazy.

He's like: 'Not when you really think about it.'

'And trust me, Alex, he's thought about it,' says Megs.

'The thing is,' Dante continues unabated, 'whatever you might say about it, the goth scene thrives on being different, on being counter to our mainstream culture. There's no surer way for that to survive that in the state of sun, surf and sand. It's completely irrational to think pale skin and layers of velvet and polyester clothing should work up here, but that's precisely why it does. Nothing screams rebellious lifestyle than being a goth in Brisbane.'

'I'll have to take your word for it,' I giggle.

'Don't take my word for it,' he says, leaning back again. 'Just look around at how much you'll get stared at for it up here compared to down in Melbourne, a city of rain and alleyways and coffee-shops everywhere.'

He probably has a point: practically every office worker dresses in black back home. Goths kind of blend in a bit down there.

Megs is like: 'On that note: I want a hot chocolate!'

We all have a good laugh at that, then go and get a hot chocolate each, despite the heat. And maybe to, like, substantiate Dante's theory.

All in all it's been a wonderful day flyer-dropping and basically learning the layout of the city, and, like, meeting some of the scene people. I've started to fit in pretty quickly. 1996 is gonna be a grouse year! Period!

FREDDY KRUEGER'S ROOM

'Let's hit the clubs, Dante,' Twix goes, springing up from the couch.

Ever since he broke up with Karen, Twix has been getting increasingly randy to try it on with someone new, and apparently he blew his chances the other night at the cemetery with some little babybat.

I've been the opposite ever since Jillian dumped me at around about the same time as Twix and Karen breaking up: I wasn't exactly feeling suicidal, but I *was* seriously contemplating hurting myself in a grand display of the internal suffering I was undergoing. But I'm past that stupidity now, and past the anger, and feel somewhat indifferent about Jillian. Not about the whole situation, of course, no. But of her, yes. I've come up with enough reasons to convince myself that I'm better off without her, namely the fact she lives on the Gold Coast and it was a pain in the arse to see each other. That and she's more interested in someone else.

As a result of both Twix and I becoming single at around the same time we've hung out together a hell of a lot more, a sort of unspoken support pact, and it's led to many on the scene to unkindly joke behind our backs that we're a married couple now. Shit like that always gets back to the butt of the joke, however, and we'd heard what was being said within days of its conception, so Twix is keen to start hooking up with girls again to dispel the rumour.

So he goes: 'Let's hit the clubs, Dante,' implying there's a variety to choose from. There's only two tonight, in fact, because there's no way I'm setting foot in a normal club, especially not with him in tow.

'Fucking suit up, Batman,' I go, holding a finger in the air and striking a pose.

'You beauty,' he grins, and dashes through to rummage through his wardrobe.

Therapy is one of the two club choices on offer, upstairs at the Oriental, so I suggest we head there because Twix has a better chance of scoring there than if we head to the straight-up goth club where most of the girls are with their boyfriends. At least at Therapy it's not strictly a darkwave club; it's more of an alternative, slightly riot-grrrl venture started up by two lesbians who play an eclectic mix of music across genres.

About an hour into the night we've managed to get friendly with this group of girls – 'normals' as Twix likes to call em – here for the novelty of being immersed in the goth scene so they can boast about their daringly adventurous night out to their boring workmates come Monday morning. Straight off the bat I notice the little gold cross and chain around the neck of the shortest of the girls, whose name is Julie, though I highly doubt Twix has clocked it yet. They're equally fascinated and repulsed by Twix's fangs, which are always a good conversation opener. He'd want to fucking well hope they would be, too, since they set him back an arm and a leg last year. Wanna earn a mint? Become a dentist.

Twix buys everyone a round of drinks; probably in the hopes of getting em inebriated enough to buy his bullshit. Fuck, but is he laying it on thick. I've never understood why he thinks it's necessary to try and charm people with pompous stories of bravado. For example, right now he's crapping on about being trained in the kinds of combat moves that are normally reserved for the SAS. Not only is this utter horseshit, but he pointedly ignores one girl's repeated request to inform them precisely how he came into possession of this elite training.

'You ever need any protection,' the stupid cunt actually boasts, fishing his idiotic business card from his wallet and giving it to Julie, 'just give ol Twixxie a call.'

There's that variation on his nickname that he insists on dropping constantly in the vain hope it'll catch on and further remove him from the embarrassing origins of a moniker that was initially thrust upon him against his will. I know deep down he's always hated being called Twix, yet his pride won't allow him to admit it. Well, it's fully stuck now.

'I work in security these days, so...' he's blabbing on.

'So you're the man to call,' smirks one of the other girls, and they all start sniggering as he hands them a card each.

I can't believe he's pulled extra out. It's just his name and phone number. They're cheaply printed at some machine up in the Transit Centre of all places, but he acts like James fucking Bond when he's got em out. Makes him look even more desperate than he already is.

Julie reads the card aloud. '*Twix. Stud.*' She looks at him, barely able to suppress her laughter. 'Thanks, I'll keep you in mind next time some bloke won't leave before breakfast.'

Twix smugly raises his eyebrows at me like he's just shown me how it's done.

'Why's your name Twix?' one of the other girls goes before I can cut her off at the pass.

Twix's eyes light up, and because I've seen this routine a hundred times it's like watching him in slow motion as he brings his hand up and waggles his extended thumb and pinkie, uttering that brainless line: 'One for the pink and one for the stink, so pick a side.'

They stare at him in horror, unable to ascertain if the dumb cunt's actually joking or not. He grins at them, oblivious that their stunned silence is not one of awe. He'd have been better off going with the real story of how he got the nickname.

Julie's fingers are wet from the condensation on her glass and suddenly the ink on the card is all over her hand. She looks very fucking unimpressed by this and drops the card onto the table like it's poison. I note with some small satisfaction that the S in STUD has smeared into a unreadable blob, the ink running in an arc across the rest of the lettering until it simply reads DUD.

'I'm headed to the ladies to clean up,' Julie says, and the other girls automatically follow her. I bet my bottom dollar they'll be in there bitching about Twix.

With the girls gone, I take the opportunity to let Twix know that he's losing them.

'You've got to lay off those stories, man, I'm telling ya.'

'I think the short one was a bit impressed, ay,' he insists. 'That Julie.'

Fuck, but he's painful.

'She could be,' I shrug. 'Did you see the gold cross on her neck?'

'Gold, eh?' Twix slaps his forehead, because he knows full well that no self-respecting goth would adorn themselves with gold for a night out. 'Dammit. She's a Christian! There's no chance she'll be up for it.'

'Are you kidding?' I laugh. 'Christian girls'll bang like a dunny door in a strong wind, given half the chance.'

'It's alright for you,' he suddenly snaps, 'but some of us have to work for it.'

This cracks me up, much to his irritation. 'Work for it? Fuck, Twix, just be yourself. Tell them real anecdotes, not bullshit ones.'

When the girls get back Twix is finally playing it cool again, so I offer to get another round in, even though I can nil afford to. I might have to get financial remuneration from Twix tomorrow if the evening proves fruitful for him. It'd be the least he could do for me.

When I get the drinks back to the table, Twix has got our company enthralled with some tale, pointing through the leadlight windows to the street beyond. I set the glasses down and strain to hear what he's saying, but I swear he's dropped his voice so I have to shuffle closer to hear him. This is, in fact, an old trick of mine, where once I'm satisfied a girl is engaged in my story I'd drop my voice incrementally so that she unconsciously leans in closer and closer until she's in my personal space.

'...and then the roof caught fire and he didn't know if it was his bed or not,' narrates Twix, and I realise with horror that the sneaky cunt is recounting a tale about me, one that I had personally shared with him and wasn't meant for public consumption!

'Oi, cunt, you telling them about the Atcherley?'

Atcherley House used to be a big five-storey concrete Anglo Dutch building with flaky white paint and river-view balconies at the back that were crumbling away, filled with squatting musicians, punks and cockroaches. It was where the Queen, Ann and Adelaide all met (so the joke went), and I also used to squat there at one point, albeit in the basement levels away from everyone else.

There was a room that the staff had either forgotten about or never had need of. In any case, I'd barricaded the door for good measure and used to come and go through a little window high on the wall. There was an old boiler in the room, but being beneath ground level meant that the room was comfortably warm in winter and had no need of it being fired up. Besides, I didn't know where it fed to, if anywhere, and didn't need to give away my secret room for the unnecessary warmth of it. I had a thin roll of foam and a sheet for my bedding, and kept my backpack of clothes tucked away behind the boiler.

The main bar of the Atcherley was managed by a gay guy called Roger, who was pretty breezy about who came and went in the rooms, if truth be told. He never questioned why I was always hanging around day and night and why I never ventured upstairs.

It was the perfect sleeping place until one day I came back from roaming and found the door had been forced open. Nothing was touched: my bed was still there, and my backpack. But I wasn't going to risk staying there any longer and grabbed my backpack and took off.

The building was unceremoniously knocked to the ground on its ninety-ninth birthday, much to Roger's chagrin, I'm sure, as he'd been planning a big celebration for its hundredth year of standing.

But before my spot had been found out, there was one particular Wednesday night – a night reserved for the metal bands – where the paint flakes on the ceiling caught fire thanks to some halfwit trying to demonstrate his fire-breathing abilities. Because the gig was in the basement, too, I'd been worried that the fire department might find my camp and so had watched anxiously from across the road where I'd been taking in the night air because there was no fucking way I was getting any sleep when the metal bands were on. At least the punk gigs were upstairs in the Stardust room and the likes, so it was usually less of an annoyance. Eventually the fire was put out.

This is the story that Twix is regaling the girls with, pointing out the leadlight window of the Oriental and down the road to where the Atcherley used to be, the traitorous cunt. He's effectively trying to better himself in their eyes by painting me as a homeless bum.

'The fuck you think you're doing, Twix?'

'Calm down, Dante,' he says, giggling nervously, trying to appease me but keep his newfound sense of cool in front of the girls. 'I didn't tell them that you were squatting in the boiler room.'

One of the girls, Julie with the big sad eyes, forms an O with her mouth. Despite the distraction of confronting Twix, I can't help but imagine this must be what Julie looks like during an orgasm.

'You didn't, huh?' I ask facetiously, watching Twix's face change as he catches on to his error. I'm gonna scull his beverage as well as mine since the cunt's clearly lost command of his tongue.

'Wait!' goes Julie, holding her hands up for time out. 'Did you used to stay in that boiler room?'

That boiler room? She knew it?

'Yeah, at the Atcherley?'

'Yeah!' she laughs. 'Holy shit! You're Freddy Krueger!'

I'm not sure whether to be flattered or insulted by the comparison. He's a funny guy, but also ugly as sin. The ultimate back-handed compliment.

'I used to work there,' she explains, 'as a barmaid.'

'You worked for Roger, then?'

'Yeah, he was my manager. I was with him when we busted in the door to the old boiler room. Your bag and bed there.'

'No shit?' I'm actually intrigued.

'We didn't even know there was a room there until we got the door open,' Julie says. 'As soon as we saw it I just looked at Roger and said: Freddy Krueger's room.'

Everyone bursts into laughter, including Twix, but in a turnabout Julie and her mates declare it's the coolest thing ever, and nickname me Krueger.

'How's about that for a twist, bitch?' I grin at Twix, trying to imitate Freddy Krueger's gravelly voice.

He smiles broadly and nods his head at me as if to say *you win again, Dante.*

When I was in grade 3 at primary school me and this other kid were inseparable. His name was Kristian, and he was Yugoslavian. He'd tell me all these weird customs his family did and I'd be amazed by it. We went everywhere and did everything together. He was pretty pudgy and used to get picked on a lot, and I was always coming home with scrapes and bruises from fighting other kids in his defence. But where he was unpopular, I freely mixed with the other kids quite easily. He was disturbingly jealous of this, though I didn't know it at the time. One lunch time I was summoned to the classroom by some of the other kids cause Kristian had organised a competition. He wanted to race against me and paint a scene, and had already set up the art easel and paints from the back of the room. I really wasn't interested in competing against him, solely because he was my best friend. But he was insistent, and so I'd reluctantly agreed to it. So we got to it, the task being to copy an image from the book *Possum Magic,* but the little weasel had already been hard at work for the first half of the break working on his own painting! I'd only realised this when I saw he wasn't madly splashing paint around. I didn't protest the injustice of it, or question anyone when he was declared the winner and the kids cooed over his efforts while they disparaged my tawdry effort.

Kristian was the popular kid for the remainder of the day, and I felt some measure of what it must be like to be him for the rest of the time, always living in the shadow of a kid more enigmatic and liked. The next day, however, he was back to being the fat kid, the previous day's glory washed away into mediocrity overnight. I was reluctant to resume the friendship as before, and kept him at a cool distance. In fact, if memory serves me correctly, I arranged to meet him on the oval where we'd play red rover with some others but went and told some older boys that Kristian had been badmouthing them and was currently alone on the oval. I watched from the hill as they chased him around, toying with him until they finally grew bored and simply beat the shit out of him. I felt tormented playing silent witness to their savagery, compelled to run and help him fend them off, but the little cunt had done me a grave dishonour and I thought maybe now he'd learn to never backstab a loyal friend.

In some ways, Twix reminds me a lot of Kristian. The cunt gets surly when things run smoothly for me. The guy hasn't a fucking charitable bone in his body sometimes, I swear.

Three Little Birdies Down Beats by The Chemical Brothers comes on, so I round the girls up for a dance out on the floor, half-expecting Twix to join in. When I glance back at our table by the window, he's still sitting there in the dark watching us have fun. For fuck's sake, that cunt really needs to loosen up.

The rest of the night goes alright, and Twix manages to get over himself at last, perhaps helped in part by copious amounts of alcohol. I give it a rest for a bit, pacing myself, and by the time we're all ready to leave Twix is out on the footpath puking into the gutter. I tell the taxi driver where to drop him off and bundle him inside the cab.

As for me, I'm headed back to Julie's place to fuck her senseless, and I've no doubt whatsoever that when I see Twix next he won't mention tonight, nor ever again. That's his way.

TWIX SQUARES UP

'What for do you need to look in there?' the manky woman spits, reacting like I've asked her to lift her skirts and flash me when all ol Twixxie here did was mention needing to see inside her handbag as she leaves the store. Just a cursory glance is all I need to be seen doing my job. I haven't even mentioned the other two bags she's carrying that are stretched to transparency and clearly have boxes of whitegoods in them.

But she's gawking at me with wild-eyed indignation.

It's not my fucking desire to be gawping through other people's stuff; it's what the manager has hired me for so it's what I gotta do. He wants me standing at the entrance of The Big Block and bag-checking. If he whinges to Gary that I'm not even doing this one basic task then Gary'll pull me from this shift in future. It's not the best of shifts because I get abused all day by chicks who think I'm being nosy just for doing my job or think I'm accusing them of being thieves, but the way I look at is that I get paid to check out the talent all day. Tig bitties galore in designer fucking outfits. That's why I like working in the city: the chicks are miles above the trash I have to settle for in the Valley.

'It's just routine, miss, nothing more,' I sigh, folding my hands behind my back so that if she tries to say I planted anything in her bags the security cameras will show my hands were nowhere near her fucking stuff.

'Fine,' she growls and upends her handbag onto the floor. Shit scatters everywhere, bits of makeup stuff and tissues floating down, keys and tampons and all sorts of stuff, some it rolling it out the door into the Queen Street Mall and under the feet of passersby.

For fuck's sake, I always get the crazy ones. Customers are staring down at her as they go round her, and the stupid cow doesn't even clock that I'm barely glancing into their bags as they leave, doesn't realise that's all I'm about. She's too busy getting hysterical on the floor.

'I suppose you want to go through this stuff now,' she wails, holding up the bags with the boxes in them.

'If you're up to it,' I say with a small smirk.

I'm stunned when she shakes the boxes loose and starts yanking out all the bits and pieces and adding to the pile at my feet. To be honest, she probably could have had anything hidden inside those boxes and I would've let her just walk out. Gary doesn't pay enough for me to take this job too seriously.

These two young lads start walking across the Mall straight towards me, staring at me with intent. I'm trying to place how I might know these jokers, but I'm drawing a blank. The smaller kid, who has a head of bouncy curls, comes up and asks if I'm called Twix.

'Affirmative. Who wants to know?'

'I do,' he says with hostility, stating the obvious.

The other kid, a bit taller and dumpier, is staring down at the woman on the floor who's now scattering the parts of a blender and going on and on about how unfair it is that she's being made to do this.

'Who are you and why should I care?' I say to the kid with the curls.

'I'm Mick Buchhorn, Yvonne's brother,' he says, jabbing a finger at his chest for emphasis.

I shrug, joining index finger and thumb to form a hole. 'Care factor zero, mate.'

'Can you believe this?' the kid says to his mate who's engaged the crazy woman in conversation and hasn't heard any of what's being said. 'Pay attention, doofus. He's acting like he doesn't know.'

'Maybe he knows her as Ursula,' the doofus says, and the penny finally drops. I *do* know what he's talking about. The little chickadee from the failed séance at Toowong Cemetery.

'Wait, so you're Ursula's brother?' I go. 'Older or younger?'

I already know the answer, of course. She still had her puppy fat whereas this lad's starting to get fluff on his top lip.

'Older, you fucking spaz,' the kid spits. 'If you touch her again you're fucking dead.'

'I barely *got* to touch her,' I say. 'More's the pity, because she could go all night I reckon.'

The curly-haired kid's eyes stare at me with pure hate and his temple pulses like he's right royally pissed with me. I'm just winding the lil fella up, as Ursula clearly wasn't into me at all. She seemed more interested in those other two dropkicks that wanted to steal that street sign. Fuck knows what she told this shit-stain happened that night, though.

'I'm warning you,' he growls.

'He needs to be locked up,' yells the manky woman on the ground, scooping her pile into the boxes and the bags.

'Sorry, but there's no law against getting it on with your sister,' I say smarmily.

'Yeah there is,' the kid goes. 'She's only fourteen!'

The woman looks at me like I'm a monster, clutching her bags as though she feared I might renew my search on them afresh.

'Just go,' I tell her, tired of her shit.

'Big brother out of control, that's what I see,' she says, pursing her lips as she hurries out the doors, struggling to hold her bags together.

'Not so fucking smart now, are ya cunt?' says Ursula's brother, and I'm about to tell the little prick where to fuck off to when the manager of the store appears next to me and wants to know what's going on.

The Buchhorn kid's in for it now, harassing store staff like this!

'It's no problem,' I tell the manager. 'Part of the job is having to put up with the public just coming up and randomly being abusive. Time to go now, right lads?'

That's how it's done: be diplomatic, look like the sane one in the conflict. Manager's respect that kind of tact. The last thing they want to have to deal with is hassle in their store.

'A word, Travis,' the manager says, beckoning me to a corner away from the other two shit-stains.

Again, the tact of the professionals where we strategise in private.

'Don't worry,' I assure him when we're out of earshot of the others two, 'I've got this totally under control. They'll be on their way quick smart.'

'Travis, I'm running a business here. My store's not the time nor place for you to sort your personal problems with your friends. Is it?'

'Oh, they're not my friends. Off the record, though, the one with the curly hair–'

'There's no *off the record* here,' he goes, cutting me off and doing air quotes with his fingers.

'Yeah, right. But just between us blokes, that one's little sis has a fantastic set of–'

The manager holds his hands up. 'Travis!' he nearly shouts. 'You're missing the point here. You have a job to do, right? Just stick to that and save the rest of the muckaround for knockoff time.'

'Sure, no problem,' I say quietly.

I hope those two jokers aren't witnessing this dressing down, but then the manager calls over my shoulder: 'Be off, you two!'

I go back to my post at the door as the kid and his doofus mate walk away with grins on their stupid fucking zit-covered faces.

At closing time Raven's waiting for me out front.

'Thought you might want a ride home,' she says cheerily.

I'm still feeling pissed off about being told off by the manager earlier and how Ursula's brother got up me, and I was hoping to walk it off on my way home.

'Everything okay?' says Raven.

'I'll tell you on the way to your car,' I say, figuring at least I can vent to her on the way home even though it's probably the same distance to walk back to the Prozac Palace as it is to get to her car, which is undoubtedly parked down behind the Uni at Garden's Point.

But on the way I don't feel like reliving the shame of that kid getting one up on me, so I tell her about how I went out with Dante last night. At least with Dante it's half-expected that he'd humiliate me, even if it's indirectly.

'I was only telling the girls the story of the Atcherley to win em over,' I explain after I give her the rundown of the night's events. 'But he's a sore loser and just had to rub it in my face. Still, the laugh's on him, because none of those chicks were even attractive, especially that Julie he went home with. How funny is that?'

To be honest, she was definitely more Dante's type except for her chesticles. I only wanted her big tits and her vulnerability.

But Raven's not amused. She doesn't even look interested by it.

'Rightio, not funny,' I go as we turn onto Edward Street, 'I get it.'

If that'd been Dante telling the story, he'd have at least got a grin out of her.

'Hey, remember that Ursula chick we took to Toowong?' I go.

'Of course,' she says, because her and Jess were the ones who knew the kids somehow.

'She got a brother?'

'Bloody hell,' she laughs, looking at me sideways. 'Batting for the other team, now? Dante's really done a number on you this time, huh?'

'Piss off,' I say, shaking my head. 'What's his name, though?'

'Dick Fuckhorn,' she says. 'Nah, only joshing. It's Mick Buchhorn, but apparently the kids at school tease him all the time. He fucking hates it, Ursula says.'

At the lights next to the Embassy Hotel there's a couple getting a bit frisky. He's got his hand up her skirt and it's giving Raven and I an eyeful of her knickers and arse in the process. You little beauty!

'Geezus,' says Raven, rolling her eyes, making a point of looking away as if to suggest I should too.

The girl timidly giggles, which goads the bloke on. Clearly she's not into excessive PDA as much as him.

'Time and a place, huh?' I murmur to Raven, then realise with a wince that I've just paraphrased the little lecture the manager at The Big Block gave me earlier. Go figure.

The green man comes on and we start to walk across the road, but even though her boyfriend goes across with us the chick stays behind. I glance back and see she's standing next to the traffic pole looking white as a ghost.

'What's with her?'

Raven looks back and when she sees the chick's expression she stops in the middle of the road.

'Oi, Raven, lights are changing in a minute.'

She runs back to the chick, so I quickly follow, and just in time, too, because the lights change and the unforgiving traffic tears past.

The chick looks like she's in shock, and I'm wondering if she just got dumped the split second before her lad took off across the road.

'Are you okay, sweetie?' she says, and the chick looks at her and shakes her head in the negative. 'Is your boyfriend coming back?'

'I don't know who he is,' she goes, turning on the waterworks.

'Fuck,' whispers Raven to me, and starts to rub the chick's arm.

When the chick's tears turn to great racking sobs, Raven hugs her and starts cooing like a pigeon to soothe her. She's good at this sort of stuff, Raven is. I guess that's why she's studying Youth Affairs or whatever it is that she does at Uni, so that she can go into counselling and therapy and shit.

'Who was the bloke?' I ask.

'I don't know,' sobs the chick. 'He just started touching me.'

'That bastard,' I growl, feeling my blood pressure go up. 'So what were you giggling for?'

'Twix!' snaps Raven, frowning at me. 'Stop it. She was in shock. She still is.'

I know about that, how some people react to shock in different ways. Like, they'll laugh at the news of a death, or a divorce, or something terrible. But at the end of the day, it's about action, direct action. And for some arseholes, like the bloke that's done this to this poor girl, direct force is the only course of action.

'I'm goin after the bastard,' I announce, and Raven grits her teeth and gives me a look.

'Don't be stupid,' she says.

'Tell that to her,' I say, pointing at the chick.

'Tell her she's stupid?' says Raven, looking at me in horror.

'No, I mean tell her it's a stupid idea,' I say, but Raven just shakes her head at me like she still thinks I'm stupid. 'I'm serious, Raven. I'm gonna smash that prick! You stay here.'

The green man comes on again and I run across the road and down a couple of blocks, trying to work out where the arsehole would have gone. It's a bit of lost cause, though, since that was easily a few minutes ago and he could've gone anywhere by now.

Except he's not. I find him across from Festival Hall, just around the corner of Gilhooley's, laughing obnoxiously with a couple of other blokes. Probably about the assault. I've found the prick!

But what to do now? I'm tempted to go up and confront him, but the bastard obviously has more front than Myers and won't mind squaring off. That wouldn't normally be a problem, but there's about five of em now and I don't like my odds. In the end, when I think about it, all I'm trying to do here is fight other people's fights. At the end of the day, it's got nothing to do with me, when I think about it. I've had a shit day myself and just wanna get home.

I start heading back and bump into Raven coming my way.

'Where's the chick?' I go.

'She went home,' Raven says.

'What? On her own?'

'Don't give me that look,' snaps Raven. 'She said she was okay and wouldn't hear of putting me out when I said I'd give her a lift. I did what I could.'

'Yeah, well, I did what I could do, too,' I bluff, 'but I couldn't find the prick. Negative contact. Could be anywhere by now.'

'That's kind of good news, but,' Raven says. 'He could've been dangerous, Twix.'

'Sod off,' I scoff. 'I'd have taken the motherfucker down. If I see him around he'll be frigging sorry, that much is on the cards.'

Raven stops and smiles at me, like she's heard a familiar joke but still likes hearing it.

'Well, I still think it was a dumb idea to try and find him,' she says, 'but you're brave for sticking up for the girl like that.'

Too right it was brave!

Me and Raven laugh and jostle each other as we continue to head down towards the Uni, but as we pass the Irish pub I peek in and see the bloke and his mates roaring with laughter at something, and am just thankful that Raven doesn't notice them.

ABI AND THE WATER BOY

The ceiling fans go *whup whup whup* slowly. I got that from an ex of mine, that sound effect for fans that rotate slowly. Girls don't have the same fixation for describing things in sound effect as guys do.

Whup whup whup.

'Christ alive!' yells Henry, one of the oldies with a mild condition of Coprolalia. It could be worse: the other day he told a group of visiting student nurses that they had a 'fucking Dot Knot in yer lot,' humiliating both himself and the Indian girl in the group. Henry can't help it, though. He's been that way since a major stroke ten years ago.

The minister's totally not impressed, though. He briefly stops his bastardisation of the morning mass to give Henry a dirty look, then continues to put us all to sleep with his monotone liturgy.

No-one's paying any attention to him, least of all us AIN's, because the heat has sapped our concentration or because some of us have been on shift half the night, so it's a fucking great relief when he finally skips straight to the dismissal – or the closing prayer – and we can finally wake ourselves up again with some refreshments. He's meant to do communion and all that other stuff, but he stopped doing it long ago and even though the likes of old Margaret get edgy about its absence, we've all come to expect that his version of the Mass is going to be sparse. In place of the old Gawd-botherer performing communion, me and Trish already brought down from the kitchen some jugs of chilled water with lemon slices in them and some Sao biscuits, and we're mobbed as we pour out cups for the residents and give them a biscuit each.

The sweat rolls down my back and chest and soaks the waistband of my pants. A new air-conditioner would be well out of the question what with the Breakfast Creek View Aged Care's rising profit margins to think of. The one currently stuck in the wall gave up the ghost a couple of weeks before Chrissy after months of appropriately making a noise like someone being choked but who refuses to cark it. I'm coming to the end of my shift soon, having started at the witching hour last night, so it was blessedly cool for most of it, but Trish is stuck doing the pre-breakfast to post-lunch shift today and it'll probably be a stinker.

The minister is over chattin up Sandy and his eyes keep dropping to her tits, not that she seems to care. She probably figures as long as she doesn't have to wipe up any more drool or stop Gladys from raiding the cupboards and squirreling shit away into her orifices. I found half a box of rubber gloves up her moot last week.

'I need to use the toilet, Abigail' says Rose, holding onto my arm.

'You know where they are,' I nod in the direction of the loos.

They get co-dependent quickly, the residents, if you let them. It's better that they learn to do it for themselves, although the vegetables lined up against the corridor wall stuck in their wheelchairs couldn't do squat for themselves even if they had the will to. They just sit there in their bedsores and piss and shit in those gross adult nappies. Twenty bucks says I'm the one changing those afterwards. Last on shift usually has to.

'Here, Abi,' says Trish, passing me a video tape. 'Friday's episode.'

'Fuck yeah!'

We're both big fans of *Home & Away*, though where Trish genuinely likes the storylines I watch it mostly for taking the piss and for that Shane Parrish, who's a total fucking hunk if I say so myself! I know he's tanned and not alternative at all, but that smile and those abs more than make up for it. He's the ants pants! Because we're shift workers, it's inevitable that me or Trish are going to miss an episode here or there, so if one of us is off-duty when it comes on we tape it for each other.

Braddles watches our exchange with eager eyes, certain I've got something for the horny little bugger. He'd be right, but it's not this video tape, and he knows it.

'Did you get a Sao and a drink, Braddles?'

'Yep,' he smiles.

Bradley Carter, a permanent resident at the Breakfast Creek View Aged Care Hostel at only fifteen years old, the poor kid. He's in here because as a result of his schizophrenia he has something called Psychogenic Polydipsia, which basically means he's addicted to drinking water. He can't get enough of the stuff. It's not just schizophrenics it happens to, but of all the mental illnesses it affects them the most likely. About eighty percent of all people with Psychogenic Polydipsia are schizophrenics. Basically, if left alone near a running tap Braddles will drink himself to death, leaching the serum sodium from his body in such vast amounts that he'd die, probably from a heart attack.

He's staring at my waist. 'Have you got anything for me?'

Trish laughs. 'You little bugger! You need a girlfriend.'

'I already asked Abi but she said no,' he smirks playfully.

'Way to break a guy's heart,' says Trish to me, and winks at Braddles before she goes over to old Margaret who's been calling Trish's name out for the last five fucking minutes. That old bitch thinks the world revolves around her.

'Right, you,' I say to Braddles through my teeth, hugging him around his shoulders, 'rein it in for ten minutes, for Christ's sake, or you'll get me caught out.'

'Sorry,' he says sheepishly, taking a leaf out of the minister's book and trying to sneak a peek down my top.

I let him get his jollies out of it, it's the least I can do for the kid. He's stuck in this home for old people on death's door when he's actually a perfectly healthy teenage boy apart from the fucked up part of his schizo brain that wants to drown him. He's got all the urges and impulses of a growing boy, but instead he spends his days not only surrounded by all these whinging old fucks in here but the poor kid is usually confined to the lock-up ward, where we keep the extreme dementia cases. His mum died of cancer just over a year ago and his dad fell apart, and the rest of his family didn't want anything to do with a high-maintenance kid, so there was nowhere else for him to go. There're no facilities in place for a teenager that is fully functional but needs around the clock monitoring, so he ended up here. Child Services worked with Don and Marg, the owners, to safeguard the dementia ward against Brad's Psychogenic Polydipsia. They took off all the tap heads and replaced them with removable anti-vandal tap keys that are kept in the nurse's station, so that when we go in to shower anyone in the dementia ward we need to take the key with us. As part of the regular rounds of the lock-up ward we carry a bottle of water and a cup and push fluids, since we can't leave a jug of water in the ward where Braddles will get his hands on it.

Josh Baird – one of the registered nurses here and whom I've been seeing occasionally, when I'm not fucking Twix – comes in and looks peeved by us all standing around not tending to the oldies. Funny how the RN's don't have to stick around for these boring-arse church services in the activity's room.

Margaret immediately seizes her opportunity. 'It's too hot, Josh! The air-conditioner needs replacing.'

This in turn only serves Josh an opportunity of his own, namely to show off some tricks of the trade he's learnt over the years that some of us relative newbies might be impressed by. He makes us gather around and shows us how to help cool the oldies down by pressing Chux soaked in chilled water over the top of their ears. He reckons it cools their blood down quickly and makes them feel refreshed. Sandy tries it and the water's dribbling down Margaret's cheek, who starts whinging about it like Sandy's tried taking her head off or something.

Suddenly there's a loud bang and a *whoooof* sound, coming from outside. The oldies freak out, essentially thinking the world's about to end. We rush to the windows and in the fields across the road, near the abandoned gas ring, there's a car on fire. Black smoke is climbing from its smashed windows into the sky.

The oldies are really starting to shit themselves.

'What if we get attacked?' Margaret posits for absolutely no fucking reason at all except to start drama.

'Calm down, calm down,' says Josh, motioning for everyone to settle. 'Abi will sort it out, don't worry.'

'Me? What the fuck am I supposed to do about it? Run across the road with a hose?'

'The fire brigade, Abi,' Josh smirks, as if I'm a retard. 'And the police, while you're at it.'

If he thinks speaking to me like that is going to get him laid again anytime soon, he can think again.

The cops and the fireys both say they're on their way, and warn me to not let anyone go and investigate on their own. As if.

Maybe the car self-combusted in this infernal heat? One of the other AIN's says there's no water in those fields, but the trucks will have some to put the fire out at least. This segueways into tasteless jokes about how there's no water in part of the south wing of the facility.

'Speaking of which,' Josh says, interrupting, 'I believe you're still rostered on for lock-up this morning, Abi? Shift's not over yet.'

'Yeah, yeah, getting to it,' I say, giving him some cheek.

What he means is that I have to escort back our more difficult residents. Of course the poor things don't wanna go, it being the lock-up ward and all. The way they see it, all the fun happens out here. They're like little kids who have to go to bed early but think the adults party on once the coast is clear. If management would pay for the extra supervision they'd be able to stay out here no problem.

It's the same ward that Braddles stays in, although at the moment he, unlike the others, is pretty keen to get back there, on account of what I have for him. When he first arrived at the centre he was vomiting a lot but still pretty overweight from fluid retention because of his hyponatremia, and he had three seizures in the first few days. Scary shit. I can still remember those days clearly. We treated his hyponatremia, bizarrely enough, with a course of antidepressants. He's done us proud with his recovery, so I have a soft spot for him.

Trish reckons we're violating all sorts of human rights by even having a lock-up ward, but the owners insist it's the only way to cope with the level of attentiveness they need. Apparently, an AIN that used to work here, older lady called Janet and before my time, challenged this rule by saying we were understaffed for such high-maintenance care; next thing she knew there were official complaints about her conduct with the residents. Don, the co-owner of the BCVAC, told Janet there were a list of complaints so serious levelled at her that charges were probably going to be laid. Trish reckons Janet was so stressed by the whole thing her hair started falling out. They found fistfuls of it in the kitchen bin one day and eventually Janet resigned. The charges, as we all understand, were never followed up on. I doubt they ever existed.

I take Gladys by the hand and tell her in a loud voice that we're going for a walk. Most of the time she's *non-compos mentis* so over-explaining shit is not only a waste of time but confuses the crap out of her. Braddles walks beside me, and I ask him how his program's going.

'It's alright,' he shrugs. 'Mister Merriam thinks I'll be okay for less supervision soon.'

'Holy moly, Braddles! That's brilliant news!'

He's on a PSR program – which is psychosocial rehabilitation – with the RN's and Merriam, the visiting psychiatrist (who only comes around twice every week), undergoing both medication (risperidone mostly) and behavioural therapies (although Braddles reckons the psych catches up on his backlog of report writing rather than actually administering therapy). All in all, if he plays his cards right my mate Braddles here might be hitting the town in search of true love soon enough, if Merriam gives him a clean bill of health in time. Christ knows the kid deserves some good stuff in his life. In the meantime, he's got me. I try and give him a break from all this stuffy shit and sneak the odd joint to him as long as he smokes when I'm on shift monitoring him on walks around the gardens. I also bring him other goodies, such as what he's keen to get his hands on right now, the horny little bugger.

He tugs at my coat as I'm guiding Gladys through the security door into the dementia ward.

'Get out of it, you bugger,' I say, slapping his hand away.

Once we're safe inside the ward and it's just us and the walking braindead, I yank the rolled up porno mag from my waistband and toss it at him. 'There ya go, Mister Eager Beaver.'

'Eager for beaver, more like,' he quips, flipping through the glossy pages like he's doing an inventory check of the girls featured within.

One of the behavioural therapies we use with Braddles is called a token economy, where we basically reinforce his management of his condition with rewards, such as longer walks in the garden and such. Giving him porno mags is essentially following that treatment, as far as I'm concerned, although it'd cost me my job if anyone found out.

'Make sure you hide it under all your socks and jocks,' I remind him.

'Don't worry, they won't find it,' he says, priding himself on his stealth.

I can't believe that the selfish pricks who run this place, and the likes of Merriam who's an idiot in my professional opinion, have never bothered to address the sexual needs of a teenage boy cooped up twenty-four seven in a cell with a bunch of old farts who've probably long forgotten sex even exists. If it didn't feel like cradle-snatching I'd probably be inclined to throw the kid a freebie out of pity. Knowing my luck, he'd be too excited about it to keep his trap shut and would blab to one of the other AIN's. They'd be quick to snitch, no fucking buts about it.

It can be a tightrope act working here, because even though the residents try and pull a fast one and get as us to do more than we need to for them, at the same time we're meant to be here to assist in providing a quality care of lifestyle for them. The trick is not to get precious about it, even when they whinge that they don't like your attitude. Gardens don't grow without shit, so they gotta learn to take the good with the rough and accept that that's life, and that we're not their fucking slaves jumping to every whim they get into their stupid old heads.

They're lucky, to be honest, because there's a lot worse out there. My sister relies heavily on the community health services system to combat her mental illness and addictions, getting methadone treatment at the Binkinba Drop-In Centre in New Farm. But the longer she stays in the system the more addictions she seems to accumulate, hooking up with a bad crowd and getting worse and worse. She's not kept in a hostel like these old biddies, but she'd be better off if she was. Instead she floats through the system, exploiting it and conversely being failed by it, changing psychiatrists as regular as some people change their underwear.

Our parents have given up hope on seeing her again anytime soon. It used to break their hearts when she'd visit with dilated pupils and mumbling incoherently, and they knew her veins were full of smack. I've washed my fucking hands of her. She was meant to be my big sister, someone to look up to, but I noticed the dried vomit stains on the hem of her dress one time and was just repulsed by her.

Nowadays I won't have a bar of her, although that's mostly due to the company she keeps. Junkies and thieves. It's funny how I won't have anything to do with my sister who in her own right is suffering, but I'll risk my job to help this boy, of absolutely no relation, to have a tug. The difference, I suppose, is I'm getting paid to give a flying fuck here.

'Leave you to it then, Braddles,' I say. 'Shift's finishing now. See you tomorrow, kiddo.'

Poor kid now has to spend the next few hours alone before lunchtime, his door shut against the wanderers, and later tonight against the sundowners. At least he's got fresh reading material.

I hate ending a night shift after the sun has risen. It feels like leaving a nightclub on daybreak or getting stuck at a train station when everyone's going to work or the markets or some shit, and we're all just sitting there bleary eyed and wrecked.

Down on the main road I can see across to the grasslands next to the river and notice that the burning car still hasn't been doused. The flames seem to have burnt themselves out, at least. Black smoke still belches into the air, though, twisting through the girders of the old gasring. Where the fuck are the fireys and the cops, then? I called them maybe an hour ago. I can just imagine Margaret and Rose sitting at a window and giving Trish and Sandy grief about the smoke, the old battleaxes. Gives me a good giggle.

DANTE AND THE KOALAS

I've been sleeping at a couple of different mate's places, mostly at Maddie's and then at Twix's, but I've overstayed my welcome at both and been asked as politely as possible to consider moving on. Maddie's got a lot on her plate and is trying to set up her spare rooms to support refugee families in need of emergency housing, and I hardly count as either a refugee or in need of emergency housing, so I totally understand her position. As for Twix, I think he's mostly jealous about me going home with that Julie girl the other night. He gets like that. Thing is, I didn't go home with her. We were no sooner in the taxi than we'd started arguing about who was going to pay for it, so I jumped out at the next set of lights and have been sleeping in the garden beds again since.

All in all, it's good of my mates to have accommodated me in the first place, but eventually having a non-paying tenant must get tiresome. The median income for the average Australian is roughly six-hundred bucks a week, and while I can't fathom having that kind of cash on a weekly basis a breakdown of their expenses proves that I'm nothing but a freeloader beyond a week's stay.

But I'm also a bit crap at securing anything long-term as far as a permanent residence of abode goes, and it's simply easier to fall back on my go-to plan of roughing it on the streets. I have a love-hate affair with the city, so being away from it for a certain amount of time only serves to recharge my yearning for it again.

This time of the year it's really no bother to sleep in the open, and normally I'd make my bed in King George Square over in the corner garden bed against the stairwell that leads up to the Presbyterian Church. I'm the only one I know that actually sleeps in the square; come midnight or about one in the morning and everyone else shuffles off to bunk somewhere less public. But this spot used to be great in winter because there's an exhaust fan for the underground carpark that would blow warm air during the colder months, and between that and the spindly trees above not even a light rain would touch me. Nowadays it's cold air year round, so I've taken to bunking down behind the wall behind the Uniting Church across the road – or the Gingerbread Church as I like to call it, on account of the red brick and white trimmings make it look like one. There's a stack of tables folded one on top of the other in storage around back, and it's dark, dry and safe under there. The low concrete wall deters any drunken cunts from the nightclubs from wandering in for a piss.

Speaking of churches, Mary the nun has wandered into the square to feed the pigeons, and she comes over to us and asks a couple of us how things are, wishing us well. The street kids still in their mid teens or younger gather around her and jostle to be closest. She reminds me of old drawings of saints when they do this.

Mary's elderly, and tiny, with a hump between her shoulders that pushes her head forward like a creature from *The Dark Crystal*. She's not really a nun, she just dresses like one in soft pastels with wrinkled stockings and a modern-style habit. We always greet her warmly, kinda like she's our surrogate grandmother. I'm not sure what she thinks of us. Maybe we're like her untouchables to her Mother Teresa, who I've also heard isn't a real nun.

And her name isn't really Mary, either. I just call her that after the Virgin of the Bible, because I'm sure that as a nun Mary here has never had a root. I could be wrong, of course, especially since she's hasn't actually taken the habit for real. Alex reckons nun's costumes are popular in the S&M scene. I try and imagine this bent over little old lady writhing on a stage as she slowly peels her habit off, and dismiss the thought as too crass even for me.

As for the nun's outfit she wears, it's said that the convents and churches are well aware of Mary and her attire, and leave her alone. As the cunts well should, too. She's not hurting anyone. And she's become something of a fixture to the local landscape, as everyone in the city knows of her, not just us homeless folk. I don't think I've spent enough hours of the day in the city if I haven't seen Mary at least once, usually zipping through the Mall on her little legs or here in the square feeding the pigeons.

She never preaches or anything either, unlike that crazy Asian lady in West End who carries the huge wooden cross around on her fucking back like she was Jesus Christ or something. I first ran into her at a photocopy shop there on Boundary Street where she was spending a small fortune on printing these little bible tracts she had cut and pasted herself, and which she handed out to people on the street. If she thrust one at you, you took it; otherwise she'd scream and get abusive.

Mary never does any of that, she just enjoys the crowds and is pleasant to talk to.

'God bless ya, darl,' says Old Graham through his gappy smile where his teeth fell out or were knocked out in his youth. He was wild as a younger man then, having joined a band of carnies as a performer after he got back from the Vietnam War. He's travelled Melbourne to Darwin and back again plenty of times, he reckons. He's also not that old, only in his forties, but his hair and beard went white ages ago so he looks old.

'You, too, Grae,' says Mary, patting his big, scaly hands. She turns to the rest of us and with a wink says: 'Happy hunting.'

We all crack up, even though she tells this joke every time. I guess it's just polite to. She wanders over to have a chat with the insecurity guards in the Town Hall, which she also does every time she comes here, and some of the younger street kids trail after her for company. *Happy hunting* refers to the task of trying to swindle a few dollars out of pedestrians as they pass by. We'd never hit Mary up for money, though. We've got boundaries.

And those boundaries are sometimes what keeps us from tipping over into complete madness, as I found out one night about a month ago.

Some of the others here in the Square stay at squats down the back of the Valley or over at West End, abandoned buildings that have long been places for the homeless to crash in. I stayed at the West End once for a couple of days. As with all places where humans gather together for too long, politics and territories develop and an unspoken law settles in between the longer-staying tenants which can develop into real problems. Like the alcove at the West End squat where Dirty Bill stays.

That part of the shelter is a scorched mess. The timber is half-burnt and the night wind whistles through a massive charred hole in the wall. It used to be a cosy spot until Dirty Bill found some blow-in sleeping there one night so he set fire to the mattress. The trespasser made a run for it with their duffle bag on fire, and the rest of us tried to beat out the flames before the entire place burned to the fucking ground. Bill didn't help; he went after his intruder, chasing the cunt off to make sure he didn't come back. We got the fire under control but no-one has since bothered to try and repair the damage done. Maybe come winter they'll have no fucking choice.

Either way, I won't return there. Some of these other bastards have the right idea by finding several spots around the city and alternating between them. So I have my garden bed in King George Square, under the tables behind the Uniting Church, and the bamboo thicket near the front gates of the Botanic Gardens. There's very few homeless people down in the gardens, surprisingly, with just a few transients opting for the ridiculously uncomfortable park benches or the hard stage of the aptly-named Riverstage auditorium down beside the Gardens Point Uni.

The kids have come back now that Mary's wandered back over to the Queen Street Mall. One of them has nicked a large decorative bauble from the thirty-five foot high Christmas tree still standing in front of the Town Hall doors, even though it's now January.

One of the older guys called Johnnie, who has started selling some magazine called *The Big Issue* right on the very street corner itself, is telling us how the tradition of the Christmas tree started in 1954.

'For the Royal Tour,' he insists. 'They put it up, but it was a real tree then. I remember we came to see it, my father and me. Was a road back then in front of the Hall, and they put the tree there in a hole. My father would grab us a coupla Downyflake Donuts and we'd sit and watch the lights on the tree.'

The kids jibe the old timer, making fun of his tales until I kick one of them hard fair up the arse to shoo em away, because I like hearing Johnnie's stories.

'Fuck off, Dante,' the brat curses as he dances away rubbing his bum. 'I'll fuck you up.'

There's no need for further retaliation from me. The little shits know I'll flip out on them if they try anything. They're all well aware I walk around armed with a knife.

'More hide than Jessie,' grumbles Johnnie, waving a rolled up copy of one of his little magazines in the air. 'I get my hands on them I'll give em the rough end o' the pineapple.'

'No need,' I tell him. 'They fucking know to stay clear for a bit.'

'Little mongrels,' mutters Old Graham absently, stroking his beard over and over again for want of something to do with his hands.

Being homeless is often about waiting: waiting for the next dole check, waiting for the street missionary food truck to come around, waiting for the weather to get better, waiting for the day to end, or to begin, waiting for something to happen. If it wasn't for the books I steal to read I'd go fucking mad, but for others there's the hustle for money or the rants about God that make up their days. Religion plays a big part in the lives of many homeless people for precisely two reasons: they need to believe that there's salvation for them, because that's all they've got left to look forward to, and because religion is a fucking great tool for leverage when you need to guilt someone into handing over their cash.

I've seen it a hundred fucking times. Right now, Micko is trying it on. He's this Aboriginal guy who sleeps over in the parks along Roma Street, near the transit centre, usually under the lip of the water fountain.

'You're an artist?' he asks this guy who looks only a couple of years younger than me. Micko's going for the empathy angle on this mark, a card he played on me when I first met him and he didn't know I was sleeping on the streets.

'Yeah, mostly oils on timber, portrait stuff of interesting characters I meet,' this sucker is going on while Micko nods enthusiastically.

'I used to be an artist,' Micko interrupts, cutting the poor cunts verbal diarrhoea about how he has applied to get into Griffith doing an arts degree. 'Up Darwin way, ay? You woulda liked my stuff.'

'Oh, really?' goes this art kid, looking lost for thought. I can tell he thought the conversation might centre solely on him. But Micko's just warming up.

'I painted alla time, in the morning *and* in the night. You know? But my little girl died. One minute she was okay, completely fine, and the next–' Micko snaps his fingers for emphasis, '–gone! Just like that, the Lord took her away. One minute I'm a daddy, next... nope.' Micko shakes his head sadly. I'm convinced he'd produce tears at this point in the story if he could, and perhaps if he'd ever really had a daughter and she had indeed died then perhaps he'd be able to summon a flood of salty outpourings that would melt the hardest of hearts. But hanging is head and looking forlorn is all he can muster.

'That's... oh my god, that's terrible,' stammers the mark.

'You bet,' says Micko sadly. 'But it's okay, coz God found me. He found me all wrecked and stuff, and he brung me back from where I was, which was in a dark place.'

That part was true, I believe. For whatever reasons, Micko did in fact find himself in a dark place in Darwin, apparently. From the fragments I've gleaned from his stories, it seems that he was married but it fell apart and she went back to live with her people, on tribal land, and Micko couldn't follow for reasons I confess I do not understand. I think it made Micko suicidal until the missionaries found him and introduced him to that omnipresent yet elusive bearded fellow in the sky.

Micko's spinning more of his tale, as far removed now from the artist origins that began it as it is from the truth, and he's leading up to the all-important part of his pitch.

'So I gave her the last of my dough,' Micko tells the art kid, describing how he'd met a young girl down on her luck and he'd parted with the remainder of his dole money just to see her through hard times. 'And that's left me out of luck, innit? And brother, as hungry as I am, I know that God looks after even the birds. The little birds, even, like me.'

I always have to look away at this point because I get the biggest shit-eating grin on my mug. The way that Micko half-pleads this last line as though it were reverent, mangling the biblical verse but retaining its meaning at the same time always cracks me up.

The art kid is more than wary by this stage. He's clocked the trap that has been laid, is eager to move on and leave Micko and his tales behind, and yet there's the doubt in his eyes. He can't trust that Micko isn't bullshitting him, knows he'll regret it if he doesn't reach for his wallet and walks away instead, only to come to the shameful realisation later that Micko was actually being earnestly truthful and is now starving in the night somewhere while the art cunt gets to sup on warm soup and croutons and follow it up with a glass of moderately-but-not-overly-priced wine with his wanky art mates. It'll be killing him right now, the dilemma.

'May God bless your days for your generosity,' wheedles Micko before the deal is even done, practically informing his mark that there's no choice now but to hand over some money.

The art kid pulls his wallet out and fishes in for a coin, and the rest of us act as nonchalantly as possible while we scope out the cunt's cash situation. Old Graham says back in his carny days they called this 'Peek his Poke'. I see a flash of blue plastic poking out, a ten dollar note for sure. Maybe one of the others can try their luck further along with the kid, but this sort of hustling isn't my thing. I've never been into spinning a sob story to tease a few dollars out of some sucker. Hang in long enough and the universe invariably presents other, more lucrative options. That's Providence.

Micko gets his two dollars and the art kid goes on his way, walking briskly toward the pedestrian crossing down next to the Town hall rather than pass the rest of us toward the crossing that goes over to the church, which is the one he was headed to originally. Going the way he's chosen will take him just slightly longer to get up Roma Street, and one of the other guys hanging out here, a shifty cunt called Wheezer or Wiser or something I've never quite caught on account of I don't like him, makes a dash along Albert Street to cross over Turbot and cut the art kid off somewhere before the Transit Centre. That's what happens when you present yourself as an easy target, arseholes like Whizzer or whatever he calls himself will swoop.

Here comes the competition. Cunts dressed up as koalas, rattling buckets to collect donations for some animal welfare charity. They've made their way slowly from the fountain over on the Adelaide Street side across to our side of the square, showing blatant disregard for any code of begging ethics and scaring off our marks, though our marks are mostly giving us a wider berth on account of we're arcing up at the intrusion from the koalas.

But the coin-collectors are unperturbed by our heckling, and the little shits are back, too, a latent childlike whimsy enticing them to follow the costumed characters around.

'Can I put it on?' says one of the street kids, tugging at the sleeve of the costume.

What compels these cunts to volunteer in this heat inside a second-rate bear costume waving around a plastic bucket and copping a whole heap of abuse for it is beyond my comprehension. Can't be money, as it's a volunteer-based enterprise.

'We do it for the animals,' one of them says haughtily when I deign to ask, its face collapsed in a fall of fur and weak stuffing. There's black mesh over its nose, and the guy's voice comes from that.

'Only the animals benefit from this,' chimes in the other koala, with matching disfigured face. This one is definitely a girl; she has a squeaky voice that almost sounds put on as if she was a cartoon character. I imagine the two of them fucking, doing it koala-style. They'd probably get people throwing heaps of money into the buckets if they put on that sort of show right here in the square.

So she reckons only the animals benefit from this? She's pretty much spot on there: the animals that sit back in their offices reaping the rewards from these dumb cunts' efforts, passing their crimes off as administration fees. The furry little critters in the forests see fuck all result from this fundraising. These cunts in the koala suits must be more touched in the head than I am.

Someone, a young guy called James I think, kicks the bucket from one of the koalas' hand and it rattles across the ground, spilling coins everywhere. The street kids swoop on it, snatching em up. The cunt in the koala suit is forced to rip his hood off and dive after the coins. His hair is plastered to his scalp with sweat, his face wet and pink with heat exhaustion.

It's said of the hundred thousand homeless people in the Land of Oz right now, over thirteen thousand of those are school-aged. And because of this sorry state of affairs in their living arrangements, most of em opt out of school altogether. There's been talk of a Government-initiated program worth millions to, and I quote, 'facilitate a support network that enables youth who are presently homeless or at risk of homelessness to utilise assistance and services' blah fucking blah blah. The poor bastards are hungry for nourishment or memory-numbing drink right now, not feasibility studies into facilitations of a bureaucratic nightmare of legalise and money-guzzling Government departments. If that bucket hadn't spilled its contents so easily, it's easy to assume one of these kids could easily knife these dopey cunts in the koala costumes to relinquish them of their booty, that's how desperate they are.

'GET OFF!' shrieks the guy trying to push the kids off the money.

'Oi!' yells Micko from his perch on the park-bench. 'Leave the kids alone!'

Old Johnnie gets a chuckle from the spectacle.

The girl has pulled her hood off now and is beseeching the rest of us to help stop the street kids.

'Control them,' she begs. 'Make them give it back!'

The insecurity guards from the Town Hall are wandering over for a look, so Micko gives a little whistle between his teeth to get the attention of the kids, who snap their heads up eerily as one unit, like a pack of wild dogs, and seeing the guards approaching make one last grab at as many coins as they can before bolting up the stairs behind us and disappearing.

The insecurity guys take their time reaching us, but they don't help the poor cunts with their buckets or coins, choosing instead to stand in the shade beside us and ask Micko what happened.

'I think the heat got to these two,' Micko says, shaking his head slowly. 'They just fell over all of a sudden and lost their money.'

'Yeah,' agrees one of the guards in a lazy tone, 'it's what we thought mighta happened.'

Johnnie sniggers and rubs his jowls to relieve his dry mouth.

We all sit around and watch as the wildlife volunteers collect up their coins, casting us and the insecurity guys bruised looks, before snatching up their koala hoods off the hot concrete and storming away.

We just laugh and laugh and laugh.

ABI AND TWIX

If I lie still the pounding in my head isn't so bad, but my throat is dry as fuck and I can feel my whole system crying out for rehydration. I shouldn't have mixed my drinks last night.

I always keep a glass of water on the shelf beside my bed. The ceramic plate that doubles as an ashtray is spilling over. I lean up on one elbow and carefully drain the glass dry. The water feels like it's spreading into my limbs and up into my head, ballooning me out to normal size again. It's no sooner down the gullet than I desperately want more, but that would require getting out of bed so I slump back onto my pillow and suffer in silence.

The morning light is peeping through the slats and beaming across my room like a laser from a sci-fi movie. It lands on Twix's calves and makes his pale skin look golden. The bed-sheets are crumpled on the floor. It's too hot for them anyway.

Twix is a fuck-friend, and more *that* than he is a friend. On a couple of occasions I've been horny enough to hook up with him, and he's not bad in bed which helps. Of course, it's between him and me and no-one else needs to know, not least of all because we started doing it when he was still with Karen.

One of the oldies at work, Mrs Francine Sullivan, died this week. Not while I was on shift, thank Gawd, but it still hit me hard because I really liked her. Francine was always so sweet, never complained, bless her, which is as rare as hen's teeth in the aged care industry. She always commented, without fail, on the size of my forehead. I normally hate people making any sort of reference to just how wide it is, which is partly because my hairline is naturally receded, but Francine was always so nice about it, saying that it was a sign of high intellect. I know that's not true, of course, but she used to be a midwife when she was my age and it's what they believed back then.

When I'd gotten in for my next shift and Sandy'd told me that Francine had passed away, I wasn't sure I'd get through the day without bursting into tears so I'd swiped some temazepams from the drug cabinet. If that's what it takes to get the job done, I'm probably better off finding another job. I might start looking around this week, see what's going.

So I'd needed a good fuck, that's all. It did the trick, got my endorphins running again, relaxed the tension throbbing in my skull.

Twix is snuggled against me, caressing my tits.

'Twixxie's boobies,' he purrs.

'They're mine, not yours,' I say flatly. 'Besides, I thought you liked big tits?'

He pouts playfully.

'I do, *au naturel*,' he says, convinced he's got his French down pat, the idiot. 'But they're mine the same way my tockley is yours.'

'Nuh-uh,' I reproach him, shaking my head. 'I like being a girl, thanks very much.'

'You know what I mean.'

'Unfortunately I do,' I say a little harsher than I'd meant to.

He looks hurt, pouting for real now, though probably putting it on more than is necessary, knowing him.

Guys like to possess a girl. Why do they need to do that? It fucks everything up. When he says my boobs are his, he means he owns me and I'm not for other blokes. It pisses me off so much that I want to go out and fuck a shit-load of other men just to prove his claim as the falsehood it honestly is. But I refuse to fall into that fucked up trap.

'I'm not yours, and you're not mine,' I lecture him. 'We fuck each other occasionally. That's it. No buts about it.'

I'm in a bad mood now, thanks to his needy bullshit. Maybe I should think about finding a new fuck-friend if he's going to start acting like this?

'I need to do a load of washing while the sun's out,' I say, getting out of the bed and deliberately facing away while I pull a shirt down to cover my tits.

'Oh, okay,' he says softly. 'Nice panties,' he adds, trying to be cute, hoping his pathetic compliment would get me in the mood again. It's a massive fail because the word *panties* makes me cringe. It makes me think of kiddie's underwear. The word was first used as part of advertising for a doll a hundred years ago. Why would that flatter me?

'Okay, go now.'

'Give us a smile first?' he says, still trying to act cute like he's the fucking ant's pants.

Fucking hell. Blokes are all studs and fuck knows what else to get you into bed, but then when they've blown their load they're either outta here or they hang around desperately yearning for emotional validation. I force a smile at him just to convince him there's no need to linger and make up for trespasses. It satisfies him, thank Gawd, and I make my way through to the bathroom to collect my laundry since I don't need to see him naked any more than I already have.

But through the gap in the door I can see he's dawdling, as usual. Last time I'd been forced to make him leave by confessing that he has a stupid cum face, which he does. I notice he's since tried rectifying that, with little success. If anything, his new cum face is even more absurd than the last one.

He finally starts getting dressed, thank fuck.

'I bid you adieu, Big Red,' he shouts.

I fly back into the bedroom, dropping the wash-basket and shouting: 'WHAT THE FUCK DID YOU JUST CALL ME?'

He looks terrified, freezing in the act of pulling his stovepipes on. I swear his dick actually shrivels under the influence of my temper.

'What the fuck did you just call me, Twix?' I demand again.

He's reluctant to repeat it but finally admits he called me 'Big Red', the childhood nickname that I've tried for years to forget and thought would never have to hear again.

'Roz told me it's your nickname from primary school,' he simpers.

My fucking sister! The bitch.

'I suppose she's told the whole fucking Palace?' I snarl.

He shrugs as if he doesn't know, but I can tell by the fear in his eyes that she has.

Fucking marvellous.

'It's not my nickname, never was and never will be,' I tell him. 'So get the fuck out of here. NOW.'

He yanks his clothes on as fast as he can, apologising ad nauseam.

'Sorry again, Abi,' he says meekly, buckling up his roachcrushers, 'I'll be off on my walk of shame now.'

Walk of Shame... why's it shameful for women to be caught traipsing home after a one-night stand but for a guy they just strut home like they're top shit? Sure enough, there's no sense of shame about Twix's skips when I peek out the window to make sure he's finally pissed off. He's strutting like he wants the world to know he's scored. Well, same here; I refuse to think of it as the Walk of Shame whenever I leave a guy's house the morning after. Everyone can just deal with it.

I lean back on the kitchen sink and pop the second temazepam I'd nicked, and stare out the window, lulled into daydreaming by the hum of the washing machine cycle and the drum-beat of a hangover pounding inside my head.

Francine once told me about how she was courted in her youth, back in the late 1920s, and how even then she thought many men were pigs. But she reckoned that the entire world was changing for women. The suffragettes had secured actual voting for women in Queensland when Francine was a small girl, and by the time she was a bit younger than I am now she was a proud voter and giving 'the boys a run for their money' while she was at it. She was always going on about how as a woman I need to make sure I get out and vote for change. I'd never bothered to before, but eventually I'd felt bolstered by her passion and jumped onto the Electoral Roll. I couldn't have been fucked voting when the elections came around and was instantly fined, so since then I've made sure I go and vote, and I tell everyone that it's Francine that inspired me, even though it's because I'm trying to avoid getting fined again.

She dated a lot, too. She said it was the done thing by the time she was twenty-one, although it was far chaster than the casual hooks-up we have now. *The Jazz Age* they were calling it in America, and the world was poised for fun times. Francine's eyes would light up when she spoke about those days, and she spoke about them a lot because she remembered them with greater clarity than she did the last sixty or so years of her life. That happens with some of the oldies: they struggle to recall their youths while they raise their own kids, and it's all they can remember when they're facing death's door.

And now she's gone to the great beyond, where all is dark and silent.

A fly buzzes against the window-sill, sounding really loud. I focus on the noise it makes, and then slowly realise that the flat is terminally silent, as though I myself had died and was in some twilight limbo where only the sound of a fly can penetrate.

The washing machine has stopped, that's why. How fucking long have I been standing at the sink staring at nothing?

As I hang the washing out on the line, I think about a story I read in the Sydney Herald yesterday about an old lady who was admitted into a hospice for a couple of months as respite but that within a couple of weeks she was drugged to the fucking eyeballs and showed signs of having been abused. It makes me physically ill to think about. I'd never hurt any of the oldies, even the ones that get on my fucking tits all the time. They're stuck in there, I'm not. I can walk away at any time.

But I'm trying to recall if Francine ever had any suspicious bruising, and I can't for the life of me decide whether the ones I saw were from falls or not. I don't know why I'm dwelling on this. She's dead and buried, at the end of the day.

I feel fucked; my brain feels like it's full of cotton wool.

I need to lie down again. Whatever good came of last night has evaporated and my hangover shows no sign of abating. I don't even have any alcohol in the flat for hair of the dog, either.

What would Francine say of my predicament, I wonder? I see her wrinkled, kindly face against my closed eyelids, and imagine her approving of all the excessive drinking and casual sex and living on my own as an independent woman.

I go back inside and stand at the kitchen sink, draining a glass of water, then follow it up with a second one.

Despite the hangover, and the sex, I still feel unfulfilled. Not like I'm feeling hollow inside or anything, but sexually. I make like the Yellow Pages and let my fingers do the walking, slipping them down between my thighs to jill myself off as I watch the neighbour feeding his chickens.

BUT FUCK, MY HEAD REALLY HURTS RIGHT NOW.

THE ROOFTOP SHOW

When I was a kid I'd always explore wherever we lived. We moved around a lot, pretty much a different school every year. Sometimes two a year. And every place, be it metropolitan or small town, got a good going over in my explorations. I'd traipse not only the streets but also the paddocks and forests surrounding whatever town we were calling home, mapping the area in my mind and noting peculiar landmarks.

I'm no different in the city as an adult. Vehicle access to basements, doorways left ajar, lifts that go up into the guts of hotels... I explore them all. Alleyways are my favourite, though. There's something about them, usually a silence and emptiness, a world removed from the hubbub of daily activity and technologies but a mere few metres away sometimes.

Telstra announced today that it was launching something called Australia Day on-line, where people can use their computers and connect onto the internet and do whatever the fuck it is people do on that thing. I don't know anyone who has used it yet, but then again I don't know anyone with a computer, either. But Telstra seem hell-bent on making sure the Land of Oz gets involved in it. The public phone booths now have the new name *Telstra* written on them, too, but me and heaps of people I know still call it Telecom because the name was only changed about six months ago and it takes some getting used to when you've spent two whole decades referring to it by another name.

That's why I love these alleys. They're a time-capsule, happy to allow me to look into the past instead of headlong into the future. I can stand in them and see the exposed rear sides of the edifices that reach to the skies, can chart their histories by aid of paint or bricked up windows or somesuch.

There're usually stairwells that snake up the walls and lead to strange doorways, access points to buildings either rarely used or entirely forgotten. There's one such example halfway up Burnett Lane, right in the city centre. Tucked away between the modern skyscrapers is a smaller and older building with peaked roofs, and there's an old wooden staircase that winds up the back of it like a broken thing. It doesn't necessarily lead to anywhere, or at least it doesn't anymore. But there's a door right at the top of the building, a couple of metres below the last step. Someone has since bridged the gap with a haphazard set of planks and rope, and I once tried to make the crossing and decided to abort my attempt. There used to be a nightclub for electronic music up there somewhere called The Sex Club which I've heard had great views of the city at night.

That's when the city's at its most impressive – the night-time – mostly I think because the array of lights creates an illusion of depth and relation between one building and the next that I don't perceive during the day. It's at night that I like to wander around before I head home, if I've come into the city to hang out or do some specialised five-finger discounting. It's also when the city pretty much empties of people, so that plays a huge factor in my attraction to the afterhours. I fucking detest people for the most part.

On Elizabeth Street I pass a tiny alley that is seldom accessible, simply because there's normally a roller-door shutting it off to the street. It's next to where Kent Records used to be before they moved up past Edward Street more. The space is only big enough for a car, and there's bins and bags of rubbish stacked at the far end. So it's essentially a garage. It's an impressive little space, rough brick walls on three sides and an opening in the ceiling at the back where the lights of the five storey Invicta House that looms over the garage.

And there's a small, fixed metal ladder going into the roof. There's voices coming from up there so I climb up for a look-see, and up on a split-level roof behind the garage space are some punks smoking against the wall of Invicta House.

'Who the fuck's there?' demands one, shooting to his feet.

'I'm on a mission from God,' I declare, rephrasing a quote from *The Blues Brothers*.

'Fuck off, ya bible-thumper,' goes the punk, tugging his tartans higher.

There's four of em all up. Well, three punks and this big Japanese-looking metalhead with a scraggly black beard and long black hair. He's probably the one I'm most worried about.

So I go: 'Can I interest any of you in a lifetime subscription to the *Watchtower*?'

This makes the big metalhead crack up, which pretty much ruins any further attempt by the others to chase me away.

I use the opportunity of the dispelled hostilities to take in the view. Elizabeth runs down to our left toward the Myer Centre, but the brick mass of Invicta prevents us from getting a view of the other end that heads towards Eagle Street Pier. Across from us is the old red-brick Embassy Hotel and next to it the soaring modernity of the Hilton, which is less than a decade old. It'd be a great spot to camp out every night up here, if that roller-door down below wasn't usually closed.

I notice the smoke wafting from their durries isn't nicotine.

'I gotta head back soon, guys,' goes the big metal guy.

'Nah nah, wait Riz,' urges one of the punks, in a DK singlet. 'Here he comes.'

They all clamber down around me at the edge of the roof.

'There he is!' the DK punk sniggers, pointing at an old cunt on the street below, arm in arm with a twenty-something blonde who looks roughly half his age.

Riz, the metal guy, stacks some cardboard at his feet and goes: 'Every Saturday night, without fail, this dude picks up a girl at a club.'

The cunt in question ambles from the direction of Eagle Street Pier and into the Embassy, grinning like a shot fox over his shoulder at us. The girl doesn't even notice us.

'You see her, Scab?' says the punk with the mohawk to the one with the tartan dacks who called me a bible-thumper. 'No wonder he took so long tonight. She looks high-maintenance.'

'He better fuckin hurry,' says Riz. 'My break's ending soon.'

'Calm down, you only work right across the street,' teases mohawk.

Scab passes him the joint, and when he's had a toke Riz passes it to me. The others don't object, so I accept. I don't normally do joints, and the dope creates a kicking cough deep in my chest that takes me a bit to snort out.

'First time's rough,' Scab mocks, taking the joint from me.

'I'll let you know if it hurts,' I retort.

The other punks let out *ooohs* and slap Scab on the back, telling him he's got a sarcasm rival at last. Scab takes it in his stride, giving me a lopsided smirk, but there's a warning in his eyes nonetheless. As if I could give a fuck.

'Don't do that, man,' Riz scolds the punk in the Kennedy's singlet, who's taken a blade to the mortar between the bricks of the Invicta. 'Fucking respect it, Chris.'

Chris the punk laughs. 'Respect it? The fuck you on about, Riz?'

But Scab can see that the big metal guy is for real, so he takes the knife off Chris and pockets it.

'What the fuck?' goes Chris, pissed off.

'Nah, man, not that building,' says Riz, looking unhappy about having to raise the issue. 'Just leave that one.'

'Whatever,' says Chris, going over and dropping spit-bombs over the edge of the roof instead.

'What's it about that building?' I ask Riz, unable to contain my curiosity. The city's mysteries are mine to crack.

He considers me for a brief moment before opening up, telling me about how Invicta House had problems first getting built, that it took ages. There was a deaf veteran from Gallipoli who got hired to work on it, but there were all sorts of union disputes around the building.

'The poor bastard just wanted to work so he could support his wife,' explains Riz. Scab is listening in to the story by now, too. 'But the union wanted him fired because he was non-union labour, so he tried to join the union but they wouldn't allow him. He was stuck between a rock and a hard place, and the whole time this building sat unfinished.'

'But why's that so important to ya?' asks Scab.

'My grandfather migrated to the States from the Philippines in the 1920s,' he reveals.

'Oh, you're Filipino?' I go. 'I thought you were Japanese, like some kind of warrior.' I run my fingers off my chin to indicate the beard and he chuckles.

'Nah man, not Japanese. But I'm part white, too, because my grandfather eventually married an American lady and that's how my mum was born. But it was fucked, because Filipinos weren't allowed to marry in California and my grandparents had to drive interstate, you know? This was during the Depression era, so money was tight, but they did it anyway. He got whatever work he could get to make it happen, but the locals hated migrants, saying they lowered the standard of living. Fuck man, shops even put up signs saying shit like NO DOGS ALLOWED, which meant Filipinos. My grandmother told me about it before she died, but it's funny because my grandfather never mentioned any of that stuff. He just told us how life was better in America and it saved our whole family from poverty. But there were arseholes who tried to stop that, you know?'

Me and Scab nod. The comparisons between the deaf veteran that the unions tried to inhibit and Riz's grandfather are vague at best, but I get it. Riz backs the underdog, an Aussie sentiment if ever there was one.

'Chris can have his knife back when we're done up here,' Scab announces in a kinda valiant way, which makes him look ridiculous.

'Show's on,' hisses the mohawk guy. 'Finally.'

'Not a moment too soon,' goes Riz, checking his watch anxiously.

At one of the arch windows of the Embassy appears the old cunt and the blonde girl we saw on the street. They're already naked and sweaty, so presumably they've been going at it out of sight. Now he's riding her doggy-style, and she's gripping the window sill for support as her hair and breasts bounce in full view of the traffic below.

'He knows we're here,' says Riz to me. 'He lives in that room and awhile ago he noticed that we come up here a lot, so he's turned his Saturday night conquests into a performance piece.'

It's weird to be watching the spectacle with these punks and the naked old guy staring back at us with a big stupid grin on his puffed face. Eventually the cunt starts bucking wildly and the girl's letting out peals of ecstasy that reverberate down to street level, either confusing or amusing the people waiting at the bus stop in front of the Embassy.

'A couple of times he's even come over here afterwards,' discloses the mohawk guy, whose name I'm yet to learn. 'He bought some weed off us once.'

I'd feel awkward about the exhibitionist coming to sit with the voyeurs. It's not right, is it? Each has its place, and should be accordingly observed.

The couple disappear from the window and the punks reach down for the cardboard sheets Riz stacked earlier. Riz produces a thick black marker from his pocket and they each take turns to write a number between one and ten on a piece of cardboard.

Soon the old cunt appears at the arch window again, a towel wrapped around his waist. I can see the girl standing in front of the bathroom mirror behind him.

Riz and the punks stand at the edge of the rooftop and hold up their cardboard sheets.

'We always score him on his performance,' explains Riz. 'It started out as a joke, but as long as we do it, we'll get a show.'

The cunt in the window seems happy with his scores, and gives us two big thumbs up. The girl enters the room behind him and is trying to see what he's looking at, peering past him as he tries to distract her. She's not easily sidetracked from her inquiry, however, and pushes past his appeals to go to the bed. She appears at the window, holding a towel to her nakedness, and stares in horror at us. The others are still holding up their signs.

We watch as an argument breaks out between the girl and the old guy, and when she quickly dresses and angrily storms from the room, the cunt returns to the window and pulls a face, shrugging comically.

Chris holds his hands above his head and applauds, and the old cunt bows to us then staggers into his bathroom to shower.

Down on the street the blondie emerges from the hotel side door, and as she stomps back up Elizabeth toward Eagle Street Pier, she glances up at us with hate-filled eyes.

'You're fucking sick, the lot of you!' she screams, and we break into hysterics.

PIXIE AND THE HOMIES

The train into the city is fuckin stressful, coz there's a bunch of homies on it who I know from school. There's about a dozen of the cunts, and half are chicks. Fuckin great, not.

Homies like to dress in basketball singlets and shorts and wear shoes like Nike and shit. They pretty much literally copy American culture, even though a lot of em are actually Asians, but. When there's gangs of em like this everyone's on edge, coz they like to bully people and get violent. Most of em have grown up here, and are kids of migrants. Like this one girl I used to be friends with at school, Jenny, her parents are fuckin loaded but nowadays Jenny just hangs out in these homie gangs literally pickin fights with other homie gangs or harassin normals.

But there's one thing homies fuckin love to pick on the most and that's people from subcultures, and I'm not just talkin kids like us either. Gothics and punks and shit of all ages are easy targets. Fuck, I've even heard of em fighting the metal dudes on trains. Imp was tellin us about how once his brother KK and his brother's friend were on a train and got harassed by a gang of about ten homie cunts. They're mostly these skinny liddle Asian dudes, but when there's ten of em they're a problem. KK's friend was fuckin wasted, and when the fight broke out he was just gettin smashed but literally too wasted to notice or care. He was laughin the whole time while KK tried to fight em all off. The next day they were both covered head to toe in bruises, Imp reckons.

The homies on the train are startin to get pretty rowdy, and the girls are millin round the doors like they're gonna wait and challenge anyone who tries to get on or off. They don't, but, coz when the train pulls up at the platforms the girls don't do anythin, and that's when I get the sinkin feeling they're waitin for us to try and get off. I've noticed two of em, in particular, starin at us.

Fuck fuck fuck.

I sneak a peek at the carriage behind, and calculate that the door is only about six paces away, but even risin to change carriages might be the excuse these bitches are lookin for.

I'm saved by three punks that get on at Buranda, coz the homies target them instead.

One of the trio isn't actually punk, but; she looks moreova gothic. Or a witch. Literally bone thin and pale with scars all up her arms and a pointy black witches hat on. The other two, a boy and a girl, are definitely punks, wearin cut up denim vests and leopard-print stockings and coloured hair.

'Can't stay in here,' says one of the homie cunts, this stupid lookin slut with a huge 1 printed on the back of her oversized green mesh singlet.

The punk dude, who's short with a tiny mohawk and mong lookin eyes, gives the homie chick a liddle grin and sits down in one of the double seats.

I think normally he might've gotten away with it if he didn't also grin at the chick, coz now he's sorta got their attention and they're not stoked about bein ignored.

'Hey shitface,' another bitch says to him. 'She just told ya you can't be in here.'

The punk dude shrugs and goes: 'Too late. Here now.'

The girls with him laugh and this sets everythin off.

About five of the homie chicks charge up to em screamin: 'THINK THAT'S FUNNY, SLUTS?'

The witch girl looks petrified. The other girl, who has olive skin and her hair pulled into short pigtails all the way along the top of her head, tells them to fuck off.

'You fuck off! You fuck off!' yells the homies, jerkin their bodies at the punks like they're ready to attack em. The punk dude makes the mistake of literally pushing one of the homie girls' back, coz this makes the homie guys mad now. They've jumped up outta their seats and rush over, shoving at the punk dude who's now standin on his seat and kicking out at everyone to keep em away.

I'm fuckin shitting myself watchin all this go down, too scared to move even though I just want to get away into the next carriage.

'Watch out, Tim!' yells the punk girl, pointin at one of the homie dudes who's pulled a swiss-army knife.

Fucking hell.

The punk dude, Tim, panics and literally kicks this homie dude in the face who falls back into the seats out of view.

The train pulls up at Vulture Street Station and the conductor comes runnin down the side, peerin into the windows. There's been a lot of trouble with these gangs lately on the trains, and there's been gangs of girls targetin other girls from certain schools and beatin the shit out of them, to the point that the cops have started hangin around the train platforms durin the hours before and after school.

The conductor opens the doors but stays outside, shoutin to the homies that the cops are on their way.

I run for the open doors, desperate to get out of this crazy situation. The conductor makes a grab for us, probly assumin I'm part of the gang.

'Get ya hands off us, ya perve,' I shout.

The cunt lets us pass, refocusin his attention on the scuffle inside the carriage.

Fuckin insanity. My hands are tremblin, and I don't want to get back on board or hang around either, so I decide to walk through South Bank to the Victoria Bridge and cross over into the city from there. It's only about a fifteen minute walk, which might get some of the adrenalin out of me system.

Thankfully the homies are still back in the train and don't follow us, or else they might take some revenge out on us for what the punk dude did. I hope they're okay, those three.

I get to the city without further incident, except it's fuckin busy as with the Friday late-night shoppin, and the regulars are all there in the Square. About a dozen of us.

A lot of the older gothics call us kindergoth, or babybats. Both derogatory names we've adopted as our own. We meet here most days, and some nights, because we often can't go to the clubs on account of our age. A lot of the time we can actually get into the clubs, the gothic ones, coz they usually don't bother with any security or ID checks. No-one's mostly strict about that, but Imp reckons his brother is adamant that the State Government is lookin at policing it more strongly next year and will start crackin down on club owners or runners who turn a blind eye to underage patrons. In any sense, on the occasion when there is ID checks, we have King George Square to hang out in.

We just come here and socialise, laughin our asses off at the normals who're terrified of us.

Dee Dee's handin out xannies to everyone like they're tic-tacs. His real name's Damien, but almost no-one here goes by their real name and coz Damien's literally got depression some of the other cunts here gave him the nickname Down in the Dumps, which we've shortened to Dee Dee. I actually don't like the nickname. It's not nice. He reckons he doesn't mind, but.

It's a bit shit gettin our buzz on durin the day with all the office workers around, but hey, a high's a high and ya get it when ya can. And if Dee Dee's handin em out for nuthin, then I'm in, especially after the nervewracking incident on the train.

The only thing about xanax is that the high isn't exactly a *buzz* at all, it's more like ya get sleepy and absolutely don't give a fuck about anythin. I really should get some for home, or for work. If I didn't know better I'd swear Dougie at Dad's burger shop was on em all the time.

Forks is here, too. He's a regular visitor to the Square, even though he's so old he's practically antique. He's like a smaller, more starved version of Lemmy from Motorhead. He gets his name from that Lard song, the band that the singer's from Dead Kennedy's and Ministry made together apparently. That's Fork Boy's kind of music, anyway. Normally we just call him Forks, coz he's always givin people the forks. I think that's actually why he took the name from the song. It's like his liddle gimmick. Anyway, it suits him.

Also, Forks isn't a gothic, he just hangs around with us. If he *was* a gothic, we'd say he was one of the Ancients, coz of his age. They come after the Elders, who've been in the scene as far back as the late Eighties, at least. We've got a runnin joke here in the Square that if we piss off the older gothics too much then the Ancients will come back in and sort all the babybats out. The Sweep, we call it.

'Here she is,' goes Forks, grinning at us, half his teeth missin. 'The working girl. With fries and a large Coke.'

'Fuck off, cunt,' I go, poppin me pill. 'It's been a hard enough morning as it is.'

I tell em about what happened on the train.

'I fucken hate homies,' growls Forks. 'Scum of society.'

'Along with junkies,' I add, tryin to be clever.

'Not the same,' Forks says in complete seriousness. 'A junky just wants to go into his corner and forget the world. The homie wants to fuck your world up so that you think he's the top dog.'

'Hmm, fair point,' I say.

'We should fuck em back,' goes James.

'Sex with homies?' says Forks. 'Pass.'

Everyone laughs at his wit, even James.

'Nah, you know what I mean,' goes James.

Forks drapes an arm around James. When they're this close, old and young together, it seems impossible that Forks is still alive, although Imp reckons he's only thirty-five years old, which is still pretty fuckin ancient, but.

'An eye for an eye makes the whole world blind,' says Forks. 'They'll get theirs, don't worry. Karma is real.'

'I'm the fucking Karma,' says James, puffin his chest up. He's so skinny it's ridiculous.

'You need a fucking xannie, mate,' says Dee Dee, wavin the blister pack in front of him. 'To calm the fuck down.'

'I need to crack some fucking skulls,' says James. 'Won't say no to a xannie, but.'

'Look at those wino cunts over there,' says Forks, juttin his chin in the direction of the homeless old cunts across the Square. 'Alcohol's a fucken depressant. That's the problem with them. Chasin the low and not the high.'

'GO HOME, YOU HOMELESS FUCKS!' shouts James, cuppin his hands next to his mouth.

Forks bursts into laughter, wheezin with the effort. 'You're crazy, James.'

James grins and recounts how last week the money-collectors in the koala suits were in the Square and they were arguin with the homeless dudes so he kicked the bucket out of their hands and money literally went flying everywhere.

'Fucking all over the place,' he laughs. 'And all the streeties were grabbing it before the koalas could. The security guys over there didn't do nothing about it.'

'That's what the world is all about, but,' says Forks. 'Eat or be eaten.'

We're sittin around because it only takes about five minutes for the benzos to kick in, enjoyin the drowsy feelin and tormentin the normals who stray from the path too close to us. Despite the xannies, James is typically actin opposite to how he should be feelin, runnin around like a mong, actin like a gorilla and climbin things and hootin like an owl, even though he insists that's what gorillas sound like. It's probably his behaviour more than anythin that makes the coppers wander in and pay us a visit. I glance round and notice that Forks has literally vanished. It's fucking amazin how fast that cunt can move when he needs to, even with a couple of xannies in his system.

'Get off the lamppost,' one of the cops says to James.

James scoots about on the ground hootin still, which the cops ignore. They ask to see our ID's, write down our descriptions in stupid liddle spiral notebooks in their shirt pockets.

Dee Dee starts loudly tellin this babybat who calls herself Tanith how he used to work on a farm, which he actually didn't, and how the pigs couldn't sweat so they'd roll around in the mud to cool down.

Taking his cue, Tanith turns to the cops and goes: 'How do you keep those lovely shirts so dry in this heat, officer?'

The cop's not having any of it, but, and orders Tanith to her feet.

'Empty yer pockets,' he goes, then turns to the rest of us. 'That goes for the rest of youse, too,'

'What the fuck for?' James goes.

Dee Dee's said nuthin, but he's literally gone pale. I'm beginnin to suspect the xanax isn't prescribed to him, or that he's got somethin else in his pockets.

'This is bullshit,' I say loudly. 'How come you lot aren't out on the trains stoppin innocent people from gettin harassed by the homies, instead?'

'Empty your pockets,' the cop orders.

'How come?'

'Because if you don't I'll arrest you, you piece of shit,' snarls the copper.

'Whoa, back the fuck up,' shouts James. 'Are you allowed to swear at people?'

'We can do whatever the fuck we want,' the cop says.

James gets a funny look in his eyes. Not an angry look, but it's easy to see by his body language that he's pissed off. He's approachin the cops slowly, starin em in the eye.

'We've done nothing wrong,' he says in this low voice.

If I wasn't shittin myself on his behalf, I'd have laughed out loud at the sheer balls on him.

One of the cops is ready to pound him into the ground, I think, but the other copper puts a hand on his arm and tells him to leave it. For his part, James stops advancin on em and relaxes slightly. Weird how the benzo has made the rest of us mellow as but he's a bit wired up.

Fuck me, it's like a Mexican standoff, but they would've fucked James up if he'd tried anything. They don't bother checkin anybody else's pockets, to Dee Dee's relief, and issue a warnin that we're all to behave in public or there'll be consequences.

When they're gone, we all cheer and call James a hero.

'You okay?' I ask.

'Of course I am,' he replies.

That strange look is still in his eyes, and it makes us think there's nuthin okay with him at all.

CLUBBED TO DEATH

Dante's headed down to the Gold Coast with his punk mates to try and sneak into the Big Day Out and see Nick Cave perform, which leaves ol Twixxie here the centre of attention tonight at Megan's new club *The Hanging Garden* at the Land's Office in the city. Me and Malik catch up with Abi and Alex in the city and grab ourselves some Big Macs from the bottom of the Myer Centre on our way (Alex sticks with just nuggets) which we finish off by the time we get to the club.

For opening night the place is pretty packed. It can be a risk starting up a club for the first time, but despite our divisions and preferences we're still a pretty strong and vibrant scene and Megs manages to stay fairly neutral from all the scene politics, which is a feat in itself!

Me and Alex bee-line to the dance floor while Abi takes over from the conversation Alex already instigated with Malik about bondage stuff; people tying each other up for kicks. Kinky shit, in other words.

Abi's been giving me the cold-shoulder lately, but I'm determined not to sulk about it. She'll come around; she always does. For now ol Twixxie's got fresh meat to consider. Alex hasn't been here long, and that's a bonus when you're trying to score with chicks. When they get to know you more it becomes too complicated, like they're not sure what they want anymore, or maybe they do know and it's more than you're able to give. As far as I'm concerned – even though everyone else seems adamant suggesting otherwise – I'm single again, and that means not being tied down. Or, if I play my cards right, it means being tied up by kinky Alex here, even though she's too overweight for me on a sober night.

Truth be told, though, at the end of the day if Abi asked me to go steady right now I would in a heartbeat.

But since she's snubbing me, it's any port in a storm.

'Abi says that you and Karen are basically, like, still an item,' she yells over the Sisters, her voice barely discernible because we're two-stepping and that means every few beats she's stepping back from me a couple of paces before dancing forward again. Legend has it the dance move originated from a bar in England called The Phono where the dance-floor was so small with a pole in the middle that taking two steps in any given direction was the only dance move feasible... much like this joint really. 'Is it true you're still with her?'

'Not at all,' I reply, mentally cursing Abi's big mouth. The split between Karen and I before Christmas had been final, in my opinion, on account of the abortion, although around long-term friends like Xanthe and Raven I spout that we're just trialling a separation period otherwise they'll harp on at me about doing more to get back with her. Not that I've done a single thing to reconcile.

'We were going to have a baby,' I confess, and Alex's eyes go wide with surprise. 'But not anymore.'

'What happened?'

I make a cutting motion across my throat with my hand. 'She fucking terminated it,' I shout over the music as Alex strains to hear me, scrunching her eyes up like she actually feels my pain. 'Didn't even include me in the decision, just fucking did it.'

'Holy shit,' she says, 'that's next level!'

'Tell me about it,' I go, shaking my head, which isn't easy to do while you're dancing. 'No-one else knows about it, so just...'

'Oh, yeah, no worries,' she says, rubbing her temple. 'Mum's the word.'

'That's the thing, though, right,' I continue. 'She didn't want me telling a single soul that we were going to have a baby, but I told my old lady anyways, and she was over the fucking moon. She's always wanted a grandkid, she reckoned. It broke her heart when I had to tell her we lost it. Karen was furious at me for even telling Mum about it in the first place, but it's my old lady, you know?'

'Yeah, I totally understand where you're coming from,' Alex says.

The song's about to finish, so I make sure to grab an eyeful of Alex's tits bouncing around in front of me for the spank-bank in case I need to rub one out later. The thing about the two-step dance that goths do is that we hold our hands behind our backs and lean forward while we shuffle to and fro, so that it's quite the view of someone like Alex whose tits are pretty impressive. Karen wasn't overly ample in that department, but still a decent size, and yet when she got pregnant they ballooned out to a whopping size and that was still in the first trimester! It was probably the only thing Karen liked about the whole pregnancy, and I'll admit that I did too, but she complained they were sore all the time and worse still was that as a result I wasn't allowed to play with them.

'I'm getting a headache,' says Alex, holding her hand to her head, and not in the gothic salute way either.

Fucking hell! I haven't even tried scoring with her yet and she's already wheeling out the classic lines to avoid the prospect of sex with good ol Twixxie! The fuck?

'I need to sit down,' she goes and staggers off the dance-floor.

Turns out she really does have a headache, and it's so bad that she ends up lying down on the floor in the corner. We form a protective circle around her so no-one steps on her in the dark, and Abi gently slides her handbag under Alex's head as a makeshift pillow. She's not really a nurse, just looks after old people when they need showers and shit, but she asks Alex some stuff about medications.

'I take imitrex,' says Alex through gritted teeth. 'In my bag.'

She's lying still as a corpse, her eyes unfocused but staring transfixed at the silver skull buckles on my boots.

Abi rifles through Alex's bag and finds a small packet of pills, checking the label. 'It's a serotonin agonist,' she informs us, and I know through Dante that it's something to do with the hormones in the brain. He reckons serotonin's what's responsible for him for being a nutcase.

Malik brings a glass of water from the bar for Alex to sip as she takes the pill, and then we let her rest on the floor some more while she recovers. There'll be no rompy-pompy with her tonight, which is no loss really since she doesn't actually do it for me anyway, to be honest, but I wouldn't mind one of those pills Abi's holding. They say opening up about your problems is meant to be cathartic, but spilling my guts to Alex about the abortion has only left me with a throbbing head of my own, and it's not the one in my pants unfortunately.

'Oi, Abi,' I go, figuring she won't be up for it but giving it a whirl anyways, 'I've got a massive headache coming on, too.'

'Give it a fucking rest,' she snaps.

Right, there's only one other option left then: to get shitfaced.

'Tequilas all round,' I say as I head to the bar.

Malik nods in approval.

MCKAY PART 1

I can use my health-care card to get free psychiatric appointments, which I definitely take advantage of. Sometimes when some smart cunt gets snide or abusive with me I just shut the fuckers down by telling them I see a psychiatrist and that their tax dollars pay for it, so they're welcome to continue to fuck with my self-esteem all they like since they're paying for the privilege. The best bit is that often the tactic actually works! I wouldn't have guessed in a million years that a comeback like that would. Never underestimate the impact of striking at the working man's wallet.

McKay's office is in a tower block in Cathedral Square across from St John's, so it's always a leisurely walk from Central Station if I'm staying at a friend's place or a bit longer if I'm on the streets. As it is, I've been staying a few nights again at Twix's flat on Bowen Street just across the road. Seems the cunt finally got over his jealousy about me supposedly hooking up with the girl he was failing miserably at chatting up last weekend.

They're doing extensive renovations on a couple of floors to the tower so there's a section of the square that's been cordoned off for piles of sand and stacks of plasterboard and equipment. I casually peruse the site on my way past, looking for anything that might not be tied down too well come the cover of night and that could fetch me a few dollars at Cash Converters. There's some power tools that could be worth the return journey, but they'd probably be locked away inside come knockoff time.

The elevator's been decked with padded work-blankets, presumably so the building materials being carted up don't damage the walls. Someone's scrawled a joke in biro, or what's supposed to pass for a joke. *What do ya do if yer wife is staggering around the backyard,* it reads, then answers with *shoot her again.* Fucking charming.

One of the reno workers – perhaps even the author of the pathetic joke – gets into the lift with me, a scruffy-looking tradie covered in old plaster dust that clings to the week-old stubble on his chin.

He grins at me: 'How they hanging?'

Well, I wasn't expecting a cordial greeting to be fucking honest, much less one as cryptic as this. I actually pause for a moment, staring at him in a kind of horror which begins to make him uneasy, so I return with a slow, drawn-out: 'They're fine... I guess. Yours?'

Rather than take the exchange for what it is, which is awkward at best, the cunt relaxes and grins even wider. 'Loose and full of juice,' he goes, and we ride the rest of the way in silence until the doors open at my floor and he wishes me a good day.

Fucking weirdo.

Normally any kind of to-and-fro between me and tradies doesn't end well, and usually because they clock the puffy sleeves of my shirt with the lace cuffs and ruffle at the throat and immediately turn into complete and utter arseholes. So now I'm left sorta feeling like I was the arsehole in this exchange.

The City North Medical Centre is on the third floor from the top, but there's no GP's here, just McKay and two other psychiatrists. The misleading name means they get people up here all the time for head colds or broken fingers asking to be treated, but the name's actually intentionally misleading so that any clients uncomfortable about revealing their psychiatric histories can infer that they're coming here for general medical advice. The receptionist is a kindly old woman with peach coloured hair and massive glasses, and as much as she's always so accommodating and pleasant I've always secretly suspected she resents me and sees me as just a piece of trash abusing the healthcare system. Then again, I could be entirely wrong.

McKay's office is as bland as can be. There are no personal effects that betray who he is outside of the plaid shirts and polished shoes, but that never stops him divulging all sorts of shit about his family and taste in music in an effort to empathise.

In fact, it was music that we first discussed when I came to see him eight months ago. I'd been dressed in a loose white business shirt and black dress pants with an oversized black coat that had Chinese characters embroidered in black polyester thread along the lapels, and I'd told him that I was in a constant state of flux, changing my look dramatically every now and then. At the time my hair had been cut to just below my ears and bleached to within an inch of its fucking life so that it was actually white at the roots.

It was probably that latter that had made McKay guess that I was modelling myself after David Bowie, and as remarkable as that supposition was, it was in fact Nick Cave I was emulating at the time, apart from the hair. Although the origins of the suit wearing lay further back than that, actually, with a failed deportment course arranged by the dole office. But at least these days, it's Cave's doing.

'That was my second guess,' McKay had replied with.

Contrary to my assertion that I was changing my appearance dramatically all the time, that session with McKay became one of the last times I really did change, more or less keeping the dress pants and dinner jacket combo with an assortment of paisley or business shirts as befit my mood. Sometimes, to be ironic and mildly annoying to the working classes, I don a tie as though I'm headed to a conference. I look the part in principle, but in application I am what we call a *swampie*, a dying breed only by name. Some of the indie rockers are keeping the style alive, but other than that only the older goths tend to recall the term.

As a clinical psychiatrist, McKay can prescribe antidepressants, which is what I'm after today. It's about time I was back on them, because I've been having mildly suicidal thoughts. They're random, but when they do come they're persistent, dwelling inside my head for days sometimes. I know why I'm having these tendencies. Same old fucking reason.

'Hey, stranger,' he says with a lopsided smirk when he sees me, because I've missed the last two appointments. They're meant to charge me a fee (a fine?) for that, but since it's Medicare paying anyway I guess they don't bother. 'Been a while since we last spoke.'

'I got dumped.'

'Ah,' says McKay.

He raises his eyebrows and straightens his chair, gestures of attentiveness exhibited solely for my benefit so that I'm aware of his interest, regardless of whether he really gives a flying fuck or not.

'Sorry to hear,' he says, as expected.

'Hardly the end of the world, though, right?' I grin insincerely. I'm always making apocalypse jokes like there's no tomorrow.

'Can I ask: did you end it or did she?'

'She did,' I reveal. 'Over the phone.'

I'd been in a long-distance relationship with Jillian for about a month or a bit more. I'd known her for a couple of weeks before we decided to be boyfriend/girlfriend, and at first it'd been okay because even though she lived on the Gold Coast I could just go and stay with her for a few days each time on account of I didn't have any responsibilities tying me to Brisbane. I think she was even considering asking me to move in at one point, but hesitated. Just as well, too, because I fucking hate the Gold Coast.

'That's tough,' McKay goes, sucking in his breath for effect. 'And how are you holding up from it?'

Of course, the cluey cunt has twigged I'm homeless again, a recurring state of affairs for me when everything goes to shit, but he has sense enough to leave the topic alone for the time being, although I'm sure he's itching to discuss its possible significance, whatever that might be.

'Not well,' I answer. 'In fact, I've been having thoughts again.'

'Suicidal ones?'

'Yup.' I chuckle darkly and stare out his office window at the traffic below, chewing on a hangnail. It tears loose and now there's a stinging pain deep in the lateral groove. Some blood, too.

'Have you tried to act on them?'

'Nah,' I shake my head. 'Not this time. Yet.'

I inspect the rest of my nails, and can see that I seem to favour chewing my index or thumb nails because the rest are in varying stages of length that stick out over the ends of my fingers.

'But I'm thinking I wanna try medication again,' I go.

'Okay, sure,' McKay says, nodding slowly. 'Any particular reason?'

'Well, I've been feeling like shit, a lot, and can't seem to shake it. Not that I've probably tried to much, but still. When I first came here you had me on Prozac and that worked for a while, but in the end it didn't seem very effective.'

'Sure, sure,' he goes. 'I remember that. Well, we do have some new SSRI's come out that we can try out.'

The employ of antidepressants in the Land of Oz rose dramatically at the beginning of the 90s with about five million people being prescribed a range of drugs in 1990. There was an almost thirty percent spike in sales by last year. McKay's goes through some of the options, which makes me wonder just how readily are professionals willing to diagnose someone with depression on account of just how many medications there are available. It must passively encourage the cunts to dole em out, especially with advantages such as the increased difficulty to overdose on these new antidepressants?

'The sertraline range is proving popular,' McKay says rummaging through the sample in his drawer as though he's comparing this year's fashions against the last, 'but I'm more inclined to have you try this venlafaxine.'

He hands me a box with the word EFFEXOR written across it.

Before McKay I saw another psych called Doctor Bourne who had prescribed sertraline to me, one called Zoloft, and I fucking hated it. Sure, you could bunker down and be away with the fairies from it if you wanted to, but all it did for me was kick in if I got agitated or too emotional, and I'd lose all my energy and collapse in an exhausted heap on the ground. And it fucked with my ability to orgasm. Having a wank was an ordeal, going on long enough to warrant changing hands and when it finally came to climax not only was my dick raw from the stroking it felt like a gush of actual fire was shooting out, like the sperm had become blazing hot. One night I bumped into a girl called Amy at the park up the road from where I was living and we'd got it on right there in the park, on the swings and on the grass. The sex seemed to go on forever, and eventually she'd insisted I had cum even though it was abundantly obvious to us both that I hadn't, and couldn't. She passed my house the next morning and we had a laugh about how we had fucked for so long that she couldn't walk straight, which was actually true. She was waddling from side to side to avoid her thighs rubbing. I still hadn't managed to cum, despite wanking as hard as I could when I'd gotten home.

'Rightio, let's give the Effexor a crack,' I say, pocketing the sample box while McKay writes me a script for more.

'Hopefully it helps you straighten some stuff out,' he goes. 'Stability is what you need.' When I simply nod and scratch my head, he's unable to help himself any longer and enquires: 'How's your living arrangements?'

'Homeless again,' I confess. 'But I'm staying with Twix and Raven, at the moment.'

He knows the names of all my friends. I mention them enough during our sessions.

'Okay, good,' he says, nodding thoughtfully. He writes his home number on a card, trusting me with this vital piece of information. 'Call me if you need to. You know, if you feel everything's too much. And get your friends something nice for their flat. Show that you appreciate all they do for you.'

I thank him and get out of there, feeling the burden of his generosity. But he's right, I should get something for Twix and

Raven's flat. I know just the thing, too. Groceries. They've hardly ever got any, and I'm always eating what little they have. That's a fucking perfect idea!

I grab my dose of serotonin-stabilising drugs from the chemist down in the Valley and decide to treat myself to a bottle of vino while I'm at it. I shouldn't mix the two, but I also need something to get me past this feeling of worthlessness my breakup with Jillian has put me in while I go through a couple of weeks' worth of side-effects waiting for the venlafaxine to do its trick.

Outside the bottle-o this muscled bogan cunt says to his mate: 'Go the fucking clothes on this poof.'

I glare at the fucker and sneer: 'Laugh it up, funny cunt. I see a psychiatrist and take medication on the house because fuckheads like you pay for the privilege.'

His mate guffaws, not getting what I'm on about, but thankfully the big boofhead clues on and actually looks a bit crestfallen for it. Good.

I sweep up Wickham Terrace back towards Twix's place, ready to kill any cunt who looks sideways at me, walking so determinedly that the little Chinese families scatter as I charge through them with my coat flaring behind me. I can't wait to crack open this bottle of cheap red and drown my fucking sorrows.

LET THEM HATE

I like to organise picnics every now and then. The elder goths used to have em back in the 80s, too, and it's not a bad tradition to keep alive. And it's a brilliant excuse to get all dressed up, but.

Normally I organise our picnics for the Botanical Gardens but we decided to do something different today and have it at the Albert Park Amphitheatre. We almost never come up this way so it's an exciting change of scenery. Usually I'd tell everyone coming to 'bring a plate', but in a miracle of massive generosity Dante bought me and Twix a shitload of groceries for the flat, including a shitload of tinned Whiskas for Lunar. He must have spent nearly all this fortnight's dole check on it! Granted, a lot of it is stuff we'd never use, but it's the thought that counts. So now we've got bags full of biccies and cheese and bread etcetera for everyone at the picnic, our shout!

'Christ, Raven,' complains Dante, huffing and puffing as he carries the bags off the bus, 'can't we just meet at the Coffee Club next time?'

He's got a bee in his bloody bonnet because I've got him and Twix carrying most of the supplies. It's only a short walk past the Town Hall then up across Turbot Street and up the hill to the park, but I guess the bags *are* pretty heavy. I've got new nails glued on so I can't help share the load, or else they'll break off.

'Stop complaining, it's worth it, you'll see.'

'I'm with Dante on this one,' says Twix, whose bags are actually the lighter of the loads. I know, because I'm the one who packed them while the boys piss-farted around back at the Palace.

We're standing at the lights to cross over Ann Street when this lady pipes up and outright asks if we're Satanists. I'm not even going to bother stooping to answer her.

But Twix does. 'Yeah, we are. And I know for a fact that the Devil himself is coming after *you.*'

She looks pissed off by this.

'You shouldn't be allowed to dress like that in public,' she says, looking pointedly at me. 'If the police see you, then you'll know it.'

'Know what, precisely?' says Dante, unamused.

'Here he comes, here he comes,' chants Twix, trying to roll his eyes back and straining the muscles and veins in his neck. 'The Devil, he's coming for you.'

The green signal man comes on and the old lady hurries across the road ahead of us, but when Twix starts joshing around by ambling after her like he's lost control of his body – waving the bags around in direct contravention to his earlier complaint about how heavy they were – the old bat starts to run away.

Me and Dante are laughing our faces off.

'You oughta see a psychiatrist!' shouts Dante at the old lady, a quote from Monty Python him and Twix are always saying together.

'CAUSE YOU'RE A LOONY!' they shout in unison, cackling at her stricken face.

When she gets to the dental hospital on the corner she turns and shouts something at us, before going quickly up Turbot. We keep going straight, past the hospital and up the hill.

They crack me up with their antics. 'You dorks!' I call out.

'What'd the old spastic have to say?' says Dante.

'C'mon, don't use that word,' I tut.

'Getting all PC on us now, Raven?' Dante scoffs.

'Well, there's a reason the C stands for Correct, you know,' I say, because I'm not backing down on this one. It actually really bothers me that he insists on using that word all the time.

'Fine,' Dante relents, rolling his eyes. 'What did the wrinkly old battle-axe have to say for herself then, Twix?'

'Probably something hateful,' says Twix, back to acting like the bags are a burden. 'They hate us cause they fear us.'

'Nah, that's not true,' Dante says.

'It is, actually,' I say.

Dante's shaking his head, adamant that we're wrong.

'Okay, let's hear it, then,' I laugh. 'Another Dante theory, coming up.'

'No theory,' he says in all seriousness. 'She doesn't hate us yet, because she still fears us. She ran away because she was afraid. Like, genuinely afraid.'

'I would be, too, if that was coming at me,' I snigger, nodding at Twix. He heaves a bag up and flips his middle finger at me.

'There's a lot of people who're used to seeing goths around, now,' says Dante. 'Maybe they went to school with some, or are related to one, or just see us around the city enough. The thing is, at first they might fear us. But after a while it's obvious we're not that frightening at all.'

'But what's obvious to me is that they do actually hate us,' argues Twix. 'Those jokers that spit on me and call me a freak really fucking hate me.'

'I don't disagree with that, Twix,' says Dante. 'What I'm saying is those cunts probably *used* to be afraid of you. Or maybe not you, precisely. But of goths. And one day they realise there's nothing to be afraid of, that we're just a bunch of fucking pushovers. And guess what? The cunt starts to feel angry that he ever felt afraid, feels like he was tricked into feeling that way. The fear evaporates, replaced with a kind of shame about how he felt. The shame turns to blame, at us. Turns to anger. At us. Now the cunt truly hates us for how he used to feel.'

'Poo to your theory,' says Twix.

'The evidence stares you in the face, you dumb bastard,' scoffs Dante. 'It's in the ridicule, in the spit that lands on you. That's not fear. Fear is when that old lady ran away from us. Those ones are still too wary to take us on. But the cunts that openly mock us have stopped being afraid. I wish I could say that's a good thing, but those cunts barely have a grip on their day to day emotional stability let alone with how they feel about us. They don't fear retribution from us, do they?'

'They know there's nothing to fear anymore,' I add, finally getting Dante's point.

Twix hasn't, predictably, and the two continue to bicker all the way up to Wickham Terrace and then down to the amphitheatre, where thankfully some of the others have already arrived so the argument might stop dead. Fat chance of that happening, but.

There's about a dozen people here already, including Megs and Xanthe. Twix says the new girl to town, Alex, might come later when she's finished at her new job. I've yet to meet her, find out what she's like. Twix vouches for her, though. Malik and Angele aren't here yet. They'll be incredibly fashionably late, knowing those two, if they turn up at all.

'Grubs up!' yells Twix, climbing onto the stage of the amphitheatre and pretending to be a thespian, strutting around like Dave Vanian and striking poses. He'd be perfect for the theatre, if he could actually act. He's got more front than Myers, as he'd say.

Megs has brought some blankets which she lays on the grass and her, me and Xanthe start laying out all the grub.

Dante's still trying to argue with Twix about fear and hate, but getting nowhere. Twix wants his audience, trying to do back-flips to impress the rest of us. He's not too successful at the back-flipping, so at least I'm impressed he's able to meet my expectations on that score.

It turns out to be a lovely day, but. A few more stragglers turn up, though Malik or Angele remain AWOL, and Shadow even brings a small ghetto blaster bulked up with batteries and some Cure tapes. If I'd known he'd be bringing a tape player I'd've brought some Smiths.

There's still heaps of grub left and the sun is starting to dip down. The shadows of the trees stretch across the park and swallow us, so Xanthe lights some tea-candles and the orange glow against our faces as *Boys Don't Cry* crashes tinnily out of the speakers makes me feel magical.

Megs and Dante are deep in conversation about how her new club The Hanging Garden went, but the flow of their talk is structured so that it seems intimate, and as much as I want to join in it feels like it'd be too much of an intrusion. I swear she's flirting with him, but I don't think he's aware of it. It's my fucking picnic; I organised it. She shouldn't be having closed-off conversations. We're all here together, aren't we?

'I gotta walk off some of this food,' Twix says, patting his stomach. 'Come on, let's go for a walk.'

It turns out he's talking to me, but.

'Nah, I'm good.'

'*Mon Dieu*, come on,' he insists, grabbing my arm and dragging me off the blanket, the funny bastard. 'We'll walk round the whole park and see how long it takes.'

'Okay, hold your horses,' I laugh, and get to my feet, casting one more glance back at Megs and Dante.

Twix takes my hand and leads us along the paths up to the road.

'Two pale figures,' he observes, then slowly sings the lyrics from *The Funeral Party*. He doesn't have such a bad voice when he sings something that suits it.

Out on Wickham Terrace we see a guy across the road with a sign, as if he's a protester. He's the only person around, but. It looks weird, like he's turned up way too early for the main event.

'What's his sign say?' I ask Twix.

Twix stops and waits for the guy to stop pacing up and down.

'It says *abortion is a sin*,' he says finally.

'Why the fuck's he got that, then?'

Even as I've said it a girl comes along and when she tries to go into the building the guy he starts hassling her. I can tell by her body language that she feels quite confronted by him.

'Wait here,' says Twix as he starts across the road. Fat chance of that happening.

'Where are you going?' I ask as I follow him across the street.

'I'm gonna smash the prick,' he says.

'Twix, no,' I say.

Pointless arguing with him, but; he's dead-set determined to get into an argument with the guy.

'Why don't you pick on someone your own size, mate?' he shouts, and the guy with the sign spins around. The girl quickly runs into the building, tears streaming down her face.

'What's going on?' I demand to know.

I guess I seem the more reasonable of us because the guy ignores Twix and tells me there's an abortion clinic inside the building. 'They're killing human life in there. That's a Satanic act in itself.'

I'm a bit stunned because the building looks so ordinary. It's about six storeys high and doesn't look much different to a couple of the others here. I know there's a private hospital around the corner to the right, and another one on the hill up the road to the left, but right here it's just office blocks and a hotel. A pub up on the corner.

'You wanna drop that fucking sign ya prick, before I drop you,' snarls Twix.

'This clinic operates in direct contravention to God's laws,' the guy calmly explains.

'I'm a bit sick of hearing about God and the Devil for one day,' I tell him.

'Seriously, mate,' Twix says. 'On yer fuckin bike, right now. GO!'

Twix keeps pointing up the road and yelling GO at the guy, getting right up in his face. I'm worried the guy'll use the sign as a weapon but actually he eventually gives in to Twix's shouting and leaves. Fucking result!

'I'm proud of you,' I say, but Twix isn't buying the compliment.

There's something dark and serious about him right now that I've only ever seen in Dante when he's having one of his turns. It's something I can't relate with, and it's so alien that I feel a hundred million miles from Twix right now, even though he's standing right next to me.

'Let's get back,' he says.

'You don't want to go for our walk still?'

He doesn't answer, just goes back across the road to the park.

I'm not willing to just forget what happened, but.

'The thing is, that abortion clinic wouldn't be allowed to operate if it wasn't lawful by our law. What's God's law got to with that? We operate by what's legal, not what's holy.'

'Well, it's technically legal and it's technically not,' Twix says, finally willing to talk.

'How can it be both?' I say. 'That's stupid.'

'In Queensland, abortion's covered by the Criminal Code, not the Health Code,' he clarifies, like he's reciting from memory. 'On a legal angle, an abortion can only be performed if it's to prevent any harm to the woman's physical or mental health. But the clinics still do it for heaps of women for other reasons, like they're not ready to have a kid and things like that. Either way, it's not for self-righteous fuckers to stand outside and harass women.'

I'm proud of this idiot.

'Don't ever change, Twix.'

THE EXORCIST

Normally I prefer my solitude and just being left alone, which is surprisingly easy to do in a city because every cunt's looking out for themselves more or less. I've seen people step over my homeless brethren, who've been lying bleeding at bustops, just to read a fucking timetable. Then sit and wait for said bus to arrive without offering any assistance whatsoever.

But normally isn't necessarily *de rigueur*, as evidenced by my attendance at Raven's poxy picnic, which for all its banality has inspired in me the need for social interaction again. Shooting the shit with Twix and Raven at their apartment's not cutting it anymore.

That's when it's as simple as striking up random conversations with people on the streets, anytime of the day or night. It's not difficult at all, especially when people are compelled to be polite and listen to whatever garbage you're ready to spew out.

But I'm not an unappreciative cunt. If I want conversation and some poor fucker humours me, I make sure they go away with something to think about or chuckle at. Self-deprecation is usually a great tactic for both examples: humble oneself and deliver up all the weird and wonderful shit that you've been through, and more likely than not the recipient of these crazy tales of wonder or woe will have never experienced anything like it before. It's a trick I learnt from Micko, watching him beg for small change in King George Square and trading stories about his life in exchange. At first I never saw the significance of his tactic, but gradually I began to see this jigsaw puzzle of his life, fictional or not, by eavesdropping on his scamming. And like his targets, I came to see the wonder in what he was telling me, sharing the other side as it were, a life I couldn't have possibly lived. Perhaps a life even he couldn't possibly have lived. Either way, I got an insight into something of life beyond the borders of my own experience. They can't even teach this shit in school!

But I don't ask for money when I tell my stories, only for company. I even have a couple of regulars who now ask about my day even though there's not much to tell. So I offer them little tidbits about others I've talked with. Like for example I might talk with a stressed out mother of three outside the library who reveals to me that she once had aspirations to be a children's book illustrator, but that she gave up painting not long after getting married. I pass these stories along, embellishing them so that the husband is abusive towards her but that she confessed to me she has a secret plan to take the kids and run to her mother's place in Perth and finally pursue her ambitions of painting for children's books. People love this stuff, like it enriches their day. Something for them to mull over on that long and boring train journey home, something they might be able to drop into the silence between them and their own partner at dinnertime and get some conversation happening in their stilted marriage.

I am the harbinger of their rekindled love-lives.

Now there's hyperbolic self-regard if I've ever heard it, but that's the mood I'm currently in. It's not only random strangers I engage with while I wait for the day to draw to a close, or for the night to creep to that midnight hour of retirement, but also with the familiar. Brisbane's such a small place there's not a day that doesn't go by in the city when I don't run into someone I know.

Today it was Erina that I ran into, this fucking gorgeous girl I know from the clubs. I've long thought I'd like to hook up with her, go steady. But she always had this menacing looking metalhead boyfriend. He wouldn't talk much, at least not with me, and usually preferred to sit in the corner while Erina danced and mucked around with the rest of us. He was like her big solemn rock she constantly gravitated back towards, bringing him drinks to satiate his obvious displeasure at hanging around in a goth club all night. I convinced the DJ one night to play some Type-O for him, cause I felt a bit sorry for the cunt putting up with our trashy 80s preferences all night. He didn't seem to appreciate the gesture; gave me a filthy look like he thought I was taking the piss. Or maybe he just didn't like Type-O.

In any case, me and Erina got into a conversation today and we ended up hanging around past her lunch break. She said her boss was gonna spit chips but she didn't give a fuck cause she hated the bitch and the job anyway. She told me to meet her outside her work at five and we'd continue our chat.

'Doesn't she have a boyfriend?' asks Twix, watching me get ready in his bathroom mirror.

He's got a couple of colognes that smell like hospital chemicals, but I decide that a shower and a relatively clean set of clothes aren't going to cut it for tonight.

'Not anymore,' I wink. 'He's fucking long gone, my friend, and I'm in like Flynn.'

He looks doubtful, the dumb cunt.

'Which of these sprays should I use?' I refuse to use the word *cologne* aloud. It sounds so fucking macho.

Twix scratches under his eye while he thinks about it. 'Dunno. Maybe none of them will suit you. Try that one.'

A quick burst of the toxic-smelling shit against my throat and wrists and I'm done. I appraise the final result in the mirror. Clean shaved, hair washed and teased up like Nick Cave from the Birthday Party era. I check my teeth. Not a lot I can do about the yellow stains.

'You're not using my fucking toothbrush, Dante,' warns Twix.

'Why the fuck would I want to use your grotty brush?' I retort, but in truth I was about to reach for it. I settle for scraping my fingernails across my chops instead.

The five o'clock rush is fascinating to watch from within the very guts of it where I'm waiting outside the Brisbane Arcade for Erina to come down. Normally I'm nowhere near the Mall at this time of day, deliberately avoiding the clock-off madness by staying in the Square or down in the peacefulness of the city gardens where the lack of public transport means the lawns and paths remain relatively free of this rat-race rush. There's fuck all co-ordination going on here, though, just streams of people flowing along, and any ol Joe Blo trying to go against the stream finds themselves doing a dangerous goosestep dance to avoid being struck down. It may be a small city, but fill it with disgruntled nine-to-fivers eager to get home and put their feet up, and it becomes a fight for survival.

Erina's looking resplendent. I'm not sure, but she may have used the company toilets to spruce herself up a bit more and hide her tiredness. Can't imagine corporate goth being this regal. Regardless, her eyes sparkle, keen for the unpredictability of a new date. I'm guessing we're on a date. We didn't really give this catch up a name.

First we head to the Coffee Club across from the Town Hall for some hot chocolates. The rest of the afternoon goes well, filled mostly with walking around chatting, some urban explorations where I show her the city's hidden spots such as the rooftop across from the Embassy Hotel. When the light leaves the sky, we make our way toward Central Station. I figure if she wants to head home, potentially with me in tow, putting her within reach of the train station will prompt the suggestion.

'I've never been here before,' she says, looking around at Anzac Square in a kind of awe.

It's a decent sized park dwarfed by buildings and the high wall with the war memorial shrine atop. Down the centre of the park are two pathways that go beneath the shrine where a tunnel takes pedestrians to the train platforms of Central Station. Along both these paths are palm trees, planted for significance according to Michael Carlyon who's probably old enough to remember them being planted. He reckons they're the biblical symbol of victory, given Australia's military success in the Middle East during both World Wars. The entire park is such an ostentatious tribute to death and destruction, but at least it's actually quite pretty and breaks up the relentless concrete and asphalt of the city centre.

We walk around a bit, looking at the statues and fountains and avoiding the dark corners below the wall either side of the shrine. In one of these corners there's three guys confronting two girls, and my hackles are starting to rise. I'm considering intervening when I overhear one of the guys mention Jesus.

'Evangelists,' I tell Erina, rolling my eyes. 'Reminds me of a joke. Three Ratbags walk into a bar to meet a skunk.'

'What's the punchline?' she says so innocently my heart skips a beat. Her eyes are huge in the gloom, fascinating and beautiful.

I lead her to a park bench where we sit so close she's practically in my lap.

'Oh, it's hilarious, trust me...' I whisper hoarsely, slowly leaning in towards her, holding her eyes as if to hypnotise her. Her lips gently part and the lamplight glints off her top teeth.

This is the moment.

Our lips finally lock, and a soft kiss turns into a frenzied pash that ends as quickly as it begins.

'God, I've been waiting for that all day,' she gasps.

The confession catches me off-guard, and I immediately mutter: 'It's not that funny. Someone nearly dies.'

Her brow creases as she slowly pulls her head back to look at me.

'The joke. About the Three Ratbags,' I clarify, but the damage is done. I surely look like the world's biggest fucking idiot right now.

She's making me nervous as fuck and I don't know why. I can feel my hands trembling. I've ruined the whole, beautiful moment. The only thing for it is to kiss her again and melt my foolishness away. Thankfully, she's keen to go again, so clearly I haven't entirely fucked things up.

The kissing turns desperate, and next thing we're pulling at each other hungrily, and my mouth is on her neck and I'm kissing down over her clavicle, tugging at her top to kiss her chest. She doesn't resist, clawing her nails across my back instead. The sensation turns me on more than ever, so while I'm kissing her lips again I reach down her top and push my hand under her bra, caressing her tit. It's warm and soft, making my mind reel. I have to suck on it now. I simply cannot wait any longer.

Right there in the park, under the relative cover of darkness, I push her top up and start suckling on her boob. I've become delirious with lust, and now my hand's down the front of her skirt, fingertips pushing past her panty-line.

'Wait wait,' she says anxiously.

'Too far?'

She's looking away from me, and even as I'm processing the thought that I've once again fucked things up in my haste I catch movement from the corner of my eye, and turn to see one of those fucking Christian cunts approaching us. Is this guy for fucking real? Now of all times?

'Hey guys, how's your night?' he asks cheerily.

'Fuck off,' I snap.

He's undeterred however, and comes right up to us. Erina's quickly tucking her boob back in and shoving her dress down over her knees.

'The city looks wonderful at night-time, huh?' he continues.

'Yeah, we're on a date, actually,' I inform him sternly, finally giving it a name.

'That's great, good for you both,' the cunt says with actual joy, not getting the hint.

Any sane prick would understand the situation and move on, or wouldn't be bothering couples in parks at night-time in the first fucking place. But these spastic cunts have got fuck all concept of personal boundaries.

'Listen, you need to fuck off right now.'

He tries to act innocent, smiling in the face of my hostility. 'Aw, no need to be like that, brother. I'm just having a friendly chat.'

'Like fuck you are,' I snap. 'I know what you pricks are all about.'

'And what's that like?'

I glance over to the fountain where the other two are still talking to the girls, ready to make a point about their evangelical crusade when I notice something odd going on over there. The girls are standing dead straight in front of both men, who for their part have their palms up on the girls' foreheads and are muttering aloud. Erina follows my gaze and when she spies them, too, she grips my arm tighter.

'You're fucking joking,' I snarl.

'What're they doing?' Erina whispers.

I turn back to this intruding cunt and growl: 'You've got some fucking hide coming over here with that shit.'

'Nah, man, if you're not interested that's okay, too,' he says, hands out in supplication, still with that stupid smile on his mug. I want to remove it with my knife.

'What are they doing?' says Erina more loudly this time, still watching the makeshift exorcism over by the fountain.

'They're casting out the Devil himself, aren't they?' I go, my eyes not leaving this shifty bastard in front of me. 'Mate, seriously... you need to fuck off back over there before I break both your fucking legs. Right now!'

'You need to get your anger in check,' he offers as he retreats, telling us he's still open to a friendly conversation if we want to wander over, emphasising the 'friendly' for my benefit.

'Fuck that cunt,' I growl when he's gone, staring at him hard.

'What the hell's going on?' asks Erina, finally relinquishing her vice-grip on my arm.

'Those God-botherers aren't just spreading the so-called Good Word. They're performing exorcisms on any ol Joe Blo they can lay their hands on.'

'Is that for real? I thought that only happened in horror movies?'

'Nah, it's real alright,' I say, leading her away from the park and up the steps towards Ann Street where the war memorial flame gutters. 'I was part of a crazy cult once, when I was younger, and they did the same thing. My family volunteered to undergo their fucked home-style exorcism, where we were humiliated by dragging out any skeletons in the closet for them to dispel as demons. We were used to satisfy their fucking egos.'

'Holy shit,' Erina goes. 'That's insane.'

My vitriol towards these missionary-styled Christians isn't the run-of-the-mill disdain some goths affect in order to look cool, to look like it's a good versus evil argument or some shit. Mine is a genuine, born-of-fire fucking hatred for what they stand for. All their posturing as righteous folk is one of the most deluded fucking things I've ever come across. More deluded than any schizophrenic I've ever met.

'Don't worry about them, Erina. You stay clear of em, you'll be fine. Get into a debate with them, then you're not because that's what they want. They want an argument so they can slowly turn you over to thinking their apparent unity is something you'll want, too. I've seen it a hundred times over in King George Square. They get into debates with complete strangers, provoking them into raging or name-calling, and then they convince the same strangers to reflect on the debate and see how irrational the stranger was behaving. From there, they start to prise into the poor bastard's psyche, finding emotional triggers to break the poor bastard down until finally he starts to think maybe some sort of salvation is for him. Which is lucky for him that they came along.'

There's a little-used elevator beside the bar across the road that takes us up to the concourse for the train station.

'Those arseholes back there have taken it to the next level. The laying-on of hands, calling forth demons and exorcising them away to leave the sinner without sin. That's the final seal.'

It's ironic when I think about it: I was sucking on Erina's tit and about to finger her pussy on a public park bench under a date palm that stood as a symbol of biblical victory. We're the ones that left the park from that simple confrontation, so I guess in a way that's somewhat of a victory for that Christian cunt, even though I'm sure he'd have preferred to cast my demons out and claim *that* victory instead.

I can sense Erina's not ready to head to the train station, either reluctant to end the night or reluctant to invite me back to hers. Given I'm only currently crashing on Twix's couch in between sleeping on the streets, that's not an option. I lead her up some more stairs to a concrete plaza behind the train station, flanked by shabby retail and office buildings and the QR headquarters. It's quiet in here; hardly anyone uses this place at night.

We start kissing again, groping at each other's bodies, so I lead her behind a dried up water fountain that they turned off because it was leaking into the carpark below. Cigarette butts litter the ground from where the day workers got their fix.

Erina hikes up her skirt and places her hands against the wall.

'I can't wait anymore, it's killing me,' she pleads.

Fair enough. It's killing me, too. My boner's returned big time, so I waste no time dropping my dacks (carefully placing the knife on the fountain edge behind me) and mounting her from behind. It's so fucking good. We fit like a glove.

I think she cums fairly quickly, because her body soon relaxes, but I'm yet to get there myself. She hasn't told me to stop, and she still feels well lubricated, so I keep pumping away. It's not that it doesn't feel good. Since Jillian broke up with me I haven't even masturbated much, so shouldn't I be more than ready to go? I only started last night on the meds that McKay gave me, so it's hardly like I'd have any adverse side-effects from those yet.

I wonder how Jillian would feel about me fucking a random girl in public. Would she feel bad for me, bad about the lengths she's driven me to? And what would Erina's ex do if he walked past now and caught us, given his boyfriend rights to protest have been revoked?

The thought of that big lunk copping an eyeful of our pale bodies grinding against one another here in this dirty corner makes my balls tighten. I can feel the familiar build-up and then the tickle shooting through my cock toward that delicious bloom of pleasure at the tip.

'Not so fucking fast,' snaps Erina, pulling away before I can blow my load up her.

The air feels cold around the wetness on my shaft, and before I can control it the semen starts pumping out. Erina's dodged it by sliding across the wall, her skirt pulled back down to protect her skin from scrapes.

'Oh my fucking god, yes,' I gasp.

Erina laughs. 'Careful calling on God like that, those crazy Christians might come back and catch you jizzing on the city.'

Her words have no effect on me; I'm lost to the orgasm. But as soon as the spunk stops dribbling from my dick, a kind of shame descends on me.

'That's what I needed,' says Erina. 'You fuck so good. Kissing not so, but the fucking is a hell yes.'

Releasing the build-up of lust returns the brain to its faculties, and the cigarette butt-strewn corner of a shitty looking office courtyard behind the train station seems like a less-than-ideal place to begin a relationship. But if Erina's happy, then I am too. I aim to serve.

'Shit, I better get going,' she says, glancing at her watch. 'Last train's soon.'

'You want me to come and make you breakfast in the morning?' I joke, hoping that the answer is firmly in the affirmative.

Erina looks apologetic. 'Sorry, Dante. This has to stay as a one-off thing.'

She can't look me in the eye now, hurrying down the steps to the gates of the train station.

'A one-off thing?'

'I have to get home before my boyfriend finishes his night shift,' she says firmly, still avoiding my eyes.

Fuck. I don't know why, but I was sorta hoping for something more, and I definitely assumed her and that stupid boyfriend must have split up. Otherwise, why'd she agree to hang out with me?

'Sorry, we've gone through a rough patch, is all,' she explains, rushing through the unmanned gates and down the escalators to the platforms.

I remain outside the station, feeling a bit shell-shocked at the abruptness of both her departure and her confession. Even if she'd explained to me she wanted something casual, I might have been up for that, too. But to do this? It feels... weird. Explains the sex in public somewhat, then. I thought she was just being kinky.

I head back to the Prozac Palace, resisting the temptation to go back to Anzac Square and get into a physical altercation with those Christian cunts. It'd be rewarding, confronting those fuckers with a knife, scaring the shit out of them by telling em I'm gonna cut the demons from them. It'd be fucking glorious watching them shit themselves. But I need to get back and sit down. Find some sleep.

I slam the front door shut when I get back to Twix's, a childish act of defiance to wake everybody in the building up so that I'm not the only cunt feeling put out.

'The fuck, Dante?' grumbles Twix sleepily as he staggers out into the lounge, shielding his eyes from the light. I'm guessing he's not long home from one of his late shifts because the manky cunt's still wearing his insecurity shirt. 'You gotta make so much fucking noise?'

'She's still with her boyfriend,' I moan miserably.

'Why'd you think she wasn't?' goes Twix. 'I tried to tell you that before you went out.'

'I don't need the I-told-you-so lecture,' I go. But he's right, he did warn me, and I should have listened.

He sits down next to me. 'You okay?'

'I dunno. It's just been so shit lately.'

'I thought you were just rebounding with Erina,' he confesses.

'I should have been, ay?'

He nods.

Raven comes out of her bedroom tying her gown shut, rubbing at her eyes. Lunar shoots out from behind her like a shadow and leaps up onto the couch next to me. I'm actually allergic to cats but animals really like me for some reason. Lunar starts stroking her head against my arm, carefully tiptoeing into my lap and curling up.

'What if she really has broken up with him?' I wonder aloud. 'Maybe she's just using him as an excuse to avoid something more serious right now?'

'Don't even do that to yourself, Dante,' Twix says sympathetically.

'Who the fuck is slamming doors in the middle of the night?' Raven goes.

'Sorry, Raven,' says Twix gently, 'Dante's had another blow. He met up with Erina tonight.'

'Ah, so she's single now, yeah?' I don't care for the edge in her voice. Raven scuffles across the messy floor to sit next to me. 'Bonk her?'

'Oh, fer fuck's sake, Raven,' goes Twix. 'Do you have to be so crass?'

He's probably hoping I'll answer her all the same.

'As if you guys never are,' says Raven harshly, then clocks the state that I'm in. 'You'll be okay, sweetie,' she says, using that woman's intuition to divine the gist of my night without even hearing a single detail of it. She kisses the top of my head before shuffling back to her room. 'Look after him, Lu-Lu,' she smiles at the cat.

'You right, mate?' asks Twix as I lie down on the couch and pull a blanket across myself.

'Yep.'

Lunar mewls loudly then goes off in search of adventure.

Twix turns off the light and staggers back to bed.

THE JUNKIES

One of the great things about being a security guard is that I work nights quite a lot. That's good for ol Twixxie's complexion, at the end of the day. Keeps me pale as a vampire for the chickadees.

The reason I get mostly night shifts is because the company I work for, NiteWorks, subcontracts to bigger firms such as Cubby Security Ltd who dole out to NiteWorks at a much reduced rate any shifts that require penalty rates, thereby skimming a heftier cut than normal from the contract with the client. NiteWorks, in turn, must also take a hefty cut cause I've heard that it's a considerably large gap between the contracted rate as per Cubby and what NiteWorks pays us guards to be on site. The client, those who fork up the dosh in the first place, have no idea about this arrangement, nor need to know anyways. But it stands to reason that if they did know of it, they could cut out companies like Cubby and come straight to NiteWorks and insist on paying only what Cubby subcontracts us for anyway, thereby saving themselves a considerable amount. They don't, though, because of NiteWorks' low profile. No-one's heard of NiteWorks outside of the industry itself because we're always wearing the uniforms of the contracting company. The only ones getting short-changed here are us guards (who are paid a flat rate with no penalties), but one look at the quality of guard on offer quickly dispels that notion.

They're a fucking sorry lot, mostly, my peers. Lots of washed up has-beens, ex plumbers, failed photographers and skilled migrants with degrees worth shit if the work's not here. And then there's the downright inept, the overweight, the toothless, the witless. Shockers, the lot of em. *Allez!* There's plenty of the latter on the company's roster. It makes me, by comparison, one of the more presentable lads in their cache, so I'm always sent to the sites where a visible presence with customer contact is required. Unfortunately, that sometimes means working the day shifts.

Such as today, in the Valley.

I patrol the shops around the McWhirter's building and the Valley Centre over the pedestrian bridge. This shift's easier to pass the time on because of the amount of people I can interact with, such as Megan for example. She works in the pawn shop on the corner before the pedestrian bridge over to the plaza, so I drop in heaps for the usual shits and giggles.

I prefer the night shifts, though, because even though I don't get paid more for them, they're always on remote sites off-limits to the public, so I can usually sneak in some naps. It's a bit risky, because the contracting company will send out a duty officer to check on us, and they'll mix up their rounds so you won't know which nights and at what time they'll turn up. Even our supervisors have been caught out when they sometimes get rostered on for static duties. I heard about how that useless tosser Robert Heeley, one of our supervisors, was sprung sleeping in the mechanic's workshop out at the Mount Gravatt Community College, a portable telly on the table in front of him. He was meant to be patrolling the grounds and making sure people didn't use the college as a thoroughfare because they'd had too many break-ins. He'd shot up out of his chair when the duty officer banged on a metal rubbish bin, declaring he was on break. Except the duty officer had been watching Heeley for about a half hour and we're not meant to have breaks on those night shifts.

I heard that story from the horse's mouth, the duty officer from Cubby, when he came out to one of my jobs and stayed for a chat. It sounded like a warning to me. A kind of morality tale. But the other guards at NiteWorks confirmed it did actually happen.

Speaking of useless tossers, a bunch of em at nine o'clock and heading in my direction.

A pack of four: three lads and a chick. All dressed in that ghetto fashion, Adidas or Nike clothing but trashed looking, like they're homeless but they're actually not. Just fucking grots. Bum bags on, goatee tufts, dark bags under their bloodshot eyes. Spot the fuckers from a mile off. Druggies.

They don't so much as walk or stroll about as they do dart. They're like those minnow fish that shoot forward in straight lines, pause, then shoot straight in a different direction. Always moving. Fidgeting. I'm committing to memory their habits, their mannerisms. They've clocked me and bee-line in a different direction, one joker with long white hair scraped back into a tortured ponytail watching me over his shoulder with the expression of a disgruntled child.

I casually stroll in their direction and slow down as they leave the centre and push through the glass doors at the bottom of the stairs and into the harsh sunlight outside.

They'll be back through here several more times during my shift, guaranteed. They've got no-where to go, and will dart back and forth across the middle of the Valley, touching upon all their connections like battery terminals, lighting up a whole network of druggies and criminals. Maybe there'll be action today, maybe not. There usually isn't, unless one of them tries to shoplift and I'm called in to try and stop em leaving the store while the police come.

I meander into the pawn shop because Megs's in today. Sometimes it's the owner, sometimes it's her. Either way, there's that creepy ever-present statue of a Roman centurion looking up at the ceiling and holding up a wooden cross, which the owner keeps up next to the ceiling rafters behind the desk. I've asked Megs about its significance in the past, but she's got no idea either. She's happy to see me, and says she saw me strolling past earlier.

'Ol Twixxie's always on duty, ay,' I go.

'Sure you are,' she giggles.

'Nah, for real,' I protest, but then remember that I like to sleep on the night shift sites, so leave the protestations at that. 'Dante's been at my place again for a few days.'

'Ah, I thought he was at yours since around New Years,' she goes.

'When you had your little séance at Toowong.'

I feel myself blushing. 'Oh, you heard about that, huh?'

That's probably what those two were talking about at the picnic. No doubt Raven blabbed it all to Dante who in turn's blabbed it all to Megs. Ol Twixxie, the big fucking joke, as usual.

'Yeah,' she grins. 'Off Xanthe.'

Oh, fer fuck's sake.

'She needs to learn when to shut her cakehole,' I go, wondering what else she told Megan, hoping my friend will spill the beans.

But apparently it's not a lot, because Megan says nothing about Ursula. 'So no spirits, no angel?'

'Nah, but we gave it a whirl all the same,' I go, even though she's just teasing me. 'You should come out one night.'

'No thanks. Spookies can stay in their place, and I'll stay in mine.'

'Suit yerself.'

Behind us the four druggies wander in, and even though they clock me, they approach the counter anyways, like well-meaning customers. One of em, the young bloke with white hair and pale skin like an albino, is sniffling and has a fucking horrible blister in the crook of his arm. *Allez!* Fucking junkies.

'Do youse buy CD's?' asks the pack leader, a guy only a bit older than me but who looks at least twice my age, possibly on account of the handlebar moustache.

'Sort of,' goes Megs, screwing her nose up doubtfully. 'We have them, but they're not our top sellers,' and she gestures toward a side wall that has a shelf full of CD's, cassettes and VHS tapes of movies.

'These are brand new, but,' crows this joker, pulling a huge stack out from his greasy knapsack and stacking them on the countertop in front of Megs. The top one's *Ceremony* by The Cult.

'No scratches,' the chick with them arrogantly points out.

Megs opens the cases and peruses the booklets, checking the surface of the discs. They're right, no scratches and they look brand new. It always begs the question of how they acquired them, but Megs knows not to bother asking.

'Well,' she begins with a tone of dubiousness, just to set the lay of the land, 'we can probably take the Marilyn Manson off your hands, and the Rolling Stones ones. I can give you four bucks each for those. Two dollars for the rest.'

The bloke's outraged. 'Are you taking the fucken piss? '

I inch closer to Megan's side, let em know I won't tolerate any bullshit.

'Can we get four bucks for all of them?' chimes in the sniffling albino prick with the infected blister.

'Four for the lot can be arranged,' replies Megs with a deadpan expression.

They start to panic.

'Morlock means four bucks for each CD,' growls the pack leader with the handlebar moustache.

'Nah,' says Megs, shaking her head.

They stare firmly at her, as though she'll change her mind. Megan stands her ground, smiling sweetly back.

'This is a fucken joke, ay,' decides the leader, giving me the forks. 'We'll take em down the fucken road to the other pawn shop, then. He'll give us what they're worth.'

The prick glances around the store and scoffs as if to say it's all worthless anyway, then all four of them storm out.

'I was ready to give them what frigging for,' I grumble.

'Don't worry, they'll be back,' says Megs. 'They won't get a better offer than that around here.'

'Wouldn't have minded that Cult CD. Didja see one of the sods had a gross sore on his arm.'

'I saw that,' she says, and pulls a face. 'And they stunk.'

'Like they were homeless,' I agree.

That gets us back onto the subject of Dante.

'I don't know how the hell he does it,' I exclaim. 'He doesn't have a home, sleeps in gardens half the time, and yet he can pull a chick faster than me.'

Megs laughs. 'Yeah, it's a mystery. But there's something about him, don'tcha think? I mean, he's not super attractive or even that charming, really. But there's something about him that I guess girls must respond to.'

'It's his energy, I reckon. There's a real stamina for life, enduring it despite his mental illness and his living arrangements. Or lack thereof.'

'Could be it,' muses Megs.

'Or maybe it's because he hooks up with sluts like Erina,' I shrug.

'Ew,' goes Megs.

'You know, I've really got no idea why you and Erina hate each other so much.'

'We don't hate each other,' Megs retorts. 'I just can't stand the skank. Besides, you're the one who called her a slut.'

'On account of she has a boyfriend and is still sleeping around.'

'Well, there you go,' grins Megs smugly. 'Another reason not to like her.'

'Oh, I give up,' I go, smacking my hand over my face dramatically.

'Speaking of which,' says Megs, 'what about you and Karen? I heard you guys were taking time apart.'

Jess, or Xanthe, really didn't fill Megs in on much, did she? I thought chicks were meant to gossip every last detail to one another, but seems Jess didn't blab at all about me trying to get it on with that underage chicky at Toowong Cemetery.

'Nah, I think we're over for good,' I confess. 'Abi told me last week that she saw Karen out with some bloke, who definitely wasn't me. I rang Karen and asked about it, but she denied it and said Abi must have mistaken her for someone else. Total bullshit, of course.'

'Of course,' says Megan, watching me carefully.

I could be wrong, but I think she's looking at me expectantly, like maybe she's secretly delighted that me and Karen are finally finished.

I decide to test this theory and plunge right in.

'You know, maybe you and I should–'

'No,' she says flatly, then starts laughing at my stunned expression. I gotta admit, when she's laughing free and easily like this, she's pretty cute. 'I'm sorry, but yeah, let's not go there.'

'Fair enough,' I nod.

The junkies from earlier have returned, just as Megs said they would, and they're acting a lot more humble than last time. Two of these jokers are even hanging their heads as if in shame!

'Hey, back again,' says handlebars, dropping the CD's onto the counter like they're not such hot property after all. Well, they're probably definitely hot property, but nothing special is what I mean.

'No luck down the road, eh?' says Megs, putting on that sweet smile again, the one she reserves for difficult customers.

The motherfuckers are mute while Megs sorts the CD's into three piles.

'I'll give you a dollar for each of these,' she goes, placing a hand on the stack with Manson and the Stones in it, 'and fifty cents for these ones.' Then she slides the third stack, about a dozen CD's in total, back at the jokers. 'Those, you can keep.'

I can see the rage develop in this bastard's eyes, old handlebars. The deep creases on his face smash into each other as his face distorts. He wants to explode, call her out on the deal, but he can't. Megs is his last hope of a quick cash injection.

'But you said you'd take these ones for four bucks each, not one,' he whines, his voice straining.

'That was before,' Megs goes. 'The market's taken a downturn since then. I can shift these at only about four bucks myself. Not much of a profit margin.'

The bloke turns to his mutts and confers.

'Bitch is givin it to us right up the clacker,' the shit-stain moans.

'Look, I get this isn't the time or place,' the albino says to him, 'but it's not okay to talk about women like that.'

'Will you shut the fuck up with that PC shit,' Forks goes, rolling his eyes.

'Is it awright for me to say it?' the chick wants to know.

'Of course, you're a woman,' the albino says.

'Bitch is givin it to us right up the clacker,' she repeats.

The albino shrugs. 'It's her right to inflate the prices if she's so inclined.'

This convo's starting to get on my tits, I must admit. I glance at Megs and discreetly point at the junkies, as if to ask her if she's ready for me to turf the motherfuckers out. But she's enjoying herself too much, it appears. She shakes her head at me.

'Awright, just do it, Forks, ploise,' mumbles the chick. 'Sell em and let's go, fer fark's sake.'

The bloke with the handlebar moustache, Forks, turns back to Megs and grumbles that she's got a deal.

Megs opens a baggie of coins under the counter, wisely forgoing opening the till, and deposits a handful of gold coins onto the counter top. She slides each across to him, counting out thirteen coins.

'There you go,' she chirps. 'Fifteen dollars and no cents.'

The bastard glowers at her with pure hatred, and scoops the dosh from the counter into his dirty palm.

Megs hands me the Cult CD, free of charge.

'You beauty,' I go, turning it over to read the track-listing.

The handlebars joker gets a bit narky about this, demanding that I give him a little extra money for the CD.

'Not your transaction any more, mate,' I tell him.

'Just leave em be, Forks, honestly,' goes the albino, motioning his mate away. 'Thanks for your time,' he says to Megs, earnestly.

Forks and his pack of junkie mutts stalk out of the shop, arguing amongst themselves about how much they've raised.

'What a frigging life, eh?' I muse, thinking about the lesbians on the top floor back at the Prozac Palace, who are known heroin addicts. I've never seen them shit in their own nest, so to speak. Everyone at the Palace gets along with them fine, and we haven't had them try and break into our flats or steal our shit to sell it for drugs. Takes all types, I guess.

'It does get tiring,' admits Megs, 'but it's fun to make em squirm.'

She takes out a pricing gun and rolls the rubber wheel until it reads $15.00 and starts stamping price stickers onto the fronts of every CD she just bought.

'I thought I was gonna have to step in and deal with the bastards for a moment,' I confess. 'They're lucky Dante wasn't here. He'd have probably pulled a knife on them.'

'I don't need either of you two going around defending me,' she says sternly.

'Four junkies isn't something to sniff at,' I remind her. 'I'm trained to deal with this sort of thing.'

'I've worked retail for years now,' she goes, haughtily. 'I suspect my abilities at conflict resolution are considerably more sharpened than yours by now.'

Sounds like a dig at me over Karen.

'Really?' I snap. 'Anyway, I got work to do.'

'Twix, sorry,' Megan says as I go. 'I didn't mean it like that.'

'Yeah, no bother,' I mutter, without turning around.

It's not Megan's fault, though. It's those fucking junkies. They wind everyone up. We're all just trying to get on with life, gainfully employed in work we're not thrilled about by any means, and those arseholes swan about stealing and begging for enough money to get wasted. And for what?

I should probably go back and apologise to Megan. She's a good sort, and I might've been a bit out of line treating her like that. If I think about it, she *can* look after herself. But you can't trust people these days. The world's slowly going to shit, and I worry about the likes of Megs believing they can stand in the face of that.

I'll grab us a cinnamon muffin later and butter her up with that.

Megs's great. She'll be gracious about the whole thing and act like we're cool. First I'll do the rounds, check on all the fire ext doors and make sure they're closed and the alarms are still on, check the toilets and make sure no-one's passed out or dead in them.

Over in the food court of the Valley Centre, outside the train station entrance, T-Rex Tony's being hassled by some little curly-haired bogan kid, a geezer who looks like he's still in high school. This seems completely in my jurisdiction so I wander over and stand behind the kid while he goes off at Tony.

I've known Tony for a couple of years now, mostly through the clubs but I see him out occasionally as well. We're definitely not friends, just acquaintances. I don't think we could become friends, anyways, because Dante hates him for some reason.

'I don't give a fuck,' this kid is hissing at Tony, 'I'll beat the shit out of you if I see you again.'

Tony's actually looking a bit scared, even though he's almost twice the height of this little toe-rag and probably twice his age, as well. That's why we call him T-Rex Tony, because he's such an old sod compared to the rest of us on the scene. That, and his bright blue eyes are all boggly like that crap dinosaur in the movie last year with Whoopi Goldberg. Can't think of the name, but the dinosaur geezer was a T-Rex, too. Called Teddy. Anyways, there's a few oldies still around, but not many attend the clubs as regularly as Tony does.

'What's up, fellas?' I say in my best authoritative tone.

The kid spins around, his curls bouncing across his eyes crazily, and Tony looks relieved that I've gotten involved.

'Nothing,' the toe-rag goes, his face pinched.

Then it occurs to me I know exactly who this kid is. The little shit bailed me up on the job in the Queen Street Mall not long ago, when I was working shift at The Big Block. Accused me of being involved with his sister, or trying to be. The latter's true, except she wouldn't have a bar of me. Ursula her name was. Can't remember *his* name, though. Raven said it was Dick something or other.

'Sounds like you were threatening my mate, here,' I say sternly, satisfied to see his eyes quiver as he begins to understand the situation he's now in. Two against one.

He's looking at me funny, like he knows my face, too.

'He's been messing with my sister,' the kid goes.

Seems the little minx gets around, and this kid's making a habit of trying to defend her honour. What she has left of it, anyways.

'Name?' I pull out my Spirax notebook and pen that I keep in my breast-pocket. Essential tools in this job. Looks a bit official, too, even though it's only one of those yellow-covered notebooks found in every newsagency.

'Yvonne,' the kid goes.

'Your name's Yvonne now?'

'Nah, my sister's name's Yvonne.'

'Yeah, righto,' I scoff. 'But I want your name, lad.'

'Michael Bucchorn,' he offers. 'But you already know that.'

So he does remember me. Why wouldn't he?

'What's this, then?' he snaps. 'A pedo's club? You all sticking up for each other, or what?'

I point directly at him, a little technique designed to command compliance. 'Listen here, Michael. The truth is that your sister's a bit of a whore, but the other truth is that I've never touched her. Neither has my mate here. Yeah, I can see you want to believe otherwise but that's on you. Not me.' Then remembering what Megs said about not needing me constantly defending her, I add: 'You've gotta understand your sister's growing up and doesn't need her precious big brother protecting her all the time.'

The real truth is that I'm worried that Tony has actually done the deed with Ursula and will get us both into trouble if this kid goes squealing to the boys in blue. If I recall, in my last encounter with Bucchorn here he said his sister was only fourteen. Well below legal limits.

The kid's obviously mindful that I called Tony a mate, and that I'm in a security uniform, so he gets a bit nervous. 'But she's younger than me,' he whines.

'I couldn't give a rat's arse,' I tell him sternly. 'You can't just go around threatening people. This bloke's much bigger than you, for a start.'

Tony grins at me, impressed with how I'm handling the situation.

I see some police officers walking through the plaza. Not good.

'Go on, fuck off now,' I tell Michael Buchhorn, shooing him away with my hand.

'You're dead, pedo,' he hisses at Tony, then as an afterthought includes me in the threat before running off full-pelt down the plaza towards the back carpark.

'Leave him,' I say to Tony, even though he wasn't making any move to go after the kid. 'He's not worth it, ay.'

What wouldn't have been worth it is those officers coming over to see what's up and finding out I'd grilled the kid and taken his name. Might've gotten me into a bit of trouble for that, not to mention the trouble Tony could've been in.

'Thanks, Twix,' gushes Tony. 'I owe you a drink next club.'

'Yeah, no problem. So, how's his sister, then?'

We grin at each other and Tony tells me she was unreal.

'Tight as a frog's arsehole,' he goes, shaking his head. 'That was a wild thirtieth birthday do, that's for sure.'

'Nice, nice,' I nod, curiosity getting the better of me. 'How old was she?'

'Fourteen,' he grins sheepishly. 'Both of them.'

I feel a jealous twinge inside me, but force the smile to stay on my face.

'Sodding hell! *Two* of em?'

'Yup,' he goes, looking bashful, or pretending to. 'Or nearly fourteen, at least. Fuck, we were all so wasted.'

'How the hell does an old sod like you get two fourteen year olds?'

Perhaps there's an edge in my voice, but whatever it is he senses some outrage in me and starts toning it down a bit.

'Dunno,' he shrugs, less grin now and more awkward rictus. 'Michael did it, I didn't even know them.'

He's referring to his best mate Michael Carlyon, obviously, not the young lad whose sister was part of this dubiously drunken *ménage-a-trois.*

'Fair enough, I spose. Better not go that way, then,' I suggest, indicating the carpark where the kid had run off to.

'Nah, better not,' he laughs. 'Gonna go see Meggie-Meg. Always good to see that rack,' he adds, making as if to squeeze imaginary mammaries on his own chest.

Tony strides off, his gait bizarrely paced because of his incredibly long legs.

I can't argue with his delineation of Megs, because she does in fact have amazing tig bitties, but at the same time I'm feeling like I've betrayed her by letting it slide with Tony. She's meant to be a friend, after all. But what I can do? Blokes will be blokes.

After all the excitement I deserve a little me time, so I bee-line for Dark Obsession to have a quick squiz at any new stock they've got in but I've taken no more than a few steps when the radio goes off.

Barry from Centre Management comes on and goes: 'Travis, some businesses saying there's suspicious activity in the south exit rooftop stairwell. Probably just kids. Go flush em out, yeah?'

'No worries, Bazza,' I reply.

'Good man,' he goes, the line all static. It almost sounds like he calls me a wanker to the bloke sitting next to him in the control room, but it's just the static. Happens all the time.

I race up the south exit stairwell and round the last bend to find a group of people huddled at the top in the darkness.

My heart hammers fast, and I just freeze and stare up at them. I broke my own rule, which I'd adopted from an old security guard I'd trained with when I'd first got in the business. He told me the pay we're on wasn't worth risking our necks, and whenever he had to go into a warehouse while on patrols he'd make as much noise as possible, even yelling out that he was on the premises. He said you never knew if someone had broken in and would attack you if caught by surprise, so he always gave them the opportunity to hear him coming from way off. Give em enough time to escape or hide, you know?

One of the jokers in the dark stairwell above glances around and straight away I clock him as that fucking junkie Forks that was in Megan's shop earlier.

I pull my maglite torch from my belt. I hate wearing it because of the weight, ay, but it doubles as the perfect weapon when needed without the police hassling us about carrying an actual weapon. I brandish the maglite up in front of my face like a baton.

'Easy, easy,' I murmur to them.

They're not having it, though.

'Shit, it's the security dude,' bellows the albino lad. What'd they call him before? Morcock? I need to remember for when I tell the police later.

'Fuck him up, baby,' spits the chick.

In response, the older bloke called Forks takes a couple of steps down towards me. 'Fuck off outta here, cunt,' he says.

'You lot shouldn't be up here,' I tell them, finding my voice, and my balls, again.

'Cunt, I told you to fuck off,' says Forks, waving his arm around in front. Only now can I see the syringe full of murky blood in his hand.

'Whoa! Whoa, easy,' I go, backing off slowly, feeling cold all of a sudden.

The albino's telling everyone to stay calm.

The Forks bloke follows me down the steps, keeping pace, telling me over and over again to fuck off while he waves the syringe at me.

When he gets to the bend in the stairwell he stops advancing. I keep my eyes trained on him and that dirty fucking syringe, and only when I get out into the plaza again do I feel the weight of the maglite torch in my hand. I'd forgotten all about it after he threatened me with the needle.

I duck into the nearest store, a shoe repairer's, and tell the bloke behind the counter to call the police.

I should've dealt with those pricks back in Megs's shop when I had the chance. The junkies, I mean, not the police. The police are okay in my books.

When the boys in blue get down here, the stairwell's empty but the alarm on the fire door hasn't been tripped.

If it wasn't for how shaken up I am, I don't think the cops would believe me about being threatened, so we all head over to centre management, where one of them takes my statement while the other gets Barry to check the cameras. Sure enough, while I was in the shoe repairer's, those junkie mutts snuck outta the stairwell and made their way past the big Chinese bingo hall and through to the McWhirter's building, doing that fast speed-walking that druggies always seem to do like they've always got urgent business somewhere.

'You're lucky you weren't stabbed,' goes one of the officers.

I think three cinnamon muffins are now on the cards, ay.

LITTLE SISTER

'It's either go for the job or get suspended from payments indefinitely, Alexandra,' says John Flaherty, the unemployment officer at the CES.

It feels like blackmail, but, like, I've got no choice, right? They obviously see my move up from Melbourne as a chance to improve my job prospects, which isn't why I came up at all. The truth is that my ex became my stalker. He couldn't cope with the break-up, and I was afraid he was, like, going to go over the edge and maybe hurt me for real. The police said they weren't able to do anything because all he'd done up to that point was verbalise the threat. I inform Mister Flaherty all of this but it hardly matters to him the real reason I've moved here.

'I've got a job to do here,' he shrugs.

'Beggars can't be choosers, right?' I reply, and he half-heartedly agrees with a grim smile. So mote it be.

So, like, I get a cheap skirt and jacket from Best and Less and head off to the interview right in the heart of the city at a solicitor's firm. I've got absolutely no experience in this field whatsoever, and will likely sink like a stone in the interview process.

The Indian lady at the front introduces herself as Prita and buzzes me through to an office off to the side for the interview. The bloke conducting it is an old guy whose gut basically hangs over his baggy trousers.

He's like: 'I'm Mister Calthorpe, one of three partners here.'

I imagine he's got no first name.

He tells me all about his firm and the work they do, most of which goes straight over muggins' head here, but when he says that my role will be filing their papers and, like, answering memos and stuff, I don't feel so overwhelmed. I mean, it sounds simple enough but it's still all new to me. Last job I had was in a factory picking orders for a book distribution company in Melbourne.

Calthorpe shows me around the office which is mostly staffed with women. Everyone seems grouse, and I, like, start picturing myself slotting into this complex little machine like a well-oiled part, helping to push along the gears of industry as it were.

'And this is my assistant Jennifer,' Calthorpe says, introducing me to a beautiful girl a couple of years my senior.

She smiles at me but, like, doesn't extend her hand. Her eyes are strangely calculating.

She's like: 'You'll fit in well here,' emphasising the word *fit* as her eyes flick down to my chest where my boobs threaten to burst the buttons of the cheapie shirt. I'm going to have to get something custom-made to fit the girls, I guess.

I'm like: 'Thanks, Jenny,' but straightaway the smile evaporates from her face and her eyes go sharp, like they were slightly unfocused before but now've become crystal clear. There's something frightening about the change in her.

Unbelievably, Mister Calthorpe thinks I'm perfect for the job and tells me he's going to let the CES know that I'm hired. My heart sinks as I was really hoping to take my time finding a job, not rush into one, especially one where I'm basically out of my depth.

'As soon as everything is sorted paper-wise,' he says, 'we'll see you back here. Should only take a day or two, I expect.'

So it's with mixed emotions I return home to my little Gillingham Street flat and phone Twix with the news.

He's like: 'Such a coincidence! I've got a couple of lawyers myself.'

I'm intrigued. This'll have to be something security-related, which means top secret, I bet.

'Yep, one's pro-Bono and the other can't stand his music.'

It takes me a moment to realise that it's meant to be a joke.

'You idiot,' I laugh. 'Anyway, the girls from the office are going out tomorrow night and told me to come. A kind of orientation. I was, like, wondering if you'd come along? Like a celebration, basically.'

'Don't wanna be picked apart by the wolves, eh?'

I sigh. 'Something like that. They seem nice and all, right? But, like, I don't really know anyone there yet. It'd be good to have a familiar face, of sorts.'

'Yeah, no problem,' he chuckles. 'Where they headed to?'

'Hogies,' I say. 'Dollar drinks all night.'

'Fuck that,' Twix snorts. 'Ten bucks entry to be fucked around by a bunch of normies?'

'Ten dollars? That's pretty steep!'

It cost me ten dollars for this shirt alone.

'It's to keep us from mixing with the ruling classes,' Twix says.

'I hardly think they're the ruling classes,' I laugh, thinking how, like, the girls at the office probably have the same everyday problems as me.

There's a dull beeping noise in the earpiece.

'Hang on, Twix, I've got another call coming through. I'll find out who it is and be back in a jiffy.'

I press the button on the keypad to change the lines, and find out it's my mother.

'Just phoning to see how the job interview went, dear.'

'Well, I got it, Mama!'

'Oh, that's lovely,' she gasps, and shouts the news to Papa, repeating herself twice because he's half deaf. 'You must be so thrilled,' she says when she returns to the call.

'Kinda, I guess,' I reply. 'Can I call you back because I've got –'

'You don't sound too happy about it,' Mama says, interrupting me. 'This is good for you, Alex, after all the troubles you've had down here.'

'That was hardly my fault,' I say sourly. 'I was stalked, remember?'

'I'm just saying sometimes it's best to keep busy,' she persists. 'Idle hands and all that, as they say.'

'I was just hoping for some time to, like, get used to things, that's all.'

'Oh pish-posh,' she tuts. 'You get used to things as you go. Look at Lisa and her business. Do you think she rested on her laurels to make it happen? Of course not!'

'Do we really need to bring Lisa up?'

I fucking hate it when she, like, compares me to my sister.

'I only do so in order to motivate you, Alexandra,' she says in clipped tones, sounding offended. 'Don't you think it's time you left all this gothic nonsense behind and start getting on with life?'

'It's not nonsense, Mama. It's my lifestyle, it's who I am. It doesn't mean I'm not getting on with life at all.'

'If you say so, Alexandra,' she says in that belittling way that means everything I'm saying is crap, and that, like, nothing I *can* say will excuse being a goth.

'Twix is waiting on the other line for me. I've gotta go.'

'What sort of a name is that?' she scoffs. 'Sounds like a chocolate bar.'

I'm like: 'Love you too, Mama,' pressing the button back over to Twix. 'Fuck, she really, really bugs me sometimes!'

'Do I really?' Mama says, to my absolute horror.

The button on the keypad didn't press down hard enough. Reflexively I slam the receiver down in the cradle, ending the call, and just, like, stare at it with my hands over my mouth in case I say something else stupidly clueless and she miraculously hears me.

DANTE AND THE HI8

'Film this, ya mad bastard,' yells Nathanael right into the lens, then spins around and snorts a line of coke off the drumkit.

The party's taken a decidedly darker edge, but it's making for great footage. I've borrowed Roshan's Sony Mini Hi8 Handycam, promising him that I'd take care of his baby. He was more than reluctant to loan it to me, and understandably so: it took him a year and half of scrimping from his restaurant job to save up the dosh for it. I've actually borrowed it to film an anti-French nuclear-testing protest at Musgrave Park on the weekend, but thought it'd be a laugh to bring it with me tonight and get some footage of the party. Might be able to use the footage later down the track for a project. Roshan would probably shit himself with worry if he could see this scene right now.

The only thing is that there's not a lot of light here, and everyone's relying on either the dull kitchen light or this intense garden spotlight Nathanael's tied to the balcony guttering with a coat-hanger.

Someone's left an empty bottle of absinthe by the glass sliding door, but Nathanael holds it up to the light outside and declares: 'There's just a drop left, but we can make this work.'

'Fuck it, it's yours,' I go, but he insists we share it.

'We'll snort it,' he grins, his eyes like fucking saucers in the gloom.

He measures half into the lid, then presses one nostril closed and puts the lid up to his nose.

'Fucking hell, smells toxic,' he goes, before tipping his head back and snorting deeply at the same time.

He sounds like a pig having a heart attack.

'WHOA!' he screams, dropping the lid on the floor.

He stumbles backwards, blindly flailing his arm out for the wall.

I spill the rest of the absinthe into the lid. There's barely a half teaspoon left. I follow Nathanael's lead, snorting the absinthe up my nose. It shoots up and suddenly I feel my brain get hot. It feels like there's a fire inside my fucking head, ready to blow it off. Then it occurs to me that I can't see fucking thing. I feel my eyelids to make sure they're open, and they are.

'Holy fuck, Nate,' I say. 'I think I'm blind.'

'You are, cunt,' he laughs. 'I was, too. But I'm alright now. By fuck, but *can* I see!'

He sounds higher than he was after the coke, laughing his head off. Probably at me, stumbling around blind as a fucking bat. I hold the camera tight with both hands, in case I drop it accidently. It doesn't take but a moment for my vision to return, though, and when it does I feel fucking great.

'Whoa, who knew absinthe up yer nose would be such a trip?'

'Oi, oi, oi,' Nathanael goes, grabbing me by the shoulders for balance, because the cunt's about to fall sideways. 'Let's get some reaction shots.'

'Lead the way,' I say, making sure he doesn't knock the camera from my hands as he tumbles away into the darkness of the corridor.

Turns out by reaction shots he means me filming people while he throws a glass of water in their faces. He's calling it a higher-concept art than what the conceptualist's produce, whoever the fuck they are. I swear he's making half this shit up.

'Get fucked, cunt!' one of his mates bellows after he's copped a face full of H20.

Nate's unapologetic. In fact, he seems slighted that no-one's appreciating his efforts. They might be his friends, or friends of friends, but I can see this turning wrong for him if he keeps it up, so I half-lie and tell him the lighting's all wrong so we may as well stop.

He goes off with a couple of girls, calling out for any Joe Blo who's got some absinthe to follow him.

'What'd you fucking film that for?' Nate's victim wants to know, water dripping off his chin.

'Whoa, don't blame me, mate, it was all his idea. I just pointed the camera where the action was.'

It's obviously not a satisfactory answer, because he makes some idle threats about taking me on. The party's now definitely lost all appeal for me, so I go and join Nathanael's girlfriend Dezzy and the group she's chattin with. Her real name's Destiny, but it sounds like a stripper's name so I always call her Dezzy, and it's kinda stuck with a few mutual friends as well. I'm just sitting here with Roshi's camera turned off when Nathanael suddenly appears in front of me with a glass of water. I look up at the cunt, and clock his dead expression, and he suddenly tips the glass and pours water all over the camera.

'FUCKING HELL!' I bawl, leaping back and wiping the water off it with my shirt front.

Nathanael stands there for a moment with a dead coke look in his eyes, then saunters off like he's possessed. Dezzy's calling for him to get back and explain himself, but he just joins the two girls in the kitchen, one of whom is waving around a bread knife.

'Fucking cunt,' I curse, for Dezzy's benefit. She can pass onto him later on just how pissed off I am. 'This isn't even my camera.'

One of Dezzy's mates suggests I open all the compartments and put the camera directly under the spotlight, try and use the heat to dry out the inside. We wrestle the spottie off the guttering and place it in front of the camera on a table. Everyone starts moaning how there's no proper light now, as if I could give a flying fuck.

Nathanael yanks his t-shirt over his head, hiding the top part of his face so only his mouth is visible, and creeps out of the kitchen pretending to be an alien or a monster. He's brandishing the bread knife, and the two cunts behind him in the kitchen doorway are giggling at his antics. He's actually doing his Hunter S Thompson walk, as me and Dezzy call it, where he walks around bow-legged and buoyant.

Thing is, he's got an obsession with Hunter S Thompson and models himself after his hero. The old crowd he used to hang out with from his school even nicknamed him Hunter, but thankfully that didn't carry over when he met Dezzy and formed new friendships. He has the same erratic behaviours as Thompson, the same mental distractions with higher concepts than what's going on right in front of him, although in that regard Thompson always had an eagle eye for the details of whatever he covered journalistically. Thompson's political observations were second to none. Nathanael, on the other hand, has more of an emotional response to the political field, using his gut instinct to determine the validity of a pollie's worth.

I can actually appreciate Nathanael's modelling on the gonzo writer, even when others think it's a gimmick. By fashioning himself after his idol he's managed to streamline his identity, even if it's not a genuine one. But that's not important, because he's wholeheartedly embraced it to the point that it *is* him. It's not a weekend disguise; it genuinely has become his identity. Most of us don't even see Hunter Thompson in him anymore, truth be told. We just see Nathanael.

Right now, though, I just see a coked-up arrogant cunt.

'Oi, Dezzy, I'm gonna be off. I gotta get this camera sorted out.'

She apologises profusely about Nate and offers to pay for the taxi, which I gladly accept. Fuck knows if this camera will sort itself out, and if it doesn't I'm gonna need all the charity I can get. There's no way I'm handing Roshan back a fucked camera.

The next day I've slept in way too late, on account of getting back to Twix's place in the early hours of the morning and pleading with him or Raven to open the door for me. They'd refused to get out of bed so I'd ended up sleeping in the stairwell, which wasn't half bad actually. I just had to make sure the camera was up inside my shirt so if any cunt tried to steal it I'd wake up first. When Twix finally did open the front door, I'd stumbled inside and passed out on their couch, so it's about two in the afternoon when I finally wake up.

My head's throbbing from the booze last night. Maybe even more from that one sniff of absinthe alone. Twix has already gone to work, but Raven's home and forgoes the textbooks to cook me some fried egg on toast with melted cheese.

The camera's on the end of the table, so I scoot over and press the ON button. It starts to whir into life then goes completely dead. Fuck, this is not happening. I try the button again but nothing. Dead as a doornail.

'Maybe it's the battery?' suggests Raven, scooping the eggs out of the pan and onto the toast.

'Either way, what can I do? They cost a small fortune. Money I certainly don't have.'

'Maybe get an advance loan off the DSS,' she says, putting the plate of food down in front of me. She's fried herself a bum-nut, too, no toast or cheese.

'Christ, it's only January and I'm already asking for an advance,' I groan.

The dole office can give out loans of up to five hundred bucks, and then they deduct the repayments out of your weekly pay, whatever amount you think you can afford. Everyone always pays back the bare minimum of five bucks a week, of course. I hate relying on that method so early in the year in case an emergency comes up later on.

'I'll take it into Dick Smith's first and see what they say. Maybe it's fixable without buying all the doodads like a new battery.'

Because it's Roshan's camera and I can't risk copping a hiding from any normals for being a goth, I decide that a disguise is in order. The only clothes in my backpack that aren't strictly goth in nature are still pretty swampie, so I call on old Bernie down in flat one and ask to borrow something of his.

'Cashing in your goth card, are we?' he smirks, the weirdo.

'Nah, mate, need a fucking disguise so I can pass as one of you cunts, ay,' I smirk back.

He laughs at the thought. 'Yeah, good luck with that!'

He pulls out a blue polo shirt, which I instantly reject.

'No polos.'

He rolls his eyes. 'Fussy, fussy.'

Next he pulls out a hideous, Mambo-knockoff from Kmart or some shit.

'Pass.'

He's got a dark blue t-shirt poking out, and I tug at the sleeve.

'What's printed on this one?'

'Nothing,' he goes. 'Plain. Bit boring.'

'That's the one then,' I say, reaching past him and pulling it out by the hanger. Yup, a plain blue t-shirt with no crap logos or jokes on the front. Hopefully this with my usual black pants and Docs will suffice as presenting a relatively normal front to the world at large. Anything to get into town and back again on a Friday night with Roshi's Hi8 safe and sound.

Raven thinks it's a fucking hoot and wants to take my photo, calling me the world's biggest dork. Funnily enough, we dress daily in a way that most people think is photo-worthy whereas we're just blasé about, then whenever one of us dons a suit and tie for a job interview or somesuch we think it's an occasion to preserve.

'No fucking way I'm being photographed in this,' I protest.

She takes it anyway, with my hand up in front to hide my face.

'Blackmail material,' she goes.

By the time I walk into the city the sun has set. I head down Edward and left onto Elizabeth, where DSEs is situated about half-way up, across the road from the back of the Hoyts. As I'm about to cross the road, though, I notice the people hanging around outside the Sushi Train, just where the entrance to the McDonald's and the comics shop is, are carrying on like headless chooks.

'How's that then, fucker?' this big boofhead's yelling as he runs at the wall. It looks like he's kicking something.

Inching further down the footpath I can see some legs poking out where the boofhead's laying the boot in. Leaning against the window of The Daily Planet comics shop is another boofhead, his arms folded. So I pretend to just be casually passing by, and cop a better view of the entire tableau: Old Mate is kicking the shit out of a couple of punks, or more precisely, the male of the two. More than that, I actually recognise the punk as Scab! His mohawk's a bit bent out of shape, but I suppose that happens when someone's kicking the shit of you.

I'm about to yell out to the boofhead and tell him to lay off when I remember the camera in my arms. If I try and intervene, maybe Roshi's camera will get busted up.

'One more, one more,' boof-braindead goes when his mate tries to tell him that Scab's had enough. His mate's glancing in my direction, at the camera specifically, and it occurs to me he thinks I might be secretly filming them. What he doesn't realise is that even if I was I'd be picking up squat in this shitty light. These Hi8's aren't made for candid night shooting.

I suppose I better do something to help Scab out. Cops aren't an option in my books, ordinarily, but in this instance it might be his only chance.

I jog up around into Albert Street and up to the police kiosk in the middle, telling the cops they need to get someone down behind the Hoyts quick smart.

'An officer has already been despatched,' the cop on duty goes.

I wonder how the fuck that's possible when I didn't pass one on the way up.

'Magically fly over, did he?' I say snarkily.

'Nah, mate,' the cop says, looking at me blankly. 'We radioed for one.' He touches the walkie-talkie on his chest for emphasis.

Ah. Fair enough.

As I'm about to head back down, I see Scab coming towards me. He's bleeding from his head and mouth, and together we try and tell the cops what happened, but seems they're not much interested. They jot down some details and say they'll check the cameras for where the aggressor has gone to, then get back to their chit-chat about their home lives.

'Where's your girlfriend?' I ask Scab.

'She's back there,' he says listlessly. I don't think he's clued as to who I am yet. It's probably this t-shirt. And the video camera.

'I don't think it's safe for her to be alone.'

'Adelaide's alright,' he goes.

I'd believe it, actually, because suddenly the guy that attacked them is headed our way. We're only about twenty metres from the police kiosk, but that doesn't seem to mean anything to the boofhead. He comes right up to us and asks if Scab's okay.

'Yeah, man, doin okay,' says Scab.

I'm fucking lost here. We're all friends now?

'Sorry about before,' the boofhead goes, hopping from foot to foot, unable to keep still. Fucker's on something. 'I got carried away, took it out on you. But don't worry, you guys are okay by me. You get into any trouble on these streets, any at all, you just say my name. OJ. You tell em you know OJ and they'll leave you alone.'

I've never heard of this cunt before, and I've literally lived on these streets.

'What if we tell *you* that we know you?' I ask, but he doesn't clue what I'm asking and just enthusiastically repeats the instructions to namedrop the dumb cunt if we get hassled by anyone.

Then he charges off, up into the mall and rounds the corner of Hungry Jacks and out of view.

The cops are just standing around outside the kiosk, oblivious to everything.

'So wait, did you know that cunt?' I ask Scab as we walk back down towards Elizabeth Street to check on his girlfriend.

'Kind of,' he admits.

How is it I've never seen or heard of any of these people before? When you hang around the streets long enough you get to know all the local identities. Do they just avoid King George Square and Roma Street most of the time? That's where I spend most of my time, I figure, so it's plausible.

We're chatting away and rounding the corner when a gang of homie guys coming towards us stops and points at Scab.

'You!' the prick at front says angrily.

This guy I do know, but not the rest of them. I've seen him around heaps of times, just a fucking thug wannabe, delusions of being an American-gangster when he's actually Aboriginal or Islander. I've seen him with the Murri kids in the mall, essentially trying to stir trouble. Seems he's moving up now, got himself a posse.

'You been talking shit about us, Scab?'

Scab's pleading with the cunt, telling him he's heard wrong and people are just out to make it sound like Scab's been talking shit. The other guy's not having any of it, though, and without warning he boots Scab so hard in the stomach the poor bastard is sent flying backwards into the mouth of the alleyway, where he stumbles into some wheelie bins and falls on the ground. The gang advance on him and stand over him, taunting him.

I'm out on the edge of the gutter, and two of the fuckers have stayed out with me. One's really tall and the other's about my height, but he's wiry and muscled and glaring at me with all the hatred in the world. The veins on his neck and forehead are popping, and he hisses at me through his teeth: 'Are you with him?'

So fucking ridiculous does this cunt look right now that I start chuckling, while confessing I don't really know Scab at all. Which is essentially true. Right now what matters most is that this Sony Hi8 camera comes out of this unscathed.

'Something funny, cunt?' the nutter goes, puffing his chest up and taking a menacing step towards me.

I haven't stopped chuckling, but I'm very aware that this cunt is about to wipe the floor with me and there's probably not much I can do to stop him. I'm not even armed, for fuck's sake.

'He's awright, Ben,' the tall guy behind his says, pulling on his arm.

The nutter death-glares me for a moment. I simply turn my attention to Scab and his tormentors. They, too, seem to have relented on dispensing violence and are helping Scab to his feet. I can't help but wonder if he namedropped OJ. That'd be funny.

'Look, I'm not really a part of this,' I tell the two wankers next to me, 'so I'm just gonna leave you boys to it.'

'Righto,' says the tall one, while Ben-the-fucking-nutter continues to bulge his veins. Cunt's OD'ing on steroids or something.

A few doors down I'm about to cross the road to Dick Smith's when I notice Scab's girlfriend, Adelaide, still slumped against the wall behind The Hoyts.

'Your boyfriend'll be down in a bit,' I say. 'He's just catching up with some mates. And maybe karma, too, it seems.'

'Cheers,' she smiles, her eyes half-lidded. I can't tell if she's drunk or drugged.

In the electronic's store one of the sales reps takes a look at the Sony camera for me, going on about how they only sell the little camcorder varieties these days.

'Could be the electrolytic capacitor, or could be the condensation detector needs to be shorted,' he explains, playing with various buttons himself.

'Shit, that sounds serious,' I go, wondering how much this is going to set me back. 'It's not even my camera! I just borrowed it for the protests this weekend.'

'Don't worry, shorting the detector can usually get em going again.' He flips open a panel, peering at what's under it. 'I already assume you've tried the reset button?'

'Reset button?'

He stands straight and smiles goofily at me. 'Oh no, you didn't try the reset button?'

He takes his pen out of his shirt-pocket and presses it into a hole under the control panel. The camera makes a whirring sound, then the noise of a tape rewinding.

'Oops, silly me, pressed my finger on the rewind button by mistake,' he goes.

'So it's all working again?' I ask hopefully. The last thing I need is Roshan trying to kill me.

'Appears so,' he says, pressing the play button and peering into the viewfinder to see how it's working. He quickly clicks it off and nervously stutters: 'Yep... good, all good. It's no... I mean don't worry about any cost. Camera's workin fine.'

'Cost?'

'Yeah, no worries,' he says, waving the thought away. 'Alright, have a great night... Friday night.'

He quickly strolls away to help someone else, looking nervously back at me.

Considering all he did was press the reset button, I had no intention of paying him for anything. Cheeky fucker.

When I get outside I can see that the homie gang and Scab have disappeared, as has Scab's girlfriend from across the road. I lift the video camera's viewfinder to my eye and press play, and the black and white image of Nathanael snorting cocaine off a drumkit comes on.

Shiiiit, heavy stuff for a simple retail clerk to have to deal with on a customer's camera.

Then a thought strikes me like lightning.

I don't know what the fuck's going on between me and Erina, but despite feeling crushed after our so-called date the thought of filming us fucking crosses my mind. Now Roshan would positively fucking faint at the thought his precious camera was used for homemade porn!

DALE DONGER

I'm fucking over the Millennium already. I've got no interest in all this gadgetry and promise of robotic futures like how I used to see on *Beyond 2000*, that TV show my family used to watch when I was a kid. They promised all sorts of marvels, stuff like CDs and mobile phones and ATMs that've been slowly introduced into our lives and we now think no more of than the stuff we grew up with back in the 80s. Even though I've got fuck all interest in embracing the internet and mobile technologies, I know it's inevitable that our futures will be full of the shit. But I'm not interested in the world changing in small increments. Just get it over with, already, or don't do it at all.

Dale Donger's always goin on about *The Celestine Prophecy* ever since he read it a couple of weeks ago. Him and every other wanker within earshot, it seems. I've done my time with the new-agey stuff and left it behind a couple of years ago, but it seems some people are still playing catch-up. I think fairly highly of Donger, but occasionally he still stumps me.

'I get it, Dante, you're a cynic,' he says in response to me telling him I've heard it all before. 'But this is an entirely new direction of thinking.'

'It's really not,' I sigh, shoving a whole kofta ball into my gob. 'And I believe in providence, not angels.'

'It's divinity, not angels,' he goes, as if that changes anything. 'But what you're saying, *this* says too.'

He's now convinced we're going to evolve into an improved and ethereal species, maybe with a new set of steak knives thrown in for good measure. Alien and angel cults are old news to me, as there's practically one in every town between here and Toowoomba, but there's no need to burst the poor cunt's bubble. Fuck knows we need a little hope these days, although economically it's been a vast improvement the last couple of years since the days of the recession *we had to have*, as our then-Prime Minister had called it, when there were massive cutbacks to manufacturing and thus to employment aplenty. Although it'd hardly been as dramatic as some people like to recall.

Markets crash and rise again all the time, and the latest trends are hardly a fucking exception. Mexico's turn now. I don't confess to understand it all, but you only have to ask around and see that there's a turning tide in the way our labour force will operate in future. I've got friends that tell me the job market is evolving, not the human species, and that youth employment opportunities have shifted from an emphasis on full-time to casual part-time, which of course sounds horrible for the poor cunts that are caught up in the job market, but I'm told it actually works perfectly for their needs. They're more able to maintain soul-destroying work while enabling them to pursue equally soul-destroying degrees and all that shit.

So on one hand I do agree with Dale about his *Prophecy*, but I think he's mislaid what he's casually perceiving in the world and giving that fucking book way more credit than it's certainly due.

'Closing now, guys,' says the bald guy with the clay smudge on his forehead behind the counter, switching off the bain-marie and beaming at us with all the universe's wonder in his eyes. I think his name's Bhakta, from memory, and he's as white as a ghost. There's your new-age fixations, Dale: makes mince meat of your mind.

'Rightio, dude, Namaste,' grins Donger as we exit, waving a hand at the Hare Krishna who graciously accepts Donger's err in place of the requisite *haribol*. 'See ya next time.'

Dale Donger and I are definitely not a part of the new-wave of the youth labour force. We're at the other end of the spectrum, blissfully untouched by the downturns and upturns of the economic landscape, except wherein it affects the regular cash injection into our bank accounts courtesy of the kind folk at the Department of Social Security. To this end, given the pitiful amount doled out to us by the Government for our generosity to stay clear of stealing gainful employment away from more needy cunts, we often find ourselves short of moolah and thusly using our almost constant state of impoverished dress and hygiene to pass ourselves off as homeless people at the Hare Krishna's on Brunswick Street. To be fair, Dale in his time has been homeless and I technically am, so by very little stretch of the definition we're entitled to the free food that the Hare's have on offer. Always after two o'clock, of course, when the paying customers have gone.

Actually, I remember Donger wanted to join them once, go down to Northern New South Wales and work on their farm and everything. He used to walk around grinning his head off like a shot fox and singing the Maha Mantra, one of their chants. He was fully into it, but then he found out he'd have to give up booze and that was him gone. 'Beer is my lifeblood,' he'd whined, and I had had to point out to him that he if couldn't uphold one of their most basic tenets then it really wasn't for him at all. Since then, he's happy to just go and eat the food. For free, naturally.

'I feel bad about not paying for that food, but,' Donger goes when we're out of earshot of the Hare Krishna's. 'I did some cash-in-hand work on a construction site last week, in West End. So I'm cashed up. Was over feeling like a prossie all the time.'

He pauses as a means to prompt me into asking what he means.

'You know, fucked for cash,' he chuckles before I can ask. 'Good money in construction. Shame to give it up, but.'

'You must've had your reasons, I guess,' I shrug, not sure what else to say, because it seems pretty obvious to me. Eight hours a fucking day being told what to do. Fuck that for a joke.

Talking about work – the getting of it and the doing of it – has to be one of the most mind-numbing topics of conversation working people love to indulge in. I'm convinced that they're so blinkered by the menial tasks of their jobs that they've got fuck all time to absorb the world around them and thus can only make banal small-talk about how their bosses are cunts or going on about crappy customers.

'We found a dead woman on site,' Donger reveals casually, like it's nothing. 'Gave me the heebie-jeebies, so I chucked the job in. Coppers interviewed us and all.'

'Holy shit,' I say. 'They found the body in the construction site?'

'Nah, in the grass outside the squat next to it,' he goes.

It's assumed I should know where the squat is, and by chance I do. I've stayed there before, the same one that Dirty Bill set fire to.

'The one on the corner of Montague Road and Bouquet,' I nod. 'I know it.'

'It was no fucking bouquet, but, the smell of her body,' Dale goes, scrunching his nose up as though he's still got a whiff of the stench.

'Fuck, what is it with people lately? There was that family murder in Hillcrest just last week, too!'

'World's going to shit, Dante,' he shakes his head. 'That's why I'm telling you, we gotta evolve into something more celestial.'

'Again with the fucking angel talk! You don't even believe in angels, Donger!'

A young girl in a mini-skirt and a stretch fleece jumper walks around the corner and pointedly ignores us staring as she passes us.

'Do I fucking not?' leers Dale, craning his neck to watch her walk up the street.

'What I want to know is how the hell is she wearing that jumper in this heat?' The warm spell began the same day as the Hillcrest murders in fact, sparking a thought that the heat had precipitated the tragedy. It was a full moon just a few nights before, just to add to the mix.

'Oi, when do you think the old lady in West End was murdered, then?' I ask Dale, nudging him to snap his attention away from the skirt.

'I dunno. She smelt fucking awful, but, they reckon. Maybe a few days, maybe a week.'

'Right on the full moon, probably!' I crow.

Dale snorts. 'And you think I'm the one that's all new-agey.'

Two copper-cunts come out of the Valley Plaza and one of them eyeballs us as we stroll past.

'Piggy Run?' Donger says quietly to me.

I pat my hip, just to make double sure I didn't bring my knife with me today. Thankfully, one of the rare occasions I haven't.

'Gotta work the grub off somehow,' I go, and we both glance over our shoulders being as suss looking as we possibly can, well and truly catching the attention of the two coppers.

Donger does a double-take and grabs me as he tries to piss-bolt, and we career wildly before finding our feet and bolting down past the cheap Asian stores towards Wickham Street. The cops waste no fucking time at all in coming after us, not even bothering to yell out for us to stop. They're enjoying the chase as much as we're savouring what's to come.

We nearly bowl over a bunch of schoolkids on the corner as we charge down Wickham towards the escalators that will take us up into the Plaza. My estimation is that's about where they'll nab us, but we've underestimated our foes and one of coppers slams Donger up against a pylon almost at full run. Holy fuck! I've got no choice but to about-turn and make sure Donger's brains haven't been spilled all over the place.

The copper on my heels nearly shits himself when I skid to a halt and duck under his flailing arms. Turns out Donger's alright, just a bit sore, but he's already laughing his arse off the stupid cunt. Naturally the cop thinks it's because he's on drugs.

'What'd you take, mate, eh?'

Considering Donger can't stop cackling I oblige the officer with a reply on Donger's behalf. 'He's not on anythi–'

OOOOOFFFF!

I'm down for the count, the schoolkids all cheering on. I was just standing there but I guess the bruised ego of the copper pursuing me called for a fucking rugby tackle, because next thing I know we're both on the fucking ground scraping our hands and cheeks on the concrete.

'Get off me, cunt!' I snarl.

The cops tell the schoolkids to move on then stand me and Donger against the pylon and order us to empty our pockets. They're stumped when there's nothing to be found, so they frog-march us into Overells Lane for a strip-search.

'What's so funny?' they ask of Donger, who's grinning from ear to ear, but he just shrugs and continues to grin like a spastic.

'Drop your dacks and lift your shirts,' the cop goes.

Again, there's no contraband, no weapons, nothing to hold us on.

'So why'd you run for?' the other one grumbles as we pull our pants up.

Donger shrugs. 'Just felt like it, dude.'

They've got no choice but to let us go, though they're not happy about it.

'We'll be watching you two,' they warn us.

'Through the bedroom windows late at night, no doubt,' I call back, and me and Donger hightail it out of there and wait diligently at the lights for the little green man. No fucking way we're about to jaywalk now, with those two cunts watching us.

That's *Piggy Run*, our little game we like to play sometimes.

We get across the road with all the other law-abiding civilians, with Donger singing a bit of Razar with '*Task Force, Task Force, how we love you,*' and check the damage done once we're out of sight. No need to add insult to injury by showing how bothered we are by the scrapes and cuts. My knuckles and jaw are scraped. Donger's shoulder hurts where he was slammed into the pillar. Listing off an inventory of our injuries reminds me of when the Dead Kennedy's came to our fair city in 83.

'Jello words still ring true about these pricks, ay,' I go. 'Remember when they got hassled by the cops and he reckoned Brisbane was the closest thing to a junta state he's ever been in it?'

'I don't need to remember cause I lived it, mate,' Donger goes.

I often forget that Donger was a teenager at the end of Bjelke-Petersen's reign of terror, so he saw firsthand what Jello Biafra was on about.

Up at the other end of the Brunswick Mall someone yells out 'Oi Donger!', and we glance around to see two skinheads and this dopey-looking cunt with an undercut sitting at a table outside one of the pubs. We were so fucking close to turning left on Ann Street and disappearing down toward the op-shops, but no, we need to be recognised by fucking skinheads of all people. Especially ones that look like they're paid up members of the Hammerskins.

'Hey, Sean,' goes Dale, heading over, so I follow.

As a ye olde punk from way back, Dale knows a lot of people, and by rote not all these clowns are gonna be savoury. If these two are the kind of skins I'm guessing they are, then they're also known as *boneheads* by the skins who, oddly enough, are anti-racist. The ones that prefer the acronym SHARP. There's not that many skins around nowadays, but you still get the die-hard revivalists. I've never hid from Donger my feelings about skinheads, on account of the trouble they've given me or my friends in my time. But they're his mates, so a civil tongue is called for.

'Grab a pint with us,' says Sean, making eye-contact only with Dale, like I was an apparition barely worth noting. He's wearing a fucking Fortress singlet, a renowned RAC band, so I'm hardly gonna cry about the slight.

'Fuck it,' says the undercut guy, 'I'm nearly finished. Gonna head in and grab us a jug.'

'Righto,' goes Dale, pulling up a stool.

I'm inclined to just tell him I'll meet him at Saint Vinnies, but it's actually a great day for a drink outdoors and the bench-top they're seated at is half in the sun, so I pull up a stool just inside the shade of the pub awning. I'd prefer a wine but beer it'll have to be.

'This is Dante,' Dale says, and Sean grunts at me in what I assume is meant to be his version of a cordial greeting.

The other skin extends his hand and as we shake, he goes: 'Me name's Pez.'

Pez looks like a fresh-cut; meaning a recent convert to the boot boys and their fascist ideologies. He's scratching a swastika into the timber of the bench-top with a pair of scissors, but the arms of his handiwork are pointed the wrong way.

'You should make it thicker,' I suggest. 'You know, so's they can't remove it.'

He grins. 'Fuck yeah!' He gets to work with renewed vigour.

The guy with the undercut comes back carrying the jug and a couple of extra glasses.

'Donger, Graham; Graham, Donger,' says Sean, omitting me in the introductions.

'How's it goin, Donger? Here, get some grog inta ya,' says Graham, passing me a glass. He's got that high nasally Australian twang most of us only do as a piss-take of how we think other countries perceive our accent.

'Thanks, Graham,' I go and lean over to shake his hand. 'Dante, by the way.'

He nods and passes the jug around when he's topped his up. I press the icy glass against the grazes on my hands. Feels good.

'Oi, you get in on that construction job my cousin set up?' goes Sean.

'Yeah man,' Dale says, nodding. 'Had to give it up, but.'

'Eh? That was a fuckin solid opportunity, but,' Sean bleats.

'Yeah, but get this right,' Dale says, leaning in closer as if to confer a secret, prompting Sean to lean in as well. 'They found a body there. Old woman. Murdered.'

'No way!' bleats Sean, slapping his hands down on the bench-top. 'That's fucked up! Jody didn't say nothing to me about that.'

I'm guessing Jody is Sean's cousin, who must've got Dale onto the site.

'I know, right? Dead a week, all rotten,' elaborates Dale.

He describes the scene in far more graphic detail than what he'd originally told me, which makes me think he saw a lot more than he'd first let on. To Sean's credit, he finds it as tasteless as I do. Hopefully about as tasteless as this fucking beer.

'Come on, man,' he opines. 'Stop with the disrespect. She's dead, someone's mother.'

'True,' Dale nods, dropping the subject in favour of job-hunting.

He and Sean start swapping stories about what's available and what they've missed out on, so I outright ask Graham if he serves any Dragons. The question stymies him, so I assume he's not an active member of the skinhead movement. Just a dimwit caught up in their social circles.

Pez finally finishes digging his swastika into the table, and blows the sawdust away to admire it. He's been going at it this whole time, and looks quite proud of his efforts.

'The arms are facing the wrong way,' I tell him quietly.

'What?'

'The arms on the swastika,' I go, nodding at the defaced tabletop.

He stares down at it, crestfallen.

'You coulda told us before,' he sulks.

'I didn't fucking know before, did I?'

This elicits a softly-spoken apology from him, for which I bask in. Nothing like compelling a fucking skinhead apologise to a goth for a change.

Sean gets a bit uppity, though, and says to me: 'Watch yer fucken tongue.'

I actually start to chuckle out loud, brazenly trying to egg the cunt on, casually dropping my hand down to the waistband of my dacks then realising I haven't got my fucking knife on me.

Dale's telling Sean I'm alright and not to worry about it, but Sean *can't* not worry about it.

'He's a bit fucken mouthy, this friend of yours,' he says to Dale, but never taking his eyes off me.

'And that's a bit hypocritical coming from a boot-boy,' I retort, whereupon the cunt stands up so suddenly his stool flies back and his hand knocks over the jug, spilling the last of the beer.

'Aw, good one, you spaz,' whines Graham.

The veins on Sean's forehead are popping.

'You want a fucken go, you poof?' he snarls at me. 'Huh? You fucken poofter cunt?'

He actually kicks the leg of the table-bench in a manner meant to intimidate, bulging his eyes out at me.

'Whoa whoa whoa,' goes Dale, jumping up and trying to subdue his mate. 'Fucking chill, dude. Dante's cool.'

'Too cool for this dropkick school,' I mutter, pushing off my perch and walking away.

Normally Adelaide gets most of the neo-Nazi action and revolts, but a few years ago in 1993 the local chapter – the Australian National Socialist Movement – graffitied a synagogue on Margaret Street. Apart from that, most of the unrest from the skin-heads in Brisbane is bestowed upon Asians and us goths. I theorise that we're typically regarded as the lowest rung on the subcultural ladder by all other subcultures, and thus good for a kicking. That and black people. My mate Alan, who is Aboriginal, often has black eyes and says he gets them from scuffles with racists like these skinheads.

But their mindset isn't exclusive to the skins. Ordinary rednecks share their dangerous philosophies, and some of those are even ambitious enough to pursue a voice in the political arena, as we saw last year with Pauline Hanson's emergence, who was then mostly anti-union but is now saying the pollies are causing a racism crisis by doling out money to the Murris. If she hadn't been booted out already of the March election, I could clearly envision these cunts voting for the fish and chip bitch from Ipswich given she's insisting on the abolition of Government support for Aboriginals. She's right up their proverbial alleys.

The skinhead subculture is one of the most persistent of the subcultures, never ceasing to exist since its inception in the Fifties. Personally, I wish it'd just fucking die out. You never see the kind of wanton hatred from the other subcultures as you do the skins, which is unsurprising really given that their entire philosophy hangs on hatred of the foreign but conversely entirely fucking surprising given that within the origins of their subculture is an appreciation for ethnic music brought into Britain by immigrants! These dumb cunts can't even sort themselves out when it comes to race-hate, doing their wild chicken-dances to ragamuffin-inspired ska while dishing out a few serves of abuse to the poor bastards at the local Indian takeaway.

Donger catches up to me where I'm waiting over by the traffic lights, and he's deeply fucking apologetic.

'It's not you that needs to be apologising, Dale. It's those backward cunts that would suck the week-old spunk from Hitler's shrivelled cock.'

'He just gets a bit worked up, but,' Donger says of Sean, who is still standing outside the pub glaring my way despite Dale having spent an extra few minutes calming the cunt down. 'It's just for show with them.'

'Seriously, Dale, stop apologising for the cunts,' I admonish him. 'They can dig their own fucking graves. I fucking know you, Dale. I know that shit doesn't sit with you.'

'Yeah, you're right,' he mopes, but it's too late. I'm starting to feel like maybe Donger can go get fucked, also. Now there's an anger inside me that's as much directed at him as those fucking white supremacists cunts. After all, if he's apologising for them isn't he in effect condoning them?

'I'm telling you, when your celestial prophecy does finally happen, those three wankers will be like lumps of coal sitting on the face of the fucking Earth. Trust me on that one. You want to be a part of that, do you?'

'Sooo,' he smirks playfully, 'you *do* think there's a chance we're going to evolve?'

I roll my eyes.

'Not a fucking chance.'

Sean and the other two are heading back inside the pub to continue drinking, doubtlessly.

Then a thought begins to bloom inside my brain: what if Donger has it right and the problem isn't Sean and his dickhead friends, but me? What if I'm just a supreme arsehole?

Dale and I head on down to the op-shops, but I'm not in the mood for it anymore. I'd prefer to just go back and knife that useless cunt Sean until the neo-Nazi fuck is dead.

THE GOD OF FUCK

It's fuckin hot and the vents on the bus keep blowing warm air. The window rattles, and won't slide all the way back, so I've pressed my head against it to stop the rattling but the vibrations from the motor and the potholes come up straight into my fuckin skull. At least the wind blows on my face. Small comfort.

James, Imp and me are all heading into the city after spendin the night at James' house, but before we get there I want to go and chew Dad out about not coughin up my pay for working at his poxy shop the last few weeks, so we get off the bus at the Gabba, across from the abandoned cop shop. I notice with satisfaction that my hair spray has left a greasy spot on the bus window.

It's fucked, but, coz Dad'll literally donate a huge fuckin chunk of his monthly profits to this Christian charity in India who rescues liddle kids from sex trafficking but do ya think the selfish cunt'll cough up to get his own daughter, his own flesh and blood, one measly fuckin concert ticket for the Chilli Peppers in a couple of months? Like fuck he would.

The whole way up to Dad's shop Imp complains about the heat.

'It'll be heaps worth it, but,' I go. 'Just wait and see.'

Dad's not in, of course, but thick-as-a-brick Olivia is. This is even better. I tell James and Imp to distract her, so they start grabbing all the straws and serviettes on the front counter, makin Olivia crazy. While she's distracted I head out back into the prep area.

Doug's back here and so's some other young tool I don't know. Another one of the many casuals Dad has at his disposal to fuck over if the dude doesn't 'pull his weight'.

'Hey, Prue,' goes Doug.

'Pixie,' I correct him, ignorin em both and headin straight for the peg hooks around side of the freezer door where staff bags and coats get hung up.

'Oh yeah, sorry,' he goes, soundin stoned.

'Ya got any?' I ask, but he looks bashful.

'Nah, nah,' he says, 'I'm not high right now.'

'Ya fuckin look it,' I accuse, convinced he's got some and is holdin. The other cunt doesn't look blazed, but, so maybe Doug's tellin the truth. Be a fuckin first.

'Nah, man,' he says, doin his best to look straight. 'I'm trying to cut back, hey.'

'Whatever.'

I find Olivia's stupid lookin handbag, a fancy *vachetta* coloured thing with LV patterns all over it, because callin it beige or some shit is obviously too ghetto. It's actually her mum's bag, from what I've heard, who got it from a business trip in Melbourne. There's a stupid liddle Christian fish symbol keychain on it. Fuckin vomit!

'Is she going through Olivia's bag?' the other dude says to Doug, who tells him to shut up and mind his own fucking bees-wax.

I fish Olivia's purse out, just some pink vinyl thing from Kmart. There's about eighty bucks in it. Mine! I toss the purse back into the handbag, and think about takin the whole thing. I'm sure it's worth more than eighty, but I doubt I can sneak it past the dumb bitch without her callin the cops on us.

Me and Doug fist-bump and I tell the other cunt to keep his fuckin mouth shut or I'll make sure Dad fires him.

Out front, Olivia's face has literally gone red coz James' climbed up on a dividing wall with his bare ass hanging over the edge. He's so unco he looks like he's havin a spaz-attack. The sight makes us crack up somethin shockin.

'When Mister Lang hears about this,' she warns us, as if threatenin me with my Dad is literally gonna work.

'He'll what?' I thrust my face into hers, making her stagger back worried. 'Fucking sack us? Later, bitch.'

I give her the middle finger and James climbs down with his ass still hanging out of his shorts and him, me and Imp stroll out like we own the fuckin joint. I can hear Olivia havin a hissy fit behind us, and yellin for Doug to help clean up the mess the boys made. It's a great fuckin day!

We get another bus into the city and I figure it's my shout so we grab some Burger King in the Mall and then go down to the Record Exchange down past the Birch Carroll & Coyle cinema. We pick out a shirt each with Olivia's cash. Imp gets a brand new Ministry *Filth Pig* shirt by Nice Man, which the guy says they got in just that week; James gets a Marilyn Manson shirt by Winterland that has a photo of Manson with a lippie-smeared mouth and lyrics on the back; and I get an ace Manson shirt by Tultex with *Antichrist Superstar* on it and a picture of him from the *Beautiful People* video clip. Fucking score! Maybe even enough left for that Chilli Peppers ticket!

James gets his shirt on straight away, tucking his old navy tee into his back pocket where it hangs like a mechanics rag from the 50's. I'll save mine for when I get home.

We head back up and hang with the crowd on the corner, where there's these wide concrete garden tubs that the council put there to make the place look nicer. But it didn't work, coz the plants died from either the heat that comes off this huge fucking concrete wall behind us, which is part of the Birch Carroll & Coyle, or we crushed them by sittin on em or puttin our bags on them. Now the garden beds are just dust bowls filled with used ciggie butts. It's a mixed crowd here, but it's mostly made up of punks, homeless people, a couple of drug dealers and some gothics.

James is struttin around like a rooster, showing off his shirt, and me and Imp also pull ours out of the bags to show em off. Some of the punks scoff at us, the snobby cunts, saying Manson is shit. The younger gothics are impressed, but.

'How'd you bastards get the money for all that?' asks one of the punks, a guy called Scab.

'I fucking earned it, cunt,' I boast.

'Bullshit,' he laughs, but doesn't press the issue. He's probly guessed how, anyway.

Suddenly everyone's gettin wet and scramblin away from the wall. Those cunts inside the cinema have turned the sprinklers on again, which they do occasionally to put us off from sittin here.

James kicks one of the sprinkler heads to break it but just ends up gettin more wet. He does manage to break it a liddle bit, but, and the fuckin thing points towards the traffic and keeps shooting out jets of water at the cars waitin at the lights. One tool on a brand new Suzuki motorbike – an R-something-one-fifty says Imp – starts swearin his head off as the water's splashin him. I'm literally laughin my fuckin head off at him. The cunt swerves his bike over to the kerb like he wants to say somethin to us, but I guess he sees just how many of us there is and changes his mind and rides away instead.

James is fuckin soaked, but. The water is pourin down his body and squeezin out through the holes in his jungle boots.

'I'm gonna go dry off in the dunny,' he goes, so we go across the road to the Myer Centre to use the hand-driers in the dunnies.

We're stopped, but, as these two security guards who had been watchin us the whole time come over and tell us no entry.

'Why the fuck not?' demands Imp.

'You're all wet,' says one.

'And that t-shirt isn't allowed,' says the other aggressively, pointin at James.

'Nothing wrong with it,' challenges Imp.

The guard goes: 'What's written on it is.'

James turns around like a dog chasin its tail, trying to look at the back of his shirt, basically bein a bit ova smart cunt.

'Right there,' I go to James, pointin at *I AM THE GOD OF FUCK* written across his back in big letters. He pretends not to know what I'm on about, and keeps twirlin around, deliberately bumpin into these wannabe cops, and I keep pointin at the back of his shirt to persuade him to keep twirlin.

The security dudes are getting real pissed off, and Imp keeps gettin between them and James, getting up in their faces. 'It's just a Marilyn Manson shirt, who cares?'

Then one of the security guards goes: 'Is that the bloke who got a rib removed to suck himself off?'

'That's the one,' says the other guard. 'The kid off *The Wonder Years*.'

'No he's not,' I go, but they just go: 'That shirt's banned here.'

'Whatever,' I say, rollin my eyes.

'Step back, shithead,' goes the other guard, pushin Imp back a step.

'Get your fuckin hands off me,' growls Imp.

'Okay, no problem,' says James finally, 'I'll just take it off.' He strips the shirt off, squeezin more water out in the process. His ribs jut from his skinny body like a starving Ethiopian kid. The security fucks are gettin really agitated now. I'm just hopin James doesn't lose his cool like he did with those cops that time in the Square.

'Put it back on,' one of em demands.

Imp seizes the opportunity. 'Take it off or put it on, make up your minds!'

'Right you three,' they go, their voices gettin really mean, 'just fuck off now.'

They sound like the really mean it now so we decide to do just that. James twirls his shirt around above his head, flinging water at the security wankers. They get more pissed off, literally yellin at us now to fuck off. I hope someone reports them for swearing at the public and they lose their fuckin jobs. We've got them so worked up that when some older gothics, probly elitist cunts, try and go inside the security guys head em off and start gettin stuck into em about where they're goin and shit. Typical.

The sprinklers have been turned off and a few people've wandered back to the wall and are sitting on the garden beds again. James goes back over to sit in the sun and dry off a bit.

Me and Imp go across and say hi to a bunch of street kids and punks hangin out in front of the Greater Union. Amongst them is this guy called Mick who used to go to our school. I don't really know him, mostly Imp knows him. He doesn't fit in with this crowd, and is just hangin around them until someone he knows comes along.

His full name is Michael Buchhorn, but literally everyone at school used to call him Dick Fuckhorn, even to his face. He hated it, and one time he screamed at us about how Dick is short for Richard and that Mick is actually short for Michael, and Stuart Greene joked 'so your dick is short?' Fuckhorn gave Stuart a blood-nose for it, and it was the first time we ever saw Mick get violent. In some newfound respect for him, a lot of people started callin him Mick after that.

He's alright, I guess.

'What're you losers up to, ay?' says KK, coming down the mall with his mates.

KK is Imp's older brother, but only by a couple of years. His name's Kenny, and he reckons the first K stands for Krazy. He's a high-school dropout but gets paid shitloads workin in construction. He's still a skinny cunt, but, even though his normie mates are literally built like brick shithouses. They don't want a fuckin bar of us gothics and punks, which is good coz they look like total tools.

KK grabs Imp by his ponytail and they start wrestlin. Even though he's bigger, Imp doesn't fight back much. Probly after seventeen years of it he's learnt to put up with the abuse. As an only child I can't really relate, but.

'What're you hangin around the streets for?' says KK, tryin to get Imp onto the ground and havin a hard time of it. 'Ay? Ay?'

'Fuck off,' spits Imp. His face has gone all red from being bent over in a headlock. 'What're *you* doing?'

KK lets go of him and grins at his tool mates. 'Me, Grubber and the other boys from work are headin to Fat Louie's. Comin?'

'No,' says Imp in a childish way. Funny how KK brings that out in him.

'Suit yerselves,' KK disses, struttin down the street laughin. 'Looks like fun hangin outside the cinema all day, ay.'

He's pretty full on, like the cunt has no off button, but I reckon he'd be the more fun brother to hang out with. He'd probly be less crazy towards us as a girl than to his own brother, I reckon.

'KK looked like he was wasted,' I go to Imp.

'He probably was,' Imp says. 'That's all he does, is smoke bongs when he's not working.'

Mick's eyes light up.

'My Dad has a stash of weedums at home,' he says excitedly. 'In a secret spot.'

Obviously not secret enough if Mick could find it.

'Good for him,' Imp goes.

'He's at work,' Mick reveals. 'You guys should come around.'

'What? Now?' asks Imp.

Mick laughs: 'Of course, cunt.' When he says *cunt* it sounds forced, not like when me or James says it. He's a bit ova try-hard, but we're eager to get blazed and an Aboriginal protest march is headed our way from the Queen Street Mall and flushing everyone out in its path, so we head up with him to Central via Elizabeth Street, leavin James with the others outside the Birch. We slip into the station without the ticketies seeing us, which is heaps easy to do.

Mick now lives in Zillmere, a shit suburb on the Caboolture line.

'Prudence, yeah?' he goes, and I tell him it's *Pixie*. 'Oh yeah, course. The gothic thing,' he adds, looking us up and down. I can't tell if he's undressing us with his eyes or not, but if the cunt tries anything dodgy Imp will literally fuck him up.

They start talkin shit about school last year, and who's doin what now or more correctly who's literally doin who, and it reminds me ova dream I had the other night. I always remember my dreams coz as soon as I wake up I start goin over the details again. This was one I'd had before. I dreamt of going to school naked, just wearin me shoes and socks. I hate those dreams. In them, ya always feel like ya didn't get the memo and everyone else did. Ya feel fuckin stupid, the same as people who turn up to parties in a costume when it's not a costume party.

'Paw paw shoots?' goes Mick, his mouth hangin open.

'Yeah, man, I'm serious,' laughs Imp. 'My brother swears by it. He says that way you don't get the plastic toxic smell of the rubber hose.'

They've moved on from school talk to bong talk.

A seedy lookin guy with a bum-bag and a cap pulled down over his eyes forces the doors apart between the carriages and runs past us.

'He's also experimented with apple bongs or potato bongs, too,' Imp boasts, Mick's eyes goin wide with amazement.

I lean out into the aisle and look into the carriage the seedy guy just came from, to see what's up.

The ticket inspector cunts are on the train.

I interrupt the boys. 'We're gonna have to ditch at the next station,' I go, noddin in the direction of the ticketies.

'Shit, only if we get there before they get to us,' says Imp.

We're in luck, coz we roll into Northgate station. Imp forces the doors to open faster just as the ticketies get into our carriage. Mick's lookin back at them grinnin like a fuckhead, so I literally shove the cunt out the doors, and he starts moanin about it.

'Stop whingein, ya fuckin sook,' I snap. 'Ya nearly gave us away, ya cunt.'

We head round the other side of the station office and hang there, where we'll wait for the next train. The Caboolture train starts takin off just as the city-bound one comes screechin into the station, so we figure we're home free, but the ticketies literally walk round the corner and start hasslin us.

'Where's your tickets, guys?' one of the cunts says all smug. It's the security guards in the city all over again. Fuckin hell.

Imp just leans against the wall with his arms folded across his chest and avoidin eye contact, and me and Mick fidget about and try out a couple of lame excuses. They ask to see our school ID's.

'Don't have one,' I admit.

'Why not?' goes the cunt.

'Left it at home, with my purse,' I lie.

'How's that any good to you?' He looks at the plastic bag from Record Exchange in my hand, as if to make a fuckin point.

'That way I know where it is,' I go.

The cunt snorts. 'Yeah, well, no good to you now, is it?'

'If I have it out here, maybe it'll get stolen,' I protest. 'Least now I know it's safe at home.'

'Doesn't make any sense,' growls the other ticketie, lookin pissed. He keeps glancin at Imp, sizin him up.

'What about you?' the first guy says to Mick, who looks like he's shittin himself.

'I left mine at her house, too,' the stupid cunt says.

'Bullshit,' says the second inspector. 'What's yer name?' He pulls out a ticket book, ready to write up a fine for Mick, or maybe all of us, coz he's had enough of our bullshit.

Mick goes: 'It's Peter.'

'Peter what?'

'Peter Evans,' he says, and the ticketie snaps his head up and stares hard at him, then glances down at the liddle name badge pinned to his own chest. The ticketie's last fuckin name is EVANS. Mick must have panicked and copied it, the stupid dickhead.

'Must be related,' sneers ticket inspector Evans.

A dude's voice yells out: 'Hey, Dick Fuckhorn!' and Mick spins round in the direction of the voice, which came from the city-bound train in front of us still stationed at the platform. There's a gothic dude hangin out the doors givin us the middle finger, with a big grin on his face. His canines literally look like they're fangs, which reminds me of that fucking security guard at that stupid school dance me and Imp went to. But I'm sure I've seen this guy at the clubs, hangin out with that Dante Halloran; not sure who he is, but.

'Fuck off, you pedo!' Mick yells back, givin the gothic dude the finger back.

The dude ducks back inside the train as doors close it starts to take off. The ticketies are grinnin their fuckin faces off.

'Dick, eh?'

Mick gets snappy. 'Dick isn't short for Michael, stupid!'

'Righto, Michael,' says the first ticketie, writin in his notebook, 'how about you give us your surname, now?'

'Good one, dickhead,' goes Imp, finally breakin his silence and slappin Mick up the back of the head.

PAINT THE TOWN RED

It's a bit bloody warm in this jacket out here in King George Square despite the weatherman saying it's cooler now than this time last year. Alan's got the right idea wearing a cut-off denim jacket covered in patches of various punk bands, although I'd never be caught dead in denim.

We're here for a forum that's been arranged to highlight how the Queensland Indigenous Land Tribunal bureaucrats are being highly fucking incompetent, although I'm mostly here as moral support for Alan. He's quite passionate about these issues. Maybe if the cunt can get some land out of it we can set up a massive homeless shelter and get everyone in for a piss up every night. Right now some cunt has the microphone and is going on about how the tribunal employs sixty people a year, processes about one claim a year and all to the hefty tune of a million bucks. I wouldn't even need half of that to set up our shelter come rave.

'And we have issued the both the State and Federal Governments with a log of claims calling for a properly managed Indigenous Lands Fund,' the guy says. 'Mundingburra matters!'

Alan roars his encouragement along with the crowd, taking their cue when the speaker pauses for breath.

'Fuck, this sun's belting down on me, Alan. I didn't even put any sunblock on.'

'Not long,' he snaps, eyes trained on the speakers at front.

Cunt's acting surly with me because I didn't bring the Hi-8 along to film the protest. Hardly my fucking fault, though: I fessed up last night to Roshi that some water had been spilled on it and he got the shits and came to take it back. I showed him it still worked, but his mind was made up. I did my part to try and hang onto it, so Alan can get fucked if he thinks I'm gonna stand around feeling sorry about it.

Speaking of, we've been out here too long already. I'm gonna burst into fucking flames any second if I continue to stand in this heat. I'm meant to be meeting Twix later on who probably won't even recognise me because I'll be so roasted.

Some of my homeless mates are in the square and spotted me. I gesture for Micko to come over.

'What's going on?' he says, looking confronted by the multitude of people here.

'Your mob's on the rise again,' I smile. 'You should join us. Take you for a pint after.'

'Yeah?'

'We've gotta start creating our own agenda, our own policies,' shouts this guy up front into the mic, 'and we gotta stop toeing the Government's line!'

Everyone yells and cheers as Micko peers around anxiously. Donger, who's a bit of a know-it-all when it comes to clashes with

State Government and its police force, told me once about how Old Joh, the Hillbilly Dictator of the 70's, decreed that marches and demonstrations were banned in Brisbane and only allowed in King George Square, but that still didn't stop the coppers from attacking a big bunch of Uni students who were against Joh's pro-uranium mining legislation. This very town square we're standing in turned to mayhem, Donger reckons, when the students refused to give up their megaphone and kept passing it around out of reach of one of the cops. His old maths teacher from high-school was one of the students who held onto the copper's ankles after he tried stomping them while the rest of the force tried to pull him free. The whole thing backfired because it galvanised the underground protest movement here in a way that made Old Joh decry them all as commies. Wouldn't see any Uni cunts doing that these days, the fucking soft bellies.

The guy up front passes the mic aside, shades of the protest in the 70's, and gestures for the crowd to follow him as he steps down and proceeds to walk towards Queen Street.

Thank fuck, finally we can get out of this sun. The top of my head feels hot under my palm.

'Let's go,' I say to Micko.

'Where we goin to?' he says, following like a puppy.

'Where're we headed?' I ask Alan.

'Down this way,' the surly cunt says. 'Just follow.'

'I've never been very good at just following, you know that, Alan.'

He gives me a severe look. 'We're gonna go tell that mob at the Aboriginal Affairs Unit what's what.'

'As long as there's shade, I'm happy.'

'What's what?' asks Micko, looking bewildered.

'You know it brother,' winks Alan, pointing at Micko like the poor cunt's actually got a clue about anything.

We march en masse across the Queen Street Mall and down Albert Street and the Union Cinemas where the babybats are hanging out. We keep on down to Charlotte Street and stop outside this plain looking building. There must be nearly a hundred people here, but a lot of them are cops and reporters. Micko's looking pretty excited by it all now.

One cop is shouting at one of the speakers who helped lead the march down here.

'Your rally permit is for King George Square only,' the cunt says.

'We don't need to follow your rules,' the Aboriginal guy shouts back. 'This is all our land.'

The cop shakes his head and turns to confer with his colleagues.

The crowd takes up a chant.

'NO MORE DEATHS IN CUSTODY! GIVE US BACK OUR LAND!'

The photo-journos get in close to capture some dramatic angles.

'Let's get up there, get in the papers, ay,' says Alan rather too enthusiastically.

I'm all for supporting the cunt, but a life of petty crime has made me invariably shy of being caught on camera, especially in the act of committing the actual offence. If what that cop was saying is true, then technically we're all breaking the law right now. Pig City's finest may not react too kindly to that.

Suddenly there's a ruckus and predictably the cops have produced batons. It looks like they're trying to arrest the leader of the protest.

'Get fucked, copper!' yells this skinny black guy who the cops drag out of the crowd. His hands are scarlet and I assume he's bleeding.

'Holy shit, look at that, Alan!' I point at the cops wrestling with the man, but Alan's surged into the crowd and taken up position next to some other guy who passes him something small and round.

The journos are being shoved around by both sides at the law tries to contain the crowd. For its part, the people are no longer chanting but are yelling insults at both the building and the police.

Alan lobs something towards the building but it misses the mark and hits an officer of the law standing near the entrance. Bright red paint explodes against his noggin and sprays against the wall behind him. For a moment I think Alan's thrown a rock and brained the copper but then realise it's a just paint bomb.

'RED FOR ALL OUR BROTHERS AND SISTERS WHO HAVE DIED IN YOUR CUSTODY!' screams this young woman next to me, her nostrils flaring with rage.

More paint bombs are hurled, little water balloon sacks wobbling through the air before bursting against their targets.

I hold onto Micko's shoulder in case the poor bastard bolts like a spooked horse and gets himself snaffled by the cops in the process.

'Don't worry, mate,' I assure him. 'I'll get you out of here.'

He looks pretty frightened, truth be told. The crowd presses around us as they shirk back from the encroaching cops. Alan's still up front throwing paint bombs with the others. Fuck the cunt. If he doesn't have sense to see it's all gone to shit, then he's on his own.

'Let's go, Micko. This way.'

I lead him through the crowd away from the Aboriginal Affairs Unit building, and the crowd starts to thin. The cops let us pass as they can see we're clearly not causing any of the trouble.

'Fucking hell, Dante,' Micko goes, breathing heavily. Even for a black guy he looks pale.

'Just breathe, mate, it's okay.' I pat him on the back gently.

'Where's your friend gone?'

I get onto tippy-toes and try and spot Alan in the crowd, but it's too messy down in the front line. I can't see shit. He better not have got arrested, the stupid prick. He's got a baby and all on the way. If he's in the slammer, Suzie's gonna kill him. Or she'll kill me. Usually girls blame me for their partners' shortcomings.

'I dunno, Micko. I hope he's alright.'

We move further up the street to Festival Hall and sit in the shade of its awning, watching the melee die down fairly quickly.

Paddy wagons draw up and I can see the cops have cuffed a few people and put them in the back. The rest of the crowd are ordered to disperse and go home.

Even from here, I can see a few of the journos and their cameras are splashed red, as too are some of the cops and the walls of the building we'd marched on.

As to Alan's whereabouts, there's no clue. I can't see him headed the other way and he's not coming this way either. When the paddy wagons rumble past us I do my best to see if he's in the back, but the caged little windows on the sides are impossibly dark.

'Shit,' I say. 'I think he got arrested.'

'No more deaths in custody,' murmurs Micko.

I glance at the cunt to admonish him for his tactlessness, but he's fearfully watching the wagons disappear around the corner. Then he glances up at me and his face changes into one of hope and yearning.

'So, about that beer you promised me...'

VALLEY BOYS

'Now there's a vision of love, me lad, a real little beauty,' says Twix, uncrossing his legs and leaning forward as he spies a girl with big frizzy hair strolling down Brunswick Street. I'll never understand his fascination for hair like that. 'Nice legs, too. Shame about the face.'

'I wouldn't have clocked you for a Dave and the Derros fan, Twix.'

'Who?'

'Nevermind.'

He cranes his neck as the girl stops to scrape gum off the heel of her shoe.

'Same hair as Mariah Carey, dontcha think?' he says excitedly.

'I wouldn't know,' I go, sucking down a milkshake. The California always does a great milkshake.

'Oh, come off it, Dante, you know the videos I'm talking about. The one from yonks ago where she's in that window of the big arse mansion singing about...'

He's stops mid-sentence, because of course he didn't watch those music clips for the lyrics.

'About what?' I prompt.

'Some shit or another,' he goes, shrugging. 'But can't you imagine fucking her?'

He's talking about the girl with the frizzy hair, of course, currently turning the corner of Dooley's, and not Mariah Carey. I couldn't look any less interested in this banter if I tried.

'Oh no, my dear lad,' he patronises, catching on. 'Don't tell me you've got eyes only for Erina?'

I shrug, feigning indifference. She had fantastic tits, and her pussy fit me like a glove. What can I say? But I'm not in the mood to dissect this thing I've got going on with Erina, whatever it is.

'Hey, did you know that back about a decade ago the AIDS Committee of Queensland did a survey in that very pub right there?' I go, pointing at Dooley's. 'Hard to imagine that place with all the shit Irish decorations being home to a research campaign on HIV cases among the gay scene in Brisbane, huh?'

Predictably, Twix is irritated not only by my sudden change of topic but also the subject matter itself. I don't know if he knew that Dooley's used to be a gay place called Hacienda's, but I know that in his opinion AIDS and homosexuality are synonymous, like the cunt is still living in Bjelke-Petersen's ignoramic 80s. The then-Premier was actually convinced that the moral fabric of our society would be at risk by condom vending machines in public toilets, for fuck's sake.

'*N'importe quoi,*' says Twix without enthusiasm. 'That's French for whatever.' He's itching to continue the topic of me and Erina, whereas I've got zero interest in that line of scrutiny.

'Get this, right, and you're gonna love this bit,' I say undeterred, 'it was called Operation Vampire!'

'Who cares?' he snaps.

'Just thought it was funny, is all,' I scoff.

'I couldn't give a toss about poofs and junkies,' he says moodily.

'Fucking Mariah Carey is all you *do* care about, yeah?'

I'm only stirring, playing with him, but he's not biting. He sits there sulking, not touching his food. He keeps this up and I'll eat it for him. A milkshake was about all I could afford, after bailing Alan outta the watch-house, but it hasn't filled me up.

'It's a lot better than worrying about junkies all the fucking time,' says Twix.

'I'm certainly not worried about the cunts,' I go. 'Why? Are you?'

'You should be,' he goes, stabbing listlessly at his sandwich with his fork. 'They're lawless, Dante. They'll think nothing of infecting you with their shit blood.'

I can't say I've ever felt intimidated by their 'shit blood', as he puts it. Junkies are hardly a secret breed that keep to the shadows and rarely seen, I'll grant, but I hang around these streets a hell of a lot and for the most part don't get hassled by them. It's the fucking drunk bogans and the homie gangs that I'm wary of.

His homophobia is getting on my nerves, however, so it's only fair I get to stir the cunt up a bit.

'Well, you might want to consider staying out of the inner-city areas in future,' I suggest.

'What for?'

'The Tenant's Union is trying to get the RTA to make boarding houses follow the same rules as rental houses do, in order to protect both boarders and the operators is their excuse,' I tell him. 'But the Boarding House Owners Association says those rules will probably force a lot of boarding houses to close down.'

'Sounds like the boarding houses are probably operating below standard, then,' he replies. 'They deserve to be shut down.'

My mate Alan actually lives in a boarding house, and with a kid on the way he can ill-afford to be out on the streets. He's been trying to cut down on the drinking so's he can save for the baby, and being homeless will almost certainly see him turn to the booze with a passion. Micko managed to wheedle two pots out of me the other day before I had to put my foot down and use the excuse of bailing Alan from the watch-house in order to avoid dishing out for a third pint. That poor cunt's got fuck all else to do but drink away reality. I'd hate to see Alan go that way, too.

'Think about it,' I say. 'Those boarding houses are where a lot of addicts currently hole up. If they close down there's no way those dirty cunts have either the social skills or the financial means to move into other accommodation. They'll be right here on the streets, sharing needles and leaving bloody cotton balls all over the ground where you walk. Actually, forget about these streets, mate, they'll be all around the Prozac Palace itself! There's shitloads of boarding houses in Spring Hill.'

Twix visibly shivers. It's not the homosexuals he's got a problem with, so much as needles or blood. Typically, like most bigots, he doesn't distinguish between junkies and gays when it comes to being prejudiced. But I narrowed his forthright fear down to either needles or blood some time ago when I told him how I'd read in *People* about some crazy fucker in America – a so-called self-confessed vampire – advertising on his local community notice board for women to send their used tampons so he could extract the blood to drink. He was apparently cautioned by the cops for soliciting, of all things. I don't know why, but for some reason talk of needles and blood is giving Twix the heebie-jeebies more than usual.

'I'm done eating,' he says, flipping off the top layer of bread from his chicken sandwich.

I lunge across and grab what's left on his plate. 'Waste not, want not.'

We head off straight down McLachlan Street because Twix reckons there's something he wants to check out.

'She's gone already, you sad case,' I tease him.

'Not the chick,' he says exasperated. 'I wanna see who's working this area now. One of the guards I used to know, lad called Stevie Harris, got caught last year doing the dodgy by towing cars that weren't illegally parked, but there's a rumour he's got his shifts back on the sly.'

We check the car-parks in front of the offices where he'd got the cars towed in the first place. I've seen insecurity guards walking around these areas in the past but mostly only at night. When the sun's beating down like this I know for a fact that the lazy cunts retreat to the pub up on the corner or hide out in the shade of Saint Patrick's Church. I've seen em do it heaps of times.

'Hmm, no-one's around,' says Twix, absent-mindedly digging the point of his roachcrushers into the cracked gutter. 'So anyways, Stevie was getting people's cars towed and they'd have to ring him on his mobile and pay him off to bring em back.'

I've never trusted insecurity guards, present company somewhat excluded, but cunts with mobile phones are definitely not to be trusted. What's so important that it can't wait for a payphone to be found, especially since there's one on practically every corner? I'm suspect of that level of immediacy required, like the world hinges on their fucking word. Plenty of others evidently feel the same way: the fucking things have now been banned in cinemas, restaurants and hospitals, and even Ansett's jumped on board and made mobile-free airport lounges. I swear, cunts keep using them on the street, I'm gonna start grabbing them by those little antennas and flipping them under the traffic.

'This Harris prick get done for nicking the cars?'

'Yeah,' says Twix, still scanning the street for the presence of a fellow guard. 'Got stung over seven grand in the courts the other day, and told he can't work here anymore.'

'Ouch!'

'Yeah,' chuckles Twix. 'No-one's here. Let's head off.'

Thank fuck. The sun is getting way too much. I already had enough of it the other day at that protest rally in King George Square. Today is my make-up day to Twix since he was pissed off that he'd cut short his visit with his mum up in Caboolture to hang out with me in the city the other day and I'd stood him up. It didn't matter to him that one of my mates had been arrested and I was a bit worried about the dumb bastard. As far as he's concerned people only get arrested if they deserved it, and so they warrant no sympathy. By that logic, he saw my preference for a jailed friend over him as a terrible insult.

Twix has this unhealthy fascination with the law, and with all its myriad branches like the military and shit. He's the kind of guy who subscribes to magazines about the SAS, combing the pages for details to regurgitate ad infinitum in hopes of impressing all and sundry. I used to find it hysterical, but thankfully the more you get to know him the less he does it, because there's no fucking way I could tolerate hearing that horseshit anymore.

On the way I'm telling him about this guy I read about that lives in Victoria who's decided never to marry and have kids and is using a shitload of credit cards to live on.

'He's got a fucking mansion, multiple cars, the fucking lot,' I go, making sure to project my voice so the two middle aged women in front of us taking their fucking time like it's a Sunday afternoon stroll in the park get the hint and move aside so we can get past. They're still dawdling, so even though this bit's not true I nonetheless loudly blurt: 'Prostitutes every fucking night of the week, no shit.'

This gets their attention. One of them half-glances back sourly and purses her lips like a cat's bum. All for eavesdropping but still not taking the hint to move her fat arse.

'And they don't work?' says Twix, who looks confused by the whole concept.

'They don't need to,' I go. 'They just max out their credit cards and then get more credit cards to cover the interest on the first lot.'

'I don't get it,' he sniffs. 'Can he pay any of em off in time like that?'

'Nah, it'd take the cunt ages,' I go, 'but that's not the point.'

Finally the old eavesdropping biddies waddle to the side, but as we overtake one of them fixes me with her muddy eyes and goes: 'If he's contagious then he shouldn't be giving it to those poor women.'

Me and Twix look at each other wondering what the fuck she's on about. She tuts some more and her friend nods stupidly, adding: 'That's what they get for selling their bodies, though, Janet.'

'That's a bit random,' Twix mutters, staring back at the ladies, then turns to me and goes: 'So how's this bloke getting away with living the high-life on a bunch of credit-cards?'

'As long as he keeps the annual interest paid off on the cards,' I continue, 'the banks are satisfied. In fact, his credit rating's through the roof, now. Then one day he'll be dead and no-one will inherit the debts. The banks'll reclaim the house, the cars, fucking everything, and that'll be the end of it.'

I'd try my hand at the scheme myself if the banks would but let me get my hands on a fucking card in the first place! But I've got less than zero credit history; it's like a red flag comes up on their computers screens screaming DO NOT GIVE THIS HOMELESS CUNT ANY CREDIT.

Twix looks dubious, like he's trying to find a way to refute the veracity of the story, when he says: 'But where's his sense of pride?'

Fuck me, but this cunt. I start laughing. 'Who needs pride when you've got a mansion, mate?'

I always forget that Twix is very pro-work. Funnily enough, it's also made him classist. Like, I know at times he really looks down on me, as if having a friend from far below the poverty-line makes him feel more accomplished. He won't admit it, but he's actually obsessed with class division. It comes from when his dad was a member of the unions in the eighties and a supporter of Bob Hawke, and his dad's union contacts kept the family pretty well off financially. But when his dad injured his leg in a work accident and couldn't prove he was grossly negligent, his union buddies inexplicably turned their backs on him. The whole family became pariahs up in Caboolture and suddenly Twix (an only child) wasn't popular at school anymore. Got bullied a lot, as a result. So ever since he's been obsessed with class identity.

As we're walking past The Beat a car passes us and a boofhead leans out the window and shouts that we're both poofters. It's not uncommon for a goth to get called a poofter or a faggot – or some other name meant to be derogatory – in broad daylight. No cunt ever comes to our defence, either: they just stand there and watch slack-jawed, as if this was prime-time TV and we're merely entertainment.

But the lights up at the intersection of Ann Street and Brunswick have turned red, so in no time we've come abreast of the car full of boofheads.

'Go fuck yourselves, ya cunts!' I yell out as they sit grinning at us with their small, piggy eyes and their thick fucking necks. 'You're thinking about giving it to me up the arse so badly I can practically see you panting at the very thought!'

'You what, mate?' snarls the stupid fucker out his window.

The lights turn green, but they sit there revving the engine in some pathetic attempt to try and intimidate us. Unfortunately it's working on Twix, who whispers for me to stop stirring them up. Eventually they tear off up the street just before the lights turn red again. Typical.

'One of these days, me lad, you'll come a gutser from stunts like that,' Twix whines, thoroughly unimpressed. 'I won't be around to back you up when it does.'

'You mean you won't stick around, full stop,' I joke, wondering if he'd really stand up to those monkeys in the car if it came down to it.

He's not happy still, looking all mopey-faced about the whole thing, accusing me of being addicted to drama. The fucking sook. Sometimes it makes me wonder how we're even friends.

'Maybe I won't be around at all,' he says, obviously goading me.

'Cause you'll be dead?' I posit, heading into the Brunswick Mall, forcing him to follow. I trot at a slightly faster pace, making the cunt unconsciously try and keep up. I'll see if I can't make him break into a sweat.

'I could be living in Melbourne,' he chirrups.

Here we fucking go, the Melbourne pipe-dream again. For as long as I've known him Twix has been harping on about moving to Melbourne, the dream destination for every goth in this fucking city.

'Everyone wants to move to Melbourne, and go to England for a holiday,' I sneer.

'Oh yeah, where would you travel to, then, lad?' he challenges, expecting me to be stumped for an answer.

'Armenia,' I shoot back without hesitation.

'The US of A isn't that original, either,' he says smarmily.

'Armenia's not in America,' I retort. 'It's above Turkey.'

He screws his face up. 'Why the hell would you wanna go there for?'

'Legend has it that there's a vampire living in the mountains there, called Dakhanavar,' I go, squinting my eyes and hunching over to act all mysterious. 'It drinks from people's feet, apparently.'

'Eww, gross,' Twix says, and we both laugh.

'I know, right?'

He grins and in a squeaky goes: 'You oughtta see a psychiatrist–'

'TWIIIIIXXX!!'

This chubby lil girl with ruined two-tone hair and equally ruined mascara comes running out of the McDonald's at us. It's like she's possessed, her flabby arms in the air as she slams into Twix and gives him what I think is meant to be a hug but looks more like she's trying to squeeze the shit out of his body.

'Holy shit,' gasps Twix, 'trying to stay standing here.'

'I've missed you!' she squeals, being as positively annoying as possible. 'You don't have to worry about Mikey anymore. I told him I'm not into you so he's gonna leave you alone now.'

'Yeah, fucking great,' Twix coughs. 'Hope he's not too pissed by the train fine, either.'

She's puzzled by this – as, too, am I – and she finally relinquishes her death-hold on him and flaps a pudgy hand towards the golden arches where a group of teenagers sit devouring burgers and shakes. 'You'll never guess what! Me and Jeremy are engaged!'

'Congratulations!' I cheer.

I can't tell which horrid little cunt is Jeremy. They all look alike, and they all repulse me.

Twix doesn't look too impressed, either, although I'm guessing it's from the news of the delinquent engagement judging by the sly way he keeps looking at her tits. She was clearly meant to be a conquest at some point, and she's slipped though his fingers.

'What are you grinning at?' he says to me.

'So, who's your friend?' I go.

'I'm Ursula,' she booms, extending her hand. I take it and bow, which delights her.

'I've never been bowed to before!' she squeals.

It always makes them feel like royalty the first time.

'So, you're Twix's lil friend, eh?'

'Yeah, course,' she says, then starts pointing out all the cunts at the bench, listing their names in turn.

'Fascinating,' I drawl, jerking my thumb at Twix. 'But tell me, Ursula, just how well do you know this shady character?'

'Knock it off, Dante,' says Twix.

'Pretty well,' Ursula says, absentmindedly kicking at Twix's boot. 'We went looking for the Angel of Death together!'

'Did you know he was in the SAS?'

Twix goes to roll his eyes, but then he obviously thinks better of it, perhaps curious about how Ursula might react.

'What the fuck is that?' she laughs. 'An STD?'

Before Twix can get a word out I quickly confirm: 'It certainly is!'

The girl's eyes go wide and she actually steps back from him, to his horror.

'No, it's not,' says Twix. 'He's just fucking around...'

But she's not listening. She runs back to her mates screaming: 'He's infected! He's infected!'

I wasn't sure where I was headed with my playful little joke, but this is a delightful outcome for sure.

'Who is?' goes one of the other runts, scowling in our direction.

'Both of them!' screeches the trashy lil bitch. 'They got it fucking each other up the arse!'

'Happy now?' grumbles Twix, shaking his head at me.

'She's got it all wrong,' I call out. 'I've got nothing to do with it. It's all him.'

Now they're all yelling at us to fuck off, calling us AIDS cunts and all sorts of shit. Their voices are echoing back and forth across the mall, and every other fucker has turned to see what the commotion is all about, staring at me and Twix like we're the fucking worst, as if contracting HIV wouldn't be enough of a sentence for somebody.

'God, you're a dickhead, sometimes,' sighs Twix as we both beat a path down the mall.

'Yeah, that didn't quite go the way I thought it might,' I admit.

'Everything's a fucking joke to you, isn't it?'

I grab him by an arse cheek. 'You'll be right mate, as long as you've got me.'

'Fuck off,' he snaps, shrugging my hand off. 'You oughtta see a psychiatrist...'

Then in unison we both go: 'You're a loony!' and burst into laughter as we push people out of the way and head up Wickham Street.

CAROUSEL

I've got all the Gailey papers in order. I just need Mister Calthorpe, boss *numero uno*, to sign all four.

I leave them on Jennifer's desk since she's, like, his PA. She catches me doing it and gives me a severe look; not that I've done anything wrong, but ever since my first day the bitch has basically been, like, making out that I have. No proof or anything, just snide and insinuating remarks that undermine my confidence, and even if I were to challenge her on it she'd come back with how I'm being, like, oversensitive and basically taking my work too seriously. Which is her way of putting me down and basically saying I don't do anything important.

It's pointless saying anything to any of the three partners about it, especially Calthorpe.

No-one has really twigged yet, but I have: he has to be fucking her. Surely. She's a witless *kargiola* and passes so much of her workload off onto me, and the other two partners don't have personal assistants, so why's Calthorpe need one? Her role has become a vague collation of tasks that have no follow-up but seem to have consequences for me if I don't get them done for her.

At first I assumed she was, like, being told to pass this work down onto me, and by the time I sussed that that wasn't the case, I'd already been doing it for so long and so well that the big bosses said they were quite happy for me to continue without actually reviewing what I currently have on my plate! That left Jennifer pretty much swanning about, and the worst part is she doesn't even hide the fact that she has little work to do. It's become a source of pride for her.

I've got a bob cut now, like a sort of Cleopatra style cut, which I treated myself to just the other day and is good in the Queensland heat. It invokes that whole silent-era temptress thing, I guess. Next morning when I walked in Calthorpe clucked at me: 'If I was twenty years younger, Alexandra!' I felt good about myself, appreciated. Not that I'd have, like, done anything with him, even with him being married and too old. Not my type, right? But Jennifer was there and she gave me this fucking death-stare like she wanted to kill me.

Now I just think Calthorpe's a fucking creep. Period. If I saw him at a club or something I'd avoid him like the plague. And his bitch of a mistress – as I'm pretty bloody certain she is – further enhances this new aspect of him. I can imagine Jennifer in high school, one of the popular girls that basically made life hell for the rest of us; especially, like, for the overweight and nerdy girls like me. Going goth was one way of sticking it to skanks like her, of saying I don't need to admire you or hope to conform to your ideals because I've basically rejected them outright, and if any further proof was needed then my newfound fashion and musical tastes should set the record straight.

Before going goth I'd actually been friends with a group of popular boys, and I'd enjoyed the immunity it had afforded from the scathing attacks girls like Jennifer would normally have dished out. But, like, even that hadn't lasted. The boys proved no better, at the end of the day.

Jennifer charges over to her desk and doesn't look straight away at the papers, instead pretending to sort something else out in front of her. It's an old ruse, one I'm already well acquainted with from this whore, but I've no choice but to go through the motions.

I turn away and begin to head back towards my own desk, the muscles in my shoulders beginning to, like, tighten in anticipation. I can almost hear her pause and consider the Gailey forms as if for the first time.

'What's this?'

It's always some asinine opening.

It says what they are on the fucking top of the sheet, for pity's sake.

It's a cheap move to wrest control in our exchange. And just like that, Jennifer ('Not *Jenny*. Only my father calls me Jenny.') swings the balance of power. It seems so effortless, and I, like, seem so powerless to avoid it. Maybe I should have beaten her to it, addressed her with the papers and tried to parry my way to some sort of stupid victory between us. But it's pointless and tiring. I can't bear to initiate any discourse with her, and so here I am once again obliged to play her game.

'Papers for Mister Calthorpe.'

My voice sounds thin and reedy. I hate it. I hate what she does to me. The strain is so bloody evident.

'Yeah, I can see that,' Jennifer says, her voice snippy. 'I mean, why are they here?'

I've no idea where this is going, but already she's managed to turn such a simple thing into an accusation. I feel my face flush, evidence of some (non-existent) nefarious wrongdoing on my part. Before I can even respond, she's into me again.

'They should've been through yesterday.'

'Yes, but, like, there was a delay from the courts–'

'What delay?'

'Um, from the barrister for the Gailey case. Mister Calthorpe said you'd get them–'

Again, she cuts me off, with a wave of her hand. 'Fine, leave it. I'll take care of it.' She says this with a tone of resignation, as though I've somehow burdened her with my own workload when in fact it most certainly was her own to begin with!

So I go back to my desk feeling defeated, right? Wondering why by the grace of the Goddess does she even have to do this to me. I've done nothing to her, nothing at all, period. I've basically walked into some sick pecking order and I wasn't quick enough to see it, and now this is my lot in life. Apparently the other girls in the office weren't slow, though, and saw the threat this new personal assistant would be when she'd first arrived, which was not long before me. They, like, kept their heads about them and then as soon as I came along they shouldered me front and centre and got themselves better rungs to perch upon, while bloody muggins here is collecting the shit on her head!

Later I'm ready to, like, do the rounds of the city, where essentially I save this shitty firm the small expense of a bike courier and walk our papers over to the courts up on George Street.

While I'm out, I'm also expected to, like, deposit our cash into the bank and also pick up Calthorpe's dry cleaning on the way, which isn't, like, on the way at all as it's a fuck of a detour on the opposite side of the city. But Megan's friend Dante showed me a neato trick using the City Loop service, the free Council bus that goes around the city circumference. Mostly only Uni students use it, it seems, to, like, get from Garden's Point up to Central and back again. From the courts I can leap aboard at the top of Adelaide and basically be down to the dry cleaner's on Edward in next to no time, without exhausting myself or getting all sweaty, thank Gaia. It pisses Jennifer off, I know, that she can't work out how I get back to the office so quickly and calmly, but I'll be damned if I'll let that bitch in on my secret.

But when I walk back into the office, Calthorpe's, like, sighing and telling me he's disappointed that I didn't get the Gailey papers through on time and that Jennifer says she asked me to do it first thing this morning.

He's like: 'I had to find them myself amongst all this,' waving a hand across my desk which has papers stacked on top of one another in a way that makes me appear disorganised. What the hell? It's a fucking mess! It's certainly not how I keep my desk! I shoot that bitch Jennifer a dirty look, who just raises one eyebrow and turns away in mock disappointment.

Calthorpe's like: 'Don't worry about it. I got Jen to do it.'

I bet you fucking did, you cheating arsehole.

'Oh, Lyndon,' Jennifer says as she pokes her head around the corner with a shit-eating smile on her face, basically showing off by calling Calthorpe by his first name, something the rest of us are, like, strictly forbidden to do in the office. 'Mister Mannington's here to see you.'

The news brightens Calthorpe, but not before he gives me a look like he wonders what the hell he's going to do about me.

'Scotty, boy!' he says cheerily, pumping the other man's hand like he's trying to shake loose change from him.

'Lyndo, me ol' mucker,' Mannington returns like they're old school buddies, despite the age difference.

I catch Jen's eye watching me from the fax machine. She looks like an evil queen from a Disney movie, smug with villainous ambition.

When I sit back down and start tidying my desk, it's all I can do to, like, hide the tears that start welling up. I just want this day to be over. This whole fucking week. I need a couple of days to recuperate from this bullying.

Thing is, I can't quit. I'm stuck. I wish I could just go back on the dole and, like, stay at home. At least it would buy me time to find a better job than this. I could try and work somewhere like Jitterbug Perfume or one of those cool shops in the Elizabeth Arcade. It'd be much less stressful than this place, I'm sure. The CES forced me into this job, though, and if I quit they won't let me back on the dole, period.

Beggars can't be choosers, as I keep telling myself, so I need to keep plugging away at this awful job with these awful people. Well, they're not all awful, actually. A couple of the other secretary's are nice to me, and we've even caught up after work a couple of times for a coffee before heading home, mostly to, like, bitch about work and Jennifer.

At lunchtime, Jocelyn's like: 'You know she's just jealous of your boobs?'

'No way!' I gasped. 'Seriously?'

'Fucking majorly,' Prita sings in a faint Indian accent. 'She is more than green with envy; she is all the colours envy.'

'It's like being stuck in a *Melrose Place* episode,' I groan.

Imagine finding out that your workplace bullying can be diluted down to basic jealousy of a body part, the size of which I have, like, absolutely no control over whatsoever? To add to the injury, these bloated balloons make my back ache by the end of the day! Copping it from all sides, right?

Even before the elevator doors open, I can hear him singing in the Mall.

On my first day working I made friends with a street busker called Chromedome Les, who dresses like a knockoff of Bruce Springsteen and even, like, covers a few of Springsteen's songs. He calls himself Chromedome because basically he shaves and polishes his head until it shines.

His voice always heralds the close of another shitty day, hoiking me out of the office and back into real life. Like, it marks the transition.

I like to drop some coins into his guitar case, and he likes to pay me a compliment. It's become our thing. He's not here every day, as he moves around the city trying out, like, different spots, but seeing his big friendly smile always makes me feel welcome after the hostilities of Jennifer.

'Have the public been kind to you today, Chromedome?' I needn't have asked: the evidence is plain to see when I drop my coins in. Basically, slim pickings.

'I get by, lovey,' he says, falling into a repetitive strum so he can chat but still, like, keep the vibe going. 'Fantastic hair, by the way.'

'Grouse, right? I got it done the other day.'

'Suits you,' he says with a wink, flashing his teeth.

If he was closer to my age I'd probably go for him. I think he's nearly fifty. Unless he's just seen too much sun. Or hard drinking.

'Okay, blessed be,' I say, about to head off.

He's like: 'Hold up,' keeping the strum on the strings even as ever.

That's my line, lovey.'

'What is?'

'As a god, I'm the one that does the blessing.'

I start to chuckle, just humouring him, but he's dead serious.

'You think you're God?'

He's like: 'Not *the* God, but *a* god, yes.'

Oh, here we bloody well go; the male ego at its most ridiculously illogical.

'I create,' he says, loudly brushing his fingers across the strings to illustrate his point, 'therefore I am.'

I haven't the heart to stress that he's just mimicking a real artist. He wouldn't hear me anyhow, I think. There'd be no room for that kind of rationale in his delusion.

'Okay then, see you tomorrow, god amongst gods?'

'I'll be here, lovey,' Chromedome says, and launches into song, his deep voice booming up and down the Mall. It stays with me the entire way down to Edward Street, and is basically like a comfort to me. Not exactly the voice of a god, but more like a strong, nurturing father-figure. As close as we can expect to a god, I guess, in this day and age.

Then I realise I'm being followed. I can, like, feel my stalker's eyes drilling into me from behind, and when I turn around at the lights he's right there staring up at me.

It's a dwarf, or near-enough to one since he only comes up to just above my belly-button.

Facially, he reminds me of Rod Stewart with his big bouffant of dyed-black hair tied up by a red bandana. I can't be certain, but there appears to be khol smudged around his eye-line. He just stares at me, or rather at my boobs, so when the pedestrian light comes on I hurry across the road and, like, try and lose him in the crowd by squeezing onto the escalators in the Anzac Square building.

The crowd sweeps through the food-court and into the tunnel under Ann Street, where we squeeze onto another set of escalators that climb forever up to the concourse for the train station's main entrance. There's a gap amongst the people below on the escalator where, like, a tuft of black hair sticks up. If I crane my neck I can just see that ridiculous red bandana.

I practically push a bloke off the escalator when it reaches the top, and power-walk to the gates. The back of my ten-trip saver card has the dates and times I've travelled printed on it, and at the end it says * 2 TRIPS REMAINING * which is good news for me; I don't have to stop and, like, fuck around buying another ticket. My miniature stalker is plum out of luck.

I insert my ticket into the machine and the lady smiles me through.

Once I'm inside Central Station I make straight for the stairs to platform one, passing the glass barrier to my left. I can see in my periphery the dwarf is standing at the window staring at me, but I keep my eyes downcast and bolt down the stairs to the platform. It's not until I'm down there that I realise I've been holding my breath as much as possible, only sucking in small intakes that have left me feeling lightheaded.

That little so and so. What a creep.

There's a hot guy down on the platform who notices that I keep glancing up the escalators nervously.

The hot guy's like: 'He better hurry up.'

'Who better?' My voice is squeaky with distress, as my mind starts to try and work out how this man and the dwarf are, like, working in unison, I guess.

'Your boyfriend,' he says with a little smile. 'I assume that's who you keep checking for?'

Bloody hell, turning all paranoid here. Need to calm down. He doesn't know the dwarf at all.

'No,' I blurt, too forcefully.

'Oh, sorry,' the guy says, and faces the tracks.

I feel bad now, because, like, I didn't mean to be short with him. I'm still a bit shaken by the stalker, is all.

'I didn't mean to snap, sorry,' I offer, and the guy screws his nose up in this cute little way and says it's okay. 'I've had a bit of a rough day.'

He's like: 'At least yours is over. You get to go home and put your feet up.'

'Are you, like, off to work, then?'

'Sorta,' he shrugs. 'It's volunteer, but it's still work.'

I notice there's a rolled up paper and a torch sticking out of his backpack.

'Are you an explorer?'

He laughs openly and without conceit. He has amazing teeth.

'No, no I'm not exactly,' he says. The corners of his eyes up crease with his laughter, so they're basically like dark slits made from his beautifully thick lashes. 'I'm working with a group called Creek Freaks. We're trying to rehabilitate some land next to Norman Creek.'

I know that creek! It's the one down the road from me, where all the mozzies breed then, like, come and terrorise me at night.

The train screeches into the station and when we get on board we, like, sit across from one another in a double seat. Under this new light I notice his eyes are hazel, and they sort of glimmer like there's crystal shards in them.

He's like: 'Council re-directed the creek to stop flooding in what's called the Moorhen Flats, but now it looks like a bit of a wasteland. It's just flat earth, some gum trees. Our group's lobbying to change it.'

'By basically sneaking around at night?'

He laughs again. He seems to like laughing, judging by the crow's feet at the corner of his eyes. I like it.

'This is a map of the area and I'm headed out to see what the nocturnal fauna is like,' he explains, unrolling the paper from his backpack for me to see.

Lots of lines and markings. Doesn't make much sense to me.

'It'll form part of our environmental impact study that we use to present to the Council for funding,' he says.

It all sounds quite interesting, or maybe it's just those hazel eyes drawing me in. Even identifying as a pagan I've never really looked at gardens or council land as anything but boring space with plants in it, but this guy really seems into all that stuff. I wonder if he ever goes clubbing and drinking?

'You know, you could get a job with the Green Corps,' I suggest enthusiastically, hoping to weigh in on this topic with something I heard on the news and, like, look at least a little bit credulous. 'It's part of the Coalition's billion dollar environmental policy. Perfect for community groups like yours.'

'Well, for a start they're not in Government yet,' he brashly informs me, 'and secondly, that scheme would replace the current Working Nations one and we'd lose twenty-two thousand jobs in the process.'

Fuck. Bad topic to try and look clever with. I'm sure I've turned red as a beetroot now.

'Thanks for the thought, though,' he adds, a little less cockily. 'So who's Zak?'

My stomach sinks, like when the roller-coaster does a sharp dip and you feel your insides drop.

'How do you know Zak?' I ask carefully, wondering if this guy is an old friend of my ex.

'It's tattooed on your arm,' he points out.

My stupid fucking tattoo on the inside of my wrist. I turn my hand over to hide the stupid thing.

'He's no-one.'

Not anymore.

The topic gets dropped, thankfully.

The lights of South Bank have come on early, and as the train whizzes past I'm reminded of the night when we all left Megan's new club at The Land's Office and, like, walked across Victoria Bridge to the South Bank lagoon for a late-night swim in our underwear. I'd been wondering if Twix and I were going to, like, make out when we were swimming, but he'd seemed to lose interest sometime around me nearly blacking out from a headache. I'd thought maybe he didn't want to be seen taking advantage of me in my state, but he hasn't asked me out or made any moves since, either.

'My name's Jai, by the way,' the guy with the hazel eyes says, jolting me from my memories.

'Alex.'

'Alex the goth.'

'Just Alex.'

An awkward silence descends.

'Have you ever seen a dwarf version of Rod Stewart?' I suddenly ask, partly curious if he's ever seen the little stalker around town and partly to keep our exchange going.

'You know what,' he says with a weirdly amused expression, 'never really considered that one! Didn't even know he had a dwarf version of himself, to be honest.'

Bloody hell, now he thinks I'm a complete weirdo. Way to go, Alex!

'Any reason you ask?'

I just shrug; yet another topic that needs dropping. I'm getting pretty nifty at raising them.

To my horror, Jai decides to follow me off the train at Buranda Station.

'What're you doing?' I ask in mild panic, wondering how I can ask him to politely *not* follow me home.

He's like: 'Heading off to Moorhen Flats,' pointing toward the end of the platform.

Of course, at the back of Woolloongabba! It's just down the road from here.

I feel like such a fucking dingbat now. Gotta laugh!

'Take care, Alex-not-a-goth,' he says with a big grin.

I can feel myself dying inside.

When I get home I dial Abi's number. We've also caught up a few times, after that first time I met her when I was flyer-dropping with Megan. She's pretty cool, and we're getting along like best mates. She took me to the Valley markets and as a house-warming present bought me some really cool hand-printed fabric with, like, cute little bat silhouettes on it, which I've turned into curtains for my windows.

She sounds like she just woke up.

'Sorry, Abi, I forgot you do night shifts.'

I tell her all about Jai, about his eyes, his laugh, the absolutely humiliating conversation about politics and how I thought he was, like, basically trying to follow me home.

I can positively hear her fake drooling on the other end. She's like: 'You should be so lucky.'

Then I tell her about the creepy dwarf and it turns out she knows exactly who I'm referring to! Turns out he's harassed some other girls she knows, too, like a girl called Raven who studies in the city.

'I'm going to kick that little cockwomble in the balls so fucking hard next time I see him,' she growls, then yawns down the receiver.

She makes me laugh. That's why I like her. She's not afraid to, like, say what's on her mind.

'Don't worry, he'll get his,' she says. 'I tell you what, let's have a get-together after your work tomorrow. I'll invite a friend of mine. Chantelle. You'll like her, I think.'

'I don't know...'

'No buts about it,' she says sternly.

'Okay then, it's a date,' I smile. 'Thanks, Abi.'

'Brilliant. I'll see you outside your office at five.'

Once I'm off the phone I hear someone whispering outside my window. Damn it, it's the crazy neighbour again. I swear she, like, hates me or something. I poke my head up to the window and see she's sitting on the steps with a coffee, looking straight at me with those demented eyes.

'Sorry, Jackie, did you say something?'

She's like: 'I heard you mention a dwarf.'

'Do you know him? He was harassing me in the city after work–'

Jackie cuts me off. 'Is that part of your witchcraft stuff, your black magic? Dwarfs?'

'I'm not into black magic,' I say sternly, really hoping not to have to have this conversation. Get it all the time. 'I practice Wicca.'

Sort of. Not really. When I have time to, basically. None of which I need to explain to this clueless mundane. Although it's weird that I should think I have to, because, like, her coffee mug has what looks like a cartoon of a goth on it, with a dragon and a monkey. Like those puppet monkeys we had as kids where the arms would wrap around us three times and hold together with Velcro on the hands. Looks like something you'd get at a medieval faire, where heaps of pagans and wiccans go.

'Saw your sacrificial altar,' Jackie sniffs, but it's more like she's accusing me of something. 'In your bedroom.'

'Bloody hell, did you break into my house?'

She shakes her head. 'Back door was open.'

I race through to the back and find it ajar. The louvre window next to it is pushed open. So much for security when, like, anyone can simply open the window and reach in to unlock the door. Great, a fucking psycho for a neighbour. Now I'll have to call the real estate tomorrow and see if I can get something done about these bloody louvre windows!

PARTY BOYS

Twix met this young gothling at one of the clubs up here and is dead set keen on getting on with her. She's having a party tonight and we're invited, but she's from the Gold Coast so of course it's all the way down there. We've got fuck all means to get there so he's begging Raven to borrow her car for the night.

'I dunno,' she goes. 'Can I trust you not to smash it up?'

'Of course,' crows Twix indignantly.

It's a laugh, though, because her car looks like it's already been in a dozen accidents and is always the one most worst off for it. There's not a flat panel on it, two windows barely close and there's gaffa tape holding the headlights in. She has to replace the stickytape every now and then when it starts to melt off. One night ages ago her and Malik, pissed as farts, spray painted white Satanic emblems all over the roof and bonnet, and have never bothered to clean it off. Needless to say, cops are always pulling her over.

While Twix is doing his level best to get the keys off her, I go wait out front where the old guy from unit one, Bernie, is sitting out on his deck chair watching the stars while he has a smoke.

The first time I ever met Bernie he was very fucking amused by my name. There's no Italian in my ancestry, and I can't count the amount of times I've had to explain to people that the name Dante was given to me only because my father loved books, the only bogan within coo-ee who did apparently, and he'd happened to be reading *The Divine Comedy* at the time of my birth. I fucking loathed the name when I was younger, but then I read *The Divine Comedy* when I was about fourteen years old (or tried to read it, at least) and had no problem with the name after that. That Dante Alighieri was alright.

'Chuffed' is the word Bernie used to describe his amusement at my name, actually. It was such an odd word that I instinctively slipped into my own syntax. I used it in front of my grandmother once and she remarked to Mum that I'm like the black-sheep of the family because of all these old-fashioned words that I come out with. I took it as a compliment, naturally. I was quite chuffed by her observation.

'Waitin on Twix,' I tell Bernie when he looks me up and down.

He snorts derisively. 'Could be waiting a while, then.'

He passes me a cigarette.

'Hey Bernie, you've been around a while,' I go.

'Gee, thanks,' he scoffs good-naturedly. 'We're only as young as the person we feel,' he says, making a grab for my groin.

I dodge the cheeky cunt, surprised by his effrontery.

'Nah, what I mean is, you know a lot of things, from ages ago,' I continue, keeping my distance in case he gets cheeky again. 'Do you remember a ship called the *Helena* from the late 1800's?'

'That's a bit before my time, thank you very much,' he jibes. 'How old do you think I am?'

I shrug, mindful to avoid referencing his joke about feeling young people. 'About a hundred? But you're a history buff, yeah?'

'I like to think so,' he says. Then he thinks for a moment, but long enough for me to think he's lost interest and is cold-shouldering me for not letting him cop a feel. Finally, he goes: 'Thank you, Carl.'

I look around for this Carl cunt, but it's just me and Bernie out here.

'There's wreckage of a schooner called the *Helena* up near Tin Can Bay, below Hervey Bay,' Bernie says. 'Crashed there in the late 1800's. Sounds like it's your ship.'

Certainly does.

'Anyway, the other day I was having some drinks with a homeless guy I know, called Micko,' I go, 'and Micko reckons his grandfather's from the South Sea Islands and used to be a slave on the sugar cane plantations up north. Got there after being kidnapped onto that ship. *Blackbirding*, he called it. I thought you might've heard something about that?'

Bernie shrugs. 'Dunno.'

That's about the best of my understanding of how the story went. Micko gets sloshed pretty quickly and two pints was all it took for him to start being slightly incomprehensible. Normally I just dismiss his wild stories as outright bullshit, but there were details about this particular one that sounded way too legitimate not to have some truth to it. Bernie's always a reliable source of info, apparently, and he's not let me down, I must say.

'Thanks for the info,' Bernie goes.

'No, it's I who must be thanking you,' I say.

He looks at me apologetically. 'Sorry, I was thanking Carl.'

Twix bounds down the stairs, holding Raven's keys up like a trophy.

'We are on our fucking way, lad,' he beams excitedly.

'Catcha, Bernie,' I go. 'Thanks again for the info.'

'Have fun,' he says with a little wave at us.

'Fuck he's a funny one, isn't he?' I say to Twix when we're in the car.

'Bernie?' he goes. 'Yeah, dunno if I'd say he was funny. Bit of a bludger, more like.'

'Isn't he meant to be schizo?'

We make our way over the Story Bridge and down the motorway.

Twix shrugs. 'Who knows? What I do know is I have a feeling, deep down if you know what I mean, that Cecilia is pretty partial to nibbling on a Twix.'

I slap my forehead. 'Fucking hell, whatever you do, don't use that line. I'm serious.'

He just laughs. 'Trust me, I won't fuck this up. She's too stunning to make a half-arsed crack at.'

A commodore revs up past us packed with dickheads who hang out their windows hooting insults. Me and Twix death-glare the cunts, raising our fingers up into the devil's horns normally reserved for concerts by metalheads. It's a great go-to device to make normals think you're hexing the cunts, but rarely does it illicit the kind of reaction it does with these arseholes in the commodore.

'They're fucking Satantists,' one of them yells, fairly shitting himself, and they all duck back inside the car while the driver floors it. The car rips up the motorway, and I'm fucking dying for the old red and blue to start spinning inside some undercover cop car, but the commodore screams away unchallenged. Who knows if they honestly thought we were Satanists or not, but it's happened enough times for me to think they honestly thought we were on the level. Especially if they were pissed, which I think they were. I know a couple of actual so-called Satanists, one of them Malik's older brother, and they're right cunts. I think the genuine article would've done more than just throw a few gestures out the window.

'Did you see the big-arse sticker on their rear window?' says Twix.

'What was it?'

'It was one of those idiotic NO FEAR stickers. Yeah, right!'

This cracks us both up.

Eventually we reach the turn off at Surfer's Paradise, and Twix starts preening himself in the mirror every time we stop at a red light.

I pretty much fucking detest the Gold Coast. Not for the usual reason most people I know do, which is generally the locals there. It's the space I can't tolerate. All that sun-drenched flat wide space with wide open streets and those abominable warehouse-like storefronts. It makes me think of bulk buying, like they're storing stuff away for some apocalyptic event, which in my opinion has already arrived and made of this place the current suburban wasteland I see out the window. Although at the moment it's more tolerable down around Cavill Mall because it's night time, when the lights shatter the night in a hundred spectacles.

We arrive at the address of the party, and I'm not at all surprised by the place. Rendered brick townhouse affair squatting in a sandy-loam soil with the obligatory wind-damaged palm trees and sun-fucked shrubbery gasping it's last in the periphery of what I assume is the fence-line for want of just such a fence. Up the side of the building we can see shadows cast by a garden-variety spotlight.

'How do you know her again?' I'm not even trying to disguise my misgivings.

'Met her at The Playroom,' says Twix.

'Wait a minute, that's down here on the coast,' I go, looking at the cunt suspiciously. 'I thought you said you met back in Brisbane?'

'I knew you wouldn't come if I'd told the truth,' he says. 'Don't worry, we'll see what's up and just sod off if it's too tragic.'

'Yeah, let's not stay too late either way,' I go. 'I'm going around to Erina's tomorrow. She's calling in sick while her boyfriend's up visiting his mum in Hervey Bay. The old bat's in hospital for throat surgery. Probably too much...' I make a motion with my hand like I'm holding a dick and shoving it in and out of my mouth.

'That's a friggin shit plan, Dante,' scolds Twix, unimpressed by both the plan and my joke with the imaginary dick.

'Yeah? Let's see how you fare morally at this party full of... how old is this girl again?'

'Shut up,' he sniffs, conceding defeat.

We round the corner of the house and are greeted by a squad of teenagers, all smoking like it's their first puff and giving us the evil eye. I sneer at them as we push past.

'More fucking goths,' I hear one of them dribble to his mates.

The place looks trashed. It's only a small unit, and sure it's full of people drinking and whatnot, but it really does look like a dingy squat. Shit furniture pushed around in every direction, and hideous tagging spray painted over all the walls and even on some of the windows. There's a pretty hefty plastic chandelier hanging in the centre of the room, but it's not working, which is disappointing. The light comes from this big-arse outdoor spotlight propped on a coffee-table, and is pointed directly at the door. It gives off a bit of heat, so it's also the only spot in the room nobody is loitering around in.

Most of the people here look like they're still in high school. And they dress like shit. One kid wearing a Creed shirt with clusters of red spots all over his chin and at the corners of his mouth actually has the fucking gall to laugh at us behind his hand.

I'm looking at Twix who sighs and gives a little shake of his head. I follow him across the room and from a corner, in amongst milk crates stuffed with books and other stuff, a thin girl in a long black slip of a dress leaps up squealing, hugging Twix.

'Twixxie's in the house,' he beams at her stupidly.

He introduces her as Cecilia but she prefers Celia, and she's as stunning as Twix said she was on the drive here, with huge crystal sharp blue eyes circled by smudged kohl and a vivid cobalt shadow reaching up into her pencil-thin brows. She has an almost perfectly round head, I note. She reminds me of something Tim Burton might sketch in his notebook. She's yelling something to us about her party, but I'm not hearing it much because she's waving her arms around as she does so and keeps spilling her drink, so I'm standing well clear of her. I've seen a lot of cheap beer here already, some UDL and other bogan brands, and I don't fancy having any of that shit on me.

We sit down, refusing a can but happily accepting a bottle of red that some other fat shark-toothed girl has with her. She passes it over with a grin and stares way too hard at me. Twix's chattin away with the Celia girl.

'Taylor,' goes this fat girl, thrusting her pudgy hand towards me after I've accepted the bottle. I shake her hand and introduce myself. She's asking about how I know her friend Cee, as she calls her.

'I don't,' I declare, taking a swig straight from the bottle and pointing it at Twix. 'He does. I'm a total stranger here,' and then instantly regret saying that because she's got this sudden glint in her eyes, like I'm game on a savannah. Her hair is all teased up like Robert Smith, and she's still got that stupid, drunken grin on her face that shows all her crooked teeth. She looks like one of those witches from that movie *Hocus Pocus*. I can't remember her name, but the one that sang that song *Wind Beneath My Wings*. The girls on my old school bus made a mixed tape from *Rage* one morning and would force the crotchety old driver to play it over the speakers every morning, and it was on that.

'What the fuck happened there?' I shout to Taylor over the thumping music, pointing at the walls with all the graffiti on it. She laughs, and I'm reminded even more of those witches.

'You don't like it?'

'It looks fucking terrible.'

'Her ex did it, last night,' says Taylor, and she points at this kid outside who's standing over by the back fence. He looks like one of those little arseholes that like to try and give me shit in the city and always end up wishing they hadn't.

'What? She let him?'

Hearing me, Celia leans forward and shouts to us: 'I don't want to feel constrained, you know? I just think we try and live in these idealised homes and it's all shit. So I break the boundaries, you know?'

No, I don't fucking know.

'Yeah, and what's the landlord gonna say when he gets an eyeful of this?'

She shrugs. 'Fuck him.' She and her fat friend are giggling like the schoolgirls they probably still are. I give Twix that look again, and he's swaying his head and smiles back at me, raising his eyebrows. Oh for fucks sake, just get it on with her already so we can be out of this stupidity.

Suddenly, and to my mild horror, I hear somebody saying my name. *Actually trying to get my attention.* I peer past the legs of some people standing next to us, and there's a familiar but unwelcome face. Michael Carlyon. He's sitting cross legged on the floor against the couch, his tangle of black hair hanging down across his grizzled face. I can see the roots showing, about two weeks' worth to judge. He's bobbing his head and trying to make small talk with me. I've got no idea why, because back in Brisbane the cunt never seems to want to know me and the feeling has quickly become mutual.

Against my better judgement, and maybe not to cause a ruckus, I deign to return his chit chat, though I can clearly hear how guarded I sound. This dumb fucker must be wrecked or something, cause he shows no indication that he's aware of how closed off I'm sounding and has launched into a conversation mid-way, it would seem. It sounds like gibberish, but it slowly dawns on me he's trying to tell me about some film that he was in.

'Yeah, just finished last month. Amazing experience, man. Just amazing.'

Cunt knows I've been trying to break into the movie-making game with my mate Roshan, who I met on a film-making course at TAFE last year. We've had some interest in getting a couple of projects up and running, but nothing's come of it yet. I figure Carlyon's trying to fluff his own ego by reminding me of my own paltry efforts.

Then I see that old prick T-Rex Tony coming from the toilet, of course. These two fucking dinosaurs have somehow, somewhere, heard of young Cecilia's little party and snaffled themselves a couple of invites. They're a pair of old cocksmen as ever there were, as close to a fucking rock-spider as they're going to be, and I'm well aware of the pompous circle they like to hang around in: fat-bellied and bearded renaissance re-enactors in their thirties using their years of tail-chasing to woo barely legal kindergoth. Fuck it, maybe Twix and I are no better, but these two old twats have backstories that make even us cringe. And I realise that with the years stacked upon them, they need a conduit sitting somewhere in the age-range between them and their prey to help lubricate the gears of their game.

Billy Muggins here fits that bill nicely, it would seem.

Tony falls onto the floor beside Michael, clocks me and gives a big stupid grin.

'Fancy seein you here,' he enthuses.

'Fancy, Mister Lament,' I sneer, using his dodgy scene name and can barely contain my satisfaction when I see his mouth twitch.

I used to like the guy until I had the misfortune of working with him on a project once. Cunt barely did any work but took all the glory: signed his name to a council-commissioned mural that took four of us to do, after we'd all agreed to let the mural remain authorless to lend it a certain mystique. He'd snuck back later, before the council had sealed it, and painted his fucking name across one corner in letters larger than were fucking necessary. I tried scrubbing it off with turps once, but whatever the council guys sealed it over with had the better of my cheap turpentine.

'You tellin him about that movie you were an extra in, Michael?' Tony persists, and I'm thinking if Twix doesn't step in here in a minute I'm going to smash this cunt in the face.

'Yup,' Michael goes, looking bashful because he'd been playing his role up as if it were something more vital than just a background extra. He quickly tries to divert my focus. 'But what have you been up to anyways, man?'

I might've been inclined to accept this as a sincere inquiry had that prick T-Rex Tony not come into the picture. He's like that niggling aftertaste you can't quite put a finger on but has nonetheless ruined the meal.

Twix's getting cozy with Celia, and not wanting to intrude I tell these other two cunts that I gotta use the facilities and remove myself from their circle, leaving the half-downed bottle of red next to the leg of the sunken couch. I'm in a foul mood now, and I'm death-glaring every little cunt I pass, willing him to look at me wrong and start something.

I actually do end up heading into the dunny, if not for anything but to extricate myself from the atmosphere of the party and get a breather. I sit down on the seat and breathe deep, trying to settle my mind and the rising temper in it. The music is ended abruptly and the thump thumping is replaced with Duran Duran's *Girls on Film*. I feel more tension ease out with the change in song, but a small paranoid part of my brain can't help but think that those two old cunts have changed the music to stir me up some more.

An argument breaks out in the corridor, and someone's banging on the toilet door. A whiny voice comes through: '*Open the fuuuging doooor...*'

I get up and unlatch it, and the door suddenly swings inwards, with it a blonde girl. She falls into the wall and starts to propel forward, but I clumsily catch her and try and help her stand.

'I'm gonna farking puuu–'

I quickly sidestep and drop her as she staggers towards the toilet bowl and spews up all over it. The seat is still down from when I was sitting on it, and the contents of her stomach hit the lid and spills over the sides, filling the cubicle with a rank acid smell. Her hair hangs in it, soaking some of it up.

I hold my breath and get the fuck out into the noise and bustle of the party again before I likewise chunder everywhere. The dinosaurs are still sitting across from Twix and Celia, engaged in conversation with that shark-toothed Taylor. *Sure, boys, but which of you will claim the prize and risk his junk in that eager and dangerous mouth?*

When I get back to my bottle of wine, that cunt T-Rex Tony screws his nose up at me and pulls his head back, as if I stink or something. I'm starting to think this is the last fucking straw, when Twix leans over and goes: 'Get out back and clean your shoes, ya manky sod!'

I stick a foot out and see that my Doc's are spattered with vomit. This is just fucking great.

'That's fucking gross!' screams Taylor.

T-Rex Tony's still looking at me like I'm a leper, but that other cunt Michael Carlyon is sitting there grinning up at me, and there's something so maligned in that toothy leer that I just fucking snap right there and then, and shove my boot straight into his face, glancing off his cheek and pushing into his hair, where I make sure to rub as much puke into his precious locks as possible.

Tony shouts in outrage, but Michael starts pin-wheeling like crazy right there on the floor, kicking his legs and arms out with abandon. I side-step his spastic little performance but trip over the bottle of red next to the couch. It falls and rolls under my foot as I'm trying to balance myself and I go arse up, falling into some cunt behind me who in turn is knocked sideways into a couple of girls.

Michael's on his feet now, pulling at his hair, stumbling sideways.

'You dirty fucker!' he's yelling.

'What's your fucking problem?' yells Tony. He's up and coming straight at me, so I start kicking wildly at the fucker trying to get him in the shins.

No need, as Twix is also up and he's shoulder-barging Tony aside and straight over the back of the couch. As he goes over his foot somehow catches on the plastic chandelier above and nearly pulls the fucking thing down on top of Twix. The sight of that old fossil going over and his legs still sticking up from the other side sets me to laughing my arse off, but Twix kicks me and gestures that we should go. Behind me some of the younger punters are getting restless. The promise of violence seems to have whet their appetite, and I can see by the dark looks in their eyes something's gonna kick off here in a minute.

Twix hauls me to my feet, and I stop to snatch up the wine bottle, whirling it to make sure there's some left. We duck and slide out through the restless crowd, telling em there's a couple of paedophiles back there and pointing in Michael and Tony's direction.

We make a run for the car, and it occurs to me that we're a couple of hypocrites for indulging in criticism of Cecilia's graffiti decor when we ourselves are in a car that's been similarly vandalised.

I glance back and see crazy shadows on the wall of the house facing Cecilia's front door, and we can hear boys whooping like wild animals and the sound of the plastic chandelier being torn from the ceiling.

'That's definitely our cue to leave,' says Twix, and I notice there's one of the plastic shards from the chandelier stuck in his hair like a big fat drop of crystallised semen.

I try and contain my laughter, because I want to see how long it takes him to notice it's there.

'Just try and make me stay,' I go, sliding down the passenger seat.

We get the fuck out of there, pronto.

Then by the light of the dashboard I see Twix's face drop as something dawns on him. 'Frig. I didn't even get any rompy-pompy with Celia.'

And so I have to put up with the cunt being mopey all the way back to Brisbane.

JUJU

As promised, Abi arranges post-work drinks at Eagle Street Pier with Chantelle, a friend of hers who brings another girl called Raven, the one Abi said my Rod Stewart lookalike stalker has also harassed. Apparently Raven lives in the same building as Chantelle, the place everyone keeps referring to as 'The Prozac Palace'. It's difficult not to imagine in my mind's eye some gaudy faux-Greek temple with, like, bowls full of antidepressants being passed around by humourless goth girls in black togas.

'So wait up, why's it called a palace?'

Chantelle smiles like I'm basically speaking an alien language.

'Alex is new to town,' explains Abi.

'You gotta see the Palace, then,' says Chantelle. 'One of Brisbane's undiscovered gems.'

The way they all laugh tells me it's quite the opposite.

Abi's like: 'It's where Twix lives.'

So it turns out I've actually, like, got the address written down at home for this infamous Prozac Palace! Twix gave me a dodgy looking business card on New Year's Eve, when he came down to Melbourne, writing his address on the back so that we'd stay as pen-friends. He'd basically gone on about the Prozac Palace then, but we'd dismissed it along with all other the bombastic bullshit he was coming up with that night. Poor guy; he really was, like, judged wrong by the scene down south. Next time I chat with any of my old scene mates I'll have to, like, set the record straight on his behalf; let them know he's not the so and so we all thought.

Raven's like: 'We're having a party there next month. You girls should come. I'll get Twix to send you an invite.'

'Cool beans, will do,' I chirp. 'I need to find out what all the fuss is about.'

Chantelle wants to head into City Rowers for the drinks but Abi and Raven won't hear of it, adamant that we need to steer clear of the place and instead head to a bar in the Italian restaurant nearby. It's got a nice view of the river and the Story Bridge, so basically I'm pretty happy with this place.

Before we head inside we go down to the where the ferries dock and take in the view, watching as a storm blows across New Farm and the winds whip at the trees under the Story Bridge. The yachts anchored to the pier gently rock on the waves.

'Gedoutovit,' snarls Chantelle, fighting against the wind whipping her hair across her face.

'My uncle was on the Queen Elizabeth II from Sydney when it got hit by a wave,' says Abi, turning her face away from the gale.

'Bloody hell!' I say as we wander the pier. 'I hope he's alright?'

'Yeah, he's good,' sniffs Abi, the wind making her nose run. 'Not some other passengers, though. Still, could've been worse, because the same ship got pounded by a wave last year that was as big as it was!'

'Bullshit,' scoffs Chantelle.

Abi's like: 'No, seriously. The captain was on the news saying he thought they were headed into the white cliffs of Dover, it was that fucking big.'

'I used to think that whenever I went down on my last girlfriend,' Chantelle jokes, making us all laugh.

'Oi, wait up,' Chantelle suddenly says, basically scooting off to catch up with a guy that's lurking nearby. He looks a bit suss with his dark glasses and beanie, until I realise he's as pale as a ghost. He's an albino! Must be tough with their lot in life, always being treated like a criminal because they've got to dress to be protected against the sun all the time.

Then I notice that Chantelle slips him some money in exchange for something that he deftly presses into her palm. She pockets it. Bloody hell, I think they've just done a drug deal right here in the open!

'Catchya,' she says to him.

He turns to the rest of us with a big, beaming smile. 'You ladies have a lovely day. Mind the wind, now.'

Then he saunters off until this boy coming the other way stops him for, presumably, another drug deal.

'It's cool, let's go,' Chantelle says when she catches me watching the albino.

There's a mundane dressed like an office worker pointing a camera at us, and while I'm inclined to just look the other way, Chantelle's having none of it. Probably feeling paranoid now that she's carrying contraband.

'Why're you taking our fucking photo, cunt?' she says.

The bloke looks frustrated, and drops the camera.

'You wanna get out of the shot?' he snarls, and it's only then that I notice the woman and the teenage girl standing by the pylon, fighting to keep their hair from blowing everywhere, too. I figure they're his missus and spawn, and bring them to Chantelle's attention.

She's like: 'Fuck, sorry mate, didn't mean to yell at ya. Me Aunty Flo's visiting.'

'I don't give a hoot about your aunt,' I hear the buttmuch mutter to himself.

We scoot out of their way, heading up into the restaurant, laughing our arses off. The bloke looks pissed off still, as if we could care. Gotta laugh! We order some drinks and grab a table, watching as the family head down the boardwalk to the Botanic Gardens, giving us dirty looks as they go.

'I've really had it up to here with men, lately,' says Chantelle, holding her hand above her head. 'Self-entitled cunts who think it's all about them.'

It makes me think of Jai and how he's committed to fixing up the Moorhen Flats. He's as about as far from self-entitled as you can get, I'd say.

'But it *is*, isn't it?' says Abi sarcastically. 'It's the possessiveness I can't handle. I bet that wanker out there probably sneaks into his daughter's room at night because he thinks he owns her.'

Raven's like: 'Whoa, that's a hell of an accusation.'

'More a generalisation,' says Abi, and Chantelle taps glasses with her, compadres in bitterness.

'That's why you girls've gotta come over to the dark side,' winks Chantelle. 'Only a girl can truly fulfil another girl's needs.'

'I thought you were AC/DC,' counters Raven smarmily, meaning bisexual.

Chantelle grins. 'Emotional fulfilment is a girl's only true needs. Anything can replace a dick.' She thumps her knees on the underside of the table to simulate a penis banging against it and we all laugh at her antics. Some guys in blazers on another table look at her like she's scum but quickly look away when she grins lasciviously at them. Their discomfort thrills me.

'It always seemed to me that bisexuals are, like, the bastards of the sexual preferences,' I offer, trying to be clever. One of my old friends in Melbourne used to say it.

'What's that supposed to fucking mean?' demands Chantelle.

She's pretty intimidating, I'll admit. Now I know how the guys in the blazers feel. 'I just mean it always seems to me that, like, heteros and gays alike look down on them. Like they're accused of not choosing a side. It's just jokes, though.'

'Fucking spot on,' says Chantelle, pointing her finger at me. 'I've said the same thing before, haven't I, Raven? We're fucking damned if we do and damned if we don't. Spot on there, Alex.'

She smiles at me with genuine approval.

'But that's their loss,' she continues. 'I get the best of both worlds. I prefer girls, but a cock is nice every now and then. I just don't care much for what they're attached to.'

People like Chantelle operate on such a face-value agenda that I doubt there's much hidden from view if I cared to look. Whereas I'm like the moon: part of me is always hidden from view. That makes sense when I think about it, because the moon's supposed to be, like, our emotional side, our feminine side, and aren't we girls always suppressing some internal part of ourselves in order to appease men? Chantelle being bisexual makes sense in that regard, because, like, I suspect most men couldn't handle her frankness, so she gets to fulfil her holistic self by not confining herself to fucking just one gender.

'Boys are definitely over-rated,' agrees Abi.

I wonder if she's trying to send a secret signal to Chantelle, but I honestly can't tell. Abi's a hard person to read. More or less the opposite of Chantelle. It wouldn't surprise me if she's bi, too. I think girls are less concerned with sexual orientations.

'When you want pillow talk, there's none,' says Abi, 'and when you want commitment they're all talk.'

I've heard a rumour already that, like, she and Twix might be on together, and if a newbie like me's already heard it then basically there's probably some substance to it.

Raven's like: 'I couldn't agree more, Abi. It's like Dante says: action is character.'

I've met Dante quite a few times now. I think he must live in the city, because that's where I normally see him and it seems to me he's always in there. He's definitely interesting to be around.

'Oh puh-leeze,' scoffs Chantelle, rolling her eyes. 'Dante's another loser, too.'

'He's not that bad,' says Raven a little sullenly.

'But not that good, either, or is he?' grins Chantelle evilly which makes Raven blush.

The way that Raven talks about Dante makes me think she's got a crush on him. I couldn't blame her if she did, of course, because he's not bad looking, though, like, he could use a shower more often. She catches me giving her a knowing smile and looks puzzled.

'What?'

'Dante, eh?' I say, resisting the urge to reference that time they had to censor out the answer card on *Blankety Blanks* that said HAVE SEX. I remember the woman next to Ugly Dave Gray held it up, and I'd asked Mama what was on it, but it turned out she was as clueless as I was, even though she'd obviously done it heaps of times. Papa loved watching *Blankety Blanks* during tea time. He thought Graham Kennedy was the bees knees.

Raven, like, just flat out denies it so I drop the subject. I wonder if Dante has clued in on it yet? Probably not; that, or he's stringing her along. In my experience with guys it's one or the other.

'Shit, I just remembered!' says Raven all of a sudden, glancing at her watch. 'I've got a Uni thing on!'

'What thing?' says Chantelle, confused. 'You didn't mention this before.'

'I forgot, that's why,' says Raven, sculling her drink dry. 'Meeting them at Her Majesty's bar. I'm gonna be late! Might be able to sneak into the Wintergarden Tavern later with all the army guys, ay?' She winks and rushes from the bar.

'Touched a fucking nerve, there,' says Chantelle matter-of-factly, sipping her beer.

'For sure. And *a uni thing* is another way of saying *having a piss up*,' chuckles Abi. 'Trust me. We'll see her later on as she's pub-crawling around with a bunch of yuppie kids, pissed off her tits.'

'Uni-shmuni,' snorts Chantelle. 'She's attracted to damaged people, that girl. That's why she's studying that Youth Services or whatever it is.'

This older bloke at the bar in a blue polo shirt with, like, a blonde moustache strolls over to us, a freshly poured beer in his hand. I saw him earlier hitting on a woman who was all for it until the bloke motioned for them to head off and she'd admitted she was actually married and headed out on her own. He'd gotten a bit mouthy as she left, typical of some men when they're rejected. Now he's standing over us. With his moustache he looks like a fat-headed PI Magnum, and his bloodshot eyes have that groggy distraction to them.

'Afternoon, ladies,' he says, pulling out Raven's empty chair and sitting down.

He's got a solid barrel of a body with meaty love-handles and no neck to speak of. It makes him look like a cane-toad, like when you look at them from above and they've got those, like, big flat backs with the bulging glands on the side.

'Oh, don't mind us,' snarls Chantelle sarcastically. 'Take a seat.'

The bloke laughs and is like: 'Don't mind if I do. You ladies want another round?'

'Nah, we're good, man,' replies Chantelle, then stares hard at him until she says: 'That goes for the company, too.'

'Righto, ease up,' he says irritably. 'Just tryin to be friendly.'

It suddenly occurs to me that I know him from somewhere. I can't tell if I knew him in Melbourne or not, but wherever I've seen him before it wasn't here in Queensland.

'We're not interested.' Chantelle's getting really pissed off now, but she's trying to keep it in check, that much is obvious. Thing is, the bloke seems to be getting pissed off, too, because he's, like, dropped any pretense to charm and his bloodshot eyes are staring obstinately at Chantelle.

'You speak for yer mates, do you?' His voice sounds mean, choked with anger. He's turning out to be a real *munga*.

'Chantelle, it's okay,' I say softly, hoping if we just let him stay he won't cause any trouble.

'Is it?' she says to me, her eyes blazing.

'Yeah, it is,' the bloke growls. 'Like your friend says. At least she's got some fucking respect for people.'

Abi's like: 'Can you please not swear at my friend?' but looks away when his big, heavy head swivels in her direction.

I remember now where I've seen him! On the TV. He's in one of the footy teams up here. I don't know which one, and I don't know his name, because when I watched football it was always the AFL, and even then I only watched it if, like, my old boyfriend or my papa was watching it. But I've seen this guy on the sports part of the news.

I glance around the restaurant and notice that everyone's having a gander at what's going down, probably partly because of this bloke's celebrity status and partly because the air is so thick you could cut it with a knife. Even the guys in the blazers on the next table are openly staring at us, grinning at the argument that's now breaking out.

'I couldn't give a flying fuck who you are, mate,' snarls Chantelle when the bloke tries on the celebrity status line. 'We're tryin to have a private chat here.'

'A private lesbo sesh, more like,' bellows the bloke, standing up and deliberately knocking my drink over. It splashes down over the edge straight onto my dress, soaking through to my knees.

'You should try getting up an hour earlier every day, mate,' spits Chantelle, jumping to her feet, 'then you can be a right cunt that little bit longer.'

Holy shit, suddenly it's on!

The big bloke's spluttering and turning red, balling his fists up. But Chantelle's not noticed yet. She's getting stuck into him while she still can, believing she's kicking him while he's down, proverbially speaking.

She grins, jutting her jaw out at him, and's like: 'That number you cunts wear on your backs when you're out on the field? That's your IQ number, yeah? Or is it your place in the queue to bum the hooker in the locker room?'

The bloke roars like a gorilla and flips our table, which crashes over the chairs at the next table, thankfully unoccupied. He steps towards Chantelle who raises her arms up ready to receive a blow. Abi screams Chantelle's name and I just freeze. So, too, does the big bloke, thank God. But his hands are still formed into fists, clenching so that the veins in his wrists pop out.

'No trouble!' calls a guy from behind the bar, inching out carefully. Probably the manager.

Chantelle steps away from the football player, glaring at him with a mixture of fear and hostility. Even in the face of abuse she's willing to tempt fate.

'Easy, buddy, easy,' says the guy from behind the bar, his hands out in a gesture meant to calm the rage but absolutely futile in its actual measure to do anything against such bristling anger.

'I'm right,' snaps the bloke, twitching his blonde moustache. 'I'm not the fucking problem here.'

'I know, mate,' says the manager, locking eyes with the beast. 'No worries. We'll leave the girls be, okay?'

The big bloke turns like he's about to spit on the ground, and says to me: 'Shame about your dress.'

I can't speak. I can't even look into those angry eyes. I'm ready to start crying and I hate it.

Then he storms out of the restaurant, and the manager turns to Chantelle.

'Everything good?' he says a bit harshly.

'Yeah, I'm okay,' says Chantelle, her voice a bit shaky. 'He just–'

'Right, well you lot better be off, then,' the manager says sharply, looking around at us angrily.

'The fuck?' says Abi.

He's like: 'If you don't leave, I'm calling the cops.'

'Oh my Gawd,' Abi groans, shaking her head and rolling her eyes.

'Have you got cock in mouth disease?' Chantelle growls at the manager. 'Coz you sound like a dick right now.'

The lunch-order girl appears at his side, cautiously sidestepping the broken glass on the floor.

'Do you need a hand, Bill?' she says, to which the manager replies that he can handle us.

This is utter bullshit! We didn't even do anything and we're getting kicked out.

'You know what this world needs?' Chantelle yells in the sod's face. 'A GREAT BIG FUCKEN ESTROGEN BOMB!'

She presses her fingertips together up in front of his face (I note with satisfaction that he flinches like he thinks she's going to hit him), then opens them like a lotus, making a hollow noise with her mouth like an explosion going off.

Outside, Chantelle is fuming as we toddle along the pier towards the Valley. Suddenly she turns around and asks us if it's all good 'back there'.

I know what she means, straight off. I check the back of her jeans for signs of period blood.

'All clear.'

She's like: 'Thank fuck. That coulda been even more embarrassing otherwise.'

The only thing worse than the inevitable wet feeling in your knickers when you're on your rags is the thought that it's actually leaked out all over your clothes. One of the pluses of being goth is that blood isn't as noticeable on black clothing.

'Imagine if guys were as grossed out by women getting harassed or raped as they are about menstruation,' Abi ponders.

'That's the thing, though,' Chantelle continues, hocking up a big lugi onto the footpath. 'You girls've got my back now same as back there with those cunts. You had my back then, too.'

I'm not sure if she's being serious or sardonic, because we hardly did anything.

'Nope, you guys had my back,' she insists. 'That was some scary shit, but you girls still stood your ground all the same. I fucking respect that.'

'You're my new hero,' I gush, feeling a surge of adrenalin course through me now that the danger has passed.

She nods and grins. 'I like that.'

Abi's like: 'But if we can't count on each other, who *can* we count on?'

'Precisely, Abs,' Chantelle says, stopping to light up a cigarette and failing miserably against the wind.

'Guys like that need a few sessions with a dominatrix to sort out their issues with women,' I joke. 'You know, maybe learn to be, like, a bit more submissive.'

Chantelle looks at me curiously. 'I'd whip the cunts for sure,' she says, 'but I'm more of a sub.'

My ex in Melbourne was into some S&M, just really light stuff like spanking me and tying me up sometimes. I must admit, I always liked being dominated by Zak, letting him do whatever he wanted to me. Some people assume it's, like, a daddy-related issue, like I wasn't loved enough, which is stupid. Papa used to hit me and Lisa with his belt when we were naughty, but, like, it was fucking terrifying not exhilarating. The prospect of losing his approval would drive us to tears more than the beating itself, which in hindsight was far tamer than any playful strapping my ex gave me in the bedroom. With Zak, I wanted to be punished, but of course I also trusted him to be respectful towards me at the same time, and that's why there was trust in our bondage play. Shame it wasn't there in the rest of our life, in the end. Still, wankers like the blonde moustache could learn a few things from that.

'Are you for real?' I ask. 'Like a submissive?'

'Sure am,' Chantelle giggles, finally getting her cigarette to light. 'You interested in that scene, are you?'

'Of course.'

'Tell you what,' she says, stopping and looking us both in the eye. 'My birthday's coming up soon and I'm having it at this club called Inferno. It's an S&M club. You girls keen to come along?'

Me and Abi look at each other and in unison squeak out 'Yes!'

Chantelle laughs and tells us the date and address and instructs us to wear black only, which is hardly going to be a problem considering the contents of our wardrobes. 'Just you two, though,' she warns. 'Don't go telling everyone about it. The scene's not everyone's cup of tea.'

'Wait up,' says Abi, sniffling from a runny nose again, recalling something. 'Who else is going to be there?'

'Just us,' assures Chantelle. 'Don't worry, I'm not silly enough to stick you in the same room with The Beast.'

'Good.'

'Besides, she'll stay home waiting for Roz to finish her shift at the laundromat,' adds Chantelle, and the news seems to pain Abi even though Chantelle doesn't seem to realise it.

I guess whoever this Roz is she must have taken Abi's last job or something at an aged care home. I'd ask but it might seem too nosy and I've already seen Chantelle go off a couple of times today. Don't want to be on the receiving end of that, right after a birthday invite no less.

I'm like: 'Grouse! We'll be there!'

Chantelle holds our hands as we continue our walk, spreading out like paper-dolls and making it hard for the yuppies to walk along the boardwalk. Who cares?

What a bonkers afternoon. Two party invites and the day's not over yet! Blessed be!

DANTE AND ROSHAN FUCK IT UP

Hanging around the streets all day every day gets pretty fucking boring, so every now and then I go to the payphones in the arcade outside the GPO down on Queen Street, saying g'day to old Les selling his papers out front, and call various friends for a chat.

In all honesty, I've got no problem with working, as long as it's doing what I want to do, like Les out there, who used to sell the telly and the city final papers outside Curran's shop on Adelaide Street back in the 80s and would have it no other way. Still doing what he loves.

So when I chanced a call to Roshan and he said he's trying to score a gig working for Arts Axis Inc who need a film-making team and has a meeting with them tomorrow, I told him to count me in! Top guy that he is, Roshan brings me on board and says to spruce myself up, meaning make sure I've got clean clothes on and I don't smell like roadkill that's been sitting in the sun all day.

Cheeky fucker. I know that to Roshan I'm something of a charity case, since he can't fathom that I'd be homeless by choice, but it's still good of him to include me on this potential job.

Next day he picks me up and looks relieved that I've succumbed to his hygiene demands (West End Laundromat and the showers at South Bank took care of that), and we head over to the back of the Gabba where Arts Axis is located in an old substation half way between the cricket grounds and the Broadway Hotel. The lady that runs it is called Cheryl Copeland, thin and mousy with shocking white hair and horn-rimmed glasses. Reminds me of a character from *The Rats of Nimh*.

Roshan makes chit-chat with her about the old building, dripping with his usual Persian charm, and I get a closer look at some of the huge paper lanterns someone's constructed. They hang from a wooden girder, and turn steadily from the whisper of a breeze coming through the massive iron door. They're quite hypnotic, and I ask Cheryl about who made them, dropping a couple of names I know from Woodford Folk Festival, hoping they're familiar to her. The name-dropping has no effect on her.

'It's an artist called David,' she says frostily, not offering David's surname like she thinks it's superfluous I should ever need to know it or to meet him. 'I know most of the local artists, but not any of those that you mentioned.'

Looks like it's all up to your influences now, Rosh, to get us over the line and into a contract with Arts Axis.

We all take a seat and she explains that the project requires the successful sub-contractee to travel from town to town around Queensland and get video documentation, which she calls 'cultural mapping', as part of a visual aid presentation of youth mental health in the countryside.

'Specifically,' she adds, 'the aim of the project is to present a mental health map of young people in regional areas, how they feel about themselves, their peers, and their lives. The footage is to be included in an interactive CD-ROM that the State Government in a joint initiative with the Queensland Affiliation of Mental Welfare will make available for schools and councils to reference.'

She says that the State Government is working on an initiative called the *Ten Year Mental Health Strategy for Queensland* that it will release next year, and she hopes this CD-ROM project will be influential to that report by focusing on aspects that often get overlooked, specifically mental health in regional youth. Despite her frostiness of earlier, I suddenly see how I can get our foot in the door and get Cheryl to consider us the perfect guys for the job, on account of when I was a teenager I lived in the country and struggled with mental illness myself!

'Well, we're not shy of getting the hard facts,' I state proudly. 'I'm sure Roshan is with me when I say this: that we've always been willing to go where many won't when pursuing the truth. I can personally empathise with those kids, and I think we'll bring back precisely what needs to be said.'

Her eye twitches a bit, and her face turns stony. Clearly, I've said something *she* didn't want said.

'The brief for this project is to present current lifestyles of youth and their mental health responses in regional centres as positive,' she says firmly.

Her frostiness is back again, and in the hopes that this is simply her natural demeanour and perhaps only a minor setback in us getting the job, I push on.

'Right, sure, we can do that, but of course we're not gonna only film the kids who say nice things. I mean, we just film whatever it is they've got to say, right?'

Wrong.

She sucks the air in through her teeth, like she's exasperated with me already. The interview's off to a shaky start!

'The project needs an emphasis on the positive because we need to include documentation on the CD-ROM that proves our regional youth are culturally enriched, too. That's the purpose of the project.'

I'm not really sure what the fuck she's on about. She's completely biased towards the conclusion! Maybe in her position as a project administrator the outcome has set parameters, but I know for a fact that neither Roshan nor I would mould the interviews or footage to fit any specific agenda. It'd go against our principles as film-makers. I mean, they could certainly edit it that way, but then we'd have shot a lot of useless footage for them, and at cost. Not to mention having let those kids down.

The thing is, we're both fresh graduates from film college, having only done the course just last year, so we've got that 'commitment to the raw facts' type of approach to film-making. Granted, it was only a basic Government-subsidised one at the local TAFE that cost me less than a quarter of Rosh's weekly wage to attend for the entire year. Fuck, I didn't even technically graduate from the fucking thing thanks to a dispute with one of the lecturer's over a single, poxy assignment. But last year was when *Pulp Fiction* came out, too, and as a consequence practically every one of us in that class came out overly zealous and emboldened by the prospect of becoming the next Tarantino or Spike Lee and creating films with impact. And nothing impacts like the hard truth of youth depression.

That's pretty much the thrust behind my pitch to Cheryl here.

Roshan seems to have picked up the thread of proceedings.

'We'll get the job done, no problem, but like Dante says, if they want to say they're not enjoying living in a country town, we have to film that, also. I can't tell them to say any different.'

'You don't have to tell them to say they enjoy it,' Cheryl snaps. 'I grew up in Townsville as a small girl, and I loved it. I don't see why anyone's going to say otherwise.'

'I think you're a bit out of touch,' I counter. 'What are you? Fifty? Sixty years old?'

'How dare you!'

'I'm just saying that I grew up in the countryside, too, not that long ago, and–'

'Get out!'

'Wait, guys, wait,' goes Roshan, trying to bring us all back from the brink. 'I'm sorry if we offended you, we're just saying that if someone is shooting up in an alleyway, then that's the harsh reality of life and we need to show that, too.'

She's not having it. The junky example might have been too much. She's gone quiet; her jaw clenches, and she stares at the paper lanterns twirling gently from the girder. I jerk my head to the door to indicate to Roshan that we should leave. He drops his business card onto the table, anyway.

When we get outside, Roshan lets out a deep breath.

'Whoa, that was intense.'

'She was fucking crazy, buddy,' I tell him. 'I could see it in her eyes. Typical fucking arts toff with too much repressed-tension trying to tell the rest of us cunts that life is all roses. I grew up out there, and I'm telling you, the regional youth aren't happy. They're sniffing paint and driving stolen cars and drinking petrol cause they're frustrated and bored outta their fucking brains. No psychiatrists out there.'

'Yeah, I know what you're saying,' he says quietly. 'I just wish she did, too. We could have worked something out.'

I remember that Roshan works hard with two jobs, the film stuff being the second one that he's hoping to make his primary income. I feel bad that we lost the gig, and can't help but feel responsible for it. She didn't seem to like me from the outset, and I wonder if it'd have gone differently if I wasn't there.

'Rosh, sorry, man. I know you really wanted this gig.'

'Don't worry about it,' he smiles, slapping me on the shoulder. 'I'm glad you stood up to her. Let's go grab a bite, yeah?'

We drop into the coffee shop next to Van Gogh's Earlobe for some cake and tea. Typically, he pays for it and typically I let him cause I've got fuck all money as usual. Sometimes I feel like a leech, sucking opportunity and funds from my friends, but in the end it's all that I've got, too. The poor bastard would be better off hiring Les the paper man for these things, who mightn't know a single thing about filming but at least wouldn't fuck up the pitch.

While we're waiting for the tea to arrive, Roshan rubs his eyes. He's looking more and more tired every time I see him.

'I'm melting the candle at the wrong end,' he tries to explain, mangling the expression.

'Burning the candle at both ends,' I correct.

He repeats the phrase for memory, not at all bothered by the language lesson. He actually appreciates it, he reckons, so he can master the English language. He sometimes spoke it back in Tehran, where he was born, but it's not until he arrived in the Land of Oz a few years ago as a refugee that he's had to rely on English on a daily basis. Because his religion is Baha'i, he and his family were part of an oppressed minority in Iran, incapable of securing bank loans, good education, government jobs or even a decent living. Leader Khamane'i didn't mind enlisting Roshan and his brothers and cousins into the army, though, so they could fight against Iraq or *the road to Jerusalem that goes through Baghdad*, as was often said apparently.

Roshi once told me that some kids, barely fifteen and holding Russian machine guns, stopped him when he was riding home on his bike one day. He'd just gotten out of the army himself, then, and said the guns these fuckers were pointing at him were faulty as fuck and prone to go off just from being bumped, so he was naturally pretty fucking nervous about having them aimed at him. Turned out the little cunts were offended by Roshi whistling a song to himself, cause music for pleasure was still banned.

But Roshi got off light. His girlfriend never had her head shaved in public, his father was never executed nor his mother imprisoned. Happens all the time to the Baha'i, he reckons, due to Khamane'i's successor upholding his piece of shit Golpaygani Memorandum.

Ever since he snuck over the border into Pakistan and got his refugee status to Australia, Roshi's worked like a dog to scrimp and save for his family back home. I know that the Arts Axis gig was sorely needed.

The lady brings out our cakes and suddenly I feel too guilty to eat it, thinking of Roshan's parents and brothers and sister back in Iran, suffering under both the aftermath of a cruel regime and the current embargoes by America.

'Not hungry?' Roshi goes, forking some apple cinnamon sponge into his gob.

'Dunno, I just feel bad that your family's gonna suffer now.'

His mouth hangs open as he stares at me. 'What do you mean?'

'You know, that they can't eat cause I fucked that arts deal for you,' I whine.

He starts laughing, bits of cake crumb spilling off his bottom lip.

'You idiot,' he says. 'My family are doing fine. They have money, food, shelter. My sister has even enrolled in the Institute of Higher Education. It's not legal, of course, since being Baha'i is still a crime, but she's studying still.'

'Ah, fair enough,' I go. 'I thought with you burning the candle at both ends meant it wasn't going so well over there.'

He stirs his tea, thinking deeply, before sighing. 'Thing is, I'm trying to get some money together for another refugee family I know here in Brisbane. They need somewhere to stay but it's too cramped where I am.'

So that's it. I knew something was up. This poor bastard with a heart of gold never stops thinking about everyone else, ready to burn himself down to the wick for it.

'I know what it feels like, you know?' he says, shrugging slightly.

Waste not, want not. I dig into my own slice of cake, deep in thought, when it hits me.

'You should meet my mate Maddie,' I go. 'She's just got involved with some underground group that finds homes and clothes for refugees. There's a whole network of people all over Brisbane doing it just on donations and shit.'

Roshi's more than interested. Suddenly my appetite's back, and I scoff into the cake somewhat guilt-free.

SCHOOL'S OUT FOR TWIX

The school year's barely begun and already the buggers are having a dance.

Once every few months we get the school disco gigs which are a piece of piss so I'm always keen, and besides there's always plenty of eye-candy. It's an all-boy's school and the Principal invites various girls' schools to participate in the occasion. I don't recall my school having this many dances on when I was a young tacker, but that's probably the difference between a public education and these private colleges.

I always arrive about a half hour early to these things in case I've got the wrong address or the entrance is way over on the other side of the school through its labyrinth of walkways and demountables. There's three other guards on duty with me tonight, the usual number for these events. We're not really expected to do anything, as we're only here to fulfil the insurance purposes for the school board.

'Heya, Travis,' nods Daryl, one of the other regulars from NiteWorks, the security company I work for. I usually see him on jobs like this where contact with the public is minimal, because he's not the most presentable guard on the books. He always looks dishevelled, half his teeth missing and his eyes bulge like that Doctor Who actor, the one with the scarf and the jelly beans. 'You still working the Valley, mate?'

'Always,' I tell him, shaking his hand. His palm is cold and dry, with big creases in it. It makes me think of an albino gorilla's hand. 'Who else is on tonight?'

Daryl glances back toward the gymnasium, where a hand-painted banner hangs over the doors: TERM 1 INTER-SCHOOL DISCO 1996. I can see a couple of figures smoking in the shadows underneath.

'Pieter's here,' Daryl says, 'and some other young cunt whose name I don't know. He's from Waverly Security, I think.'

We get to know many of the guards from other companies through working subcontracted jobs like this one, but there's such a high turnover of employees due to the shit pay structure and the shift work that sometimes we're at a complete blank as to who we're working alongside. But as for Pieter, I already knew him from one of these school dances last year and a New Year's Eve gig where we made sure people watching the fireworks at Southbank didn't accidently walk into the river or whatever the fuck we were there to prevent them from doing. Pieter's a dumpy looking bloke with a bulbous nose who originally came from Holland, as I recall, back when he was just a kid. He's lost the accent completely, sounds as Aussie as, but he still eats all that weird Dutch food like chocolate sprinkles on toast and stuff. That's how I remember where he's from. I've never liked him much.

A Nissan 200SX screams into the parking lot and spits out a silver fox who struts confidently across to us, extending his hand and introducing himself as Terry, the Principal of the school. I've met him before, of course, but he looks at me like he only thinks he recognises me. When he's dealing with so many students and their parents it'd be hard to keep a mental track of faces and where you know em from.

'There's only two of you?' he says quickly. 'We asked for four.'

I point to where the other two lurk in the shadows like a couple of predators. 'Four, as requested.'

'You blokes know the drill by now, yeah,' he says, rubbing his hands together in anticipation of the night ahead, as if this was going to be an enjoyable experience for all involved and not just the young lads trying to get their rocks off with the little chicks. 'Perimeter walks, stop the little shits who haven't paid from coming in through the fire exits. Usual thing.'

'No worries,' goes Daryl, and actually gives a tiny salute. Terry looks Daryl up and down like he's taking the piss, then moves off to open up and get ready, just as the DJ for hire drives past us.

'Gonna be a long night,' I groan. Five hours of standing around in the dark listening to crap music thump through the walls of the gym. Inevitably we'll start to group up and talk shit amongst ourselves until we see the Principal or one of the other teachers doing a check up on us, making sure we're doing our jobs and not slacking off. It's like *we're* the naughty students out in the dark, kept a watch on.

The lads arrive first, excited to see the familiar grounds of their school at night time, following their teachers around like they were celebrities. There's no way they'd do that in school hours, I'm sure, but there's something about seeing your teachers outside of the classroom environment that makes them more likeable.

We're not needed yet so we wait out on the lawns beside the front fence, watching the gym slowly fill up.

Soon the parking lot is choked with vehicles dropping off kids left, right and centre. The chicks seek each other out, and from what we can gather there's about three different girls' schools invited along. The parents are forgotten about immediately those car doors open, and they're often left unheard as they call out last-minute instructions about waiting close to the teachers at pick-up time and whatnot.

The students aren't the only ones distracted. I saw this doco once where these hawks were next to a lake that filled up with sparrows or finches or something, and the little birds were whizzing all over the fucking place and the hawks had no clue where to look first! Well, me, Daryl, Pieter and the other guard are like that: there's so many sweet young things running around in their disco gear, which consists of trying to dress as skimpily as possible in Lorna Jane stuff or mostly pleat skirts and boob-tubes. Us blokes are spoilt for choice!

'Fuck me,' whispers Daryl hoarsely, 'what a fucking smorgasbord. They didn't dress like this at school when I was a young bloke. I gotta keep reminding muhself over and over: they're too young, they're too young, they're too young...'

The dirty old fuck's about fifty years old, as far as I can tell!

'Yeah, but I can't help it,' he complains when I point out that he's old enough to be their grandfather.

He reminds me of my old neighbour, Jim Farrell, who wasn't as old as Daryl but when you're a teenager anyone over thirty seems that way.

At night I used to go out into the backyard and sit in the only tree we had because it had the perfect view of the house behind ours. The daughter of the family that lived there was Ellie, who I knew from school but didn't really speak to because she was a couple of grades lower. That and everyone used to bully her a lot because she had curly hair that shot out in all directions like an afro, calling her Poodle or Shirley temple. I felt bad for her but could hardly defend her in case I got picked on for it.

Well, Ellie's room was at the rear of the house, facing towards the back fence where I'd be sitting in my tree, and after her shower she liked to and change into her nightie (or flannel pj's if it was winter) without closing the curtains, shaking loose the water from that beautiful head of curls and making her titties jiggle in the process. Even at such a young age, they were a proper handful, and sat against her chest in defiance of gravity as young tits sometimes do.

I didn't know what an exhibitionist was back then, only that I was sure she was doing it on purpose. And she became my ritual, the one thing I anticipated most nights, where climbing into that tree was like an act of spiritual devotion, giving myself over to a voyeur's delight.

Jim was a married man in his thirties and used to sometimes come out for a smoke and watch her, too, standing on a discarded besser brick leftover from the shoddy-looking barbecue he built.

'A fucking sight to behold, alright, Travis,' he'd say, his eyes boring across the yard at the Ellie's body. 'Too young for me now, but. Too young for me.'

Just like ol' Daryl.

I couldn't admit to Jim that every night I'd be in my room having a wank to the memory of Ellie naked, but he didn't mind confessing he'd done it while pretending to take a dump so that his wife was none the wiser.

'Mate, when you get to my age and you only get a few roots a year outta the missus, you'll really appreciate what a moment like this means to a bloke. In fact, you should take a crack at it,' he'd nodded in Ellie's direction, 'and fill me in later on all the juicy details.'

I'd thought that was a bit fucking much, as if I was a performing monkey for some married bastard fantasising vicariously through my own early sexual experiences.

Ellie would always take her time patting down that slim body, in such a careful and measured way, posing as if for a camera. Or an audience. She had to know we were out here, watching. Would it matter who it was, I used to wonder? Like, if she saw our faces leering from the darkness, would the free shows come to an abrupt halt? Would she yell at me at school, and tell people I was a Peeping Tom?

One night Jim was out alone, watching Ellie getting dressed. What he didn't know was that Ellie's daddy was out trying to fix the aerial, and saw Jim watching from over the fence. Daddy came round to see his daughter in the window naked, and he leapt over the fence and gave Jim such a hiding that Jim's wife heard the commotion and called the cops. Ellie's old man got arrested, charged with assault, but after they found out why he did it they let him go, charges dropped.

Jim's wife stood by her husband's story – he was a doctor on a good wicket, so why would she jeopardise her comfy lifestyle? – but they soon moved out anyway.

The sound of heels clopping on concrete across the street catches my attention, and Pieter notices me look up at a woman walking past on the other side of the street, wearing jeans and a tight top. A 'prowler' is what I've heard the boys in blue refer to hot chicks out for a jog as. The others go quiet as they watch her, the light of Daryl's cigarette reflecting in their wet eyes.

'Go the fucken knockers on that, ya cunts,' says Daryl, breathing heavily. I can't tell if he's putting it on or if he's really been left breathless at the sight of her.

Pieter says quietly: 'Oi, Dazza, go you halves in a rape charge.'

There's an uneasy round of sniggering at this, and I force something like a laugh from myself as well so that I'm not singled out by the pack. The woman glances swiftly around at us then looks away just as quickly; the prey assessing the proximity of the predators. It makes me feel like shit to imagine how worried she must feel, but even worse that I laughed along with their sick joke. I can feel it twisting in my guts, and I wonder if the others feel it in their guts, too.

'Goin for a piss,' announces Daryl, heading over to the trees across the driveway.

'Probably a wank, more like,' sneers Pieter, eliciting another round of sniggers from the others, although he sounds especially venomous, like he's decided Daryl's the weak link and is ripe for bullying. This encourages me to join in, hoping that if anyone does become tonight's target for backstabbing sentiments it'll be that old prick and not me. There's something sinister about Pieter's personality, like he could actually be evil incarnate. It would explain the massive scar on the side of his face, like he was used in a sacrifice and a demon got into him and has taken over his body.

Terry, the Principal, waltzes over and claps his hands together. 'Ready, fellas, let's go!'

He's got so much energy this bloke that it puts us four to shame as we drag ourselves after him across the parking lot to the school hall.

The noise is already unbearable. These kids are no different tonight than when they're at school during recess, shouting over each other and all talking at once. Competing with this racket will be the DJ for Hire, spewing out mindless tracks from Shaggy, Alanis Morissette and East 17. Without a doubt, Coolio's gonna get a couple of spins tonight with his gangsta song, which might actually manage to induce me into slitting my own wrists out the back of the hall.

So far the kids are still grouped together by gender, stealing glances at each other and whispering to their mates about who's hot and who's not. The boys all look like they're auditioning for a Take That music video, but the girls are something else. They're far more sexualised than when I was a just a lad at school, that's for sure.

And what high-school dance wouldn't be complete without the goth contingent? Here they are now, decked out in whatever black clothes they've got at home, skulking in the corner, now playfully pushing each other around, as if they don't get enough of that without the playfulness in the playground. At the end of the day, they're just kids like the rest of the crowd here.

A beat-up station wagon pulls up in the drop-off spot next to us and another babybat gets out, this trashy looking chick who's rolling her eyes for the benefit of her mates when her mother goes: 'Make sure you're in this spot when the disco finishes, Prue. I'm serious.'

'Whatever,' the chick, Prue, snorts. 'And it's not a disco, either.'

As soon as the mum's down the road the chick grabs one of the lads by the arm. 'Let's get the fuck outta here, Imp,' she goes. Obviously doesn't want to be caught dead at a school dance. Who can blame her?

Daryl fronts up, though, trying to do his duty by preventing them from leaving through the front gates.

'Just leave em, Daz,' I call out. 'They're only headed into King George Square, probably. Or maybe into those bushes across the road for some rompy-pompy, ay?'

Daryl beams his toothless grin at the thought.

'Fuck off, cunt,' the little tart snaps at me. Got a mouth on her like Dante, the little shit!

No respect for their elders, these kids. I bare my fangs at her just so's she knows who she's dealing with. It's funny, because even when we're dressed like normals, goths can always spot another goth a mile off. But these babybats haven't developed this intuition yet.

Daryl lets em go and they disappear up the street. No worries, in walks a suitable distraction for us.

A gang of fresh meat toddles past in matching black leotards and and cat-ear headbands on, with black triangles drawn on their tiny noses and whisker lines across their cheeks.

'Lookin good, girls,' I whistle, my heart hammering in my chest as I chance a little flirt with them. 'Nice pussies.'

'Pussy cats, actually,' one of the chickadees snaps.

'Yeah, righto,' I go, smiling benignly. I'd probably be fucked if they reported me. Can just imagine Gary copping an earful from *le Directeur* over it.

They race up the steps into the hall, looking for adventure, their youthful breasts bouncing around in their tight leotards. Still haven't got the hang of those wayward puppies yet, poor things.

It makes me wonder where Ellie is these days, and if her boobs got any bigger?

PLAYGROUND TWIST

Chantelle's birthday is today, so me and Abi head into the Valley dressed to the nines, looking for a club called Club Inferno.

Normally it's called Hellbound, but the organisers are calling it Club Inferno on account of, like, the State Government basically putting a ban on Hellbound operating in Queensland. Apparently they had no problem with an S&M club being held, just so long as it wasn't Hellbound. Chantelle said the guy organising it was always running into strife with the authorities for, like, pushing envelopes. Apparently he'd tried to get a lesbian film festival up at the Wickham but Soorley tied it all up in red tape and that was the end of that.

Despite the name change, the organisers aren't taking any chances with being hassled by the law, so we've, like, gotta walk from the train station through the Brunswick Mall and all the way up to the warehouse area of Roberston Street in our four and a half inch heels, well away from the established party district of the Valley. This means that we're getting hassled by every second group of blind-drunk party boys commenting or, like, whistling at us in our PVC thigh-highs with shaggy faux-fur coats hoiked protectively around our shoulders. One so and so even starts jogging backwards in front of us, basically egged on by his wanker mates to get a gander at our cleavage. He's lucky Chantelle's not with us; I'm sure she'd chew him up and spit him out after the way she stood up to that celebrity footballer last week.

He's like: 'You girls working tonight, or what?'

Abi's like: 'Or what.'

'Don't talk to him,' I tell her. 'It just encourages them.'

'Hey,' he sort of pleads, focused only on her now, 'I'm not trying to be funny here.'

'Get her number!' yells one of his mates, who stayed back where we first passed them. I check to be sure, and only two of them are even showing interest in their friend's chances. The others have grown bored and headed over next to Rics Bar.

Our funny-man gives his friends a pained expression and starts apologising to Abi. 'Naw, don't listen to them, they're just being dickheads.'

'Fuck off,' she says.

He slams into a light-post outside the Royal George, cursing at the pain in his back and doubling over. Talk about laugh! Me and Abi crack up and carry on, and we, like, vow to try and distract any more wankers to self-harm for the rest of the journey, but it's mostly trouble-free except for the cat-calling when we pass the Irish pub.

It's downhill once we get onto Robertson Street and if I thought walking up the gradual incline of Brunswick was difficult in these heels, then going downhill is worse.

Thankfully, the club isn't too far down; close to The Playground. It has no advertising, and basically just looks like a windowless little warehouse with a roller door down bottom and, like, a rickety stairwell leading up to a red door on the second floor. There's a muscled bloke up there dressed head to toe in black, and, like, a couple of punters also in black climbing the stairs. Chantelle hadn't been joking about the dress code.

The muscle lets us in after checking our ID's, and the door bitch takes our money. Inside, it's pretty much just like the goth clubs we go to, but amped up with a heavy emphasis on, like, bondage and bondage play. There's a table with a topless girl on it and another girl dripping wax across her tits from a candle. There's A-frames and hobby horses and all sorts of stuff. But there's also just a lot of people basically, like, standing around drinking, and over on the far left wall are some couches where Abi spies Angele, who she says is Malik's girlfriend.

'Ugh,' she groans, 'judgement daggers at nine o'clock. And she's wearing a short skirt, go figure.'

Abi says how Angele's been known to go up and abuse young goth girls at the clubs for wearing anything above the knee, citing it's not proper goth fashion.

We're like cats or something, us scene goths, getting all territorial with each other when every other mundane bitch is welcome to stay. I'm feeling pretty nifty about getting away from that whole scene and mixing in with another crowd, to be honest.

'There's Chan,' says Abi, nodding towards the bar.

'Where? I can't see her.'

'In the cage,' Abi says into my ear, with a small smile.

On the floor a few feet away from the bar is what looks like a wire cage for, like, a dog or something. And sure enough, Chantelle's in it, basically down on her hands and knees topless with a collar around her neck. A chain clips from the collar to the cage above. Gotta laugh!

I nod and break into a grin as we go over to her. She's really happy to see us.

'Bitches! You guys fucking came!' she yells out. 'Fuck yes! Thanks, man, it's so good of you.'

'Yeah, no worries,' I say. 'But what's going on with you?'

She laughs. 'My domme put me in here. I gotta stay here until she says I can come out.'

'Okay, cool beans,' I say, and Abi's having a good chuckle about it.

'I'm sorry,' says Abi, spluttering on her laughter. 'I just wasn't expecting this.'

'All cool!' laughs Chantelle. 'You guys should look around. Put your coats at front. I'll be with you in a bit. I can't really talk now.'

And sure enough, in steps this, like, oiled Amazonian of a woman wearing a black and baby pink latex ensemble, carrying a leather horse crop. She whacks the crop against the cage, demanding that Chantelle shut the fuck up. Chantelle whelps and, like, cowers down, kinda scared. It's all an act, of course, but bloody hell this woman is so domineering that even I shirk back from her. I don't know whether

I should, like introduce myself or not. Be polite, right? But thankfully Abi just hoiks me away by the arm and we start grinning at each other. I think we've found our new playground, one full of new rules and forbidden things.

The door bitch takes our coats, so that we're finally unveiled, as it were. Abi's got a hot PVC corset on that, like, squashes her small boobs out the top, while I'm wearing a strappy uncoloured-latex Kayser halter-top that I got from Peril 305 in Melbourne that sucks to my body and, like, pushes my tits up to make them look even more huge than normal. The lubricant I rubbed over the latex to remove the matte finish has made the rubber slick and slightly translucent. I can't be sure, but I think my areolas, which are quite dark, are showing through. Thank fuck for those fur coats otherwise the walk from the train station would basically have been unbearable.

'Woo, woo, woo!' giggles Abi, pointing with both hands at my chest, and I do the same back to her, then we giggle and, like, skip back to the bar for some voddies.

Chantelle's domme has hooked a heel in the bars of the cage and is pouring a bottle of cheap tequila down her leg while Chantelle, like, licks at the fluid dripping from the point of the heel. It's fucking insane! Gotta laugh!

The DJ starts playing Atari Teenage Riot's *Destroy 2000 Years of Culture*, and while, like, no-one really dances *per se* here, me and Abi start moving our hips anyway as Chantelle keeps lapping away at her dispensed tequila.

There's a couple dressed up as a doctor and a nurse, although it's definitely, like, a slutty version of the latter with her cleavage bulging out and her arse cheeks poking out from under the uniform. It's a shame the guy isn't as adventurous with his outfit. He's just got the typical long white coat on with a stethoscope. They're at a wooden saw-horse, like the ones carpenters use to rest planks of wood on while they cut them up. There's also, like, a padded section across the top, and they've just had a girl bent over it with her top off while they did things to her. Next to them on a stool is an assortment of toys and equipment basically best suited to a mechanics shop.

The nurse invites muggins here over, and compliments my top.

'Are you ready for your examination?' croons the doctor, who isn't particularly attractive but does have, like, striking blue eyes.

They must sense my trepidation, because the nurse says it's a bondage-horse and explains how it's used, then assures me: 'We'll start off small.'

Abi gives me the thumbs up and wiggles with excitement, so I think fuck it, let's do it.

'Sure thing,' I say.

They, like, position me in front of the bondage-horse and strap my ankles to it with buckled straps on a metal ring that's bolted to the timber frame. I'm firmly tied into position with my legs open. We've barely begun, but, like, already the feeling of being enslaved to the whim of this playful couple has got me horny. My muffy has that slick feeling to it and the vulva feels engorged. I can't help but wonder what the doctor's love muscle looks like and imagine him taking me from behind right here in this club full of people with, like, the music pulsing in time to his thrusts.

Abi's taken a seat a few paces away, holding our drinks. She's put a straw in mine and leans over, holding it in front so I can sip from it. Her skin is pale but she has naturally dark eyelids, like they're a sort of brown colour, like the lips of a vagina. It makes her look sleepy, or on heroin, and is dead sexy. I know she pops pills, but she doesn't touch smack at all. All the guys want to fuck her. The girls, too. If I wasn't her best friend, I probably would, too. Like, it's those heavy, dark eyelids over her big brown eyes that do it.

'You look so hot, Alex,' she breathes.

A leather paddle gently smacks against my arse, and I can feel my PVC skirt being tugged up to expose my stinging cheeks. Instinctively I squeeze my buttocks together, worried about my wet muffy being seen through my G-string.

The doctor and nurse are right into their roles, dropping all sorts of medical lingo picked up from Hollywood and bad pornos.

He's like: 'Judging by the state of her panties, the patient is ready for the clamps.'

My nurse holds up said clamps, which're basically those toothed things people use for, like, jump-starting cars.

'Fucking hell,' I whisper without meaning to.

'It'll be fine, sugar,' the nurse promises. 'You want to try?'

I nod dumbly as the doctor continues to strike my arse with his paddle. I gotta get me one of those things!

My tits are, like, ready to spill from the latex on their own, and it takes barely a flick of the nurse's finger to liberate them. They tumble out and swing free.

They've always been massive, ever since early high-school. They actually developed earlier than that, to my horror, when I was, like, still in grade six at Bayswater Primary School. They hurt like fuck and swelled up quickly, frustrating Mama who had to keep upgrading my bras throughout the year. I was teased in the playground and stared at by the male teachers. Their gaze more than most disturbed me because there was something, like, *different* in their eyes that I'd never seen before. The closest I'd seen it was, like, in the eyes of kids I'd fought with in the playground, but the teachers weren't cranky with me. How to explain adult lust to a twelve year old?

The nurse dons a pair of latex gloves and squirts a shot of baby oil into them, and to my surprise she reaches under me like she's going to milk a cow and starts basically massaging my boobs. Between that and the spanking it feels so good I can hardly object. Once she's oiled me up and stimulated my nipples, she attaches the clamps.

It hurts.

But in an amazing fucking unreal kind of way.

'Oh my Goddess, Abi,' I groan. 'You've gotta try this.'

She giggles and finishes off both drinks, the greedy bitch. Some dark techno is on and she can barely sit still. We might have to head to The Beat after this and, like, get the dancing bug out of her.

The clamps bite into the soft skin of my nipples, making them even harder. The irony of human arousal.

The nurse lets go of the chain that the clamps are on and it, like, swings down to just above the floor, tugging on my tits and sending jolts of pain and pleasure in a confused combo through my nips and down to my muffy. I even yelp a bit.

Then she brushes a leather thong whip across my back, and my skin prickles at the sensation. My libido almost goes overboard from this alone. The administrations get more forceful, and the doctor swaps the paddle for a leather switch as well, and they're both, like, whipping across my burning skin in short flicking motions.

I would fucking kill for some dick right now!

I don't know how much time passes because I have what can only described as, like, an out-of-body experience. Or it's more like a blackout. Either way, I become unaware of myself, focused only on the sensation, the whipping and the tingling skin and my nipples tugging down with the weight of the chain. But eventually it all stops and the sweet pull on my tits stops, basically hoiking me out of my meditation and into the reality of a club full of people, of the patterns in the dark carpet and the sound of the music.

That was truly next level.

I feel compelled to hug the doctor and nurse when they release me from my bonds, stopping short thank fuck of telling them that I love them.

'That was amazing, period,' I confess, holding my latex top out and bouncing up and down to, like, settle my boobs back into place. It actually feels weird having them bound again in rubber.

'You were amazing, darl,' the doctor grins, his spanking hand on my shoulder.

I'm sure I wasn't, but we're all feeling a strong connection now, the three of us, and easing away from that needs to be done gently. Basically, this is like a breakup, without the heart-wrenching loss.

'Holy shit, Alex,' gushes Abi when I rejoin her, and I break into a big grin, feeling a bit whoozy and lightheaded. 'You're my new hero.'

'Fuck you're funny,' I laugh. 'Let's get more drinks since you, like, stole mine, you sneaky bitch, then it's your turn to try something.'

'No way,' she says wide-eyed. 'To the bondage, I mean, not the drinks.'

'That goes without saying, for you,' I tease.

'Calling me a lush, are ya?' She grabs us some more vodka tonics.

'Puh-leeze,' I grin, raising one eyebrow.

The really weird bit is that when I was bent over that hobby horse I haven't felt so relaxed in, like, ages, and it's not just because of the arousal. If anything, that causes tension because I just need a cock at that moment to burst the built-up pressure. But no, what I felt being tied up and dominated was a sense of calm, like I wasn't in control and neither was I in danger, and so I just let go. I felt this complete sense of, like, release, and from that the tension inside my brain just slid away.

But I'm still horny, and only an orgasm or emotional misery is going to fix that. I don't plan on the latter, so maybe when we hit the clubs later, I might have to, like, find a bloke to take home.

Chantelle's out of her cage now, and apparently free to roam because she comes up to us with a drink in hand and wearing a long black latex dress similar to the Syren one that Pamela Anderson wore on *The Jay Leno Show*.

'Happy birthday!' me and Abi shout, and we all group hug. Our bodies press together and my sore nipples send, like, tiny currents of pleasure down over my body.

Abi's like: 'You still thinking of moving out of the Palace?'

Chantelle nods. 'When I can, yeah. Just waiting for a problem boarder at a mate's place to pack his shit and go, and I'm straight in there.'

'Does Nel suspect?'

'Not a fucking whit, thankfully,' laughs Chantelle.

Then Abi tells Chantelle all about my go on the bondage-horse, how it was, as she puts it, the 'ants pants'. Chan looks at me with such pride.

'Good on ya, girl! Slave to the scene!'

The DJ announces the floor-show is about to begin, so everyone gathers around an area near the cloak room where the floor is, like, linoleum-lined. Two girls from Sydney come out and perform a strip show, basically culminating in one of them popping ice-cubes into her shaved hole while the other, like, sucks them out and spits them into a glass of champagne.

During the performance, this bloke with long dreadlocks dressed in nothing but leather pants sidles up to us. He's got, like, shitloads of piercings: plugs in his nose and earlobes, barbells and orbital rings in ears, snakebites for his bottom lip, nipples and dermal piercings on his throat.

'Heya doll,' he says to Chantelle.

'Anyone else, Ryley, and they'd get a smack in the chops for using language like that,' she grins at him. 'Good night, ay?'

'Fucking tops night,' he says, glancing around the room. 'Don't see Nelly the Beast out much anymore, though.'

'Nah, too much of a homebody these days,' Chantelle says, miming a syringe plunging into her arm.

Ryley smiles. 'As if you don't, eh?'

'Recreational only!' Chantelle protests, playfully punching him on the arm.

I notice Abi's grinding her jaw, trying to, like, distract herself by watching a scrawny guy with a ponytail basically getting his arse whipped raw on a huge wooden A-frame. The welts are starting to bulge, ready to spill blood. The woman whipping him refuses to go on despite his pleas. Must be, like, rules about drawing blood here. Sanitation and all that, I guess.

'Coupla scene virgins for ya,' Chantelle says to Ryley, turning his attention to me and Abi.

'I wouldn't have thought it of this one,' he says, staring intensely into my eyes. 'I saw you on the horse. You looked like you were born for it. No soft limits.'

'Like a duck to water,' I giggle, thinking of how my knickers are still wet. Most uncomfortable. I should, like, duck into the toilet and get them off.

Chantelle explains that Ryley helps run Club Inferno.

'But I also organise private BBQ meet-ups for this crowd,' he says.

I'm like: 'Ah, cool beans. It's my first time here, but I'm loving it.'

'They're a great bunch of people,' he agrees. 'All walks of life, too. I'm a dental assistant, for example.'

'Really?' I glance down at his chest where, like, thick silver rings pierce his nipples and self-inflicted scars criss-cross his entire torso. 'I would have taken you for a priest, myself.'

'The flagellation, huh?' He rubs a hand across the pink scars.

'Does it hurt?' Abi asks.

'Not at all,' he replies.

I'm like: 'But, like, it must have when you did it?'

Chantelle smirks on, enjoying our naivety.

'Nah, I anaesthetise first,' he enlightens us. 'I get stuff through my job and it numbs the area. See this mark here?' He points out two blobs of deformed skin above his left nipple, about two inches apart. 'That's from a padlock, a big brass bastard. We numbed the area and my mate punctured the skin and got the padlock on. We even locked it.'

Shit. It's a fair chunk of flesh they managed to do that with. I feel a bit ill thinking about it.

'It looks like it probably went through muscle.'

'Yup,' he grins. 'It did. My mate has this massive scar tissue down his deltoids where I numbed it and used a scalpel to cut the muscle down to the bone.'

'Fucking hell!' yells Abi, then covers her mouth in embarrassment.

'They rubbed table-salt into it, after,' laughs Chantelle, enjoying our squeamishness.

'What on Earth *for?*' gasps Abi.

'To keep the wound open,' shrugs Rayley. 'That way the scars will heal slower and wider.'

Man, that's intense. On the goth scene there's a lot of, like, cutting; tiny scars that shine against pale skin so prolifically sometimes that it looks like a hundred cats attacked them, but this is another level!

I chat with him a little more about some of the stuff that he's into, steering him away from the scar stuff onto piercings, and he tells me proudly that he has eighteen piercings all up.

'How would you like to come along to our next private munch?' he asks.

'I dunno,' I say, because, like, I've got no idea what a *munch* is. Chantelle nods eagerly at me.

'It's a meeting place for like-minded people,' he says, explaining that a *munch* is a social thing he sometimes organises at a cafe, but sometimes as a private BBQ. 'Evey and I are keen to see you there. The Libido Club, we call it.'

'Evey?'

'The nurse,' Chantelle volunteers, jerking her head toward the girl in question currently packing up the toys and bondage horse.

As if sensing her name mentioned, Evey glances up and sees us looking at her. She smiles broadly at me and continues to pack her things away.

'Oh yeah, cool beans,' I say, nodding and trying to act nonchalant.

Ryley laughs at my little attempt to appear cool, but it's an easy and carefree laugh that, like, puts me at ease. It reminds me of Jai's.

I'm like: 'Actually, I'd like that.'

'Great,' he nods. 'I'll write down the details for you and leave them with Evey. I've got to help close up the bar. Nice to meet you, Alex.'

'You, too.'

He kisses Evey on his way to the bar in a way that makes me realise they're a couple. Old Blue Eyes the doctor was just another regular, I guess. I'd sort of assumed that he was, like, Evey's partner, but assumptions are obviously easily waylaid here.

'What was that all about?' grins Abi, arching her eyebrows lecherously.

'My ticket to a whole new scene.'

WE DON'T VOTE

I fucking told that cunt Lachie to pick us up a goon bag of Lambrusco but of course he's forgotten. Probably on purpose. Instead the useless cunt brings back a whole case of UDL's, as if either me or Donger is going to drink that shit.

'Where's the VB's at, Locko?' Donger goes, equally unimpressed. 'And Dante's wine?'

Donger's stretched out on the banana-lounge, the base of which is dodgy and won't crank up to support his legs anymore, so he lies with his belly bulging up. He looks preggers.

'They ran out,' Lachie says, the lying prick.

'Could of got something else,' Donger says.

'Could've come and helped carry it, ya lazy bastard,' says Lachie, without any hint of joking around.

'Righto, righto,' Donger goes, repacking the bowl on his bong. 'Calm ya tits.'

'I want my money back, then,' I demand, reaching across for a can anyway.

'No change left,' the sneaky fuck goes. 'Consider yourself lucky we don't charge you rent for stayin here.'

'I've only been here a few nights, you petty bastard,' I remind him, and Lachie simply smiles and cracks a can open.

M.A.S.H. is on the idiot box but suddenly it flicks over to a news announcement to talk about the federal election results, and they cut to a room at the Wentworth Hotel in Sydney all decked out with blue curtains and a podium.

None of us could be fucked getting up to change the channel.

John Howard comes on to give a speech and the writing at the bottom of the screen says he's now Prime Minister elect. Where's Norman Gunston when you need him?

'Oh for fuck's sake,' I spit, partly from rage and partly from the shitty taste of the beer, 'who the hell voted the Libs in, then?'

'What's wrong with him?' Lachie goes.

'Don't look at me, I didn't vote for im,' says Donger, reaching down for his bong again. 'So it's not my problem.'

Lachie looks at us like we're spastics. 'Neither of you fucking vote,' he goes. 'Youse two *are* part of the problem.'

'Fuck off,' I snap. 'If you think your vote even counts in the long run, you've got your head in the fucking sand. It's all rigged.'

'Spoken like someone who refuses to enrol,' the cheeky cunt rebukes.

'Now, now, kids,' says Donger, pressing his lips to the juice bottle and lighting up.

'Look, even if by some miracle your vote *does* count,' I argue (Lachie immediately retorts 'and it does'), 'why give it to that shifty lil cunt?'

'The alternative didn't appeal,' Lachie says loftily.

'I'm not saying Keating was ideal, either, but at least he was for telling the Queen to get on her bike and let us work out who the fuck we are as a country. This cunt,' I point at the telly, 'he'd have us still kow-towing to the Monarchy. He's got his nose so far up Edmund Burke's decayed arsehole any Joe Blo with a skerrick of concern about staunch conservatism in politics should feel a shiver going up their spine.'

'Don't give me the Republican argument,' Lochie drawls, rolling his eyes.

'I don't need to,' I fire back. 'Both our economy and our society before Labour was conservative and unsustainable. Labour's always had to fight against the senate and the courts and backward State Government's like Joh's in order to get things like, oh I don't know, a consistent healthcare system in place. I mean, there's plenty to be in favour of a Labour leader.'

'But Keating didn't start that on his own,' scoffs Lachie. 'Sorry, but he's conniving as fuck. Like signing the agreement with Indonesia in January and not telling anyone until it's done.'

Yeah, that was a bit sly, I'll admit. Instead I say: 'And he went to Malaysia at the same time and mended relations there. He knows how important Asia is to our trade and security. Does Johnny?'

'Nope, sorry, can't believe our foreign policy is to be sneaky about treaties,' Lachie goes, trying to crush his empty can with one hand and nearly cutting himself in the process. 'Fuck these things are sharp!'

'Roll us over a can,' says Donger, but Lachie's too busy trying to stop the blood leaking out of his hand.

'Lachie, our foreign policy is pretty fuckin basic: don't get invaded, maintain our democratic system, and make a shit-tonne of money as possible from Asia's growth. We rely on the ANZUS Treaty for the first two and on China for the last. Soon, on South-East Asia.'

Recently Samuel Huntington has suggested that Australia's already trying to define itself as an Asian country, an opinion which will probably piss off lil Johnny to no end.

'What about Timor?' goes Donger, and gets no response from either of us.

'When Keating was our treasurer he put us into a recession,' says Lachie. 'The one we had to have, remember? Time for a change, I reckon. End of story.'

A fucking change alright. Lachie's obviously ignorant about our past politics, but in the late eighties Howard said we'd have more harmonious communities if we restricted Asian migrants from coming over. When your childhood's marred by Cattle Tick versus Proddy conflicts I guess you grow up with a sense that division is crucial in society. Yet he was on *Four Corners* the other week saying quite the opposite, goin on about how the Land of Oz is a unique intersection that includes Asia. Anything to turn the spotlight away from a fucked ideology and focus, as Governments are wont to do, on the failings of the opposition, which was pretty much how he ran his campaign. Not hard to see why he brought that former Ipswich independent Pauline Hanson aboard and played her like a puppet for his own agendas, who obviously harbours similar sentiments about minority groups when she revealed in a letter to the Queensland Times that she thought the Government shouldn't be dishing out money to Aboriginals. Fuck knows what she was on about, but it's something to do with the Minister for Aboriginal Affairs and the issue of black deaths in custody, as the Royal Commissioner someone-or-other Dodson dubbed it I believe. The Aboriginal Affairs minister is the same one who fucked up a couple of years ago when he got a bridge built to Hindemarsh Island and apparently desecrated a sacred site. In any case, for penning the letter Hanson was disendorsed before the election, a great big thanks-but-no-fucking-thanks from the guy who clearly shares her attitude and has now taken the highest office in the country. Talk about walking all over the people you used to get there.

'Righto, forget the fact that Liberal's always rode the coat-tails of Labour's ideas, claiming them as their own at the last,' I go, unable to resist getting a dig in then swiftly changing tact, 'but let's see if Howard continues things like the Wilson-Dodson inquiry into how Aboriginals were separated from their families. That investigation's gonna get the chop, you watch. This is what you've voted for, mate.'

'He's only just got into the role for fuck's sake, Dante,' whines Lachie. 'Give the man a break, ay? You're goin on like he's got a racist agenda.'

'I reckon he has,' I boldly posit. 'He's the one, let me remind you, who reckons you can argue a racist position without actually being a racist. Unless he means playing the devil's advocate, then...' I shrug.

'But even playing the devil's advocate, you're still making the argument,' says Donger, finally joining the conversation.

'That's what I mean,' I go, nodding at Donger, unsure if he was backing me up or disagreeing with me.

Now Howard's saying on the idiot box that the major wins his party secured are an endorsement of his philosophies. Sadly, he's probably right. Lachie here's lapping it up, that's for sure. Donger's just wasted, struggling to follow the conversation. Always hits the maryjane too hard, that boy.

The phone goes off next to Lachie, who huffs and puffs to reach it without getting up, the fat cunt. He says it's for me, then claims the cord's too short to pass the phone thereby forcing me out of my seat.

'Change the channel while you're up,' drawls Donger.

Alan's on the other end of the line and says he's at the hospital now because Suzie's been in labour for hours, on and off.

'Suzie's mum and dad are on their way, ay,' he says. 'Mine can't make it down yet.'

His folks are out west; up in Murgon or Cherbourg, I can't recall which one.

'You want me to come in?'

He sounds relieved, unwilling to ask me outright out of politeness, the funny bugger. 'No hassle?'

'Fuck off, you're a mate! A first time dad! Of course I'll be there!'

He thanks me profusely and hangs up.

'Alan's gonna be a dad,' I say to Donger. 'You know Alan, singer from Sodomy Finger.'

'Oh yeah, nice one,' grins Donger.

'Out with the old and in with the new, ay?' says Lachie, drawing an insipid parallel between the Labour party's defeat and Suzie's contractions. He hoists a fresh can of piss in toast. 'Here's to Alan and Suzie.'

'Hear hear,' me and Donger go, him pulling on another bong and me thrusting out my hand to Lachie for my change so I can get the bus over to Herston and visit Alan in the hospital.

'Fucking recession in my bank account now,' the cunt whinges, pulling a tenner free from his wallet.

Of course I have no intention of buying a train ticket. I just want the booze money back. I'm too fucking poor to just let ten bucks slide. Conservatives like Lachie can only measure wealth by the poverty of others, and engineered poverty is the chief prerequisite to the social failure that allows conservatism to persist.

There's a knock on the front door.

'Oi, take Spaz with ya,' goes Donger as he struggles to get off the banana-lounge to answer the door. 'Wake im up. He's meant to be playing at Van Gogh's Earlobe tonight.'

Spazza's room stinks. It's not even a room really. It's a closed off veranda space next to the dunny, accessed only by first going through Donger or Lachie's rooms. Fuck all privacy, although at one point they had up to six people living here. It's just a modified worker's cottage, not meant for that many occupants.

'Spazza,' I say, kicking his foot. 'Carn Spaz! Wake up, ya cunt!'

'Fuck ooorf,' he bellows and hides his head under a doona.

'Spazza, it's four in the fucking afternoon, get up already.'

'YOU GOT A GIG, YOU STUPID FUCKER!' yells Lachie from the loungeroom.

Spazza springs up, his eyes screwed shut against the light and his pale pink hair sticking out to one side like a galah's crest.

'Cunts,' he mutters, then stumbles into the dunny to shake hands with the unemployed, slamming the door shut. It bounces back open since there's no latch on it anymore, so I head back into the lounge to wait because Spaz has a tendency of dropping his dacks all the way to his ankles when he takes a leak, and his zit covered arse is the last thing I need to see.

I notice there's a couple of copper-cunts at the front door, talking to Donger.

'Fuck, Lachie,' I hiss, jerking my thumb at them.

Lachie's eyes nearly pop out of his head when he sees them, and he runs and grabs the pedestal fan and aims it at one of the windows to try and blow Donger's bong smoke out. There's nothing for me to grab and use as a fan, so feeling inspired I yank Donger's prize piece of carpet off the wall and start fanning the cloud of stagnant smoke. The shag pile is crusty under my fingers from years of built up vomit and spilt beer but I've got no choice but to keep fanning. I know Donger's gonna have a conniption fit when he sees I've pulled it from the wall because he got this as a memento the night Funkyard closed down. It was before my time but he always reckons it was one of the best clubs we've ever had here.

'Fellas,' one of the coppers says, peering through the doorway at us madly fanning smoke towards the windows. He gives us a little nod then turns away, following his partner out the front gate.

Donger closes the door and makes a dramatic gesture of wiping sweat of his forehead.

'That was a close fucking call,' Lachie snaps.

'No worries,' Donger says, sauntering back in and flopping back down on his lounge. 'Just a follow up to the murder I witnessed.'

'You didn't witness any murder,' I point out. 'You were present when a body was found.'

'Same diff, dude,' he goes, looking around for his bong.

'It really isn't,' I snap, then realise I'm still waving around his treasured piece of carpet, or the *Dutchman of History* as he likes to call it. I quickly stash it under Lachie's chair with the intention of re-nailing it to the wall when Donger's not around.

When Spazza finally comes out from the dunny – shaking droplets of urine from his fingers, I notice – he wants a beer, so Lachie throws him one and he misses the catch. It lands on his foot and he hops around screaming all sorts of profanities at Lachie. Everyone cracks up at him. The poor bastard, he snaps the tab and beer pisses out all over him, shooting high into the air over his head.

'Cunts!' Spazza goes again, then dips his head into the geyser as it drops down. He flattens his wet hair back, licking his chapped lips as the booze dribbles down his face.

'You feral prick,' laughs Lachie.

And that's it. Spazza's ready. He's only wearing a pair of hippy pants and a patchwork vest, no shoes or nothing, and is ready to go. He plays drums for Foetal Cake, who actually have a song about me and Donger called *Piggy Run*, so named for that little game we like to play with the cops. Fortunately, we don't have to worry about lugging Spazza's drum kit with us because the rest of the band won't trust him with any of the instruments, wisely so I might add, so they transport it to all the gigs for him. All he's gotta do is turn up on time and play. He never fails on the latter task. Can't always say the same for the first one.

We follow our shadows down Station Road to the train station, while I tell him about how Alan's having the baby. Not for the first time am I struck by how Spazza looks like an old man, with his receding hairline and little beer belly. Even his face looks more like a wizened old man rather than the braindead twenty year old that he really is. He's a couple of feet shorter than I am, more like my Great-Nan, who's in her nineties now and is shrinking every day the way that really old people tend to.

Coming off the Ipswich-bound train are two familiar faces. The first one is a nasty piece of work called Joss Hansen. The other guy is Martin Tadlow, Malik's older brother, although he's dwarfed by his younger sibling. The cunt's even shorter than Spazza is. According to Matty, it's why they used to call the cunt Tadpole back in high school, and defending himself for it turned him into a fighter. Unfortunately it didn't stop there; the cunt now has a reputation for getting pretty violent. And heaven help anyone who calls him Tadpole to his face.

Megs went to the same school as Joss, and is still on social terms with him, but she reckons she's wary as fuck of him. He's not tried anything with her, but she says they're both known to get particularly deviant with girls, getting em drunk then sharing them whether the girls like it or not. Megs once told me how they've got a fondness for Aboriginal girls especially, and make weekend trips up to Murgon with some mates and flash their money around like kings, turning their motel rooms into a smorgasbord of sex. Bareback, doubtless.

'Where you two gayboys off to then?' sneers Joss.

'Gonna suck each other off down the end of the platform, ay?' Tadpole joins in.

I'd tried steering Spazza towards the opposite end of the station, but we kinda stand out in the crowd.

'Martin, Joss,' I acknowledge. 'City packed, is it?'

Malik reckons his brother's actually pretty smart, but obviously not smart enough to catch onto the opportunity to lead with a fudge-packer inspired insult because all the cunt can come out with is: 'For you pussies, it is.'

Thankfully, Spazza's bewildered by the whole exchange and just stares at them stupidly. He has a real aversion to hostility, and just kinda shuts down when it rears its ugly head. He's been that way ever since he found his brother Dylan hanging by an electrical cord from the family veranda last year. Dylan had been on and off a methadone program for yonks but couldn't stave off the inevitable depression that comes from heroin withdrawal. Even though it was a suicide, Spazza now equates the death with all violence in general, and gets squeamish around aggressive people, the poor bastard.

Joss leans in and sniffs at Spazza. 'What'd you do, Al Dente, piss on him?'

I've heard stories about these two and their network of deviant mates beating the shit out of punks and gays. They're stout supporters of fuckheads like that shit for brains Bruce Ruxton, the old cunt with the embarrassing rap song that says it's forty-two degrees but there's a nip in the air, even though his supporters say the song's meant to be a jibe at his detractors. But Ruxton's a racist old prick who's got issues with Asian migration and 'poofters' apparently, saying they never served in the army. I've news for that old cunt: if they drafted people against their will in his hey-day, then they undoubtedly caught a few closet-boys in their nets, meaning he'd have been bunked down with a couple of them for sure. In any case, I can only assume these two halfwits have issues with migrants and gays, too, if they're big into the antediluvian old fart's rhetoric. They're pretty gung-ho on being Australian, whatever the fuck that truly is these days, and they love nothing more than proving it by stomping on anything or anyone that challenges that identity.

There's another part to their makeup that they freely express to all and sundry, and that's as self-confessed Satanists. I've plenty of experience with whacko Christians and their crazy cults, but not with this other end of the spectrum. As far as I'm concerned, though, it's all a load of shit. I mean, I don't doubt that there's some people in the world who could probably really mix it up with the Devil himself, but I think these two posers are all show. Hence the use of fists, so that once again no-one will challenge the facade.

No worries, boys, you're welcome to your delusions.

The inbound train's coming over the Walter Taylor Bridge, thank fuck.

'Well, take care, fellas,' I go, all smiles. 'Me and Spazza gotta go suck each other off now.'

'Yeah, you do that, Al Dente,' Tadpole hisses in my face.

I'm very fucking tempted to push the cunt onto the tracks and watch him get crushed by the train. That'd send out a message to his dickhead network of fucktards, wouldn't it? Don't mess with Dante.

'Yeah, rightio,' I mutter, and they laugh as they saunter off, death-glaring other pedestrians who're mostly oblivious to their presence anyway. When they're out of ear-shot I quietly add: 'Captain fucking obvious.'

'No worries, Dante,' Spazza goes, slapping me on the back. 'Relax man.'

It's a bit hard to relax. I can feel my blood boiling, like my anger is a volcano. I've got visions of those two cunts bleeding on the fucking ground, begging for mercy. An inventory of weapons flashes through my mind, quickly narrowing down to a small list of things I might readily find here on the street: sandwich boards, bicycles, shopping trolleys, even skateboards. My mind races through these all options, processing their potential to do damage.

'Fucking stupid nickname, too,' I spit. '*Al Dente?* I'm not even Italian you fucking dumb cunts.'

'Easy, mate, they're gone,' says Spazza, looking worried. 'C'mon, train's gonna go.'

The conductor blows his whistle so me and Spazza make a last minute dash for the doors as they close, and even though I manage to clear em Spazza gets caught between them, struggling to free himself and get aboard I yank at the handle, forcing the fuckers to open just enough for Spazza to slip through before the train starts moving. We can see the conductor hanging out his door watching us through the window, shaking his head. I give him the finger.

'Cunts,' I snarl.

A family with little kiddies in strollers decides to move a few seats further along, vacating the prime position on any carriage.

'Fucking choice,' Spazza grins. 'Double seat to ourselves.'

It's no fucking victory, you dumb cunt, I think to myself. That poor family with their kids are scared of me, but it's those other Satanist-wannabe cunts that are the problem, not me.

'Tell Alan congrats from me,' Spazza goes, already emotionally moving on from the scene at the train station. I envy how easy it is for people like him to do that. For me, it'll probably play on my mind for days.

I smile as freely as I can. 'Will do, Spaz, will do. And you have a great gig, too, buddy.'

He glances sidelong at my enthusiasm and beams back, but his eyes the same scared-rabbit wariness as that family whose seat we took.

EVERYDAY DEVILS

Joss chuckles.

'Did you see that cunt Halloran? I thought he was gonna cry, the fucking baby.'

'Pussies, the both of them,' agrees Martin. 'One of these days I'm gonna fucken destroy that cunt.'

Joss grins, imagining the scenario in his mind.

The sun shines straight into their faces as they walk up Station Road, blinding them, so that when they get to the crest and swing right onto Stamford Road it's a relief to be in the enormous shadow of the Westfield Shopping Centre, gaining the gift of sight once again.

Martin spies a cat resting beside the path, close to where the cars are parked. When he was a teenager he was renowned for killing cats, and in a whole variety of ways, too. The more creative he could get the more renowned he became. The girls that lived next door hated him and would scream at him for it, but he didn't care because he thought they were ugly bitches anyway.

He finds a rock and hefts it at the cat's head, narrowly missing it. The rock glances off the side of a car inside the parking lot. The cat hunkers down from the near-miss, but when it sees Martin reaching down for another projectile it bolts straight across the road behind the Stamford Tower.

'Shit throw,' sneers Joss.

'I was aiming for the car first time,' Martin lies, 'to shoo the cat closer to us.'

Joss just shakes his head doubtfully at his friend.

There's a hole in the fence where the underground parking and Westfield's wall meet, and the two boys duck through it, scooting back alongside the building in the direction of Station Road. At the end they're met with a high bluestone rock wall and an old door to their right, which Joss reaches out and yanks it open. It used to be secured shut once upon a time, but security hasn't bothered locking it anymore since vandals keep shattering the lock anyway.

It's dark and musty inside, and the path slopes down steeply. The bluestone rock wall is still to their left, but overhead is now concrete. They're under the south end of Westfield. The earth to their right tumbles away into darkness (a yawning gully that experience tells them is full of trash and abandoned shopping trolleys), beyond which is a long besser brick wall with locked doors at key points. Halfway along their path is a small bridge across a service corridor that leads into the guts of the shopping centre.

This is what local delinquents call The Cave.

At the other end is a burst of daylight where the path angles past the exhaust fans around to the west-facing side of the shopping centre into the multi-level parking flanking Musgrave Road.

Except there is a gang of silhouettes blocking their way, about halfway along the path.

'Heads up boys,' a voice sounds out, and the silhouettes shift to form a line along the width of the path.

Joss and Martin are unperturbed. They sincerely believe in their ability to overcome this obstacle, certain the Devil walks with them.

'Youse are lost,' one of the silhouettes calls out.

The sound of a chain rattling. A weapon?

'We're home,' Martin calls out, his breathing shallow. He's excited.

'Fuck off, poonce,' one of the silhouettes yells out. 'This ain't no-one's home, motherfucker, cept ours!'

'Homies,' mutters Joss contemptuously, and Martin echoes gist of the sentiment.

The silhouette gang starts to break apart, some disappearing into the shadows of the bluestone rock wall. The rattling sounds increase, but rather than instil fear in either Joss or Martin as it is intended to do, it makes them eager. They could have beaten the shit out of Dante Halloran and his stupid punk friend Spazza down at the train station, but there'd been too many people. Too many witnesses. Besides, Halloran and Spaz had been shitting bricks. Comparatively, this is a dream rumble: no witnesses, outnumbered and weapons.

'Let's go, cunts,' snarls Martin, breaking ahead of Joss to charge into the pack ahead.

Joss takes the rear, ready for the fuckers hiding in the shadows of the wall. They'll spring out after Martin's passed, try and flank him. But that's when Joss will strike.

'Here he comes,' a voice roars as Martin ploughs into the group.

He hears the chain rattle and clink as it is swung, but these guys are amateurs. The chain goes wide of the mark and he collects one of the idiots with a clothesline hook, dropping the cunt into the dirt. Typically, the rest of them jump away as Martin continues ploughing forward. He's seen it a hundred times: their self-preservation kicks in and instead of standing their ground as a group they spread out and fail completely in their defence. They're wide open now, with Martin on one side and Joss on the other.

'Who shall I take to be the human sacrifice?' calls Joss.

Someone jumps at him from the darkness to his left, but he's fast, and collects their jaw with a quick and powerful jab. Joss can feel it connect, feels how his hand tries to drive through the cunt's face. Hears the body land on the ground behind him, moaning in agony.

He doesn't wait for another strike. He runs into the shadows and up the angle of the bluestone wall. He's been down here so many times, practicing his martial arts against the darkness and the rocky terrain, the dusty path and the shaky hand railings. He knows the land here. He thumps into someone and they both roll down onto the path, bumping against legs. Feet try and stomp his head, but it's an uncoordinated attack, every bastard striking out randomly in the hopes of meeting their mark.

Martin ploughs back through the bodies, knocking several from their balance. A dust cloud is starting to build around them now, with everyone, including Joss and Martin, choking on it.

'OI!' yells a voice from far away, and coming around the west corner are two figures.

'Security!' one of the homies calls out, and they scatter, sprinting in the direction of the busted door and Stamford Road.

Martin stretches out, helping Joss to his feet. 'Thank God you guys are here,' he says innocently to the approaching security guards. 'We got attacked.'

Torch-light is flashed across their faces.

'Sure you were,' laughs the guard holding the torch. He tells the other guard it's okay and that he'll handle it from here on. The other guard is wise to the situation: these boys are known to his colleague. He leaves them to it, taking the service corridor into the underbelly of the shopping centre, whistling a song as he goes.

'Smoke?' the remaining guard offers, holding out a cigarette pack.

Martin and Joss take a fag each. The guard reaches his lighter out to each in turn, sparking up a flame.

'Cheers, Pieter,' says Joss, patting the guard's rotund belly. 'How you doin, big fella?'

'Knock it off,' laughs Pieter. 'You cleaned those lil chinky cunts up, eh?'

'Yeah, we sorted em out,' grins Joss.

'Fucked em up good,' says Martin, his face like stone. He blows twin jets of smoke from his nostrils, like a B-grade movie demon.

Pieter glances down and kicks something with his boot. It twirls in the dust with a distinctive rattle.

'Little shits were tagging again,' he says. He peers up at the pillars and the bluestone walls. 'Yep. Up there. Fucken cunts.'

Joss reaches down for the spraypaint can while Martin takes a closer look at the graffiti. Funnily enough, the word UP is painted on the rocks in pink and green, but Martin knows that piece is the work of a girl called Coralee who he knows of from around the traps.

'It's white,' Joss tells Martin, studying the paint can.

'Then it's that useless shit over there,' Martin says, pointing at a scattering of crappy looking tags further along.

Joss climbs the wall and holds the nozzle close to the surface, releasing a steady burst of paint slowly across the rocks, slow enough to build the paint up so that it drips. Like blood, if blood was white.

'*Deus meumque jus,*' he says without any hint of irony as he climbs back down. It is the only phrase in Latin he's ever memorised.

Martin and Pieter admire the massive Thaumaturgic Triangle with a 33 in the middle that Joss has spray-painted. Even in the gloom it's clearly discernible, partly for how large he's made it. Joss tosses the spray can down into the gully where it rattles around for a moment then stops abruptly. It becomes deathly quiet. The hum of traffic on Station Road is faint.

They smoke their cigarettes, admiring how the paint drips inexorably creep down the bluestone.

'You boys headed up to Murgon tonight?' asks Pieter hopefully.

MISTER FREEZE

The baby's stillborn, them doctors tell us.

'Sorry Alan, but your baby is stillborn.'

That means it's born dead.

I'm fucking gutted, man. I feel like someone's gone and put a huge block of ice inside my chest and it's expanding, pushing all the warmth outta my body.

The doctor's saying something to us, but I can't hear im. Even his face is kinda blurry.

Dante'll be here in a jiffy, he reckons. And my cousins; there's a mob of em stay out Kingston way, so they're comin in, too. It'll be good. Have a support network, ay. Like the doctor says.

'You need your family and friends around you at this time,' he says.

Now my fingers and toes are gone numb. Soon the ice in my chest will either freeze us completely or make us adapt, like that bald cunt with the red eyebrows on the old *Batman* reruns who becomes as cold as ice and takes revenge on the world. Wild.

Suzie's lyin in her bed, exhausted, but using the last of her energy to death-glare us, like she blames us for the baby.

I just keep getting colder n colder.

MURGON BOUND

Alan and his long-term girlfriend of three years were expecting a child. Suzie, that's his girlfriend, went into hospital with contractions on Monday afternoon and now me and Alan are headed on a Brisbane Bus-Ways coach up to Murgon for the funeral. The baby was stillborn, which wasn't expected until Suzie had gotten to the hospital. As can be expected, Alan is fucking gutted. There's two things he's been wanting lately: to win a Deadly award, and to be a father.

'I couldn't hold him,' says Alan. 'The baby. I couldn't hold him, Dante.'

I just nod. Not sure what to say. There's a fat woman sitting a few seats away eating a whole roast chicken, but the meat smells off and the rank stench is starting to piss me off.

'I wish I did, though,' he continues. 'I wish I spent time with him like Suzie did. She held onto him after he came out, held him like he was a real baby, but I couldn't cope with it, man. I just got out of there. Went and got drunk.'

I get where he's coming from, but even to me this seems like a shitty confession. Even I would have stayed with my girlfriend and the baby in this circumstance. But we are who we are, so I keep my judgement to myself and let him spill his guts.

'I didn't like the look of him. He was a dark purple colour and his skin was starting to peel off. It didn't look like what me baby should, ay.'

'Yeah,' I say noncommittally, even though I don't know what he's on about. Why would its skin be coming off? Cunt's clearly tripping from grief.

'When Suzie pulled open them baby's eyelids, that was it for me, ay. It was too bizarre. We had a big fight about it at home, when she got back. She said she just wanted to see the baby's eyes. Fuck, man. See the baby's eyes?'

I wince, knowing I can't keep quiet any longer. I'm gonna have to tell him he fucked up and Suzie sounds more sane than he does.

'Suzie's just trying to get a handle on it,' I say. 'That's her way of coping. She has to know who her baby was.'

He just shakes his head, gritting his teeth.

'You should talk to her about it one day,' I offer gently. 'Talk about that baby, and his eyes.'

He lets out a deep sigh. 'Yeah, maybe.'

I'm trying to get the image of a purple, peeled baby out of my mind, but I have an overactive imagination. I picture the baby riding the bus with us, sitting in the opposite seat and staring at us in silent condemnation as its bruised skin slowly peels off layer by layer and drops to the floor with a soft plopping sound.

Suzie's already in Murgon. Her parents came down for the birth, and the next day she went back with them and the body of the baby to arrange a burial. She didn't want it to be interred on Brisbane soil, says Alan, and on that at least he agrees. But her parents had sat quietly in the next room while he and Suzie had argued, and that's also eating away at him, knowing he'll have to face them again at the funeral.

Alan's fumbling now with my Walkman, inserting an unlabelled tape into it and offering me one of the ear-plugs. I'm expecting some Suicidal Tendencies or Black Flag, but instead it's a simple and sweet acoustic guitar with a strong vocal. He sees my curiosity and tells me it's Kev Carmody, a Murri singer.

'This is gunna be our soundtrack this trip.'

We watch the dry landscape fly past and try not to choke from the smell of rancid chicken meat. The miles slip by and soothe our souls in the way that only road-trips can do, like you're putting distance between you and your problems and they can't get any traction to keep up. Except we're headed straight toward them, toward that purple little body that must be put in the ground.

We get off the bus at Murgon and Alan's dad Jimmy greets us. Him and Alan hug and slap each other's backs and his father openly cries. Not for the baby so much, I guess, as for Alan. He takes us across the road to the funeral home and the funeral director greets us solemnly, speaking softly to Alan in reverent tones.

'Huh?' Alan keeps going, cause the poor bastard is half deaf from too many punk gigs. He likes to be up close to the action where the speakers pound his head with noise.

'One of the first steps we need to do is to have you sign this form, Alan,' the guy says in louder tones, slipping a sheet in front of Alan. It has PR13 marked at the top in bold lettering, and PERINATAL FORM OF INFORMATION OF DEATH written beneath that. 'You just need to sign your name here, next to where Suzie has already signed, and then we can begin.'

'Never mind all the forms, mate,' I butt in, swatting the form away. 'We're just here to bury his baby.'

The guy actually gets stroppy with me. 'But you need this form for the files, for the Government,' he says, directing the info at Alan but glowering at me.

'It's alright, Dante,' Alan says, emotionless. He takes the form and a pen off the guy and scrawls a signature where the guy's finger is pointing. I'm sure that's not actually Alan's signature, but I doubt anyone's going to care at this stage, as long as there's a mark on it.

Alan turns away and pats my arm. 'You got my back, brother.'

I'm filled with such warmth for the guy. I wish I could take his pain away for him.

Jimmy then drives us around to his house in Cherbourg, which is the next town over. He tells me proudly that the little bridge that links the two was once nearly burnt down by him and a big mob in protest. I look for scorch marks as we cross over but don't see any.

Cherbourg isn't big, just a dozen or more streets in a grid, and red soil dusting the walls of the homes.

'We haven't had rain in a long time,' explains Jimmy. Suddenly he starts singing. *'But good ol' Cherbouuurrrg, thaaaat's my home!'*

'That's from a local song,' says Alan, shaking his head and rolling his eyes. 'Dad and my uncles sing it all the time at get-togethers. It's bloody embarrassing, ay.'

'Heeey,' tuts his dad, but he's only ribbing. He smiles to himself despite the reason for our visit, clearly happy to have his son by his side again. 'Dead echidna back there. Microwave him up?'

He sounds serious, but glances across and starts cracking up at the look on my face.

'Don't worry about him, Dante,' says Alan. 'He's crazy.'

'We've done it, but,' insists Jimmy.

'Really?' I'm not asking his dad, I'm asking Alan. I'm keen to find out if my friend's eaten road-kill.

'Yeah, fraid so,' he admits. 'Tastes alright, actually.'

'Geez, is it even legal to eat them?'

'Fuck yeah,' goes Alan irritably.

'But not for you white mob,' jeers Jimmy, cracking up again.

We pull up next to the community hall, an awful looking besser brick thing painted white with a cool mural down the side of a black snake dotted yellow, white and red. From the hall emerge a parade of women and children. The children are smiling and jostling each other, rough housing each other to the ground, but the women look forlorn. A couple of them regard me with some suspicion, looking warily at my swampie get up, even though I kept it basic: Nick Cave shirt and old suit. On second thoughts, the *Murder Ballads* shirt was probably a poor choice.

'Look who's back,' announces Jimmy as we climb out of his truck. He slaps Alan on the back and gives him a squeeze on the shoulder.

Alan makes the introductions, but I've already forgotten half the names by the time he's done. He assures me I can just call them all Aunty.

Suzie's here, too, so I go give her a hug.

'It hurts so bad, Dante,' she says.

Her voice is fractured, in real pain. I feel my eyes sting, and tell her everything will be alright, which is fucking stupid cause it's already far from alright, but I don't know what else to say. I notice the body of the baby isn't here. It must be back at the funeral home.

After the catch-up's, we have lunch in the hall where the women have prepared a buffet style spread. Mostly it's cold roast chickens, buttered bread and some tubs of coleslaw and potato salads straight from the supermarket. I notice Suzie's not eating; she just stares at the light in the doorway. From the community hall we all bundle into an assortment of vehicles and head back over to Murgon for the *sorry business,* as they've been calling the funeral.

It's at a cemetery, not the funeral home. By the time we get there, the sun is blazing, and the funeral director has had a shade sail put up with some fold out chairs under it. There's not enough, however; it's a big turn-out, with even more people arriving than were at the lunch.

Jimmy's tasked me with handing out the order of service cards. It's got a picture of a cartoon baby near the top and some clip-art of angels in the corners, with a poem in the centre. I skim through it, the usual shit about Heaven and God. Neither Alan nor Suzie are particularly religious as far as I'm aware. There's a list on the inside of the people who will talk at the service, including the funeral director himself.

I hand the cards out, smiling as I go, figuring it's better than looking all dour-faced. Just about everyone here is Indigenous, and I don't want to come across as an unfriendly cunt.

But then this official looking car turns up, and out gets these white guys in uniforms and frumpy faces, followed by an Aboriginal boy only a few years younger than me and wearing a one-piece orange jumpsuit with cuffs on his wrists and ankles. This must be Alan's cousin Rocko, from the prison. He's in for aggravated assault and burglary, apparently, and must've been allowed out for the funeral on special permission.

The wardens trundle Rocko over and sit him down at the edge of the gathering, where the family chat quietly with him. I was going to hand him a card on his way past, but the sight of the wardens got me edgy. As far as I'm concerned they're in the same boat with cops, and my feelings about them have never been uncertain: I hate and distrust the cunts as far I can throw them.

The funeral gets underway, so I join the family beneath the sails. I'm probably already sunburnt.

The coffin's pitifully tiny. We're all giants by comparison. It hangs suspended above a small rectangular hole that's quite deep. The dirt's piled to one side, covered by a satin sheet. It's a desperate looking graveyard, all barren soil and cracked tombstones, but I'm impressed with the dignity of the service that the funeral guy has put on. It's exactly what Alan and Suzie need right now.

Alan's a fucking wreck, sobbing uncontrollably, hanging his head down between his knees. His father rubs his back, stoic in the face of this tragedy. It's the complete opposite from his earlier shenanigans. Always curious how different people react to death.

At the end everyone throws a fist of dirt onto the coffin, including Rocko, who brushes his palm clean on his prison jumpsuit. As they shuffle him back toward the car, I sprint over and hand him a card, ignoring the baleful stares of the wardens. Rocko thanks me, smiling generously. I can see the sadness in his eyes for his cousin and the whole family at the baby's death, and a stab of regret gets me in the chest that I didn't give him the funeral card at the beginning of the service.

Alan breaks away from his family and approaches me.

'Thanks for all your help, Dante,' he goes, giving me a hug. He looks numb.

'No problem, buddy,' I reply. 'Just wish it was under different circumstances, you know?'

'It's just how things are,' he says, getting this strange light in his eyes. It sorta unnerves me, not because it's sinister or anything, but it's like his thoughts have found a new way to formulate and its showing through his eyes, changing him. Windows to the soul and all that. It's not really the muckabout Alan I'm used to. 'Oi, turns out my uncle Noel is headed back to Toowoomba in about half an hour, ay. You can head with him if you want, man, and bus it back to Brisbane from there, coz the bus don't go from here til the mornin. I'm gonna stick around here for a few days.'

I figure Alan doesn't really need me hanging around like a third wheel while he does family business, so I take Noel up on the offer of a ride. On the way I tell him how charismatic his brother is, careful not to make it a comparison with Noel's own dour character.

'That's not charisma,' Noel grumbles. 'He's a dead-set loon.'

'Some of the best people I know are loons,' I muse, undeterred.

'Nah, but he's rubbish, eh. A bunch a gubbas come up from the city way and carpetbag im, take the fucking lot,' he says. 'That makes him a loon.'

I'm stymied as to what Noel's on about, and more than certain he has no fucking idea what *loon* actually means.

'What does carpetbag mean?'

He leans over the steering wheel and casts a disparaging glance at me. 'Means he's being ripped off. Gubbas, the whities, come up and they buy his art, but they buy it all and for cheap. I seen it in the gallery down your way, selling for big bucks.'

I remember Alan said his dad was an artist, but I'd forgotten. I wonder what kind of art he does, and why he lets it go for so little? If what Noel is saying is true, then it sounds like some arsehole back in Brisbane is taking Alan's dad for a fucking ride.

'Do you know who they are, Noel? Their names?'

'What you gonna do, eh?' he nearly sneers at me. I'm trying hard to believe that Noel's animosity is toward the world in general, and that it's not personal, but I'm struggling with that concept. 'You gonna go make em pay up?'

'I don't know,' I admit. 'But I can sniff around for a start. Find out where the art is, check with some people. I have a mate who's in the art scene. Nathanael. He might know who they are. Maybe we can do something about it.'

'Sniff around? Too much humbug outta you,' he says and goes quiet.

This is gonna be a long fucking trip to Toowoomba, that's for sure. It's only meant to be about a two hour drive, but with Alan's uncle brooding at the wheel it's going to feel five times that.

PARTY AT THE PROZAC

Raven and I are having a party tonight at the flat. We've invited the whole building, and got word out to everyone we know (and want) along, including a bunch of Raven's Uni mates. Booze and snacks have been procured well in advance, thanks mostly to good ol Twixxy here.

Raven's got The Smiths playing really loud, but I'm not a fan so suggest some Sisters. She responds by turning the volume up even louder. She won't be budged because she's a mad Smiths fan. Her room is decked out in Morrissey posters and rare LP's. She stopped talking to me for a whole two days last week because as a joke I cut out pics of Robert Smith's face, sticky-taping them over Morrisey's face on all her Smiths posters. Unfortunately, some of the posters ripped when she tried to take the tape off. As a result, I'm not allowed in her room anymore. Fair call, I guess.

The bogans in the house next door start blasting what sounds like Midnight Oil. Either way it's fucking horrible, and their stereo system is obviously bigger and better than Raven's because she gets into a volume war and immediately loses, so we're stuck finalising party preparations with Aussie pub-rock thumping away at the windows, drowning out *Strangeways, Here We Come*. Even Lunar the cat can't handle it and bolts out the front door.

'What the sodding hell are we going to do about that fucking noise when everyone starts turning up for the party?' I want to know.

'Dunno,' shrugs Raven stubbornly.

Her mood is getting shittier as the countdown to the party gets nearer.

'Not helpful, Raven.'

She goes through to the kitchen and starts loudly tearing open chip bags and tipping them into bowls. This is gonna be a fucking travesty of a party.

Then from upstairs we hear Nirvana blasting out a window. Roz, presumably. Someone else in the Palace puts on Cocteau Twins, and that's followed up by what sounds like The Church. The Prozac Palace becomes like a giant stack of powered loudspeakers, a wall of noise that hits the house next door like a tsunami and forces the bogans to yield. Despite all the noise I can tell that the Oils has ceased, and one by one the music coming from the Prozac Palace dies down again until all I can hear is Morrisey moaning on.

Me and Raven are staring at each other in disbelief.

'Fuck, that was amazing,' she goes, like she's witnessed a miracle.

'Power to the people,' I crack and thrust a fist into the air.

We get on with the preparations, using a box of old Halloween decorations Megs loaned us to spruce the place up a bit. We've got a fair amount of this stuff ourselves already up on walls and doors, as a result of raiding the two dollar stores last Halloween. It's funny, because apart from the clubs and some band gigs, that's probably the third place you'll find the densest gathering of darkwave people: the post-Halloween sales at the discount stores.

I've already cracked into the beers, so not to be outdone Raven gets into the West Coast Coolers early. Malik and some others come down and we all sit around eating chips and lollies until everyone starts turning up. At one point Raven heads into the loo so Malik changes the music over between tracks as quick as lightning, getting some new Inky Sucky on, a ripper of a song called *Heartbeat of the Earth*. Raven doesn't even seem to notice when she gets back. Too sloshed, I suppose.

'There's just no fucking way I could endure a night of Morrissey for entertainment,' whispers Malik.

'No argument here,' I reply. 'I know this song, actually, because Meggie's always playing it in the shop.'

He grins in recognition of Megs' habits.

'Get this right,' Malik says, 'you know that Mark Little, the Brissie boy that used to be on *Neighbours*?'

I shrug. I don't watch that shit.

'Missus Mangel's son,' says Malik, staring at me like he's dropped a massive clue, then he gives up. 'Anyway, he's on the TV in London nowadays, doing this thing called *The Big Breakfast*, and one of my old mates over there emailed the other day to say Inkubus Sukkubus was on it and Little's doing this ring dance with a bunch of normals and the smoke machine guys are pumping way too much smoke out until everything disappears.' He cracks up. 'Worse than the smoke machines at the Alliance, he said.'

The party's in full swing by now and there's no protest from the bogans next door. It's all going swimmingly. Amai-li turns up with her boyfriend Clem, handing me a case of stubbies for the esky. Thankfully we got two backup eskies and ice, too, so between those and the fridge we should be okay.

I've known Amai for just over a year now, and we get along really well, but her boyfriend Clem's still awkward around me. Or maybe it's that I'm actually awkward around him? Not sure, could be mutual awkwardness. Either way, as nice a guy as he is my conversations with him are always a train wreck. I just hope he's not jealous about me being friends with Amai, which is highly possible actually. One night a few months ago she had a nightmare and immediately rang me to talk about it. I was out on a job where I basically had to stand outside the gates of a construction site overnight, so it was hardly like I had anything pressing to do at the time, like sleep for instance. But our conversation had woken Clem in the bed beside her, and she had dashed through the flat to open the line in the lounge-room before running back and hanging up the phone in the bedroom. Christ only knows what poor Clem made of his girlfriend calling blokes in the middle of the night.

'I think we should have worn black,' Amai-li says over the music, glancing around the room of mostly goths.

Her and Clem are normals, dressed like sci-fi geeks actually. He's much taller than her, about my height, where the top of her head only comes up to my shoulder.

I point a few people out and give her and Clem a few names to work with when they mingle.

'And which one's this Cecilia you've been going on about, then?' grins Amai.

'I've hardly been going on about Cecilia,' I object.

'Oh, come on,' laughs Amai. 'Every time I've spoken to you on the phone lately you've mentioned her.'

'Yeah, *mentioned*. And that's it. Hardly a testament to how I feel.'

She jabs me in the ribs with her elbow, smirking up at me.

'Piss off,' I laugh. 'Really? Every time we've spoken?'

She closes her eyes and nods exaggeratedly.

'Damn, I'm more transparent than I realised.'

'Guys always are,' she snorts, which elicits a moan of protest from Clem. 'Even you, babe.'

'Anyways, she's not here yet,' I go, noticing Abi and Alex's arrival. 'Scuse guys.'

I first met Alex in a goth club down in Melbourne when I was visiting that brilliant city. We hit it off, and I thought about hooking up with her even, but she's a bit overweight for my taste. Big tits, although I try not to stare at them much. Chicks apparently hate that even if they do have em out on display. I wonder if Abi's mentioned that we're fuck-buddies?

I grab them both a beer and before I can get a word in I clock these two manky jokers – a man and a woman – strolling into the flat and going over to grab some beers from the esky. They look familiar, but at the same time they don't look like they're at the right party. They're thin and malnourished and belligerent looking, wearing dirty Adidas tracky dacks and rugby jerseys up top. They park themselves in front of the telly, and despite the excessive volume of the stereo system, proceed to watch one of my videos, not being too fucking careful with the tape either when the bloke inserts it into the VCR.

'Oi, Raven,' I say, interrupting her conversation with one of her mates. 'Who're those two?'

She squints and wracks her brain before she twigs who they are. 'Shit, they're from down the road. The derros that live in that housing commission near the corner.'

'Fuck me, they just walked in here and took our grog.'

'The hell?' Raven screws her nose up.

Time to lay the law down.

'Hey, mate,' I say to the bloke, who's irritated I've interrupted his movie. 'What d'ya think you're doin?'

'Watchen *Highlander* with the missus,' he goes, checking the video case for the title. 'Why?'

'This here's a private event, ay,' I inform him and his neanderthal girlfriend. 'You jokers weren't invited.'

He actually has the nerve to get indignant. 'That's not very civil,' he goes.

'Youse got any UDLs?' the woman pipes up.

'Listen, you two are leaving right now,' I say in a terse voice.

Malik's noticed and comes over to stand next to me, crossing his arms. 'Want me to give him the bum's rush, Twix?'

'Why the fark should we?' the bloke argues. 'It's a pardy.'

'It's *my* fucking house,' I go, almost shouting. 'Get the fuck out now!'

Malik points to the front door, jutting his jaw out to look tougher.

The bloke struggles up from the couch, pulling his girlfriend with him, moaning on about how he just got here and how we shouldn't leave the front door wide open if we don't want people wandering in. A ridiculous argument, of course, because first he'd have to enter into the building's hallway, then come up the stairs to get to our flat.

Me and Malik usher them all the way to the street and tell them to fuck off. He stands out on the footpath for a full minute, his middle finger raised in front of him the whole time, sucking on the stubby he stole. Eventually he and the troll wander off down the street.

'This is something I definitely won't miss when I get into a new flat,' muses Malik.

I envy him. I wish I could afford to find a decent place instead of this shithole. Maybe even one in Melbourne!

As we're both heading back into the Palace, I notice three chicks approaching. They look almost as rough as the couple we just got rid of, with only the fringe left on their shaved heads (except for one with dreadlocks), wearing nighties, Docs and an assortment of piercings in their faces. Fucking riot-grrrls.

'Hold up, girls,' I announce, raising my palm in the international sign for STOP. 'Private function. Turn around and be gone.'

Then I notice that one of the girls is Sabrinha, who works at the radio station I often help out in.

'Sabrinha! What're you doing here?'

'I'm here with Maddie,' she says simply, flicking a thumb to the other bald girl whose babydoll dress is so short it's more like a shirt.

'That's weird,' I snort.

'Dante invited us,' she says.

That'd be sodding right.

'He's not here, though,' I tell em, though they look unfazed by the news. 'He went up to Murgon.'

'For Alan's baby,' the one called Maddie says to Sabrinha.

'We've got beer,' goes the tall girl at the back, the one with the dreadlocks, hefting a slab on her shoulder.

This changes everything.

'Rightio then,' I smile, waving them in like I was a fancy waiter. 'In you come, girls.'

They pile up the stairs ahead of me, affording me the opportunity to check out the arse of the chick with the dreads. Not bad. Turning out to be quite a selection of available young ladies at this shindig. Shame about Amai-li, though, with Clem and all. I wouldn't mind being more than just friends with her, to be honest.

Speaking of, when I get back inside I notice that Amai and Clem have joined in with another group on a drinking game of sorts, and Amai must be on a losing streak because she's knocking the drinks back hard and fast.

Amara and Megs are admiring the finish on my coffin-shaped bookcase that I had commissioned last month. It's the perfect pretext to jump in and strike up a conversation. They're both good looking sorts, though I don't know Amara all that well. I'm beginning to think anonymity is to my advantage with chicks.

'Great bookcase,' enthuses Amara.

'Is this the one you were telling me that Tony made for you?' asks Megs.

'Yup, and I painted it myself,' I say proudly, leaving out the bit where I didn't wait for the paint to cure and some of my Somtow and Rice novels got stuck to it. Black enamel paint glued some of them shut forever, unfortunately.

'Yeah, you're good at that,' she smirks good-naturedly, referring to the time she left her old Docs in Raven's car and I'd decided to give them a scuff with my boot polish to rejuvenate some of the cracked leather on top. She'd gone ape-shit when she'd got them back. I should have known better than to ruin her goth-cred by making her Docs look newer than they actually were.

The drinks have gone to Amai's head fast, quite literally: her face is as red as a beetroot. She reckons that's what happens to Asians when they get drunk. Looks like she's been mixing them, too. There's all sorts of spirits and even wine bottles around the throng she's with. She clocks me watching her from across the room, and starts cackling.

'I WANT TO SUCK *HIS* DICK!' she yells, pointing at me.

Frigging hell, she's smashed, and poor Clem's just sitting there looking like a complete dickhead. He must be pissed at me, and her of course. Everyone else pretty much ignores her, including the people playing the drinking game with her. Standard fair at a piss up, I guess.

I'm about to turn away when I see Amai stagger to her feet, and a rising dread fills me as I think she's about to lurch toward me and continue screeching her fantasies, but she runs for the loo instead, a hand clamped over her mouth like she's about to spew. Clem rushes after her. The lad's devoted, I give him that.

'Interesting friends you have,' smiles Amara.

'Amai's cool,' I reply. 'Just gotta learn to handle her drinks, ay.'

A roaring noise from outside gets everyone's attention and we poke our heads out the windows to see the bogans from next door in their ute tearing up the street doing a burnout. Smoke is belching from their rear wheels as they fishtail along the bitumen.

Me and the girls hurl abuse at them, derogatory shit about the size of their balls and whatnot.

They squeal back past the Palace, giving us the finger out the window, and hook down onto Turbot so fast I actually expect to hear a horrible accident. The sound of their car hurtling away towards the Valley diminishes and I decide I might go and check on Amai and see if she needs anything. Maybe offer a half-arsed apology to Clem even though I haven't done anything wrong. He must feel like shit coming to my house and then his girlfriend acting that way about me.

The bathroom door is slightly ajar and Malik passes me in the hallway.

'Dude... fair play to em, but,' he grins, shaking his head as he rejoins the rest of the party, the shifty bastard.

I knock on the door, announcing: 'Hey Clem, everything alright?'

I shove the door open and Amai's got her face in the toilet bowl, her pants slid down so her bare arse is on show. Clem's behind her, holding the hair away from her face so she can vomit freely, but his strides are also down around his knees, and it takes a moment for me to understand that he's actually fucking her from behind while she's spewing up.

Clem smiles weakly up at me. Then Amai turns her head, and when she sees me she grins widely, bits of carrot and spew in her teeth, and she slurs: 'Traaaavissss...'

The way she says it, though, is like when you finally catch up with your mates at the club and everyone's happy to see each other.

'What the fuck?' My voice sounds small, swallowed by the music behind me.

'Stay and watch,' chuckles Amai, as vomit drips off her chin.

I quickly back out and pull the door closed. Manky fucks!

I charge through to find Raven and tell her what's going on, but she's disappeared.

'You alright?' asks Megs.

'Yeah, fine,' I go. 'Where's Raven? We got a situation.'

Megs shrugs. 'What's wrong?'

'I dunno,' is all I've got. 'Everything's a little bit fucked tonight, if I'm honest.'

Why'd they have to root in our bathroom in the middle of a party? Frig's sake. Sabrinha and the riot-grrls file into the kitchen behind me to raid the fridge for beverages.

'That's because Mars entered Aries the other day,' explains Megs, trying to be helpful. 'Everyone's feeling uptight and impulsive.'

'Impulsive is right,' I moan. 'People fucking in the loo, for Christ's sake. It's too much.'

Megs giggles. 'Really? Who?'

'Just mates.'

'Well, that's also because of Mars. Gets people horny, hungry for the chase.'

'Bullshit,' snaps the tall girl with the dreadlocks.

What was her name again? Can't remember.

'What?' goes Megs, a bit stunned.

'All that astrology shit,' says dreadlocks, twisting a top off one of Raven's coolers. 'It's all bullshit.'

'How would you know?' asks Megs defensively.

'The burden of proof isn't on me,' laughs dreadlocks. 'It's on you.'

Sabrinha and the other girl, Maddie, are tearing up an empty beer carton while all this is going on.

'You sound like a Taurus,' retorts Megs with arched eyebrows. 'Or a Capricorn.'

Dreadlocks smacks her own forehead with the palm of her hand. 'Fuck me. That's the single most predictable aspect of your religion.'

'Religion?' Megs pulls a face.

'It's the card-trick you people use to bait the vulnerable,' continues dreadlocks, and I'm disinclined to intervene on poor Megan's behalf because mentally I'm still dealing with the situation I witnessed in the bathroom. 'You lot are always asking what star-sign we are, and whatever it turns out to be is also miraculously exactly you already figured it was, going on about how we exhibit all the classic traits.'

'Whatever,' sniffs Megs, and her and Amara waltz off to the lounge shaking their heads.

'I thought you *were* a Taurus,' says Maddie to dreadlocks, tearing the cardboard so small it looks like confetti.

'I am,' goes dreadlocks. 'But that's beside the point.'

I'm glad this chick didn't stumble upon the séance me and Raven and Xanthe had at Toowong Cemetery that time. Christ knows what she would have had to say about *that*.

'Enjoy the party, girls,' I say, grabbing a beer and heading through to the lounge.

'We're about to,' grins Sabrinha, patting me on the back as I pass.

She was always a sodding weird one, that chick.

Where the hell is Raven?

Chantelle, from upstairs, is out in the main hallway making out with some random chick who must be one of Raven's Uni mates, because I've got no idea who she is. Maybe this other chick is bi and I can interest them in a three-way? I could try both, and pick a side.

'If you girls want some privacy, you can use my room.'

Chantelle casts me a smarmy smile. 'No strings attached, eh, Twix? I'm fine right here, thanks.'

'Shit, you're not into exhibitionism too, are you?'

'The hell you on about, cunt?' growls Chantelle, looking at me the way some people look at disabled people.

'Never mind,' I go. 'Just don't use the loo any time soon.'

The other chick breaks into a giggle. 'We'll just take a dump right here if we need to.'

Fucken classy. It's such a turn off when chicks talk like that.

Malik rushes up to me. 'Oi, Twix, you got a fiver I can borrow?'

'Yeah, maybe. What for?'

'Some girls are selling acid for five bucks,' he grins. 'Can't pass that up.'

I storm through into the flat and find Maddie and Sabrinha handing out bits of ripped up beer carton in exchange for a Stuey Diver. Right now they're about to convince Abi to shell out for one. Worse than that, the victims of this scam are carrying on like pork chops saying that they're hallucinating.

'You're not tripping, you stupid prick,' I say to this young bloke when he tells me there's colours swirling in the air in front of him. Is he for real, or just going along with it because he's too fucking embarrassed to admit he got conned?

I race across the room, trying not to trip on legs and empty bottles, and confront this Maddie chick.

'What the fuck do you think you're doin?'

She snaps her head around, caught by surprise.

'Free market enterprise,' Maddie goes. 'What're you willing to cough up?'

'Stop that,' I say, swiping the cardboard confetti from her hand onto the floor.

'What the fuck?' yells Abi. 'You're fucking wasting them, Twix.'

'It's just cardboard, you stupid–'

I leave the sentence unfinished, but Abi seizes it.

'Stupid what, Twix? Stupid *bitch?*'

'Get the fuck out of my house before I call the cops,' I tell Maddie and Sabrinha.

'Your party's lame, anyway,' says Maddie, before her and Sabrinha walk out.

'Jesus Christ, you have some issues,' says Abi, shaking her head at me.

'YOU'RE NOT FUCKING HIGH,' I yell at a couple of fuckwits acting like they're tripping. 'It's just beer carton with ink on it!'

But there's no reasoning with the idiots. Stuff it, let em all check themselves into Binkinba in the morning and make absolute fools of themselves.

'There goes your grog,' says Abi with a big grin, pointing towards the kitchen.

Maddie, Sabrinha and the girl with the dreadlocks are carrying one of the esky's from the kitchen out the front door.

'Malik!' He looks around at me, and I point at the door. 'The beer!'

He spins around and begins to run through the flat after them but slips on a fucking bottle on the floor and crashes into the wall instead. The useless prick falls down holding his head and moaning out loud while everyone around him cracks up.

Am I the only bastard here making any sense?

Then Clem and Amai sneak past and out the front door, too. Amai glances at me over her shoulder, looking a little more sober and definitely a little bit embarrassed.

'Fuck this, I give up,' I go, throwing my hands up.

My room's blessedly free of revellers. I close the door, but it's not exactly quiet since the party's right on the other side. At least it's dark and I'm alone.

I go to lie on the bed but get a shock by the sight of someone crouching next to it, in the gloom. Immediately I assume a defensive position, ready for an attack, until my eyes adjust and I see it's only Raven sitting on the floor with her knees tucked up and her head in her arms.

'Hey, are you okay?'

She looks up.

'Yeah... just cramps. Alcohol and period pain don't mix well.'

'Fair enough.' I lie on the floor next to her. 'Some party, huh?'

'Sounds like it's going well out there,' she goes, with a lopsided grin. 'Sorry I didn't help out.'

We both start laughing quietly. 'Yeah, it's getting crazy.'

'Better in here, huh?'

I nod.

We both sit in silence, listening to the music and the shenanigans through the thin walls. Something metal glints under my bed. I pull it out with my foot, rolling it into full view: a can of tinned minestrone. I bought that ages ago, and it went missing around about the time Dante bought us heaps of food and we had that picnic at Albert Park. I'd always assumed Dante had eaten it on me.

'Did you put it under my bed?' I ask, but Raven shakes her head.

I peer into the darkness under the bed and can see the shapes of a few more cans under there. Baked beans and stuff.

'What the fuck?'

THE BEAT

Noel dropped me off at the McCafferty's terminal and I was glad to be rid of the cunt. He was a misery-guts all the way down, moaning about practically everything, not just his brother, but that was the subject he tried returning to again and again. I'd given up resisting in the end and just let him drivel on about how Jimmy always got everything he wanted and never appreciated anything, contradicting his earlier assertions that Jimmy was an idiot being conned by white cunts from the city.

The lady behind the counter in the terminal tells me the last bus for Brisbane just left about ten minutes ago. Fuck that prick Noel. He was adamant that the buses run later than this, and had insisted on stopping off along the way for a pint in Crows Nest.

I don't have enough cash for somewhere to stay, and I don't know anyone in Toowoomba, either, as my folks live much further south in Stanthorpe. I'm a bit fucked now, because it gets viciously cold up here at night. Maybe not so much this time of the year, but still. I wander around for a bit and decide I can spare a few dollars for some hot chips, which come wrapped old-fashion style in newspaper. I take them to Queens Park and perch on a park bench, scoffing down the chips, idly reading parts of the paper. There's a small column that actually impresses me: it talks about how one of the first initiatives by Johnny Howard's new Government is to set up a task force to tackle the issue of youth homelessness, called the Youth Homelessness Pilot Programme. Not that that's of any help to me right now, even if I wanted it to be. I'll sleep here tonight. It's a pretty big park, so I should be okay.

I should have got more chips, though, so I could keep some left over to warm my hands with.

There's another section of the park across the road called Park East, with an old oak tree surrounded by hedge. It's unusual and out of place here, I love that it's an oak tree, because my heritage goes way back in England to the Celts and the Druids, so this seems fitting. On the inside of the hedges are a ring of park benches, and it's kinda dark in here, even with the sun out. I decide this is the perfect spot to kip for the night, on account of it's enclosed from the cold and from prying eyes. Safety is paramount when sleeping out, cause there's too many wankers that like to beat the shit out of the homeless knowing they'll get away with it. There's precious few who really give a fuck about some homeless turd copping a few bruises or broken ribs.

I wander around the city some more to kill the boredom, getting ogled and heckled by the locals. Standard fare for here, really, and I glower back at the cunts or tell em I'll be round to their places tonight to burn the house to the ground while they sleep. Standard fare from me, too.

When the sun finally sets and I've had enough of wandering and getting abused, I hoof it back to my hidey spot in the park, looking forward to sleeping in my brilliant new shelter, but even from a distance in this gloom I make out shapes moving amongst the hedges. Some cunt's only gone and snaffled my spot! I shouldn't be surprised, as it's a good one and why wouldn't the local homeless already be onto it. Still, it's a shame.

So I walk back into the main part of the park, thinking about where to camp out next, when I see this sneaky looking fuck acting suspicious around the dunny block, slipping into the ladies' side.

Fuck that, I think I've got myself a rapist on patrol here, waiting for some poor unsuspecting girl to wander in!

I sneak up to the door and listen for sounds coming from within, but it's deathly quiet. Only the sound of my heart beating hard. The cunt is obviously lying in wait, otherwise I'd hear signs of struggle or something. If I charge in now, not only can he say it's all a grave misunderstanding, but the cunt might even overpower me and that's me fucked then. Maybe for real.

So I creep back a distance and sit down beside a bush, using it as a kind of camouflage. From here, I've got a good view of both doors to the dunnies, and I'll see when some woman comes to use it and then I'll spring into action, using her presence to further confound that rapist fuck.

After a while of waiting, though, I start thinking there won't be any women along here at night anyway, at least not on their own. Then a dark shadow slips from the women's door and into the men's. What's this cunt's game?

From the direction of my oak tree I can see another guy ambling this way, taking his time like he was on a Sunday stroll around the park in broad daylight. This guy gets over here and sees me sitting by the bush, so he nods at me. Clearly I'm not as hidden as I thought. Maybe the guy in the dunny block's already seen me, too?

'Hi there,' goes this new guy, testing the waters for something. Maybe he thinks *I'm* a would-be rapist, and he's gonna try and do something about me. I better clear the air before he makes trouble.

'There's some fucker hiding in the men's toilet,' I warn. 'If you need to go, I'll come in with you. We'll sort him out together.'

He thinks about it for a moment, glancing first to the dunnies then back to me.

'Hmm, I'd prefer one on one with you, if that's alright?'

Oh, for fuck's sake! I don't know why I didn't see it sooner. This is a fucking gay beat.

'Nah, mate, you've got the wrong end of the stick,' I say flatly.

'Okay, sure,' he says, and I can hear the smug smile in his voice.

'Nah, seriously, mate,' I growl. 'I'm just looking for somewhere to lay my head.'

He just nods and continues to linger close by.

I'm fully aware that this isn't my turf. I don't know the layout of the park, who these guys are (especially the lurker inside) or whether I'm putting out the wrong signals by staying here. So I decide to get a move on.

Once I'm on my feet I can see from this new vantage that there's about a dozen bachelors hanging about. The headlights from the cars down on the Margaret Street roundabout pick them out easily.

'Catch you cunts later,' I quip to the smug bastard, and hoof it across the park to the road.

The chill night air has finally fallen, damp as fuck. I can't sleep out anywhere open cause I'll catch a fucking cold. As I'm trudging up the street trying to work out a solution, I pass a modest size motor inn. It looks like something from an old American movie, but it's right here in the middle of suburban T-bar, as some of the more dipshit locals like to call Toowoomba.

Sneaking around back I find a tiny window left ajar, clearly a dunny window. They don't have the crime problem yet up here that Brisbane has, thankfully, so they're less prepared for a sneaky fuck like me. I grab an aluminium bin and prop it under the window, hoisting myself inside. I scrape my elbows and knees doing it, but it's worth it cause instantly I'm feeling warmer now the chill night air is off me. Turns out the room's empty, so I deserve a pat on the back. I could have been sleeping in that freezing park on a metal park-bench, but thanks to the guys creeping around the dark I'm tucked down for the night in a big bed with pillows and blankets. The fucking works!

As soon as the sun is up, I flip back the blankets and peer through the curtains. The cars parked outside the other rooms have a layer of frost on their windshields, and not a soul is stirring. I crack open the door and gingerly slip outside, briskly walking to the street and away. Easy fuckin peasy.

NICOLA

The bus ticket back to Brisbane turned out not be as expensive as I was dreading, and that meant I was going to have a little money for food when I got back. Always a bonus.

This bus station is tiny as fuck, and just about everyone here is either a local or someone from along the way to Brisbane, hick towns like Gatton and Marburg. There's way too many oversized cowboy hats and R.M. Williams boots for my liking, but then like an angel she's suddenly there: an olive-skinned girl with dark eyes and a broad face, wearing a long tattered negligee as a dress and an equally tattered leopard-spot faux-fur jacket. Her old Docs have no shoelaces. What really appeals to me is her badly dyed orange hair with the two inch dark regrowth, pulled into six little pigtails across the top of her head in rows of three.

Instantly that song from the Presidents of the United States of America pops into my head, the one about Carla the stripper. But not because I think this girl's a stripper; far from it, I think she's a fucking angel!

This goofy looking guy with pronounced front teeth and a scruffy blonde mohawk yells to her from the vending machine: 'Oi, Nicola! Coke or Fanta?'

The girl, Nicola, screws her face up, shaking her head.

Then another girl, in a slip of a black dress that covers her ankles but barely sits on her shoulders, emerges from the dunnies behind the Coke machine. A floppy black felt hat droops down the sides of her head, and coming from under it is her long, straight black hair. She looks like a cartoon witch.

When I glance back at Nicola she's looking straight at me with the cutest little smile. It kinda curls her top lip up until her teeth show. On anyone else it'd probably look like a sneer, but it's strangely fetching on this girl.

Jesus Christ, *fetching?* I fall hard and fast like a fucking idiot, always. But the attraction between Nicola and I is obvious straight away, watching each other across the small terminus and exchanging bashful smiles when we board.

Her friend Darcey, the witch girl, chooses a seat close to mine and strikes up a conversation about where I'm headed. The answer is all the way to Brisbane, of course. It'd be hard to imagine a swampie with lapel badges and straggly pink pigtails getting off anywhere else along the way.

'Are you from West End?' she asks.

I confess I'm transient, currently sleeping in King George Square or the Botanical Gardens when I'm not crashing at friends' places.

They tell me about Tim's stay at the Toowoomba lock-up, which is why they're up. He'd been busted driving a stolen car with some local yahoos up this way, although technically he was only the passenger.

The cops still banged him up in the watch-house anyway, but fortunately for him they didn't charge, focusing only on his shit for brains friend who stole the car, who remains in the lock-up. Nicola and Darcey came all the way up from Brisbane to get him, the lucky fuck.

'What was it like in there?' I ask him.

'A nightmare at first, coz of my hangover,' he goes, cracking open his Fanta. 'But when I got over that it wasn't too bad. It was a bit of a bummer to leave, actually.'

Darcey slaps his chest. 'Don't say that,' she chides. 'Me and Nik travelled two hours by fucking bus to come and get you, and turns out you're having a great time?' I notice her thin, pale arms are scored over and over again by nubby scars. They're paper-thin, unlike some of the fat, pinkish ones on my arms, but she makes up for it numbers. There must be a hundred of the little white bastards along her forearms. They stand out because of her black dress.

Tim tells us about how he made friends in there with two guys, one of which was a small Asian guy who hated Asians and was actually in there for beating the shit out of one at one of those shitholes Toowoomba calls a nightclub. He and Darcey get into a debate about if it's okay to be racist against something that you already represent, like can a punk hate punk, which just sounds stupid. It gives me and Nicola a chance to talk alone. She moves over into the seat next to me.

'I like your pigtails,' I tell her lamely, because I'm feeling a bit shy and can't think of anything else to say. In truth, it's something I really want to say, anyway.

She laughs and her brown eyes crinkle up and sparkle from between her lashes. 'Thanks. I like yours, too.'

There's a little spark between us but the small-talk is awkward as fuck, so I'm grateful when Darcey butts in and commandeers Nicola's attention.

I content myself with staring out the window at the passing countryside, counting the towns down to Brisbane, but the whole time I'm thinking about Nicola and her radiant smile and sparkling eyes, and those little orange pigtails.

It's a wonderful and refreshing feeling to be struck mute by this girl. I spend so much time feeling cynical and snide toward the world and along comes this punk angel and it's like I'm fifteen again.

Oddly enough, we don't exchange details when we arrive in Brisbane, not that I have much to exchange. We part ways at the Transit Centre and I head into King George Square with everything I own stuffed in my backpack.

I have a love-hate relationship with the city. If I'm in it for too long, I feel a pressure inside my head and start getting irritable. If I get up into the countryside for a bit, staying with friends or my folks, then I unwind and become sort of zen like, I suppose. Megs reckons whenever I come back, I seem at peace. Makes sense, because within a couple of weeks of being back here, I'm agitated again and feeling a hatred towards people in general. But I can't stay for long out in the countryside, either, because the exact same thing happens to me there! Mum reckons whenever I return home I've got this restless energy about me, sorta can't sit still for one moment. But after a week or so I become languid, and then I start getting snappy with her and Dad. I don't mean to, but I've always been that way with my folks. I guess they're too familiar, or just forgive me easily. Either way, it seems I'm not content to be in either place for too long.

Feeling the vibe of the city again, I set out for Elizabeth Arcade, to a this little bookstore called Zephyrs. It's an overcrowded, dusty shop brimming at the seams with books, and there's a tiny mezzanine that can only be reached by an impossibly narrow, spiralling stairwell. Its so pokey in here that when some cunt needs to get past you gotta flatten yourself against the shelf.

It's all really wonderful actually.

I spy a thick omnibus edition of Lewis Carroll's works so I snatch it from the shelf, holding it just inside my coat and leaving the store in such a way that it's mostly hidden from the old guy at his tiny cash register.

I head into the Valley, walking via the Eagle Street Pier to take in the river on my way. I stop a few times to rifle through the pages of my new book, dwelling on the magnificent old etchings of the Turtle Dove and The Mad Hatter. Good stuff.

The Valley is a bit of a shit-hole, full of drunks and addicts and cunts who want to get in your face for no reason. But otherwise I like it. It's a hodge-podge place that works of its own accord, and has its own rules, a sort of law-of-the-jungle mentality. It's easy to step out of place here and find yourself in an altercation with somebody. But once you've found the rhythm of it, the Valley can feel like a haven from the stifling mundanity of the suburbs.

There's an Italian cafe in the mall, next to the newsagents, and the plates haven't been cleared. I spy some leftovers, bit of spaghetti and some garlic bread, so plonk myself down for some free grub. The pasta is lukewarm at best, but I doubt it'll give me food poisoning, so I hoe into it. It's good to have something in my belly. I hadn't realised how hungry I was.

As luck would have it, Nicola and the other two happen past! They see me and take a seat across from me. Darcey and Tim go inside and order a pasta dish to share between them, leaving me and Nicola alone.

'What's your book?' she asks, grinning from ear to ear.

I hold it up, feeling the same bashfulness on the bus. I fucking love this feeling. Whenever we make eye-contact, I understand what people mean by when they say they could melt from someone's eyes. There's a warmth and cheek to Nicola's that I find too endearing.

'*The Collected Works of Lewis Carroll*,' she reads aloud. 'Like *Alice in Wonderland?*'

'The very one.'

After we've all eaten, Darcey and Tim head home to West End, but

Nicola opts to hang out with me. We head into the city, aimlessly wandering around. When it gets dark, we go over to the Riverstage in the Botanical Gardens and lie down on the grassy hill, surrounded by the trees and the stars overhead. It's quite beautiful.

Nicola snuggles close to me, and we rub our noses together, which then leads to that heart-stopping moment in every courtship: the first kiss. We're tentative at first, almost shying from the contact, but Nicola leans in more and takes the lead. It's amazing, under the stars, making out. When we're done we're both content to lay hugging each other and watching the stars.

What I've had going with Erina's been fun, but this is far more fulfilling. I feel elated. I feel like a small void inside me is being filled. I could get addicted to this sensation.

For some reason, I start telling her about Alan and the baby and the funeral I went to.

'It was weird seeing him there, with his family in his hometown and his baby gone. I mean, it all seems out of context. It's not how I know Alan. He's a punk who dances like a crazy rooster and gets into fights with skinheads and is always drunk or on his way to it. And suddenly there he is, a grieving father with a whole slew of relatives in what felt like a completely different world.'

She seems touched by my concern for my friend, although I don't interpret my babbling as concern. I feel alienated, rather. I'm not sure how to emotionally connect to Alan's predicament.

Nicola leans across me, kissing me tenderly again. I'm not sure if I should try for something more. I can't read her at all. Thing is, I'm happy to keep it at this for now.

After a while I'm feeling knackered and tell Nicola I'm heading off into a garden to sleep, and she follows me. I was expecting her to wish me well and head for home instead, so the prospect of being with her all night fills me with such contentment as I've not felt in a long while.

My favourite spot in the gardens is under inside the bamboo thicket near the front gate. Bamboo grows outwards, in a ring, so after it's been there for yonks it forms into a kind of circular fence that's perfect for hiding inside. The other thing is that it only drops soft leaves, so the ground's soft and spongy. The birds and bats hate sitting in the branches above, so there's no chance of the bastards shitting on me while I'm asleep. And the street-cleaning trucks always come by about five in the morning and make such a fucking racket that I've got no choice to get up before the city has a chance to.

The perfect spot, all in all.

I pull the Lewis Carroll book out of my backpack and slide it under Nicola's head like a makeshift pillow. I kiss her forehead.

'One time,' I murmur in the darkness, 'I was in here and woke up because a baby possum climbed on top of me, the cheeky fucker. You alright? I went, and it looked at me then ran off.'

Nicola's quiet, and when I hold my breath I can just make out her softly snoring. I concentrate on the gloom in front of me and can just make out her face, her eyes closed and mouth slightly open. She looks so peaceful.

The whine of mozzies get closer, the fucking things. It's just that time of the year for them, and the main pond is close by so they're probably breeding in there. They buzz closer, so I wave my hand around in the air above Nicola until the little bastards fuck off. It soon becomes a regular routine, however, as they keep returning, but I keep it up as long as I until I finally succumb to sleep.

As usual, the street-cleaning trucks trundle up Alice Street dead on five o'clock, waking us up. The sky barely begun to lighten. Best time of the day, this.

There's a couple of mozzie bites on me but all in all I've survived the night.

'Yeah, me too,' smiles Nicola in such a delightfully sleepy way that it makes me go delirious.

The rest of the day is spent wandering around the city, stealing breakfast leftovers from the plates at a cafe under the Wintergarden where fake plants poke out of the walls. We take turns suggesting shit to do, in that way that couples are doomed to repeat until they've exhausted themselves to death from constantly asking 'What do *you* want to eat?' or replying 'I'm up for whatever *you* feel like.'

At lunchtime we head to Topps in the Myer Centre and throw the Maltesers that I snaffled from a newsagents at the cunts riding the dragon rollercoaster, trying to hit them in the head. We come across the shoeshine guy in the cap and dirty white sneakers and harass cunts to get their boots polished, making sure they tip him big, while we dip our feet in the fountain on the stairs of King George Square. Some of the street kids have got hold of a bottle of washing detergent and tipped it in and there's bubbles foaming up above our heads. The shoe shine guy thinks it's a fucking riot and nearly falls over from laughing so hard.

We're ready to call it a day and walk over to West End to Nicola's flat when I spy that cunt Matty Boy, or Malik as he prefers, sitting in the middle of the Mall, hunched over his art book and scribbling away. He keeps glancing around at this big bunch of Greek bastards who're yelling down the phone at someone. Or more precisely, at a petite lil girlie with them, a bit fuckin young really but not a bad looker, and here's Matty already with a girlfriend and all back at the Palace.

I *tsk* loudly, but the fucker keeps his nose in his book, his hand darting back and forth across the paper, leaving behind a series of disjointed lines that begin to form a face. 'Wandering eye,' I admonish the cunt, finally getting his attention.

'Oi, Dante,' he says suddenly, a bit too anxiously which betrays him. As if I could give a flying fuck that he was checking some girl out. He notices Nicola but quickly averts his eyes back to me. 'How's tricks?'

'Tricks are fine,' I go. 'Whatcha doodling there?'

'Just stuff, random people,' he goes. 'Do it sometimes after the classes.'

That's right, I forgot. He's studying computer technology or something here in the city at one of those private institutions that're popping up all over the place now that businesses and nerds are starting to get the internet. I don't fucking get it myself. What's wrong with pen and paper, calculators and all that? What good's a computer in a blackout? Besides which, they're a corruptible influence on the arts. Last year on my film course they tried to teach us how to edit our raw footage on a fucking computer! I mean, it was kinda interesting, I suppose, from a technological viewpoint, but it had no heart and soul, not like yelling at the old analogue machines and having to coax the buttons to make the cut because the gold filaments underneath had been flattened from fucking years' of use and abuse. I just fucking fail to grasp the attraction to computers.

We get into an argument about politics, with me basically trying to tell Matty that trying to study and get a good job is a waste of fucking time because this new government's already set to shaft our entire fucking generation. But do you think the cunt is convinced? Nah, he's been sold too much on the capitalist's dream, working his arse off to acquire more debt and become a slave to society. Fuck that for a joke.

It's pointless arguing with him about it, especially since he's now got a face on him like he's the cunt that's been made to eat the soggy Sao, so Nicola and I push on, grabbing a bus instead of walking all the rest of the way.

The next couple of days are spent at her Dornoch Terrace flat at the back of West End, technically Hill End. It's a one-bedroom thing with peeling paint in a large subdivided house, and Nicola's got an old single mattress plonked on the floor of the loungeroom, if you could call it that. The kitchen is a travesty, so I avoid going in there altogether.

Because there's no electricity, the shower's cold water only, and there's no soap, so I wash as vigorously as possible to both try and get clean and to stay warm. It might be March weather but it's still cold enough at night that without hot water I'm shivering in the shower.

When it gets dark, we all lay around talking shit. At one point I notice that Nicola's boob's fallen out of her tank-top when she's lying down, but she hasn't noticed cause she's yammering away about the time she got it on with this old guy who claimed to be one of the replacement drummers for The Gun Club when they toured Australia in the 80s. I know I should pull her top up, especially before Tim notices, but some perverse part of me holds back. I'm not sure why, though, and can only conclude that I don't want Nicola to think I'm being possessive by trying to protect her dignity or some such shit. Basically, I think I don't know this girl at all.

Finally it's so dark we're just voice in the gloom,. After a while even those die down until it's just silence, and I'm left wondering if everyone else has fallen asleep or whether they've simply become ruminative.

In the morning we head over to Woolloongabba on the hail n ride because the girls want to grab a stash of drugs from this GP called Doctor Death, who apparently gives you whatever you want, no questions asked. Not to be confused with the new Griffith MP Kevin Rudd, who shared the same nickname back when he was running the cabinet office for Goss.

Nicola's elected to go in and get their order from Doctor Death. This isn't really my cup of tea, so I leave em to it and head down the street, mostly cause I don't want to hang around out front with Tim. He's acting pissy with me, and Nicola told me on the bus over that last night Tim wanted a threesome between her and Darcey, despite my fucking presence in the flat. The fucking nerve. Fuck that cunt.

So I walk up the street and duck into the Railway Hotel to see if Maddie or anyone else is in. They're not, and the place is fairly deserted but for a few of the locals who glance at me scornfully, so I head back out into the sunshine and wait.

Nicola should be out from the Doc's soon but I need a bit of a break from them all, as I've been hanging around them twenty-four seven for the last three days. I might head back to her place and forgo domesticity for a few nights of roughing it. Nicola's probably going to be too wasted on whatever cocktail of pills she procures to even care if I'm there or not.

Nicola and the other two are coming towards me, absorbed in rummaging through the pharmacy bag she's holding. I fall into step with them but they barely notice. The drugs hold sway now. We get down near the Mater for the bus, getting off near the Museum so we can jump on the hail and ride back up to Dornoch Terrace. It's good to finally plonk down on Nicola's mattress after all that transit, but I'm feeling a twinge of jealousy that I'm the odd one out here and that Tim is a card-carrying member of this pill-popping party. As a result he's probably got one foot in the door already, *vis-à-vis* his *ménage à trois* fantasy.

I sniff my armpit, and it's so rank I know I'm going to need a proper shower and get these clothes washed too. My skin feels oily and gross. I weigh up the possibility of grabbing some soap from Jack the Slasher's in West End – inside the old Tristram factory which is incidentally the saddest little shopping complex I've ever been in – and taking a shower at the toilet block by the lagoon in South Bank. I can stop by the laundromat on Boundary Street on the way and get a change of clothes done there. The thought of freshly washed clothes and clean skin starts playing on my mind like a lurid vision until I'm almost desperate for it. Scrubbing myself raw again in Nicola and Darcey's cold shower holds no appeal.

I say cheerio, promising Nicola I'll be back. She actually looks sad to see me going, but I'm sure that's a short-lived emotion. Darcey tumbles the drug cache out onto Nicola's mattress and Tim's already popping a xanax from a blister pack as I'm pulling the front door closed behind me.

MALIK'S A BIT SKETCHY

I like to spend about an hour hanging out in the mall after class before heading home. Some days, like today, I pull out my sketch book and just doodle stuff, trying to unscramble my brain after a day of learning coding and programming. Me and Angele decided we'd get proactive about getting off the dole before it's too late. Can't wait around forever to win the Lotto.

Living at the Prozac Palace has been alright, but it's not forever, you know? In truth, the Prozac is a dump that should be condemned. If the council only knew there were people living in closets in the stairwells they'd be all over it like a rash. One of the flats even used to have no door, because they burnt it one Winter. Angele told me how she once saw the scummers inside rooting on the floor in full view of the open doorway. They're just dogs. No way for my girl to have to live. But we need money to move on, and during the recent Federal election the coalition (Liberal and National parties united) pledged to slash six billion dollars for welfare, tightening up the entire unemployment sector like they're fixing a loose bowel. Further reason to think about getting off the dole.

On top of that, there's been a six percent drop in job adverts and on the news one of the big banks was saying that there'd be no job growth until the middle of the year. Normally such figures would mean squat to me, but like Angele pointed out, if it worsens and we wanna do something about our futures later on, it'll just be harder to achieve. To which end, I've signed onto an IT course because I know a lil bit about computers, so its right up my alley.

Still, it's been tough going, especially because I'm not used to being classroom environment for six hours straight, learning the arithmetic's and the engineering computations of Fortran 90. Going straight into that from being able to do my own thing at home has been exhausting, so sketching freestyle is a good way to unwind, you know?

The college is in the building next to the Record Exchange, which is where I go on my lunch breaks and sift through all the records and CDs. Just down the hall from the college, on the same floor, is the New Age bookstore where I got Twix his copy of the Necronomicon. I think he believes he can actually use it to summon demons, too, the dumb scalliwag.

It's not really a college in the traditional sense, but; just a coupla rooms with big whiteboards and computer monitors on every desk. We keep the towers down under the desks so there's more room for our paperwork. I would've never guessed just how much paperwork would be involved in a computer course!

There's a woggy guy spitting the dummy something fierce at a phonebooth behind me, surrounded by a group of men all built the same as him: robust, thick necked, big bellied. They're probably

Greek, about a half dozen of them, looking seriously pissed off.

'No, no, you tell him from me!' old mate yells, going rank into the receiver while one his mates, much shorter than him, jostles to get up to the mouthpiece and shout something himself. He keeps getting pushed back by the others, but, who hold fingers in front of their lips to shush him.

Then I realise that holding onto woggy guy's arm is a teenage girl, slim with mousey-brown hair, looking at me with an amused smile on her face. If I'm not mistaken, she's flirting with me, the little minx. Not frigid at all, this one. Bit young, more Twix's type. Still, can't hurt to have a lil flirt back, boost the ego, you know?.

'NO, YOU FUCKEN TELL HIM!' screams her father into the phone. 'TELL HIM, I FUCKEN KILL HIM!'

There's nods of approval at this from the other men, and shoppers and tourists passing by divert their courses to be as far from the group as possible. The girl continues to makes eyes at me, smiling in what's probably meant to be seductive. Near enough for me for all the effect it's having!

I'm literally flirting with danger here.

I get back to my sketching, imagining if Angele caught me flirting with the minx she'd kick my arse. It's one thing to smack a bottom or whip someone at a fetish club, entirely another to flirt with teenage girls in the middle of the city!

'Tut tut,' someone says loudly nearby, 'wandering eye!'

I snap my head up so fast I nearly lose it. Dante, the motherfucker, is standing there smirking at me, glancing sidelong at the girl and the gang of wogs going rank.

Last time I saw him he'd been perched bird-like on the edge of the gutter outside the Underworld Realm arcade, talking to the road as far as I could tell. He'd been having a full-on conversation with it, too, or whatever he was imagining was in the gutter. I don't know, but when I'd tried getting his attention it took him a moment to snap out of it. He'd looked up at me with sheer hatred, but once he'd realised it was only me he came good, you know? He's a fucking head-case and a half, no two ways about it. Simple.

Beside him's a grotty punk dog, hair as orange as Ginger Meggs. Both barefoot, carrying their boots by the laces, with sticks and leaves in their hair like they've been sleeping in our public parks, which knowing Dante they probably have been. Probably at it like root-rats, too. Fuck, imagine catching an eyeful of that on your morning walk?

I don't get why he doesn't flat with someone. It's not that fucking expensive to share and try and look a bit more presentable. I just see this thing he does, living like one of the street scum, as having a really fucked up perspective or attitude to life, you know? He's not even trying to be a better person. Right now he's probably up to some scam where he's gonna fleece this punk chick, the thieving bastard, although it's hard to imagine she's got anything worth nicking.

I'm caught off-guard, like I'm being cross examined here. 'How's tricks?' I go.

He asks what I'm up to so I explain how I'm unwinding after class by doing some traditional style art, and this sets us up on a fucking debate about robots and the future of all things, which is typical of trying to have a simple conversation with Dante. He's either snide and cynical, or he's sympathetic. I can't keep up with his inconsistency! Currently he's being sympathetic.

'Don't worry too much about a degree, Matty,' he says, addressing me by my real name since he almost never calls me Malik. 'Just go and have fun with it. It's only a matter of time before the whole system collapses on itself and we're back to our primal roots.'

He puffs his chest up, clearly proud to be the one of us dispensing advice, such as it is. Bit hard to take someone serious when they walk around the city with no shoes on, especially because if I didn't know any better I'd swear he was blazed. It's stoner talk, but he's stone cold sober. Dante's not into drugs, Twix reckons.

Ginger Meggs is staring at the Leviathan Cross tattoo on my arm, so I discreetly pull my sleeve down to cover it up. I'm not actually into all that Satan shit, but my brother Marty is and I got a matching one with him back when I was still an impressionable teenager who thought he was cool. Turns out he's not. Whenever anyone asks about the tattoo nowadays, I just say it's a symbol off *The X-Files*.

'The future will be a game of wits where we try and outsmart each other for food and other resources,' Dante continues lecturing me, 'and computer degrees will mean fuck all if those of us with the street smarts get the upper hand all the time. But that's way down the track, so chin up.'

Only Dante could see such a prospect as a positive outcome. This isn't the first time I've heard him waffle on about his visions of an apocalyptic future. What he doesn't realise is that his version of the future isn't coming and mine's already here: dole bludgers like him already suck the resources from those who work hard for a living, and while I currently engage in a similar fashion via my Austudy, once I've got my degree then the plan is to sit high and pretty where the likes of him will be wanting handouts from me.

It's one thing to say that, but it's another thing to try and imagine that as a reality, you know? I've still got another twelve months of study before I graduate mid-next year, and maybe by then it'll be too late. Who knows, I might just end up an overqualified bum watching all his dreams wash away down the drain. Maybe I'm doomed to spend forever in the Prozac Palace, growing fat and lazy with all the other losers?

The woggy guy at the phonebooth finally relinquishes the receiver to one of his entourage, who currently negotiates in a much calmer way, using precise hand-gestures that make it look like he's karate-chopping someone. The minx's got her back to me. It's seems more and more that these thugs are the ones that do well in life, with their gold chains and big fancy homes in the housing estates. They've probably got down payments on small mansion-sized places out at that new one, Forest Lake. They're already putting bricks and mortar distance between themselves and the likes of me and Angele.

'Maybe you're right,' I shrug, not entirely convinced Dante is but willing to play the devil's advocate. 'Maybe I've got buckley's chance of getting something out of this course, what with the recession and all.'

'Backpedal there,' Dante says, making a motion like his hands are on the pedals of a bike. 'I didn't say *don't* do the course. There'll still be jobs. I've heard that's not too bad if you're looking for casual stuff. The problem is that small businesses are stuck in their ruts and acting like we're *still* in a recession.'

'But we are,' I point out.

He shakes his head. 'Change of government means a change in everything. I'm no fan of John Howard, don't get me wrong, but that Beazely fucked his chances to contain the national budget and now Howard's gonna have to prove himself after a decade of Labour in the driving seat. That means the cunts are gonna shake things up, for better or worse, but straight off the bat lil Johnnie needs to be seen doing it for the better, at least. Short term that's great news, and we live in the short term, do we not?'

'And after that?'

Dante shrugs. 'We try our best to cope with it. That's the lay of the land. You do your course, get your degree, and join the bread queues.'

Ridiculous.

I guess that's how it is when you're one of the street scummers, only dealing with things when they pop up, even though I see him staying over lots at Twix's flat. So much for him dealing with it, huh? But it's not how Angele are gonna live much longer. When we've got degrees and good paying jobs, we'll be fucking outta there, out of the Palace and into a decent flat. That's a start at least, you know? It's not a mansion at Forest Lake but at least it's a step up. Maybe one day we'll even get to go on holidays to London, experience where goth and punk started.

'Don't look stressed out by it, Matty,' says Dante.

'I'm not.'

'Thing is, right, they'll axe funding left, right and centre, fuck the entire system, then they'll reintroduce a whole new set of fucking programs and all sorts of shit to accommodate the shortfall in jobs growth. That'll mean blowing out parts of their budget again, for which of course they'll be heavily criticised and for which they'll promise to axe again come the next election. It's a popular cycle with those toffs in parliament.'

Fair play to him, but, because for a homeless bastard, Dante sure knows a lot about politics. I suppose someone who uses newspapers for a blanket would be. Twix reckons he's just well read, that he hangs out at the State Library a lot. I wonder if that's true for a lot of street scum?

But then again I'm not even sure that Dante even knows what he's talking about, so I nod anyway just to keep him happy. The last thing I need after hours of staring at a computer screen trying to decipher the specifications of IETF's (or rather, the HTML Working Group's) HTML 2.0 publication is to start debating politics, and with the likes of Dante of all people. Don't get me wrong, I don't mind the guy, but fuck man; he's a bit much sometimes.

Like, for example, how he's always going on about the end of the world, his apocalyptic future. As in, the world's *actually* ending soon. There was a discussion in class this morning about how there's a fear going around the IT community that come the New Year in four years' time computers are going to set themselves to the date of 1900 instead of 2000, and the resulting glitch could entirely wreck pensions and insurance policies and all sorts of stuff. Our tutor, Mark, reckons it could cost governments and the global IT industry over seven billion dollars to prepare for! Dante would go ridiculous mental for that kind of scenario.

His girlfriend or whatever she is looks bored by all this talk, or wasted, and complains about the heat. Dante waves his hand in front of his face as if he can feel it, but the thing is we're in the middle of a fucking cold spell at the moment. Ridiculous. It's not nearly as hot as it was in February or as a humid as it was in January!

They choof off up the Mall, boots swinging from their fingers and their soles slapping on the concrete. Fucking derros.

Man, after that painful conversation I definitely need to get into this sketching and clear the ol head. But I've no sooner started than a shadow blocks the sun and I glance up to see the angry woggy man from the phone-booth looming over me with his meaty arms crossed and a fucking foul expression on his face.

Yea, though I walk through the valley of the shadow of death...

Fuck, but he looks angry as! Around him are his mates, scowling at me and my sketchbook, and the girl behind them, peeking around with a mischievous smile.

The fucking minx. I bet she ratted me out.

'You draw?' her father says. Sounds like a statement rather than a question, but.

'Yes.'

Without asking, he grabs my sketchbook and flicks through some pages, mostly thumbnail sketches of random people on the streets or crappy attempts at drawing Gillian Anderson. He drops it back into my hands and goes: 'Draw me.'

Shit.

'Sorry?'

'Draw me,' he repeats, pointing at the blank page he's flipped over for me. The other men continue to scowl at me.

'I can't really,' I start. 'I mean, I don't really...'

They all continue to stare, and from the corner of my eye I can see the girl smiling at me still. I'm doing my fucking best not to make eye contact with her, you know? Who the hell knows what this guy'd do if he thought I was making eyes as his precious lil daughter?

'You do others,' old mate states, 'you do *me*.'

I want to make a joke at this point but besides being inappropriate he'd probably kick seven shades of shit out of me for it. I continue to defy him as politely as I can, making weak excuses for why I can't do it but he continues to demand that I do it until finally I just cave and do the fucking thing.

Thing is, I don't do these things on demand. It's not like I can draw everyone.

The worst bit is, is that because it's a portrait, I have to keep glancing up at him to get his details right, you know? He's got a characterised face, thank fuck, which would be easy to draw, but it'd also look quite comical and therefore farcical. Again, I can't see that ending well, either. Suddenly being stuck in a room for six hours doing a relentless amount of coding doesn't seem like such a bad way to pass the time.

I stall for as long as I can, and because it's quite the sight – the gorillas in the mist lording it over this industrial kid – there's a crowd gathered to watch. This is the last thing I need! It's turning into a fucking performance piece... I'll be lucky if the Council don't fine me for not having a busking permit!

The woggy bloke clears his throat, as if to give me the bum's rush.

Fuck it, it's gone on long enough. They're not going to get bored and wander away, so I've got no choice but to finally announce that it's finished. Besides, the portrait is at that point where if I add any more details it'll be lost. Looking at the picture I realise that all my attempts to avoid doing a caricature have failed: I've unwittingly lampooned the bloke.

'It's finished.'

He yanks the sketchbook up close to his face, scowling. The others crane their fat necks for a squiz. Only the girl doesn't bother to check it; she's ducked under her father's arm, looking at me approvingly, all the better, I bet, to get a decent view of the pummelling that is about to follow.

'YES!' yells the fat bastard.

I nearly jump out of my fucking skin!

He grins broadly at his entourage who're all nodding their heads and stepping forward to slap me on the back. It still takes a sec for me to register that they're pleased with the drawing. The crowd around us breaks into applause, like I've done a trick.

What a fucking relief.

I'm intentionally avoiding eye contact with that lil minx, hoping everyone will fuck right off now, including the onlookers.

'Here,' the woggy guy goes, digging a fiver from his wallet and thrusting at me.

'Oh no, I couldn't,' I say, feebly waving it away.

Now the motherfucker *does* look legitimately rank. Ridiculous!

'Take it,' he growls, so I oblige by snatching it from his meaty fingers and stuffing it into the pocket of my jeans.

He holds the paper up to admire it again, a stupid smile on his fat head, and they all amble away. The girl trails behind, smiling at me meaningfully. May she have a fruitful fucking life, geezus.

Some of the audience have lingered, as if in expectation of more.

'Sorry, show's over,' I announce, my head down so I don't have to look at anyone anymore. I cram my sketchbook into my backpack, aware that the corners are being dog-earred by my carelessness but really not giving a fuck at this stage. I just need to get out of here.

Then two cute Japanese girls slide onto the bench next to me, close enough to reach out with a soft, dainty hand and tap me on the arm.

'Please, you do us,' the girl says softly, her accent almost mangling her English.

An offer too good to refuse, but if only I could act on my deliberate misinterpretation. Would Angele understand, given she's whipped enough arses at the clubs in her time? Like fuck she would. She'd cut my dick off while I was sleeping.

But how can I say no to those big black eyes?

Fuck it, I cave and pull the sketchbook back out. But after these two, no more. In fact, after these two I might have to detour via the Valley for the dollar peep-shows, you know?

A crowd starts gathering around again as my pen-hand deftly gets to work. Maybe I'll raise enough cash to buy Twix some new paint for his coffin-shaped bookcase? The poor bastard totally flipped out the other morning when he found me crashed out in it after some others at the party had buried it down the side of the Prozac as a joke. I don't know how I got in there but there was buckley's chance that I'd dug a hole and dragged his bookshelf around the side of the building in the state I was in. At least whoever did it had the sense to respectfully pile his books and shelves in his loungeroom. I'd woken up with Lunar burying a shit on me followed by Twix shouting at me, the hangover amplifying his tirade about how the rocks and dirt had scratched the paintwork. Even though I said I didn't do it, I was the one found in it so he's been holding me responsible ever since.

Can't blame the guy, but.

It's that fucking building and the people in it, you know? They're a shit influence.

'Nice work,' says this guy in a No Fear shirt and colourful happy pants, giving me the thumbs up. 'I'm next in line.'

MCKAY PART 2

Doctor McKay (I just can't bring myself to call him Gary) greets me in his usual style: 'How is the Divine Comedy of Dante, lately?'

It's tiresome but it's also routine. It's a little joke that's no longer funny, and in its own not-funny way it's the perfect opening for our sessions. Tied up in the quip is the flair for the dramatic and the literary that are both me to a T, but it also pinpoints precisely how I have viewed my life: as a divine comedy, because not only do I think that my adventures in the world are funny, but that they are providential. That is not to say I'm especially religious, despite my time in a crazy cult when I was younger, but I *am* inclined to think I'm a child of the universe, a kind of stray human that will be catered to when and if it is needed in order that I may endure my trials long enough to present my life as a tragic farce for the universe's own amusement.

McKay thinks that's horseshit, but he did get a good laugh out of it when I first told him; which pretty much validates my avowal.

I begin our session by revealing how I've met a girl called Nicola and that I might be in love.

'But I dunno, I think maybe it's not going to work out,' I confess.

'Why would you say that?'

I'm thinking about how that cunt Tim sees me as a roadblock to his threesome with Nicola and Darcey, and how I'm sort of getting the cold shoulder from him as a result. But I'll be fucked if I'm bringing that up with McKay.

'Well, I like her a lot, obviously,' I say, 'but I don't think she'll make the effort in the long run.'

'Are you sure you're talking about her, and not yourself?'

I screw my nose up. 'I'm pretty sure I'm talking about her.'

McKay's in one of those moods today where he doesn't want to fuck around. Normally he lets me steer the course of the discussion because he knows I can get a bit temperamental and clam up, but occasionally he likes to take the reins and get some actual progress happening.

'You fear commitment,' he assesses.

'That's a bit suss,' I counter. 'I come here once a month, for a start. Even without a home to live in. That sounds pretty committed to me.'

He lets that one slide, because we both know full well that I've missed a few appointments, and despite the sign above reception that says otherwise I haven't been charged a fee for my lapses.

'As much as we share experiences or insights here in this room, you're not invested in me emotionally,' he says. 'But neither do you go to your friend's' weddings, or their engagements. Or see the ones anymore who've had babies. They're all starting to settle down and you're still drifting.'

I roll my eyes derisively. What's all that got to do with anything?

'Well, there was the funeral for Alan's baby,' I counter.

He nods but smacks his lips like he doesn't fully agree.

'I think with death you're different. It's the close of the emotional investment, not its start. You can finally wash your hands of it.'

'But I'm still emotionally invested,' I argue. 'Alan and Suzie and their families are still grieving. I faced all that.'

'How long did you stay up there with them?'

'You *know* I left straight after the funeral,' I say sourly. 'But that's not the point.'

'Isn't it?'

He looks smug. Point-scoring. He's trying to challenge me to look harder at myself, but sometimes he takes to the task with a proverbial crowbar. I confronted him about it once, as diplomatically as I could, and he told me that it was my *language*, that I was always engaging with the world head-on, and that it's the only way I'll listen.

I ruminated on that over and over for a couple of weeks and finally concluded that it was a fair assessment.

Still, the self-indulgent smile is uncalled for. So I point that little detail out to him.

'You're distracting from the issue again,' he parries. 'I only smiled because I knew you'd come up with something to avoid talking about your fear of commitment. And you did,' he laughs. 'You used my smile.'

'It was more a smirk, I'd say.'

'You're still doing it, Dante,' he says, raising his eyebrows.

He looks tired, like his eyes are too small and he's straining to keep them open. I often reflect on how exhausting his job must be, listening to us loonies whine on about our issues and fears and inabilities that seem so inconsequential to what are probably his real-world problems. Sometimes I feel like suggesting he just rest his head on the desk and sleep for the entire duration of our session, gratis of Medicare and the tax-payer (of which I do realise he is one), but even contemplating the suggestion feels like crossing over a line that I'd prefer stayed in place. He tells me anecdotes about his kids sometimes to illustrate a point, because he can trust me with the stories and he knows I learn through anecdotes. And clearly I tell him personal stuff, also. But extending the hand of compassion in such a demonstrative manner would feel just too weird.

'So what are you saying?' I go, exasperated. 'That I won't commit to this girl because I can't?'

'You could if you wanted to.'

'I do.'

'Then do,' he shrugs. 'You just have to do it. But if we're totally honest here, you also have a chequered history for love.'

'It sounds a bit like you're suggesting I'm responsible for all my relationships falling apart.'

'Well, in a way...' he spreads his hands, succouring the ultimate point score.

So we examine my so-called past relationships, and the exercise, as enlightening as it is, proves fucking embarrassing:

Sharon Lang from Canberra. Engaged to her long-term boyfriend. Worked as a prostitute. I met her at the Winter Solstice Festival in West End the year before last when she was up visiting family (one of whom I have since gotten to know through the club scene). Hardly a whirlwind romance, but my first at least. She was here for a month, and might have stayed longer, but her stay (and the relationship) was cut short by her sudden departure when her cunt uncle inadvertently learned of her chosen career path after he saw her nude photo spread in Piccie magazine at his work. She went back to chilly Canberra and we kept in contact for a while, making absurd promises to each other, but naturally she resumed both the whoring and the engagement.

Next was Kaelen Walle from Sydney, who I met at Woodford Folk Festival. We became a long-distance couple, pouring our feelings out in letters every week. Finally I went down and stayed with her at Glebe in her mum's house, because she was actually only sixteen at the time. And already had a boyfriend, so I found out the hard way one night. But he put up with me being around, fuck knows why. Eventually I had to face the fact that I was being ridiculous and head back to Brisbane all hangdog.

Jillian Oldacre from the Gold Coast followed. No boyfriend, but had recently lost her virginity to the school stud and used me as a temporary surrogate for her feelings. We saw one another for a couple of months, commuting back and forth when the funds were available. I was turfed out as soon as the school stud had come to his senses and saw Jill for the catch that she was. It didn't last, I've heard.

Then there was Simone, an airy-fairy artist-wannabe from out just past Ipswich, who has since moved to West End. More her kind of people there. I still see her around, occasionally. There's no bad blood between us, even though I thought the end of our fleeting relationship turned pretty volatile, mostly because I couldn't swallow the fact that she still lived with her ex at the time. Share house of five, mind. But still. Some people, and Simone's one of them, just find it difficult to hold a grudge, I guess. So we've remained acquaintances.

And finally Nicola, of Brisbane.

'Bit of a pattern emerges,' he says, sucking on his teeth.

I address the elephant in the room: 'They've all had boyfriends at the time. Or close enough to it.'

He simply nods, raising his eyebrows meaningfully.

'Except Nicola,' I add.

I don't bother mentioning Erina, since I've never brought her up before. No need to pour petrol on the flames.

A sad list of credentials, all in all, with a series of casual hook-ups scattered between.

'At least they're getting closer to home, too,' says McKay of the progressively shortening distances. 'It seems kind of convenient, don't you think, that there's such a prominent obstacle to the relationship for each: the distance.'

He looks at me, almost sadly.

'What to make of it, huh?' I shrug.

'The divine comedy at play,' he goes, falling back on his go-to line.

'Yup,' I agree, wagging my head from side-to-side like a clown.

I'm forced to concede his point about the fear of commitment, of course.

'But what I don't get,' I say, 'is why would I bother even trying for a relationship in the first place if I have this fear of commitment that you reckon I have?'

'Because you're in love with the idea of love itself,' he says cryptically. 'You've got an idealised Hollywood romance in your mind, which is not how it generally goes. You've got to work hard at love, and not chase after it when it's not there.'

'And that's what I do?'

'I have no doubt you genuinely liked these girls,' he says kindly, 'but what you *truly* felt for them is something only you can answer. All I can say is that you set up some mighty big hurdles for yourself, knowing you'd get tripped up and not have to follow through.'

'I agree it's certainly sounding that way.'

'But like I said before, Dante, the fear of commitment runs all through your life, not just your love-life. You have these tenuous friendships that you end or renew on a whim. There's nothing very solid going on there.'

We've discussed in previous sessions how my folks moved around all the time when I was a kid, which resulted in an 'invalidating environment', as McKay calls it.

Essentially, he posits, that as children themselves my parents got to grow up in relatively stable households, able to call the same neighbourhood their home for years and years on end, but as young adults they typically rebelled against it all with parties and booze and pot around the time Rory and I were born, moving up and down the east coast of Australia so many times we barely spent an entire year in the same school. McKay's adamant that when it came time to put aside their transient ways it was easy for my folks to do since they'd had stability instilled in them growing up, but for my brother and I we'd had transiency psychologically ingrained into us all throughout *our* childhoods: constantly changing schools, homes, friends, curriculums, the lot. We'd grown up in a constant state of flux, and considered it normal.

Never mind my folks kinda had no choice to settle down, but that's a whole other story.

The result of this transient lifestyle, McKay reckons, is what he calls an invalidating environment.

'Why would you know how to lead a stable life?' he shrugs. 'You don't know what stable is.'

'Or how to commit to it,' I grin, realising what the cheeky cunt has been driving at all along.

'Exactly!' he points at me.

'Well,' I sigh, falling back in the chair with resignation. 'That's me up shit-creek without the paddle, isn't it?'

'Not really,' he goes, making a steeple of his fingers, which he actually does a lot. 'I want you to try something. An experiment.'

I sit forward, all ears. He knows I'm always game for these psychological experiments. Simple things, really, but the effect they can wring always fascinates me.

'You need to be stable for a while,' he explains. 'Stationary. Stay put. No more sleeping in garden beds, friend's houses. No more constantly travelling back and forth between here and your parents' property. You need to find somewhere to live, and see how long you can make it last.'

'Interesting,' I murmur. 'Try and break the cycle?'

'At least try and introduce a new theme into your life,' he says. 'Convince yourself that it's possible. Give yourself that rock you can always come back to when you lose your way again.'

I mull his proposition over, mostly thinking about palatial homes with wide driveways and warm fireplaces in winter. I once walked all night from Kingston train station along the train line and then diverted somewhere through suburb after suburb, utterly lost, until I came out at Coopers Plains train station and followed it the rest of the way into the city. I'd had enough money for a bus-fare back to my folk's place and a single donut from a 7-11, drinking tap water along the way. But the entire time I'd been daydreaming about the warm homes I was passing, imagining myself cosied up inside in front of a big TV with someone to hold and warm food on a plate. It was fucking awful, and I longed to get away from the cold and the hunger and the pounding in the soles of my feet that seven hours of walking on concrete had inflicted upon me. Being homeless is no fucking rock to cling to.

'I'm gonna do it,' I announce.

'Good, good,' he says. 'Just experiment with it. You manage that; you might manage the love side of things, too. Because, you know, Nicola's right here in Brisbane. Can't get any closer or better than that, right?'

He exhales and does a dramatic show of glancing at his little clock on the desk, which he does every time. I wonder if he extricates himself from every client like this? Winding down the session and delivering some introspective homework, then looks to the clock for our cue to leave.

Outside the rush of the everyday spins me around again: the traffic shoving its way along Ann Street into the guts of the city, the bells of St John's chiming the hour, the bustle of office workers making their way from lunch and casting disparaging judgments at me. The energy of the city almost dispels McKay's lesson, so I'm forced to reiterate his words over and over in my head to retain it.

So, I need a place to live. But where? And more importantly, with who? I couldn't live with just any Joe Blo. That'd be a nightmare in the making. For a start, it'll have to be someone who is prepared to put up with my shit, with my outbursts of anger or my shit-stirring, because both of those are likely to be high on the agenda.

A pretty girl with freckles and deep auburn hair walks past, smiles as I'm talking to myself but quickly looks away when I notice her. It's been one of those days for me, the hormones on over-drive, falling for every girl on the street. It's so fucking distracting, like being a dog on heat. I need to get out of the public arena, which is practically impossible this close to the city centre, so I duck down Creek Street and left onto Queen where Raven normally works at an el-cheapo bookstore a few days a week to supplement her meagre benefits as a student.

Providence provides, because she's tending shop today, so I can hang in here and chat with her. I quickly spell out McKay's challenge, which is that I must find suitable lodgings and see how long I can stay put for. Sounds simple enough, but where does one even begin to implement this experiment?

'You know,' she says with a big grin, 'you're in luck. Bernie from flat number one at The Prozac Palace needs someone to move in. His disability pension barely covers his rent and expenses so he might be keen on you moving in.'

I've only spoken with Bernie a few times. Odd fellow.

'I dunno, what's he like?'

'You know, he's old, like fifty or something I think, so he's quiet.'

I weigh up the idea and decide it sounds like a goer; a chalk-and-cheese arrangement could be the right scenario for me.

'Can you look into it for me?'

'Sure,' she nods, 'I'll ask him after work.'

'You're the best,' I tell Raven, wondering if offering her oral under the counter as a gesture of thanks would be inappropriate. I'm sure it wouldn't be, but I'm a guy in love now, so gotta keep it in my pants.

The universe always looks after its own!

AMAI ON SET

So, even though I get a handful of shifts every week at Gus' pizza place up the road, I still go into the dole office occasionally and check their new job-search kiosks if for nothing else than just to play around on the new technology. Not many dole offices have got these kiosks yet, but the one in Stone's Corner is trialling them early. I think we're finally coming into an age where the presence of the computer and the electronic interface is big time inescapable. I mean, we've got automatic teller machines, email, the internet, the damn list is endless, isn't it? And at a super-computing conference last year, a challenge was put forward by sponsors to try and develop a computer to process at a trillion FLOPS, which is exactly a teraflop. In short, they mean to make a computer that can think as fast as a human being!

Imagine the boost to the artificial intelligence industry with that!

So, in a recent paper to the Robotics Institute in Pittsburgh, Hans Moravec proposed that robots will move beyond human command in just fifty years from now! He thinks technology will keep on expanding big time and develop intellect of its own design, and that it will eventually seek out the furthest corners of our galaxy and beyond, and that corporations will spread between the stars and humans will redesign themselves to reflect their new extraterrestrial lives and they will be biologically greater than anything we could comprehend right now!

The downside is, by the time the robots rise and we live in these utopian societies exploring the stars, I'll be an old lady and exempt from the whole damn thing. Still, the near future's just so damned exciting, but it's depressing how many people still fixate on corny TV jingles instead. Of course, the kiosks at the dole office are hardly the robots of the future, but their presence is a sign of things to come, isn't it?

So, to add a dose of reality to my daydreaming, I remind myself that I work casual for a crappy pizza place up the road called Scat Pizza, who probably only hired me because I'm Chinese and the owner assumes I'm potentially here on a work visa, even though I sound perfectly Australian. Which is a bit of a misnomer. I mean, who'd want to sound perfectly Australian? It's a crap accent, isn't it?

Agosto Scaturro, or Gus, is the proprietor and an asshole Sicilian. He says his nickname is Scat or – as he seems to prefer ever since that hideous song came out last year – The Scatman (although we refuse to call him by either name). Ergo, the shop is called Scat Pizza. Little does he realise *scat* is also the sexual practice of eating shit, and we make sure that consuming one of Gus' pizzas is as near enough to performing scat that most of his customers will ever get to. The repeat customers are a testament to the failing tastebuds of our populace. Sometimes when I'm serving them I sing that jingle 'call one-three-one-triple-eight, brings Silvio's to your door' to plant the idea of buying from the competition, but some people are stuck in their ways and keep coming back. Oh well, not my problem.

Last week the Immigration department caught up with one of my co-workers, Tamrat, and deported him back to Ethiopia because he'd overstayed his visa. So the thing is, he's been working for Gus for about three months now and Gus was well aware that Tam's visa had expired because Tam asked him for assistance to help renew it. Gus had done what he could, but the visa office didn't come to the party and Tam had been freaking out. Right before he was deported, Tam admitted to me that part of the problem was that he didn't have the cash for the new visa because Gus hadn't paid him his wages for about a month. I was so angry with them both and told Tam he should have said something sooner. Next thing I know, Immigration finds him and he's gone!

I fucking know that asshole Scaturro was behind it. The rumour is that it's not the first time he's called Immigration on his workers for complaining about being short-paid. That's why he likes to hire migrants from developing countries, isn't it? The asshole knows that no-one cares what happens to them.

He's stuffed my pay up a few times, too, and it's taken a lot of asking and patience to get it corrected. So I'm lucky I can talk my way around him. Others, like Tamrat, don't stand a chance. That's why when I saw the job for a makeup artist come up on the screen at the dole office I felt like the tide was turning.

So, I'm registered with the dole for assistance only. I don't get a single cent from them because of the means-testing. My parents are too well off for me to be eligible for payments, so the Government expects me to be financially supported by my *sìyǎng yuán*. That's just how it is. Ma and Ba pay the rent and bills for me, and give me a small weekly allowance, which they recalculate weekly so that I've only got a small amount left after the necessities. In that way they hope to curb me from buying alcohol, pot or hanging out with my friends. In turn, I try to make sure they don't know how many shifts at Scat Pizza I get, but Ma (or Lao Foye, as I sometimes call her) gets around that by calling the house as often as she can to determine my whereabouts. If Sally or Clem can't satisfactorily account for my whereabouts, Ma assumes I'm working a shift and shaves some more off my weekly stipend. She's as bad as Gus!

But I'm still allowed to avail myself of the services that the dole office provides, and that's how I'd found out about this makeup job on the kiosk. I'd printed off the receipt number and contact details and used the free phone over on the wall. The guy on the phone, Neil, gave me the position straight away. The shoot is at a fancy serviced apartment in the city, close to Central Station which is handy.

On the way in I sit my humble makeup kit next to me on the train and do an inventory check one last time. If there's anything else I'll need, I'll have to run to Priceline and use some of the grocery money. Which will mean going without some home essentials this week, because I'll be damned if I'm telling Lao Foye about any extra work I get, if I can help it.

So, it's a bit nerve-wracking because it sounds potentially like it's going to be a professional shoot and I haven't done any makeup gigs since film school. I only did it because we had to specialise in a role for the year and no-one picked makeup. Ma was furious, of course, because it was the only role the college didn't supply equipment for so I'd had to buy a lot of the stuff myself. Or rather, she'd had to buy it for me, embarrassingly settling for a plastic Caboodles from Target because it was 'best value'. The stuff to go in it, though – the sponges, brushes and other stuff – added up big time, not to mention all the consumable stuff like concealers and powders. I should've fought harder to be an editor, but my parents raised me to accept the shorter straw because that was the polite thing to do, so it's on their heads really.

Not that that argument made much of a difference in the end. Ma supplied me with such basic stuff for my kit that I had to get a job at a restaurant in the Valley just to keep restocking all the consumables. I mean, no-one on the film course had any sympathy for my situation, and would constantly ask for retouches to the makeup on the actors. If I refused to do it, the stereotypical jokes about Chinese being stingy came up.

That job was the worst. I mean, it really sucked balls, big time.

So, the restaurant where I did the waitressing was this crappy restaurant with standard Westernised dishes such as sweet and sour pork and lemon chicken on the menu. But not only was the food actually terrible, the whole establishment was a front for prostitution. Some of the waitresses did fuck all work, but were way too dolled up for the job, too! They'd hang around with Vinnie the manager and he'd introduce them to customers that didn't even buy any food. At first I was thought 'this is fucking weird' but then the penny dropped. None of my business, but then the restaurant was understaffed by *actual* table waiters.

I put up with so much shit from the customers, especially the ones that assumed I was one of Vinnie's whores. In front of all the other customers they'd loudly ask Vinnie how much I was (with the usual shitty jokes about 'five dollar, five dollar'), or they'd grab my wrist when I was putting the plates on the table and say the lewdest stuff to me. Vinnie used to laugh and try to placate them, demanding that I keep working. He was an asshole, like pizzaman Gus, but at least Vinnie always paid. He couldn't afford to jerk any of the employees around, I suppose, in case we went to the cops about his pimping.

The serviced apartments where the shoot is are amazing. The foyer has huge ceilings and the concierge's counter is marble. So the guy on the phone, Neil, already gave me the room number and told me to ignore the concierge and just head straight up.

The building is quite old and has tiny windows, and everyone is really quiet like we're in a library. The elevator takes me up to the sixth floor and I knock on the door. This big fat guy answers the door.

He's nothing like I was expecting. I mean, he looks like he should be working at a butcher's or on a construction site.

'Amy?' he says, pronouncing my name the Western way. 'Thanks for coming.'

He ushers me in, quickly closing the door. It looks like a well-maintained apartment, the fancy kind Ma and Ba always put us up in whenever we travel back to Hong Kong for family holidays.

There's another three big-bellied men, dressed head to toe in long sleeves and slacks even though the weather's unusually warm, thanks to that massive hole in the ozone above us. I'm guessing none of these gentlemen will be starring in the production.

I'm suddenly quite nervous, wondering what I've gotten myself into. I should've told someone where I was going, because apart from these three men, no-one knows I'm here.

'I'll introduce you to the talent,' says Neil, forgoing introductions. He leads me down the corridor, where I can hear a couple of women laughing, thank fuck!

So, it occurs to me that this could potentially be a porno shoot, which gets me really excited. That, or I'm still riding the adrenalin from when I walked in and thought I was alone with the dodgy brothers. I've always wanted to work on a porno, behind the scenes of course. It's illegal to make porn movies in Australia, at least definitely not in Queensland. If it *is* a porno shoot, the clandestine nature of the gig is all the more thrilling, isn't it? Except if it's something dodgy like where they abuse the girls or they pretend to be underage. Can't stand that 'barely legal' stuff.

In the bathroom are two girls in their underwear, totally pissed. An empty bottle of champers is next to the wash-basin, and a fresh one's cracked open in the hands of the older girl.

Neil introduces them as Daniella and Chantelle, although I don't know if that's their real or stage names. Daniella says to call her Dani. The other one, Chantelle, looks like a kind of goth girl, with a streak of pink Manic Panic through her hair and what looks like a bondage harness over her bra.

'What look would you like?' I say to Neil.

He shrugs. 'You're the makeup artist.'

So, he leaves the room, and abruptly I feel out of my depth. I've got no instructions, and I'm not sure what they're after specifically.

Chantelle laughs. 'You look lost.'

I notice she's got an angry red crater on the side of her nose.

'I'm not sure what I'm meant to be doing,' I confess, and tell them how I haven't ever done a professional gig.

'Don't stress,' says Dani, leading me by the hand to the toilet and dropping the seat down. I sit my makeup kit on it. 'Just make us look fabulous!'

I suspect she's had the lion's share of the champagne.

'So... face and everything?'

'Whatever you need to do, babe,' she says, resting her arse against the basin counter and flicking back her hair to expose her chest.

Even though I want to check out her body, I try not to. I can't believe I'm doing makeup on a porno!

'Make sure our toes look good, too,' Chantelle orders. 'Pedicure, nail polish, the fuckin works.'

'I'm only getting paid for the makeup, though,' I say, trying not to protest too much but eager not to be taken advantage of either, if I can help it.

'It's all part of it, trust me, girl,' says Chantelle. 'These gonzo operators love to start the camera at the chick's feet then pan up the body. They want *everything* on screen since they're paying for it.'

'I see, thanks for the tip,' I nod, checking what colours I've got in varnish. The cherry red will do.

'Twenny says the cunt with the monobrow gets his dick out for a wank,' says Chantelle to Dani, apparently resuming the conversation they were having before Neil and I interrupted.

Dani breaks into a drunken cackle big time that wouldn't be out of place on a crazy eighty year old.

'Or cries.'

They start sniggering until Dani's snorting like a pig. Suddenly, I quite like these girls. So, Daniella seems about my age, but Chantelle looks a fair bit older even she acts more like our age.

'How did you guys get this job?' I ask, laying out the brushes.

'Uni,' says Dani. 'There was a sign up on one of the noticeboards that said they were looking for models. I had a feeling it was for a nude shoot, but it didn't say.'

'Friend of a friend,' smiles Chantelle in that way that means there's more to the story but she won't let on. She dabs at the crater on her nose with a tissue.

'Pays not too shabby, and there's free piss,' Dani grins, hefting the champagne bottle. 'Sip?'

I figure it can't hurt, and might help calm my nerves a bit, so I take a few swigs from the bottle. I haven't had any lunch yet, and it goes straight to my head, making me feel pleasantly light. I wouldn't mind getting drunk right now and hanging out with the girls in our undies all day. Not with the men hanging around in the next room, though. I try and imagine what my parents would think if they saw this!

I consider the task ahead. Dani's got naturally smooth skin, so she should be a breeze, but Chantelle's going to be a bit more difficult. Her skin looks damaged and tired.

Turns out Dani's an engineering student, and thinks it's tough being a girl in the course but that she's not the only one.

'There's a couple of Asian girls, actually, like you,' she says.

My parents would fucking love to hear that. They'd probably rub my face in it. That's just how they are.

'Have you ever heard of Hans Moravec?' I say, but she shakes her head. So I tell them about his theory of ex-humans and living in space, evolving as a species, and how we won't be defined by today's restrictive stereotypes. They're fascinated, pitching in their own view points. At one point Chantelle says we sound like we're stoned, not drunk.

'Hell yeah, would kill for a joint right now,' sighs Dani as I try and cover a razor burn on her pubic area with foundation.

'After you shave, put clear deodorant on it,' suggests Chantelle. 'That's why I don't have any red bumps down there. My flatmate's a prossie and gave me the tip.'

'If you're going to remove your hair, you should try waxing instead of shaving,' I tell Dani.

'No fucking way,' she snorts. 'I heard of a woman who lost several layers of skin all down her cunt from doing that.'

I doubt that's true, but Dani's adamant it happened.

'I normally don't bother shaving,' she says, 'but my boyfriend reckons that porn is more about being bald down there.'

I'm surprised she's got a boyfriend, while Chantelle doesn't bat an eyelid.

'I mean, who cares what porn is meant to be about?' I say. 'Too much of it is catering for men. Teen fetishism is a by-product of men resisting feminism, isn't it, because they correlate body hair on women with the so-called rabid feminazis who fought for the Equal Rights Amendment in 1972. That's all. So, ever since they've been eroticising teenagers big time and now we're all expected to look as pubescent as possible for their gratification. I say fuck em.'

'Hear hear,' says Dani with a big grin and salutes with the bottle.

Chantelle rolls her eyes.

I notice there's a little bit of razor burn on Dani's chest, as well. A dab of foundation and a pat of powder will fix that up. A *pat pat* we used to joke at college. Then I see the long stray hair curling from her areola. The pores on her nipple suggests she's plucked a few more out earlier, but must have missed this one.

I tug it out just as she takes a swig from the bottle, and suddenly she spits champagne into the air and screams. The alcohol mists down over everyone and Chantelle bursts into uncontrollable laughter.

Neil appears at the doorway, looking annoyed.

'How's it going?'

'Good, good,' I stammer. 'Nearly done.'

He looks Daniella over. 'Nice work.'

'I'm not sure what I can do about Chantelle's sore,' I say, referring to the open crater on her nose. It's weeping a runny liquid that Sally once told me is called serous fluid. The advantages of being flatmates with a nurse!

'Just plug it up,' says Neil and leaves the room.

Damn it. This shouldn't be my problem. A sore like that can't be 'plugged up'. But I've got no choice.

'It's okay, man, just do it,' Chantelle says, jutting her chin out unnecessarily, angling her face in a way that makes it harder to get the job done.

I mix a compound paste of setting powder and liquid foundation. I'm sure if an actual professional makeup artist saw me doing this, they'd be horrified. Any other job I'd potentially be fired for doing this. I scoop up the paste with a brush and scrape it into the open wound on Chantelle's face. At first it doesn't stay, but I manage to make it stick by plastering more over the top and smearing it across her skin in all directions. The end result looks like a pale mosquito bump stuck on the side of her nose.

I check her over to see where else she needs makeup. Damn, her skin isn't the best, and a full body application wouldn't go astray. She's watching me like a hawk as if she can read my mind, so I put on a blasé expression. She's got some bruises and a few red spots where broken skin is mending. Something else I notice is the tiny infected spots in the crooks of her arms and inside her thighs. I definitely need to cover those up, and maybe discard the brush afterwards. If I'm not mistaken, those are needle holes for injecting drugs, isn't it?

When I'm done I step back to assess my work, and to my horror I notice the crater on the side of her nose is leaking again. The serous fluid has pushed through my compound and is dribbling down her face, scoring a trail through the thick foundation. I don't have any waterproof foundation because Ma balked at the cost of it.

'I'll just touch up your cheeks a bit,' I say, willing Dani not to say anything.

I use a new brush, lamenting that this one also will need to be thrown away. So much cost! Cleaning up the serous fluid with a tissue wipes away part of the foundation, dammit.

'Damn it,' I say through my teeth.

'Everything okay?' asks Chantelle.

'Yep, just gotta fix this one tiny little bit.'

She must be able to feel me poking at her sore, but she shows no reaction. I'm grateful that she's not saying anything about it because it's proving extremely difficult to correct the makeup again and is stressing me out.

'We good?' asks Neil from the doorway.

'Yep, ready to go,' I fib, dabbing away furiously at Chantelle's nose and cheek.

Dani saves the day by dancing out the doorway and herding Neil back along the corridor, ostentatiously singing the whole time.

I manage to contain the leak, and get Chantelle looking as normal as possible again.

So, when I look over my work again, I realise that makeup's probably not my calling, at least not on white girls. It looks flat and lifeless, the opposite of how I imagine Moravec's ex-humans would look like. With just a bit of cream and powder I've managed to completely de-evolve the species.

But it will have to do.

'Good to go,' I smile weakly.

Chantelle checks the bathroom mirror and is enthusiastic about my labours.

'Nice work, Amai,' she says, pronouncing my name with the correct inflection. 'You got my back, girl. Now to go earn my pay.'

She wiggles comically out of the bathroom, already putting on a little show.

I'm feeling flat. Useless. Both the makeups look terrible. No-one's saying so, though. I probably make a better pizza than I do a face. My dreams of being the next Kevyn Aucoin go up in smoke. I quickly pack my Caboodles, eager to get away.

'Amy's Asian,' I hear Neil say to the others when I go out into their makeshift studio, wondering if they're about to ask me to do an inter-racial porno. Dani and Chantelle are sitting on the edge of the bed that's been dragged into the living room. I'm wracking my brain for a hundred and one ways to decline the offer when Neil points at the camcorder and says to me: 'You know how to operate these things?'

The fat bastards are all poking at the camera trying to work out how it even turns on. It's an amusing sight. I imagine they're the same in the bedroom with their wives.

I went to film school for this? Not my problem.

'Yes,' I hear myself saying.

I go over and press the tiny button in, flicking the power dial up. The camera whirs into life and the men cheer.

'Don't you guys have instructions for it?' I ask nicely.

'Yeah, somewhere,' says Neil, glancing idly about the floor.

'In the box,' says the guy with the monobrow, the one the girls were making jokes about. He points to the camera packaging over in the corner of the room beside their bags but makes no move to get it.

'Should probably get you to film it, too,' laughs Neil.

Not my problem. So it occurs to me that if I hang around long enough these guys are potentially going to pressure me to get naked on camera. No thanks.

'Actually, I've got another makeup appointment to get to, so...' I fib as convincingly as I can.

'No worries, all good,' he says. He pulls out his wallet and shuffles through some notes, sliding out a fifty for me. Better than a kick up the bum. 'Again, thanks for coming along.'

'Anytime,' I say for some reason.

One of the guys rolls out a towel on the bed beside Dani, revealing an impressive assortment of dildos, vibrators and butt plugs. Damn, there'd be easily a grand's worth of toys there. A couple I wouldn't mind for home.

Daniella picks up a long, double-ended dildo and waves it around in the air. 'Super dick!'

The crater on Chantelle's face is starting to ooze again, and before it gets any worse I thank Neil for the pay and get the fuck out of there. Not my problem anymore.

I mean, I'm grateful for the cash, but first thing I'll do when I'm next in the dole office is let them know they've got amateur porn productions recruiting via their brand new job search systems. We can try and usher in the age of new technology all we like, but human beings will always bend it to be about sex.

MARY STREET

Me and Nicola are in the Valley, half-way to drunk already, although I think she's further gone than I am.

We were going to crash a goth club and get up to mischief, and I honestly thought there was one on at the Oriental Hotel tonight, but all that's on is a skacore gig. There's shaved heads and Fred Perry shirts galore. Not our fuckin scene, that's for sure.

At the back of the Oriental is a gravel carpark, carved from the ruined foundations of whatever was built here before Brisbane's own nefarious demolition brothers probably got to it. There's a couple of BMX's against the chain-link fence, and one of them isn't padlocked, so me and Nicola nab it and I dink her all the way into the city, down past the Eagle Street Pier and along Mary Street.

We ditch the bike over a barricade and hear it tumble down into a construction pit on the other side.

There's a club here that's so upmarket there's only a snowball's chance we'll get in looking like we do in our tattered clothes, lace and docs. But aloha, the doorman actually lets us in! I might have to have a word with management about getting the guy an appointment with Spec Savers.

It feels like we're in the lion's maw now: tans and bright red lipsticks and designer fucking clothes, gold cufflinks and necklaces and Italian leather shoes. Laughably orange bleach hairdos courtesy of that Sun-In shit.

But in a way this isn't that different from being in a goth club. Everyone's got garish makeup on, tailored clothing, getting sloshed and hoping to get a win on.

But there's a lot of bald guys, I've noticed. Not naturally bald, but intentionally shorn. The testosterone runs high here.

'Sure we're not still at the Oriental?' I say to Nicola over the music, who looks around at the shaved heads and grins.

And the music is fucking hideous. Doof-doof music, appalling techno loops and crap, soulless beats. They need to throw on some NIN, :wumpscut:, or even a bit of Skinny Puppy. Fuck, even a lil Gary Numan wouldn't go astray!

We shove our way through the crowd at the bar, sliding into a spot where the bartender might see us. We're getting glared at, of course, but as if we could care.

Nicola orders us a couple of tequilas each, and by the time the guy has lined up the salt and lemon for us we've downed the drinks.

'Fuck, that's impressive,' he goes.

'Is it?' Nicola says. 'Line up another if you really think so.'

The guy grins and pours us another shot each. 'Normally everyone has the lemon, at least.'

We laugh and thank the guy for the free drinks, forcing our way back through the throng to do some crap dancing on the dance-floor.

A couple of ladies next to us think we're hilarious, but they're about it. Everyone else seems offended by our dancing, which is precidely why we do it. It's turning out to be a great fucking night. Who'd have thought?

At one point I'm dancing so fast to the music, trying to mirror the speed of the beats, that this insecurity guard comes over and grabs me by the arm, nearly crushing the bone. She's shorter than I am but all muscle, her arms bulging out the way the Looney Tunes characters do when they're taking the piss.

'Calm down,' she warns me, squeezing my arm one more time for effect.

Nicola openly laughs at the woman as she strolls back to her place near the front entrance. I start dancing in slow motion and this elicits a positively hateful glower from the guard. Insecurity guards almost never have much of a sense of humour.

'I gotta go piss,' Nicola yells in my ear.

I wait for her over by a pillar where some other guys are hanging around. Making casual conversation with them proves a futile effort. They're not hostile about it, they're simply not interested, to the point of not even bothering explain so; they just point-blank ignore me. But when Nicola gets back from the dunnies, then their interest piques. Fucking typical.

'So why're you so chatty now, all of a sudden?' I ask one of them, who also happens to be bald, trying to make small talk with Nicola.

He just continues to ignore me, and so Nicola tells him she's not interested.

When the cunt persists, for a laugh she tells him she's a lesbian.

Bizarrely, the bald cunt actually gets hostile at this declaration.

'Fuck you then, you frigid bitch.'

'You fucking right, cunt?' I bristle.

'Fuck off,' he sneers at me, finally acknowledging my presence.

He continues to harass Nicola until she threatens to cut him with a knife, which I know she doesn't carry. But I do.

The guy leaves us alone after this, but Nicola's not done.

She goes to the bar and tells our bartender that the bald cunt's hassling her, that he touched her arse, even though he didn't.

The bartender spits chips and goes over and says something to this big black insecurity guard at the end of the bar who looks like he could probably snap me in half if he wanted to. There's an inordinate amount of insecurity guards here, especially considering on the goth scene we have pretty much next to none at most of our clubs and when we do it's usually one of us that happens to have a licence, like Twix.

The big black guard shoves his way steadily through the crowd until he finds the bald cunt who was hassling Nicola and has a word with him. Baldie's protesting his innocence, shaking his head and shrugging ostentatiously. The guard appears to leave him with words filled of menace, because the bald cunt blanches beneath his fake tan and looks a bit shaken. Serves the dumb cunt right.

'I'm pretty impressed,' I yell in Nicola's ear as she strains to hear me over the music. 'I didn't think no cunt would help us in here.'

'Fucking rad, ay?'

We grin and embrace, lifting our faces to the ceiling as we scream with happiness. There's a few disapproving frowns as a result, mostly thin skinny bitches with unhappy faces, but who gives a fuck about them? I'm so happy with Nicola I already know that I won't be seeing Erina again. I'm done with cuckolding her poor knob of a boyfriend.

'I love you,' I whisper into her ear, the curls of her pigtails tickling my nose and eyelashes.

'What'd you say?' she yells back.

Nothing I mouth with a big smile, shaking my head.

'You look drunk,' she laughs.

Drunk on fucking love, yeeeeeaah!

We get a couple more drinks at the bar, and notice the bald cunt from earlier next to us. He hasn't clocked us yet because he's trying to chat up this anorexic thing with peroxide hair.

Nicola calls out to our bartender.

'He just grabbed my fucking boob,' she tells him, pointing at the bald cunt who sits there oblivious to our presence still.

The bartender's face goes red and he motions the big black security guard over.

'Fucking turf him,' he goes.

So the guard reaches through the crowd and grabs this bald cunt by the collar, whose first reaction is to lash out in defence. He lands a fist on a girl's face behind him, and before he can apologise another guy steps up and warns the cunt not to touch his girlfriend. Suddenly it's on, and the crowd parts to give the brawl the space it needs.

'Holy shit!' shouts Nicola in pure glee. 'Better than I expected!'

The guard finally steps through and shoves the boyfriend back a few times before he can get the bald cunt into a head-lock. Then he grabs the boyfriend by the arm, too, and marches both through the dense crowd and out the front door.

'On yer fuckin bike!' I yell, laughing.

'It's over the fence in the construction pit,' cackles Nicola.

We're like birds of a feather, she and I. Well paired. McKay is right: I need to stop being fearful of commitment and seize the day with Nicola.

We give the bartender all four thumbs-up, and he winks at us and gets back to serving.

'You're next,' Nicola warns this guy in a pink business shirt who looks her up and down, except his face registers disgust not lust.

The big insecurity guard comes back into the club, empty-handed, to take his position at the end of the bar again. That security guard's a fucking top guy, I decide.

'Let's wait a few minutes for the coast to clear outside, then head off,' says Nicola. 'I'm bored already.'

'Sure thing,' I go, resisting the urge to again tell her I love her.

PART TWO

DANTE MOVES IN WITH BERNIE

As per Dr McKay's proposal, and because everyone figures I should stop sleeping in garden beds, Raven sets me up to live in the Prozac Palace with Bernie in flat one, who's in his fifties. Good thing she did, too, with winter approaching. Fortunately, being homeless means I have fuck all stuff to move so I pretty much just have to turn up with my backpack of clothing and books.

Mum's pretty happy about it for obvious reasons, but also because she now has a way of keeping in regular contact with me. She could hardly phone me when I was homeless, and I'm not that inclined to call her much from my end. Especially since the phonebox chews coins up like nobody's business on those STD calls.

To get to the Prozac Palace, you need to come off Turbot Street if you're coming from the City, or off Boundary Street if you're coming from Spring Hill. Then go about half way up Bowen Street where it meets Mein. There's also an abandoned little cottage with a wrap-around verandah on the corner of the T-intersection that some punks and addicts use as a squat.

We call it the Prozac Palace firstly on account of just how many people that live in here are now goths, or are associated in some way with darkwave culture. So it's kind of a joke that we nicknamed it 'Prozac' since there's also a lot of us that are, or have been in the past, clinically medicated. Recreational medications don't count in this instance, and there's a lot of that going on, too.

It's basically a shitty pre-war, three-storey timber and stucco set of flats, but either by wit or through sincerity the founders did erect, in four-foot high metal-work lettering no less, the words THE PALAIS across the front of the building up where the facade peaks in a half-arsed attempt at an art-nouveau formation. It's neither a palace, nor a dance hall as is the usual reserve of the term *palais* in the Land of Oz. But that's the second reason we call it the Palace.

There's a set of wooden stairs up the middle with a threadbare runner that leads to the landings on each level and from which run dimly lit corridors. Off each of these corridors leads four doors each, though not all doors are present anymore, some having been removed through excessive force during wild parties and another for firewood one particularly bitter winter that also saw the fire-brigade attend and get really fucking angry about a fire in the house. The property owner was less than impressed by the fine so he kicked out the offending tenants, but they just moved in downstairs with the people in Unit 3. All in all, there're a dozen flats here and two redundant communal toilets since the landlord was made to install a dunny in every unit back in the Seventies. So the communal bathrooms were turned into storage spaces yonks ago, which have since been commandeered to accommodate more tenants, who've built makeshift beds and shelving into the spaces. If they need the toilet they knock on the door at one of the other flats.

At some point in its sad and chequered history, the Palace became infested with goths. Legend has it that once one had breached its hold, securing for himself a bottom unit at the front, more and more secured tenancy via word-of-mouth with each successive vacancy. Sometimes they're already squatting across the road in the old cottage, and make the short journey over when a flat is empty. More than half the flats are now occupied by people who've a preference for wearing all-black. And some of them house more than the customary one or two occupants: there's up to six or so people crashed in some at any given time, in various stages of transiency.

But Bernie's always lived on his own, watching everyone come and go. He's never wanted anyone sharing his flat with him, and still doesn't, but the price of his antipsychotics have gone up and he needs the cash.

He's a quiet guy with brown skin, but he's not Polynesian or Aborigine or Asian or anything, like some people think. He says it must be some kind of throwback to someone in his lineage, but all his relatives are white, with his heritage coming from Germany.

In his unit everything's as anachronistic as he himself is, as if it's all from another era: his furniture is old and worn, the metal bed-frame in his bedroom is rusted, and his kitchen appliances are from the 70s. He's got an impressive collection of vintage Tupperware. You could put Bernie onto Antiques Roadshow and they'd date him as a pre-war relic.

At the same time, though, living with him is kinda cool. He knows everyone in the building and they all know him, cause he's been here for donkey's years. So long, in fact, that when he's sitting out front of the building on his little deck-chair having a smoke, he often comes back in with gifts from the little Mongolian lady a few doors up, like plates of fried goods wrapped in cling-wrap. I don't always have lot of grub in the house, so it's great cause Bernie shares it every time.

Bernie doesn't have much in life, especially ambition, and so he doesn't need much room to live in. He offered to move out of the larger bedroom and give it to me, taking for himself the poky little thing that is more like an over-sized closet. He doesn't even ask me to pay more than half the rent. He's a good guy, Bernie.

On a little shelf nailed to the wall where Bernie likes to sit in the lounge area is a photo in a cheap frame of Bernie in his younger days. He was much thinner back then. Even his face looked different. I remark about how age catches up with some.

'Nah, it's from the medication,' he says. 'The risperdal makes me fat. After I started taking it, I just ballooned.' He takes a deep breath and puffs his cheeks up.

He's still taking the meds because of his delusions, although he's told me several times that his imaginary friends still make day-to-day decisions for him. He even calls them his 'imaginary friends' without irony while still insisting they exist, at least as entities inside his own head. They've got names, too: Carl (after the psychologist Carl Jung) and Elizabeth (after the character from the TV show *Bewitched*). He calls them his anima and animus, which he says are terms that Carl Jung coined.

We watch a lot of TV, or Bernie does at least. His favourite channel is Briz 31, shows like *Lucy Lockjaw* and *Crazy Crosswords*. I go out a lot, or hang out with the others in their units upstairs. Otherwise, I'm in here watching program after program, sometimes standing in front of the window and just watching the street, noting the comings and goings of the neighbourhood. I sort of get sucked into the miasma of Bernie's being, unconsciously mimicking his inertia. We don't talk much, just make scathing commentary on the shit we see on the TV.

His cupboards were pretty fucking sparse the first day I moved in, and I thought I was gonna starve. Turns out Bernie survives on a steady diet of soup and toast, which just won't fucking do for me. I remembered that time I gave him a whole tub of groceries. I was staying at Twix and Raven's place at the time, and my psychiatrist had suggested that I get them something to show my appreciation. So when they were at work and Uni respectively, I'd called up the Salvo's and told the cunt on the other end that I was broke (which was more or less true) and in desperate need of nutrition (less true), and he came round to assess the situation. I'd had to empty out the kitchen cupboards and hide all of Twix and Raven's grub under Twix's bed. Initially I'd gone to hide it under Raven's bed, acting on the assumption that girls are naturally cleaner creatures, but her bedroom had been a fucking pigsty. All sorts of shit had been shoved under her bed. So when the guy from the charity got there it looked like the place had been robbed of food, I'd been that thorough. He was a bit suss about it, since I'd probably overdone it, but he couldn't ignore the evidence that there was absolutely nothing to eat and gave me two big plastic tubs full of groceries. There was way too much for Twix and Raven to believe I'd bought it myself so I'd hauled a whole tub load down the stairs and given it to Bernie. The old bastard had been so overwhelmed he'd barely registered any emotion.

It was fucking fantastic watching Raven get all choked up at the gesture, though. She was yanking all her cupboard doors open and reading out the inventory for Twix when he'd got home from his insecurity shift. There was so much of it that Raven decided to organise a big goth picnic at Albert Park in the city and invite a shitload of people along to share in the abundance.

'Don't thank me,' I'd told her. 'Thank Providence.'

So, one day we get some mail by mistake meant for across the street, like the postie's got his odd and even numbers mixed up. I see it's from Myers, addressed to a Mister David Leecham, who must have had a brilliantly paying job because his house across the road is pretty fucking decent. I can imagine him staring out those polished windows at the monstrosity of The Palais and wishing to God it'd burn down, and everyone inside with it. Truth be told, this old building is a bit of a blight on the postcode. Inside the envelope is a credit card statement, and he's pretty well-to do indeed judging by these numbers! At the top of the letter is his card number, and there's a glossy catalogue of useless shit that Mister Leecham can spend his small fortune on to relieve the boredom of being a rich cunt.

There's a vacant house further up the road that has been on the market for a little while. The punks that squat across on the corner of Mein broke in there once but a few days later the cops chased them out and the real estate agent boarded up the doors and windows with sheets of ply wood and large screws. In my brain-dead musings out the window I've noticed that neither agent nor landlord ever come around to the house, and the mail's overfilled the little box, scattering over the edge of the footpath where it's beaten flat and colourless by rain and sunshine.

As a little belated thanks to Bernie for letting me into the unit and for giving me the larger of the two bedrooms, I ask him to pick some music he likes from the catalogue. He thinks I'm pulling his leg because he knows I'm broke as, but he humours me all the same and picks out a Tracey Chapman CD and a Hootie & the Blowfish CD, which I pointedly ignore and change to a Smashing Pumpkins one for him, even though he doesn't much like the Pumpkins. I do, though, so there's that at least.

I pick out a couple for myself, including Nick Cave's *Murder Ballads* album, writing them down on the order form with their code numbers. I put my name down as David Leecham and give the address of the vacant house up the road. Lastly, I put down the all-important credit-card number in the box provided, and mail it off.

Next, I head up the street and clean out the overstuffed mailbox, or as I like to think of it, my new postal address. Under all the junk mail there's a build up of little granulates of millipede shit. I scrape the black shit out with a stick and my fingernails.

A week later there's a parcel on top of the mailbox, addressed to Leecham. I smuggle it home and tear it open. Hallelujah! There they fucking are, the CD's, in pristine condition with non-scratched cases and perfect mint discs. I've never owned a new CD before. I can't stop admiring the plastic casing and the newness of the booklets inside.

The Chapman and Pumpkins CDs go straight to Bernie.

'Where'd you pinch these from?' he laughs.

'I didn't steal them,' I grumble. 'It's a gift, you ungrateful cunt. You're supposed to be impressed.'

'Yes, I am,' he says, chuckling at my mood. He holds one up close to his face, because he's a bit short-sighted. 'What's this one? Smashing... what? Pumpkins?'

'Yeah, you'll love that one,' I go, snatching it from his hands and slipping the disc into our portable player that looks like a deformed bubble. Bernie's other player is an old one with wooden speakers on the side that have cloth over them and only plays cassettes, so when I moved in I used some of my dole money to get this cheapo unit from Kmart to play these CD's.

He's not at all chuffed by the music, waddling outside for a smoke.

The next week I put in another order using the form they sent with the last set of CD's. This time I double up on a couple of the titles and pass them out to the other units. Giving them free shit puts me in good stead with the neighbours. And by selecting the album titles personally, I can try and ensure that if I'm going to be kept awake late at night by loud music coming through the walls, it'll at least be something that I like, such as The Pixies.

One day I hear a commotion outside on the street. It's David Leecham, and he's arguing with a couple who live further down the street in a dump of a house near the corner of Turbot Street. They're truly scummy looking people, the great unwashed but with bad attitudes. I've never had anything to do with them, but some of the others in The Palace have said they've had run-ins with them before, like the time they just wandered into Twix's party and started watching his movies. The guy's in thongs and an oversized Rabbitohs jersey that looks like it's got blood or wine stains on the sleeve. The girl's got a mess of bed-hair that looks like it's never seen a brush, and she's barefoot. In her arms she cradles a full-size bottle of Coke like a baby, and is staring at Leecham with a lacklustre and stupid faculty.

'I can see the fucking name on it,' yells Leecham at them, his face red with fury and jabbing a finger at a package the guy is carrying. *My* fucking package, to be precise!

'Nah, we found it, carnt,' snarls the guy, gripping the package tighter.

I'm halfway across the street now, wondering how to get the CD's away from all three of them.

One of the lesbians from upstairs, Roz, is leaning out a window with her flatmate Chantelle, and calls out: 'Fuckin leave em, Dante. We're enjoying the show.'

The scummy girl looks me up and down as if she disapproves of the way I dress. Or maybe it's just the way I carry myself, but it seems as though it always comes down to how I dress.

Leecham also glances around to find the whole street's watching the argument unfold, but he doesn't care. He's the aggrieved party and will vent as he sees fit.

'The store manager said you aresholes have been using my credit card to buy CD's for the last month,' he accuses the scummy couple.

'Fark orf,' goes the guy, and starts walking off. 'C'mawn, Tammie! Get a farkin move on.'

Tammie snaps out of staring at Leecham and shuffles off after her beau, her thongs snagging on the concrete and nearly tripping her head over heels.

Leecham looks like he's about to run after them. His neck muscles are taut and the veins on his arms pulse. It's like he wants to snap a cunt in half, so I decide to cut my losses, heading back across to The Palace and watching the rest of the proceedings from there.

Bernie's on his little fold-out chair looking very amused by it all.

'A little drama for the afternoon,' he goes. 'Didn't even have to turn on *Home and Away* for it.'

MAD COW ABI

I'm on a girl's road-trip with Maddie and her friends Jane and Sabrinha, the latter of whose car it is. Jane and Sabrinha are more like hippies in their dress and style, but are one hundred percent punk in their attitudes and music tastes. Jane's got an old tape from a band called The Horny Toads playing in the tape slot, thrashing her dreads around to a song called *Rock Hard* and reminiscing about seeing them tour with The Exploding White Mice in 1989, while Maddie keeps checking the referdex to work out where our turn-off for Springbrook National Park is. We're headed to stay the night with their friend Dave, who has managed to score a position as a park ranger.

I met them all at Twix's party at the Prozac Palace where they were selling fake LSD. Funniest shit ever! Since then I've hung out a couple of times with them, especially Maddie. She's the one who invited me along, and it's been fantastic so far! Just getting out of the city and driving the sun-saturated highways with the windows rolled down and the wind whipping the hair into our eyes as we sing.

At one point Jane's telling me how her and Maddie help refugee families in their spare time because the refugees have to spend six months on review before they can even be considered for financial help from the Government if they can't get work.

'They get fuck all from it, anyway,' she yells over the sound of the wind. 'So why make it harder, hey? But the Federal Government wants to cut the programme altogether. So me and another friend, Tess, are fighting them over it, in the political arena, hey? In the meantime we're setting up an underground network of people like Maddie here who can help feed or house the refugee families. A lot of them have kids, you know?'

'I didn't know,' I say, hoping she won't ask me to volunteer space in my flat. I already look after people in my day job.

'Some of these refugees have been tortured in their home countries for the crime of having a different religion or being poor,' she continues, 'and they come here and we're almost no better to them. Immigration and the Review Tribunal need to pull their fucking heads in for the way they treat people like cattle, sometimes.'

'I know, right,' I agree, for wont of something to say.

'*Non-genuine applicants* they reckon,' she says, shaking her head and staring at the dry landscape rushing past, probably imagining what she'd do if she could get her hands on the Government officials.

The drive to Dave's place from the highway is even better, because we're going through forests up the side of mountains on roads that are often one-lane only. We're out of the city and the rat-race now, and getting fresh mountain air into our lungs. You can see by the looks on the other girl's faces that it's the break we need.

Dave's pretty cool, a tall guy with a scraggly beard and a shaved head. He has a Dead Kennedy's tattoo on his arm that looks homemade, and some others that look like they could also be band logos. There's a huge septum piercing dangling from his nose.

He basically lives in a cottage on loan by the State Government for the duration of his contract as a park's ranger. It's not a bad place at all, and he delights in pointing out how self-sufficient it is with the solar panels and water tanks and compost toilet.

'Maddie tells me you work in aged care, Abi.'

'Yeah, for now. It's alright.'

'That's great, though,' Dave says. 'In a way we do similar jobs. Some of these trees are ancient but the modern world means they need tending to. We need to look after them in the same way you look after our own eldest.'

Fucking fruitloop.

'Yeah, I see what you mean.'

Dave smiles and nods approvingly, breaking out the bong.

'Now you're fucking talking,' grins Jane eagerly. She rubs her hands together.

We all have a toke and relax while Dave plunks on an acoustic guitar. He's not bad.

'Dave used to be in a band with Sabrinha,' Maddie tells me.

'It's true,' wisps Sabrinha airily, stroking Dave's skull. 'Now I just DJ.'

I suspect they were probably more than just bandmates.

'And now I'm *el capitano* of the forest,' says Dave.

The rest of the afternoon passes in this fashion, just sitting about and feeling cruisey, hitting the bong. My eye keeps being drawn to a poster on the wall above Maddie's head which is of a drag queen *sans* wig (just the stocking over a shaved scalp) running recklessly in a street with STONEWALL in huge letters above her head. Something about the queen's eyes and posture fascinate me, but I can't place why. From what I can tell, it's a movie poster, so could be a character running to or from some disaster, like in *Daylight*. Shit movie, that one. Basically a remake of *The Poseidon Adventure*.

'We're gonna go down and look at the glow worms when it gets dark,' says Maddie, dropping down onto the bean-bag with me. 'Have you ever gone before?'

'To the glow worms? No, but I've always wanted to.'

So I'm a bit excited for nightfall now.

Everyone's chatting amongst themselves, and Jane's engaged me in conversation about hair of all things because she tells me she's fixated on my fringe and how straight my hair is. She's making comparisons between our hair-styles, wondering what we'd be like if we swapped. She's clearly baked. At least she's stopped going on about refugees.

When the sun finally sets I keep watching Dave for indication of when we're gonna head down and look at these worms. Twix was telling me once about how he's seen them and said they were so beautiful to behold that he wrote two poems about from it, so I'm pretty keen. They're down in the cave of the Natural Arch, which is called that because the creek that flows above has worn a hole through the cave roof and now it pours through into a pool, thereby creating an arch from the crown of the cave.

But Dave's got other ideas, and ushers us into the kitchen where he's laid out some field mushrooms that he's picked himself.

'No fucking way!' exclaims Maddie.

'Magic mushies?' asks Sabrinha, as excited as Maddie is.

'Yup,' Dave grins. '*Psilocybe cubensis*, found all up and down the Eastern board. Let's cook up.'

He puts an old pot on the stove. The handle's long gone, so he uses a pair of tongs to manoeuvre it around, boiling the mushrooms into a broth.

'This is gonna be fucking magical,' goes Sabrinha, looking high as a kite already.

Dave reckons that a sweet herbal tea with strong flavour is best with shrooms, as he calls them, and his personal fave is liquorice tea. It sounds pretty gross to be honest, but I have to hand it to Dave, the taste turns out to be alright. I'd never even heard of liquorice tea until now! The mushrooms make the water turn a turgid brown colour, not unlike the Brisbane River after they've dredged it for the concreting industries. Maddie forgoes the tea bags and has hers straight up with a dollop of honey.

'Oh yum!' says Sabrinha.

I suspect her enthusiasm's a bit put on. It's not *that* good.

The other thing that surprises me is that the mushrooms have totally no effect whatsoever. I was expecting to be tripping, seeing psychedelic shit whirling in front of me or whatever, but there's zilch. Nada.

'It takes a while,' Dave says, popping out some pills before he has his share of the shroom tea.

I get a look at the packaging for his pills, and notice that they're Nardil, a phenelzine drug used to treat depression. We don't use that one at the Breakfast Creek View Aged Care, but I still know of it.

'It sustains my high,' Dave says when I ask him about it. 'It's a two-fold effect. I inhibit an enzyme that will boost my dopamine levels, and my serotonin too, and I can also activate the n,n-dimethyltryptamine compound in the shrooms.'

When he sees my overt curiosity at this, he adds: 'But I wouldn't bother with it for your first time.'

'But I'm not feeling the effects at all,' I whine. 'I might make a second cup.'

He places his hand over mine to stop me. 'Whoa there, Abi. It'll kick in soon. It was only one cup but I put heaps in the pot.'

Back in the lounge Sabrinha and Jane are arguing over the music selection, and we're all sitting around talking shit and rolling durries. The eyes on the drag-queen on the Stonewall poster look odd, like maybe someone (possibly Sabrinha?) has gone up and put eyeliner on the poster. The eyes are popping.

'Did you draw on that poster when we were in the kitchen?' I ask

Sabrinha.

She looks a bit disgusted with me, like I've accused her of a crime.

'Sorry, I don't mean to be offensive,' I go, 'but I just noticed that it looked weird.'

'That's the *cubensis* kicking in,' Dave says gently. 'Just breathe deeply, and slowly.'

I didn't realise it, but I was starting to hyperventilate. It's that fucking poster. The queen on it looks like she's actually starting to tear free from the paper she's printed on. Not moving, mind, just sort of sticking out from it like in a 3D effect. When I was in grade one as a little kiddie, we'd make these pictures by cutting out animals from wrapping paper and gluing cotton balls behind them, which we'd then stick onto a ceramic tile. The effect was that our little animals stood out from the background and looked more real than a normal picture. The effect fascinated me as a child, but right now the same trickery is producing the complete opposite feeling in me. I don't want anything to do with the Stonewall drag-queen looming toward me with those bugging eyes and her twisted, desperate body frozen in mid-flight.

'Abi, listen to me,' says Dave, his face sliding into view, his big blue eyes impossibly close. *'Breathe.'*

My chest expands and my lungs fill to capacity, like I've been holding my breath. When I look around the room, the others are watching me with concerned expressions.

'I'm okay,' I nod furiously. 'It's cool.'

'That's it,' smiles Dave, and passes me the durrie.

He's laced the joint with some pot, and I'm worried that it'll make me even more paranoid, so I limit myself to two small puffs only before passing it to Sabrinha.

Shifting the bean-bag puts the Stonewall poster out of view, but I desperately need to piss. The hallucinations have abated, so it feels safe to go.

It's weird, because now I don't feel anything again, like the trip has passed, but when I reach down and flip up the lid of the compost toilet the cavernous black hole seems to stretch towards me while the walls recede, like that camera trick they do in the movies when something big dawns on a character and the world seems to shrink around them. I thrust my hands out and feel the walls, pressing my palms against them to steady myself in case I fall straight into the toilet. That'd be fucking embarrassing!

When I get back into the lounge I feel it's best not to mention the toilet incident, but do admit that the hallucinations are coming in waves.

'Yeah, best score all week,' laughs Dave.

'Where do you find them?' I ask, imagining a ring of mushrooms growing in a lush green forest, lit by a beam of sunlight.

'Some cow dung in a paddock just down the road,' says Dave. 'I was just coming back from town and I could see these spots of white out in the paddock. Stopped the truck straight away and jumped the fence. Nature provides.'

'Sure does,' grins Jane.

Sure does. Cow shit provides. The mushrooms we just ingested, growing in cow shit.

I can feel my thoughts starting to spiral, but I'm powerless to stop the descent.

'Isn't that dangerous?'

All eyes turn to me. Bugging eyes rimmed with too much kohl. No, wait, that was the drag-queen.

There was a show on telly the other night where they showed video of cattle with mad cow disease from a few years ago, and it was distressing to watch. Their knees were shaking and they could barely stand up straight much less stand still because of the shaking. Those same cows died from the disease not long after the video was taken. They shoot cattle now if they show signs of mad cow disease. But if this virus has spread into humans, what then?

'You mean mad cow?' Maddie goes, and makes a *mooing* noise which she ends in a strangled sound.

'Yeah,' I admit, my voice trembling.

'Abi, its fine,' says Dave, his voice that mellow tenor again from before, placating and assuring. 'There isn't any mad cow disease in Australia.'

'This show on TV the other night said there're cases of CJD already here, though.' CJD was the name the show gave to the disease, and people who had it got symptoms that looked a lot like those shaking cows in the video footage.

Now Sabrinha and Maddie look worried, too.

'Guys, it's cool,' Dave says, noting the concern on the others. 'Seriously. There's farms all round here, and I talk to the farmers and read up on this stuff myself. CJD's been here for yonks. It's not here because of mad cow. It's not linked.'

'But the show said that people eating the meat could get it,' I say, irritated. 'One guy already has it!'

'Abi, he got it from the meat, yeah,' Dave goes, equally annoyed. 'But that's there. Not here. Everyone's been panicking about mad cow for years here, but it's not here. Both the Department of Health and the Therapeutic Goods Admin are pretty thorough at restricting access for any contaminated goods.'

He does sound like he's looked into this, and he's right that there's been panic. Not so much in the city, but more in the countryside. We haven't had any cases here but there's been speculation that some of our farms have fed their cattle with MRM, or mechanically-recovered meat, a blood and bone mix made up of cattle parts that could include infected spinal tissue. When I was still a little girl in 1987 there were ads shown on the telly about AIDS, which I'd never heard of before, and in the ads the Grim Reaper used bowling balls to knock down kids, parents and people from all walks of life that I recognised such as builders and hairdressers and whatever. Whole families, perishing to this thing called AIDS. While mad cow disease isn't a new thing, either, the death of nearly two-hundred thousand cattle in Britain a few years ago sparked new fears of it, and we've had the first human casualties this year. The same paranoia and fear that permeated my home in the late Eighties because of those AIDS ads has once again pervaded our lives.

'Its fine, Abi,' Jane chimes in, 'Dave knows what he's doing. Park Ranger and shit, right Dave?'

Maddie comes over and puts her arms around me because she can see I'm really distressed. Sure, I'm worried about mad cow disease coming in and mushing our brains, making us into these vegetables that can't walk and will fill our aged care facilities to capacity, vibrant young people reduced to–

'Abi, shh, calm down,' whispers Maddie. She wipes at the tears that have sprung in my eyes.

I must've been ranting aloud.

Jane's switched the punk music over to something mellower, and everyone has gathered around me to hold my hand while Maddie talks me through my panic attack. Dave gives me a glass of milk to drink, saying that it seems to work for some drugs.

The thing is, right, is that practically everyone in Britain now who eats meat could potentially have this condition, this CJD. It makes my blood run cold. I've seen the oldies with Parkinson's and dementia and I wouldn't wish that on anyone, and now here's a whole nation facing a fatal brain disease that may or may not surface anywhere from now to the next fifty years! It's like a zombie movie come to life.

Eventually I come good, and feel really fucking humiliated by my freak out, but the others are fully supportive, thank Gawd.

'Don't worry about it,' Dave goes, waving away my apology and giving me a hug. 'Just happy to see you come through it. We're gonna have a great night, don't worry about it.'

I feel so grateful for their support and understanding that I could cry again, and this gets a big chuckle out of everyone. Jane whacks on some Dead Kennedy's, and while it's not my kind of music it's exactly what's needed right now. We all start dancing around the room, stomping and bumping into each other. Maddie's got hold of me, arm in arm, and we're laughing so hard at Sabrinha's weird dance moves like they're from every tacky Seventies disco movie ever made.

Dave's got some firecrackers so we go out into the empty public carpark and light them up, marvelling at the colours and profiles exploding in the night, lighting up the forest around us.

Maddie and I are in the gazebo when we decide to light one, thinking it's gonna be a little bunger or something, but it turns out to be one that fires into the air. Maddie's leaning over it when it goes off, and it shoots straight at her face. She throws her head back and arches over, almost falling backwards, as the rocket screams past her nose and strikes the roof of the gazebo and explodes. The green and orange sparks spray out across the ceiling and rain down like an umbrella of fire all around Maddie, who stands motionless, her face craned skyward at the sparks. She looks so beautiful standing there in this detonation of light.

Suddenly, we notice a car sitting about forty metres away, with its headlights pointed straight at us. We stop letting off the firecrackers, wondering aloud whether it's the cops or a serial killer. Eventually Jane's had enough and grabs a flare from our bag of goodies, strikes it above her head and rushes at the vehicle.

It doesn't move, and I have lump in my throat, fearful for Jane's safety.

She looks like a crazy woman with her dreads bouncing around her head, lit up by the smoking red flare held high above her head as she roars menacingly. She stops by the driver's side, engaging in a quiet conversation with whoever's at the wheel.

'Fuck, Dave, what do we do?' asks Sabrinha.

'Dunno,' he goes. 'I hope it's not my boss.'

Jane saunters back, twirling the flare so that the light oscillates wildly in our eyes, trailing a thick plume of crimson smoke behind her through which the vehicle's headlights cut through as it turns to exit the carpark.

'Was it the devil?' goes Maddie.

'Nah, just some lost Asian tourists,' giggles Jane. 'Scared out of their fucking wits by us, but.'

This cracks us up, our laughter bouncing around the trees.

The rest of the night is awesome. We head down to the Natural Arch, our torches failing us half-way down the narrow dirt track so we're forced to stumble along blindly, tripping on the occasional tree root. But eventually we make it down to the rock pool and the cave, deafened by the rush of the water through the hole in the ceiling. We hold each others' hands and enter into the darkness and the din, Dave leading the way.

Inside there's a wooden balustrade to stop people falling in the water.

'Look up,' yells Dave.

All around us I can briefly make something out, something green, like light. When my eyes finally adjust, the light becomes clearer, more focused, and I'm able to easily pinpoint their distinct locations, although there's literally hundreds of them.

'Glow worms!' squeals Sabrinha.

Fuck yeah. The whole cave around us is alive with them, a mass of greenish glowing bugs right above our heads.

Everything feels right with the world. There might be cows galore dying across the oceans, but here inside this cave time has stopped and we have just the glow.

Like Sabrinha might say, it's magical.

NEW BEGINNINGS

The 412 bus takes the boys up Coronation Drive, through Toowong and along Sir Fred Schonell Drive towards the University.

Dante fiddles with the air-conditioning nozzle above him, but the air that blasts out is barely cool. The wind coming from the window in the seat before them provides more relief, so he struggles to slide his own window open. It catches several times, jerking from his hands.

'See that other park across the river?' says Twix.

He points out the window when they're passing a park on their own side of the river, complete with an art deco theatre called the Avalon. Dante can, indeed, make out another park on the other bank across the river.

'That's where the Vampire Lesbians lured that taxi driver to his death a few years ago to drink his blood,' says Twix.

Dante tries to pick out the details of the park better but it slips from view as the bus rounds the bend and continues down past the new townhouses built to accommodate the growing influx of students to the area.

'We'll have to go up the back of West End one day and check it out,' suggests Dante. From behind them they hear another passenger tell their friend that the boys' suggestion is morbid, but neither Dante nor Twix think it is.

The bus rumbles all the way to the terminus at the University, about faces at the roundabout and continues back along Hawken Drive until it comes to a complete stop at some shops.

'End of the line,' says Twix, swinging from the bus doors and into the oppressive heat of the Queensland summer sun. The massive ironbark trees next to bus shelter are so tall that their shade is cast uselessly upon the house behind them, leaving the boys in the full glare of the burning rays.

'Please tell me your new place is just here,' whines Dante, who's wearing his trademark black dinner jacket with the pin-buttons on the lapels. Many on the scene like to unkindly joke behind his back that he looks like Rik Mayall from *The Young Ones*, but Dante's fond of the comparison. Even though the lining's torn open and lets a little airflow through, it's otherwise heavy and hot on his back.

'Not far,' says Twix, and leads Dante down onto the Esplanade, where there's a lush park and open access to the river. 'There's a great breeze through here so it's not as hot as living at the Prozac Palace. Just wish there was a closer train station.'

The son of a train driver, Twix gets free travel on the QR network. Now the buses eat into his drinking funds.

At the bend in the gully Twix leads Dante into a two-storey brick apartment complex, flanked either side by stately homes and their charming gardens.

'Congrats on moving into the Prozac, by the way,' says Twix.

'Cheers,' goes Dante.

'So how is it? Better than sleepin on the streets, surely?'

'It's different,' says Dante, noncommittally.

'Are you kidding me?' scoffs Twix. 'No more rats crawling across your feet and stuff.'

'Waking up with possums sitting on top of me.'

'*Géniale!*' says Twix. 'Unless now you wake up and Bernie's on top of you.'

'Piss off, idiot,' says Dante. 'But yeah, I guess it's alright. There's hot water, and TV, and I can cook toast whenever I want. Mum and Dad came up from Stanthorpe with a bed. It's only a single spring base but beggars can't be choosers, can they? And no-one's gonna stumble across me and start kicking the shit out of me for fun.'

'There's a plus,' grins Twix, opening the front door. A waft of cool air greets them. The apartment block is nestled into the belly of the hill beneath which Hawken Drive winds along, so that and the cluster of homes surrounding it keeps the building from the full heat of the sun. Add to that it's a bottom storey flat, and the temperature inside is perfectly regulated.

'But forking out cash every week for the rent is a bit of a kick in the guts,' says Dante. He looks around at the lounge area of Twix's flat. Solid, cement-rendered walls and well-kept carpets. 'Ooh, this is nice.'

Twix shrugs. 'We've all gotta make sacrifices in life, mate,' he says, referring to Dante's having to pay rent. 'But don't see it as money lost rather than services gained. All those things you mentioned – the telly and toast and security – that's what you're paying for.'

'Good point,' nods Dante.

'Just wait until the electricity and phone bills come in, too,' grins Twix, and Dante groans. 'But it's what we have to do in life, Dante. Better ourselves all the time. Malik's been going on about that lately, too, and I agree with him. This is just the first step for me to get into a flat of my own.'

Dante wants to roll his eyes because he's not the biggest fan of Malik, and so by dint is not the biggest fan of his so-called wisdom, either.

'Well, you seem to have done well for yourself, at least,' says Dante, gesturing around the flat. He notices a wooden coffee table with sheaths of paper and a biro on it, and clocks that Twix has been writing poetry. He's desperately hoping he won't be subjected to an extended recital.

'Yeah, St Lucia's great,' enthuses Twix. 'All those Uni chicks with no time for a steady boyfriend but stressed out enough for a quick root to take the edge off. I'll be swimming in pussy.'

This isn't how Raven described Uni girls to Dante. She'd said a lot of them have already got boyfriends, and they definitely wouldn't be interested in Twix if they didn't.

'So there's swimming pools there with disembodied lady parts, eh?' says Dante, deliberately hoping to ruin his friend's analogy and thus his enthusiasm for using it again in future.

'Fuck off, you know what I mean,' says Twix in a tone that tells Dante his jibe worked.

Twix shows off his bedroom, which he's nicknamed Zothecula.

'You named your bedroom?' laughs Dante. 'What for?'

'Why not?' retorts Twix. 'People name their cars, their boats.'

'Yeah, and there's a name for those people: wankers.'

'Don't you like the name Zothecula? It's Latin for *little alcove*, apparently. From a Bauhaus song.'

'It could be Pig-Latin for *den of the gods*, for all I care. It's bloody stupid.'

'Yeah, right!' scoffs Twix. 'That's not how Pig-Latin even works.'

'Not the point,' remarks Dante.

'Anyways, this is the bedroom,' says Twix, keen to move on from the topic of his room's Christening. 'The other two doors go to Billy and Greg's rooms.'

'And what have they called theirs?'

'*Fuck* and *You*,' smirks Twix and strolls back down the hallway to the lounge.

'I don't know if I could live in a place with three people,' Dante says as he joins Twix. They stare out the glass sliding doors at the big yellow flowers in the bushes across the road. 'It'd feel suffocating.'

'But you grew up with parents and a brother,' Twix points out.

'People change. I've changed,' admits Dante. 'I've started getting used to the streets, given I've been on and off em for a couple of years now.'

'It's been way longer than that,' says Twix. 'You've been homeless for yonks. It's a bloody miracle you even manage to stay on the scene.'

Dante shrugs, and watches a girl with a backpack stroll past, flipping through her text book, oblivious to being observed.

'See?' says Twix excitedly, gesturing through the glass at the girl. 'They park all along the Esplanade and walk straight past here. It's like window shopping without having to go anywhere.'

Dante screws his nose up. 'Settle down on the chauvinism, mate.'

'I'm not being chauvinistic,' argues Twix. 'It's healthy hormones, is all. As if you can talk, you slut.'

'What are you on about?'

'Come off it, Dante,' laughs Twix, heading over to the sink and pouring them a couple of glasses of water. 'You can barely keep it in your strides yourself, and you're havin a go at me?'

'Well, for a start I don't think that's a fair assessment of my sex life,' says Dante, 'and secondly, a root-rat and a chauvinist are two entirely different things.'

'Yeah, yeah,' says Twix snidely, 'pull the other one.'

He hands the glass of water to Dante and toasts him. 'Here's to new beginnings, for us both.'

'Cheers,' says Dante, raising his glass, fighting the urge to ram it into Twix's chin.

BREAK BREAD

I'm taking Nicola to lunch today, and as luck would have it, when I go to the ATM to get some money out someone has left their card in the slot and the screen is asking if I wanna make another transaction. The answer is well and truly yes, naturally, so I make a withdrawal for two hundred dollars. I'm tempted to make it more, but don't know how much time's remaining to check the account, let alone grab the cash and run. Turns out the answer is no time at all, for a yuppie guy in a pressed shirt and pants with a thick gold chain around his neck comes up behind me, peering over my shoulder. Straight off the bat I've clocked the toupee: it sits too high off his scalp to be natural. And those flinty eyes, the kind that can predict a man's death, if not personally guarantee it. I'm no gynaecologist, but I know a real cunt when I see one. Something about him fucking bugs me.

We lock eyes and I immediately go on the defensive, giving the cunt a disapproving look as he watches his card eject from the ATM.

'Sorry, mate,' he says, frowning at the cash in my hand, 'you didn't happen to see a lost card here?'

'Nah, sorry,' I go, pocketing this dumb cunt's hard-earned savings.

I don't believe in morality, or at least I don't think it pertains to me. I'm more of the belief in values, which are an entirely different thing from morality, and the personal values that I've come to endear myself to over the years are in stark contrast with what most people subscribe to when they idiotically say they follow a moral code. I'd rather tailor-make my rights and wrongs according to the things I've learned in life, and what I've learned is that when this fucker with the bad toupee and cold, flinty eyes piss-farting around at my back's not preoccupied with misplaced bank cards, he's likely more than happy to sneer at poor fuckers like me and thereby psychologically increase his own perceived sense of success. I'm rather enjoying the panic in his eyes right now, the realisation that he's lost something of great significance and that there's a possibility that a bottom-feeder like me might've availed themselves of some of it. In much the same way that this cunt might ordinarily absorb some sense of superiority from passing me in the street and calling me some fucked up name, I too now have a sense of greatness from *his* inability to cope with the situation he finds himself in, a situation that said bottom-feeders like me happen to excel in.

He goes into the bank in some futile effort, perhaps, to stop his funds from dribbling away, so I drop his card down the drain.

There's enough cash here for me to not only take Nicola to lunch, but also grab ol Twixxie a fucking whiz-bang belated house-warming pressie for his new place in St Lucia and still have loads left over. Not that the cunt really deserves a pressie, after he called me a slut. Still, I'll get him one anyway and show him up. I don't remember him getting me a housewarming gift when I moved into the Palace.

With a big shit-eating grin on my face, I stroll across the Victoria Bridge, slipping ol Ledrud twenty bucks, then continue my merry sojourn up Melbourne Street into West End to meet up with my girl.

A lunch date isn't something I'd ordinarily do, not because I'm not a romantic or anything like that, but simply because I'm actually a bit shit at dating. While I don't necessarily think Nicola's into dating, either, I'm compelled by McKay's psychological experiment challenge to try and do something that regular people do, like a lunch date at least. It feels quite good arranging the whole thing, if I'm honest, even if I did feel like a bit of a fucking idiot asking her at the time. But when I asked her there was that beautiful sparkle in her eyes that I love so much and then I knew that this wasn't a bad thing to do. As with stealing that cunt's money, I'm not arranging this date out of any sense of morality (concepts like dating before fucking spring to mind) but because the look that came into her eyes when I asked her told me this was worth it. I could probably live for that look alone, from now on.

Probably.

I don't know, maybe that's going too far.

I've arrived way too early, so I duck into the op-shop where we've arranged to meet and browse around a bit.

Passing all the shirts and coats hung alongside one wall, I hear some mumbling, but it's so faint that I don't pay it any attention, until I suddenly see this forlorn face jammed between two coats. It nearly scares the fucking shit out of me, and I feel anger rise up in me by way of response.

Turns out it's just one of the West End specials hidden amongst the clothes on the rack, staring out at me with big wet eyes and moving his lips in a whisper. I try and push down my anger.

'What the fuck are you doing in there?'

He blinks a few times, like he's just come back to reality, and goes: 'Wanna buy some xanax?'

These stupid old fucks from the boarding houses around here are always trying to palm off their medications so they can afford to buy beer and drink themselves to forgetfulness. It's an easier route than dealing with the shitty memories or brutal boredom of their lives.

'Go home and take your medication,' I order him, as if I was his health professional. The stupid old prick climbs out from the rack and shuffles out the door.

I've only just stopped taking antidepressants myself, as of last week. I'd been complaining to my psych a few months ago about feelings of uselessness and wanting to maybe top myself, and it was my idea that I go back onto medication again. I didn't mind the Prozac the first time around (last year), which is a serotonin reuptake drug, and unlike most people I know it actually did me some good, but after a few months I didn't think it was doing anything, and I'd felt my old destructive self re-emerge. My theory was that physiologically I'd adjusted to the drug, like I'd hormonally rebalanced myself to it and eventually it simply had no effect on the inhibitors in my brain that slowed down my serotonin intake.

McKay explained it like there's a grid across my brain, and each cross-point sparks an electrical current to the other points around it, spreading the serotonin around and creating a relatively pleasant version of me. But sometimes they misfire and the currents aren't making it across, and the lack of serotonin makes me a pretty fucked person to be around.

At least, that's how I'd understood what he was saying. I'd been off the Prozac for yonks, and wanted something as effective, so McKay had suggested venlafaxine. It was a new one on the market, one that he said was going to be popular, and could do what all the other serotonin reuptakes couldn't do: increase the norepinephrine levels in my brain. This would normally mean fuck all to me, but whereas the fluoxetine in Prozac dampened my sexual drive, I had no problems with that area on this venlafaxine called Effexor, and was back to wanking off twice a day.

The fluoxetine drugs some doctors are doling out are old news now that these you beaut venlafaxine drugs are available, I reckon. SSRIs (fluoxetine) were introduced into the populace in 1990, quickly dominating the anti-depressant market and replacing the tricyclic antidepressants of yesteryore, known as TCAs. They were initially considered more favourably because SSRIs are harder to OD on, apparently. Now both are old hat with these SNRIs, which is what I was on up until last week, that venlafaxine stuff. I heard recently that someone took a lil peek into the Department of Veteran Affairs' dispensing claims database and discovered that some of these old fucks, guys like the one hidden in the coats, are still taking the old TCA medication along with the new SSRI ones, which you're not supposed to do. Who says they're actually taking both, though? One down the hatch, palm the other off at your local op-shop for beer money.

The British Pharmacological Society reports that concession card holders – that is, those of us on sickness benefits, disability support pensions, child welfare recipients, aged pensioners and war veterans – make up thirty-nine percent of Australia's population but we get sixty-four percent of the prescription drugs that chemists sell. We're a viable part of our economy's growth, a one-hundred million dollar a year industry that continues to grow as more medications are released at ever-more increasing prices. This isn't something to sniff at and dismiss. Us nutjobs have become a contributing pillar to the Land of Oz's economy whether you like it or not. Ironically, a lot of the drug companies are now following industry-sponsored rules and trying to convince us that as a result of their exorbitantly-priced medications health-care cost has been dramatically reduced. What a load of horse-shit. Zoloft alone costs the Australian Government nearly forty million dollars through the fucking PBS!

I see the old coat guy hanging around the park bench outside the op-shop, so I press my mouth on the glass to do a window blowfish, banging my fist on the glass to get his attention, motioning for him to fuck off home when he looks around at me. He wobbles his jowls like a spastic walrus, shuffling off up the street with a kind of mortal fear in his eyes. Stupid old fuck.

'You shouldn't laugh at him,' says this elderly lady behind me. She's got some clothes and hangers draped over her arm. Obviously volunteers here. 'He's *special needs.*'

'Oh nah, he's okay,' I say to her, flashing a disarming smile. 'We're old friends. It's a just a joke we have between us.'

She remains unconvinced, and continues to frown disapprovingly at me as I pretend to meander around the store for a bit. I can imagine the old coat guy will get home and be thankful he's got those pills to calm his poor nerves now. See? Yet another thankless service to the community that I provide, not that the stuffy ol biddies in here would appreciate that. Their idea of Providence is turning up to church on time every Sunday morning.

In the glass service counter are piles of crap jewellery. It gets dumped into their charity bins along with bags of musty clothing by relieved middle-aged fucks who've suffered through years of their folks' waning years, waiting for the day the old fucks keel over and cough up the inheritance monies. Amongst the stacks of rings stuffed into ornamental ashtrays is a gold one fashioned into a triangle with the number thirty-three in bass relief at its centre.

'You wanna chuck that one out,' I say to the old biddy at the cash register. 'Shit-tonne of bad luck for you having that one in the shop.'

She just boggles her eyes at me and sucks the saliva dribble from the corner of her mouth. It crawls back between her lips like a reverse creampie.

The door bell tinkles and Nicola comes in. Finally. The old biddy is still casting sour looks my way, which is our cue to leave, even though Nicola says she wants to look around first.

'Can't,' I say, injecting a note of regret into my tone. 'Reservation's fast approaching.'

'Reservations?' She looks a bit stricken. 'Geez, that's a bit full-on.'

'Nah,' I go, making eye contact with the old lady behind the counter and giving her a wink as I lead Nicola out the door, 'there's a loads of West End specials going around at the moment, so having reservations is considered the best approach.'

The old biddy looks pretty ticked off now. Too bad.

We get up around the corner to a little place I was recommended by Roshan, an Indian place he works at and says is real authentic and not over-priced, not that it matters anymore thanks to the thoughtless flinty-eyed yuppie at the ATM in the city.

It's a modest little establishment, the usual trimmings and with a buffet style spread for those who prefer to try a bit of everything. The grub smells amazing, and the girl behind the counter shows us to a little table. We've barely sat down when I see Roshi, the cheeky cunt, come out from the kitchen in his work uniform.

'Rosh, you didn't tell me you were going to be on today!'

He grins. 'I'll send you my roster next time.'

I introduce him to Nicola, and he lets us know that he's going to prepare for us some of the high-end menu stuff at the regular dish prices. He's a top guy, always got my back!

But Nicola seems out of it, a bit off her face actually, so when we're ordering she seems reluctant to pick out what she wants to eat.

'I'm not really hungry,' she goes.

'Then what're we doing here?' I wave a hand at the room.

'Yeah I know,' Nicola moans, 'but I don't have any appetite.'

'Are you sick?' But I've already guessed the answer.

'Naw,' she goes, with the hint of a smile, 'just high.'

'For fuck's sake,' I say, shaking my head.

Fucking doctor death of me!

'Ease up, dude.'

She's telling me to *ease up*? The fuck?

'Yeah, right,' I snarl, 'but you know, I'm not really cashed up most of the time and I thought this might be something that, you know...'

I shrug, making sure to mope. Of course, I neglect to mention the two-hundred bucks from the ATM. That's not the point here. It's the principle that matters.

'No, I don't know,' she says flatly, looking at me like she despises me.

'I don't get it. You knew we were coming here. Why take those fucking pills?'

'Jeffrey died.'

Brilliant. Don't I look like a cunt now?

To make matters worse, I can't actually recall this Jeffrey's face. I'm wracking my brain going through all Nicola mates, and not a single fucking one of them rings any bells as this Jeffrey.

'Sorry, I didn't know,' I offer. 'Did I meet him?'

She starts to snigger but stops herself, which gets me defensive.

'Right, well, I don't get it, Nicola,' I yell. 'Your mate Jeff's dead so you get high but now it's funny he's dead?'

'No, Dante. I'm sorry. Jeffrey's the singer of The Gun Club.'

Of course. Only one of her favourite bands. But how was I to guess the correlation?

'He died yesterday from a brain haemorrhage,' she goes on. 'I just feel fucking gutted. I'm sorry.'

'Don't be,' I mutter, unsure what to do, feeling embarrassed about my outburst.

'I shouldn't have had the pills, but I just needed something to get me through it. I didn't want to cancel and let you down.'

And yet, paradoxically, by turning up high, she has.

Roshan comes out with plates of Persian-style fish on spiced rice, and other delicacies. He informs us conspiratorially that the fish is cooked in a way that the restaurant reserves for the big boss only, and that customers never get the privilege of tasting it.

'It's the best thing since grated cheese,' he winks.

Then he clocks Nicola looking dazed, her eyes dilated to the point that her entire iris nearly disappears.

When she excuses herself to head into the dunny, Roshan asks if she's okay. He's gravely concerned.

'Yeah, don't worry about it. Drugs.'

'Oh man,' he sympathises, running his palm across his scalp.

'Happens,' I shrug. 'Her favourite singer died today.'

'Dante, listen to me,' he says quite serious. 'That's no good. She's no good. You are just wasting your time.'

'Yeah, you're probably right,' I nod, not really in the mood for the lecture. 'This fish is fucking amazing, by the way.'

His face softens then cracks into a smile, filled with such warmth. 'You'd only ever get that at a special function or back in Iran,' he says proudly.

'You're too good to me.'

'I know,' he says, looking at me with something close to pity.

When Nicola gets back to the table, I insist she try the fish at least. She's more than reluctant to, and although I know that even the smell of the grub's probably making her gag, I pretend I'm none the wiser and coerce into taking a small piece by guilt-tripping her about the cost. Her face fairly loses colour as the fish slides down her throat.

'Good, ay?'

She can't hide her disgust, but nevertheless agrees.

I devour as much of the fish and rice as I'm able to on my own, and Roshi packs the leftovers into a doggy-bag, saying: 'Remember what I told you.'

'Yup.'

When we get outside Nicola's curiosity gets the better of her and she goes: 'What did he tell you?'

'Who?'

'Your friend. What'd he tell you?'

It's obvious that she's clued it was about her.

'Nah, it was nothing,' I go.

Let it eat at her.

I decide to head home, but don't invite her back, opting to pretend that I thought she'd prefer to walk back to her flat up on Dornoch Terrace. As the bus pulls away from the curb I intentionally refuse to look out the window even though in my periphery I can Nicola's still standing there. She's waving goodbye. Probably got that hangdog expression, too.

The lights turn red so we're stuck here, but a few feet away from the bus-stop. From the corner of my eye I can still see Nicola. Why won't she just fuck off home already?

On the other side of the bus I notice Uncle Kev, but he mustn't've got his eyes done yet because he hasn't seen me. Either that or he's flat out ignoring me, the old bugger.

'Oi, Uncle Kev,' I go, changing seats to sit with him, aware that I'm now completely out of view of Nicola.

'Dante?'

'The one and only,' I say. 'I thought you might've gone walkabout by now, maybe even headed back down south one last time before the cold sets in.'

'Nah, gotta stick around for these tests,' he goes, folding some TAB forms in half and sticking them in his pocket. Been gambling away his dole money, as usual. 'Buggers are piss-farting around.'

As the bus accelerates away I feel a stab of remorse, my conscience telling me that I'm being the world's biggest cunt to Nicola, but I quell the feeling, reminding myself it's not I who ruined our date.

'You want to get onto them and tell em to pull their bloody socks up, ay,' I go.

'Too right,' nods Uncle Kev.

'I've got myself somewhere to live now,' I say proudly.

'I thought you were already living in Spring Hill?' he says, and I'm surprised he's retained even that much from our last conversation.

'I was just crashing at a friend's place, but now I'm living with Bernie, this old schizophrenic bisexual guy.'

I tend to think of – and introduce – people by what differentiates them from everybody else. It helps me to remember who's who and sometimes how they relate to one another. So many young people nowadays are anti-label, and half the time I'll cop crap about how someone's 'not into labels' or some shit, like as if they're not already applying names to everything in order to communicate effectively. On the one hand I get what they mean, but on the other I find it useful.

Uncle Kev gives a little cough. I notice he's trying to imperceptibly shift away from me, shimmying his arse down the seat. A full hand span has opened up between us. The homophobic cunt thinks that because I'm living with a bisexual guy then by default I must also be bisexual. Fuck me, but some guys are precious about their sexual identity!

And here I was thinking about slipping him fifty bucks, too! Well, he can get fucked.

By the time I get home to The Palace my conscience still hasn't let up about how me and Nicola parted, and I lie on my bed feeling like utter shit, wanting to cry but unable to.

VOODOO DOLLY

Heading to the Valley at night dressed in fetish gear is one thing, but it's, like, quite another to do it broad daylight on a Monday afternoon. Two boys on the train across from me sucking melted Easter Egg chocolate off their fingers obviously think my coat looks suspicious this time of year because they, like, keep surreptitiously glancing over as if they're going to catch a gander of something for the spank-bank later on.

I follow the instructions that Ryley wrote down, basically looking incongruous as I walk up the street from the train station. It's all homes around here, like really nice ones, and a lady watering her garden glares at me as if, like, I've defiled the good reputation of her neighbourhood.

A girl answers Ryley's door dressed head to toe in rubber. Like, even her whole head's covered. Just her eyes staring from two holes and her teeth behind an open zipper mouth are all that remains of her.

She's like: 'Alex, you made it! Welcome to the Liberty Club,' and only now do I realise that it's Ryley's partner Evey, the one dressed as the nurse at Club Inferno. She notices my coat and the heeled boots poking out beneath. 'You should of just got dressed here.'

'I didn't realise.'

'It's not the Inferno, sugar,' she smiles, the sides of her gimp mask creasing up into a hideous manifestation of something from a horror movie. 'You're here by invitation. We try and do this on weekends, but most people like to go away with the kids over the Easter long weekend, so Tuesday afternoon it is, I'm afraid.'

I'm like: 'No worries.'

I give her my coat, slightly embarrassed by my zip-up PVC top and purple snakeskin patterned PVC skirt. I don't have much fetish-wear and didn't want to wear my latex halter-top again in case they thought it was the only true fetish gear I have, which it is. Hopefully my goth stuff is passable.

She takes me through the house, which looks normal, except for one room where a man dressed in a big pink rubber bunny suit is getting oiled down by two girls, one of whom has weights on chains clamped to her labia.

'That's the playroom,' Evey says. 'I'll explain the rules and the safe words for you if you'd like to go in later.'

'Is that the Easter Bunny?' I joke.

'Funny timing, huh?' grins Evey. 'That's Mister X. He likes going by pseudonyms. For fun only, not because he's trying to hide his identity or anything.'

There's all sorts of toys on tables, some that'll need explaining. To one side is a girl that's basically been crab-tied and behind Mister X (in his bunny suit) is an old man getting his nuts, like, paddled hard by an old woman who I presume is his wife.

This really is some next level shit!

Evey opens a door onto the backyard and gestures for me to join the crowd who're standing around drinking like they'd be unaware the playroom even exits if they weren't themselves already in various stages of undress or trussed up in leather and rubber. There's even a table out here for more tamer stuff like dripping wax on each other or whipping with horse crops.

Evey's like: 'Ryley's over by the barbecue. Make yourself at home. I've got to get back to my crab girl. Feel free to join in when you feel like it.'

I see Ryley over at the barbecue chatting with a couple while he turns the meat on the grill. He's completely starkers except for a leather thong that cradles his balls and goes up his arse-crack. His exposed penis hangs over the top like a big floppy sausage roll, like the kind that's been sitting in the servo warmer for weeks on end. Except there's a massive piercing going through the head of his penis, shining brightly in the sunlight.

'Hi, I made it,' I announce.

'So you did,' says Ryley with a big smile, turning to me so quickly his penis whacks against his hip before falling limply back between his legs. I'm trying my best not to keep looking at it.

He introduces the couple as his friends Mark and Janet, the latter buttering slices of white bread, and says Janet is famous in the BDSM community because she, like, appeared on a cover of *People* magazine in 1992 wearing a dog collar and positioned on all fours.

'It blew people's minds,' she says, waving the butter knife around as she gesticulates crazily. 'They couldn't handle it. It got banned and newsagencies had to take them off the shelves. Little by little we're breaking down barriers but it just goes to show you that society needs baby steps in dealing with the kind of stuff that *we* already think is fairly standard.'

'It's weird considering that, like, doggy style is such a popular position anyway,' I remark.

Janet's like: 'Exactly. Most favoured position for men!'

'Not all men,' Mark scoffs good-naturedly. 'Ball-tie is my favourite. Get in deep.'

She rubs her arse against her husband's groin and for a split-second I actually think they might start, like, getting it on right here at the barbecue. I mean, considering Ryley's choice of – or more accurately *lack of –* attire, it's highly possible, right?

'You're embarrassing the girl, Janet,' Mark says, looking straight at me with a wicked little smirk, like he's flirting not with his wife but with me. 'Naughty bunny.'

He holds up a small remote control device and says with a leer: 'In celebration of Easter, we already got an egg tucked away someplace hard to find. If she's naughty, Janet gets a clue as to its whereabouts.'

A thin cord runs from the controller down between Janet's legs, disappearing under her skirt. I hadn't noticed it before, what with Ryley's skewered sausage roll on full display.

'Anytime... she's naughty...' Mark says, pressing the button.

Janet squirms and her eyelids flutter half-closed.

'Warmer, warmer...' Mark coos.

Ryley's amused by this, but I'm not sure where to look, and settle for glancing around at the rest of the people. Basically, no-one's even paying any mind to the shenanigans of Mark and Janet.

'Enough,' Janet finally gasps. 'I've learnt my lesson.'

Mark laughs and releases the button.

Janet composes herself and gives me a playful apology. In a way, I find it really cool she just had a mini-orgasm so openly like that.

I'd always known about clubs like The Inferno and Hellfire and the Queen's Ball from reading magazine's like *Skin Two*, but beyond the recent experience with Abi and Chantelle at The Inferno my only real immersion in this world has been through my ex Zak. We used to, like, experiment with spanking and choking and collars, and even though he became an abusive boyfriend in the end, the fetish stuff we did was always really cool because basically there was still control and respect. Outside of that, when he, like, started hitting me and controlling everything I did, stopped me from seeing my friends and family, it was a like a completely different Zak to the one in bed who'd spank my arse or choke me while he pounded me. Like, the one I loved, the other I hated. My sister Lisa didn't understand that the degradation I gladly received in the bedroom had nothing in common with the fear and misery he'd induce in me in every other part of my waking life, so even though sisters normally share their private lives I'd eventually stopped confiding in her.

But that's a world away now. I finally got the courage to walk away from him, and life has never been better. Period.

Then I hear a familiar laugh. Feminine but manly at the same time.

I look over at one of the tables where the whipping and the wax is taking place, and see Jennifer from work standing there.

My blood freezes as all I can do is stare in horror.

'Don't worry,' jokes Ryley, 'we won't whip you unless you say so.'

'Oh, good,' I stammer, barely glancing at him before my eyes are wrench back in Jennifer's direction. I can't believe that *kargiola* has been invited to a BDSM party! How the hell is this happening?

'Sausage's are up,' shouts Ryley, scooping the oily snags off the hotplate into an aluminium dish. His penis dangles precariously close to the food.

Everyone comes over for a snag in a slice, and not wanting to get pressed up against Ryley's own flaccid snag, I duck out and over to Jennifer. It's only then that I realise the man climbing onto the table beside her is Mister Calthorpe! I barely recognise him in just his leopard-print jocks. His shaved gut bulges in contradiction to those wasted limbs, and his skin sags and creases with the culmination of his years on Earth. He looks like ET the Extraterrestrial.

No wonder he gave her a lift home today after work. We all joked it was so she could give him a blowie on the road, but, like, it turns out to be a bit more than a BJ.

'Why, Alexandra!' he says in shock, looking from me to Jennifer and back again. Finally he blurts out: 'Fancy running into the both of you here! Who's next, then, ay? Is Prita hiding inside somewhere?'

He's nervous as fuck, blabbing on, but Jennifer's managed to compose herself after the initial surprise.

She rolls her eyes and's like: 'Just stop it, Lyndon. She's worked it out already.'

So it's not just inside the office that darling Jenny here practically has the big boss by the short and curlies; she's barely treating him with the same courtesies she uses at work.

'Okay, okay,' Calthorpe stammers, gripping the sides of the table with white knuckles. 'Gig's up. Gig's up, eh? What're you gonna do then?'

It hadn't occurred to me that the ball would be thrown into my court, but they're both looking at me expecting an answer. Like, do I want to spill the beans to his wife, ruin his marriage, make things weird at work? Maybe I can use this to my advantage, basically leverage some respect from Jennifer and get her off my case finally?

But her face says otherwise. She's considering me with amused hostility. It's clear that I might be able to hold Calthorpe to ransom over this, but Jennifer couldn't care less if it ruined his marriage. Either way, she'd still be his piece on the side, she'd still be his favourite at work. She'd still lord it over me, piling me with more work than I can handle and timing my toilet breaks, which she pronounces as *torlet break*. More's the point, if I ruin his marriage then there's nothing to compel him to make Jennifer lay off me at work. She'd be worse than ever, with his full support.

I've got no other choice but to keep mum about this.

But there's no reason not to, like, cause him some pain in the meantime. Fully sanctioned by all present, of course. And I can still hold him to ransom in the workplace even if I never intend to reveal his dirty little secret.

'Don't worry about it,' I tell Calthorpe. 'Like, what happens at the Liberty Club basically stays at the Liberty Club.'

He smiles in relief, and physically collapses back onto the table.

'And, like, what happens at the Liberty Club,' I say, picking up a candle, 'is a shared experience, no?'

The expression on his face changes into one of glee as he realises what I have in mind. His eyes fix on my cleavage, much to Jennifer's annoyance.

A tip of the candle and the wax splashes down onto his smoothly shaved chest. I figure he gets rid of the hair for this activity alone, but whatever does he tell his wife?

He's *oohing* and *ahhing* and, like, arching his back off the table.

'Ease up, ganga,' Jennifer spits at me. 'You're doing it all wrong.'

'Am I really?' I coo, hoiking the zipper down on my top until my cleavage bulges so far out it's a wonder the girls don't just pop out. Much like Mister Calthorpe's eyes. That's it, you stupid old arsewipe, get a good gander while you can. 'Am I doing it wrong, Sir?'

'No, no, not at all,' he stammers excitedly, eagerly bracing himself for another splash of wax.

'Must be you're the ganga then,' I say smarmily to Jennifer, and dribble some more wax onto Calthorpe, making him groan with a mixture of pleasure and pain.

'You guys coming over for some grub?' shouts Ryley from the barbecue, holding up a sausage with his tongs.

'Be right over!' Jennifer shouts back, then fixes me with a dirty look while she addresses her sugar daddy. 'We done here?'

He's like: 'Sure, sweetie.'

Before he can even make a move I hoik the zip all the way down and my tits spring into view. I know this dirty old prick must have fantasised about them before. It gets precisely the desired effect: his jocks tentpole with his erection, exposing a neatly trimmed mat of greying pubes.

'Oh for God's sake, put em away, you slut,' Jennifer says, crossing her arms and rolling her eyes.

How fucking dare she talk to me like that when we're not at work!

'Are you going to let her speak to me that way, Lyndon,' I pretend-sulk.

It's a step too far, evidently. Seeing him practically skyclad with my own chest exposed is one thing, but addressing him by his first name proves to be where the boundary lines are drawn.

'You'll do well to remember who your superiors are,' he barks at me, catching the attention of some of the other invitees who begin wandering over to see what the problem is.

Without thinking, I grab his jocks and yank them open, his boner springing into full view, and fling the swill of hot melted wax from the candle straight into his underwear. The wax splashes all over the tip of his penis and into his pubes.

Instantly he screams loud enough to wake the dead, thrashing like a fish out of water before he falls sideways off the table and belly first onto the ground, yanking his underwear down and thrusting his hips as he rubs his groin into the grass in an apparent effort to, like, get the wax off. From where I'm standing it looks like he's humping the ground, his flabby white arse wobbling like a plate of jelly.

The spectacle makes me laugh out loud until Ryley appears at my side, calling for an explanation.

'He fell off the table,' I begin, but Ryley shakes his head angrily.

'Everyone saw you do it, Alex!'

I glance around and find that the whole party is standing there, staring at me with horror.

'He didn't, like, tell me the safe-word,' I mumble, not trying to be funny but just desperate to try and make this Calthorpe's fault, not mine.

'ARE YOU TRYING TO BE FUCKING CUTE WITH ME?' bellows Ryley.

'Get out!' says Evey, storming up behind her husband, no longer in the gimp suit. 'Get out now, Alex, and never come back!'

'Call an ambulance,' I hear a voice behind me say, while others call for ice, and still others for my lifetime banishment from all future fetish events Australia-wide.

'Please,' I start to sob, 'I'm sorry. It was an accident.'

Ryley grabs me by the arm and frogmarches me to the front door, my exposed boobs bouncing around as I try to keep upright in these stupid boots.

I'm tossed out after I've made myself decent again, wrapping my coat as tight around myself as I possibly can.

'You might be hearing from the police for this,' Evey snarls before slamming the door in my face.

FUCK.

I've fucked up.

Why did I do that?

I'm a wreck, a total wreck. I'm, like, bawling my eyes out on the train platform in front of everyone, hugging the coat to me tightly and sweating madly. Fuck me if this isn't the hottest day of the year so far.

A middle-aged bloke with a throat like a bullfrog lurks nearby.

'What's the coat for in this heat?' he wants to know.

'April Fool's joke,' I say flatly, hoping he'll go away.

'Oh yeah,' he sniggers, 'makes sense. Hope you got a few laughs.'

No, it doesn't make any fucking sense, I'm thinking.

He continues to lurk, sneaking peeks by pretending to be on the lookout up the tracks for the train, sighing dramatically when it fails to appear each time.

So now I'm left wondering what my options are. Do I, like, go back tomorrow and hope that Calthorpe and Jennifer pretend this afternoon didn't happen? Do I go back and beg for my position back, and hope that Calthorpe doesn't let the CES know? I'm fucked if he does tell them, because that'll be me out of a job and, like, no benefits either. I've barely saved enough to tide me over with rent and groceries while I find another job!

Thankfully the train finally arrives, but the frog-throated man follows me to the end of the carriage. There's a lot of spare seats but if I choose one of those he'll sit next to me. There's a boy about my age – sort of effeminate, but I don't think he's gay – sitting in a double seater so I gingerly sit across from him, and as I suspected the old bloke doesn't push his luck and chooses to sit across the aisle.

But he's, like, staring at my breasts bulging out of my top, so I have to pull the coat lapels over them even tighter than is possible.

The boy sitting across from me has noticed the man ogling, too, and says he used to get that all the time as well.

'Are you taking the piss?' I say angrily. The boy's the softer target here, so he's copping my pent-up emotions.

The boy's like: 'Not at all,' then checks to see if the creepy bloke's not watching. He grabs his shirt hem, yanking it up to his neck.

My instinct is to recoil, thinking this so and so's about to try and, like, get naked on me, but his chest is crossed with thick scars and I can't help but be fascinated.

'What happened?'

'I used to be a double D,' the boy says, and then it clicks: he used to be a girl!

'That's next level,' I breathe in wonder.

'Bandages came off recently, actually. There was leakage so I had to go back and get treated a few times but now it's all good, and the itching's stopped. The scars'll mostly heal over soon.'

The shirt comes back down just as the creepy bloke turns his head our way. The creep must've seen the shirt come down because he says: 'Flash em again.'

'Fuck off, you lech,' the boy growls at him. It's clear he's nervous, though, afraid of a backlash.

But thankfully the old bloke figures he's met his match and ambles off down the carriage in search of someone else to annoy.

'Thanks,' I say. 'Do you mind if I, like, ask when you had your sex-change?'

I'm fascinated only because I've never met anyone who's had the surgery before. Not as far as I know, anyway.

The boy gets a resigned look on his face like he's heard it a million times before, but happily answers anyway. 'No sex-change. Just a breast reduction. Damn things hurt my back, got me ogled and treated like an object. They did nothing for me. I hated them.'

'So you've still got a muff?'

'Of course,' she says, shaking her head.

'I'm sorry, I didn't mean to be offensive.'

This seems to make her happy. 'No problems. Most people are pretty rude about it, actually. They just don't get that someone might not identify as a gender.'

'You mean you're not a boy or a girl? Like, you're androgynous?'

The boy/girl nods, introducing themself as Phoenix.

Of course being androgynous is nothing new to the scene. At some point we've all met someone who claims to be genderless, and it's becoming more and more common, but they've usually, like, dropped the facade within a month or so. A year at most. Never to the extreme of removing body parts.

I glance down at my boobs, trying to imagine what it'd be like if they weren't there, but I'm so used to seeing them that try as I might it's impossible to think of my chest as flat.

'They give you lots of trouble?' says Phoenix, nodding at them.

'Got me fired today,' I sigh.

'Time to part ways with those useless motherfuckers, then,' shrugs Phoenix, making a scissor action across the chest.

I laugh. 'Yeah, maybe.'

'Happy Easter!' squeal a group of teenage girls with fluffy bunny-ear headbands on, bursting into the carriage and running through the train, dropping a small chocolate egg in everyone's laps as they go, giggling away.

Me and Phoenix smile at each other as we unwrap our chocolates.

THE ACRONYMS

Now that I've got a stable address at the Prozac and McKay's sorted out my medications, the CES has referred me to a Department of Education and Training for Youth rehab service that's Government subsidised. The truth is, this had been arranged before I'd even got on the disability pension on account of I'd overstayed my welcome on the sickness benefits so both the DSS and the CES thought it prudent that I go along and try my hand at what the rehab service had to offer anyway.

Of all the fucking luck.

It's just poor timing, really, since the new Howard Government has plans to eventually coalesce all these various departments into one massive entity in order to streamline the flow of information. Currently it's just too easy to rort the system, or in my current case be rorted by it. Just too many fucking acronyms trying to manage me at once when a keen eye overseeing the big picture would have seen it's not for me.

The letter from the DETY says to meet this Shirley woman at an address for one of those buildings next to the Anzac Square Park, the same park I first made out with Erina in.

They've got a pretty small space for a Government department, only a few staff members. It seems rehabilitating the disabled isn't such a big priority, and why would it be? There's several reasons, but straight off the top of my head I can imagine how much more costly and time-consuming it probably is to find us work, and something that we'd be inclined to stick at. Besides, there's what Alan reckons about the Government being not keen on rocking the unemployment figures too much. If they can siphon a whole lot of us onto disability benefits, then a department like this one surely only serves as a front to any naysayers who criticise the Government for not doing enough to rehabilitate back into the workforce. The risk for the Government on this, of course, is that they're relying totally on us fuckups to pull through on our end and maintain the employment that they do manage to find us, otherwise we'd slip back into the system and start the whole process over again, swelling those unemployment figures while the bloated figures for disability remain relatively unlooked at. It's a bit of a tightrope dance, really.

I'm not hopeful that this Shirley lady can do much for me, though, and I'll be upfront with her on that score. She greets me pleasantly and ushers me through to where her desk is, over by the window which looks down into Anzac Square. From here I can see the park bench where I sucked on Erina's tit.

Shirley explains a little bit more about her role, lots of boring shit about matching needs with clients and fulfilling support roles blah blah blah. It's all Double Dutch to me, lady. The plus side is that she's stopped speaking to me like she's reading from a brochure.

'Basically, we help you to try and get a job,' she says, all smiles.

Keating just resigned from Parliament to the envious tune of over a hundred grand a year for the rest of his life. Maybe I should likewise announce my retirement? Admittedly, the cunt's in his fifties and I've just started my twenty's, so there's that to take into account. And that I've got no job to retire from.

'Okay, sounds cool,' I go, letting a note of fatalism creep into my tone to gently massage her subconscious into readying itself to accept defeat. If not now, then later. 'I've given the situation a lot of thought myself, and I gotta say I can't see it ending in success. For either of us, to be honest.'

She simply nods, employing the tried and true tactic of any good negotiator: she hasn't agreed with me verbally, only allowed me to relax a little before she really tries to prise open my shell and expose me to her machinations. Negotiating public servants is like playing a bout of fencing. Thrust, retreat, thrust, strike.

'It's always a difficult process, I'll admit,' she says diplomatically. 'We've got a lot of people coming through, from all walks of life, and currently most of them occupy a position of employment somewhere, even if it's not full-time. And it doesn't have to be, either.'

Nice parry there, Shirley. I've picked up quickly on what you're up to, dropping words like *admit* to instil in me a sense of trust towards your veracity, and the carefully chosen phrase *from all walks of life* as a substitute for wasters and losers. You are well versed in your art; I give you that, lady.

'Well, it'd have to be a *lot* not full-time,' I counter. 'The fact is, I'm something of a fuck-up, if you'll pardon my language.' She indulges me with a patient smile. Doubtless, she's heard worse in here.

'I understand,' she goes, moving junk around on her desk in an unquestionably dead giveaway that I've got her on the back foot. 'You wouldn't be here with us, if you weren't facing difficulties. Can I play a little game for moment? Humour me, if you will.'

I shrug, agreeing happily enough.

'For a moment, don't think about what you can or can't do, or what skills you have or don't have. I want you to think about what kind of job you *would* have if you could have anything.'

The immediate answer, of course, is to tell her that me and Roshi need to set up a film production company doing all sorts of lucrative corporate gigs for high-flying clients, the kind of hideous commercial work that will financially pave the way for our more creative side projects, those of which will then go on to win accolades and garner interest from producers who demand to see feature-length stuff from us. Seems a no-brainer to me.

But it'd be a fatal blow to play that hand. *The arts* is not what these cunts want to hear.

What they want is to immerse me into the corporate world, find me meaningless work packing boxes onto a conveyor belt or cleaning out the bins from street to street, thereby depriving my homeless brethren of much sought after scrounging.

No, I know what she *wants* to hear, and I know what *I* want her to hear. I know how to make the two coalesce and still make me the victor in this tug-of-war over my free time.

I grin, standing up to face the window, watching the workers walk the streets to and fro. I don't understand anything of what they do. There's a multitude of different clothes, and some even look a bit like uniforms, but for the most part none of it means anything to me. I can't tell you what a single person down there actually does for a living. I couldn't even tell you if they were doing it right now, or if they were simply on a break. The nine-to-five routine is such an alien concept to me.

I decide I want to give Shirley a reasonable answer, to play this game with a little sincerity at least.

At last I turn from the window with my answer.

'I want to be that cunt that sits in an office somewhere, preferably somewhere high.' I glance again to the window, looking out at the black glass of the skyscraper over next to Post Office Square. 'No-one knows what I do, so I'm never asked to do anything, but I get paid a shit-load to be there. You know the type of job I mean: the ones where no-one knows what the hell it's even there for. That's the job I can do, put me in one of those!'

Shirley gives a little chuckle. It's good to see she has a sense of humour, otherwise we'd both be fucked in this forced arrangement. Suddenly I like the lady. She seems to sense that I'm half serious, but willing to be in on the joke at the same time.

'That would be good,' she agrees.

We talk some more and Shirley says that one of the ways she can work better to help me is to know what my interests are. So I tell her about my creative pursuits, like the film and video stuff. She actually seems intrigued, and tells me she'll endeavour to get me something along those lines.

'Nice one, Shirley, and for my part I'll endeavour to think of what other skills I might have hidden away inside this brain for you to exploit,' I go, rapping my knuckles against my head. I think my attitude has gone a little overboard now, because she gets a funny look on her face, like she's offended. No matter. Carry on.

We agree on a follow-up consultation in a few weeks time.

Back out on the street, amongst the bustle of the city where cars shove each other along and pigeons drop lice and shit on pedestrians, I feel a sense of achievement. It wasn't a long meeting with Shirley, but nonetheless I got through the whole thing without being told I was out of turn or on the wrong path. Maybe Shirley very cunningly guided my hand, but I doubt it. I felt like I've waded through the first of many tests to come, and I did it with my usual panache. Did I really want a job? Fuck off. I doubt very much that ol Shirley up there is going to do much about getting me one, either. And perhaps I'm being naive here, but let's say there *is* some form of employment out there that *does* involve being holed away out of sight of people and requires one to simply thumb through an index or some such shit for well more than what I currently get on the dole. Would I take it then? Fuck yes.

A few weeks later I ascend that stifling lift again, as anxious about returning as I was the first time I came here.

True to my suspicions, and to my relief, Shirley has done fuck all about finding me suitable employment. Thank fuck for her natural inclination to be lazy. To be fair, she probably doesn't get paid a lot, it being a Government job and all. At least, that's how I hear it works.

'There's just nothing going for you at the moment,' she sighs, truly believing her own bullshit.

'Don't stress about it,' I go. 'It was never going to happen anyway.'

There's a bruised look about her, like I've named the elephant in the room and the elephant is her ineptitude. Something about the way she sucks in this criticism and allows it to physically diminish her sparks a note of contempt in me. She's suddenly got an air of self-pity about her. It's quite possible that she's been bullied from one post to another in the Government sector, but that's hardly an acceptable reason to let her languish in a state of abandon.

'The thing is, Shirley,' I go, curling her name as it was an insult, 'people like me are a foreign identity to, well, people like you. People in offices.'

'I really did try, though...'

I shake my head sadly, giving her the same look my high school principal used to give us when he knew we were bullshitting.

'Maybe we need to come to some kind of agreement here,' I shrug. 'Cannot this file be closed or something?'

'We don't really close files,' she says weakly. 'The idea is we try to find the best possible outcome for you... we try and find work that suits you.'

She's resorting to those brochure hard-sell lines. She's desperate.

I twirl my finger around in the air. 'This is sounding an awful lot like a merry-go-round, though.'

She nods. 'It is, isn't it?'

My contempt for her hasn't abated. I realise now it's her job that I want. Hers is the job where no-one knows what she does, is never asked anything but gets paid a comparative shit-load to be there. Comparative to the pension, that is. I could sit up here and look down on all those cunts in Post Office Square, and come to the same futile conclusion with my clients as she has done with me, but without the inner-remorse that's currently eating away at her self-esteem.

I could probably excel in this job, outperforming even Shirley in my failure to place the unemployable into gainful employment.

Rather than wholly admit defeat, Shirley decides that we'll 'wait until the employment market improves' and try again.

'Give me a call in about a month's time,' she says, and I summarily thank her for all her hard work and take my leave, forgoing the lifts to instead skip down the stairwell and burn off some of the elation at having successfully manoeuvred myself off the Government's plans for rehabilitation.

I know full well that if I simply neglect to call Shirley in a months' time she certainly won't take the initiative to call me, and my case file will thusly be pushed further back in preference for clients much easier managed than Barry Muggins here. After all, Shirley still needs to yield results occasionally to justify her job, or else they'd probably make it redundant and she'd be back to swanning after another cushy Government sector post somewhere.

The little victories in life are worth celebrating, so I'll stop by the bottle-o on the way home and pick up a bottle or two of reasonably priced red. If that funny cunt Twix isn't working tonight I'll harass him to join me and Raven for a good ol piss up!

HAIR OF THE DOG

We're both nursing hangovers because we celebrated how Dante's rehabilitation officer has given up on him. He reckons it's a win, but I think he's just being a typical dole bludging slacker. Same diff. Still, at the end of the day he's a mate, and also any excuse to get right royally pissed, ay. So after polishing off a bottle of cheap red, me, him and Raven had hit Midian at the Normanby, then someplace else after that but it's all a bit of a blur, really.

Dante's really obsessive about eliminating hangovers and will do anything to fuck them off as quickly as possible. One of his theories for chasing them away is to walk in the sunshine, hence why we've come to West End after a big night on the town when we should be holed up at home in the dark watching the debut of that new show on the ABC, aptly called *Recovery* of all things. Especially because it's been unusually hot for this time of year, today no exception. Heat and hangovers don't mix in my opinion, especially when we reek of the stale cigarette smell from clubbing all night. But the sod tricked me when we were still pretty pissed, making me call Amai-li at some ungodly hour and arrange a catch up. She wasn't happy about being woken up, but agreed to meet me later, all the same. Her boyfriend Clem sounded even less pleased about the call; I'd heard them start arguing as she put the phone down. So I hafta follow through now or risk her fury at being stood up.

'Fucking nonsense, Twix,' goes Dante, when I'm still insisting that we should've stayed home. 'You just need some hair of the dog to get ya going.'

'At oh-eight-hundred in the fucking morning? Come off it, Dante, where the hell are we gonna find booze at this hour?'

'Leave it to me,' he boasts, heading us towards the roundabout at the junction of Melbourne and Boundary streets. 'Heyo, Jim!' he goes, waving to the guy running around like a headless chook at the little petrol station, one of few that hasn't converted over to self-service yet. The guy waves back. It's always a marvel to me how Dante seems to know everyone in Brisbane, but he didn't even grow up here. What's even more of a marvel is just how many random people Dante's on a first name basis with, given how much he generally hates people.

We wander over to a group of blackfellas, so I hang back. Dante just goes straight up to them, though, and he's making idle talk about the sodding weather and shit like that. Eventually he offers to buy a cask of wine from the manky fucks.

'This?' one goes, holding up a fat bottle of nasty looking port.

'No, no monkey's blood,' Dante laughs, pointing at a box of wine. 'That one, *Lady in the Boat*. How much?'

'Ten, ay.'

Dante comes back over and asks me for an Ayrton Senna, revealing that he's dead broke. No surprise there.

'Sod off,' I snap. 'I'm not givin them ten bucks for that rancid shit.'

For fark's sake, isn't it enough I already fork out my hard earned dosh on taxes for the bludgers to get a free hand out? Now they're dipping straight into my wallet.

'Yeah, I know, it's exy,' he goes, wincing for my benefit alone, 'but it's a seller's market, mind. Take it or leave it.'

My head's starting to really fucking pound. We should've stayed home and had greasy bacon and eggs and watched TV and slept all day. I fish out ten bucks and Dante whips it from my fingers before I can hand it over.

'Stop sooking about it,' he goes when he clocks my expression. 'It's only a measley ten bucks.'

Easy for him to say. I don't see him fishing into his own pockets for spare change.

He bounds cheerily over to the blackfellas.

'Here you are, my good man,' he goes, swapping the money for the goon bag. He shares a quiet joke with them or a 'just gammon' as he likes to call it, eliciting grins from everyone, then struts back like he's been on a long quest and has claimed the prize.

'I'm seriously not drinking from *that*,' I go, thinking of germs.

'Don't be such a fucking sissy,' he says, and holds the bag up to dribble wine into his cakehole. Fucking derro. Old habits die hard, obviously. 'Go on, just do it,' he goes, wiping his mouth on his sleeve.

I've got the nozzle as far from my mouth as possible, tipping my head back, but the wine still splashes my chin before I manage to get the aim right. It's foul stuff, rancid shit wine. A crotchety old prick sitting at a window of the boarding rooms above the shop across the roundabout watches me drink. I'd rather kill myself than be reduced to living like that. Naturally, Dante appears to know this prick, too, giving him a casual wave and getting one in return.

'They call it *Lady in the Boat* because of the picture on the box,' Dante says of the wine as I screw my face up at the taste. 'Makes it sound nicer than it is.'

'Doesn't improve the taste, unfortunately.'

We wander up Boundary taking turns at the goon, staving off the hangover as best we can, copping dirty looks from the early morning market crowds. Dante nips over to the milk-bar across from the Boundary Hotel, coming back with a bag of chips for us to munch on.

'I thought you were broke,' I go.

'Five finger discount,' he says, stuffing his mouth full of chips.

I shake my head, knowing it was on the cards. He really tests me, this lad. In my line of work I've gotta stop shoplifters all the sodding time. Once in a blue moon, if it's a cute girl, I'll look the other way. Normally I don't, though. I can't. It's the entire reason I get hired. But Dante's a mate, so what can I do?

He passes the chips over, and despite my misgivings I'm pretty fucking famished, so I dig in.

'You're gonna get caught one of these days.'

'Nah, not me,' he says arrogantly. 'I'm the Gingerbread Man. They can run, run, run as fast as they can, but they'll never catch me.'

Where Vulture Street intersects on the corner, there's some punks.

'Dan, ya bastard!' one of them, this Abo bloke, yells out.

We wander across the road, getting beeped at by a car that swerves to avoid hitting us. I give it the forks.

'Oi, Alan, this is Twix,' Dante says. 'Twix, that's Alan, that's Scab, his girlfriend Victoria, and last but not least is Chris over there.'

I say hi, but only Alan and Victoria bother responding. The other two lads, Scab and Chris, are busy gluing sheets of butcher's paper over a tobacco billboard against the brick wall, and Chris is trying to write COMMUNITY NOTICE BOARD at the top with a biro, but the stupid prick's spelt it as COMMIE NOTICE BORED.

Dante starts telling Alan about the result with the rehabilitation people. This seems like as good a chance as any to ditch him and go and meet Amai on my own. I was kind of hoping the hangover would knock Dante flat somewhere and we'd have to call the catch-up off, as I don't really want him meeting her. He can be a bit flirty.

'Oi, Dante, I'll go get Amai, yeah?'

'You're going without me?' he says, confused.

'Nah, I'll come back,' I go, passing him the goon bladder. I can't drink any more of that shit. Alan's eyes light up at the prospect of a tipple, though.

'Yeah, righto,' Dante says with a little smirk, like he's fucking onto me. But that's just me being paranoid, I'm sure.

I don't wanna be around those manky fucking punks any more than I want Dante being around Amai-li, so it's to put some distance between us. I must admit, Saturday morning in West End has a nice feel to it, in ways that neither Bowen Street nor St Lucia's got. It was always too busy at the Palace, and it's too quiet at St Lucia (except when the cyclists stream past all yabbering like fucking parrots).

At the markets I park my arse on the pine railing out front for some crowd watching. In due course I spy Amai, in a long colourful slip-dress and a white baby-tee; the complete opposite of how I like girls decking out, but it suits her. I sneak up behind (tiptoeing slowly so the skull buckles on my roachcrushers don't jangle) and in a deep voice go: 'Excuse me, miss, please submit to a thorough cavity search.'

She nearly shits herself, holding a hand over her heart. It cracks me up, but she's right royally pissed off. Not entirely at me, it proves.

She tells me about how she was riding her bike to the markets when she saw this old lady accidently spill all her vegetables and shit out of her trolley at the traffic lights on Vulture Street.

'So, it was one of those old-fashioned vinyl trolleys on two wheels that only the really old people use,' she goes. 'So I hopped off my bike and ran across to help the old lady, but when I looked up some prick was stealing my bike!'

'What, you just left it on the footpath?'

'Of course not!' she protests. 'I leant it on the wall of Mick's Nuts.'

'Same diff,' I go, though I don't mean for it to sound as callous as it does. It's just that when you hang around the likes of Dante enough you start to realise just how people take personal security for granted.

'What kind of asshole steals a girl's bike?' she goes.

'Indeed. That's the world these days. More front than Myer's, some pricks. Did the old lady see it happen?'

'Yeah!' Amai says dramatically. 'I said *did you see that?* So she shrugged and said: *I've lost my eggs and baskets.*'

She slaps her forehead in frustration, boggling her eyes. She looks so cute when she's angry and it makes her eyes as big as saucers, but I've gotta keep a straight face because she gets pretty agro when she thinks I'm patronising her.

'I mean, it's a stupid fucking thing to say when I'm the one trying to help her, isn't it?' she continues to moan. 'It's more like a trolley than a basket. Stupid old woman.'

Some people've got no clue, that's true.

'I suppose you don't wanna keep looking around the markets?'

'Not in the mood anymore,' she goes, pulling a sad face as she leans against me. It takes all my will power to stop my mongrel from developing into a fully-fledged boner. 'I just want my bike back. Ma and Ba'll just use this to berate big time if I ask for a new one. I'll have to save up somehow and get one myself, but I'm fucking broke! I just need some more makeup jobs, dammit.'

She looks at me significantly.

'Don't you have a friend who does videos and stuff?'

'He doesn't do it anymore,' I lie. Thank fuck Dante stayed behind.

Suddenly she sniffs me. 'Are you drunk?'

'Hair of the dog.'

'I could use a drink right now,' she moans.

We start walking back to the West End shops, but I take us down Jane Street towards the Boundary Hotel so's to try and avoid bumping into Dante again. Hopefully he's preoccupied with his punk mates and whatever vandalism they're currently up to. Amai thinks we're headed to the pub for that drink, but it's not even ten-hundred hours yet.

As we turn the corner there's this old Greek man walking his rat of a dog comes along the street, eyeballing Amai up and down without any sodding shame at all. Here we fucking go, another situation like the one in the Queen Street Mall that time where the old Chinaman sod wouldn't stop gawking at her.

'Look at da cute widdle dog,' she says to me, using a baby voice.

'It's not cute, it's ugly,' I say, partly because I don't like the owner.

'That's why it's so cute, because it's ugly, isn't it?' she goes.

Fuck, but chicks can be confusing!

There's very little room left on the footpath because of the council's not-so-brilliant placement of the rubbish bin, so the old man and Amai nearly run into each other, the dog trying to run ahead and tangling the leash around Amai's leg while the humans dance awkwardly side to side trying to avoid each other. Eventually, the old man deftly steps out of the way, dropping the leash to untangle it.

'Sorry, so sorry' goes Amai, picking up the leash for him.

'Never be sorry for walking down the street,' he admonishes.

'Good advice,' I nod, staring hard.

'Okay, not sorry?' says Amai uncertainly.

'But my dear, such beauty!' the old man announces loudly, holding his hands up in the air and squinting his eyes as if in ecstasy. The old fuck is quite the dramatic one, that's for sure. I can imagine he must have wooed heaps of chicks as a younger lad. He turns to me, hand on his heart like he's got angina. 'Is she not such a beautiful girl?'

'The most beautiful girl in the world,' I agree, getting in on the playful spirit, winking at Amai. The Lady in the Boat has definitely gone to my head.

But the old man looks genuinely affronted by my admission.

'Why would you say that?' he chastises me. Then dead serious, he goes: 'Every woman's as beautiful as the next.'

'Not to me they're not,' I reply, thinking that there's some fucking shockers out there and it'd take being lined up in front of the firing squad for me to think otherwise.

The old man's left eye twitches and his mouth turns down in a parody of his hideous dog.

'Pah,' he spits, waving a hand at me as if I'm trash. 'Young people know nothing of true beauty. You can't see it yet. You're blinded by your cock still.'

'Damn,' laughs Amai. 'Settle down, you cheeky old bugger! We're just friends, for a start.'

He screws his nose up at her like she's lost all allure, trudging off up the street, dragging his idiot mutt by the leash as it tries to piss on everything it passes.

Amai bursts into laughter, actual tears coming out of the corners of her eyes.

'Holy shit, what a crazy bastard.'

'Crazy as a fucking loon,' I add with a smile, unable to shake what he said, nonetheless. It's like he's saying I'm shallow, which is what Alex called me, too.

'So, did you mean that?' asks Amai as we keep walking.

'Mean what?' I'm guessing she also wants to have a go at me now for saying not all women are beautiful.

'That I'm the most beautiful girl in the world?'

She's watching my face expectantly.

Did I mean it? Does it matter?

'Why not?' I shrug, holding my chin high.

Her eyes twinkle from the sun, or maybe from something more.

Right now, she *is* the most beautiful girl in the world. I don't care if anyone else thinks that's the wrong thing to say, it's what I feel in my heart when I look down at her pretty face. But with Clem in the picture, I'm just a friend, like she told the old guy.

A panel van tears past us and a witless bogan pokes his head out from the passenger window and yells: 'FUCK HER BRAINS OUT!!'

ANKHS AND ANGST

Now that Twix is living in St Lucia, it's no longer a quick skip, hop and a jump down to the Valley to go clubbing. He alights from the bus black cheongsam and fishnets, taunted by a group of meatheads on board, lads who assume he's a goth transvestite and are giving him the full gamut of their ire as a result. They, too, are headed to the Valley for a night out on the town, attired absurdly in matching plaid shirts tucked into white jeans.

Twix waits until the doors of the bus close before he salutes them with two fingers formed into a V. Their blockish heads poke from the windows as they scream tired insults and threats at him.

Dante's waiting on the corner, staring mystified at the bus rolling by with its cluster of furious boofheads at the window. He's dressed as a priest, of all things, wearing a long coat from Velvet Web and a makeshift collar of white cardboard.

'Friends of yours?' he asks Twix, watching the bus rumble down past Centenary Park.

'Neighbours, more like,' Twix says, because most of the boofheads live in the Uni dorms up the road from his new place. 'But my days of putting up with that shit on buses are numbered. Mayor Soorley's got his fleet of new catamarans ready to hit the river at the end of the year.'

'The new ferries are gonna be catamarans?' says Dante, who tends to skip local news for more provocative articles.

'Yup,' nods Twix, a feeling of command swelling inside him as he imparts his covertly acquired knowledge. 'Stevie Harris now works security at the yards they're being built in over at Hemmant. Sweet as fuck catamarans. Imagine taking a chick home via one of those? I'll be sailing the seas with only the wind in my ears.'

'Sounds romantic,' says Dante dubiously, thinking that Twix will simply have swapped being yelled at on a bus for being yelled at on a boat.

'It will be,' says Twix, still lost to his daydream. 'You should take that punk chick of yours on it if you're still with her by then.'

Dante resents the implication that his love-life will always lack longevity, but he bites his tongue on the matter.

'But those Uni cunts seem to have more dosh than ever these days,' he says instead. 'If they jack up the prices of those ferries to recoup their cost, it'll be those arseholes with the wind in their ears while you're still thumbing a ride on the beasts of burden.'

'Yeah, we'll see,' says Twix, shaking his head because he thinks Dante hasn't got a clue.

From inside the Oriental comes a cacophony of crashing drums and thrashing guitars.

'That's not us, is it?' says Twix, peering through the windows.

'Course not,' says Dante. 'It's a metal gig. We're upstairs.'

'Fuck a duck,' breathes Twix hoarsely, his hands cupped either side of his face against the glass. 'There's a giant swastika flag behind the drummer.'

'Yeah, I know,' sighs Dante. 'It's a bad scene. I've already had a run-in with a couple of neo-Nazi's already.'

At the bottom of the stairwell that leads up to the top floor there's a couple of skinheads leant on the door-jamb in casual conversation, attendees of the neo-Nazi metal gig. Coming up the street is Michael Carlyon and some other cunts that Dante despises, so as he Twix shove past the skinheads Dante turns and gives the sign of the cross in front of them, saying: 'Bless you, my sons.'

'Fuck you say?' snarls one of the bootboys.

Dante and Twix bolt upstairs, sniggering like children, though Twix has to yank his cheongsam all the way up his thighs to run. Down below they can hear Carlyon trying to get past the skins and having a hard time of it.

Alex is happy to see the boys enter the club, some familiar faces at last. Abi hasn't arrived yet and in the four months she's been in Brisbane Alex still hasn't got to know a lot of the people here. But right now she's less interested in socialising with the familiar than getting shit-faced drunk, so drunk as to wipe away the memory of losing her job and being denied unemployment benefits for her role in the fiasco at the fetish barbecue. At least the police were never called. With her boobs pulled up in a tight and revealing top and her best attempt at a Siouxsie Sioux eye makeup, she's already off to a good start as various guys have all tried their luck so far and bought her drinks in the process. Currently in her hand is a gin and tonic, but it's getting low so she's trying to wrangle another from the hopeful sucker in the puffy pirate shirt. What was his name again?

'What did you say your name was again?' she says, unbothered by the impression this makes on him. If anything, he'll probably think it's the booze and on the assumption he's nearly got her at a compliant level will eagerly ply her with more.

'Lament,' he says with sincere gravitas, then adding with a Bond-like flourish: 'Dark Lament.'

Alex laughs, careful to keep it tinkly and not her usual guffaw. 'Right, and that's what it says on your birth certificate?'

'I was birthed in a time before birth certification,' Mister Lament informs her haughtily.

She knows the type right off the proverbial bat: a self-confessed vampire. Certainly he looks old enough to be one. She puts him at roughly her own father's age.

'Just a stab in the dark,' she begins, leaning back and closing one eye as if to appraise him like one might a painting or a fine wine, 'you sleep in a coffin, right?'

Far from discerning any mockery from Alex's inquiry, he quickly confesses to doing just such a thing. He leans in close, staring at her intensely and brushing the hair from the side of her face with the back of his hand, gestures he undoubtedly thinks are seductive and irresistible to women. He begins to wax lyrical about life as one of the undead, unabashedly stealing lines from the film version of *Interview with the Vampire*, while Alex motions another gin and tonic is in order.

Michael Carlyon approaches the bar, still fuming at the treatment he got at the hands of the neo-Nazi's downstairs. They'd nearly roughed him up until he'd had to, embarrassingly, plead to be left alone. He'd get onto the hotel manager about this and sort them right out. The bar staff will pass the message on, for sure.

'Whatcha want?' says the girl behind the bar, poised like she's about to sprint off and make his drink in record time.

'I need to get a message to the manager,' he calls across the counter right at the very moment the guitar-grinding intro of Killing Joke's *Millenium* drowns out his voice.

The bar-wench is irritated, holding a hand to her ear to indicate she can't hear him.

'There's Nazi's going ape-shit down there,' Michael yells, pointing to the floor.

What she hears – whether it's *Nazi's* or *ape-shit* – Michael can't be sure, but that together with him pointing in the general area of his crotch, the bar-wench is unimpressed and tells him to piss off while she scoots across the end of the bar to serve someone else.

'Fuck, didn't even get a drink,' moans Michael, then he notices his old mate Tony, known widely by the coarse moniker of T-Rex Tony, chatting up the fresh meat in town. She's a big girl, and far older than Michael's usual tastes. Tony's welcome to her; there'd be no rivalry from Michael for this one. 'Hey, Tony, get us a drink, will ya? Bitch behind the bar has it in for me or something.'

Tony grins at his friend, enjoying his misfortune. They have a strong competitive streak between each other.

'I thought you said your name was Dark Lament,' chuckles Alex to Tony, as she plucks her fresh gin from the bar top and makes her way through the crowd.

Tony's face falls and he glowers at Michael. 'Get your own fucken drink.'

By now Dante and Twix are on the dance-floor, engulfed by the sweetly-scented plumes of an over-exuberant smoke machine sitting jammed beneath the DJ booth, free-wheeling around various couples and groups who have clustered together. Alex admires Twix for wearing a dress, and adds him to her mental list of potential sex partners. She's not really made her mind up about anyone yet, let alone Twix, but he's got a good body for a skinny boy. She wasn't sure if there was something going on between him and Abi, because Abi was definitely giving off all the signs of someone who didn't want people to think she was fucking him, but then Abi's started dabbling in opiates and other pills so it could've just been that.

Suddenly something flashes across the dance-floor and Dante is leaping after it. The object bounces off someone's boot and Alex can see it's a knife, about the length of a school ruler, sitting right there on the floor! Dante swoops down on it and just as quick as the knife appeared it's secreted away somewhere, hidden inside the folds of his long coat. When Dante returns to Twix she can see them both laughing about it, but no-one else finds it amusing. The rest of the dancers give the boys a wide-berth, or retire to their tables mid-song.

Pixie and Imp are fish out of water. They're no strangers to the goth scene, but they're still 'babybats' as the older, more elitist goths like to refer to them. They happily embrace the term. Fortunately nightclubs are pretty relaxed about underagers getting in, especially so with the subcultures, so the door fee is all that is asked of them and they're in.

'Shit, dude,' says Pixie, pressing a hand to her stomach, 'I dunno about this roll. It doesn't feel right, but.'

'Stop freaking out, Pix; just breathe,' instructs Imp with a level-headedness that suggests he's feeling fine.

He did say it wasn't his first time taking ecstasy, but despite saying it wasn't hers either Pixie has in fact lied. She's starting to think she should've eaten something before taking it, especially since she's only had coffee and booze since breakfast time. Carlyon had warned them that MDMA on an empty stomach isn't necessarily a great idea, but she'd wanted to get the most effect out of the pill.

After the week she's had, a massive serotonin boost is just what Pixie needs. Her kind-of friend – a fellow babybat by name of Dee Dee from her King George Square circle of friends and acquaintances – killed himself a few days ago. His management of his depression had become worse lately, and the medications he'd been prescribed had produced a barrage of side-effects that while not precisely the cause of his misery didn't help clarify his feelings, either. That and he was prone to giving the pills away rather than taking them like he was supposed to. Thus poor Damien Maddington, aka Down in the Dumps, had finally topped himself.

Imp puts his hands on Pixie's shoulders to steady her, because she's reeling all over the place and bumping into people. 'Stop acting like a retard, Pixie.'

'*You* stop actin like a fuckin retard, ya fuckin mong,' she shouts back, shoving him away, just as Dante and Twix pass by with drinks in their hands. Imp staggers back, kocking the glass in Twix's hand.

'Oi, watch it, lad,' says Twix angrily, spilt beer soaking his cuffs.

Imp apologises, enthralled by Twix's fangs, while Dante asks how Pixie's going.

'Fuckin shit,' she complains. 'Coz of this mong cunt here.'

'I didn't do nothing,' says Imp sullenly when Dante smirks at him. 'A friend of ours commited suicide the other day.'

'Shit, bum luck,' Dante says, sucking air in through his teeth and shaking his head.

Pixie's over dwelling on the incident, however, and wants a night free from dark and introspective thoughts. Her eyes light up when she gets a good look at Twix, recognising his flop of dyed-black hair with the shaved part exposing little tattoos of bats.

'I fuckin know you,' slurs Pixie, pointing at Twix. 'On the fuckin train station at Northgate that time.' She turns to Imp, beseeching: 'Remember? Oi, remember? Cunt literally yelled at us from the train when those tickities were bookin us.'

Imp's face finally registers recognition. 'Oh yeah, you bagged out Mick Buchhorn and got us into trouble.'

Twix roars with laughter. 'Fuckhorn! Yeah, I remember that time!' Careful not to spill his beer any further, he does an elaborate bow. 'My humblest apologies that you were both collateral.'

Pixie and Imp crack up at Twix's theatrics, suitably impressed by his capacity for remorse.

'I fucking love those fangs,' enthuses Imp, and Twix is more than happy to show them off for further admiration, yawning wide.

'You still flipping burgers with your dad?' asks Dante of Pixie.

'No fuckin way,' she says, rolling her eyes. 'Cunt can flip his own meat. I'm not goin back there.'

'Fuck the system!' shouts Dante, which makes Imp grin widely, the E releasing a rush of serotonin into his system.

'You're the man,' squints Imp. He's got a classic case of shutter vision, like everything's being broadcast on a TV screen where the horizontal static's gone. Too much MDMA does this, converting into MDA and creating a psychedelic experience. Imp hasn't taken much of it, he's simply a probationer when it comes to drugs.

Dante glares at the boy, trying to hold him in an intense stare, but the boy's eyes have got nystagmus, or *dancing eyes*, and won't sit still. Dante realises these two are off their faces on something, but nonetheless he swears the little cunt called him *Dan*, the same horrid nickname Alan likes to tease him with.

'Hold your fucking tongue,' Dante warns him.

This gets a giggle out of Pixie, much to Imp's chagrin.

'I'm still tryin to work outta way to make money, but,' she moans to Dante. 'I've still gotta few more weeks before I can get back on the dole, coz I took too long to reapply.'

'You should give modelling a go, then,' says Dante, noting with satisfaction Imp's unease at this suggestion. 'Don't scoff, I'm serious.'

'Model for what, cunt?' Pixie laughs, caressing her pot-belly.

'Go in the nudie mags,' says Dante, addressing Pixie but looking straight at Imp. 'They'd fucking eat a young piece like you right up. I know I would.'

'Shut the fuck up,' says Pixie, laughing even harder now. 'I'm not old enough for that shit.'

Twix has caught on that Pixie is well wasted and begins to fancy his chances.

'Get this, right,' says Dante, fuelling the fire, 'Hustler magazine recently put a sixteen year old on the cover. No shit. Tits out right there on the cover on newsstands right across Australia. Woulda got paid good money, too.'

'Serious?' says Pixie.

Twix nods, backing Dante up as mates should, although it's more because he hopes she goes through with Dante's suggestion so he can grab a copy of the magazine for personal use.

'Sounds like a stupid idea,' Imp pipes up, avoiding eye contact with either Dante or Twix. He doesn't like them one bit anymore.

'Tell her about the censorship bloke,' says Twix to Dante.

'Fuck, that one's a laugh,' says Dante, turning to Pixie. 'The chief censor, right, who was dealing with the whole fiasco and jumping up and down about it in the first place? His surname was Dickie.'

'Imagine that!' says Twix with a huge grin for optimum exposure of his fangs.

Pixie roars with laughter, falling against Dante for support who in turn warps his arms around her, giving Imp a shit-stirring wink.

'Let's get some more drinks,' Imp says sullenly, hoping these two haven't killed his roll. The ecstasy set him back a bit more than he'd been hoping to spend.

'Let's get fucked up, cunt!' screeches Pixie, throwing her arms up as if in celebration.

Imp leads her over to the bar, casting a sour look back at Dante.

A ruckus from the stairwell reveals a group of metalheads from downstairs charging upstairs into the club, their faces painted in the style of their Nordic brethren in brutal strokes, stark contrast to the restrained efforts of the goth's makeup. They wave away the door bitch's demands for the door charge, waltzing deeper into the club unchallenged, a couple of them going straight for the bar and ordering up a round of pints. The rest congregate on the edge of the dance floor, surveying the goths performing a three-step waltz in two lines to the *Temple of Love*, roaring in unison as though they themselves were the Gods of Asgard. As rowdy as they are, they're the death-metal variety of metal enthusiast, and not the neo-Nazi kind, a fact that puts some of the goths at ease.

Twix anticipates some trouble that he and Dante might need to make themselves available for on the chance that these guys give the club-runners some grief if they're told to behave, but when Dante sees them he's straight over before Twix even realises what's happening.

'Okay cunts,' barks Dante, 'show's over! Especially for you!' He points directly at one of them, a guy of Asian-looking descent who turns around menacingly.

A goth couple close at hand shrink deeper into the shadows of the corner, strategically sat behind a large wooden barrel (which serves as a table) that they hope might offer some protection.

The big Asian metalhead suddenly breaks into a grin. 'Holy shit,' he says, 'haven't seen you since that night on the roof.'

It's Riz, the half-Filipino guy that Dante met the night he also met Scab, on the rooftop across from the Embassy Hotel when they all watched a couple have sex in front of a window.

'What the fuck's going on downstairs?' says Dante, referring to the presence of so many Nazi sympathisers gathered in one place.

'Don't ask us, man,' says Riz, shaking his head. 'Not the usual crowd we hang with. We're just here for the music, you know?'

One of the other guys, who Riz introduces as Davo, shouts over the music: 'Bartender down there's had a fucking gutful and told us on the sly that he's called the cops.'

Dante nods knowingly, and Riz smirks and says: 'We got out while the getting was still good.'

Davo turns around to the couple seated behind him at the barrel, regulars on the scene. The girl, Eleanor, has been furtively watching them ever since they arrived, so Davo strikes up a conversation with straight away, despite their reticence. Eleanor's boyfriend, Albert, is done up to the nines in a frock coat and frill shirt with a cravat. He wears round spectacles and a top hat. Everyone thinks the glasses are for show, but few actually realise he's blind as a bat without them.

'Check out Davo,' sniggers Riz to his mates, 'chatting up Dracula's bride.'

The metalheads aren't shy about having a squiz at the awkward attempt at courtship, and the immense discomfort of Albert is evident to everyone, so Riz offers to shout him a drink, despite Albert's protestations that Riz needn't trouble himself.

At the bar Riz confesses that they've seen Albert around before in the mall and some clubs and have always called him Dracula on account of how similar he dresses to Gary Oldman playing the same character onscreen.

'It's more than intentional, I'm sure,' says Dante, leaning on the bar and surveying the club with a drowsy sneer. 'Way too much pretension here.'

'Says the guy dressed like a priest,' laughs Riz.

'Repent of your blasphemy or you'll burn in hell,' jokes Dante.

'I'll take Hell, thanks,' retorts Riz. 'Apparently it's more fun.' He orders a round of drinks then turns to Dante: 'Hey man, you don't know anyone with a camera, do you?'

'I do, as it happens,' admits Dante. 'I work with a friend who has one. We make films when and where we can.'

Riz is more than chuffed at this, and presents Dante with the idea of filming a music video for his band Necrogore, explaining they want a dark mediaeval theme with hot pixie girls and all.

'Yeah, we can definitely do that,' Dante says, his eyes scanning the crowd. On the danceflooor he spies Adelaide, Scab's ex-girlfriend, dancing like a banshee in the billows of choking smoke.

From the stairwell emerge three zit-faced babybats, first-timers or near enough to the hallowed ground that is the goth club. They shrink under the door-bitch's baleful gaze, mistaking her boredom for scorn. Timidly they pay their entrance fee, making straight for the bar to see if their luck holds out and they won't be asked for ID there.

However, their arrival has been well and truly noted, as they'd been counting on, for the trio wear matching t-shirts emblazoned with a shitty transfer of an acne-riddled boy with buck teeth. Above the image the words RIP DD are printed in block letters.

Twix leans around as they grip the bar's edge, and says: 'That's a curious fashion statement you three are making.'

'It's our friend Dee Dee,' one of them pipes up, projecting his voice over the bar to catch the attention of the busy barmaid. 'He committed suicide the other day off the Story Bridge. We're tryin to honour his memory.'

'Must be the cunt Pixie and her mate mentioned,' Dante whispers to Twix.

'It's fully wrecked us, hey,' one of the other of the trio offers, and explains how at school they've had to band together against the kids who've been sullying their deceased friend's reputation with vicious gossip.

'Our friend died this week,' repeats first guy for the benefit of the barmaid when she comes over for their order.

'Yeah, right,' she goes, then asks them what they'd like to drink.

'Anything, really, if it's on the house,' they admit, hoping to tip the scales of compassion in their favour.

The barmaid is far from impressed. 'We're not a fuckin charity.'

She walks away and everyone who's heard the exchange giggle behind bejewelled hands, except for Twix and Dante who brazenly laugh openly at the three.

Pixie's spied them, too, and the subsequent ridicule their actions have brought.

'Oh no, they didn't,' she gasps.

Imp whips his head around and can't help but laugh out loud at their matching shirts with Dee Dee's mugshot on them.

'He would've hated that,' Imp chuckles.

'They're just attention seekers, the selfish cunts,' Pixie observes. She looks around the room and sees how many people are mocking the trio. 'Backfired, but.'

Imp suggests they vanish further into the crowd before their three acquaintances see them, and Pixie agrees wholeheartedly.

As they shove into the wall of black velvet and PVC before them, Pixie realises she's definitely feeling green around the gills now. She wonders if it's too late to find a 7-11 somewhere and stuff a sausage roll down her gob. Her guts are churning over, and there's the bitter tang of vomit at the back of her throat, so she rushes around to the girl's toilets, shoving people out of the way in her haste. Of course, the cubicles are full, but the guy and the girl at the washbasin are simply talking shit with one another while they wait, so she barks at them to move aside and straddles the ceramic with her shaking hands.

'Excuse *me*,' says the guy snarkily, glancing Pixie up and down in judgement.

The vomit gushes out of her, splashing into the basin.

'Fuck, watch it!' yells the other girl, scooting back and checking her dress for splashback.

'Just fucking gross,' says the guy, pinching his nose against the acrid smell.

Pixie washes the vomit down the drain with a quick turn of the tap, then has a panic attack that the ecstasy pill was brought up and washed away, too, not realising that it's long dissolved.

'FUCK FUCK FUCK,' she screams with such violence it silences the critics behind her.

She staggers from the toilet, feeling drained, and finds Imp. She's about to tell him she thinks her roll is gone, flushed down the drain, when a sudden compulsion to kiss him overwhelms her and she lunges at him, wrapping her arms around his neck and planting her lips on his. They're mouths instantly open, tongues encircling, the richness of passion swelling her chest, thumping in her head.

Imp pushes her away and starts spitting on the carpet.

'Fucking hell,' he says horrified, wiping at his face. 'You taste like chuck!'

'Coz I just fuckin spewed, ya selfish cunt!' Pixie yells at him. 'Stop thinkin about yaself for once!'

'We're meant to be having a good time,' whines Imp.

She can't stand him right now. He's so pathetic, standing there looking at her like he's a wounded little boy, angry and sad at the same time. *What a shit cunt*, she thinks.

Then she sees him over on the other side of the bar which forms a U shape, the old guy who sold her the pills. He's not a friend, more of an acquaintance, and she's more than aware he'd get into her panties if he could.

'Hey, Michael,' she says obnoxiously loud, slapping his arse as she comes around in front of him. He doesn't react to the slap except to produce a hungry smile.

'Are the pixies having a swell night?' Michael Carlyon purrs.

'A fuckin shit night, cunt,' she moans, snatching his drink and downing as much as she can in one gulp, washing the dregs of her vomit back down.

'Yeah, help yourself why don't you?' he says sarcastically, looking at his mate T-Rex Tony and shaking his head disdainfully.

'Buy us another, then,' Pixie says, schmoozing up to him, playing with the zipper on his leather jacket.

'Do the honours, Tony?'

The old dinosaur sighs like he's been put upon, and orders them a vodka each.

'I'm fuckin sick from those pills you got us,' she says. 'Fuck callin em ecstasy. Call em misery instead.'

'Mine's doing me wonders,' Michael smiles smugly. 'I did tell you to go easy on em if it's your first time.'

'It's not me first fuckin time,' snarls Pixie with her head resting in her arms, then quickly adds: 'Okay, it's me first time, but you don't have to literally act like such a cunt about it.'

'My flatmate had a bit of a downer on this batch, actually,' admits Michael, accepting his drink off Tony and coaxing the other glass into Pixie's hand. 'I eventually got him to chill and just enjoy the trip, but it took a bit of work on my part. We had a fucking brill time in the end, though. But I think this batch was cut with amps, which'd make them a bit crapper than usual.'

An understatement, thinks Pixie, whose only recourse now is to get shitfaced on alcohol and over-ride the effects of both the pill and her dickhead friend Imp.

Michael pulls her closer and sways gently to the music, Visage's *Fade to Grey*, as he feeds her sips of his drink in between imbibing it himself. The slow rocking of their bodies and his large hands on the small of her back draw her focus, the music clouding her head. The chatter and raucous laughter of the club seem like a million miles away to her, and yet so close at the same time. It's like she's cocooned from it all but still a part of it. It feels secure.

By the time she reaches the bottom of her own glass Pixie's feeling good, can feel the roll coming on good and proper. The sickness in her stomach has eased to a small cramp, nothing she can't put to the back of her mind. Michael's lips feel rough, his breath hot and masculine. She wants nothing more than this moment, the music and booze and the man.

'She looks like the demented lovechild of Siouxsie Sioux and Courtney Love,' observes Twix, watching Carlyon make out with the underage girl Dante was chatting to earlier. 'Trashy goth.'

Xanthe nods in agreement, muttering something disparaging about Carlyon that neither Twix nor Dante properly catch. Something about how he apparently confessed to the bar-wench that he had nasty shit down in his groin or something.

'That's not biologically possible,' says Dante of Twix's observation. 'Two wombs and no inseminating member?'

'Maybe she's cloned, then,' counters Twix. 'Like in *Blade Runner.*'

'Those were technically cyborgs.'

Twix points at Pixie, now dancing stiffly with Carlyon out on the floor. 'Look at her and tell me she's not part robot.'

This makes Xanthe laugh in a really cynical way.

'Anyone willing to get intimate with that cunt Carlyon has to be, surely,' observes Dante snidely.

Twix scans the crowd, noting Alex amongst those on the dance-floor. When he first met her he had notions of sexually engaging with her the first chance he got, but ever since her arrival in Brisbane he's not been tempted to in the least. Maybe when he's been tanked he's played with the idea, mostly on account of the voluminous size of her breasts, but she's a big girl in all regards and that simply doesn't get his engine going.

What does, though, is petite goth girls in corsets with sharp cheek bones and doe eyes. He's spotted one such specimen just now, sitting on a wooden chair by the weathered couch next to the old fireplace. Her breasts are rather small for his liking (more in keeping with Dante's preferences, who has previously voiced an aversion for larger breasts on account of how they sag), but it's both the expensive-looking corset and those big, doleful eyes that more than make up for it. Eyes like that scream *save me, Twix*. How can he resist such a calling?

'Where are you going?' Xanthe wants to know.

Twix knows she has a judgemental streak about her, so he does the Bangles' *Walk like an Egyptian* dance moves at her as he makes his way into the crowd.

As it turns out, the girl with the doe eyes in the corset has a boyfriend, one of substantial size, and he's clocked Twix sashaying through the crowd straight for his partner, so Twix has no sooner started his flirtatious administrations than he's been shut down by the boyfriend.

'We know you, mate?'

Twix does his best to ignore the sod, but ignored the sod won't be.

'You wanna leave my girlfriend alone?' the guy growls, standing up menacingly, so Twix takes the hint and moves on, doing his Bangle's routine for the girl's amusement, except it fails to amuse.

It has been a while since Eleanor went off to the toilets, Albert notes, and he's starting to get concerned. The metalheads have all but ignored him since that Dante guy was talking with them, but they've commandeered the barrel-table that was in front of him and now he sits, alone, on his stool with his and Eleanor's drinks jammed to one edge of it to make room for the overfilled ashtray and the growing collection of empty glasses the metalheads are racking up.

Watching them, quietly loathing them, Albert suddenly realises that one of their members is not present. It's Davo, the one that was making passes at Eleanor earlier. A quick panic, like a fluttering bird banging itself against a window, fills his chest. He knocks his drink over in his haste to slip off his stool, but he doesn't care. He jostles through the crowd, peering everywhere for his fiancée, heading in the direction of the toilets.

Normally he loves this venue with its various corridors that interconnect all the rooms, but in this moment Albert hates it. There's little light to see by, and each room bar the one with the pool table has a door on either side, so there's a chance that even now Eleanor is also wandering around looking for *him*, and that they keep missing each other due to the roundabout maze of the venue's design.

If only that were the case, though.

In one of the corridors he finds her, his fiancé, making out with the metalhead Davo, up against the wall while onlookers grin at them.

Albert's heart has been yanked from his chest and magnified for all to see, suspended in the air, beating and bleeding and cracking apart. One of the door-bitches, Adelaide, whom he kind of knows, sees him and follows his gaze to where the scene of his heartbreak is playing out, and she forms an O with her mouth and looks at him sadly.

Someone taps Eleanor on the shoulder and points Albert's way. Even with her pancake makeup on, it's not hard to tell she's gone crimson red from shame. That said, though, there's little else about her that expresses any remorse, or even embarrassment.

'Fuck... Albert,' she says leadenly. 'Sorry.'

That's all he's offered from the girl he's known for two years and is engaged to marry. A barely heartfelt apology. She's even still got her hands on that metalhead, damn it! He wants her to run to him, to beseech him, something, but she just stands staring at him, waiting for *him* to make the first move. *Let go of the metalhead for a start*, he thinks.

'WHY?' he screams, startling a couple next to him who stare at him aghast then crack up in a drunken fit.

Eleanor simply gives a little shrug, unable to bring herself to offer anything more significant for her lover of two whole years.

Albert turns and runs from the club just as the opening beats of the Pet Shop Boys' *Can You Forgive Her?* slam from the speakers on the walls, aptly laying down the soundtrack for his humiliation.

Michael Carlyon hates this song, hates the band, and is trying to leave the dance-floor, but Pixie won't hear of it. She grabs him by the belt-hooks of his leather pants and pulls him back, grinding her pelvis unashamedly against his thigh. It's an irresistible sight, thinks Michael, imagining the little slut naked and crawling up his leg like a sex-starved demon.

Over by the bar Imp watches with a bruised expression, imagining a punch straight to Carlyon's face and saving Pixie from his lecherous ways. He asks the bar dude for a couple of tequila shots, and thanks his lucky stars that they don't card for ID here. He's no sooner downed both and sucked the lemon and tried to lick the salt but fucked it up than he wants a couple more. The spirits are still blazing inside his throat, combusting inside his belly and making his eyes water. He's going to run out of cash pretty quickly, he realises, but doesn't care. His ecstasy trip has bottomed out and now he needs a depressant to deal with these feelings of anger and jealousy.

'I thought I fucking told you, already,' says the big bastard loudly at Twix, who has gravitated back into corset girl's vicinity again. He's fuelled up on beer and feeling invincible, ergo the boyfriend is hardly an obstacle he reckons.

'So why bother repeating yourself, then?' Twix says, grinning cheekily at the boyfriend.

The guy stands so quickly that momentarily Twix is left jutting his chin smarmily at the guy's crotch, before reassessing the situation and looking upwards and into his eyes instead.

'Calm down, lad,' says Twix, shamelessly placing his hands on the guy's chest. 'Just playing around.'

The boyfriend's far from amused, however, slapping Twix's hands away. 'You wanna play, you motherfucker, let's play. Outside!'

'Oho!' laughs Twix. 'You wanna go? I'll fucking smash you, prick!'

The guy nods and smirks with the kind of confidence that should make Twix seriously reconsider, but he's drunk and the danger signs mean nothing to him. If anything, they're like a red flag to a bull, and he imagines himself impressing the girl in the corset enough to soon be leaving in a taxi with her. If only those catamarans were raring to go now!

'See you out there,' he says, and rushes over to the bar where he slaps down two fifty dollar notes. 'Set me up with a hundred bucks' worth of celebratory drinks,' he says, instructing the bartender to put the drinks on the table in front of Dante and Xanthe.

He then motions to the boyfriend that he's ready to rumble, so the big bastard stalks for the doorway and down the stairs, with Twix in tow. On the way past Alex, who is chatting with Adelaide on the door, he crows about his impending victory. 'Just gotta sort out some business, then I'll be back to celebrate, and you girls are invited.'

Adelaide glances down the stairwell at the wide shoulders of the guy disappearing around the corner. 'Why don't you stay up here and just enjoy yourself, hun?'

Twix gives her a sloppy grin, his fangs sparkling from the light of the various candles clustered on the desk in front of her. He bounds down the stairs two at a time. The neo-Nazi's are mercifully absent from the bottom of the stairwell, so Twix bounds outside to sort this other joker out.

As he steps out onto the footpath he notices a metal garbage bin flying towards his face, then the world explodes into red-hot puddles of blackness, each wave blooming against the other and spreading across his face.

Twix drops to the ground with blood pissing from his nose and his mouth. One of his fangs has snapped off from the impact of the metal bin hitting him square in the face, and bounced away to the curb where it teeters on the edge, ready to fall into the gutter.

The big boyfriend throws the bin, now dented in one side, back around the corner into the empty lot used as a storage area for bins of bottles and piles of broken delivery pallets.

'Let's see you sweet talk my girl now, motherfucker,' he says, sneering down at Twix, and heads back inside.

From the windows of the bottom floor hang assorted metalheads and skinheads (although with this particular crowd the distinction is sometimes hard to make), whooping and cheering at Twix and raising their beers in salute.

'Fucking nice catch there, mate!'

A few of them spot the cheongsam and fishnets he's wearing, and begin hurling sundry taunts about transvestism and homosexuality.

Upstairs, Riz and his mates notice the big bastard that left with Dante's mate come back inside and beckon his doe-eyed girlfriend and other friends to the table where the bartender has set up a couple dozen drinks. Riz had seen Dante's mate order those drinks then cockily follow the big bastard outside for a showdown, so it's evident who won that confrontation. The metalheads piss themselves with laughter, even Eleanor who now sits with them, as the big bastard and his friends get stuck into the drinks.

Riz goes up to the DJ and bullies him into playing an Obituary CD he produces from inside his jacket. He knows the goth clubs aren't generally inclined to play death metal, but he figures if they can play that Marilyn Manson shit then they can play some Obituary. The boys at the table cheer in unison as they hear their kind of music blasting.

'Sir James Murphy ripping it,' one of them bellows as they charge out onto the floor, swinging their long air around in big circles. They form a ring and unanimously growl: '*Feel the blood spill from your mooooouffff...'*

Riz has noticed that the guy they call Dracula hasn't been around since he spilt his drink, and thinks the poor bastard must have left after finding out that his girlfriend has hooked up with Davo all of a sudden. He feels pretty bad for Dracula and promises himself to buy the guy a drink next time he sees him out.

Outside, Alex hunches down next to Twix and passes him a glass of beer. He takes a swig, swilling it around his mouth to wash out the blood, turning his head to one side to spit but it splashes all over someone's shoe. Beer and blood slime down over the polished black leather.

'Aw shit, sorry lad,' Twix groans, and looks up to see two police officers staring down at him in disbelief.

He recalls that just last week some wanker Dante knows – Lachie – was given four months in the slammer for spitting in a policewoman's face in West End. Thank Christ this is just a shoe, he thinks.

Twix proffers up the glass. 'I know the drill,' he says, his voice distorted by a numbing pain, 'no alcohol in public.'

'Not just that anymore,' says one of the officers angrily. 'Local Law 51 has been passed statewide, buddy. Know what that means? We're not restricted to just taking the alcohol from you and moving you on.'

'Powers of arrest, now,' sneers the other officer.

'Been that way for years,' scoffs a skinhead from the doorway. 'Never stopped you fascist cunts before.'

The other officer turns and goes: 'Yeah, yeah. We're getting to you lot in a minute. Do us all a favour and get back inside.' Naturally this fuels a full-blown argument between him and a growing number of hardcore skins who clamour at the windows.

'You're shitting me?' says Twix to the other officer still standing in front of him.

'Afraid not,' the policeman laughs, and shoves his shoe towards Twix. 'And I hope for your sake you're not wearing ladies' knickers under that dress, or we might have to book you for impersonating a woman, too. Soliciting even, maybe.'

Twix holds his throbbing cheek and moans, feeling a splitting headache coming on.

The officer isn't finished with him yet.

'Now wipe my fucking shoe clean.'

Twix turns his head to the side as the smell of his own vomit threatens to make him spew again, and he spies the three babybats emerge from the Oriental, still sporting those hideous matching shirts emblazoned with the image of their dead bucktoothed friend, as terrible a fashion statement as Twix has ever seen.

Now there's the real crime, he thinks, tasting acid reflux at the back of his throat.

TWIX AND AMAI

Amai and Clem broke up last week, and while she's not saying it's because of ol Twixxie I like to think I'm the reason.

Tonight we've gotten drunk with her flatmates, playing *Truth or Dare,* and her roomie Sally dares me to kiss Amai. It's a drunken pash but if I've ever held back on admitting to myself any feelings (or lust, at least) for Amai, I can't any longer. As soon as we've kissed, I know I wanna fuck her more than anything else.

Thank Christ no-one dares me to kiss Sally, because she's got this nasty looking infection above her eye that I reckon should've been bandaged and kept well hidden from the public. Sally reckons it's better if it's aired out, except I can't help but keep gawking at the fucking thing. It's making me feel ill. Consumption of bulk piss helps render the spectacle more acceptable, thankfully.

Everyone's so drunk that we all crash here for the night. At some point close to midnight Clem's on the phone bawling his sodding eyes out cause he knows I'm staying over (that or it's a wild fucking guess on his part), even though I'm sleeping on the couch. Amai's sympathetic to his whining, however, but it's pretty obvious that it's getting on her nerves by the end of it.

In the morning, before everyone else wakes up, Amai pads out of her bedroom in her cute little baby-blue cotton pyjamas and curls up next to me. We kiss again, delicately this time, and she stretches out against me while I stroke her fine hair. She closes her eyes as I brush my fingertips against her eyelashes.

Everyone else is still asleep, their heads tucked under their arms to avoid the morning light.

Amai's pyjamas are a singlet and shorts set that sit loosely on her frame, so in my position I can look over her shoulder and down the front of her top at her small breasts. Her skin's an even olive colour all over, not like the splotchy pale and reds of white chicks. I trail my fingers across her cheeks and down along her neck to her collar bone. Her breathing becomes shallower. I circle her clavicle a few times and let my hand slip lower and lower until I've breached the opening of her PJ's.

Checking to see if the coast is clear and the room's still well and truly slumbering, I reach in and clasp Amai's boob, feeling it's perfect softness and instantly cracking a fat. I'm embarrassed she'll feel my boner, despite circumstances. Not sure why, but I guess I'm worried she might think I've gotten hard too prematurely. Shifting my pelvis slightly helps move my boner clear of her hip.

Eventually we fall asleep and only wake again when Amai's big boofhead friend Robbo, good lad that he is, starts clanging pots and pans in the kitchen as he cooks up a fry to combat our hangovers.

For the next few days I can't get the memory of that morning out of me head, specifically of our kiss and stroking those boobs, so I call her up and arrange to meet in the city and look at a new art exhibit in the basement of the Town Hall. Art's not my thing, but I know she likes it. The exhibit is all different stuff, with one wall nothing but shelf upon shelf of pickling glass jars containing dead animals. Birds, toads, rats. Amai thinks it's hilarious. A little plaque says the animals are road-kill collected over a month long period from a stretch of tarmac out towards Cleveland. Some kind of statement, I guess.

On the way into the gallery, we were accosted by panhandlers for returned services or veterans or one of them. I didn't find out, because Amai had launched into a tirade about the irony of wars being funded to defend our cultural values and how we've failed to fund the cultural institutions we aspire to defend. Looking at the road-kill on the wall, I can't see anything here to go to war over.

Standing beside us is a nuclear family of four with rough but interesting features, and they're all dressed head-to-toe in white, like they're from a cult. They're staring in fascinated horror at the jars of dead animals, muttering quietly to each other in another language.

'A bit spooky,' I comment to them tentatively, and the parents turn to us and smile broadly.

'Ya,' they nod.

'Are you French?' Amai asks eagerly. She's got a weird fascination for Paris and for all things French, for some reason. *Allez!*

'Germany,' they go. 'We are here for a holiday. We arrived today.'

'Oh!' says Amai, feigning faux-shock which Asians do so adorably well, even though she's been here since she was ten. 'What else have you seen around the city?'

'Just this,' the father says, pointing at the wall of dead animals. 'Airport to hotel, and hotel to here first,' waving his hand through the air to mimic flying on a plane and then, presumably, walking.

'Well, just so you haven't got the wrong end of the stick about Aussies, we don't all pickle our road-kill and call it art,' I go.

They stare at me until Amai goes: 'We have lots of different kinds of art, not just this.' They register comprehension and laugh with her like she'd told a joke or something.

Amai has a relaxed way with people that I don't have, even though I like to think my communication skills aren't too bad on account of doing security work. Nine times out of ten it's about being able to talk to people in security, not arm-wrestling them into submission.

Me and Amai hang around the city eating ice-cream and discussing the merits of different movies, because Amai's a huge movie nerd, especially for sci-fi ones.

At one point we're leaning against the wall above the bus tunnel entrance that comes out on Albert Street in the Mall when these old Chinese blokes stand close us, chatting and pointing at things. At one stage one of the old geezers comes over and stands right in front of us, only a couple of feet away, just gawking straight at Amai without blinking. Amai doesn't seem to notice, and I'm glancing from one to the other wondering if she's gonna acknowledge him. He's there for a few minutes just staring at her, and it's really starting to bother me.

'Look mate, what's your problem?' I finally say to him, but he just blinks at me uncomprehending and shuffles away.

But the thing is, when he gets to the other old geezer he says something and they both gawk back at me.

'What the fucking hell are you staring at?' I demand loudly, but Amai grabs my arm.

'Don't worry about it,' she says, dragging me after her. 'Let's go to the Square.'

'What the fuck was that all about? He was staring straight at you for ages.'

'Not your problem, isn't it?' she says.

'Did you know him?'

'No,' she sighs. 'That's what Chinese men do. They stare at girls.'

'First time I've seen it,' I snort.

'Chinese girls,' she clarifies, rolling her eyes at me.

'That's weird.'

'So, that's Chinese men for you,' she goes. 'They think they own us women. Actually, that's all men, everywhere.'

We stroll across into King George Square and find a spot on one of the lawns to sit down. There're families and couples all around us doing the same, and some homeless and Aboriginal kids hanging out in front of the fountain asking for loose change off people going past. The lights on the Town Hall look cool at night. It's a great evening, despite that old Chinese motherfucker.

After some small talk me and Amai end up kissing. Her breath has an unusual but not unpleasant aroma to it. At some point she starts to freak out.

'Oh shit, I think I know them,' she suddenly goes.

'Who?'

'That couple that walked past. I think they're friends with my parents. Dammit!'

'So?'

'So I think they saw me. They'll tell Ma and Ba that they saw me kissing with some guy.'

It sounds ludicrous, but maybe only because by comparison my family wouldn't give a shit.

'That sounds really full-on,' I tell her.

'It sucks balls,' she goes, clearly exasperated. 'Everywhere I go and everyone I see my parents need to know. It's so stupid, isn't it?'

She goes on to tell me that she can't be on the dole because her parents earn too much, so she relies on them for her rent and living expenses when she's in between jobs, which is fairly often. So she feels obligated to play the good child for them, which is pretty much in contravention to how she wants to live.

She's in a shit mood now, so we agree to call it a night and she catches the train home while I grab the bus. All I can think about on the way home is Amai's little boobs in that baby-blue cotton top, and the old Chinese bloke gawking unblinking at her. I probably won't even be in the mood to rub one out when I get home. Which turns out

I'm not.

Next day, as luck would have it, all Amai could think about last night was fucking me, or so she says on the phone, so after work I borrow Greg's car and swing by Amai's place and we sit around chatting about movies and shit until Sally heads out to work. She's a nurse at Greenslopes, so she'll be gone half the night.

As soon as Sally's car's down the road, Amai's tugging my shirt off and I'm pulling at hers. She doesn't shave her underarm hair, or her legs, and the hairs are straight and soft and jet-black. Normally body hair on a chick would turn me off, but Amai's doesn't bother me for some reason, and it's barely noticeable on her legs anyways. We fall into her bed and rub our naked bodies together, kissing and groping at each other with wild abandon. I wasn't expecting to get this eager, but I think the foreplay is gonna have to take a backseat this time. Karen was the last root I had and that was months ago, so I'm keen to just sink my tockley in.

Amai's got the hint and pulls out a rubber from the bedside drawer, which I make a face at, but she says it's not happening unless it's on, so I reluctantly take the condom and slip it down over my hard-on. Amai watches me do it with a big smile on her face.

'It's so long,' she says, running her hand up and down it.

Her tits are pretty small, and hang a bit flat even though there's not much to them. Her nipples make up for that, though. They remind me of little playdough balls like I used to make as a kid.

The sex isn't great.

In fact, it turns out to be pretty ordinary, and the condom doesn't help either. Eventually I manage to cum by imaging my old neighbour Ellie and her amazing head of curls. Unfortunately, I don't think Amai climaxes and afterwards we're silent about whether the sex was good or bad. We just get under the covers and spoon until she falls asleep.

I'm wide awake, though, staring past Amai's hair at her t-shirts on the clothes-hanger. I'm wondering about her ex, Clem, who used to live in one of the other rooms. Was the sex with him as ordinary? Was it better? Or is it me, somehow? I don't know why it feels like there's a problem, but it does. I feel like she was holding back. But I can't shake the feeling that there's some piece of a puzzle missing and I'm left here in the dark knowing it's missing but with no clue as to what or where it is.

There's a Star Wars poster on one wall, and Tilda Swinton and Billy Zane in a bed on another. Her dirty Converse sneakers lie on the floor, incongruously small. They look like they belong to a child. Socks and knickers and other clothing are strewn from bed to wall, and there's a small stack of books on the side drawers. Mostly sci-fi stuff. Asimov. Douglas Adams.

I quietly leave without waking her. Sally's sitting at the kitchen table after having finished her shift at the hospital.

I grin sheepishly.

'Get over it, ya dickhead,' she drawls, crunching on her toast.

I'm not sure why she said that. Maybe she doesn't like me? Maybe she wishes Clem was still here? Thing is, she was the one who dared me to kiss Amai earlier, when we were playing *Truth or Dare*.

The drive home feels surreal. The streets are dark and empty, and while I feel relieved to be on my own again I feel a pang of regret that I left Amai's without saying hooroo to her.

'Well, the Moon was in Mars last night,' says Megs, spouting off that astrological crap she's into, when I tell her all about it the next day at work. 'Everyone was acting weird, especially sexually.'

'You know I don't believe in that stuff,' I tell her, deadpan.

'You're not in love, are you?' she goes.

'Fuck no. It's just casual sex.'

Megs tips her head and raises her eyebrows at me, pity in her eyes.

'Don't give me that look,' I say a little irritably.

'Sorry, hun, but it hasn't been that long since Karen.'

'So what? You think I'm transferring?'

She just shrugs.

NIGHT OF THE MANIMAL

So packed to the rafters is the Railway Hotel that there's fuck all elbow room, which makes it difficult to point the camera where it's needed down here in the mosh pit.

Roshan's got the second camera and is positioned on the stairwell at the back of the crowd, trying to keep out of the staff's way who're probably getting more than a bit shitty with him perched up there.

Decapitation just finished their set and are leaving the stage. When we got here and were reading the band names off the poster at the front door, Roshan pronounced it as 'Decapacitation' and didn't get why I started laughing my arse off or why the door-bitch got surly.

Next to me is a thick-set bald fucker in a shirt with holes all over it is getting pretty excited by the prospect of Necrogore coming on.

'Fuck yeah!' he bellows, turning to face the rest of us and throwing his fists into the air. 'The fucken Gore!'

I hate it when cunts shorten band names. You hear those wankers on morning radio like Triple M and whatnot doing it all the time, so that Powderfinger becomes 'The Finger' and Regurgitator becomes 'The Gurge', not that they play much if any of the latter, but that's besides the point.

'Somethin of a fan, eh?' I ask the bald fucker.

'The Manimal's their number one fan, ay,' he goes, and it actually takes me a few seconds to realise he's referring to himself in the third person, that *he* is in fact said Manimal. This cunt and Twix could hit it off together. 'Never missed a fucken gig yet.'

The stage lights dim after some tech set-up, and someone's put on the soundtrack from *Conan the Barbarian*, setting the tone for what's to come, presumably. This positively puts the Manimal into a state of near arousal as he caresses the foldback speaker, eagerly watching the stage wings.

After what seems like nearly half a song from *Conan*, Riz, Davo and the others finally stroll onto the stage with their guitars strapped on and ready to go.

The Manimal's roars at them like a beast, and the crowd attempts to match his enthusiasm. I had no fucking idea Riz's band were this popular when I agreed to shoot a music video for him. He wanted something set in a forest with girls in nightgowns swishing about but Roshan, whom I've dragged into this simply for access to his camera equipment, was insistent that we get some live footage to splice in so as to ramp up the pace of the video. He's not going to be too happy about that idea now, though, because they've just dimmed the lights down more than Decapitation had them set at, and the camera I've got is picking up fuck all detail. Just indistinct figures and a shit-load of film grain.

Strangely, the band just stands there in the dark, waiting for the *Conan* track to finish playing. It takes another half a minute before it does, but the crowd don't seem to register the oddity of watching the guys standing there looking bored as fuck with their instruments idle.

Then the drummer sets off a shimmer on the ride cymbal that rises in crescendo before smashing into the bass drum and toms, seemingly awakening the rest of the band from their Conan stupor and igniting the stage in a cacophony of metal.

The Manimal goes absolutely ape-shit, bouncing up and down and swinging his meaty arms around, matching Riz word for word. He's not wrong about being a massive fan: he seems to have all the lyrics memorised. He'd make a useful prompt.

Davo on bass grins out at somebody in the crowd, holding their eyes longer than is usual. I crane my neck over the crowd and spy Eleanor standing over on the other side of the venue, transfixed by seeing her new boyfriend onstage. I guess it really is over between her and Albert. I should probably avoid him at the goth clubs in future lest he snaffle me in some endless, self-pitying tirade. Could be awkward given my brief working relationship with the very band who've nicked his fiancé.

A couple of songs into the set and the Manimal's torn his shirt in two, dropping the them on the floor. Kinda explains why it was full of holes. How embarrassing would it have been for him in this crowd if he'd been unable to rip it apart?

I've got to get more light onto this stage somehow.

I peer round at Roshan and wait for him to glance my way, then point up at the lights and over to the guys at the mixing desk who're a lot closer to him than they are to me. He gives me the thumbs up and goes over to them, haggling for a moment. He's got this suave Persian charm he can turn on when he needs to wrangle something, and it evidently works because the stage lights brighten just enough for the camera to work. I waste no fucking time at all, whipping the camera around just in time to film the now crazed Manimal trying to brain himself against the foldback speaker. Blood's spraying up every time he slams his face down.

Riz is shielding his eyes against the light, giving the thumbs down to the mixing guys, so the lights aren't up for long. Just enough for me to get a little footage that might be salvageable in editing.

The Manimal continues to carry on like a fucking porkchop, blood streaming down his face from a nasty gash on his forehead. He grins at me, flashing a set of small and ugly teeth, his eyes crazed in that dumb and dangerous way. Blood dribbles into his mouth and when he laughs it sprays onto the girl behind me. She's not happy about it but it's the Manimal, so what's she gonna do?

After Necrogore's set I ask the Manimal if I can interview him, thinking he'd not only be a fascinating subject but that the band'll be able to use the footage in any future tour videos they possibly make. The Manimal's keen, but it's too dark and way too fucking noisy out here to conduct it, so I very tentatively enquire if the men's dunnies is okay?

'You wanna fuck The Manimal?' he growls, and when he sees I've realised the mistake I've made, he laughs his arse off and goes: 'Just fucken with ya! Let's go.'

What a cunt, ay? I thought he was gonna knock my block off right there and then.

We burst into the men's dunny and while it's still not ideal for an audio recording, it's a lot better than out in the venue and as a bonus the lighting's perfect for this crappy camera. While I set up I clue the Manimal into the kind of questions I'll ask, stuff like how long's he known the band, blah blah blah.

Some other punters look critical of our set-up here in the dunnies but the Manimal death-glares the fuckers and they quickly look away, like he's got em all trained to be shit-scared of him.

'Yeah, sounds good,' he goes, then gives me a bit of a rundown, even though I'm still setting up. 'I've known those cunts a fucken long time, mate. A *fucken* long time. Been through all sorts of shit with those cunts,' he says, chuckling at his memories, and recounts a couple of quick stories that're exactly the sort of thing I'm after.

He's got a mouth on him like a trooper, worse than me, in fact, but it really suits him, especially with the blood dribbling down his face, the hideous homemade tatts down his arms and his massive, hairy gut poking out. You can't make this shit up!

'Righto, let's get started,' I go, turning the camera on. 'Manimal, tell us about how you first met Necrogore.'

He clears his throat, then as polite as possible he goes: 'Well, I first met the boys from Necrogore at one of the four triple zed Marketdays a couple of years ago, and I've been both a fan and a friend to them ever since.'

What in flying fuck is this shit? The Manimal, scourge of the scene, has suddenly transformed into the kind of guy you'd not hesitate to take home to meet your mother. He's eloquent and mild-mannered, and even his face has lost the menace and leer, despite the blood.

I try another question but it's the same kind of response, clean cut and proper. This won't fucking do at all. I want the beast of a man back, the cunt who'll tear you apart just to see what colour you bleed. I start getting aggressive with my questioning, deliberately peppering it with obscene language but the fat cunt won't budge: he remains the perfect gentleman, answering with utmost civility.

I imagine Riz and his bandmates sitting down later on to watch the tape, wondering why the fuck their number one fan, the Manimal, is standing in the men's toilets speaking like a kindergarten teacher. This is fucked. They're gonna think I've lost the fucking plot.

'Righto, great, thanks for that Manimal,' I finally go.

He grins. 'Is that alright? Not too much?'

'Never too much,' I grimace, and farewell the cunt while I pack.

'Where've you been?' Roshan goes when I catch up to him.

'Had to use the loos,' I groan. 'Got myself a persistent shit that just wouldn't budge.'

'Not what I needed to hear,' he says, disgusted.

'Nor me,' I go, completely deadpan.

THE SHAMROCK GOES OFF

As I hook a right off Water Street towards the Valley, I see three punks with a wheelchair coming down the hill from the hospital. It's Alan with a couple of his mates. Scab's with him, his green mohawk faded to a pale imitation of its former self. I don't who the girl is pushing the wheelchair.

I jog across the road – careful to avoid the traffic cause sometimes the cunts deliberately speed up when you're goth or punk – and wait for them to catch up. Alan's wasted, wheeling a mobile IV stand alongside with a shiny goon bladder that's ready to burst in place of a drip bag. Judging from how drunk he is, there's at least a whole goon sack totally drained somewhere back from whence they came.

'Oi, Dan, ya bastard!' Alan's enthusiasm nearly tips him forward out of the wheelchair as he reaches out for a hug. I bend down and give him a half-arsed embrace, even though I hate being called Dan. He pongs something wicked.

He introduces the girl as Sarah. I notice she's got junkie sores in the crooks of her arms, and hope my friend isn't also using. 'Oi, listen, we're headed to the Shamrock. Come up, ya bastard. Them Rifles are playin, ay.'

'Yeah, sounds good, Alan. I'll swing by on my way back from the dole office.'

I walk with them up to the Shamrock Hotel, but I notice that for some reason Scab's not paying much attention to me. In fact, it seems he's deliberately ignoring me, like he's pissed off with me. I'm not sure if he is or he's just being a moody cunt.

'Check this bloke out,' Alan says to Scab, pointing ahead at a car parked on the footpath, the bonnet up. Steam hisses out everywhere.

As we pass by, this guy steps back from the engine, an exhausted and irritated expression on his mug. He gives us a pissed off look, and I know it's partly because he hates how we're dressed. People see Scab's green hair or my ragged swampie ensemble and make all sorts of prejudiced assumptions about us.

'Blow a seal, mate?' Alan asks the guy.

'Yeah, fucken thing,' the guy goes, rubbing his hands in the grass at his feet to get the grease off.

'You spit or swallow?' Alan asks, and Sarah cackles like a witch.

The guy frowns for a moment, but comprehends quickly enough and explodes at Alan. 'Fuck off, you boong bludger!' He makes as if he's going to come at us, flashing his teeth viciously. 'Go get a fucking job, you bludging pricks!'

'Have a great day, Captn Cook,' Alan calls back as Sarah pushes the wheelchair faster.

Scab gives the guy the forks and we trudge up to the lights on St Pauls Terrace, with the guy still staring after us.

'They always gotta go racial, huh?' broods Alan, looking deeply pensive, which is a bit of a fucking worry because he's one of the most carefree people I know.

'What I don't understand,' I counter, 'is how they're always quick to assume we're bludgers.'

'Well,' says Alan, spreading his hands as if the case were obvious.

'Come off it,' I say, screwing my nose up at him. The green man comes on the signal box and we all cross over to the Shamrock Hotel. 'I've always got something going on with Roshi or some other mate.'

'Oh yeah?' Alan grins up at me. 'Where you off to now, mate?'

'Fuck off, cunt,' I laugh. I leave them at the Shamrock and head on down the Terrace to the local branch of Social Security.

My twelve months of sickness benefits have come and gone so I was sent a letter to see a Commonwealth doctor, but I assumed they just meant that as some kind of ordinary psychiatric appointment and ignored their request. As per usual between me and the DSS, they absorbed my slight and continued to pester me rather than discipline me. I've known a lot of people to get fucked around by these public servants for far less than what I always manage to get away with.

Back before I was put on the sickness payment I still had to fill out the job form like every other cunt, the one that necessitates we declare at least two places we've actively sought gainful employment from that fortnight; including their contact details so as to verify we have in fact tried and haven't simply penned in any old company from the phonebook. The amount of times I used to write down my own phone number with company names like *Spike Milligan's Banana Factory* or the position applied for as a role model for Jesus at the local church, would need to be seen to be believed. Never got questioned for it.

I got put on the sickness benefits to begin with for depression. It was the verdict of the first psychiatrist I ever saw, Doctor Friedman, out at Ipswich. While that diagnosis hasn't exactly changed, McKay's amended it to 'reactive depression', meaning I have a tendency to respond to certain situations or emotional triggers with a depressive state that I find extremely difficult to shake off. In fact, shake it off I cannot, for that's not how depression works. It's like the chestburster in *Alien:* it gets inside you and feeds off you until it breaks you open and makes a fucking mess of you in front of your loved ones.

There's a section for McKay to fill out on the back of this form the DSS cunts've sent me. When he'd handed it back to me the other day, I'd noticed in the little box for *existing conditions* he'd written down DEPRESSION, BORDERLINE PERSONALITY DISORDER.

'Beef up the resume, so to speak?' I'd asked with a conspiratorial smile.

'What do you mean?'

'The *Borderline Personality Disorder* bit.'

He'd looked genuinely surprised. 'I told you about that, didn't I?'

It'd been news to me, and I'd told him as much.

'Oh, I noticed it on your first session,' he'd gone. 'You know, your identity changes. The invalidating environment you had growing up?'

So here I am now facing an interview with the dole office in order to be referred to a Commonwealth doctor for further assessment, and I've only just learned I've also got a personality disorder. Holy shit.

It's such a seedy office, this one, where sometimes fights break out. There's a fucking long queue as per usual, but I notice there's an old guy behind another counter marked PENSIONS, and there's no queue for that one, so I waltz up and bullshit him about feeling anxious on account of people staring at the way I'm dressed, and he takes my letter and confirms my appointment, asking me to take a seat in the waiting area for my number to be called.

As I'm passing back along the queue some fuckhead in an hideous Mambo shirt sneers at my puffy-sleeves and lace cuffs. 'Nice shirt,' the cunt scoffs.

'Yeah, well, it got me to the front of the queue, didn't it?'

The cunt's face loses its smugness. When will these yobbo cunts ever learn not to try and smart-mouth me?

I sit down next to this thin guy with no shirt on who's got his arm in plaster. His jaw clenches and his red eyes stare at some point across the room as he watches me from his periphery. His leg's bouncing uncontrollably off the floor as if he's on amphetamines. Everyone's giving off a bad vibe so I make sure I am too, otherwise they zero in on the weakest link and then you've got all sorts of grief to deal with.

The guy with the plaster cast asks for the time.

'It's two,' I go, glancing at my plastic watch.

'Fark,' he spits. 'Been waitin since farken one.'

'Yeah, sounds about right,' I go, deciding I'll try my luck. 'What happened to your arm?'

Being forthright's always worked for me.

'I farked it in a shop winda. Me old man was pissen me off so's I had to walk it off, ay, but I got so rank finkin about it that I punched a fucken winda. Next thing, all cut up from the glass, ay.'

'Christ,' I sympathise. 'How long you had that plaster on?'

'Happened two days ago,' he sniffs, rubbing at his nose like the cavities have been destroyed from too much speed.

I couldn't care less at what got him angry in the first place. It's not important. Sometimes we get trapped in these ever-revolving cycles where our shitty emotions just pack on top of one another like crusts upon mantle, like in the geography books at school, and after a while the reasons for being angry all the time matter less and less. In the end, sometimes it's all that some people have to communicate with. Can't even take it personally when someone like that eventually lashes out. Looking into this guy's eyes, I could see it. He had a perpetual scowl, which sorta suited him, and his eyes burned as red hot as his core.

We chat until he finally gets called up.

'See ya round,' he goes.

'Yeah, will do,' I reply, hoping he doesn't. It's only a matter of time before a cunts like that lets loose and burns those around them. It's normal for them.

After what feels like an interminable wait, where even the strange and bristling Valley specials refreshing the queue fail to hold interest, I get called in.

It turns out I know the lady I've got my own interview with. Her name's Heather Field, and she's a friend of Renata's, who is one of Mum's friends. I met Heather at Renata's place once in West End, and she had said then that she works here. I wonder if it's a coincidence that she's the one interviewing me today. In any case, she's happy to see me, and asks about Mum and if she's still doing oil painting.

'Yeah, she's not bad,' I go.

It's funny she asks that, because Mum told me once about how Heather came into an inheritance when her father died, leaving her a condo in New Farm overlooking the Story Bridge. Heather sold the condo, but kept some paintings that her father had collected over the years, including some Sidney Nolan's from before he was making prints of them. So they'd never been seen by the public, except for anyone visiting her father's condo. Anyway, she had these paintings all leaning against each other in her car one summer day while she was here at work, and apparently by the end of the day the heat had melted the oils and all the paintings were glued one to the other. Totally fucked, and never to be seen or documented for prosperity.

'Nice to hear,' says Heather, quite genuinely, also asking about me before getting to the point. 'Well, you know you're here to review your sickness benefits status.'

'I'm still pretty fucked in the head, to be perfectly honest,' I'm quick to clarify, in case she's got in mind that I'm ready to join the dole queues on a fortnightly basis again. 'Not as fucked as that Martin Bryant cunt, mind, but fucked nonetheless.'

Mention of the peroxide-haired gunman from the massacre at Port Arthur last week elicits a shocked look from Heather. Clearly we're still at the stage where glib references to the cunt and what went down is off limits. Everyone's been so touchy about it; fuck, I've even watched friends fall out debating whether the children he shot were less deserving than the elderly who'd died. Not that anyone thinks anyone *deserves* to be shot, mind. Poor wording on my part. I'm just pointing out that people have lost their fucking minds over it. We're truly a nation in mourning, which is now reflected in Heather's eyes as she absorbs and dispels my throwaway remark.

'Yes, awful, just awful news,' she says, shaking her head.

'That's true,' I agree, adding: 'I didn't mean to sound so offhand about it. Just a bit nervous about being called in, is all.'

Then she looks at me with motherly affection. 'Don't panic, we're not going to cut you off.'

'That's reassuring.'

'Don't worry,' she winks at me. 'I'll look after you.'

I think about those destroyed paintings that were in her care.

'You've been on that benefit for over a year now, but it can't be any longer than that, really,' she goes. 'So, now the next step is to review your suitability for a disability pension.'

'I don't think I want be on a pension.'

'It doesn't *sound* great, I'll admit,' she says. 'But it's no different to being on the sickness benefits, really. You'll just answer a lot less to us, is all.'

'Well, that *does* sound kinda good,' I muse, all ears now.

She goes on to explain that I'll be reviewed by a Commonwealth doctor, and after that she'll track the progress of my case and get back to me about it. Sounds alright to me, I guess, so I thank her and promise to send her regards on to Mum, whereupon I hit the streets again back up to the Shamrock, which is full to capacity. The Celibate Rifles always pack a full house, but they're not on until later and Spazza's band Foetal Cake is playing a set right now. I grab a couple of fire-engines off the bartender and push through the crowd to find Alan out back in the beer garden. The wheelchair is gone now, fuck knows where to, but the IV stand is still here with the empty goon skin sagging from it, and Alan's now got a half-full pitcher of beer in front of him. He does a little victory yell when he sees me, customary Alan greeting when he's blind and happy as a pig. Scab still seems to be ignoring me, so fuck the cunt. He can sit there and suffer my presence until he's got the balls to say what's eating him.

Alan's punk mates are thrashing their heads and jerking their bodies to the music, despite the lack of space. One of them laughs at the fire-engine in my hand, and Alan yells in his ear how I hate beer.

'Fermented wheat juice,' I nod.

The guy shrugs. 'More for us, ay,' he shouts, and I raise my glass in a salute which makes him break into this big grin.

Scab ducks away and heads towards the door.

'What the fuck's with him?' I wanna know, but Alan just shakes his head and smiles at me, like it's business he doesn't wanna get involved with. He just wants to have fun, not mediate a domestic. Fair enough, too, after everything he's been through. I tell him all about the interview I had with Social Security.

'That's fuckin great, man,' he goes, but I'm not a hundred percent sold on the idea myself. 'No gammon, mate. They're not gonna hassle you anymore. You'll be sittin pretty soon enough.'

'Is that right?'

'Too fuckin right it is,' Alan says, jabbing a finger to stress his point and spilling his beer in the process. 'Fuck's sake, now my leg's all wet.' He wipes at his jeans with his elbow, getting his jacket wet in the process. 'When they release them unemployment statistics, they don't want them fuckers from opposition pointing the finger and sayin they're not doing enough about jobs, ay? Course not. No, they wanna say that them's the bastards that got people off the dole and saved the job market. Cept they can't save it, coz they don't know how to. So it's easy, ay. Just shift a good whack of us from job-seekers over to the disability pension, and bingo! Unemployment figures are down, so that must mean they got the job market fixed up better than that last government. I'm telling ya, ay, it's all about face with them dipshits and fuck all to do with doin their job properly.'

I'm only half-listening because Adelaide's headed our way from the mosh pit, tits swinging side to side under her top.

'They just gotta keep that up until the next election,' continues Alan with vigour, spilling his beer again, 'where the opposition will both call em out for it and then immediately start doin the same thing when *they* take over.'

'Hey, there cutie,' Adelaide greets me, giving me a little hug. She takes my drink, downing the last of it, gasping with satisfaction as the vodka burns. 'How's the video looking? Bet you can't stop. Watching it, I mean.'

She's talking about a music video we did for Riz's metal band, where I got her to play one of two mysterious forest spirits that Riz insisted on having in it. Me and Roshi shot some cutaway stuff with the girls at the Botanical Gardens, where Adelaide ultimately got her boobs out even after we'd insisted it wasn't necessary. Eleanor – poor Albert's ex-fiancée and now girlfriend to Necrogore bassist Davo – was in it as well but she kept her white nightgown laced up.

When I showed the band the rushes they wanted to keep the titty footage in the video, so I ended up editing two versions for them so they got to keep one with boobs in it and we had another censored version that was suitable for screening on TV. Not that it mattered in the end, as the video was too shit and Necrogore's music too abrasive for anyone to want to broadcast on the idiot box so the whole thing ended up being an exercise in futility.

Me and Adelaide are chatting away when Scab and Sarah come back inside the pub and clock us talking, and Scab immediately goes into a rage, storming over with this intense look on his face. He's still not paying much attention to me, though, and it's Adelaide who cops the full brunt of his ire.

'Can't leave you alone for one fucking minute,' he's screaming at her, up in her face.

She immediately bristles and screams back, her face contorted with both fear and indignation.

'It's got fuck all to do with you, Scab!'

'Like fuck it doesn't!' he retorts, looking at me for the first time today. His face is screwed up in an ugly sneer, which sorta suits the cunt. He turns back to Adelaide and continues yelling at her. 'You've got no idea how much I fucking care about you, how much I do for you!'

She shoves him away, laughing at him. 'Do for me? DO FOR ME?'

I've never seen her so angry, but granted I probably don't know her all that well when I think about it. Besides clubbing, I've only talked with her a half dozen times or so, and she's acted for me in a couple of projects, one of which was Riz's music video. When you're directing someone, though, you either bond with them or you don't, and I did with her, so I sorta feel like we're closer than we actually are. Not to mention that one of those projects was a private photo shoot where we ended up hooking a dog-chain from her snakebite piercing down to her clit ring, and without thinking I'd tugged on the chain to make sure it was clipped on. She was gasping and assuming

I'd hurt her I had apologised profusely, but then she'd confessed that it wasn't pain she'd felt. Despite accidently turning her on that time, we've never fucked. More's the pity.

Scab flies back at Adelaide, bullying her up against the wall and calling her a slut and some other awful shit.

Alan's staring embarrassed at the floor, the pitiful cunt. Two of his mates step in, though, and tell Scab to calm the fuck down, but he shoves one of them off when the guy tries to lead him outside by the arm. Sarah steps up and is getting between Scab and the other punk, challenging him.

'Get the fuck off him or we'll press charges,' she says lamely.

Scab continues to call Adelaide appalling names. Adelaide's ready to cry, and the whole thing's turning ugly and I'm starting to see red. I don't know what the fuck is going on but the cunt has been out of order all fucking day, and with all the shit recently with Twix I've had more than enough of my fill of fucking drama.

With little forethought, I reach down and pick up my empty glass and I fling it at the brick wall behind Adelaide's head. It explodes with a strange muffled sound that is instantly sucked into the blast of the music coming from the band inside, and the glass disappears in a cloud of white dust and flashing slivers.

Scab reels away from Adelaide, holding his face. Adelaide looks stunned. Her shoulders hunch up in recoil from the glass exploding behind her head, and she slowly steps away from the wall, fearful of more to come.

Alan's mates stand back as I stride slowly up to Scab, who looks up at me bewildered. He sees the look on my face, and I can feel it too. I feel like my eyes are blazing, like I'm boring into Scab and I'm ready to kill the cunt just by looking at him. There's a bit of blood on his temple and his cheek, just a scratch really.

'I think there's glass in my eye,' he whimpers to me.

'Whatever your problem is,' I tell him in an even and menacing tone, 'pull your fucking head in. We all have problems, Scab. There's no need to take it out on us.'

'You're the problem,' hisses Sarah, glaring at me with hatred. Scab just stares at me timidly. He's hunched over, holding his face, looking as pathetic as he can. I can't cope with this shit.

I shake my head at Alan, who in turn shakes his head at Scab, and I turn and shove my way through the crowd for the street. It's good to get outside, into some personal space and fresh air. The sun has just set, and the lights of the traffic coming over the hill and cruising down Brunswick Street leave white hot spots on my vision. There's a deep rage in me, so I'm breathing heavily through my nose, glaring at cunts that walk past, challenging them to say something stupid and get me going.

Alan stumbles out and has a quick word with someone and says he'll catch up with them later, then he comes over to me. I feel a bit bad for him, cause Alan just wants a good night out, especially after the funeral and then Suzie and him breaking up.

'Go catch up with your mate, Alan,' I go, feeling more mellow.

'Nah, it's all good, ay,' he replies, slapping a hand on my chest. 'Listen, maybe I shoulda said somethin earlier, but Scab thinks you fucked Addie.'

I give him a tired look, and he rolls his eyes.

'Oh, for fuck's sake,' I groan.

'Yeah, I know,' he says. 'Scab can be a paranoid bastard.'

As if on cue, Scab and Adelaide burst outside, followed by Sarah. She's seething, going on about finding bits of glass in her hair. The other two are still arguing, but it's not so vicious now.

Alan goes over and tries to reconcile them. Scab throws his arms up at something Adelaide says, storming off. I didn't catch what she said, but I'm watching Scab like a fucking hawk. I haven't decided yet what I'm going to do about him, but he probably shouldn't stand so close to the road like that is all I'll say right now.

The thing is, I never tried it on with Adelaide in all the time I've known her because I thought her and Scab still had something on. It pisses me off that he'd think I would do that, but I know why he's so worked up about it, and it's actually not so much because he thinks I got with her as he suspects he can't salvage what he himself has with her. Although I'm starting to see that there isn't anything *to* salvage. The vitriol he came at her with before was too intense. It had all the hallmarks of someone who knows they've already been tossed to the kerbside. The other thing is that I heard tell from Megs that Adelaide already got it on with Radio James, of *Ignore the Machine* fame, much to Meg's chagrin since she was hoping to snaffle that one for herself. She'd told me they'd pulled up beside her at the lights on the way home from The Smashing Pumpkins at Festy Hall, and Adelaide had been straddling James as he drove. So, you know, there's *that*.

Scab wanders over to me, wary as fuck, but he's regained some of his former hostility. I stare at the cunt with a deadpan expression, conveying that he'd better keep his distance.

'We gotta get past this, Dante,' he wheedles.

'I'm not interested.'

'I haven't got any issue with you,' he goes, 'it's Adelaide. She's the problem.'

Sarah's hovering around on my right, watching intently.

'Perhaps you're both the problem,' I snarl.

'Yeah, that's true,' he concedes softly. 'Thing is, I don't know what to do. I'm tryin to save the relationship and it's like she's not even tryin, but she won't let me go, either.'

I narrow my eyes, shrugging, because I'm not sure what he's on about. He picks up on my confusion.

'We're still together,' he explains. 'I thought you knew that?'

'I know fuck all,' I go, and realise it sounds like I'm admitting that something between her and I might indeed be going on. Right now, I can't even be bothered correcting this potential misunderstanding.

'Nah,' he says sadly, and it seems like he's about to cry. The last fucking thing I need. 'We're still sort of together, sort of not.'

Out of the corner of my eye I can see Sarah stiffen and storm off inside. Scab seems oblivious to it, just going on about him and Adelaide, who's still talking animatedly with Alan over by the road. She's gesticulating wildly, arguing and pointing in Scab's direction. I start to feel a bit sorry for the stupid prick.

'Scab, mate, maybe the last thing you need to be doing is trying to save something that's unsalvageable,' I say. 'Trust me, I know,' I add, thinking of Nicola.

He looks at me with something like gratitude, all the hostility in his eyes nullified. He nods in agreement, mulling over the situation.

From my periphery I see a hulking figure lumbering towards us quite quickly. It's some big bastard in what are probably steel cap boots, with a scraggly beard and huge lugs in his ears. He looks like that Jaga cunt from the *Thundercats* cartoons in the mornings. With a belligerent expression on his face, Jaga charges right at me.

'Wait up,' I protest, raising my hands in submission. The cunt's a hell of a lot bigger than me, so when he brings his fist down on my shoulder I'm surprised it only hurts a little. But he's already gearing up for another swing when suddenly Scab jumps in between, waving his arms in front of Jaga.

'Back off!' Scab yells at the big guy, who easily shoves him out of the way and comes for me again.

I start scooting backwards, going on about how there's no need for this bullshit. I've got no fucking idea who he is or why he's after me, but Jaga keeps his pace up, forcing me to make a hasty retreat down Brunswick, eyes trained solely on the bastard. Behind him some other big cunt has started out after me, too, but Scab wrestles with the guy, demanding that they fight him instead, to which the cunt obligingly does. Where the fuck was this fighting spirit the night he was getting the shit kicked out of him behind the Hoyts that time I got Roshan's camera fixed?

Beyond the scuffle between Scab and the other monolith, Alan and Adelaide stand looking on in confusion, and over at the door of the pub I can see Sarah amongst some of the onlookers. She's grinning at me like a shot fox.

Fuck this. I tell the big cunt to go fuck himself and start jogging down the road, deciding that's me done for the day. Down past the Valley Plaza I glance back and see Jaga the giant Thundercat's given up on me and is trudging back up the hill to the Shamrock, where the his mate has Scab on the ground and is kicking the shit out of him. Alan's coming down the street, so I wait for him to catch up.

'You alright?'

'Those cunts need to sort their shit out,' referring to the situation between Scab and Adelaide. 'It's got fuck all to do with me. I'm still dealing with how I feel about Nicola.'

'And they gotta do it without all this violence, too, ay,' he says, casting me a sly look.

'You can't judge, ya cunt,' I shoot back, remembering how he got locked up for paint-bombing those coppers. 'You're always getting yourself into scraps.'

'Nah,' he goes.

'Bullshit. How many times have I seen you covered in bruises and black eyes?'

He goes really quiet, hanging his head as we walk. He's struggling with something big.

'What's the matter?' I probe. If he's got something to get off his chest, he may as well do it.

'That was Suzie,' he says softly.

'What was?'

'The bruises and shit, man,' he says slightly irritated. 'It was Suzie. All of them. All them times I told you I got black eyes coz of fighting racist bastards and skinheads calling me boong or some shit, it wasn't true. I don't fight them arseholes. Nationalism just teaches you to take pride in shit you've never done and to hate people you've never met, on stolen land that was never redeemed by a treaty. I'll fight them with words, not fists.'

He's starting to distract from the confession already, so I cut him off at the pass.

'Suzie used to hit you?'

He screws his nose up and smiles bashfully, thrusting his hands deep into his pockets. Nervous gestures.

'Shit, Alan, I didn't know.'

'No-one did,' he smiles. 'Why would they? She didn't do it in front of you mob, anyways.'

'I didn't even know she had it in her,' I admit.

'No-one fuckin knows, Dante. Fuck me, man. You think them people who beat each other up go round with a neon sign over their heads sayin they do domestic violence? But, you know, it happened. It's in the past now. I'm a free man again, ay.'

And then the penny drops. Alan's been partying it up and getting pissed all the time recently, and here I've been thinking that he was trying to deflect the reality of his baby dying when in fact he's been celebrating his severance from an abusive partner. You don't see this shit coming, and I'd never have guessed that Suzie was beating the crap out of Alan, especially because his cover story of fighting with racists stands up. Cunts are always hassling him because of his skin colour.

'I was gonna go straight home,' I tell him. 'But now I'm thinking another drink is in order.'

'Yeah I reckon, but you got the right idea, ay,' he says. 'Too many dumb fucks out tonight. We'll swing by the bottle-o and get us some takeaway. A night in on the piss with you's gotta be better than a kick up the arse, Rifles or no Rifles.'

A PERFECT CIRCLE

We're out of sodding milk again. I'm sick of picking up the slack after these lads all the time. Work has got me on rotating shifts again and it's killing me, so I don't always have the time or energy to go grocery shopping, but one of these jokers works regular hours and the other geezer doesn't work at all. The one who works, Billy, is saving for a deposit to buy his own apartment, but that's no frigging excuse to shirk his responsibilities here.

And now it's State of Origin night so of course there's no way either of them will budge from the couch to go up to the Foodworks on Hawken Drive and get some, even though it's only a five minute fucking walk! I just got off a gruelling day shift in the Valley, and as much as I just wanna collapse into bed it's off to the bloody shops ol Twixxie goes to make sure everyone's got milk.

To make matters worse, because Greg's a semi-hippy he insists on drinking this curdled milk called *kefir* every morning. There's a large vegemite-jar of it sitting in the bottom of the fridge, with a redundant DON'T TOUCH written on it in black marker. Who'd wanna touch the hinky shit, seriously? He absolutely has to have it every day, and will use up a good portion of our milk supply topping it up. But do you think the bastard will shift his arse to replace what he uses? Yeah, right!

I've been packing on the weight lately and my stomach's starting to bulge out my security uniform, so I make sure to only take enough money for milk alone and nothing frivolous like choc-chip cookies or ice-cream. I'm gonna have to start giving those up for a while, if I can. The problem isn't so much what I'm eating, it's the lack of actual physical activity my job requires.

The nights are starting to get chilly, dead of fucken winter for sure!

I never walk on the side of The Esplanade that's got the houses on it. I always cross the road first then walk along the park, preferring the shadows. Tonight in particular. Looks and sounds like the house a few doors up is having an Origin party, and there's groups of likely lads milling about out front of the house in their maroon jerseys. The kind of normals best avoided when in packs, more so when they're tanked on grog.

But this car pulls up and a pizza delivery chick hops out. The blokes at the party've noticed her, too, and start howling and jeering at her as she climbs the stairs in the block of flats next door.

'Do you deliver blowies?' one boofhead yells, and encouraged by the guffaws of his shit-stain mates he continues to catcall in hopes of a response, apparently.

The girl tries to ignore them, but at one point she acknowledges them with a lopsided grin, shrugging her shoulders. But I'm familiar with that lopsided grin; I've seen it plenty of times on the job. It's a grimace, a look of fear, of hoping to placate a domineering force. And she's still gotta come down yet, back to her car where these apes are starting to drift towards.

Time for ol Twixxie to step up.

There's a few choice stones by the roadside, so I fling a couple at the house where the party is. The sound of the stones ricocheting off the roof tiles can be heard even from where I'm standing, over the *thump thump thump* of their stupid music coming from the backyard. The guys have heard it, too, and momentarily give up their heckling of the pizza chick to locate its source.

I'm grinning to myself, safe under the cover of darkness, when one of those motherfuckers points across the road and goes: 'Over there! It was that cunt in the Halloween costume!'

One bark orders for the others to go inside and grab backup. I could make a run for it, but the pizza chick's coming down the stairs. I can't well leave her to deal with the hostilities on her own. The front door of the party house bangs open and a stream of burly looking blokes exit, heads swivelling around and finally fixing on me.

'Let's sort that fuckhead out,' they roar, all twenty or so of them charging across the street toward me.

I don't like my odds and I've got no backup plan for dealing with this. It's quite likely they play footy themselves up at the Uni. They'd outrun me easily, especially with my own physique having gone to shit recently. Damn those choc-chip cookies!

I've got to stall these bastards somehow.

'STOP!' I shout, holding up my hand like a traffic warden.

To my astonishment, it actually works. The entire lot of them grind to a halt, halfway across the tarmac. Go figure, right?

'Why?' one of them growls.

I feel inside my coat pocket and finger the fifty cent coin, barely comforted by its dodecagonal corners.

'I'm armed,' I declare, intending that if it comes to the crunch I'll try and brain one of them with the coin and then make a run for it.

'With what?' says one of them, a guy with a swollen forehead. Has to be a football injury, surely?

I'm reluctant to show my hand, have them all laugh and then jump me and beat me to a pulp. So I stay silent, hoping for another avenue of inquiry that gives me a better advantage.

'Maybe it's a knife,' one of the apes suggests, without any hint of sarcasm or irony.

'Nah, it's a gun,' adds another, so now they're reluctant to get any closer

Is this really frigging happening?

The pizza chick drives off without further any further hassle.

Yet I stand here, armed only with a perfect circle, and accused of holding a gun. It's not like I can wristlock the lot of them! I just wish a car would come whizzing over the hill and scatter everyone. I could try and get away in the confusion, then.

More people from the party have come out and joined the crowd, to inquiry as to what's going on.

'This cunt's armed,' one of them says.

'He was throwing rocks at your house, dude.'

The lad in question is a small prick with a big nose.

'Is this your house?' I ask him, and he confirms it. 'Isn't your mum a lecturer at the Uni?'

'Yeah, she is,' he says, getting my point. 'She's not home but she knows I'm having a party.'

'Oh, she'd be happy about these losers threatening the neighbours, eh?'

The lad's ashamed, to his credit. The blokes that started the whole thing have grown bored by the outcome, and of me, shuffling back across the street to rejoin the party.

'I don't actually know most of these guys,' the lad sheepishly admits. 'They just crashed from the dorms up the street.'

At the top of the hill are several so-called 'colleges', which are really just a series of student dormitories for out-of-towners. Ten to one a lot of the apes that have gate-crashed this poor bastard's party are from Gatton, out near Toowoomba. Probably never seen a goth before. No wonder they jumped to the conclusion I was packing heat.

'Get rid of them,' I snap. 'Just tell them to fuck off.'

'I've tried,' he whines. 'They won't go.'

'Then get the sodding police in here,' I retort, unable to hide the exasperation in my tone. 'Geez.'

'You guys are fucking boring,' comes this voice from behind me.

There's a dropkick lounging against the pine-log barriers that circumnavigate the park perimeter. He looks like he's wasted, high as fuck. I don't know how he got back there, as I was pretty vigilant about that crowd. I guess my instinct's not as sharp as I'd thought.

'Well, it's a fucking disgrace how your guests are treating your neighbours,' I again address the lad with the huge nose. 'Invited or not invited.'

I leave them to it, standing around in the middle of the street mumbling amongst themselves or perhaps wondering about the gun I don't really have. How fucking drunk are these wankers to think I'm walking around with a gun in St Lucia? Last week or so the Howard Government announced their new gun-control initiatives because of the massacre at Port Arthur a few weeks ago, so maybe that's playing on their minds.

On my way back from the Foodstore I'm again on the park side of the street, and this time the music is down a few notches because the police are now on the scene. As I stroll by with the plastic bottle of milk hooked on my finger, the little joker with the nose is out front discussing something with the boys in blue, and both he and the officers look over in my direction.

The wasted dropkick's still leaning on the treated pine barrier.

'Don't you fucken spill that now,' he says to me with a chuckle. 'Don't need any more tears tonight.'

'Go fuck yourself,' I propose.

THE BIG CHEESE

Mum's friend at the DSS, Heather, called me the other day to let me know that the appointment for the Commonwealth psych is all set up for Thursday, which is today, so off I go in my Sunday best.

Bernie suggested I mess myself up a bit to try and trick the psych into believing I can't look after myself. For some strange reason I rejected his advice, perhaps on the notion that it's simply too obvious a move. Isn't that what the cunt would be expecting, after all?

But I do try and tone down the goth stuff, which actually proves impossible. I thought I'd nailed it, picking out a simple black button shirt with long sleeves, dress pants and my trusty black coat. I even removed some of the buttons to look less ostentatious. As per usual, I got shit from some boofheads down the road and had a mother pull her child away at the traffic lights on Wharf Street as if I was some depraved child rapist ready to commit the deed right there in broad daylight. By the time I get down to the Adelaide Street office of the psych, I've reconsidered my position on looking toned down and a quick appraisal in the reflection of the glass doors corroborates my new suspicion: I don't look like the *normal* I'd been aiming for.

Oh well, no matter. Wing and a prayer and all that shit.

I head inside and take the elevator up to the third floor where a receptionist confirms the appointment and gets me to wait for the doctor. Apparently, he swings into town only every now and then, reviews a whole slew of cases in a very short amount of time, then choofs off to his next port of destination.

Me being here has got to be a shitty outcome for Cheryl the CRS lady, whose sole job where I was concerned was to get me off the sickness benefits and into the workforce. The fact is I was never going to allow that to happen. And yet, fronting up to the Government doctor I'm ready to do my level best to appear as sane as I possibly can. Perhaps not the right terminology, of course, because even mad cunts that have butchered their families and eaten them for breakfast can fail to convince the courts that they're actually clinically insane. Which reminds me of Donger's suggestion that I murder my family on Roshi's Hi8 camcorder and play it back to this doctor and attempt to convince him that it was in fact he, the doctor, who killed my family. In Donger's mind that's me certain for the disability pension then.

The funny thing about being mentally ill on the goth scene is that the stigmas we face in mainstream society are significantly reduced. This is in large part due to goths being openly inviting towards being different to mainstream society, so that we actively embrace the things considered taboo or undesirable. For example, the cutters have got no problem showing off their multitude of scars, and if they aren't wont to boast about them (and most aren't) then they certainly don't bother hiding them, either. McKay once suggested that I stop cutting my arms on account of if I did manage to procure gainful employment in the future, the sight of scars criss-crossing my body parts in a manner that suggested they were self-inflicted would go against me. I joked that I'd just say they're from doing fencing out on my parents' farm, and as much as that excuse would seem highly dubious coming from an inner-city gutter goth, I have actually used it a couple of times with people and they seem to believe it. Not that I intend to procure gainful employment, in any case. So his point's kinda moot.

Ask any Joe Blo on the scene if they suffer from a mental illness and half the cunts will straight up tell you they have bi-polar or OCD. Those two alone are the go-to self-diagnosis that crop up all the time, bandied about like badges of honour. The older goths who confess to an affliction usually have the right to the claim. It's the younger ones – particularly those still in school or fresh from it – who think being mentally ill is an impressive marker that further sets them aside from mainstream society and thereby elevating their status of worthiness in the scene. In many of the examples wherein the illness is boasted of, in the same breath the afflicted will lament how much people don't understand their suffering and how that makes them reticent about confessing it blah blah blah. I see fuck all of said reticence and suffering, however.

It's only about one in a hundred people in the Land of Oz who're bi-polar. Perhaps as goths we're pre-disposed to mental illnesses; or rather, we're more likely to embrace this subculture because of it. But that doesn't make one whit of fucking sense, in all honesty. But it *is* how we think. We describe ourselves as intellectuals, as artists, as people who find beauty in the ugly. As fractured people.

Sounds so fucking pretentious.

In the girl's dunny at the Oriental once I saw written on the wall: GOTHICS ARE THE INDIVIDUALS OF SOCIETY. I nearly fell off the seat with laughter. It's that kind of naivety that compels many of us to make wild claims about being fucked in the head.

The club is the perfect place to promote what you're about, or what you want people to think you're about, as evidenced by that scribble in the ladies'. I once saw a girl pretend to pass out not from too much booze but from a sort of seizure or something. I don't know what the fuck she was doing, but most of us were pretty sceptical about her little performance and left her slumped at the table in the pool room, certain she'd miraculously recover and lay claim to some debilitating condition.

Which is precisely what she did.

I can't say she didn't actually have a mental illness lest I contradict my own assertion that the stigmas we face outside of the subculture are significantly greater than within, but i do know that drunk cunts don't deliberately act drunk: they try and pass themselves off as sober. I don't go about decrying the state of my brain at every opportunity I get. I'm more inclined to hope that that side of me isn't manifesting, and that if it is, it isn't too noticeable. I mean, when my personality disorder flares up, I can be a bit of a cunt. No-one truly wants to be thought of that way. Do they?

But this girl that pretended to pass out from her unspecified illness, I wondered what she got from that stunt? I mean, I assume she was hoping we'd all fuss over her, but we didn't. Not even when she came to and was ready to receive our concerns (or praise?). The general consensus, of course, was that she faked it, and so the reaction she got from us was quite the opposite of what she'd hoped for. You could see it in her face. We didn't outright shun her, but we were snide in our dealings with her for some time afterwards. I mean, we're at a fucking nightclub, right?

So, it makes me wonder about stigmatisation and how it can be perfectly acceptable on the one hand for us to try and lay claim to something that seems to be relatively shunned by the greater society, and yet we're ready to secretly dismiss one another for it. Or rather, not so much dismiss but diminish its impressiveness by outshining it with our own debilitations. *Oh, you have depression? Well, I have bi-polar. Oh, you have schizophrenia? Okay, I fold and you win.*

That kind of competitiveness seems really childish to me. Being childish is something many goths seem to fucking excel at, to be honest.

The psych, the Big Cheese of all psychiatrists, is now ready to see me, says the receptionist. The poor girl leaving his office has a face wet with tears. Looks like this is going to get pretty brutal.

He's nothing like what I was expecting, so there's that. He looks more like a garden-variety GP than someone who makes executive decisions about the mental wellbeing of the nation. He's thin, liver-spotted, balding, bespectacled and rather congenial. I don't know why, but it's the last one that surprises me most.

The whole affair becomes like a watered down cross between my regular visits with McKay and those hideous visits I used to have to make to the dole office. He asks about my condition and how I live, but without any real depth, taking notes. Like he's ticking off the boxes, almost. I ramble on about myself, the usual shit about hating people in general and my sense of self-loathing, cross-examining at length my own confessions and deviating as necessary in order to further enlighten certain points. He's nodding away patiently until it becomes clear to me he's lost interest and is simply filling out his official looking forms.

'Look, none of it really matters, does it?' I finally go, in all earnest. 'With all this rain we've been having lately, the Big Flood's probably on us soon anyway.'

I clue that he must feel the same way about seeing the continents going under, because he has a little smile at this. But it's true: just in the first week of May alone we've had non-stop torrential rains and flooding. It's just getting started, I reckon.

All in all it's not quite clear what this cunt thinks of me, or whether he thinks I'm ill enough for a disability pension, but lately there's been a bit of heat on the Federal Government when disability advocacy groups accused it of backing down on disability support even though more than a billion dollars was going to be allotted to new buses and whatnot that would cater for the disabled. While the Government seems keen to pump a billion into transport changes, it's more than willing to cut eight billion over the next couple of years to social security services in a scheming effort to further diminish the plight of the fucking poor, a cuntish move that compelled one of the Democrat's to declare as flying in the face of Christian values. Tricky fuckers, aren't they?

On the other hand there's also been new calls from a senator in parliament to pursue so-called welfare cheats, which has become a favourite game for pollies after two dumb cunts recently got three years in the slammer for swindling a hundred and sixty grand off the dole. That means we've all gotta start treading more carefully in case we're made an example of. After more than twelve months of sickness benefits, that could well mean my head on the chopping block, so the timing of this Commonwealth doctor's assessment couldn't be better.

Satisfied with my answers, he wishes me well and I'm on my way already. Feels like I only just got in there and I'm already being turfed out, so I can only assume I'm getting the big fat rubber stamp marked SANE smashed across my file.

I swiped the cunt's pen as a souvenir of our meeting. It's a hideous pen with a swirly black and white plastic casing like it's meant to be made of pearl. Or sperm. Imprinted on the side of it are the words: PARKER DUOFOLD NORMAN ROCKWELL LIMITED EDITION. Even more limited now that the cunt won't be able to find it, ay!

I wonder if this is the kind of pen that those pollies sign off on billion dollar ideas to make the poor even poorer?

TWIX'S CANDIED CASHEWS

Amai and I have been casually seeing each other a couple of days a week, but have only had sex again once since then. It was a pretty piss-poor performance from us both, like there was a spark missing. I don't know what it is. She did say she wanted to be free to see other men, especially since she was with Clem for so long. I'd demanded rather hastily if she had seen anyone else yet, and she'd said no but was pretty put off by the question, telling me she didn't need me getting possessive.

Fair call, I guess, but I'm really starting to like Amai in a way that's more than just friends. I was telling Alex all about it and her suggestion is that I need to also go out and meet other chicks and not limit myself to waiting around for Amai when she's not willing to commit to anything more at this stage. Sounds like a solid plan. So me, Dante, Alex and some others are gonna hit Black Sunshine tonight at the Treasury Hotel and then crash back at Alex's place for a big breakfast in the morning. She reckons she's an excellent cook, but we've all gotta chip in because she's pretty broke from working only casual shifts.

So, because a root's on the cards tonight, only my Sunday best will do, but the velvet frock coat I wanna wear still has splatters of dried mud all over it from the downpour at the Mediaeval Fayre in Musgrave Park a couple of weeks ago. I've been meaning to get it dry cleaned because Alex reckons sticking it in the washing machine won't do it any good. To be honest, I've never actually washed this particular item since I don't wear it that often. So I'll have to head down to the cleaners soon and ask them if they can get it done before they close today.

This full-length mirror on the wardrobe door is so old there are black spots and flecks of rust all through it; and on the underside, too, where I can't get to it to clean it or whatever. I stand before it stark naked and decide the reflection isn't too promising for my root-to-be. My legs are hairy as fuck and there's a nest of unsightly pube bushel around the base of my old fella. That's going to have to go, for sure. No chick wants her nostrils tickled by this mess. I want to try and get a bit of an androgynous vampire look happening. Gotta make the effort if we expect the chickadees to do likewise.

I drop my dacks and sit on the closed lid of the loo, with one leg propped up against the bog-roll so that my balls dangle freely over the edge. Using the tweezers from the window ledge above, I grab hold of one particularly long hair growing off from scrotum and give it a yank.

FUCKING HELL, THAT HURTS.

It plucks off alright, but I'd had to give it a pretty hard tug and now there's a spot of blood on my sack. My stomach turns at the thought of it and I quickly dab some toilet paper over the spot, trying not to think about it in case I pass out. I don't know how the hell my ex used to do it. Not pluck pubes off her balls, of course, because she didn't have any. But Karen would pluck her eyebrows, her top lip, her legs, everywhere. Not her vag, though. She said plucking meant the hair didn't grow back as thick.

Well, fuck that for a joke, there's got to be a better way to do this.

In amongst all Billy's exfoliants and special shampoos for his chlorine-ruined hair, is a tube of body-hair remover. He uses it on his arms and legs, which are baby-smooth and look like the limbs of an alien, so that he can swim faster. So he reckons, anyways.

There's only half a tube left, but I want to do my balls, my arse-crack and my legs. I'll have to owe Billy-boy a new tube when pay day comes around.

I lather the cream all over my legs, laying it on thick and flattening down the dark hairs along my shins. They remind me of long grass along riverbanks that's been flattened by a flood. I smear it all over my balls, where it globs all the hair together and makes them hang in a point like a Misfits fringe. I never realised just how long the hairs on my nuts were!

And then I wait, because if I walk around the cream squishes around as my balls rub between my thighs, and the instructions specifically say not to massage the stuff into your skin. Even though it's all over my arse, I find the best position is to sit with my legs spread on the loo with the lid down, just on the edge where I can let my junk hang over, free to dangle and not rub on anything. It almost looks like I'm on display.

Here it is, ladies!

I can imagine sitting on a throne-chair, naked except for my royal robe and a crown, the court wenches lined up down the stone corridor to ascend the steps and kiss the royal jewels, perhaps have a little sucky while they're at it. I'm just sitting there completely on show, my cock out for all to see but who the fuck's gonna say anything? It'd be off with their heads while I continue to get head.

My old fella starts to respond to the fantasy, and lifts off my balls. I can see a string of the hair-removal paste stretching between the two. The packet says not to put it on the genitals, and there's a smear of it on the underside of my helmet, so I tear off some toilet paper and wipe my tockley clean, then pat a fold of paper over my testicles in case my old fella flops down onto it again.

The hairs on my legs have turned squiggly. They look like wriggly little worms or leeches.

Time is up, and I jump into the shower and wash it all off, sluicing the gunk off my body. Amazingly, it takes the hair away with it, leaving my skin as smooth as a baby's bum. My legs look and feel like a chick's legs and it's all I can do to stop touching em. The hair on my balls pulls away in one great clump, which I fling against the shower wall. It lands with a splat, the cream dribbling away slowly from the overspray of the shower water. I rub away the reminder of the pubes from my nuts, digging the rest out of my butt-crack until my fingers can feel only smooth skin and the crinkle of my starfish.

Back in front of the mirror the effect of de-hairing my body is remarkable. I look thinner, though my shins are weird with their sharp, angular ridge. I need to make sure I hook up with the gothiest of chicks tonight, someone who can really appreciate the effort I've gone to. The thing about some goth chicks is that they dress in funeral rags, but man, underneath is a two-hundred dollar corset that looks five-hundred! Often it's not even underneath, these days, thanks to the riot-grrrls popularising wearing lingerie as normal clothes.

I can't help but slip my hand under and feel my balls, and they're so smooth. They're hanging a bit, like the skin is loose and stretched, but they should tighten up later when action is called for. All around my groin feels as smooth as a girl's body, the way they always feel soft and easy to run your fingers along. It's strange thinking this is my body. The sensation has me immediately hard, and I rub one out while I stroke my perineum. My balls tingle when I cum.

I can hear movement in the flat, so Billy must have got home. Thankfully, I hid his depleted tube of hair-remover behind his special shampoos. I'll wait and see if he notices, and if by payday he hasn't then he can remain none-the-wiser.

I slip on my jeans and shirt since it'll be a while before I head to Megs's to get ready with everyone, and the feel of my jeans against my legs is weird. It's good, but weird. I'll have to get used to that. The tingling sensation in my balls hasn't gone, either, so I'll have to get used to that, too!

Actually, it's less of a tingle and a more of a heat sensation now I think about it.

I whip down my dacks and see that my testicles are a deep maroon colour, and starting to feel a bit hot.

I recheck the tube, once again skipping over the warnings to read the time-lengths. Check. I read over the instructions. Warning: Do not apply to genitals. Uncheck.

Fuck.

My nuts are starting to cook now. They look like candied cashews: dry, red, shrivelled.

The rest of me's fine, it's just my balls that are suffering. My poor balls.

Although my anus does feel a bit raw and weepy, too.

A quick perusal of the stuff on Billy's shelf in the bathroom comes up empty for a solution to the situation. The burning in my balls has intensified, so much so I rip off my jeans and splash some cold water on them for relief, but it doesn't work.

The burning sensation gets so bad I've got no choice but to fess up and ask Billy for advice.

I can't get my jeans back on much less close my legs because any friction on my burning balls is like fanning the flames, so I waddle stiffly out to the lounge in just a t-shirt trying not to slap my testicles against my thighs.

Billy looks up from reading his mortgage brochures from the bank and sees me half-naked, my junk swinging between my legs and a pained expression on my face, and nearly falls off his chair.

'Geezus, what the fuck are you doing, Travis?' he cries out.

'I need your help, Billy,' I whine.

'No fucking way,' he shakes his head. 'I don't swing that way.'

'It's not that,' I moan. 'I burnt my balls. I'm in pain.'

'Burnt your balls?' he screws his face up, looking at me in total bewilderment.

He thinks I meant with fire.

'I used your cream,' I confess. 'Sorry mate, I should've asked.'

'Yeah, you should have.'

'I'll replace it, I swear,' I go. 'But right now I'm in trouble. They're on fire, see?'

I flip my old fella up to expose my red raw balls.

Billy turns his head and holds a hand up. 'Please, put em away.'

'What am I gonna do? They're on fire!'

'Cool them down, dude.'

'HOW?' I scream, doubling over.

Billy looks around the flat for some soothing gel or aloe vera or something, but comes up empty handed. The despair on my face must be pretty persuasive, because he yanks open the fridge door and passes me a jar of mustard.

'Cool em on that,' he offers.

The cold glass definitely helps, but the pressure of the hard surface makes me wince.

'Wait a minute,' he says in victory, grabbing the bottle of milk and rummaging through the cupboard.

He produces a ceramic cereal bowl. He's always eating soggy weet-bix despite being into activities like swimming; has cereal whenever he can instead of a sandwich or pasta or any kind of proper meal. He admitted once he's jealous of babies cause they just get soft, mushed foods all the time and it's considered normal for them. He'd buy jars of baby food, he reckons, if it wasn't for the price. Lazy bastard.

'Hardly the time to be fixing something to eat,' I snap. 'I'm fucking dying here.'

'Hold yer horses,' he grins, pouring a generous amount of milk into the bowl.

He places the bowl on a chair, and stands back folding his arms, a big shit-eating grin on his face, looking at me expectantly.

'You want me to drink that?'

'No, you retard,' he chuckles. 'Dip yer gonads in it. Cool em right off.'

Sounds pretty kinky, all things considered, but when there are spots of jellified skin on my scrotum I'm not going to quibble over the integrity of his solution. Straddling the chair, I lower myself into the bowl. To Billy's credit, his idea actually works! My balls feel the same relief as with the cold mustard jar, but without the weight of the glass. The milk soothes the inflammation and I feel the fire in my groin dying down.

'I wish I had a fucking camera,' Billy says, pissing himself with laughter.

'Yeah yeah, poonce. How long do I need to stay like this, you reckon?'

'Dunno,' he shrugs. 'It's a chemical burn, dude. You might need to go to hospital yet.'

'Shit shit shit.'

After a half hour my thigh muscles start killing me, so I sit milk-free for a bit. Billy's gone back to his magazine after standing around laughing at my expense, so I've managed to recoup some dignity.

There's a pitter-patter as the milk drips from my burned balls onto the linoleum.

'You done?' Billy yells out from the lounge.

'I think so. It doesn't burn anymore.'

But even through the coating of milk on them I can see the scrotum is red raw still. Billy comes through, still managing a smirk.

'We're throwing that bowl away,' he says.

I go to tip the milk down the sink.

'Wait,' says Billy. 'I've got an idea.'

He gets Greg's kefir jar from the fridge, the one Greg tops up every second day or sometimes daily.

'No way,' I gasp.

Billy unscrews the cap on the kefir jar and instructs me to tip in the milk I've been dangling my balls in.

'Fuck him,' Billy goes. 'Serves him right. Always whinging when there's not enough milk but he won't go buy any.'

Fair enough, I suppose. He can't complain now if there's a shortage of milk for kefir; we're doing our best to help out.

When the milk tips into the jar, I notice there's some slimy dregs sliding out at the end. Maybe that's bits of melted scrotal sack?

Billy's laughs his arse off, screwing the lid back on and carefully placing the jar back on the shelf, turning it so the DON'T TOUCH written in Nikko on one side faces the front, just the way Greg always obsessively places it. Billy wipes a tear away from his eye when he closes the fridge door.

'Now go put some dacks on, you pervert.'

Billy seems pretty relaxed about our prank. It makes me wonder if this joker has fucked with *my* food before?

My balls are still too sore for clothing, the poor lil sods, so I just lie spreadeagled on the bed and let them air. My frock coat isn't going to be cleaned today, after all. In fact, I don't think I can leave the flat full stop. I'll have to cancel going to Black Sunshine tonight, which also means missing out on the big breakfast at Alex's in the morn.

THIS UNREST

'The bible-bashers are at the foot of the fountain, as usual,' says Dante as we cross through King George Square, interrupting himself mid-story about getting on the disability support pension in order to point out a bloke screaming stuff. 'This especially vocal cunt always gets riled up whenever he sees a goth or a punk. As if he's not fucking loud enough as it is without the sight of us provoking him.'

I can't disagree with that. The bloke, a stocky little guy with his button shirt tucked deep into his trousers, is bloody loud but now that he's seen us coming he starts to, like, fume even more. Some next level aggression.

'At least he's not doing any exorcisms,' Dante says cryptically.

'IT IS SIN! SIN!' the evangelist screams. To his credit, even though we're the prompt for him to start turning red from a lack of oxygen as he rants and raves, he doesn't seem to single us out for eye contact. 'A SIN TO EMBRACE THE DARK AND TURN YOUR BACK ON YOUR LORD!'

Dante's like: 'I'm not into all this sin malarkey.' He's distracted by a cop car parked over near the Town Hall doors. 'According to the Good Book the first sin committed was eating a fucking apple and the second sin was murder, so I find the Bible to be an unreliable source of information to live one's life by.'

'That sounds fair enough,' I allow, intimidated by the evangelist. He's but a few metres behind us as we wait at the lights.

'The interview was a piece a piss,' Dante continues, picking up so suddenly from where he left off before that I almost question him as to what interview he's talking about. He's been talking non-stop the entire way into town and jumping from subject to subject that it's, like, wearing me out. But then I remember pretty quickly that he's been talking about an interview he had with the Commonwealth Doctor. 'A couple of questions, blah blah blah. Done. And here I am, holder of the little blue and purple card that instantly gets me cheaper transport, discount movies, all the fucking perks.'

He seems pretty pleased with himself about it all, even though I recall that he was a basically indifferent about going on the disability pension before. Like, I'm not sure if I'm meant to be impressed, but hope that's not the case because I struggle to think blokes being on the dole's a good thing when they seem quite capable of working. It's definitely not an attractive quality, period.

On the plus side, he did chip in for Twix's share of the breakfast stuff for this morning since Twix couldn't make it over last night (he said his flatmate was vomiting a lot from bad milk so he was staying home to look after him). I've heard a lot of things about Dante and how he's light-fingered, but he's always paid his way from what I've seen.

It's a shame Twix couldn't make it, though, because I haven't seen as much of him as I'd like to. He works shifts and can't always make the clubs as a result. I was hoping to use last night as a means to, like, test if there could be anything more between us than just friends. Abi was screwing him on and off for a while there, she told me, but definitely isn't interested in him anymore. She says he's good in bed (not that she'd ever boost his already swollen ego with that info, she reckons), which sounds grouse to me.

'Now there's a fucking ambulance headin in,' Dante mutters.

'In where?' I say, glancing around, wondering if he's capable of seeing things I cannot. I wouldn't doubt it, he's that strange.

'From the other side of the Square,' he says softly, turning on his heel.

The bloke waving the bible around and losing oxygen sucks in a deep breath and steps back, like he thinks Dante's about to come after him. But I can see the ambulance now, coming alongside the front of the Town Hall from the Ann Street side. Its lights are flashing but the siren's turned off.

'Back in a moment,' Dante says and dashes up the stairs past the evangelist and straight for the scene of the crime, as it were.

I'm not sticking around here to get yelled at, so I follow him.

The ambulance has pulled up near the police car and I can see everyone fussing over a body under a tarp.

'Oh my gosh,' I gasp when I've reached Dante. 'Is it a murder?'

Dante grinds his jaw. 'I don't think so.'

From out of nowhere this smelly Aboriginal man appears for a gander. His body odour is making me choke.

Dante nods at him. 'Who's under the sheet, Micko?'

'Johnnie,' the Aboriginal guy, Micko, says. His big, dark eyes look wet and sad looking.

'Fuck,' whispers Dante. 'What happened?'

'Ambos says he froze,' Micko says, looking at me warily. 'Found im huggin them Big Issues, ay. Probly to keep warm.'

Dante fishes out twenty bucks, handing it over to Micko. He's like: 'Next rounds on me. I'll bring everyone some doughnuts later on.'

The Aboriginal man smiles grimly and the money disappears before I can even see where he stashes it.

As one of the police officers approaches, presumably to get some info on the deceased, Micko turns heels and Dante suggests we do likewise.

'Don't you want to tell the police you know him?'

Dante shakes his head.

'But you can help identify him, for his family?' I persist.

'He doesn't have family, Alex,' Dante says, glancing back as the police officers give up trying to get his attention. 'He's just another homeless bum that no-one gives a fuck about. Best left at that.'

That's too sad, and I can't believe Dante would be so heartless, especially since he seemed to know the poor man. It reminds me of a poem, which although I can't exactly recite word for word, for Dante's sake I try to, as some small comfort: 'Wild things won't feel sorry for themselves. A bird will drop frozen dead from it's branch without feeling sorry for itself.'

Dante rolls his eyes, obviously not willingly to budge from being a bit of an arsehole.

'Don't make the mistake of over-romanticising the homeless,' he snaps. 'So many people already do. Sure, when the old fart froze to death he wouldn't have been bitchin and moanin to every cunt about it. But no-one would've listened anyway. So why would he bother?'

'That's sort of what I meant,' I say, feeling ashamed, because it's actually not entirely what I meant when I, like, quoted the poem. 'It's just sad, is all.'

He looks at me intently, and agrees. 'It is, I suppose. But what's done is done. No changing that. The guys over there will divvy up his stuff, and that'll be that.'

For the first time I notice a group of homeless people, that Micko amongst them, sitting in the shade of the trees in the corner of the Square, behind the big fountain. Funny how, like, I never seem to notice them unless they're in my face asking for spare change.

The evangelist is still on the steps at the fountain, giving it his all. I figure Dante's not in the mood now for talk of damnation so spare him the brunt of the preaching by walking on his right side. At the lights Dante just steps out onto the road without looking, forcing a car to brake suddenly. It blares the horn but Dante just flips his finger at the driver. I'm not risking my life and wait for the signal.

By the time the lights change and I've crossed over to him, Dante's noticed something else down the street. I'm, like, dreading that it's another dead homeless person.

He's like: 'Slight detour,' nodding in the direction of a punk guy with a tall mohawk slipping into the doorway of Rocking Horse.

I follow him down to the record store, not unlike Missing Link in some ways I guess, and we take the stairs up to the second floor where all the, like, second hand CD's are and stuff, and where Dante talks with this scruffy punk guy who smells of bad BO. The same one we saw on the street. Dante neglects to introduce me to him, but I gather from the conversation that his name's Scab, and if it's not then Dante keeps calling him one.

'They did a number on you, alright,' says Dante, checking out the bruises and scrapes on the other guy.

'No thanks to you,' the punk says sourly.

Dante just laughs. 'No need to thank me, Scab, it had nothing to do with me. Be grateful, you're faring a lot better today than some people I know. So everything's good between us?'

'Of course,' Scab the punk says, accepting Dante's handshake.

'As it should be,' says Dante, with a cheerio.

We bound back down the stairs and out onto the street, heading around the corner. Dante's meant to be showing me where Baroque Sienna is, apparently a mixed all-sorts shop of, like, clothing, art and weapons somewhere in the Elizabeth Arcade. I haven't been able to find it on my own, somehow.

'One of your friends, huh?'

Dante shakes his head. 'Cunt's a dickhead. I just needed to make sure things were cool between us, especially after the other night. I think he's gotten the picture, now.'

I hate the C word, absolutely loathe it, but Dante always insists on littering his vocab with it. I don't even get why that's necessary.

As we're about to cross over the Mall, this short *munga*-looking bloke and his missus passes us. He's built like a brick shithouse, obviously roided up or something, with thick veins bulging on his sunburnt neck. His missus is equally gross, looks like a trashy crack whore *kargiola*, and as they pass us I hear Dante grunt and move aside a bit, and then he, like, glances over his shoulder and suddenly it's on.

The brute has also turned and is now yelling at Dante.

'Why don't you watch yer fuckin self!'

'You need the whole fucking footpath do you?' retorts Dante. He sounds pissed off.

The *munga* starts marching back towards us, his massive arms rising from his sides like they've begun to levitate away from his body. He's screaming at Dante now about punching the shit out of him, and Dante's threatening to throw the brute over the side and into the bus tunnel that comes out from under the Queen Street Mall. We're walking backwards and the brute's, like, getting angrier and angrier.

'Who the hell is this *munga?*' I ask, but Dante's preoccupied with dishing back the insults.

The brute makes a swift dart towards Dante who scoots back just as quickly, so I jump between them and hold my hands up. 'Wait, wait! Just leave us alone.'

The brute ignores me, but at least he's stopped chasing after Dante. I'm, like, standing in front of him and he's looking past me, hissing through his teeth. 'If I see you again you little cunt, you're fucking dead.'

The crackwhore is behind her man now, sneering at me. I feel like poor muggins here is the only one trying to, like, hold this situation together, right? I can hear Dante behind me somewhere goading this brute on further, for pity's sake.

Eventually the bloke storms away and his *kargiola* missus follows, patting his arm like he's basically a good boy. I turn and see Dante glowering after them.

I'm like: 'No, seriously. What the fuck was that all about?'

Dante ignores me, just stares at the brute walking off, working his jaw muscles. He breathes hard from his nose and finally looks at me. 'That cunt seems to need the whole fucking footpath. Fucker thumped into me when I gave them plenty of room to pass.'

'And that's why we nearly got into a fight, right?' I start walking away, and Dante follows.

My hands are shaking.

'Fuck him!' Dante spits. 'Why the fuck do we always have to give those cunts everything?'

'Who cares? Why not just get over it, instead?'

'Get over it?' There's genuine menace in his voice. 'Really? He threatened me with violence and that's your response? How about if someone says they're going to rape you, and I was to just tell you that you should get over it? Would that sound like an okay thing to say?'

I nod and feel a bit shit. I take for granted the threats of bashing and punching and stuff that blokes throw at each other, because it all sounds like hollow machismo to me. It wouldn't be if the brutish guy had actually followed through on his threats, I figure.

Over in the middle of the Mall is a little information kiosk, but down the side of it the police have a tiny setup, like at the back of it. There's a small roller-door and counter, so I go over and explain to the police officers what's just happened, and how Dante was threatened. The woman writes down my details and I'm expecting her to put a call out, but she just looks at me blankly and's like: 'What would you like us to do about it?' There's something about the way she says it that tells me I needn't answer, but I do anyway.

'Get him on camera. He's headed towards Central Station.'

The woman is unimpressed. She arches her brows slightly, and tells me there's not much they can do.

Dante is leaning against the wall, listening in, slowly shaking his head.

'What'd you expect these cunts to do?' he says to me, and the policewoman shows the first sign of, like, real animation at last and pipes up with an indignant 'excuse me?' which Dante ignores. We walk back into the Mall, and I see two uniformed officers walking across the Mall towards Adelaide Street. To my amusement, they're each carrying a bag from Dunkin' Donuts.

'These are the ones you want,' I tell Dante, who doesn't look too convinced. The ones we want, alright. The male officer is looking pretty fit, especially in that uniform. 'Come on.'

We go around the corner and the police officers have been stopped by some backpackers who're struggling to converse with the female officer. So I go up to the male officer who's standing aside and, like, get his attention, right?

'Listen, my friend here was attacked by some bloke who looked like he was pumped up on drugs. Said he's going to kill us if he sees us again.'

The officer nods, but looks Dante up and down in a judgemental way. 'Uh-huh. And where is he?'

I point towards Adelaide Street and tell the officer that his quarry is headed towards the train station.

He's like: 'Well, steer clear of that area, then.'

He turns from us to listen to the faltering English of the tanned girl talking to his companion. I'm, like, a bit gobsmacked, and throw my hands up in frustration. Dante sighs and gives me a tight smile.

'No, but seriously,' I say to the officer, feeling flustered. 'The bloke seemed really dangerous.'

The officer shrugs and actually says: 'What do you want us to do about it?'

Is this something they're all instructed to, like, fucking well say when they couldn't be bothered doing their job?

Dante's like: 'I got an idea,' and when the officer turns to him and wrinkles his brow doubtfully, Dante's like: 'Why dontcha shoot him?'

'I beg your pardon?' says the officer, squares up to Dante.

For his part, Dante acts as if he hasn't noticed the police officer's sudden aggression, and assumes a relaxed posture. I know him well enough by now not to be deceived by his apparent feyness. A knot is forming in my stomach.

'Yeah,' Dante carries on. 'Just take that gun there and blow his fucking brains out.'

The officer tightens his grip on the bag of doughnuts and his other hand shifts to his hip, close to the same gun Dante just pointed at.

'It's what you cunts do all the time, isn't it?' Dante continues, unfazed. 'Lest we forget Joe Gilewicz? Yeah? Fucking empty cartridge indeed. You guys always like shooting dead us mentally ill people, why not go after some of these other fuckers for a change?'

I vaguely remember the incident Dante's on about. The bloke held a siege, if I recall correctly. Basically asking for it, acting like that.

The officer stares steadily at Dante, who stares back. But there's a twitch going across his face. He seems genuinely upset, and I think the officer's noticed it, too, because he relaxes and's like: 'I don't need to talk to you.' Then he turns to the other officer and they walk off.

'Shit,' I say quietly, feeling a tremble in my legs.

Dante looks at me so I, like, smile weakly. I don't know if he'd let me hug him or not, but fuck man, I know I need it right now.

Instead, we walk back up the Mall, where I meekly suggest that, like, perhaps the police have got a point, that maybe there's not much they can do. Like, I don't know what else I can say at this point. But this sets Dante off to ranting.

'Not much they can do? They can do anything they fucking well want, obviously! Shoot people dead, eat a fucking doughnut, tell you there's fuck all they can do about anything. A dozen people, Alex. Twelve fucking people with mental illness shot fucking dead by cops in the last five years in the Land of Oz because these fuckers choose to kill rather than opt for something less fatal.'

Dante's voice has gotten pretty loud, so when we cross over the intersection at the heart of the Mall, people are, like, making a wide berth around us. His arms are waving around as he punctuates each point.

'Cunts like that other guy walk about like they own fucking the place, and what do these tossers with their stupid fucking uniforms and a licence to kill do? Nothing. Go to them for help; they can do nothing. Have a breakdown; you're fucking dead.'

We pass Hungry Jack's and the roller-door to the little booth the police were sitting in before is hoiked down. But an empty patrol car is parked just behind the booth, and without any warning Dante rushes over and starts kicking at the side mirror. It takes only a few go's at it to bust it completely, bits of glass of flying up in the air and falling back down onto the windscreen and bonnet.

People all around have stopped to watch as Dante destroys the mirror. Faces appear at the windows of Hungry Jack's, astonished.

When he's done Dante walks back over to me, looking at another car parked behind the patrol car. I didn't really see this car before, but inside it are two men in suits staring out at Dante. On the passenger door I can see the State coat-of-arms of the deer and stork or whatever it's meant to be. *Oh fuck.* Detectives.

But they don't move, and Dante, calm now, says we're good to go.

'There's some detectives in that other car,' I say quietly. 'Coat of arms on the door, see?'

He glances over his shoulder and is like: 'Fuck em.' Then he starts to chuckle darkly. 'That's a fucking red deer on that coat-of-arms,' he says, turning away and stalking down the mall towards Elizabeth Street. People are quick to move out of his way. 'There's a colony out my folks' way. The farmers reckon they're a pest and should be shot on sight. Telling, isn't it?'

We're at the traffic lights outside the McDonald's and Myer Centre entrance, but I'm too scared to check behind us to see if the detectives are, like, coming after us. When the green man comes on and we're crossing over Elizabeth up towards the arcade, Dante gets his mentor voice on.

'Alex, think about this,' he says with the measured tones of a sane person. 'You gave them your name and address, three of them saw our faces. We're on heaps of cameras in the Mall, and I kicked the crap out of their car in front of two detectives. And we're not done here. We've still got to cross the Mall again later to get home, and if by tonight I haven't been arrested for what I did to that car, you think about that. Think about if they can't be bothered to come and get me after I insult them and break their mirror, what are they gonna do when you're in trouble on some train or something late at night cause Mister Steroids back there feels like ripping into you.'

It's a pretty heavy thing to say, but I get his point. I can't believe they haven't arrested him (or us) yet.

I follow him in silence down into the Elizabeth Arcade. Halfway along there's some stairs, a sort of blink-and-you'll-miss-them affair. I knew the shop was in here somewhere and couldn't find it before, but I didn't realise I had to, like, go *above* the arcade.

'Hidden gems,' Dante winks, back now to his former, jovial self.

I smile back as genuinely as I can muster, but I'm feeling as crook as Rookwood.

At the end of the corridor where no daylight gets in there's an open door with glittery moons and stars painted on it, and the words BAROQUE SIENNA painted so floridly I almost can't read it. The door belies my expectations of the room beyond. Actually, cavern would be a more appropriate term. It's a massive space with pillars sectioning it off into rudimentary rooms. Each section is devoted to a theme, with one being about medieval stuff with, like, suits of armour and swords, another more gothy with dresses and corsets on racks, and another devoted to wiccan stuff. There's shelves of tarot cards and books and crystals in the latter.

In another corner there's a couple of easels and a girl sitting at one, painting. There's tattoos coming out of sleeves down both arms almost all the way to her wrists. They're extraordinary, large blocks of green with, like, inca-styled designs. Puts my paltry tattoo to shame, which is of my ex-boyfriend's name in Melbourne. *ZAK*. On the inside of my forearm, where I see it every time I raise my hand. He insisted we get them, mine on his and his on mine, except I went first and then he chickened out. Said that level of commitment made him, like, second think our relationship, right when I was getting his name permanently inked onto me, but the prick waited to tell me until the tattoo was done. 'At least you'll have something to remember me by,' he'd said, as if that was something to look forward to! The tattooist felt so sorry for me he promised to do a picture over it for free when it had healed, but I'd, like, forgotten to go back because this was in the days just before I'd decided to turn my back on all the shit and come up here to Brisbane.

'That's Simone,' says Dante, and the girl looks up at the sound of her name. 'An artist like Nathanial.'

'Who?' I've got no idea who he's talking about.

He yanks his head back incredulously. 'You don't know my friend Nate?'

I shrug. He hasn't actually introduced me to anyone, not even the homeless guys or that punk. Why would I know this friend of his that I've never heard of before?

Dante and Simone hug briefly, then he wanders around giving everything a cursory glance as if he was a security guard checking for something out of place.

'Hi, I'm Alex,' I say, and to my surprise the girl jumps up and hugs me, too. 'Are you an artist?'

She's like: 'More like an interpreter,' and I hear a snort of derision from Dante as if he doesn't believe her, but when I check he's actually holding a crystal up to the light of a window, peering at it sceptically.

'What do you interpret?' I ask.

I'm sure she's an artist, though, because there's, like, paint both wet and dry on her fingers. I notice a floor-length mirror over near the corsets that I'll have to use and check there's no paint on my back from when she hugged me.

'People,' Simone says, pointing at the canvas on her easel. It's a riot of colour and brush-strokes, with only a vague hint of the human form in it. 'It's the real them, do you see?'

I don't.

'When someone sits for a portrait,' she explains, 'they have to sit for a pretty long time while I paint, and what happens is that they start meditating without even realising it. At first they're stiff and awkward, asking me how they should pose and what kind of face they should pull. I just tell them to relax, and after a while they let go of their ego and their inner-core comes out.'

I study the canvas again but struggle to see a face in it. 'Is this one finished?'

'It is,' she smiles. 'It's their true selves. At first I only pretend to paint them until they've relaxed, and then once they're truly relaxed I can see inside them, I know who I'm really painting. They're always amazed by the results, and a little embarrassed. It's hard to confront that part of your inner self so openly.'

My thoughts are that it'd be hard to confront something so, like, abstract and colourful. Where would anyone even put such a rainbow creation without an attic to hide it in? Maybe yuppies would be into this, but it'd clash with all the bat decor in my place.

'Now, there're some people that get frustrated by the process,' she says, which I don't doubt. 'They've got no patience for the world and need things done on *their* time. Sometimes I can't even paint those people, and other times I just end up painting what I see, which is an impatient and angry exterior. Usually those people hate the painting because they didn't give me a chance to see inside them.'

It sounds like she's saying everyone, whether they open up oir not, hate her paintings. I wonder if she's cottoned onto that at all?

'Maybe they don't want you to see inside them?' I venture.

'Dante is one of those people,' she grins, looking over at him. I get the feeling there's, like, some history between these two. 'They're full of a relentless energy; always need to be engaged in activity. They don't have quiet souls, so I can't paint those people properly. The paintings look like shit.'

I nod as if I understand and cop a gander at her other paintings on the wall, hoping to, like, find one I can enthuse over, but come to the conclusion she must be only painting those frustrated people because basically all the paintings look like shit. Maybe they're all of Dante?

'What's so funny?' she says when she sees a smile play on my lips.

'Oh nothing, I was just, like, thinking how good your work is,' I lie.

She beams and thanks me. 'Take a look around and yell out if you need a hand.'

I join Dante over by the sword stand, where he runs his fingertips down each one, apparently admiring their craftsmanship.

'Touching swords with your fingers and not cleaning them after will eventually make them rust,' he says, pressing his fingertips all over the shiny blades. 'The guy who makes these is a right cunt.'

I'm compelled to touch each of the swords, too, although I don't share Dante's disdain for someone I've never met.

But I really like this store. It's so quiet. It feels so removed from the crazy world outside, just far enough down the arcade, up the stairs and down the corridor to feel like the madness and aggression and ranting can't touch us here. I'm surrounded by beautiful things – Simone's paintings notwithstanding – and the sun streams in through the dirty glass and highlights the dust motes drifting lazily in the air.

It's so grouse I could basically just curl up like a cat and, like, sleep forever here.

As if reading my thoughts, Dante's like: 'I like it in here. It feels like everything has stopped moving. Like time has stopped.'

I stare at him, not willing to break the peace by enjoining my voice to his, and he looks at me funny until he simply wanders over to the racks of medieval dresses and admires their lace sleeves. Or maybe only pretends to?

Eventually some kindergoth stumble in, noisy as hell, giggling at each other's inane jokes. They've broken the spell the store held over me as their voices echo around the space. Dante gives them only a cursory glance as he chats to Simone about how he's now on the disability pension.

The presence of the noisy kindergoth has brought the chaos of the outside world into this sanctum of peace, ruining the atmosphere. I feel flustered by their quick, jerky movements and their shrill shouts and giggles.

When we finally leave, I ask Dante if we can walk slowly. He's always in such a rush, charging about like he's got deadlines to meet.

'Slowly?' he says in surprise.

I nod dumbly in the dimness of the corridor, and we take our time like we're walking down the aisle to be married. The darkness is a comfort, and that Dante is willing to, like, indulge me in my simple request means more than he could ever realise.

And sure enough, later on we pass back across the Mall, Dante making sure we do it at a leisurely pace not for my sake but because he wants to make a point about how, like, the cops won't arrest us. He even goes over to the Dunkin' Donuts shop and gets a couple of bags to share with his homeless friends after I've gone. We get up to the train station (via the Square again where thankfully the evangelist has packed up and already gone) where Dante skips past the ticket checkers and sees me off on the platform.

As the train pulls away, I watch him standing out on the platform with his hands in the pockets of that oversized dinner jacket he always wears and the bags of doughnuts at his feet, and it seems to me he's at peace. What is it about a day like today that still has me rattled but can, like, soothe a soul such as his?

PLACEBO EFFECT

So I might've been wrong about Twix not being into me, because he asked me around to his new place in St Lucia where we're, like, sharing a joint, lying around on his bed and talking crap for a couple of hours. I keep thinking at any moment he'll initiate a kiss but he doesn't.

His bedroom's decorated in posters of his favourite bands, but wedged between one of Robert Smith and another of Specimen is an Erika Eleniak in her red *Baywatch* togs. He grins bashfully and says he's had a celebrity crush on her for years.

'She's got kinda sad eyes, huh?' I note, which makes him really curious.

So he gets up and pulls one of the posters down to get a better look, holding it up to the light from the window.

He's like: 'Nah. Normal eyes.'

They're definitely sad looking, in my opinion. I think Twix has a white knight complex, because Abi told me Twix's ex, Karen, had sad eyes, too.

Maybe remembering the night we all snuck into the lagoon at Southbank after Megs' club before Parklands security told us to get out of the water, Twix suggests we go for a swim at the Spring Hill Baths, up the road from the Prozac Palace.

He's like: 'One of the things I'll miss about the old place.'

'In the middle of winter?' I say with surprise, but he says it'll be kind of warm because the water's, like, really salty.

We have to get the bus back into town, which is easier said than done when you're half-stoned, but we finally make it into Spring Hill, promising ourselves a visit to the Palace afterwards for a catchup with everyone. Except for Malik, he says, who's, like, on holidays in England with Angele. We both agree that they're pretty lucky.

It turns out the pool's in this beautiful little building with old-fashioned seats around it, changing booths either side divided into a men's side and a women's side in reflection of, like, days gone by, and most impressively a roof overhead with a small section cut out to show the sky. Perfect for the goth complexion.

While he's in the men's taking a leak I quickly change into my togs and jump in the pool before he's finished. I hate my potato body, so it's only natural that everyone else probably does, too. It's only fair that I spare them the sight of the monstrosity that is my figure. Stupid Greek genes.

I get a sneaky gander at Twix's body when he comes out and drops into the water. Not bad. Bit of a belly but otherwise pale and lean, like Pete Murphy. Drooool!

'*Yeeeow,*' he hisses. 'That stings my balls! Just what they need, though.'

'What the hell?' I laugh.

'Nothing,' he says, suddenly coy. 'Just feels good, is all.'

He says such strange things sometimes, so, like, out of the blue. It kind of fascinates me. I can see why he and Dante are such good friends, even if they don't always act like it. They're both basically weird.

We float in silence, listening to the water lapping at the side of the pool and echoing around the viewing gallery. There's only, like, one other patron here, an old lady doing gentle exercises in the water at the shallow end. Otherwise, the whole place is basically ours.

Twix floats on his back, totally still, staring up at the sky through the hole in the roof.

The sight unnerves me more than it should.

I got a call from the police the other night asking if I'd had any contact with Zachary. Afterwards I got calls from both Lisa and Mum, both cranky as hell. The police stormed Lisa's house looking for me, and nearly arrested Darren for obstruction when he tried to make them leave. That's what happens when having dated the son of a Deputy Commissioner of the police force, I guess.

I told the police that I hadn't seen Zak since we'd split up down in Melbourne, which isn't, like, exactly true. Zak had gotten wind that I was planning to move to Brisbane and had turned up drunk at the rents' place one night, outside my bedroom window, pleading with me to stay. Papa got the Vic Police to move him on. I'd stood in the dark, watching them take him away, unsure if he could see me.

A crow's feather floats through the gap above, spiralling slowly down. It lands softly on the water with the barest hint of a ripple.

The police said they'd found Zak's body floating in the Brisbane River. Evidently he'd followed me up here, perhaps to, like, win me back or maybe to find and punish me. Either way, I've not heard from him or seen him since Melbourne, so it was a total shock to me to find out he was up here! Dead, no less!

I tread water across to the feather, thinking it'll make a blessed addition to my little altar at home. I can mark this moment, use its magickal energies to inspire my spiritual growth, my magicks.

The police said they'd found heroin in Zak's system. He'd started using on and off when I was still with him. I hated it, but if I'd said anything he'd get abusive, tell me how my moping around the house had basically driven him insane and heroin was the only thing that helped. When I'd finally suggested maybe he could cut ties with me and devote himself solely to drugs he'd cried and told me he couldn't live without me. I'd wanted to leave him but when I'd seen him in that state, so vulnerable and broken, I couldn't bring myself to do it. I'd felt guilty even just thinking of leaving him. The next week he'd be back to abusing me again, like insulting me and blaming me for everything wrong in his life.

I pluck the feather out of the water. It's grey with white bands.

'Lotsa pigeons nest up there,' Twix says, pointing at the metal beams criss-crossing the inside of the roof.

I don't want a diseased pigeon feather on my altar!

I try and fling it out of the pool but it drops straight back into the water and, like, just floats beneath the surface. Like a dead body.

'Dante says he took you up to Baroque Sienna the other day,' Twix suddenly says, his face still poking out of the water as he floats on his back, his lips barely above the water level.

'Yeah,' I reply.

Twix sounds a bit jealous, I hope, but it could just be that his voice comes out weird because of all the water. He jerks up into a standing position, flinging his wet hair back from his face.

He's like: 'I heard he kicked a cop car.'

'Yes! Bloody hell, Twix, it was next level bonkers, I'm telling you.'

'I can imagine,' he grins.

'He needs a chill pill! What the hell's wrong with him, though?'

I don't mean to come across as sounding so rude, especially about his best friend, but Twix just laughs and is like: 'He can be a mad bastard, alright. There's so much crazy in the lad you could bottle it and make your fortune. But he's a loyal friend, at the end of the day.'

'I guess so,' I agree. 'A bit scary, though. Like, really shook me up.'

'You get used to it,' Twix says simply, swirling his palms across the surface of the water like he's a wizard. 'Not sure if that's a good thing or not, though.'

The old woman finishes her exercises, making her way out of the bath-house. Twix idly watches her go.

'I've seen her in here heaps of times,' he muses. 'Always alone. Probably widowed. Bit sad, huh?'

'Maybe she prefers it like that. Being alone, I mean.'

'I dunno, not with that generation anyway,' he says. 'Bet she's still got hubby at home, slowly decomposing in the marital bed.'

Ew, horrible thought but still funny. We're both chuckling at this.

'Would you?' he says.

'Would I what?'

'If you had a boyfriend and he died, would you root him one last time even though he's dead?'

I'm dumbstruck, back-tracking on the whole day trying to recall if I'd told Twix about Zak being found in the river, but try as I might I just know I haven't brought it up. That's freaking crazy, that he just said that, like, just out of nowhere.

'I don't think so,' I shiver. 'What if their spirit gets attached to you somehow because of it?'

He sucks something from between his teeth, and is like: 'I reckon I'd give Amai one last bang.'

Fucking stupid Alexandra.

I forgot about Amai, his, like, sort-of girlfriend. He talks about her like they're together, but I've also heard him say she won't commit. Gotta wonder if they're even an item, right? So if he's with this Amai now, does that mean he's not interested in Abi anymore? Good time to find out...

'What about Abi? Would you have sex with her corpse?'

His head snaps around and he looks pleasantly surprised.

'Good question, good question,' he grins. 'The answer, naturally, is who wouldn't? She's sex on a stick.'

He's staring at me with a playful little smile, trying to, like, figure me out.

'How'd you know about me and Abi?'

My laughter tinkles over the water and around the bath-house. I hate my laugh. 'We girls are, like, pretty intuitive about these things. Also it's, like, the worst kept secret on the goth scene up here.'

'Yeah, well, I wanted to go steady, but she's not that into me I guess,' he says softly, kind of regretfully.

I want to ask about Amai, for reasons, but instead I go the more direct tact: 'What about me? Have you thought about dating me?'

'I have,' he says without hesitation, catching me off-guard.

The pigeon feather floats past and gets stuck to my arm. I scrape it off and splash it away.

'So you probably would, then?' I venture.

'Nah, not really,' he says, sniffing. 'I'm not really into fat chicks.'

I'm stunned, staring at him hoping he'll at least start laughing or say it's just jokes, even if it is in poor taste, but he continues to skim his palms across the water's surface like what he's just spewed out couldn't possibly be worming its way into my guts and twirling over and over like a fork in a pile of spaghetti.

'Just jokes,' I hear my small, strangled voice say, and he looks at me strangely.

I feel like shit.

No.

I feel worse than shit.

I slowly sink under the water, trying to reach the bottom and kick away from him, put a bit of distance between us. When I resurface I notice he's not even paying any attention to me. Two skinny girls have come in and he's, like, submerged his face until he can blow bubbles, watching them with that obvious-as-fuck discretion guys do that they think we don't notice.

When I first started high-school and my boobs were starting to balloon out, I'd decided that girls were no fun to be around. They'd always seemed to be bitching about each other, pulling each other down for how they looked. The boys were more easygoing, and didn't give a fuck about how I'd looked, except for the swelling bumps on my chest. They liked those. But even that I was able to put aside and just get on being friends with them. We'd joke around with each other, teasing each other about our hair or whatever, or in my case my boobs. But it was just, like, friends teasing, not the spiteful shit that the girls always did.

However, over time it occurred to me that the joking had changed. It was probably after two years that it dawned on me that the boys and me no longer teased each other about how we looked, but rather they mostly focused on me and what they'd do to me if they'd been so inclined to. Which they made obvious that they weren't. It was, like, all sexual stuff.

I'd become the butt of my friends' jokes without seeing it coming, and it'd felt like a kind of assault, because it had turned into a daily banter about doing shit *to* me, not *with* me. I had no involvement in these scenarios beyond being the object of the fantasy, which was clearly what their boy's banter was. A sexual fantasy.

Initially I'd laughed along with it all because, like, I didn't realise just how my friends had turned on me. But once it was more obvious, like, I couldn't ignore the truth behind it any longer, and I was super embarrassed, unsure what to do about it but frightened by the threat that I was feeling from my so-called friends. They seemed so sexually aggressive. So I'd confided in one of the boys, Jimmy Cho.

'Why're you so scared?' Nathan had wanted to know when Jimmy went and snitched. 'You know we wouldn't touch you, right?'

I'd heard the sly inference, that nasty undercurrent, but needn't have bothered trying to question its sincerity because then Jimmy had voiced straight away what they'd all been thinking: 'You're not rape material.'

Fucking hell.

The paradox is, it was Nate that I'd lost my virginity to anyway.

They'd laughed at me after that, and I'd laughed along with them because I hadn't known what else to do.

I was a joke to them, the butt of their sexual innuendo's and their supposedly insincere threat of sexual assault. It had felt like they'd already raped me by intent.

I'd stopped hanging around them after that, which hadn't bothered them at all. With me out of the way more and more attractive girls started hanging out with them. I'd started hanging out with, like, the rejects instead, the nerds and the goths and grungies. For the first time in years I actually had friends who were basically, like, interested in who I was as a person. It was a strange but grouse feeling that took some getting used to.

Without being conscious of it, I've drifted to the other side of the pool and balled myself up so that the skinny girls won't see my body under the water if they come past. I suddenly feel cold, even though, like, the sun's still out.

Eventually Twix calls across the water to see if I wanna head off, but I can only nod in response.

'You okay?' he asks.

'Yup,' I nod, offering a small smile. The old reflex. It never truly leaves. Period.

I won't get out... no, I *can't* get out of the pool until he has.

Fortunately he climbs out and goes into a booth to get his towel is.

As fast as I can I climb out, detesting how my body revolts against this simple act and, like, makes me struggle in front of the two girls who have now emerged from their own booths.

They give non-committal smiles as I trudge past, but in my mind I, like, imagine them sneering behind my back, scoffing at how girl's like me dare think they can ever be attractive to guys like Twix.

So mote it be.

ABI THE AIN

We have to wear these hair nets for a couple of weeks to get the oldies used to it, on account of we're having an inspection here soon to keep our accreditation. Don and Marg run the centre, the Breakfast Creek View Aged Care, and are too stingy to buy supplies like food-handling gloves and hair-nets year round, so we never bother using them until an inspection happens.

Because the old folk never see us in hair nets, if we simply wore them on the day of the inspection these busy-body fucks would keep piping up with questions about why we're suddenly wearing them, so for the next couple of weeks we're easing them into accepting it as normal. Once the inspection is done, the nets and gloves will be back in the cupboards until next inspection. Or until ol Gladys, who has dementia, shoves a handful up her moot again and we need to fish them out. Stupid ol biddy barely knows who or where she is most of the time, but still manages to get into those cupboards like she was a master locksmith.

The name Breakfast Creek View Aged Care is a real misnomer, because not only is there no view of Breakfast Creek itself, there isn't much of a view anyway unless you count the paddock across the road with the skeleton frame of an old gasworks. There's the river off to the left of that, but it's mostly obscured by the treetops growing below us on the cliff.

It can be a cruisey job if you approach it with the right attitude and not freak out about every little thing that happens. Some night shifts the staff on duty just sit around and laugh at the stuff we find in the resident files, stuff you'd be too embarrassed to tell even your closest loved ones but for which these helpless sods have had prised out of them and recorded for all prosperity.

Right now, I've just served everyone up a plate of baked beans and they're all slurping away, sucking the mushy stuff through shrivelled lips, trying to tongue stray beans from underneath their dentures. It's a traumatising sight. If I close my eyes, it sounds like I'm in the middle of an orgy. Lots of moaning and slurping.

I thumb the volume up on the TV, trying to drown out as much of their sexualised dining as possible. Sandy's meant to be in here minding them with me, and we're supposed to be either helping them with their food if they're incapable or mopping the floors while they're all confined to the table. But the stupid slag has hooked up with Greg who's on shift on another wing, and they're both banging away in the pantry, huffing and puffing. A couple of the oldies, Margret and her shadow Rose, are staring in judgement through the kitchen at the darkness of the pantry. They'll probably dob, but I'll cover for Sandy and say the old girls are stirring shit again. Not like that, mind; I'll say it proper. But they do it all the time anyway, these old folks, stir trouble and spread lies because they're bored shitless.

Their families never visit, most of them can't go anywhere.

As if reading my thoughts, Margaret deliberately drops her spoon onto the table with a clatter, splashing sauce across the vinyl tabletop. Fucking marvellous, Margaret. As if I don't clean up enough around here.

'I can't eat this muck a second more,' she whines.

'Then starve,' I mutter.

'What was that noise?' says Ethyl shrilly, who's legally blind and can only see blurred shapes and colours at the best of times. I realise she hasn't even touched her food. Probably didn't even know it was in front of her.

'Just eat your din dins, Ethyl.'

'What is it?'

'Baked beans.'

'Ugh, *again?*' Ethyl screws her face up, which makes her look like one of those old Muppets that're always giving Kermit the Frog shit.

Margaret pipes up again, the bitch. 'It's always baked beans! We want proper food.'

'Baked beans is the legal requirement,' I sigh, as if I haven't told them a hundred times before.

'Surely not for breakfast, lunch and dinner!' scoffs the old biddy, looking around the room as if to rally support. She's met with the sounds of slurping and gums smacking.

'It is,' I remind her. 'As long as they're giving you this, they're covered by law.'

'Disgusting,' she snaps.

I hear ya, lady.

'You could always protest march against it,' I offer, chuckling a little.

Groans all round at this. I've told these old invalids countless times to march the streets for their rights whenever they've got a gripe, and they're sick of hearing it. Makes me laugh, though.

At the end of the day, however, I feel sorry for them eating nothing but these tasteless slops. Don and Marg would never expand the menu to include anything beyond these slops, the penny pinchers. Occasionally, besides the odd porno mag, I'll sneak an apple pie or something in for Braddles. He's got family that visit, at least, so he's not stuck on this fart-inducing diet twenty-four seven unlike these poor old sods. Poor kid's locked in his ward during dinner time, though, like some kind of felon, because we don't have enough eyes to keep on him out here in case he makes for the water taps.

'I want to die,' whispers Ethyl, right on time.

When I started working here, she freaked me out when first time she said it. I'd been helping her to eat, spooning the tomato-sauce soaked beans into her gob, and she'd dribbled them out and hoarsely whispered her entreaty. The other staff had laughed and admitted she says it all the time. Ethyl's quite serious, by the way; her daughter carked it several years ago and no-one's visited Ethyl since. No-one interacts with her, on account of her blindness, even though at heart she's actually a lovely lady.

'Abi,' says Margaret sternly, her head eerily stock-still but her eyes sliding from pantry to me and back to pantry again. 'Abi, I think the pantry door is open.'

'Yeah, we're letting it air so the bean tins don't galvanise.'

I know she wants me to go and investigate and catch Sandy and Greg in the act. For residents that carry on like this, we immediately diagnose them with *elevated porcelain levels*, meaning they're a crock of shit.

'Really,' Margaret scoffs indignantly, insulted at the improperness of everything. 'I think the door should be closed.'

Rose nods sagely.

I ignore them, watching John Burgess and Adriana spin the Wheel of Fortune instead.

'I'll buy a vowel, please, Adriana,' says this cockwomble in a suit with what looks like a toupee on top of his noggin.

The best part about being an AIN is the access to all the oldies' drugs. They've got a treasure-trove of pills that we hand out, although there's some only the RN's will administer, schedule eight drugs and such, like oxycodone, which is my favourite. It's an opioid analgesic used to treat acute pain in some of the residents here, and I just love it! Takes about an hour to kick in, and when it does, none of the shit these oldies dish out bothers me anymore. I just feel like I'm floating in space with Major Tom.

I was actually planning on quitting until Josh the RN shared some with me. I guess his plan was to hook me so I'll stick around, because he's pretty keen on me. It's a Gawdsend this stuff. It's tricky, though, because the other RN checks everything and is anal about how the drugs are managed. But Josh covers his tracks like nobody's business. If Don and Marg ever did find out, it'd have to be because someone snitched.

Josh is addicted to the oxycodone, though. He admitted that to me one day after we had sex back at his place. He said he's finding it hard to manage without it some days, and mixes it up with Paracetamol all the time now. He reckons he needs to keep taking it, because the chills are always at his heels, and when he tries to ween himself off he starts feeling like shit. Like depressed shit, you know? So, now he maximises its effects by washing it down with grapefruit juice, which he reckons boosts the oxy and thus his dopamine levels. He has to maintain those levels, because the amount of oxy he's taking these days means the crash is ever stronger. As a joke I said he should check himself into Binkinba for treatment, but he got real stroppy with me, going on about how he'd never shoot up and junkies are the scum of the Earth. My sister Roslyn is an on-and-off again junkie and on a methadone program at Binkinba, so it fucked the mood and I left him to it and went home.

We haven't had sex again, but we do still take the oxycodone together if we're on the same shift. We egg each other on to try new ways, just out of boredom, like crushing it to snort or drink. He dared me once to ingest it vaginally, but I just laughed and told him to fuck off. Thing is, I keep wondering now how different would that high be if I did do it?

Greg and Sandy come back out, leaving the pantry door open, and Margaret's head snaps round at them, her eyes boring into them. Greg waves to me and heads back to his wing, a slight spring in his step.

'Woo-ee!' says Sandy, pushing her hair back and flopping into a chair across from me, a shit-eating grin on her face. 'That boy knows how to make a girl happy.'

'Ha!' I snort. 'Who needs a boy to be happy?'

'You're off ya face, Abi,' chuckles Sandy, tugging her hair net on.

'Piss off! I only had a half one.' She's the only other person at work who knows I'm using the pills.

'Your eyes look fucking huge!' she says, leaning in to check my pupils. 'You still constipated?'

'Yeah.' I've been backed up for a couple of days now, and can't seem to shift it. I tried some of the prune juice we give to the oldies to keep them regular, as if the beans aren't enough, but I hate the taste of the stuff and spat it out after two mouthfuls. So much for that.

'Dude, seriously,' she sniffs, lying across her arms on the table, pushing Ethyl's half-eaten baked beans aside. The old lady startles at the sound of her bowl scraping across the table top. I think she was dozing off.

'Yeah, yeah, yeah. I've got three days off after this shift, so I'll stop for a bit.'

Thing is, I've actually been taking them pretty regularly myself. Not enough to be called an addict, but if I haven't got any in me I get a bit agitated with the world, you know? I remember Josh saying he got constipated and couldn't sleep much, either. It was sometime after that he thinks he was addicted. I should be worried, I guess, but truth is I think I'm a lot smarter than Josh is, even if he has gone right through medical to become a Registered Nurse. That means fuck all, really. If I wanted to commit to years of study, I could do it too, but I couldn't be arsed. I have a life, thank you very much!

'Like fuck you will,' snorts Sandy. She stares wistfully through the glass doors toward Greg's wing. 'Damn that boy's got some moves on him. He has just the right amount of thrust and holds it there, doesn't alter it. Drives me insane. It was all I could do to stop from screaming in there.'

'Yeah, Margaret and Rose were onto you,' I say.

She guffaws and says they can go fuck themselves, and Ethyl gets the hint of a smile on her face as she sits and stares at nothing with those dead eyes.

'They keep it up and we can just write em up for something and kick it up to the day supervisor. Eh, Ethyl?' I nudge the old lady gently on the arm, soft enough to leave no accidental bruises.

Ethyl grins and hides it behind her hand, bless her.

'You checked on Sylvia yet?' asks Sandy.

'I've been out here keeping watch while you were having all the fun,' I declare indignantly.

'Rightio, keep your knickers on,' she says, pushing out of the chair and strolling towards Sylvia's door.

'I should say the same to you!'

She flips her finger at me, grinning as she slips into Sylvia's room.

Sylvia is a cranky ol crone who is bed-ridden, and that probably accounts for some of the crankiness. She has emphysema and was still smoking up until a month ago, wheeled outside on her bed, but she's really weak now and the RN (Rachel, not Josh) has cut her off the cigs, so she's pretty much been in a foul mood ever since, cursing us occasionally. The emphysema is basically drowning her from the inside, and her legs are black and scaly like she's been charred by fire. Rachel the RN says Sylvia doesn't have long to go now. I think it's cruel that she's been denied her habit, given she's on her way out already. I thought we were meant to make things easier for them, not frustrate the fuck out of them right before they check out?

So when Rachel's not on duty, because the RN's aren't round the clock like us AIN's, then I like to wheel Sylvia over to the window and aim a fan at her so the smoke doesn't blow toward the detector. Someone usually has some cigarettes in the office, and I give her one of those, because I don't smoke and I'm not going to spend the little I earn on this cranky old bitch. But I sort of like Sylvia, too, cause she has these sharp blue eyes that penetrate everyone and there's so much intelligence and vitriol in them. She's like a wizened witch with those eyes. The shame of it is that she has moderate dementia, or what we call CDR-2 which is a scale on the Clinical Dementia Rating and means that she slips in and out of a lucid state. Sometimes she has no clue where she is or who we are, and other times she tells us all about her days of married life over in Indonesia, slipping in and out of Dutch but telling some amazing stories about her time living in Java.

Sandy comes back out. 'Potty time.'

'Is she lucid?'

Sandy gives a smart-alec smile. 'About as much as you are.'

'Hardee-fucking-ha,' I say, grabbing the sliding sheet from the PPCE cupboard.

We use the slide to get Sylvia across to the wheelchair, who gives a little shout of surprise when we sit her down. She's obviously lost where she is or what's going on, looking at us with confusion. It's actually a bit distressing when she does it, normally freaks me out. Her eyes lose her mean edge, and her face slackens as she relaxes. She looks like Sylvia still, but not the Sylvia I know. Today I'm okay with it, though, because I feel like her and I are kindred spirits, losing our minds to entirely different causes but still on the same wavelength.

The bathroom is cold, so I punch the button on the wall for the heater above the door. We've been warned about using the heaters too much, with instructions to only use it once in the mornings during Winter when we get the residents up at five AM for their shower. It's a fucking joke, because even clothed I can feel the bitter chill of these tiled cubicles, and these poor oldies have no collagen left on them and are just skin and bone. They must be freezing. But, you know, there's the electricity bills to think of, isn't there Don and Marg?

Sandy wheels the chair into position while I lift the lid and ready the toilet. We take our places and nod; no need for communication: we've done this so often it's well-rehearsed. What we do know, from experience, is that we have precious little time to get Sylvia from the chair and onto the toilet seat. When she's not lucid like this, her brain interprets her body folding up when we lift her as being in a seated position, and can direct a defecation reflex to Sylvia's bowels, with instructions to directly proceed on a course of ejection. So we work fast, scooping our arms under her and supporting her back, lifting her from the chair and across to the toilet seat in one swift motion.

Swinging her across like that, though, nearly makes me pass out. The oxycodone can cause dizziness and nausea, and my head swims and stomach lurches. I even taste bile in the back of my throat.

Sandy's face looks panicked, and with good reason, as I hesitate for the barest moment in lowering Sylvia onto the porcelain.

The old woman's anus makes a burping sound and a slurry of hot shit spews across our arms, dripping down over the toilet seat onto our shoes. It's soaking into my sock, which is black, thank Gawd. The stench is unimaginable, and though we're not supposed to show any reaction because it hurts the resident's self-esteem, I can't help but shout out: 'I'll buy a bowel please, Adriana!'

We drop Sylvia onto the toilet seat and hear the rest of it gush into the bowl. Sylvia looks petrified, probably from our reactions. She's still clueless about where she is and what's going on. I wish I was, too. This oxy isn't doing me any favours right now, but it must be worse for Sandy, who's in the corner dry-retching, holding her arm out like she wants it chopped off and incinerated. The shit drips off her arm and splatters onto the tiles into a runny pool of the stuff, and finally my tummy flips and I chunder straight on top of poor Sylvia, emptying my lunch and stomach acid into her hair and down over her shoulders.

After this experience I'm going to need a little more than the oxy I took earlier. I'll grab a sandwich baggy from the kitchen and treat myself to an all-sorts mix of Demerol, Tramal, and of course the trusty ol oxycodone. I'll steer clear of the anti-psychotic drugs, which we have for the Alzheimer and dementia residents, because there's crap all recreational use in those.

Should be a good weekend, once I get this shit and vomit cleaned off me. Gawd bless old people!

FIVE BUCKS

There were over two hundred and fifty of us at the women's forum the other night, where we tabled a proposal to the State Government to continue funding for sexual assault services and domestic violence programs, with an emphasis on re-educating police in how to deal properly and sensitively with women reporting rapes, and to request the Government's Office of Women's Status to research the rights of coppers to perform strip searches without a warrant. There was more stuff, also, that we discussed and drew up key points on, but that was essentially the crux of the seminar. It was an amazing night, full of ideas and vocal women who really knew their stuff, like this one girl with dreadlocks who introduced herself as Jane. Holy shit, she was super informed on the current State legislations, police practices and reforms not being met, etcetera etcetera. She could probably run for council and win easily, I reckon.

I went there with a group of girls from my Uni course, but not all of them got into it as much as I did. In fact, a couple of the girls seemed bored, but.

I'm telling Malik all about it, my voice getting higher with excitement as I recall how that Jane girl stood up and gave a speech that was like an old hellfire-preacher giving a sermon full of anger and righteousness. Even though he and Angele recently just got home from holidaying in England and are probably bored by my dorky seminar, Malik indulges me with a smile as I recount everything, but stops me when he sees someone coming up the stairs of the Palace.

'I can't fucking believe it,' he says in amazement, staring down at a younger guy grinning up at us.

He's got dark blonde hair but Malik's same thick, black eyebrows. Bright blue eyes sharp with intellect shine from beneath them. He's a little bit breathtaking with that dazzling smile. There's a TV set in his arms, too.

'Beau, ya bugger, whaddya doin here?' laughs Malik. 'Come to see how the other half live?'

'Nah, come to give you this,' Beau says, hoisting the TV set up for Malik to examine. 'Mum said you might want it coz we got a new one now. A bigger one.'

'Is that right?' Malik says a little less enthusiastically.

I knew Malik had two brothers, one older and one younger, but I've never met the younger one. He never visits. Until today. He's a dead-set cutie! I can imagine all the girls at school would gladly drop their panties for him. I'm half tempted drop mine and drag him into my bedroom, myself, but. Naff, I know.

Beau comes up the rest of the stairs just as Dante appears at the bottom.

'That's a nice lookin TV there, Matty,' he says, and bounds up behind Beau, pulling the TV around for a look which forces Beau to do a pirouette. Beau frowns disapprovingly but Dante's too absorbed in flicking dials and pressing buttons to notice.

'Here, take it,' Beau says to his brother, swinging away from Dante's poking and prodding to dump the TV into Malik's arms. It's much bigger than the one he and Angele currently have. 'That's my second good deed for the day.'

'What was the first one? Gettin this outta mum and dad's hair?' says Malik wryly.

'Nope,' he says proudly. 'I saw this homeless guy when I stopped for petrol on the way here and gave him five bucks. A whole five bucks.'

'What, are you made of money now that you can just hand out wads of it to street-scummers?' Then maybe because he remembers Dante used to be homeless, Malik adds: 'I mean the homeless people, of course.'

'No offense taken,' grins Beau, misinterpreting who Malik's self-censure was meant for. 'But it feels good to help out, you know? Especially in the dead of winter. You'd know all about that, yeah, after your hols?'

'It's summertime in England right now,' Malik says. 'Still cold, but.'

Angele pokes her head out of the door and when she sees Beau she skips out and gives him a hug. 'England was ahhhmazing, Beau!'

As if still starstruck from her time away, she's still got the travel bag from Ansett slung over her shoulder, although she's already tried turning the star on the logo into a pentagram using a texta.

'We want to go and live there now,' she gushes.

'Correction: we *will* go and live there now,' says Malik with odd conviction.

'What do you mean?' I ask as Lunar strolls out and curls around my ankles, purring loudly.

'We've changed our savings plans and we're not gonna buy a flat now,' Malik announces. 'We're gonna move to London.'

Dante sniffs and says: 'Isn't England just like here but wetter? I don't get the attraction.'

'Anyway, thanks for the telly,' Angele gushes, all smiles.

This is the most animated I've ever seen her. Don't get me wrong, I get along with her, but she can be a bit frosty at times. It's like Beau's put her into a thermonuclear meltdown. I wonder how Malik feels about that?

'And good on you for being so charitable towards the people on the streets,' Angele says with another big smile, although it lacks the sincerity it should have. Her and Malik have strong opinions about poverty, even though they're hardly affluent themselves.

Beau shrugs, a casual gesture that makes me think he could easily command the room if he wanted to. 'They don't have a lot in life,' he says, 'but maybe with my help that man can now get a nice cup of coffee. Realise the world's not totally against him, you know.'

'Yeah, I see where you're coming from,' I nod, getting in before

Angele can. 'That's really nice of you, Beau.'

'Thanks...' he holds his hand out.

'Raven,' I giggle, taking his hand and shaking it, trying not to drop Lunar who's cradled in my arms now. No peck on the cheek or kissing my fingers here. We're equals. Hardly women's forum stuff, I suppose, but it's a start. 'Dorky I guess, but that's what everyone calls me.'

'I like it,' he says with a big smile, then tickles Lunar under the chin. Result!

'Fuck's sake,' groans Dante, shaking his head.

'So wait, giving me this TV set's like giving a street... I mean, a homeless guy five bucks?' says Malik indignantly.

'Nah,' laughs Beau breezily. 'Mum said I had to give it to you. I'd've dumped it curbside if I had my way.'

Malik laughs. 'Of course you would, ya prick. Wanna stay for a cuppa?'

'Would love to,' says Beau reluctantly, probably sensing he's about to be subjected to a show and tell of holiday photos instead, 'but the grand tour will have to wait until next time. I gotta fly.'

'No worries,' says Malik.

Beau playfully slaps his big bro on the arm and takes the steps two at a time down to the entrance door.

'Bye, Beau,' I say, waving flirtatiously.

He gives a wry grin and goes out to his Torana, peeling away in a cloud of dust and stones. Probably to impress me. Boys.

'Someone's in luuuurve,' croons Malik, putting the TV set on the floor and sitting on top of it.

'Shut up,' I sulk, pretending I'm about to punch him in the arm.

'It's cool,' smiles Malik. 'He's a good sort. Unlike Martin.'

Martin's the older brother and a self-confessed Satanist according to Malik. Beau's a far cry from Martin, or Tadpole as we used to call him in school. It's hard to imagine Tadpole being as kind or generous as Beau.

'How's he a good sort?' demands Dante. He's got a bee in his bonnet about something, judging by the tone of his voice.

Malik stares at him, obviously unimpressed with being spoken to like this. It *is* pretty rude, I'll admit!

'You think he's a good sort because he gave money to a homeless guy?' continues Dante.

'Yeah,' shrugs Malik. 'He does it all the time. So?'

'He does it all the time,' scoffs Dante. 'How the fuck do you know? Do you follow him around?'

'Dante,' I say, giving him a look so he knows he's overstepping the mark. Do you think he gets the hint, but? Fat chance of that.

'You know because he goes on about it all the time, right? That makes him a wanker in my book.'

'Come on, Dante, Beau's alright,' I say, half because I believe it and half because Malik's still not saying anything. He doesn't look happy, but.

'Fuck Beau!' snaps Dante loudly, shocking me. Lunar's head snaps in his direction. 'Cunts going round handing out a pissy five bucks to the destitute so they can brag about it to their mates don't deserve any praise. They're a fucking abomination.'

'Ease up, ya bastard,' Malik finally says.

'No, Matty, fuck yer brother and fuck his Samaritan acts,' retorts Dante, his voice booming now. 'If he was really keen on helping the homeless he'd do it quietly and no cunt would know about it unless they were there to see him do it.'

I'm worried the boys are going to start fighting. It's getting a bit intense.

'You're out of order, Dante,' Malik says, standing up.

'Don't worry, I'll see myself out,' Dante barks, even though we're all still standing on the second floor landing.

When Dante's gone, I ask Malik if he's okay and he lets out a deep breath, dragging the TV inside his flat.

'Yeah, but he shoots off at the mouth too much, that derro,' he says.

'I guess he's pretty passionate about homeless issues, kinda like I am about women's rights,' I say.

'But are you?' Malik says, and when he sees I'm affronted by this question he looks at the floor. 'I think what Dante doesn't understand is that because of my brother's generosity some homeless person can now have a cup of coffee.'

I forget how thin the walls are here, and how easily our voices can travel up and down the stairwells. From down below we can hear Dante clapping sarcastically.

'Oh, praise be!' he yells up to us. 'Praise be for a cup of fucking coffee!'

TWIX ON AIR

The last caller's yabbering on too long, ol Twixxie now realises. We're talking about how Specimen influenced the birth of the subculture, you know, on account of starting The Batcave and all, but Ben (that's the caller) is insisting it's Bauhaus who started it all.

'Fucking heresy,' I go. 'The Batcave sound was deathrock, for a start.'

'Which came from LA, with Christian Death, didn't it?'

This joker's winding me up now, surely?

'Rubbish, mate,' I fire back. 'Jonny Slut developed that sound, end of story. Murphy and the lads, for the record, didn't want anything to do with the goth label. But, you know, it sells albums now.'

'Fuck off,' Ben goes, getting stroppy. 'No-one was even calling themselves goth in those days, including your precious Specimen. Get your facts straight, Twix. And even when the name started to stick, just like any self-respecting goth these days no-one freely admitted to being one. It was the media that gave them the name, same as with deathrock. Sartorially, Specimen paved the way, I'll grant you that.'

Touched a damn nerve there, ay? Stiff shit. And he wants to be sarcastic about Specimen paving the way for the goth movement? Cheeky bastard! Time to end the convo, anyways. Too much air time devoted to blabbing on about music and not enough playing the actual stuff.

The port's not helping me keep track of the time, either, especially since I've already downed a good measure from the bottle, so by the time our debate's wound down it occurs to me that I haven't played a song in ages. It's turned out to be more like talk-back radio than the weekly goth programme!

I want to drop 'satorially' into a future convo, because it sounded pretty spiffy, but I better bone up on its exact definition so I don't look like a right arse. I find a beat up dictionary in the office that's been defaced a million times over by idiots drawing tockleys all over it in biro, but fortunately most of the S section's intact. And will you look at that! Turns out it means 'style of dress'. I thought it meant to be sarcastic. I guess I had the wrong end of the stick with ol Benny boy. Oh well. C'est la vie.

The thing with graveyard shift, especially when you're filling in for a sick friend, is that it goes on for fucking ever. I've co-hosted for James a few times now, but with the station empty save for me and the in-house ghost who I never seem to see or hear from, it's just boring as hell. To make it up to both the listeners and myself, and to rub caller Ben's nose in it, I slip in Specimen's *Batastrophe* EP and press the repeat button, heading outside to grab something to eat.

My balls are still sore to the touch in spots, so when I walk it's with a swagger to stop them from brushing against my thighs. It gives me a cocky and wasted attitude.

The Valley clubs are in full swing and the streets are crawling with the drunk and disorderly. Thanks to the on-air dispute that went on for ages, I reckon I've bought myself plenty of time to get over to the mall and grab something to eat, so I bee-line in that direction, passing a standoff between some young skinheads and some Abo kids.

'Leave em alone,' I yell to the skins. 'They're not hurting nobody.'

'Fuck off back to faggot land,' returns one of the bald little freaks.

'No, you wait there, Shakespeare,' demands another, referencing my puffy-sleeved pirate shirt and pointing at me. 'You're next!'

Normally I'd rise to the insult, but with a belly full of monkey-blood I couldn't give a toss. The port's warmed me and loosened my limbs, so I'm feeling relaxed. Just gotta get through the next hour or so and can hit the clubs myself. It'll have to be a club for normals, cause the darkwave stuff is only on Wednesday, Friday or Saturday nights. It's still only Thursday. The Tube seems promising, at least.

On the corner I bump into Abi coming outta The Den, stuffing some porn mags into her handbag.

'Whoa, there,' I laugh. 'Salutations, fair maiden. What's this then? *Barely Legal Tarts?* I hope the sex wasn't so bad I turned you gay, Abi!'

'Hardee-fuckin-ha, idiot,' she says smarmily. 'It's not for me.'

Who the hell buys porn for other people? Seems pretty sodding weird to me!

'Calm your tits,' I smile with my hands in surrender, because her attitude can be pretty peevish, now being no exception. 'If you wanna take some edge off, ol Twixxie here–'

'First off,' she goes, interrupting me, 'you're drunk and even if you weren't the answer would still be no. And secondly,' she steps back, waving a hand down her body, indicating quite clearly that she's not dressed goth.

'You gone sartorially normal now?' I ask.

She rolls her eyes and actually slaps her own forehead. 'I'm going to work, you nob. Night shift, remember?'

'Oh yeah, I knew that.'

'Sure you did,' she sneers. 'Sharp as ever, Twix. Catcha round.'

Abi storms off before I can bid her adieu, telling the skinheads to get fucked when they tell her to flash her tits.

Well, that went smoothly, but who cares? I've a tum full o rum and a spring in my step!

I keep going down the road and into the Brunswick Mall, where it looks like a dystopian future. There's neon lights and strippers in doorways and all manner of nightlife. Yuppies, Yobs, Goths and Punks. Everyone's drunk and belligerent. I don't see much difference between any of them, to be honest. That's what being a security guard has taught me: that we're all just selfish, argumentative children who throw tantrums when we don't get our way, except as adults those tantrums can get nasty and need people in uniforms to keep em in check. In this respect, goths are just Bogans in Black at the end of the day. There's a bunch of them now, walking past and giving me wary sidelong gawks. The mall is full of people who harbour barely-concealed desires to punch our heads in for being sartorially mostly black, but when we see one another we treat each other with caution and disdain. Like me, I'm sure they're not ignorant to the possibility of threat around them, but until it surfaces I'm the one they keep an eye on, in the same way that cats get suspicious of each other or little kids stare at each other when they cross paths in public.

Go figure, right?

Suddenly this raver chick leaps out in front, yelling my name, a baby's dummy sticking from the side of her gob. I nearly fall over trying to avoid the silly bitch until I realise it's only Angele, Malik's girlfriend. She's off her fucking chops.

'Twixxy Twixxy Twix,' she goes, grinning her face off, but there's no smell of booze on her. 'I haven't seen you in ages, man.'

'Yeah, I should pop round again for a visit.'

'Too fuckin right you should!' She spits the dummy out, which swings down into her cleavage on twine slung around her neck, and gets me into a hug which she holds forever. This is the most animated I've ever seen her.

The port's put me in such a good mood I feel my old fella start to respond, so I've gotta angle my hips so that it doesn't give me away against her leg.

She pulls away, staring into my eyes like she's trying to hypnotise me. 'You been good? How's your new flat? You should come clubbing with us!'

She's with a group of girls done up in a mixture of fetish and rave gear who're bugging some lads over by the bank. It's funny seeing this progression of darkwave into rave-culture because we always kid about how we either grow out of being goth or we turn into ravers. It's a joke, but there's certainly a lot of truth to the adage. By the New Year those girls will have probably totally chucked off their darkwave personas in favour of fluro colours and popping E's.

'Can't, gotta get back to the radio station,' I tell Angele. 'Doing graveyard shift.'

'Awww, you work so hard all the time,' she pouts, still holding me by the arms.

Suddenly we're engulfed in an awkward silence, just staring into each other's eyes. I lean my head down to kiss her but she let's go of me, laughing.

'Sorry, Twix,' she goes, apparently registering the weirdness of the situation, finally. 'I'm not into you. It's the mollys. Hence the binky,' she adds, holding up the dummy.

So they *are* high on ecstasy pills. Fucking drugs. It's hard enough reading chicks at the best of times, let alone when drugs mix the signals all up. Hate being led on.

She seems to find it amusing, at least.

'We're out looking for a toilet, actually, coz the fucking bar we were in only had one with a massive queue,' she says, switching from sour face back to perky in an instant. 'The molly's've accelerated our metabolisms. Some of these girls over here need to shit real bad.'

'Sounds charming,' I reply, only half-arsed hiding my sarcasm. 'There's the public loos down next to the police beat.'

I bite my tongue so's not to suggest checking into Binkinba for some rehab.

'You're a life-saver,' she says, giving me a quick peck on the cheek and accidently brushing against my hard-on. 'Oh, hello!' she squeals, glancing down at my crotch, then runs over to tell her mates about it. They crack up and begin their constipated advance down the mall in their chunky soled boots, looking ridiculous.

I tuck my hard-on under the waistband of my jeans, out of sight but not out of mind.

As usual, the all-night convenience is packed with all walks of life volleying for preference of service at the counter. There's ravers and street beggars and week old sausage rolls, dimming fluorescent lights and harried cash-register attendants. There's the hum of life in here, a crossroads of cultures and classes all here for the same pre-packaged sustenance or fix of nicotine. The junkies hang around out the front wheedling and cajoling the rest of us to part with as much cash as possible for their own fucked up brand of fix.

After the solace of the radio station, my spirits are lifted by the commotion and activity of human life. And more than that, I'm in the mood for one-on-one interaction, as I'm sure most of the people in here are too. But I don't have the luxury of hanging about in a club and testing the waters just yet.

The doughnuts are sitting in a pool of stale treacle, but I couldn't give a toss. I'm hungry and the thought of some spongy doughnutty goodness is too hard to resist, so into a bag a few of them pop. A large slushie tops off my order and I wait in line with the rest of my night-time brethren, munching on a chocolate-glaze while I do so.

In stumble some feral punks, raucous as hell and grabbing at the loaves of bread, throwing one around like a football. The security guard part of me wants to step forward and tell them to lay off the goods, but then I'd probably lose my place in the line. Punks are manky grots who smell and don't wash, and the thought of them pawing everything in sight just gets ol Twixxie's goat, so I glance at the big bastard behind me to secretly signal to him I'm not done with my place in the line.

'Watch my spot for me, mate,' I say all buddy-like.

'Fuck off,' the big bastard grumbles, screwing his nose up as he glances at my crotch.

Fuck! The tip of my tockley's poking out of the waistband. I shove it to one side, out of sight, figuring a slight bulge in the front is better than the tip of a hard-on actually showing.

The punks are throwing bags of chips at each other now, so I can't resist. I leave my position in the line and the big bastard closes the gap, the prick.

'Come on, lads, give it a rest,' I snap at the punks.

They stop laughing, sizing me up, obviously wondering about my sartorial choice of black jeans and puffy white pirate shirt combo.

'Who are you, the strippergram?' goes a boy shorter than me with a septum piercing dangling from his nose. I heard those things get boogers stuck on them all the time.

I consider admitting that I usually *am* a security guard, scare em a little bit, but one of the chicks isn't looking at me like the rest of them are, which is like they think I'm just funny and should fuck off. Nah, she's smiling in this really sweet way and even for a punk I guess she's kinda cute with her pigtails. Her face could be improved with a paper bag, maybe, but after the encounter with Angele I'm actually a bit raring to go, so any port in a storm. It's like old Bernie back at the Prozac Palace used to say, anyways: who looks at the mantle-piece when you're stoking the fire?

'Nope, I'm a radio DJ, actually,' I declare proudly. There's a round of snorts, because I forgot that punks prefer live music and generally diss DJ'ing. So I add: 'But on the radio, you know? Not like in clubs or anything.'

'Right, coz if you really were a security guard it would've made them doughnuts even funnier,' says the septum kid.

'Yeah, I guess so,' I agree, but looking at the girl with the pigtails. The port's doing the trick, because I completely ignore the rest of em to offer this chick a tour of the radio station. If one of these jokers is her boyfriend then stiff shit, I'm trying my luck here.

'For real?' she goes.

The rest wanna come, too, and I figure that'll at least get her back up there so we're all headed back to the station, passing the Abo kids from earlier who mock us as we pass. After I stood up for em and all! Go figure, right?

Everyone's impressed by the station, checking out all the rooms, the ones that aren't locked at least. I tell em about the ghost, bringing a new round of derision from them, but then one of them, Dave, admits he used to work here last year for a couple of months and he remembers there was talk of a ghost then. His confession of working here casts me in a new light, especially with the girl I'm flirting with, Nikki.

'But what's this fucking noise?' goes the lad with the ring in his nose, whose name is Chookie.

It's the CD I left on rotation, and judging by the track I'm guessing it's into at least its third rotation. Maybe even its fourth.

'Fuck, I gotta fix that!'

We go through and turn the music off and I pull a coupla mics up and put us all on air. There's not enough seats so I suggest that Nikki sits on my lap, which she does. Her arse feels nice and warm on my legs.

'Night's nearly over, folks,' I announce into the mic, using a lower baritone than I use off-air. 'You've been listening to an epic session of Specimen.'

'Spasticmen, more like,' says Chookie, muffling his words because he speaks too closely into the mic, his beer-breath wafting across the mixing desk.

'It's not often we do that for ya,' I continue, biting my tongue so I don't get into another long-winded on-air debate about the merits of Specimen. 'But now we've got a special past presenter in with us for the moment. Say hello Dave.'

'Hello Dave,' he goes, to a round of sniggering from the others.

We talk some shit and eventually they request a song by local act Blowhard, something we'd not normally play on Ignore The Machine, but never say never, right? We've gotta hunt around for it, leaving the radio with dead air for a spell which isn't the best thing to do. But its volunteer radio at midnight, what do people expect?

'Thing with these ska bands,' I joke when I finally find the CD, 'is they're never short on members, are they?'

'Let's see how short your member is,' Nikki smirks mischievously, making her mates squirm and cringe.

The CD goes on, skipping to the track *Sexual Deviant*, whereupon everyone else shuffles out of the booth on the pretext of going out back for a smoke. Nikki grins at me and without a word she warps her arms around my neck and we start making out. I guess neither Dave nor Chookie are attached to her, after all.

I start necking her, but her skin smells a bit musty from the lack of bathing these punks do. So instead of wasting time inhaling her funk I just get down to business, hooking her skirts up, searching around for the hem of her knickers, which is pointless cause I soon realise she isn't wearing any. For some reason this gets me hard enough to pop a cast-iron hymen so I hoist her up onto the edge of the desk and hold her legs open while she unbuckles me.

'Careful of my balls,' I go, arching my arse so that my healing ballsack is out of harm's way.

With my tockley out of it's cage it's time for action, and no amount of port's going to drown this erection. I barely aim as I sink it in. A hole in one! You fucking beauty!

'Oh my god, Nikki, your pussy feels so good!'

She laughs and tells me how it's been a while since she had a good solid fuck, which encourages us into a vocal sparring match, trying to out-dirty each other. It turns me on hearing her talk like this, and it seems to be getting her motor running hotter, too. In no time we're bandying about the filithiest obscenities at each other. Hanging out with Amai's got me into good practice for this.

'Fuck that whore cunt, you fucking arsehole,' she yells in my face, so I respond with name-calling in kind. I'm getting ready to blow.

I try and do a mental calculation of when the next shift is up, an experimental electro show called BuzzKill hosted by Sabrinha. I've got to try and finish with the punk bitch before Sabrinha gets in, but the thought of her walking in on us bumping uglies and peeping on us puts me over the edge, and I yank my tockley out just in time to shoot cum all over Nikki's skirts and thighs.

'Ew, don't do that ya fucking bastard!' she goes, kicking me away, aiming for my leg and not my jewels thankfully. She pulls a disgusted face as she looks down at my spunk. Between her reaction and having unloaded my balls, I'm a bit miffed by the dirty bitch, now.

'It's probably the only way to get you to wash up,' I say sourly, instantly regretting my words.

She looks hurt, and instead of waiting for me to get something to clean herself off with she just flips her skirts down and storms outta the booth, snatching up a bunch of CD's and tapes as she goes.

'Oi, put those back, bitch!' I yell, struggling to get my dacks back up without knocking my sodding balls, pursuing her up the hallway. 'Wait, Nikki. I didn't mean it.'

Out back she's got her arms loaded up with stolen stuff, telling the others what an arsehole I am. They're looking pretty pissed off with me. When Chookie goes and picks up some empty bottles from next to the bins, I run back inside and swing the door closed, just in time. The glass smashes on the other side, three small explosions, and then a volley of abuse from the three of em. When it's gone quiet I peek through a crack in the door and see that they've left.

The phone's ringing inside. More requests, probably, but it's too fucking late. Shift's nearly over.

Indeed, here comes Sabrinha with a box of CD's and tapes in her arms, hair grown longer since my party. She always brings her own stuff in instead of playing the station's catalogue, cause she's into the cutting edge, she reckons. Just another music wanker.

'Those people didn't give you trouble, did they?' she says to me as I hold the door open for.

'What people?' I know full-well who she's talking about, but I'm hoping she hasn't twigged that I had em in here. It's against company policy, although it's not uncommon for presenters to bring mates into the studio after hours.

'That lot down the road,' she says idly. 'Looked like they came from in here.'

'Nah, all cool,' I say. 'Got the last track on now.'

'Different for you guys,' she goes, cocking an ear to Blowhard as we descend the short flight of stairs down to the studio.

'Oh yeah. Listener request,' I laugh, noting that it's no longer the song I put on. Must've been porking that punk bitch longer than I realised.

'All good,' she smiles. 'I like Blowhard.'

She would. 'Well, I'll leave you to it, Sabrinha.'

I head through into the booth to grab my backpack while Sabrinha piss-farts around outside the studio, checking the front door lock and whatnot. I notice my fly's undone.

The phone starts ringing, and oddly enough it sounds like we've got two phones because I swear I hear the echo of it ringing out in the hallway. Thing is, though, we only have the one phone.

Sabrinha comes into the studio with a frown, looking at me as if I've done something weird.

'Why's the microphone on when you're playing a track?'

She reaches down and flicks the mic button off.

That's odd.

She picks up the receiver and has a lil convo, then looks at me in horror.

It's then that it dawns on me what's happened. The sound of the other phone was this one playing on air, and the speakers out in the hallway were echoing it back to me.

The weird thing is, I turned the mic off when we put the Blowhard CD on. So why's it on now?

Sabrinha slams the phone down, and as soon as she does it rings again, so she picks it up and slams it down once again to silence it. She's glaring at me in real anger. The CD switches over to the next song.

'You had sex on air?'

Fuck, no, this isn't happening. But yes, it is. I start praying that Sabrinha's just guessed, somehow.

'That listener rang in to say they heard you having sex with a girl in here for the last twenty minutes,' she says, her voice shaky.

'It wasn't that long, Christ.' I can hear a similar tremble in my own voice. This bitch has been on my nerves ever since her and her mates tried to spike my party with fake acid. 'Who the fuck are you to judge?'

'The mic was still on when I came in here, Travis!' she yells.

She starts laughing, holding her hand over her mouth.

'Oh, you're fucked, me boyo,' she goes. 'Really fucked, too, not just some floozy-impressed-by-the-radio-DJ fucked.'

She's right. It's not just me that this effects. There's James to think of.

'Sabrinha, please,' I plead.

She uncases one of her CD's and whips out the Blowhard one mid-song. She gets her show underway without announcing herself, and turns to me with her hands on her hips.

'What the hell is wrong with you? And James, what's he going to say?'

'He'll be royally pissed with you for ratting us out,' I suggest. 'You just want his timeslot, you uppity bitch.'

'Oh, I want it alright,' she sneers, eyes wide with indignation, 'but I'm not ratting anyone out. The listeners won't be silenced on this.'

As if on cue, the phone rings again, and she answers it, staring at me meaningfully.

'No, he's not a fucking legend you sick pervert,' she snaps into the mouthpiece before slamming the phone down. She turns on me with renewed ire. 'Get out. Just get out!'

I trudge out of there, feeling my shoulders bunch up with stress. James is gonna be in so much shit over this. There's no way him or I can talk our way out of it, out of me having sex on air for nearly half an hour. Fuck, and the things me and that punk chick were saying to each other!

I remember the half bottle of monkey blood is still in my bag, and unscrew the cap and swig from it on my walk home. By the time I get to my bed, I'm fucking smashed, and drop into a deep sleep.

Sometime in the morning James calls, and the ringing of the phone bashes into my hangover. But I must confront this as much as I don't want to, especially right now.

'James, I'm sorry, mate,' I groan, holding my head in my hand and closing my eyes against the brutal morning light.

'The fuck happened?' he says, his voice hysterical and tinny down the line. He starts repeating the shit he's heard, which is pretty much exactly what happened.

'Listen, don't worry about what they say,' I drawl. 'When we talk with management, we'll sort it out in a way that makes it look way more innocent.'

'It was management that told me,' he screams, making me nearly drop the receiver.

'Fuck, don't yell.'

I can hear him huffing on the other end.

'James?'

'Ignore the Machine is gone, Twix.'

He falls silent, letting it sink in. Honestly, it was all I could think about on my walk home last night, so the impact he's after right now isn't as dramatic. But I fake it all the same.

'Shit! No! Oh my God, James, I'm so sorry mate.'

'Yeah, they took me off graveyard shift and now I've got nothing.'

'Fuck, I bet that fake bitch Sabrinha with a H grabbed the spot.'

There's a pause at the other end, and when he finally pipes up his voice sounds razor-thin. 'Why's she a bitch, Twix? Huh? Sabrinha's a great girl, and guess what? She didn't say anything about last night until management asked her. You've got serious problems with your relationships with women. You know that?'

I don't need a fucking lecture.

'What'd you say?' he snaps, sounding furious.

Shit, I must've said it out loud. I can't tell, I'm too hungover.

'I'm sorry,' I say lamely. 'About everything. About your show.'

'Not my show anymore, Twix,' he says flatly. 'They've given it to Michael Carlyon now.'

Then he hangs up.

I don't know what's more deafening: James yelling at me or the insufferable silence that accentuates the pounding in my skull.

And I must've got pretty drunk on the way home last night on that port and forgot to walk with my legs bowed apart, because my balls are burning like fuck again.

PART THREE

COUSIN SHARON

Me cousin Sharon, or Shaz, from Canberra is a prostitute, and the whole extended family knows about it. It was actually me fuckhead Dad who first found out coz Dougie had a magazine lyin around out back of the burger shop and Shaz was in it, completely starkers! This was a couple of years ago, but, coz if I'd of been working there at the time I wouldn't have let that thick-as-a-brick cunt Dougie leave the mag lyin around for Dad to find in the first fucking place!

He's such a spazzo cunt, that Dougie. And I reckon Dad would've been pervin his eyes out and beatin one off over his own niece, too. After the whole thing with the magazine happened, Shaz wrote to me and said there's a sayin amongst her co-workers that goes cunts'll wank with one hand while pointin with the other. She was talkin about Dad bein a fuckin hypocrite.

Since it happened the whole family's disowned Shaz. So Mum and Dad don't like us talkin with her but we keep in contact every now and then anyway, but.

I'm shit at writin letters to people, but at least with Shaz I make the effort to put pen to paper every six months or so, mostly coz of how she gets treated by the family. She's literally one of the most interesting people I know. I might be the black sheep of my close family, but she's the black sheep of our entire family tree.

About a month ago she wrote sayin she was comin up for a visit. Shaz always puts a fake name on the back of the envelope, which is her working name of 'Jessica', and coz Dad is such a dickhead, when Mum told him about the letter, he literally thought I have an actual penfriend named Jessica in Canberra. As if. I think Mum suspects it's Sharon, but she won't dare open it to check coz she holds fast to the principal of respectin privacy. I've opened her mail heaps of fuckin times to find out how much is in her bank account and all that. I use the steam from the kettle to soften it open and then just glue-stik it closed again.

Shaz gets off the bus and gives us the biggest hug until we lose our balance and literally fall on the ground, laughin and screamin out coz we're so fucking happy to see each other. Everyone is lookin around and starin but we don't give a fuck. She's only four years older than us, so we're more like friends than cousins. Unlike the rest of me family, she has the decency to call us Pixie, not Prudence.

Her bag's in the luggage section under the bus, so she shoves a couple of people over to get in first, crackin us up as the fuckers look at her all shitty. Then we get down the escalators, past the shitty food court and get the fuck out of there.

Out front are all sorts of low-life smokin or doing drug deals. One of the guys nods at us, coz I've been here a couple of times with Imp to score some weed. It's funny, coz right across the road is this big-ass police headquarters and up from that is the courthouse, which we pass coz Shaz has a room booked up at a backpacker joint called The Ridgie-Didge Hostel on Liddle Roma Street. If ya didn't know Brisbane, ya'd think she was going to some perfect liddle Italian place coz of the name of the street, but it's just this crappy liddle side road that looks over the railway line and Suncorp Stadium.

She throws herself on the bed, pulling off her bra from under her shirt, buggered from the bus ride which she says was shit. She can diss it all she wants, but the idea of takin a long-distance journey to literally anywhere sounds like fuckin heaven to me, just to get away from the everyday shit and the everyday people and go to another city where no-one knows ya, knows ya past.

'It's fuckin ace to see ya,' I tell her again for the hundredth time.

She's like an enigma to us, coz when I try and picture what a prostitute would look like, me cousin Sharon isn't what comes to mind. She has amazin eyes, big and almost saucer-like with different shades of browns that intersect, but the rest of her is kind of ordinary. Her nose is long and thin, and her lips are thin, too, and so's her boring brown hair that hangs like octopus tentacles down past her shoulder-blades. Her body is slim and petite, smaller than mine even though I'm younger, and her tits are pretty small. She has long thin fingers that makes us think of those freaky elf creatures in that old kid's movie *The Dark Crystal.* She has lots of dark freckles that join all across her nose and cheeks. I love those.

She reckons it doesn't matter what ya look like, coz guys are interested in all sorts of girls, all shapes and sizes and colours.

'And I still get carded at bottle-o's or clubs all the time,' she says. 'Coz I look young, right? That's a plus in this game. Especially in Canberra. Those pervy fucks like them young, let me tell you. When you come out of high school, basically think about heading to Sydney or think about joining a brothel. The whole system down there for youth employment is made to encourage as many new bloods as possible into brothels so the pollies can make out they're fucking a minor.'

'So there's a better job for us out there, after all,' I giggle, thinkin maybe it's better than workin for Dad in his crappy burger house.

'You're *too* young, cuz,' she says, unzippin her suitcase. 'They'd love that for sure, though. And it's possible, of course. Happens all the time. But it'd fuck you up. It's a messy business, bad bastards running the whole thing. That's why I stick to a brothel. At least down there that's legal and properly regulated. Same as in Melbourne. You poor bastards up here are still behind the times, where the brothels are still illegal.' She pulls out a gift-wrapped parcel from her suitcase and gives it to us. 'I got you something.'

Squealin, I hug her again. She smells so good, but not of perfume just her skin.

The present is soft and when I carefully open it there's a gorgeous black crushed-velvet dress inside, with a lace front and spidery bell sleeves. It's not the sort of thing I'd normally wear, but I love it and can't wait to try it on. Off comes me shirt and skirt and on goes the dress, careful but, treating it like it was priceless. Shaz helps to do the ribbons up on back. There's a mirror on the inside of the wardrobe door, and by standin on the bed I can get a full view of myself in the dress. With my pigtails and Docs, I look super fucking cute as.

'I loooove you!' I shriek, huggin her again, not lettin go this time.

We sit down on the bed, flattenin out the creases in me new dress with our hands.

'Ya should come and live up here for good. We could hang out all the time.' My voice sounds small, hopeful. Maybe a bit sad, even.

Shaz smiles softly. 'That'd be nice, wouldn't it?'

'Dante's still single,' I go, wigglin me eyebrows.

Shaz looks a bit shocked, coz I've never mentioned to her before that I know her and Dante used to have a thing a few years ago when she came to stay with us for a while. I was literally about twelve or somethin and only met him once, but I still remember him.

'Dante Halloran? Holy shit, how'd you know about him?'

'I know him through the clubs. He doesn't remember me, but.'

She laughs at how Brisbane's like a small town where everyone knows everyone else. 'There's no privacy up here, not that Canberra's much better in that sense.'

'I've never been interstate before,' I admit.

'It's freezing down there.'

'Hot chocolates and cafes and cute guys in scarfs,' I go, picturin myself hangin out in small alleyways and drinkin coffees served by hot Italian waiters who know us by name. I don't even know what Canberra looks like, if it even has tiny narrow alleyways filled wall-to-wall with coffee houses.

Even though she's tired as fuck, Shaz wants to go out and look round the City for a while, maybe take us to a late lunch somewhere. I keep the dress on, coz I feel amazing in it. On the way, she tells us about one of her clients last year.

'He was really high profile, and didn't hide it either. Sometimes they do, like this one guy who said he was a dentist but later I saw his photo in a posh mag and turns out he's a famous photographer. This other guy didn't hide it, just told me who he was. An hour after he fucked me, he flew to Sydney and met the Pope when he got off the plane. Hope he washed before shaking hands with the holiness.'

We're arm in arm, laughin at her stories, like two friends who have grown up together. And we probly should have, coz our father's are brothers and used to be close, but her dad was shady as fuck and got into all sorts of criminal shit, constantly using aliases and movin around a lot. He was in hot water up here and Dad apparently washed his hands of helpin, typically, so me uncle and me aunt and Sharon all moved down to Sydney first, then to Canberra. I guess me uncle finally got tired of doing dodgy deals and runnin. He's dead now; heart attack five years ago.

I take Shaz round all the usual places, like King George Square where I usually like to hang out, and the shops like Rocking Horse and Underworld Realm and all the stores that I like. Down behind the

Hoyts we run into some of the street kids and the punks hangin at the entrance to the all-night McDonald's. Sam and his girlfriend are here, who I know from school, and some of the older punks like Scab. Shaz gets a kick out of meetin them, and I'm proud to show her off as me cool cousin from down south.

We go inside to get burgers and fries. It's a long corridor ya walk down, which then turns into the inside of McDonald's and the walls and floors are white tiles so it feels like going through to Heaven. I imagine this is what *all* McDonald's in Canberra must look like. It's the same on the other side, and there's some stairs that go up to the Mall. Along that corridor are props from Movie World like a Gremlin and some stuff from Batman, but in plastic cases so we can't touch em. It's still really cool, but.

While we're eatin, Shaz asks if I know anyone who works in the care hostels up here.

'Not really. There's a woman I know called Roz who works the streets mostly, but. Over in the Valley.'

Shaz giggles. 'I mean the aged care hostels, silly.'

'Oh, right. Not really.'

'I want to check some out and see if they're suitable for Mum.'

I forgot that Aunty Lorraine's in a mental hospital for literally bein a total schizoid. She's been in there for yonks now. Poor Shaz, putting up with that!

'How come you'd send ya mum up here for?'

Shaz says she's up to check out what business is like in Brisbane, as she's gettin a bit old for Canberra now and is thinkin about a change to warmer climes anyway, but she'd also have to transfer her mum from a hospital down there to one up here. I can barely hide my excitement.

'I thought it's illegal to work up here, but,' I go, chewin on my Big Mac.

'It is and it isn't,' she says.

'How can it be both?'

'Well, there's no legal brothels up here, but you can work from home as a private enterprise,' she explains. 'However, you can be the *only* sex worker on the premises at the time. More than one, and it's a brothel, which is illegal, of course. It's also illegal here for a prostitute to network with other prostitutes. This all started in 1993 under your State Premier at the time. Ol Gossy boy.'

'Wait up, are ya saying there's literally brothels here in Brisbane?'

Shaz nods.

'Naturally, and there's a reason for it. Supply and demand. Do you think the blokes in Queensland are celibate? Course not. And they're not all relying on casual or marital sex, either. A lot can't be bothered, or are too busy. The reasons for employing a prostitute are numerous. So there's demand here, it's just the supply is flying under the radar.'

It's a whole new world I've never even thought about, and here's Shaz saying it exists right now in the city I live in!

'So how will ya find the work up here?'

'Easy,' she goes, shruggin casually. 'I can either advertise myself for massages in the papers, or I'll just join a massage parlour. That's where loads of it happens, even in the regulated states. The problem with up here is that there's fuck all protection for sex workers. The Australian Institute of Criminology actually released a report a few years ago suggesting that it be decriminalised and properly regulated because the laws surrounding it at the moment endanger us. And I agree.'

'It's dangerous?'

'Can be,' she says, washin her nuggets down with a lemonade. 'Not for me. But there's a guy who visits some of the other girls in the place I work at, and he's roughed them up. The madam knows about it, but he's a regular, so.' Shaz shrugs. 'I just refuse to take him. I've got the right to, at least.'

'God, it sounds complicated,' I say.

'Not really, it's sort of like any other job really, when you think about it. They come in and tell us what they need, we quote them, get the job done, and if they're happy, it's a repeat customer. All I gotta do is give them what they want, and bring them to orgasm.'

A dude and his girlfriend walk past us with a tray of food and nearly run into the wall when they overhear our convo.

I laugh and Shaz goes: 'Serious. That's all.'

'Is it easy?' I think about the gobbies and sex I've had, and it *is* pretty easy, unless they're drunk then it just gets boring and takes forever or not at all. Otherwise, it's fuckin hard to imagine gettin paid for it. Seems almost criminal.

'Believe it or not, the young clients are better,' she says as if it's a liddle known fact. 'The old ones take ages to get it up, ages to blow their loads. It's so much more work. The younger the better, coz they get too excited too soon, and I can make them cum easily. And once they unload, that's my job done. Services rendered. Time to cough up the moolah.'

'Wow!' I had no idea. 'Just to make a dude cum.'

We have a good laugh.

Funnily enough, and I haven't told anyone this, but I often fantasise about bein a whore, or at least being used by hot guys like Manson and Twiggy however they please as if I literally was a whore. I remember the teachers chucking a massive wobbly when I was in Year 9 coz Jenny Spiers showed everyone this article, probly from *Sassy* magazine or one of the others we used to read, that said it's a common for women to fantasise about bein a whore. I reckon that's probly true, coz the Bitch Clique at school've literally been livin that fantasy for years with the jocks on the footy team, the PE teacher Mister Hoges, and probly more that no-one even knows about. Or so everyone says.

'Yeah, but making guys cum is the easy part,' Shaz says. 'I reckon it should be the other way around. They should pay to try and make *us* cum. Now there's a challenge.'

'Fuck, that'd be decent. Can't remember the last time a guy got us there.'

'Oh really?' She looks at us with pity, and I raise me eyebrows as if to say *yeah-can-ya-believe-it?* 'Oh honey, do you orgasm at all?'

'Sometimes, with me fingers or the shower hose.'

'You don't have a vibrator?' She's almost shocked.

I'm sorta embarrassed to admit that I don't. Am I meant to have one? How could I afford one anyway?

'We gotta change all that for you,' she says defiantly, and I don't bother arguing. She's the pro, after all. 'You have the right to orgasm.'

'I have the right to orgasm!' I shout, and we both literally start sayin it over and over again on repeat until some old wino cunt in the corner and the normal couple from before start givin us judgmental looks. Then we crack up and decide to find a sex shop. Luck's on our side, coz just a few doors up across the road there's a new adult store, which only opened in the last month or so, I think. That's where we go after we've finished our food.

It turns out the shop is run by two women and they tell us they wanted to create a store that catered for women as well as men, since they reckon so many other adult stores are androcentric, meaning they're more suited to the needs of males. Fuckin selfish cunts. Men, I mean, not these women. These women are pretty fuckin cool, in my books.

The shop's a new experience, but. I've never seen so much porn in one place before. There's heaps of magazine shelves with everythin from schoolgirl to granny, anal to bondage. It's like a newsagent's but for sex! And then there's four whole walls of VHS movies, again with every desire catered for, it seems.

'This is nothing,' Shaz whispers to us. 'In Canberra when you go to buy porn, it's in, like, warehouses. I don't mean stored in boxes, but shelf after shelf of the stuff. They're fucking ginormous. The pollies can't get enough of it, and the sort of stuff that's banned in the rest of the country, too, because of the Constitution. In January they pushed up the classification fees five hundred bucks per title just to make it more costly for porn companies to distribute, but it's barely made a bloody dent in what's being stocked down there.'

But we aren't here for any of that. We go straight for the sex toys and I must admit I'm a bit out of me league. There's whole racks full of stuff I have no idea what they're even for. What I do recognise clearly, but, are all the dongs. There's dicks of all sizes and colours in silicone, some with suction caps or double ends, some with bits not natural to any real dick I've ever seen. Like wiggly wormy bits comin off them. They tickle when I brush my fingers over em.

Shaz and the ladies start debating the pros and cons of each brand, askin if anythin stands out to us. I wanna keep away from the realistic lookin dildos and go for the smaller, hard-cased vibrators that are only a *bit* shaped like a penis. But then Shaz points out this one that is anatomically correct but is a pale greenish colour.

'That one glows in the dark,' she says. 'Imagine using that at night and seeing it glow inside your cunny?'

We all laugh and I stare hard at it, imagining just that. It's not too big, either, like a lot of the realistic-looking vibrators.

'Go on, Pix, get that one,' urges Shaz. 'It's not gonna pound against your cervix, at that length.'

'It's a lot of fun when the lights go out, that one,' says one of the ladies encouragingly. 'And it vibrates nicely, too.' She demonstrates by puttin some batteries in it, which she says she has to do anyway before she sells it to us to make sure it works, since there's a no-refund policy on the toys.

It shakes all over, and when I press me hand against the shaft there's amazing tiny vibrations goin all in me hand, almost numbing my fingertips. Thinkin about that on me clit almost takes my breath away.

'Ace,' I grin like a motherfucker. 'I'll have that one.'

Shaz puts up the cash for it, tellin the ladies it's me first toy. They're delighted.

'We're so happy that you came here, then,' they go, puttin the vibrator into a liddle pink paper bag.

Shaz tells us that those two are really great sales staff, and that sometimes ya can get impatient store staff which would be a bit off-puttin for a first-timer.

On the way back to the backpackers, she asks if I know anywhere to get some weed.

'Of course,' I smile. 'The Transit Centre, where ya got off the bus.'

Out on the front steps nearly everyone from before is still hangin around. A lot of them will spend all day here, wanderin in and out. This skinny guy with long hair and a lazy eye asks us if we're looking for any grass, and we nod and do the deal right there on the steps, our backs to the police headquarters across the road, not that it actually matters. Almost symbolic, I reckon. Lazy Eye gives us 5 grams of leaf wrapped in foil and Shaz hands him the cash, the equivalent of doing two shifts for Dad in his stupid burger shop. But for Shaz, this is nuthin.

Back at The Ridgie-Didge she grabs a couple of cold stubbies from downstairs, flashin her ID, and the guy says she has to drink them here, house rules, but he's eyeballin us as if to say that I shouldn't be having a beer at all. Fuckin spaz.

I wander outside while Shaz keeps arguin with the cunt, and these backpackers from fuck's know where are pointing at the shit load of fruit bats flying across the sky. 'What are they?' one of em goes, a tall guy with hair like straw, as if it's not obvious that they're fuckin bats. 'They're wombats, doofus,' goes another, 'haven't you ever heard of Australian wombats?' I fuckin piss myself with laughter!

Finally Shaz sweet-talks the bartender cunt and he lets us take the stubbies up to her room. The door to upstairs is actually outside the building, so Shaz comes out with the bottles.

'Open em when youse get up to yer room, not out there!' yells the bartender.

'Yeah yeah, I know the fuckin law,' mumbles Shaz, grinnin at me.

'Wombats,' I go, pointin at the sky.

'Ah, the rare flying ones,' she jokes.

The backpacker with the straw coloured hair turns round to us and looks impressed. 'So this is like a special treat, then?' he goes, pointin at the sky.

'Sure is,' smiles Shaz. I fuckin know that look. She's flirtin big-time with him.

He's got golden skin and a goofy smile, rollin a durrie like it's the most important thing in the world. Shaz gets into conversation with him and asks where he's from and stuff. He's from Croatia, which is fuck knows where, maybe Russia? He has that kind of accent, like from the movies. When he shakes my hand it's in a poofy way, not like Aussie guys all aggressive and shit. Anyway, he says his name is Luka, like in the Suzanne Vega song.

Shaz asks him for some papers to roll a joint, and invites him up to her room for a toke.

'If that's okay?' he asks, specifically lookin at us.

I shrug. 'Sure.'

'Okay then,' he goes in that weird accent. I want to hear him talk some more, coz I kinda like it, but don't know what to ask him. No need, however, as Shaz is right in there.

'When did you get here, Luka?'

'I arrived one week ago,' he replies as we start climbin the stairs. He insisted we go first, like a gentleman, but I wanted to be behind him to check out his ass. His eyes look even paler in the darkness of the stairwell.

'Straight into Brisbane?'

'Yes, that's true,' he says. 'And soon I will go to Sydney and then to Melbourne also.'

'You should also come to Canberra, too,' she winks. 'The nation's capital. That's where I live.'

He seems interested, and for a moment I think he's just puttin it on, but he's actually for real. I don't know if that's a Croatian thing or not, but when he listens and responds it's with real curiosity, not just to humour us. Most of the people I hang out with couldn't give a fuck about a proper conversation; we just talk *at* each other, not *with,* like it's a game of one-upmanship. *Oh, ya dad threatened to hit ya if ya swore at ya mum again? Mine did slap us for it. Oh, yours went fucking mental on ya? Well mine put us into hospital.* We just talk shit. But Luka doesn't even try and do that. He genuinely hears what Shaz is sayin and asks more about it. It makes us afraid to speak, in case I talk the same way as me friends do.

The room is warm, despite the window being open, so Shaz pulls her shirt off and throws it on the floor, not botherin to cover her bra. Luka doesn't stare; he looks around the room and makes comparisons to his own, which he says he shares with three others.

I tuck me pink bag out of sight of Luka and crack open the beers.

'We have bunk beds,' he explains. 'You're lucky to have one bed.'

'Not lucky,' laughs Shaz, rubbin forefinger and thumb together.

'Takes more moolah.'

'Moolah?' Luka looks so adorable being confused.

'Money,' winks Shaz, sittin herself on the bed and openin the foil.

'Ah yes,' says Luka with a chuckle, takin a swig from her beer. 'Moolah... moolah...' He's soundin the word out, gettin used to it. He smiles lazily at us, pattin the bed next to him. 'Relax, Pixie. No stress.'

I feel the heat of his body when I sit down, and me arm is resting against his. The touch is sendin liddle jolts of excitement straight to me crotch. He's got nice arms. Smooth, slightly muscular, with curves where his biceps – or whatever they're called – bulge. Normally I hate tanned dudes, can't fuckin stand them. But Luka's skin doesn't look tanned, it looks more natural. Like olive skin.

They roll the joint and light it up, and Shaz goes first, suckin it back with pursed lips. She exhales and passes it to Luka, but looks like she has somethin on her mind. She gives a liddle cough.

'Something the matter?' he says.

'It's grass,' she says, raisin her eyebrows and shakin her head.

'Good?' goes Luka, but I've cottoned on already.

'Actual grass,' she goes, and starts to laugh, which sets us off, too.

Luka looks confused for a moment then he gets this big grin.

'Fuck,' says Shaz, still laughin. 'I paid sixty bucks for that.'

It occurs to us that I could've used that money for somethin more. Somethin a bit stronger.

Luka shifts himself up behind her on the bed, resting against the headboard, and rubs her back.

'Don't worry,' he smiles, 'I will get some real, tonight. We can do it again, later.'

Shaz grabs the rest of her beer and leans back on him, and with the sunlight comin from the window behind them it makes the tops of their heads glow. They look like the old paintings, somethin ya'd see in the art gallery.

'You can smoke the cock, if you want,' goes Luka, slowly strokin Shaz's hair.

'I haven't got the foggiest of what that means,' she says, smirking, 'but I'm open to interpretation.'

They kiss, smackin lips which I normally hate but right now is a bit ova turn on.

Before I know it, she's got his fly undone and he's wigglin his hips so she can push his jeans down. I don't know if I should leave or not, but Shaz gives us a wicked grin and neither of them tells me to go, so I decide to stay and watch what happens.

Shaz pulls off Luka's undies and tugs his penis free. It's beautiful, quite long and smooth looking with the same olive skin as the rest of him. And it's cut, too, which is better. I don't like the pinched liddle openin of skin that some dicks have. Looks like a choco starfish when they're like that.

I'm still nervous about bein an observer, so I get stuck into the last of the beer to calm me nerves.

Shaz has eyes only for Luka's dick now, runnin her hand along his shaft. She doesn't hesitate, but literally opens her mouth like a whale shark ready to swallow the whole friggin thing, and at the last second she only takes the tip between her lips.

Luka pulls his shirt off and fuck me his chest and abs are perfect. I don't think he works out in the gym or anythin, it just looks natural. I guess the backpacking and all the shit they do with hikin and surfin or whatever the fuck they get up to tones their bodies more than most people. Whatever it is, it works. His tummy's flat and hard, with liddle ridges of hot muscle.

Shaz glances at us and obviously reads my awkwardness. So does the dude.

'What's the matter, not sucked a man's cock before?' he goes, kinda cocky.

'Course I have,' I snap back, rememberin how I sucked off Michael Carlyon a coupla times coz he said he'd share a shot of heroin with us, but the cunt was all talk. Never kept his end of the bargain. He'd be too chicken-shit to touch that stuff, anyway.

'Well, get into it, girl,' grins Shaz, and Luka does that thing guys always think is super impressive but is just stupid, where they tense their pelvic muscles to make their dicks twitch around on its own.

I scoot across the bed and sit beside Shaz.

'Here, hold it,' she goes.

His penis feels warm and soft. Not soft like flaccid, but the skin moves when I stroke it and feels soft like a girl's skin does. He's fully erect now and the veins on the shaft have popped. It's probly literally the most beautiful dick I've ever seen. Luka's eyelids are heavy, and he's watchin us with a lazy smile, his hands crossed behind his head.

Shaz stands over him, tuggin her shorts and undies off. Her ass is small and tight, not like mine. I'd kill for an ass like hers. She squats over his head, and Luka breaks into a big grin, guiding her down with his hands on her thighs until she's on his face, grinding herself into his mouth. He moans but I don't know if it's coz he's eatin her or if it's from me handjob. I'm not really doin a lot, so I guess it's coz of her. I decide to see if I can do better. This could be fun, seeing if I can beat a whore at her own game.

So I start strokin him as best I can, dribblin saliva onto the head of his dick then spreadin it all over, workin me hands in a piston-like action but squeezing just a liddle bit at the same time. He responds by revolvin his hips slowly, and Shaz keeps grindin her pussy onto him and squeezin her butt cheeks. She's got hold of the headboard and I can see her forearms are tensed up, like she's gonna cum soon.

So I tighten me grip and pump a liddle harder, lickin at his helmet and tastin his salty pre-cum. I think I'm getting him there. This is gonna be a close finish. His helmet's gone tight and shiny and a deep purple colour, and he's groanin loudly even though it's muffled by Shaz sittin on his mouth.

There's a violent jerk to his hips, but only once, and I see the hole of his dick literally expand, ready to unload.

But it's not cum that shoots out.

Blood jets out of the end of his dick, and suddenly Shaz is yelpin, springin from the bed and holdin her crotch, doubled over in pain.

'FUCK!' she screams. 'Fucking cunt bit me!'

The blood's jettin out of his penis in spurts all over me arms and neck, splashin onto me new dress.

My scream nearly shatters the fuckin windows!

Luka thrashes around, shoutin in a way that doesn't sound like it's his voice. It's like an animal sound.

I'm stunned, just sittin there with me hands frozen in mid-air while the blood squirts outta him and soaks into the sheets. It gets all over his fingers as he tries to stop it flowin from his dick.

'Fuck fuck fuck,' I stammer.

'Get the fuck out!' Shaz screams at Luka.

But he's not hearing her, he's just moanin and yellin in another language that sounds a bit like: 'Boli me kurac!'

'I'll go get help,' I say, as Shaz keeps yellin for Luka to fuck off.

I sprint out the door and fly down the stairs, leavin blood marks on the rails and walls as I go. I race round into the bar area of the backpackers and scream at the guy behind the bar.

'We need fuckin help up there! His dick's bleedin!'

But the useless fucking cunt shouts at me to piss off. He's pointin at the door and gettin angry with us.

'Get fucked cunt!' I yell back. 'Call a fucking ambulance!'

These two girls come runnin in, askin what's happened to Luka.

'His dick is like a fuckin fountain,' I go, holdin me hands out so they can see there's blood all over me.

'Whadja do to him?' demands one of em while the other one starts arguin with the bar-dude about callin an ambo.

'I didn't do nuthin,' I tell this bitch, who looks at us like I'm trash. She's the one with her tits nearly fallin outta her impossibly thin tank top. How the fuck is that fashion?

The guy finally calls the ambulance, then him and the two girls follow me back up to Shaz's room, bringin towels to stop the blood and for cleanin up the mess.

Luka's out on the landing with his jeans half way down his legs, which are literally fucking saturated in blood. It looks weird, coz only a liddle bit sprayed up onto his abdomen, but from his groin down it's just red. He looks like he's in agony, but he's able to talk clearly so I think most of it's just a reaction to seeing the blood come from his dick. He should try goin through that once a month and then come back and whinge.

Sharon's sitting on the edge of the bed, with her crotch hanging off the edge and her heels diggin into the floor. Her pussy's completely shaved, somethin I've never seen on a girl before, and her labia is still extended from the growling she got. There's a nick of blood on one of her pussy lips, but otherwise she seems okay.

'The fucker bit me,' she goes, throwin a pissed off look toward the doorway. 'It feels hot. I'm just cooling it down.'

'What happened?' I ask, glancin back at Luka. The girls are fussin over him, staunchin the blood flow with towels.

The cunt from the bar's standin in the doorway, frownin at the whole scene: Sharon with her pussy on show and nearly the entire bed drenched in blood.

'I don't know,' says Shaz. 'What'd you do to him?'

'Maybe his balls broke or somethin,' I suggest, coz that's all I can think of. I'm hoping it wasn't from wanking him too hard. That might be considered assault.

'You need an ambulance,' says the guy at the door.

'Yeah, maybe,' snaps Shaz, madly fannin her vag with her hand.

The guy gives us a dirty look, like he's holdin us responsible for this drama. Fuck that cunt.

Finally the ambos get here and take Luka to the hospital, tellin us he'll be fine.

'It looks much worse than it is,' says the female ambo. 'A vein in his prostate probably tore.'

'Worse than it is?' I go. 'There's fucking blood everywhere!'

'Not as much as you'd think,' the ambo says. 'There's a lot less blood loss than it appears.'

They treat Shaz's labia by dabbing some sterile wipes on the bite and makin her curse like a motherfucker, givin her some salve for it. It'll heal quickly they reckon, coz the skin round vaginas always does apparently.

Then the cunty guy from the bar tells Shaz to pack her things.

'Go stick it,' she says. 'I've done nothing wrong and I've paid up front. I'm the victim here. I'm not going anywhere.'

'I'll tell the cops that you supplied a minor with alcohol,' the cunt goes, pointin at the empty beer bottles on the side dresser.

'Piss off,' snaps Shaz, but then she tells us she's better off movin on coz this prick won't let up.

I wanna take her back to me new flat, but the bitches I live with are super fuckin anal about guests stayin over, and Mum's place is out of course.

'Don't worry, sweety,' she goes. 'I'll find a hotel.'

She packs her suitcase up pretty quickly coz she didn't get a fuckin chance to unpack it completely. I pull my shirt on over me new dress, which is fuckin ruined thanks to Luka's blood, the cunt.

Out on the street I see the asshole from the bar is leanin out of the stairwell window on the first floor.

'You left something behind,' he shouts down, throwin my pink bag out, literally aimin it at us. The wind catches it part way and twists it, pullin the bag in one direction and the contents in the other, so that the vibrator hits us fair in the fuckin noggin and bounces around on the ground, kickin into life and buzzin madly.

Some of the backpackers crack up somethin shockin at the sight of it, so Shaz gives em the finger and calls them assholes while I quickly pick the vibrator up.

'Great,' I mumble quietly to Shaz. 'It could be rainin titties and I'd still get hit with a dick.'

REBOUND

Even though Dante's actually notoriously anti-drugs, him and I popped some valiums last night and slept in the same bed together.

He's been so on edge about his breakup with his girlfriend – the punk one that he never even introduced anyone to, although Malik claims to have met her one time after his IT class – that I talked him around into popping a pill. It wasn't hard, because I guess most of us don't consider vallies to be a hard-core drug, unlike the shit the lesos upstairs get stuck into. It's more like taking paracetamol, really. Even Morrissey took them regularly, apparently. Return to Valium!

I freaking swear, but, I was trembling at the thought of touching him when we were in the bed, but the Valium soon saw to that and feeling like I was drunk I reached out and stroked his back until I got the nerve to shuffle over and spoon him. Then we both passed out.

Even though he can't sing for shit, he'd sung softly in faltering bits and pieces: '*While empires burn down... ever and ever... I'll be your... I'll be yoooouur... lovermaaaaan...*' So cute and dorky!

In the morning we're just lying here with our vallie hangovers, like our heads are full of cotton-wool. It's better to just keep sleeping it off, which is what we do. At some point, but, I wake up super horny and can't help myself anymore. I run my fingers down his back, across his hips. Even though it's freezing bloody cold in the flat he'd kicked off his dacks before climbing into the bed, so he's only in his jocks now. My fingers glide down his thigh, through the hairs on his leg.

The morning light is a dull blue out the window, the lovely gloom before the sunshine breaks and ruins everything with colour. I love these winter mornings cozying up to a warm body in bed. I'm gonna give Uni a miss today. I can always get notes off someone else. I brush my fingertips over the ridges of old pale pink scars on his arms: relics of his self-harm days. Dante almost always wears long sleeves, so I've never seen these scars before.

It's been so quiet in the flat since Jeremy and Ursula moved out. Jeremy – or Jermy as we affectionately call him nowadays – has gone moved in with Nel and Roz. I suspect he might be using, and I tried to convince him to stay here with me and Ursula but they've been fighting so much that I guess he just needed some space away from her. Ursula took this pretty bad and pissed off back to her parents' place, but she still comes round sometimes to hang out with Jermy, so hopefully with their own spaces now they can patch things up to the way they were before.

My hand glides around on Dante's hip and down over the curve of his bones. He's so thin. He needs to eat more. I can hear his breathing getting heavier. My hand dips down across his belly then down more, finding him hard. So I'm not the only one that's horny, then.

He rolls over in the dark, his lips finding mine, and for the first time – a moment I thought might never come – Dante Halloran kisses me. It could melt winter from the world, it's so good. His kissing gets hungrier, and his tongue darts into my mouth so I suck on it, fevered with lust. My whole body has gone tense.

The love-making is fast and furious, belying the Valium still in our systems, but it's still everything I've ever wanted. He opens me up like the dawn sun splitting the sky in half, and when he cums I'm in love with his moans, with the sound of his voice in my ear.

I could spend days in here and not need to go anywhere. Probably quite literally. If I don't eat – and I'm not hungry so it's a possibility – then I don't need the toilet. With those two needs struck off the list, the only thing I do need is to be made love to again and again. If I'm totally honest, Dante's not the best lover I've ever had, but he's not bad either. There's no-one I want more right now, put it that way.

He rolls back onto his side of the bed, and when he finally speaks it's like he's only just now woken up to some horror.

'Christ, Raven, what have we done?'

Fuck.

Fuck.

Fuck.

'What do you mean?' My own voice sounds shaky, on the verge of a breakdown. But surely I've only misunderstood him. He's gotta be joshing, surely?

'What the fuck is this?' he wails, sounding distressed. 'I shouldn't have done that. I'm sorry.'

'No, don't be sorry!' I reach out in the dark and place my hand on his back. 'Dante, it was lovely. It's what I've always–'

'It was wrong,' he says simply, his voice hardening into hideous resolve.

What the fuck??

'Fuck!' he snaps. 'I feel hung-over.'

I want to tell him that it's the Valium, that it'll pass soon. I can't, but. I'll break into tears if I speak. I'm still feeling shell-shocked by this sudden turn in him, but the shock is starting to wear off. I need to get the fuck away from him ASAP!

I tear off into the bathroom, for some reason grabbing his knife from the floor on the way.

'Raven!' he calls out.

I slam the bathroom door shut and lock it. My hands are shaking, the knife wobbling like crazy. It looks weird in my hands. Dante's knife, the one he always carries around for some stupid reason.

'Raven, open the door,' he says on the other side.

In my mind are two memories playing side-by-side: our love-making, which was wonderful, and then Dante's response afterwards, which was horrible. One memory keeps tripping up the other, over and over and over again.

I could cut my veins open. Run a cold bath and sit in the water shivering, waiting to see which takes me first: hypothermia or blood-loss. I won't be like those idiot cutters, either. I won't cut across my wrist. It'll be straight up the centre, with no hope to seal it shut.

'C'mon, Raven,' he says again, 'open the door.'

He sounds annoyed I'm in here. He doesn't give a fuck about me.

'Fuck off, Dante!'

I test-run the knife across my skin, but it doesn't do anything. Not even the hint of a freaking scratch. When I run my thumb over the tip I understand why: it's blunt as shit. Why the hell does Dante carry around a blunt knife for, anyways?

'I'll break the door down if I have to,' he says, his voice coming from the bottom this time.

I lean to one side and can see his fingertips and nose at the crack below the door. I quickly open it and race out while he's still down on all fours, giving him no chance to stop me. His knife makes a loud clattering noise when I throw it across the room on the floor.

'Raven, Raven, I'm sorry,' he says, coming after me.

I fall onto the bed and start bawling my eyes out, pulling the blankets over my nakedness.

'Listen, I don't know what to say except you're a friend and that's all,' he says.

My heart is torn in two, and his words keep on stinging.

'Why would you sleep with me, then?' I sob.

'The Valium's fucked my head all up,' he says.

What a fucking dead-set shithouse excuse, but.

'You can't blame it on a couple of little pills, Dante,' I sniff. 'That's weak.'

'What happened shouldn't have happened,' he continues, flogging his dead horse. 'I shouldn't have said it was wrong. But it shouldn't have happened, either.'

'You're that repulsed by me, is that it?'

He sighs and stares at the floor for a long time.

The light outside is getting brighter, when all I want is for it to get darker. I wish I could will the sun to stop rising. I want it to stay cold right now. I want to be freezing cold.

'We're just mates,' he finally says, real quietly. 'I like you too much to wreck that.'

Fucking hell. I've heard that line a hundred times from guys after they've popped their load. I expected something a bit more original from Dante.

So we sit and make small talk while the world wakes, and the traffic gets progressively busier outside and the Prozac starts to wake up, with its boards creaking and kettles whistling and footsteps thumping across the ceiling above.

Eventually our conversation becomes a dull drone in my ear, the cotton stuffing inside my head absorbing the sounds on my behalf. Has the vallie gone straight to my head or is life just cruel instead?

'I can't do it,' his voice says, suddenly crystal clear.

I realise I've just asked him if he'd think about committing to me, despite everything that's already been said. As in, be my boyfriend. I didn't even mean to ask it... it just came out when I least expected to.

I don't even have the emotional wherewithal right now to regret it.

'You should really think about what you do in future,' I say with a hint of meanness in my voice. 'You know, so you don't hurt anybody else. Because, dead-set Dante, this really fucking hurts.'

He looks pained by my words, as he should.

'You're right,' he says, nodding soberly. 'You're right, and again I'm sorry.'

I can hear his stomach growling. We skipped dinner last night. We'd been up late talking about life, about friendship and how some pan out the way they do. He'd been looking to get some resolve on what had happened between him and Twix – actually mostly he just kept talking about getting revenge on Twix next time he saw him out, which is going to prove difficult because I've heard Twix has stopped clubbing completely now – and we'd completely forgotten to eat until I finally got the Valium from the cupboard and we went to bed at some ungodly hour because we were freezing. If only I'd just told him to go downstairs to his own bed, instead. Then I'd be spared all this heartbreak and humiliation.

'Jesus Christ, my belly feels hollower than a politician's promise,' he says, a note of irritation in his voice.

'I can make us some breakfast,' I offer.

'No, it's okay, I should get going.'

He gets dressed, facing away from me. That exact gesture itself, after we've had sex together, is hurtful. But he could break my face with his fists and it wouldn't change a thing because I love him.

I feel gutted and completely raw, but, as he walks to the door. On the one hand I'm hoping he'll stop and say something, anything, but on the other hand I'm hoping he'll be utterly cruel and just walk out without another word.

'You gonna be okay?' he says, hand poised on the door-knob.

I nod, trying to will the tears to stop from falling. I can't.

To his credit, it appears to upset him seeing me cry. But it's cold comfort.

'I'll check in with you later, after your Uni.'

'Okay,' I say, sniffling. 'I'd like that.'

He goes out, closing the door ever so softly behind him. His knife is still on the floor but I deliberately didn't tell him because it'll give him an excuse to come back up later if he's already decided to pike out on checking in on me. I kick it under my bookcase where I don't have to look at it.

I flick through the The Smiths CD in the stereo until I get to *How Soon is Now*, because it's the perfect song for right now. I press the repeat button, pop a few more Valiums and head back to bed to cry myself to sleep for the rest of the day and maybe even the night.

...and you cry and want to diiie.

SOLSTICE

Matty's big into computers and everything technological, and he's in with this crowd that hold experimental noise nights in basements around the city, constantly shifting the location around as if they're oppressed or some shit, which they're not. It's just a wank they do so's they feel like they're into this completely underground scene. Matty even tried to start an experimental outfit with Twix once, in the same vein as Einstürzende Neubauten, but they didn't have any power tools for the ear-splitting clamour they insisted was music to their ears. Twix – being the pompous and obviously two-faced cunt that he is – was just into it so he could woo impressionable groupies. Fucking loser.

So despite all that, and the fact that he and Angele's entire music collection consists mostly of industrial and dark EBM stuff, I was surprised when Matty agreed readily enough to come along with me to the Winter Solstice Festival at Davies Park, knowing full well it'd be full of world music and maybe even graced with the presence of the ubiquitous Morris dancers.

'As a favour to you, but,' he goes, spilling his coins over to the bus driver. 'And I'll ask for a similar favour down the track.'

'Okay, but no fucking blowies, though,' I warn him, getting a shit-eating grin for my efforts.

My interest in world music started after we moved to Queensland and my parents – who'd been bevans, or bogans as people like to call em up here – went through this complete turnabout in lifestyle and became Christians, shutting out any alternative influences the world offered up. It was our neighbour, old Jaromir Ristovic, who started taking Rory and I to the Maleny Folk Festival (before it moved over to the Woodford site). Jaromir used to play a *domra* – still does, Dad reckons – which is a kind of lute or something, I guess. Apparently back in Europe he and his wife used to be in bands and would travel around, but she's got cancer these days and doesn't play, so old Jaromir loved taking us boys to the festivals and introducing us to all the different music and cultures that performed. He'd stay up late in the Chai Tent playing like crazy, dancing around as the drummer's circle would bang on into the small hours. Me and Rory would fall asleep on the hay bales, watching old Jaromir's silhouette jumping around to the beat of the tabla.

Mum and Dad didn't mind, so long as there was no heavy metal music present.

One year there was this crazy old fucker with wild hair and even wilder eyes that gave me a cassette tape in exchange for imparting some words of wisdom which he'd scribble down in a recycled-paper notebook that he reckoned he was taking around the world. That kind of oddity was common at the Folk Festivals. I was still just a clueless teenager then, at odds with the world even more than I am now, and so all I could give him was: 'Spooning leads to forking.' It just sort of popped into my head, and at first he was a bit disappointed by it, but after a moment he roared with laughter and gave me the tape. When we got home from the festival I found the tape in my backpack and put it on. All this weird fucking music came out, nothing like the stuff we'd heard at Maleny. It sounded like children speaking in tongues, but the sound was relaxing, and beautiful.

So I kept the tape and played it often, always remembering that if we give then we receive, that the world will always provide if we're willing to do likewise. It was the germination for my strong belief in Providence, a belief more spiritual than religious, the irony being that the old hippie had imparted this to me rather than the religious cult my family had been absorbed by years earlier. My brother Rory never shook off the Christian stuff despite our subsequent exposure to the folk scene, and eventually he got sick of going to the festivals with me and Mister Ristovic, calling poor ol Jaromir a stupid old fart. Not to his face, thankfully. But he hated that people knew we were friends with this old geezer who played weird instruments, I think. People talk in small towns.

Last year I played the tape – the one the old hippie had given me – on my Walkman for a woman at the art gallery in South Bank, just this random stranger who'd been intrigued by the noise coming from my headphones while I was looking at the installations. Turned out she was a cultures expert from the Uni, and before the first song had even finished she'd told me it was a recording of Amazonian pygmies singing. I was fucking floored! I'd always assumed it was made up by a bunch of hippies high as kites and sped up just a tad to make their voices squeaky.

The bus doors slam open and we tumble out onto Hardgrave Road, following the sound of bongo drums down to Davies Park where the Winter Solstice Festival's well under way.

In a way it's a bit like Woodford but smaller. More like Maleny when it first started. I was here a few years ago when it first started, which is how I met Sharon Lang, the first girl I ever got with. Twix is always going on like I've been at it for years, but the fact is I'm a late bloomer with sex. A lot of BPD's are deemed promiscuous, but I developed a snob's taste early on and had a disdain for most of the girls where I grew up. Not hard to, when so many of them were eager to whip their panties off for the school bullies.

I scan the crowds for Sabrinha.

We'd bumped into each other the other night in the Valley, where she's taken over the timeslot that Radio James and Twix had for their goth program (Michael Carlyon's got her old spot and is doing the new goth show). She said the station managers were incensed by Twix's actions. She didn't think it was funny, like some do, even though she's the one who caught them out. But she said it wasn't her that snitched on Twix. I couldn't really care if she did or she didn't. It's the fucking betrayal of that cunt that I care about. Whatever issues me and Nicola might have had – and they weren't very fucking major, rest assured – it doesn't excuse what he did one fucking iota. We had an unspoken rule that we didn't fuck each other's exes, let alone each other's current girlfriends. Fucking cunt. That's why I wasn't keen on introducing them in the first fucking place. He was always panting after my love interests as if he couldn't be fucked finding his own girls.

Anyway, it's Sabrinha who clued me in that the Winter Solstice was on this weekend, otherwise I'd have totally missed it again (I missed last year's one), so she should be around here somewhere. Unless she's still at the Bohemian Cafe up the road. She practically lives in that place when she's not at the radio station.

Matty lights up a smoke and sniffs, his eyes following a feral girl in fluro green faux-fur bikini and leggings.

'Fuck me dead,' he mutters, shaking his head in disbelief. 'Could do with shavin her armpits once in a while, at least.'

'Judge not,' I tut.

It's funny, because when I first met Matty I didn't much care for the cunt. He sorta annoyed me, and I thought his nickname of Malik was way too fucking pretentious. We've even had some really fucking intense arguments in recent times, but he's started growing on me since I've moved into the Palace. While I wouldn't go so far as to say we're mates, it's still weird how all of a sudden he's become like a surrogate friend in place of Twix. In the same way that me and Twix were like chalk and cheese on our differences of opinion with politics, Matty are I are on technology.

Lose one mate, gain another. Providence provides again.

The sun's started setting already and the festival has that magical feel with all the lanterns coming to life and the various tents glowing like caves. Viola and piano and acoustic guitar fills the air, and the people are the far cry from the suits and blouses of the city: there's hand-painted overalls and top hats with sunflowers stuck in em, gum boots and fairy wings and furry leg-warmers. The fruit bats screech and squabble in the ficus trees. The night's perfect. For the first time since I heard what happened at the radio station I feel some sense of peace, and I'm not dumb to the part that nostalgia plays in it, given how I feel like a teenager again back at the Maleny Folk Festival.

This is what having a Borderline Personality Disorder does to a person, apparently. It soaks up every possible trace of nostalgia it can and amplifies it, as if we're reliving the moment again. Our memory of a place (or, in this case, an event) triggers the emotions associated with it and nearly drowns us in it. Fortunately, my time spent at this festival in the past has always been enjoyable, but it doesn't stop the flood of memory, or from me rabbiting on about them to Matty, who seems to tire of being the brunt of my reminiscing pretty quickly.

We head to the bar area and grab some booze in plastic cups (beer for him and wine for me), then wander around for looking at the craft stalls. One of them is full of different essential oils and burners and stuff. Matty suggests I buy some scented oil to mask my body odour.

'Ease up, cunt,' I go.

'Nah, serious, buddy. You smell like a derro. Did Bernie bust the shower nozzle or something?'

'Fine,' I snap.

There's tiny bottles for fourteen bucks or bigger ones for only eight bucks. Seems a no-brainer to me. I trade my eight dollars and douse myself on the spot with the stuff.

'Whoa! What're you doing?' says the lady who owns the stall. She looks startled.

'It's my deodorant.'

'It's lamp oil,' she goes. 'It's not for pouring all over yourself.'

I check the label and sure enough it says it's lamp oil.

'He'll be fine,' goes Matty, waving her concerns off with a chuckle. 'Smells a lot better.'

She still looks flustered, but that's her problem.

We settle down on some bales of hay, across from the entrance to a marquee where a girl on guitar performs on a small stage. Her voice is deep and strong, her lyrics provocative and sassy, and she herself is petite and sweet-looking. A brilliant combo, in my books.

I'm still too sober to properly relax as it turns out, and my mind (and my mouth) keep returning to the topic of Twix and Nicola. Matty seems unfazed that the conversation has returned to these shores.

'I should kick seven shades of shit out of the cunt next time I see him,' I go, borrowing a phrase I've heard Matt use a few times. 'I'll break his fucking teeth.'

Matty rests his head against the marquee pole and watches the girl sing. 'He's a toey little bugger, but. I've seen him in a scrap before, and he can definitely hold his own.'

'Like fuck he can,' I growl. 'He's got a snowball's chance in Hell with me. I'll disembowel the cunt before he knows what's what.'

'Well, he's laying low for the time being, he reckons, so you might be waiting a while for your chance to, as you put it, disembowel him.'

'He can run but he can't hide,' I say, embarrassed that such a trite adage actually slips my tongue.

'Don't put it past him to stay low long enough, but, since he's pretty cluey, actually,' Matty goes, of course. Maybe they don't see each other as much as when Twix still lived in the Prozac, but they're still mates. 'They're thinking about bumping him up to a supervisor role at his security job, apparently.'

'That means fuck all,' I retort testily, because the thought of that cunt succeeding anywhere in life right now just gets my goat. 'Middle management's just the reward for those who kiss enough arse. Crap place to be, being shafted from both ends. The workers hate your guts and senior management's always one push away from crucifying you for one of their own major fuck-ups. Actually, now that I think about it, that's the perfect place for the cunt. A nice little pressure-cooker environment for him to stew in, before I get my hands on him.'

'Yeah, well, while you're waffling on about revenge, a beautiful girl serenades the audience,' says Matty, and he reaches across and pats my arm. 'Drink up, buddy. Tonight, we be merry and hopefully not hook you up with any frigid doggers.'

Sex is the last thing on my mind, which is clouded with constant flashes of Twix's face and mental reconstructions of what he and Nicola probably looked like on the control panel of the radio station. The other mental image that keeps flashing up – and it's the one I'm trying to suppress even more than that of Twix and Nicola together – is Raven's hurt expression, holding the bed-sheet over her nakedness. I toss back my cup of red, immediately suggesting we get a refill.

We head back to the bar for our drinks, then duck into this small marquee just as the rain starts pissing down. The corflute sign out front says DIALOGUE TENT, so I guess this is where all the spoken word and the political essay stuff happens. There's a tall girl with dreads on stage at the microphone, going on about feminism in film and pop culture. Behind her's a large cardboard sign strung between two potted palms. BE NATURAL it reads. According to a blackboard side of stage, this is Jane and she's presenting a talk that she's calling *The Uterus on Celluloid and the Scopophilic Gaze*. Fuck me.

'No chance of a root from this crowd,' Matty surmises.

Matty doesn't believe in feminism. He reckons the stats on men getting higher pay is because there's more men in dangerous jobs that pay better, or they're working longer hours than women. He thinks the movement's an elaborate prank being played out to undermine the modern economy, the dumb cunt.

'You know, there's more to life than sex,' I suggest, to which he gives me a sceptical look. 'Seriously, though. What the fuck is wrong with our generation? We're obsessed with shitting it all up the wall, ready to sit down and give up and let all this pointless shit define us.'

'I think you'll find that's the case with every generation, but,' he says. 'But it's also a bit of a generalisation. I'm definitely not letting it define me. To which end, Angele and I have got it all worked out: the money we saved for the flat's going to our London plan, instead. We're gonna fly over and try our luck there. I'll try and get a job in I.T., but until then I'll pour beers to pay the bills. When you plan properly, it's possible. Simple.'

'Really? You're drinking beer from a plastic cup in the rain hoping to get me laid. Aspirations aplenty there.'

'Keep that talk up and you'll be on your own,' Matty warns. 'You gotta kick the negativity and look on the bright side.'

If he starts whistling and singing that Eric Idle tune, I swear...

'Do you two mind?' a voice booms from the speakers, and me and Matty glance over our shoulders to see the dreadlocks girl with the microphone glowering at us, the rest of the audience turning to see what the fuss is. 'There's a discussion in progress here, so if you've got more important things to talk about, maybe another venue would be more suitable?'

'The music's shit anyway,' Matty yells at her, adding 'frigid bitch' under his breath, and we duck back out into the rain and race across to another marquee where people are dancing to a jug band. A much better atmosphere all round anyway.

We're no sooner in there than we're being followed by a girl from the Dialogue Tent. One of the speaker's fans, doubtless, come to give us the what for over Matty's insult. She nearly runs into us as she charges in from the rain, and I immediately recognise her as Sabrinha.

'Dante! Malik! You guys came,' she says, brushing the water off her shoulders and hair. 'I saw you as you were leaving the other tent.'

'The entertainment was a little on the dull side, but,' says Matty.

'Jane's alright,' says Sabrinha, a bit put off by Matt's snarkiness. 'She's actually a really good speaker, if you'd hear her out.'

Ordinarily any other time I might be inclined to, although I tend to be wary of gender-focused themes from either side of the genitalia divide. People always get this stupid notion that having either a donger or a snatch makes for a deciding argument, when all it does is muddy the waters of true intellectual pursuit.

For example, when I was studying film and TV at TAFE last year our design tutor once asked us what film we really liked, and since I had an obsession with Giger at the time I'd said *Alien*. She'd latched onto that with typical fervour, suggesting it might be the role of an empowered woman in the lead that inspired my admiration. Without missing a beat I'd confirmed it indeed was, to her smug satisfaction, and then added that the dual aspects of powerful femininity being terrorised by the relentless phallus was an irresistible image. Just to annoy her.

Of course, she'd been displeased by my analysis, which was fucking stupid because not only is that exactly the underlying symbolism of the film, but the unquestionable outcome and perhaps the take-home significance was that endurance against the emasculating masculine is attainable. I was, essentially, in my own cheeky way, confirming that indeed the central character was an empowered one and that as much as her sex was irrelevant to her survival against the odds it was nevertheless noteworthy in the film's design. There'd been positively no reason for the tutor to get shitty with me.

I couldn't actually give a flying fuck about the gender argument. It seems so irrelevant to me that one need be more successive than the other. I've met plenty of women who'll always be considerably way more financially, intellectually and emotionally triumphant than I am, and I've met plenty who are not. I hardly cry foul over the state of things. All manner of cunts get wound up debating each other about the finer points of it, falling out of friendships and harbouring bitter resentments.

We already know there's no equal pay or opportunity between the sexes, nor for the homosexuals, the transsexuals, pansexuals and the damned androgynes. It's all been explored before, is being explored, and will again. There's rampant hostility toward the poor fuckers for being honest about who they are, for wanting the same footing as their peers, no question. But that's not me. I'm just a thieving dole-bludger who likes *Alien* because artistically it's pretty cool. I'm not interested in being dragged into a discourse about how the things I enjoy inhibit the self-respect of some insecure cunt who can't simply crack a fucking skull open for being slighted, and be done with it.

None of which I communicated directly to my design tutor, of course. 'I just like the alien,' I'd said.

'Oh yeah, that's rad, too,' she'd agreed, which was really all that had needed to be said in the first place.

'Sorry, Sabrinha,' I interject, back to reality. 'I guess I wasn't really in the mood for a lecture today. Meaning the talk over there, not you.'

'Yeah, I get it,' she says. 'So how've you been holding up?'

I shrug. 'One day at a time and all that crap, you know? Processing the betrayal.'

'Yeah, the depressing thing about betrayal is it doesn't come from our enemies, huh?' she goes.

Malik screws his nose up, looking at her like she's talking shit.

'Well, everyone's the enemy now,' I go. 'Some of you just haven't made your moves yet.'

'That's a depressing outlook,' Sabrinha says, pouting.

'Dante'll be all right,' Matt says. 'He just needs a good roll in the–'

'Hey, don't worry,' Sabrinha goes, playfully punching me on the shoulder, 'you'll meet the right girl someday.'

Matty's got a shit-eating grin on him.

'What's so funny, Malik?' she says, hands on her hips. I can't tell if she even likes him or not. Sabrinha's always been difficult to read.

Matty sniffs. 'This guy's always finding the right girl,' he goes, getting me into a playful headlock and patting my chest. 'That's his problem, but. A vicious cycle if ever there was one. Ridiculous!'

I think Matty's driving at how I seem to fall for girls quite easily. That's something Twix could never see. He always thought I was just a sex maniac, interested only in fucking and nothing more. The cunt even had the cheek to call me a slut, once. I'd thought about glassing him for it, kinda wished I'd had now. The thing is, I didn't have sex with Nicola straight off the bat like I did with my other girlfriends, and not because I didn't want to but because of that same shitty impression people have of me as someone who can't keep it in his pants.

McKay reckons it's my BPD coming into play, that the condition can make us promiscuous. But I know that's not the case with me. Maybe in the past I've been quick to move a relationship into a sexual one, but that's because I'm not really able to make the distinction between love and sex. Although the first person right now who'd step up and try and tear that argument apart would be Raven. I do feel bad about what happened between us, and the thing is she's still talking to me so it couldn't have been that bad, right? Besides, love's just a neurochemical con-job anyway.

'Regardless of what either of you think,' I interject as they begin to argue, 'I don't really need any ol Joe Blo trying to discern where I've gone wrong in my love life.'

'I know that,' says Sabrinha. 'Don't look at me like that. I'm not trying to be smart, Dante. It's that Maddie swears you're one of the most self-aware people she knows.'

I've always thought Maddie to be pretty astute, so if she really said that then it's quite the compliment, because I truly believe I've spent enough years' soul-searching to have arrived at just such a conclusion.

We wander over to a forty-four drum with a fire in it because the rain's stopped now and we chat for a while, or at least those two do. I've turned my thoughts to the eternal question that haunts me: what kind of person am I? I might be self-aware, but I'm still as fucking clueless as ever as to what I'm about. I couldn't even describe myself beyond a physical representation and a list of my interests. The fire's warm on my outstretched hands, and it dances on the faces of the small gathering clustered around the drum. There's a girl with messy braids on the other side smiling directly at me. I can only assume the inner turmoil of my self-identity crisis showing on my mug is perhaps mistaken as being a tortured artist. Which I probably am, too. I'm sure this girl is internally wired to respond to that, just as I'm internally wired to recognise this in her and take advantage of it.

'Watch your hands there, Human Torch,' says Matty, reminding me of the lamp oil I'd doused myself in earlier. I take a step back from the flames, noticing the fumes wafting from my sleeves as the heat dries the rain drops from the fabric.

Matty's done for the night and suggests we head off.

'Nah, I'm gonna stick around here a bit longer.'

He smiles knowingly at me, saying cherrio to Sabrinha. I wonder if he'll detour via the Valley first? Hardly anyone knows this about Matty, but he likes to go to the one dollar strip booths on Brunswick Street and jack off to the girls behind the plexi-glass. He says they get really curious and will come right up close and watch him unload. He doesn't consider it cheating, but he hasn't told Angele about his dirty lil habits, either.

'I feel like dancing,' Sabrinha beams at me, twirling on the spot.

She's got too much energy for me.

'I'm just gonna hang here with my thoughts for a bit.'

'Okay, I'll be over there,' she goes, skipping across to the biggest marquee where some energetic bluegrass fusion blasts out.

'Your girlfriend has nice hair,' says the girl with messy braids from across the fire, holding her breath. I can tell she's holding her breath by the constrained muscles in her neck. They loosen when I tell her Sabrinha's not my girlfriend. She nods at my hands. 'Crazy nails you have there.'

I'm not in the mood for this small talk. It's painful at best. The others around the fire are watching on with amusement as the girl makes eyes at me, until one of the guys pipes up and goes: 'There's heaps of stars, ay.'

A few of us glance at the sky; the rain clouds from earlier have cleared. Still, there's fuck all stars up there, especially compared to what can be seen out in the countryside. The city lights smother the fuckers here.

He makes some quick small talk with the messy braids girl and quick as that she diverts all her attention to him, going off together when he suggests a dance. They head for the same tent that Sabrinha went to but the girl smiles back over her shoulder at me. What the fuck does it mean? I feel my heart lurch, like I've been summarily rejected, and with it comes a sudden, burning hatred for the dipshit with the pathetic small talk. Fucking stars, of all things.

'What a tart,' goes this petite girl next to me, screwing her nose up at the departing couple.

'I know, right?'

I'm happy someone has voiced aloud some disparaging remark or another. I need it right now. I'm not feeling very charitable about the human race, least of all myself.

The petite girl brushes her hair back with her fingertips and binds it with a rainbow-coloured knitted headband. It makes her forehead look huge, and with her big eyes and small mouth and button nose she kinda looks like a Roswell alien, like the ones in Matty's *The X-Files* videos. It actually suits her in a weird kind of way.

'I'm Rosie, by the way,' she says, 'as in ring-a-ring-a-rosie.'

'So, you're like the plague?'

She snorts from her nose as she bursts into laughter. 'No! What a thing to say to a girl!'

'That's what the nursery rhyme is about,' I point out. 'The Black Plague, killing millions of people.'

'Well, I'm not going to kill millions of people,' she says, making a face to be funny.

'Thousands, then?'

She cackles and bumps me with her hip. 'You're funny!'

Fuck, here we go. Am I just bleeding pheromones out here?

After some small chit-chat I've sorta warmed to Rosie, or more like her persistence and strangely charming geekiness finally breaks my resolve at being antisocial. We wander over to the marquee with the bluegrass playing in it, and I notice that the girl and guy from the fire drum earlier are gone. Probably already rooting like rabbits in his tent out on the football oval.

Rosie pulls me into a wild spin and we start jumping around to the music. It takes me a minute to break out of those rigid goth dance-moves and find my old festival self, the fun one that used to dance without inhibition. It's not the most graceful of sights, but it gets my blood pumping and I actually start to feel really good. Rosie's grins are infectious.

An older woman with short, cherry-red hair sidles up next to us, smiling broadly at me. Christ, it really must be pheromones.

The girl throws her arms around the woman then introduces us.

'Mum always took me to festivals when I was younger, so I made her come along to this one for old time's sake,' Rosie explains.

'Nice to meet you, Barb,' I say, and she hugs me.

'You smell...' she pauses, searching for the word. 'Flowery.'

'Frangipani oil,' I go. 'It's all over me.'

'And why not?' Barb laughs, then introduces a guy who joins us as her boyfriend Tom.

He's started balding so he's buzzed his hair down as short as he can without shaving it totally bald. He's very standoffish. A man of few words, though he shakes my hand readily. Tom seems more content to just soak in the atmosphere rather than join in the tedious small-talk. A man after my own heart, but I'm now obliged to indulge the women in their conversation, which at the moment is about how jealous they are of the length of my nails.

Turns out Rosie's camped out at the oval as well, sharing a tent with Barb and Tom, but she's keen to know if I've got a tent pitched or whether I'm headed home somewhere nearby.

'Dunno, I might just do what I used to do at Maleny, and find a stage to sleep on when everyone's gone home.'

Her eyes light up.

'That sounds so cool!'

I guess it does have a romantic bohemian ring to it, but like so many lifestyle choices I make it's one born from necessity, mostly on account of how disorganised I usually am. I'm also partial to the idea of waking up to the dawn preparations of festival life, of joining the other sleepy stragglers in sourcing out the only breakfast option available, usually a noisy fry-up by a die-hard festival stalwart. It's living by the seat of my pants, and even though I'm now sharing a flat at the Palace, there's just no denying the pull of this lifestyle for me.

Barb and Tom call it a night while me and Rosie lie outside on the damp hay bales and look at the night sky while we talk about random stuff. She opens up like a meat pie being dropped on concrete, telling me her fears and dreams and all sorts of shit, a lot of which revolve around her upcoming trip next week to see her biological father in America, whom she hasn't seen for a few years now. She's going to stay with him until after Christmas time and see how she likes it over there. Again and again I have to resist the urge to talk about Twix and Nicola, and finally concluding that it's a topic too tricky steering clear of, I suggest to Rosie that she head back to her tent as I'm going to find a spot to curl up in to hit the hay.

The disappointment on her face is obvious. I've guessed already that she was hoping for a entire night with me, potentially for sex, but my heart's just not in it. Whatever Matty says I'm just not up for mindless sex right now. I'd rather dwell on being bitter and bruised, for which I need to be alone, no matter how cute this alien girl is.

'I might see you around for breakfast,' pouts Rosie, slinking off in the darkness in the direction of the oval of tents and canopies.

My clothes are soaking up the water from the wet hay bales, and I'm wondering if I should head back to the fire-drum to dry off before finding a spot to sleep. It could get pretty fucking cold tonight and I don't have a blanket.

The festival's died down now to just that one marquee still going, but it's only a die-hard crowd in there dancing away feverishly to the music. The bluegrass band's become possessed, pretty much playing for themselves now as some musicians are wont to do when they get into that headspace. I've known of some who could go all night just jamming one long continuous song, feeding off each other.

I choose a tent on the far side of the festival space, able to still hear the fevered music in the distance and glad of its company. The stage is made of sheets of ply timber painted black and slotted onto a metal framework. There's sandbags flung around the bases of the light and amp stands, and one of them makes a good – if not hard – makeshift pillow. I curl up and left myself drift off to the music, ignoring the discomfort of my hip and shoulder bones jutting into the stage floor.

Sometime during the night I'm aware there's someone creeping across the stage toward me. The night is deathly quiet, the music apparently long since stopped, and the boards creak under the weight of my intruder.

'You're going to die,' I snarl into the darkness.

The figure stops advancing.

'That's not nice,' comes Rosie's voice from the shadows.

'Christ, what the fuck're you doing sneaking around in the middle of the night?'

She creeps forward again, running her hand along my body to orientate herself with where my head is. Satisfied with the result, she snuggles against me. I hadn't realised how cold it was, but suddenly I feel warmer now she's against me, even though her hands are freezing cold. She tucks them under my coat, against my chest, and I yelp like I've been burned.

'They're cold,' I hear her pout.

'Yeah, trust me, I know!'

She giggles.

I can smell her breath, sweet and warm, drawing my own mouth toward hers. Our lips lock and suddenly I couldn't give a fuck how cold her hands are as she wraps her arms around me and thrusts her groin against mine.

Oddly enough, when we get down to business I imagine I'm with Raven, that we're making up. I don't know if that's a good thing or not, but either way it's not enough from preventing a premature ejaculation. This girl must really work her pelvic floor muscles out, because she's as tight as a frog's arsehole.

'Shit, I'm gonna cum!'

'No,' she demands, but what's the use?

As pleasurable as the orgasm is, it's offset immediately by the disappointment in her voice.

'Should I be flattered?'

'Christ, I'm so sorry,' I moan, wincing as she frees herself from my still-hard dick, her vice-like grip no less powerful post-coitus.

'I have something of yours,' she says as she kneels above me, rolling her hips forward.

Cooling blobs of spunk splat down onto my groin and belly as she squeezes my cum out. I'd have a fucking go at her about it but after my poor performance I've hardly earned the right to complain.

THE POWER OF LOVE

The wind howls around the Prozac Palace, beating at the thin glass in the window panes and flapping a loose bit of roofing iron above. The noise of the gusterlys ripping around the corners of The Palace sounds supernatural. It brings a chill with it, too, and even with two pairs of socks on and a blanket etcetera etcetera, my legs and toes are dead-set frozen numb.

Frankie Goes to Hollywood's *The Power of Love* echoes through the hallways and stairwells. It's coming from unit number ten, and has been on repeat at excessive volumes for nearly an hour now, heard even above the sound of the wild weather outside. It's pissing everyone off, so a couple of us bang on the door only to be greeted by a bashful Roz.

'Sorry, Raven,' she says, nearly in tears. 'Jeremy's holed up in his room and won't open the door. He's playing the same song over and over again.'

'Ursula dumped him, that's why,' goes Nel from the couch, looking so forlorn it's as if she was the one that got dumped.

I know how poor Jeremy feels, but.

'Fuck, weren't they together for ages?' I ask.

'Since February,' nods Roz, gesturing me inside.

It's crazy how we think four months seems like a long time for a relationship. A lot of people I knew in high-school are now married with kids and own their own homes, and then here's the rest of us struggling with love like we're still in highschool, breaking up and rebounding off each other like it's nothing.

Bernie comes up the stairs, looking at us each in turn.

'Jeremy's holed himself up and is making the racket,' I explain.

He pulls a face. 'Well, we've got to get him to stop,' he informs us. 'Dante's down there getting really worked up about the noise. It was all I could do to calm him down.'

I feel like telling Bernie to go back down and tell Dante to go fuck himself. This is a serious situation up here. Hearts have been broken, though fat chance of Dante understanding that.

I call through the locked door to Jeremy. 'Sweetie? Jerm? It's me, Raven.'

No answer.

I feel for the poor boy. The young ones take heartbreak so much worse than we do, and sometimes it seems to hit the boys the hardest. I'm worried he might do something severe. In my Youth Studies at Uni it's said by the ABS that hanging, strangulation and suffocation have become the prominent methods of suicide in young men this year. I'm beginning to dread the music is to cover the sound of just such a thing.

'JEREMY, SWEETIE!' I bang on his door with my fist.

'Raven, watch out,' warns Nel.

I spin around just in time to see Dante storming into the flat with murder in his eyes.

'No, Dante!' I yell, but he ignores me.

The stupid prick is carrying a bloody great big knife. We all back out of his way, none of us game to initiate a citizen's arrest. He storms across to Jeremy's door and starts kicking the door handle.

'Who whoa whoa!' screams Nel, still keeping her distance, but. 'I want my fucken bond back on this place!'

Dante continues to kick at the door until eventually Jeremy opens it to see what all the fuss is about. The poor darling looks like he hasn't slept in days, but he's just been crying heaps is all. Thank god he's alive, is all I can think. But it must be barely, because the window is open and the room is like an ice-box.

Dante pushes past Jeremy and before anyone realises what he's about to do, he picks the stereo up off the desk and tosses it out the bloody window! The power cord yanks out of the wall socket and *The Power of Love* is silenced mid-sentence.

'What the fuck, Dante?' I yell.

He just spins around and storms past us, muttering something that's probably vile and hate-filled. Nel squares up at him ready for a fight, but Dante just brushes past her and disappears back downstairs.

'That's my fucking tape player,' yells Nel into the corridor, turning to us and staking her claim again. 'That was my fucking tape player.'

Jeremy simply stands in his doorway, showing no reaction to losing either the stereo or the song, but the rest of us are shaking our heads and agreeing that Dante went too far and should buy a new stereo as replacement.

'A CD player, even, and a Frankie CD to go with it,' I add, rushing over to shut the window and stop the freezing wind whooshing in. Maybe it'd teach Dante to be more careful about how he treats other people's stuff. Other people, even.

'It was my tape player,' Nel says again.

'I bought the bloody thing,' Roz says snippily.

'Yeah, right,' agrees Nel, nodding frantically. 'Belongs to the flat, ay? It's *our* fucking tape player. Either way, but, it better not be broken or it's not worth anything now.'

'Wasn't worth anything anyway,' Jeremy says quietly.

'I'd've let it go for five bucks still, but,' Nel says with a little laugh, half-joshing.

The comment about the stereo's value is concerning. They always seem to be getting rid of furniture and whitegoods in this flat, almost faster than they're replaced, which only seems to be when someone new moves in.

'I don't know how you live with him sometimes, Bernie,' I say, meaning Dante.

'It's a test of wills,' says Bernie with a sad smile. The wind howls so loudly it almost swallows his words. He glances nervously at the windows. 'This reminds me of the tornado in 1973 that ripped across Brisbane.'

No-one knows what the hell he's talking about, so he gives up and heads back downstairs, too.

'Christ, we need to get you warmed up,' I say to Jeremy, hugging him and shivering at the coldness of his skin against mine.

'You're freezing fucking cold,' says Nel, touching his skin. 'It's not worth dying over some silly girl. Use yer brain, Jermy.'

Roz narrows her eyes and her chin quivers. 'Get some blankets for him,' she says to Nel.

'On it,' says Nel, and heads into her room.

I notice through her doorway that there's little plastic spoons and foils on the floor, but decide to keep my mouth shut. We all know her and Roz use heroin, but I hope they've had the fucking common sense to keep it away from Jeremy. He's still a high-schooler. If he *is* using, I'll blame myself, but, since I'm the one who encouraged him last month to move into a flat downstairs with Malik and Angele. That hadn't worked out, unfortunately, mostly because of how anal Angele is about hygiene and the dishes, so after tensions down there Roz had offered Jeremy a room up here. It was kind of her to do so, but I'd had my reservations. Still do.

'Just ducking into the loo,' I announce, where I check the toilet paper. I was up here last week and decided to unroll some of it and leave a lipstick smudge on one of the sheets. Of course, when I unroll it two turns now I find the same lipstick smudge. They've barely used this roll, if any, in the last week. Every single person in this flat is obviously constipated from heroin use.

Back in the loungeroom Jeremy's murmuring something to Nel, who replies: 'No worries, we'll get you some soon, matey, just hang in there.' She looks at me guiltily.

I can't really face this shit so I tell them I'm headed downstairs to look for Jeremy's tape player.

'Righto, love,' says Roz from the kitchen, filling the kettle. 'I'll make us all a hot cuppa. Jermy's gonna need some heat in him.'

The boy has been through a lot these past six months. He got into his first ever relationship with Ursula the night after I took them to Toowong Cemetery, so I feel like I helped make that happen. The same night, incidentally, that Twix was trying to get on with the poor girl. At his age that would have just been creepy. Then Jeremy's parents split up and sadly his dad didn't want anything to do with him. Never said why. Then, perhaps for the same reasons, his mother began beating the poor boy. Not vicious attacks, but hitting him around the head and telling him how useless and unwanted he was. He told me about it and I was determined to get him away from there.

Like a fucking mother hen I was. But you just need to look at him to know he's broken and in need of nurturing. First his father, then his mother, and now his girlfriend. He's losing everyone he ever loved and the year's not over yet.

It's really fucking dark outside and I can't see squat. There's very little light coming from the windows of the Palace since it's full of goths mostly and we've put up makeshift curtains of black bed-sheets etcetera. The only light comes from the bogan neighbours' windows, and they're not home, so it's pitch black out here.

Bernie comes outside with a torch.

'This might help,' he says.

'Ta. I think it probably went over here.'

'Getting colder,' he says.

'Don't hang about here, Bernie. You head inside where it's warm and I'll find the stereo.'

'Not me,' he says. 'You. You're getting further from it. Elizabeth says it's over by that fence, under that plant over there.'

Elizabeth is one of the voices in Bernie's head, that's no secret. We can't converse with them as such. He's not got a split personality or anything. He says the voices are parts of his psyche and that they guide him. Advise him and stuff. Of course it's all in his mind, but I humour him when he gets like this, especially when it's just me and him out in the dark. So I go over to the bushes further down.

'Warmer, warmer,' he says as I kick around the branches with my foot.

Sure enough, the cassette player rolls into my torchlight. Result!

I glance up at the window on the top floor and it's hard to imagine how the cassette player made it over here when it went straight out the window. It should be at least about twenty feet away. Funny how that always happens when you drop things. In any case, Elizabeth was right!

'That's amazing, Bernie!'

'Not really,' he shrugs, genuinely unimpressed with how accurate his guess or whatever it was is.

Inspecting the cassette player I can see there's a bit of scuffing and a crack across the shell. Not sure if it still works.

'Better get out of this wind,' suggests Bernie.

I pass him back his torch and we head inside.

'Please don't be too angry with Dante,' he says to me at the foot of the stairs.

'You know I'll always forgive him,' I say quietly.

He grins and winks at me. 'Oh, I know.'

I feel myself going crimson, so I hastily wish Bernie a good night and run the cassette player back up to flat ten.

SURRENDER

Amai and her mates are headed out to the Valley for the night and she wants me along. I haven't shown my face at any of the clubs since the disaster at the radio station, especially since I've heard Dante wants to kill me. It won't be the first time he'll have pulled a frigging knife on me, I'll say that now. He's got a screw loose somewhere upstairs.

Hanging out with Amai might do me some good. Sally's here, too, and her eye is mostly healed. There's just a red blemish where the infection used to be. As a bonus she's acting totally fine with me, unlike last time I saw her when she called me a dickhead. That was a weird night. Or as Megs said, moons and planets all messed up.

We sit ourselves in the garden area out back of Pulse, and get the drinks happening. I'm sticking to good ol regular beer, but some of the others are trying out the cocktails or pre-mixes. Amai's downing the pre-mix like she's dying of thirst, and soon she's tanked.

I go order my third beer, and the gay lad behind the bar twists the cap off and licks the rim. More sodding front than Myers! He grins as he hands it over, so I rub the rim with my sleeve and the grin's gone.

The others are cracking up when I tell them.

'You could've had free drinks all night, maybe,' wheezes Allan, Amai's skinny nerd mate from her Uni days.

'But it wouldn't be free, would it?' I wink at him, and he jumps back in his seat laughing his head off. I've never seen anyone crack up so animatedly before at something so unfunny.

'It'd only cost a root,' chimes in Amai, a big drunken smirk on her face. 'Would it be worth it, though?'

'I dunno,' I shrug. 'I've never fucked a poof, but I've fucked a guy who has.'

I'm on fire tonight, whipping out the jokes to impress her mates.

'But would it be worth it?' Amai says again rather obnoxiously, falling off her chair at the same time. She's just playing around, drunken revelry stuff, but there's a little voice in the back of my mind that says she's actually taking a shot at me.

'Would *you*, for another pre-mix?' Sally asks of Amai, standing up to go get some more drinks.

'Fuck yeah!' screams Amai. Her eyes are slits and her face burns red from too much alcohol. 'I'd fuck him straight.'

Yeah right, I think, but hold my tongue. After the dud lay the other night it's hard to imagine Amai keeping straight blokes straight. As soon as I've thought it, though, I feel bad. She's a mate, has been for a long time. I shouldn't be feeling resentful toward her. If I think about it, the sex was okay.

'So, I want to fuck right now,' Amai declares for all and sundry, and her mates snigger. 'I want to fuck Twix.'

Allan stares right at me with an expression of amusement. 'Why, I think you're blushing, Twix.'

On your bike, ya poonce.

'Who's bigger?' says this chick called Tifany with one F. 'Twix or Clem?'

Amai gives this some thought, and while I feel like running and hiding because her friends are a bit intimidating, I'm also extremely curious to hear Amai's answer.

'Twix is longer,' she finally says, 'and Clem's is fatter, isn't it?'

Everyone grins, exchanging glances, but no-one, including Amai, delivers any insight as to which is preferable. Longer or fatter?

Amai knocks a bottle from the table when she swings her arms wide and throws her head back, groaning out loud: 'I just wanna fuck Twix right now.'

Bugger me, girl, get a fucking grip. She wasn't this bad the other night, as far as I could tell, but now I'm starting to form the opinion that Amai can't handle her alcohol one iota. *Allez!*

'Ease up, girl,' cackles Tifany. She takes Amai into the toilets for a freshen up, probably to gossip about me although they don't seem to have much issue doing it to my face.

Allan sits closer to me, cradling a bottle of pre-mix voddie. 'Amai says you're a security guard, right?'

I nod in the affirmative.

'Do you guys have cuffs and stuff like that?'

'Nah, no equipment,' I admit. 'It's all wrist-lock and that sort of thing.'

'Ah.'

'Why's that? You thinking about getting into the industry?' My beer's nearly done, so if we get chatting in-depth it'll take my mind off it.

'Not really,' he chuckles. 'Just if you had some you could use them, you know,' and he nods his head in the direction of the loos.

I shake my head in the negative. 'Not following.'

He sniggers, peering around at Sally to share the joke, but she's deep in a drunken debate with some random lad about the infection that used to be on her eye.

'Herpes on your eye? Fuck off!' the lad bellows.

'It was, I kid you not!' she screeches good-naturedly. '*Herpes simplex*, it's called. I should fucking well know, mate, I'm a nurse.'

'She really is a nurse,' says Allan, peeping over her shoulder.

'Ooh, kinky,' grins the lad, and Sally slaps him on the arm.

'*She* might not be,' Allan grins conspiratorially in my direction, 'but our Amai sure is.'

'She's what? Kinky?'

'Yeah,' he nods, sitting back down across from me. 'Yeah, man. She loves that shit. Deprivation of liberty and all that.' He sculls the rest of his bottle and offers to get me another beer.

Deprivation of liberty... I roll the words around in my head. It sounds like a fancy way of saying rape, at the end of the day.

'Yeah, rape fantasies, dude,' Allan confirms. 'Clem never told you?'

Yeah, right. I'm sure he knows Clem's not my biggest fan.

It's a fucking weird place to find myself in, because I've always had such a strong reaction to rape stories in the news. When I used to live with my parents, I swore to my mother once that I'd find the bastard who raped a high school chick the next suburb over from us and make him pay. A few years later Mum confessed to me she was frightened of my anger and often thought I'd turn vigilante. 'Leave it to the police, Travis,' she'd always say.

But I was talking to Dante about it once, back when we used to get along still, and he observed that I never reacted as strongly when it was older women that were reported as raped. He noted that the older the victim was, the less riled I became. I told him that it was bullshit, and asked what reason could I possibly have for reserving my wrath for younger victims only, and the prick actually had the front to suggest that I was sexually jealous. Of rapists!

'Not jealous that they're getting to be rapists and you're not,' he'd elaborated, 'but jealous that they got to have sex, by whatever fucked up means possible, with a girl you'd probably find desirable. In a way, you feel protective of the victim as though she could have been a potential partner, and now someone has violated that possibility.'

What a fuckhead, huh? Who'd want to be friends with a prick who'd say that to your face, anyways?

Allan returns from the bar with a beer for me, and Sally screeches at him to back her up on some point she's trying to make against the random lad.

But there was one thing Dante was definitely spot on with: I *did* feel kind of protective of those chicks in all the news reports who got victimised. I really would bash the rapist fucks' heads in if I could. I think any normal bloke would.

But now I had this mate of Amai's trying to tell me she's into rape-fantasies. I find it a bit hard to believe, and more than that, a bit offensive of him to suggest it. How's this hinky prick know anyway?

I watch him through narrowed eyes, watch as he giggles away at something Sally's said. I wonder if she knows what a sick fuck he is? Has this little weasel been with Amai, has he? Is that? Is he jealous of me, of my long tockley, and wants me to fuck it all up with Amai?

The girls get back from the toilets and I can tell Amai's too wasted to keep drinking, even though she demands more and even tries to steal Allan's drink out of his grubby little hands. She settles for groping at my crotch, instead. It reminds me of that time I found her and Clem in the loo at my party. I know she was pretty wasted and he reckoned he'd thought the door was locked, but ever since I've always felt there was something exhibitionistic about that incident.

'Take her home,' Tifany whispers to me, as much to stop Amai from drinking I suspect as to sate her unbridled lust.

I sneakily tip the rest of my beer into the plants behind me, and not much liking the present company, any of them, I use the opportunity of finished drinks to say farewells and take Amai with me. Trudging down the stairs to the street reveals that Amai's actually not as pissed as she was making out upstairs.

'Back to mine, I guess,' I go, and she agrees.

In the taxi home she leans against me with her hand tucked under my shirt, her fingers making circles on my chest.

'So... thanks for enduring my friends,' she murmurs.

'Nah, they're alright,' I say, and she laughs.

'Piss off, fibber,' she goes, sitting upright and smirking at me. 'I mean, you were soooo out of place back there.'

I get the urge to deny it, and then the thought comes to me to just be honest. Care factor zero, right?

'Yeah, I was,' I admit with difficulty, but she looks perfectly fine with the confession. So much so, that I feel emboldened by it. I don't know why I have to be so constricted all the time. I guess I grew up with a lot of rules; work in an industry where there's even more, where there's serious consequences for disregarding them. Amai's bound to her parents financially, but she's constantly fighting against it with a brazenness and openness that belies her upbringing.

I pull her across the seat to me and we start making out, noisily and with no thought of the driver and his mirror.

Back at mine, Amai races through to the toilet and I'm thinking about what Allan said. I don't want another night of half-lame sex. I want to show her I'm up to the challenge of fulfilling her. So if Allan's not bullshitting, then that's where I gotta go. Not sure how to broach it, though.

When she comes out from the loo, Amai's only wearing a t-shirt. Her smoo's hidden by a silky tuft of jet-black pubic hair, but I can't tear my eyes from it. She comes over and rubs up against me, like a kitten. Like a sex-kitten.

Greg's gone on some new age retreat thing in the countryside, and Billy's dancing it up at Options or sucking knobs in the alleyways of Spring Hill, probably, so we've got the flat to ourselves for the night.

'Put your uniform on,' Amai purrs. 'I'll wait out here.'

I whip into the bedroom and shuffle out of my clothes, pulling the strides on that I normally wear for the job. They're not standard issue or anything, just these crap looking things from Target, but they do in a pinch. The only part of the uniform we get given is the shirt. Since we subcontract a lot to a larger company, Cubby Security, we have two shirts: one of theirs and one of ours. The NiteWorks shirt is just a basic navy polo shirt with SECURITY printed across the back, but the Cubby shirt is a crisp long-sleeve shirt, like a business shirt, with their logo on the pocket and navy epaulettes across the shoulders. I choose that shirt for our role-play, and top it off with a generic navy tie and my black Altama combat boots.

Back in the lounge Amai is sprawled on the couch, her legs open, madly fingering her smoo. The inside of her thighs and the bulge of her butt are wet. Her eyes are barely open as she peers up at me.

'Damn! Oh, fuck yes,' she pants. 'Arrest me, officer. I've been bad.'

I feel like a fucking clown standing here in my uniform, expected to play the part, but I give it a whirl anyways.

'Get to your feet,' I tell her, and she crawls off the couch, pouting because she's not masturbating anymore. She kneels in front of me, and though that wasn't where I was headed with this, I decide to take advantage of it. I unzip my fly and carefully inch my hard-on out, trying not to scratch it across the zipper teeth.

Amai falls onto my tockley and half swallows it. It catches me by surprise, but the feel of her warm mouth quickly evaporates any other reaction than sheer pleasure. You fucking beauty! I actually groan aloud. I can't remember the last time I got head. Karen hated doing it.

Amai's really into it, in a way that surprises me.

'I fucking love sucking dick,' she says candidly, before ducking under and taking my balls in her mouth. Thank Christ they've fully healed now.

I command Amai to her feet, which is the direction I was initially going in with this role-play. She stands to attention in front of me, looking delighted by this turn of events.

'Get that off,' I demand, hooking a finger under her shirt and flicking it up derisively.

'Yes, sir,' she says demurely, pretending to look sullen. She pulls her shirt off and drops it to the floor. Now she's completely starkers.

I walk around her full circle once, like I've seen generals do in army movies, glaring at her, giving her bum a smack. I grab one arm from behind like they taught us in the security course, though I've never had to use the manoeuvre, but then reach up with my other and grab her under the chin and lean in so my mouth is up to her ear.

'I'm going to rape you,' I say, whispering so that if Allan's fed me bullshit and I've got the wrong end of the stick, I can always deny it, pretend I said something else. She stiffens, and I'm fucked if I can tell whether I've overstepped a boundary. That sodding Allan prick!

'Say it in French,' she moans.

I pause, slightly shocked that Allan was right.

'You speak French, yeah?' she gasps sexily, practically begging.

How can I say no to that?

'Yeah, no worries,' I stammer, wracking my brain for something that sounds convincing because in truth I only know a few French words.

'Servir le poulet, s'il vous plait,' I mutter, struggling to recall a line I'd learnt in my phrase book. Can't remember exactly what it means, but it was in the restaurant chapter, not the relationships bit. Same diff, at the end of the day.

'Yes, yes, rape me,' she gasps. 'Do some *servir le poulet* on me.'

Now what do I do? I'd much prefer to just drop my dacks and get down to business, but Amai's gone crazy with lust at this foreplay. So I march her into the bedroom and tell her to get onto the bed.

I go down on her, tasting her slit for the first time, relieved that it tastes good. She grinds her pelvis into me, but soon gets frustrated.

'No more,' she goes, yanking me up by my hair. We get into the missionary position, and I guide my tockley to her slit. 'Whoa, whoa, whoa,' she goes, pressing against my chest.

Have I stuffed up already? Am I being too vanilla, as Alex calls it?

'Are you forgetting something?'

'Oh yeah,' I mumble, fishing in the litter of shit in my drawer for a condom. 'Forgot.' I snap the franger on, even though I reckon this invalidates the forced fantasy aspect, doesn't it? My one consolation in all this snatched away by the foresight of unwanted pregnancy.

When we get back into it, rubber sheath securely fastened, she tells me to talk to her. Specifically, she's adamant, about raping her.

Oh, come off it. I'm really not comfortable with this, but I'm also too horny to deny the lady what she wants, so I give it a whirl.

'I'm going to tie you up and then... and rape the shit out of you,' I begin.

This is so fucking stupid. It's obvious I'm an amateur at this. I sound so insincere, for a start.

'No, not you,' she clarifies. 'I mean about other men raping me.'

Oh, fer fuck's sake. What is this? A wind up?

'Do it,' she demands.

Honestly, I feel like *I'm* the one being raped here.

Eager to please, I give it a shot, but the story comes out staggered and deadpan, just useless words falling out of my mouth. Does the trick, though, because Amai's panting and gasping in no time. I'd rather just get down to fucking and grunting, to be honest. All this story-telling shit is exhausting, trying to think stuff up. Eventually I just put myself on repeat, kinda like that CD that night with Nikki.

As soon as Amai cums, I'm gonna call this quits. At least she can't go back to her mates and have a good chuckle at my expense if I get the task done.

But my hips get sore thrusting in this position, so I lift myself up like the cobra position in yoga that Raven used to do. It gives me a good view of Amai's body beneath me. I'm a bit over the rapey talk, so stick some good ol fashioned sex for a change, closing my eyes to imagine Amai with bigger tits.

Suddenly there's a slap across my face, the shock snapping me out of my daydream. Amai bursts into laughter at my expression, which right royally pisses me off. She looks so amused with herself, like she's just being a bitch for no reason.

'Not enough forcing,' she smirks.

'Serious?' I pant, realising that if I don't take charge in this game, then she will.

She rolls her eyes. 'That's just how it is.'

I pull out and she looks disappointed.

'Get up,' I demand.

'Oh, so in charge,' she coos, grinning. 'I love it.'

I push her down onto the bed again, face down this time with her arse in the air. In this position, it looks huge. Spreading her cheeks roughly, I lick my fingertip and tickle her puckered browneye, which produces a little giggle from her. Deep inside me I feel a beast rise up, a powerful lustful urge to take Amai and do to her whatever I want. I snap the condom off.

I position myself over her rear, stretching my leg out and planting a foot on the side of her head, pinning it to the mattress. Her hair feels like super-fine spaghetti on my sole.

'Oooh,' she purrs.

The spit dribbles from my mouth and lands in bubbly globs right onto her sphincter. Bulls eye! I take my tockley in hand and lower myself until it presses against her butthole, sliding myself in with the aid of my own body weight. Amai lets out a long moan, and beneath my foot I can see her scrunching her face up. I wait a moment for her anus to adjust, then I slowly pull back and plunge back in.

'Fuuuuck yessss,' she hisses.

'Shut the fuck up and take it, bitch,' I growl.

She chuckles into the doona. 'Bitch,' she repeats.

The way she says it makes me feel like a poonce. Like she's just taking the piss out of me.

I can't maintain this much longer, and Amai's groaning and crying out in equal measures, encouraging me to go faster and deeper. I've abandoned her rape fantasy for a good hard fucking in the arse, and the sight of her arse up and her face pressed under my foot finally does it, and I start pile-driving like crazy into her as I feel the spoof pump out of me.

We both collapse onto the bed, and if the rawness of my tockley's anything to go by, I can only expect Amai's anus to be really feeling the battering I just gave it. She shows no sign of discomfort, instead lolling about with sweat dribbling down her tits and belly, her fringe plastered to her damp forehead. She's got a big grin on her face.

'Damn, boy,' she gasps. 'You were an animal. Big time.'

After the weirdness of the role-play, it feels good to hear that. It validates me, even though I know she's specifically referring to the brutish way I fucked her in the end. Maybe that's what she needed on top of the talking stuff? Maybe those two things need to get mixed together? Either way, I feel spent emotionally. I don't think I could do this again. It's a sodding monumental effort to go from zero to a hundred in the fast lane like that, to pull up from the depths the kind of shit she wanted and deliver it at a moment when all I wanted to do was enjoy the sex, the sight of her body and her hair and the feel of her pussy on my tockley. Some people need more boost, I guess.

Her arse starts queaving, and I see the bulkhead of my load appear at her sphincter, glistening under the bare bulb on the ceiling.

'You better get to the bathroom, quick,' I suggest.

Amai laughs. 'I thought I'd let you have it back.'

'Not here on my fucking bedspread!'

She cackles and carefully gets off the bed, holding a hand under her arse in case the sperm falls out, and shuffles up the hallway to the bathroom. I don't hear her close the door.

I swing off the bed and face the mirror inside the wardrobe.

Is there a darker look in my eyes now, something others will see?

Nah, it's still just regular old Twixxie, but a bit more exhausted looking.

From the other room I can hear Amai farting and the sound of my cum sploshing into the toilet. Then Amai giggling.

I wonder if that poonce Clem ever fucked her like that. They were together for about four years, she reckons. In all that time it's not possible that he didn't know about her predilection for rape-fantasy. In which case, I wonder how he fared with it and whether or not he indulged it. Cause to be honest, the sex tonight, despite the effort involved, makes the sex the other night very sub-par by comparison. I imagine the dumb bastard couldn't do it for her, unlike me.

It takes a special kind of person to rise to that challenge.

Looking at myself in the mirror, imagining different scenarios of Clem begging or crying about his inability to satisfy Amai when the fact is that I, too, struggled to do it, it occurs to me that maybe that prick Dante is right, that I'm sexually jealous. And of a lad that's not even on the horizon line anymore.

Amai stands on tippy-toe in the doorway, backlit by the lounge light. Her pubic hair hangs down between her legs in a point, like those Misfits blokes, with droplets of water clinging to them, catching the light.

She looks like a work of art, and I can't wait to fuck her again. Just vanilla rompy-pompy this time, though.

DMX PIXIE

The sisters, Jules and Frannie, have headed into the city to hit the clubs so the flat's all ours for the night, which is perfect coz me and the boys have got a fuckin ace night lined up.

James unbuckles the nikko-scrawled flap on his canvas haversack and pulls out a couple of bottles of Robotussin. He puts the bottles of cough syrup down on the floor between us like they're literally holy relics.

'Two? Isn't that a bit much?'

'No, it's not, Pixie,' he goes, talkin like as if he's bein told off by a parent. 'There's three of us. That's how much we're gonna need for a decent trip.'

'Can't argue with that,' says Imp.

'Fair enough, I guess.'

'Get a glass,' James says, unscrewin a cap and sniffin at the lip of the bottle. 'Actually, get one each and we'll go at the same time.'

We pour the fluid into our glasses, and it really does smell like the awful fuckin cough syrups I had as a kid when I was sick. It makes us think: did it really help soothe our liddle coughs or were we literally being made high so we'd forget our sufferin and just trip off our tiny brains, seein Scooby-Doo and Sailor Moon sittin on the ends of our beds and discussin Nietzsche while snappin Smarties in half between their teeth?

The bottle's label says the active ingredient is Dextromethorphan. Just the stuff we need.

'Bottoms up!' calls Imp, and we try and down our drinks in one hit like shots, but neither James nor I can do it, literally gaggin on the smell before we've drained the glasses dry.

'Fuuuck, that's fucking horrid,' whines James.

'Pussies,' smirks Imp, his lip twitchin and giving away how much he's tryin not to show he hates it, too.

'Don't think about it, cunt,' I holler at James. 'Finish it!'

We hold our noses and swallow the last of it, sittin back and gaspin in triumph.

'The shit we do,' laughs Imp.

'The shit we do,' I agree.

We turn the lights off and talk crap for a bit, waitin for the effects to kick in. Imp is the first to feel it.

'What the hell is that?' he says in horror, pointin at a pale-green glow behind us.

It's just me vibrator shinin in the dark on me makeshift bookshelf. I'd stood it up on its end so it could point proudly upwards. That these cunts didn't see it before shows the level of attention they have to their surroundings.

'Looks like a radioactive dick!' says James, uncertainly.

'It is!' laughs Imp.

He grabs it down and waves it round like a lightsabre which gets a chuckle from the room. Then he sticks it in his gob and pretends to blow it. We can see it glowin inside his cheeks. I'm not too keen on the idea of it being inside Imp's mouth of all people, but.

'Oi, cunt,' I go, 'I used that this mornin and didn't wash it.'

'Ew,' says James, 'that means you just went down on Pixie.'

Imp throws it across the room and it shoots through the darkness like a meteor. It crash lands on the other side and disappears behind somethin, probly a pile of old clothes.

'Watch it ya stupid prick,' I snap. 'That's not cheap.'

Imp spits and faux-gags onto the floor.

'And don't spit on me floor, dickwad!'

I kick him in the shin and he cries out, fallin over dramatically and holdin his leg.

'That hurt,' he wails.

'No duh,' I go, rollin me eyes.

'Not by much, though,' he goes, thumpin his own leg with his the heel of his hand, then pinching it with his fingers. 'I can't feel much.'

I test the feeling in me own fingers, and sure enough there's next to no sensation there. Neither hand can feel the other. Me body's gone numb as fuck.

'Fuck!' yelps James, who stuck a finger up his nose and accidently put it too far, the unco cunt. 'This is freaking weird.'

A familiar voice outside calls me name. At the door is Roz, pantin from walkin around even though it's cold outside. Sweat literally soaks her skin, makin the liddle red sores on her neck and arms look disgusting. I imagine them leakin ooze, even though they're not.

'I was in the neighbourhood,' she says.

Roz rarely leaves The Prozac Palace unless she needs to, and I do owe her some money for some maryjane I'd got from her a few weeks ago. I didn't have any money at the time, coz Dad was still being cunt about those withheld wages from ages ago, but Mum has since gotten it from him for us. She was worried I was going to spend it on drugs or somethin but I'd convinced her that now that I was renting I had responsibilities, and she'd handed it over. Stupid bitch.

'Come in,' I giggle, which makes her tilt her head questioningly.

'What're you kids on?' goes Roz, then she comes into the lounge and sees we're sitting in the dark. She sees the bottle on the floor. 'Drinking youse some DMX, huh?'

'Want some?' I ask.

'Nah, can't,' she goes. 'On the methadone.'

'Ah, okay,' I go, figurin the two must clash or somethin. I don't know, we didn't really do our research before gettin the cough syrup. What are we gonna do, let the pharmacist in on what we're up to and get some friendly recreational-drug advice? Of course, the stupid bit is Roz here is probly exactly the person we could've asked.

She laughs and calls us amateurs, but last I checked she was always moanin about how fuckin awful the methadone that she got for free from the clinic in New Farm was compared to heroin. At least the DMX is kinda fun, even though I've always been curious about heroin. She can keep the methadone, but.

The boys know full well who Roz is, coz I've been excitedly telling them stories about her, Nel and the Prozac Palace. Their credentials as lesbians and junkies were enough to elevate us above me usual lot, but knowin an actual working prostitute had gotten us full street cred points with the others we hang out with in the city.

'How about a blowie?' goes James with a stupid grin, actin like a complete retard.

But Roz just smiles like it's meant to be funny, like she's literally heard it all before.

'Don't be stupid, James,' I say.

'Nah, serious,' he goes, actin put off by my scorn.

'Hey, it's just business to me,' goes Roz, holdin her hands up in the air. 'If you boys have got the moolah. Fifty bucks, mate's rates.'

James and Imp exchange furtive glances, the wankers.

'Would you, if I did?' goes Imp, with a nervous tickle in his voice. What's this cunt playin at?

'Sure,' goes Roz, reclinin back with a smug smile. She drapes her arm over the couch behind her, the ciggie danglin loosely between her fingers.

'I've got thirty,' Imp says.

'Bullshit!' I snap. 'Where'd you get thirty bucks from?'

'I worked for it,' he says without makin eye contact, which means I know the lying cunt stole it from his dad's wallet.

'Thirty it is, then,' Roz goes, challenging Imp.

'You gonna do it?' asks James of Imp, a bit doubtful.

'Maybe,' Imp says quietly. 'Sure.'

'When you're done with the sweet-talking over there,' Roz sneers at them both.

'Okay,' Imp goes, and starts undoing his fly.

'Not here, fuckhead!' I shout.

He zips back up and looks flustered.

'Duh, in the fucking bedroom,' I go, shakin me head. I point at Jules' bedroom. 'That one there.'

'Oh yeah,' he goes.

'Alrighty then,' says Roz, hoistin herself up with a grunt, usin the couch for support.

I don't know how old she is, but she looks like she's about thirty, although that could just be all the drugs that makes her look older. And she's a bit overweight, but still, when she tries to stand up it's like watchin an old lady.

Imp follows Roz toward the bedroom.

'Yer not gonna even feel it, Imp,' I scoff. 'The DMX has made ya numb, ya dumb cunt, so why bother?'

He hesitates at the door to the bedroom.

'Something wrong, hunny?' Roz's voice is like warm syrup, but it's tainted with a mean edge, too.

'I dunno,' Imp says lamely. 'I was gonna use the money for some new Docs, but.'

'Docs cost more than thirty bucks,' I say in me deadpan voice.

'Nah, these ones are from Deano,' he says, and when he sees us shrug, he adds: 'From year twelve. Robert's brother.'

I shrug again. I know who Deano is. I just couldn't give a shit. I'm pretty sure he doesn't have any Docs he's parting with, either.

'Your call,' Roz says.

'I better not,' Imp goes, and shuffles back into the lounge.

Roz just saunters out matter-of-factly, movin like a massive ghost, and drops back down again in front of the couch.

'Would ya have done it?' I ask Roz.

'Course,' she goes, poutin her bottom lip out in place of shruggin her shoulders.

'We're still in school,' laughs James.

'I don't know that,' says Roz, winkin at us with a smirk.

Imp's lookin awkward, embarrassed from makin a tool of himself. I'm embarrassed, too, for callin him a friend.

'Is that how much they cost?' I ask. 'Gobbies?'

'What? Thirty?' Roz laughs. 'Nah, but I get what I can.'

'Me cousin Sharon's a prostitute,' I go. 'Down in Canberra, but.'

'Yeah, I think you've mentioned that before.'

'She was thinkin about comin up here for work,' I say.

'She should,' Roz agrees eagerly. 'It's warmer. Easier to get going.'

'She says it can be dangerous,' I continue. 'The clients, I mean.'

'Nah, not really,' Roz says, stubbing out her ciggie butt and pullin out another. The glow of the burnin end draws my attention, sucks me into it believin it's the centre of all things. Fire has that power. 'It just is what it is. Although I've had some close calls, but. It's better off belonging to a parlour for safety. Compassion's the key, but.'

I nod, thinkin how Shaz said somethin similar.

'Why?' she goes, narrowing her eyes at us suspiciously. 'Are you thinking about giving it a go?'

'Of course not,' growls Imp.

'Piss off, cunt,' I snap irritably. 'Ya don't speak for us.'

'You're not serious, are you?'

'Oh, it's alright for you to get ya dick sucked by a prossie, is it? No offence, Roz.'

She puts her hands up in mock surrender and grins, showin off half rotted teeth. 'Hey! None taken.'

'That's different,' Imp goes.

'How come? Coz you're a dude? Fuck ya double standards.'

Roz cackles like a witch, then coughs roughly before regainin her composure. Spit dribbles down her chin. Gross.

'You tell em, girl,' she wheezes.

Imp starts sulkin and James looks petrified that we'll start baggin him out next. They both sit there quietly while the grown-ups talk.

Roz tells us I should think about ditchin these two wankers for some serious playtime.

'Like what?'

She grins wickedly. 'Adult stuff,' she goes, pretendin to jab a needle into her arm.

Fuck, she's talkin about heroin! It has a pretty bad rep, but Roz and Nel have been doin it for yonks and they're okay. Roz reckons the media blows it all out of proportion. I feel really fuckin excited by the prospect, not least of all coz then the guys will tell everyone how I've moved on from shit like cough syrup and xannies. I can literally just picture everyone outside the cinemas on Elizabeth Street talkin about how I used to hang out there but I'm with a cool new crowd now, in a much darker scene. They'd be too chicken shit to even dare doin it themselves.

'Fuck yeah,' I go, and Roz smiles broadly.

Imp's heard our liddle conversation and is lookin at us sullenly, like a fuckin child that's been rejected.

It's clear to me that I've outgrown me friendship with Imp and James. It's time to ditch these losers for some more mature friends, like Roz says.

BR'ER DANTE AND BR'ER TWIX

So apparently that cunt Twix has been mouthing off, saying I've over-reacted to him fucking Nicola and that I'm the one who jeopardised our friendship. Just when I was really trying to let it go and put it behind me, that mouthy cunt just has to go and fuck it all up again.

Why I was friends with that tosser I'll never know. It's probably more like I just put up with him. But that's not true, either, if I'm to be honest with myself. Of course we were friends once, there's no denying it. We had similar interests, got along with each other like a house on fire, more or less. But his arrogance was always something that gave me pause for thought. He'd always boast about his tepid accomplishments like a motherfucker and it really annoyed me in the end. I'm actually glad to be rid of the backstabbing cunt.

But this is just too much, after what he's done.

Megan had told me he'd been mouthing off, and I could tell she'd immediately regretted it. Maybe the look on my face changed and made her rethink the wisdom of making me wise to the cunt's actions, but it's better that I know now so I can confront the bastard and put a stop to it. Which, of course, I will do in due time.

First, I'll have to find out where he's working, make sure that whatever plan I have in mind incorporates a job loss in the process. I've always hated insecurity guards and their bloated sense of self-importance, and Twix is no different in that regard. He swans about in those fucking ridiculous costumes – his security uniforms – like he was The Man, using them to try and score with girls. But fuck me, it actually worked once or twice, though I never knew who they were. Just normals from his workplace, he reckoned. Probably doped-up junkies ready to perform any depraved act for an Ayrton Senna, the fucking sad-case.

'Are you sure there's no hope for reconciliation between you two?' Megs had asked hopefully, and naively.

'Is that a fucking joke?' I'd snapped, feeling a tad bad when she'd flinched. It wasn't her fault.

As far as I'm concerned, Twix crossed a line when he did that with Nicola. He fucking *knew* how I felt about her, knew I was hoping to find some stability in my love-life and make a proper go of it. I'd told the cunt often enough. So, naturally it feels like his betrayal was almost calculated, although Megan tried to reason that Twix couldn't have possibly known it was my Nicola.

'Brisbane's hardly New York,' I'd retorted. 'This is a small city. In scenes like the punk and goth crowds, we're hardly strangers to one another.'

Still, what if he'd not known it was her? But of course he fucking must have. Nicola, punk girl, got rows of small coloured pigtails along the top of her head. Hardly a dime-a-dozen description.

I haven't been going out much lately, just staying at home reading books and trying to lose myself in their worlds. I re-read the Titus Groan books twice over. Stared out the window a lot. Begrudgingly went into the Valley with Bernie to get some grocery supplies. Other than all that, barely showering and eating shit food. Staying up most of the night and sleeping most of the day.

That latter's working in my favour right now because I'll be out on the town all night. I haven't seen Maddie for fucking yonks, and she dropped in today to see me and insisted I come out with her to see the Blitz Babies perform at Crash n Burn. I'm not even into them, but Maddie wouldn't take no for an answer. I suspect her other mates have prior engagements. Certainly I know Sabrinha's starting earlier on the radio now that she's got Ignore the Machine's old spot.

We start the night at the Vic, where the jugs are cheap and the stares are aplenty. Maddie's shaved her head bald now, and has four snakebite piercings and wears faux-fur coats over. Even though she looks like a riot-grrrl, she swears she's not which leaves me thinking she's leaning towards an anarchist influence. She denies that, too.

'How many anarchists does it take to change a lightbulb?' I go, testing her. 'It can't be changed, only smashed.'

She's not amused, which sorta confirms my suspicion she's joined the resistance.

'That joke's meant to be about Marxism, not anarchism,' she goes.

'Works either way,' I shrug.

She lays out her tarot deck and does my reading while I paint my nails with her fluro green nail-polish. It's mostly straight wankers in here so we're a bit fucking out there for the cunts to get a handle on.

'There's some big opportunities for you coming up,' Maddie says, studying the layout of the cards.

'That could mean anything,' I go.

'It's something you've been planning, or will plan, with someone close to you,' she appends.

The only thing I can think of is Roshan, but I've not heard from him for ages. He's either had no projects come up or has been reluctant about including me after I helped him lose that Arts Axis gig. Unfortunately, there wasn't any money in doing that music video for Riz's band (unless the ol 'good exposure' line counts as capital), so that doesn't tally as a favour returned. The other possibility is Alex. She's been doing some photography work through her sister's shop. Maybe I could get on board that as an assistant. I'll have to check with Alex about that possibility next time I see her.

'*Planning* might not be the right word,' she sniffs, sipping from her pot of beer. 'More like *engaging*.'

'I definitely have no intentions of getting married anytime soon, that's for sure!'

'You're not getting any younger, either,' she goes.

'That's all a matter of the mind, though, ay?'

'Like, you're crazy so it doesn't matter?'

She's so flippant sometimes.

'No, but seriously,' I retort. 'Say, for example, if you wanted to go somewhere and there was something in the way, like a great big fucking wall, and the only thing stopping us from getting past it is ourselves. Our own minds. We have the potential to be anything, but we never do. The likes of me, however? No problem. I'm not bound by that attitude.'

'So you turn around and go back?' she goes.

'Go back where?'

'Away from the wall,' she says, packing up her tarot deck.

I shake my head. 'I'm not talking about a literal wall, just using it as an example. But if you wanna get smart, then yeah it's a real wall, solid as shit. But why can't we just walk straight through it?'

'Because we can't.'

I'm thinking back to a time when the likes of Donger and Bernie could've influenced me easily, back when I was actually convinced I just had to believe strongly enough that I didn't need the density of my atomic form and that I'd be able to disintegrate and reintegrate after passing through solid objects. Like walls. I tried to do it a few years ago, convinced when I pushed on the wall of the National Bank in town that the solidity of the stone was giving way and that my hands were sinking through the wall, as if through mud. It was really early hours in the morning, and an insecurity guard across the road heard me laughing with joy at my revelation and stood there shaking his head. It'd broken the spell and I'd been locked out of my revelation, standing once again in front of a solid stone wall.

'We have the possibility to tap into abilities we can only dream of,' I say, 'but none of us ever will. We're too convinced that it can't be done.'

'Except you,' she says sarcastically.

'No, even me. Otherwise I wouldn't be here. I'd have vanished long ago.'

Fuck, I really am starting to sound like Dale Donger now, spouting his *Celestine* shit.

Maddie's pissing herself with laughter.

'The invisible man!'

'Nah, I reckon I'd have become a vampire,' I grin.

'Don't you already think that?' she goes, obviously referring to me being a goth. There's this erroneous belief that all goths wanna be vampires, when in truth not only is that not the case but it's also true that not all goths even like vampires.

'All I'm saying is that if we have the conviction, then it's possible. Take your example,' I indulge her, 'if someone believes they're a vampire strongly enough, then perhaps they are. They may develop behaviourally and physiologically to conform to the rules or whatever you wanna call it that the vampire lore dictates. If I wanted to walk through a wall and I believed a hundred percent in dissolving atoms to do it, it *could* be possible.'

You see, I believe in the concept of things like this, but I doubt the possibility of them. As a concept it's sound; in practice, it's flawed by the constant presence of human doubt. That's why I disagree with

Donger about his theory on human evolution. When I look around, despite this notion that we could become anything we want to be, all I see is us becoming the exact opposite. Striving to be what everyone else is, and making sure we don't stand out. So we constantly limit ourselves to blend in more than the dumb cunt behind us, who's got no ambition to stand out either, so they try and blend in even more, and so on and so on. In the end it's just this great big homogeneous mess of people doing their best to limit their potential so as not to be noticed.

I sometimes think of mental illness as being like a superpower in this regard. Many of us are unaware that our conditions make us stand out, or we're unable to control how much it makes us noticed. We constantly fuck up, lash out, or lose control of both our emotional and mental faculties; sometimes of our bodily functions. We're reviled and feared and locked away, not because we don't *fit in* but because we *stand out*. If Donger ever wanted to try and support his theory that we're evolving into a more open species or whatever the fuck it is that he believes, I reckon he needs to start his evidence with the psych wards, or a trip down to Binkinba. Either he'll think of us nutters as the new and improved version of the human condition, or convince himself that the way we deal with the mentally-ill proves just how backwards people really are.

Maddie grabs me by the wrist and checks my watch.

'Enough chit chat,' she says, 'let's go.'

We finish our drinks and, ignoring the jeers of the other punters, hit the streets. Crash n Burn's just down the other end of the block. Trying to get past the crowd hanging around outside the Metro Arts building means we need to step out onto the road, and some arsehole in a Valiant deliberately swerves to make out he's gonna hit us. He and his dickhead mate in the passenger seat laugh their fucking heads off. I will the traffic lights to turn red so they're forced to stop, but they cruise on down all the way to the turn at the Botanic Gardens.

'How about leaving some room for other pedestrians?' I yell at the Metro crowd, who just stare at me all mopey-faced, the dumb cunts. There's a yellow poster with a picture of what looks like a dead girl on the door that says the movie's called *Parental Guidance*. This mob need a bit of that, I reckon.

They're boggling their eyes at me and Maddie, who for her part is unabashedly picking her nose, one of her favourite things to do to annoy yuppies when she's out in public.

We round the corner and the bouncer takes one look at my nails and scoffs. 'Why're your nails so long?'

'Why've you got no neck?' I immediately shoot back.

Maddie shits herself. We're both fully aware what a mean crowd this can be, but I couldn't give a rat's arse if this guy is built like the proverbial brick shithouse and is covered in tattoos with biker's leathers on. Good manners aren't too fucking much to ask for.

The cunt bristles up. 'The fuck you say?'

Maddie knows me well enough to know I'm simply going to

repeat myself verbatim, so she quickly interjects: 'It's so he can scratch the girlies eye's out when they try and win onto him,' she goes to the bouncer, dragging me inside before the stocky cunt thumps the living shit out of me.

Fortunately, I'm in the kind of mood where I can quickly drop my petty grievances, and allow myself to soak up the atmosphere. The crew from Groovy Gravy comics are here playing pool, and there's a shitload of punks of all descriptions come to see the Blitz Babies. I perch myself up atop a stack of speakers just to be out of everyone's road, so I can get a spot of crowd-watching in. Behind me there's tiny windows with bars on them that look out onto the street. They're up near the ceiling in here, but outside they sit at footpath level, so I can see straight up the skirts of any girls that walk past. I'm checking out what's on view when I recognise a pair of roach-crushers scoot past. They've got distinctive silver skull buckles on them.

Maddie's confused when she sees me leap down and run for the door.

I shove past the punters trying to come in, some of whom look like they'd happily stomp my head if I stayed still long enough. I sprint up to the corner and look up the street, and sure enough, there's the cunt right there.

Twix.

He's arm in arm with a little Asian girl, and they've joined with the crowd outside the Metro, who're starting to pile into the cinema.

He's a dead cunt.

I start running up the street.

The Asian girl notices me and points me out to Twix, who turns and inexplicably begins laughing. He no sooner starts, though, than he freezes and his face looks very fucking frightened.

That's all the satisfaction I need, to be honest, so I come to a stop just a few metres short of him, sliding my knife out of my waistband and letting it dangle in my hand where he can see it.

'This your girlfriend, ay?' My voice is like the rumble of a beast. I flash my teeth in a nasty smile.

The Mercy Seat is waiting, cunt.

'Now just hold on a second,' Twix goes, his voice crackly.

I start to roar as if I really am a wild thing, something voracious, and just as I'm about to make a run at him – to really scare the living bejeezus out of him one final time – the world suddenly explodes in blotches of darkness as something cracks the back of my head. There's a falling sensation and I can feel the ground, I can feel that I've landed on the ground. It takes only a moment for my vision to come clear again, and all I can see is a sideways view of the road and the lights of the cars going past. The building with all those Scientologist cunts is across the road. Where the fuck are they and their street surveys when you need backup, ay?

I try and move but I must be paralysed or something, because I cannot fucking budge a muscle.

'Drop the fucken knife,' a voice demands, right in my fucking ear.

I recognise it. It's the bouncer with no neck, and he's on top of me, the fucking cunt, holding me on the ground. The fucker must have chased after me and king hit me from behind.

'Get the fuck off me!'

'Drop the knife!' he yells again, banging on my arm.

I let it clatter to the concrete. 'There. Now get off me, cunt.'

But the fucker remains where he is. I can hear people gasping and asking what happened, telling each other how they saw me running up the street with a knife in my hand with the big man chasing after me. The other stuff they say suggests they think I was running away from the bouncer. I can't hear Twix's voice amongst them, but I bet he's standing by and watching, like a fucking voyeur.

'Can you call the police?' the bouncer goes.

'GET THE FUCK OFF ME!' I roar.

'Get off him,' Maddie's demanding of the bouncer.

'Call the police,' the bouncer says again, more urgently.

'On it,' someone from the crowd says, running inside.

'Just stay down,' the bouncer warns me. 'Don't move.'

I'm fucking trying to, I can guarantee it, but the cunt's got my left arm twisted up behind my back and is squashing it with his body. The pain in my shoulder is starting to turn white hot.

The cops arrive and the bouncer finally gets off me. By this time I'm a snivelling mess, crying on the concrete, wondering how Twix could have betrayed me and what's become of me. At first the police don't even touch me, and I can hear them hassling the bouncer about why he attacked me until the cunt explains that I was armed so he'd made a citizen's arrest.

Cunt thinks he's fucking Arnold Schwarzenegger or something.

Then the cops talk to me about what happened, and ask where the knife is. The bouncer made me drop it, so there's little point bothering to help the blind fuckers trying to find it. Let some other dipshit do that.

'Where's the knife?' this one copper asks me.

'In my back,' I reply, but I'm being serious. Twix stuck it there.

'Marcel Marceau put it there, did he?'

'Fucking hilarious, funny man,' I snarl viciously. 'Come closer and say that and I'll bite your fucking nose off.'

This sets him off chuckling, but I'd bet if I didn't have these cuffs on and he didn't have the gun on his holster the cunt wouldn't be laughing then.

'Where is it?' they ask the bouncer about the knife, who says he made me drop it on the ground and it should be right here. The dipshits are looking all around for it but can't find it, which doesn't bode well for the bouncer. Then some cunt from the cinema crowd corroborates his story that I was, indeed, armed when I was running towards them.

The cops cuff me from behind and leave me sitting there. Snot's hanging from my nose in strings, so I ask one of the cops if he's got a tissue, but I'm ignored. When Maddie tries to come up and wipe my nose she's warned to stay away from me.

'Are you with him?' they ask, point blank eyeballing her shaved head and fur jacket.

'I'm his friend, yeah.'

They grill her about what happened, asking if she knew I had a concealed weapon. She denies it.

I just hang my head and wait. That's all I can do now.

I wonder if Twix is still standing there, watching everything?

I wonder if he's gloating?

The police haul me to my feet and I immediately go limp, trying to make out to any newcomers on the scene that I've been brutalised. It must be an old trick played out a hundred times, because this older cop just says: 'Give it a rest, mate.'

They put me in the back of the paddy wagon. If I thought the cuffs were uncomfortable, digging into my wrists with even the slightest of movements I make, then the floor of the wagon is killer on my knees. There's rungs running the length of it, presumably so any vomit or piss can drain off the back. There's no padding or nothing, just cold hard metal that digs into my bones.

There's little grilled windows with thick plastic over them on the side of the wagon hard top, and I can see everyone on the footpath but can't make anyone out. The plastic's too thick.

'Righto, see you fellas back at the station,' one of the cops says to his colleagues, and I can make out two officers walking round to the cabin of the paddy wagon.

I'm fucked. They're gonna take me to the watch-house where the other inmates are gonna take one look at my painted nails and think I'm their new bitch. I've got only one trick up my sleeve, so hopefully it's all it takes.

'Not the hospital!' I call out through the mesh window. 'Anywhere but the hospital again! I can't go back there!'

One of the cops turns his head, so I know they've heard me. I read this in a Br'er Rabbit book when I was a kid, where the rabbit tries to avoid getting eaten by the fox by telling him that eating him is okay so long as the fox doesn't throw him into the thorn bushes. The rabbit reckons that'd be worse than being eaten, and because the little cunt's been tormenting this dumb fox all his life the fox thinks throwing the little bastard into the thorns will serve him right. Of course, rabbits live in these bushes, make tunnels all through them where foxes can't fit. So when ol Br'er Fox throws Br'er Rabbit into those bushes, he's fucked up. The rabbit gets away.

Whatever happens now, I've got to try and avoid getting locked up in the watch-house. Fuck, I'll even take infamous old Wolston Park Hospital out at Wacol over that.

The wagon lurches forward. In an effort to stay upright, I've tensed my whole body up and the floor dug deeper into my knees. These fucking cuffs are eating into my wrists, scraping bone, surely. All I'm aware of now is the motion of the vehicle and the agony in my body, with strings of snot stretching from my nose down onto my knees.

PIXIE SHOOTS, SHE SCORES

I'm gonna try smack for the first time ever.

Nel's made the call around, settling on one of her regular dealers, a dude called Brett.

'Fine by me, good sir,' Nel says cheerily to him, hangin up the phone and turnin to us. 'Hope is on its way, gang. He can't come up, but, coz he's got other shit to do. So he's gonna honk three times.'

I want a toke to pass the time, and help me nerves, but Nel's dead against it.

'You don't know what kind of reaction you'll get mixing hammer and choof,' she goes. 'Some people reckon it's okay, others get the shakes and shit. But most of all I don't need anyone getting fucken paranoid when Brett gets here. Got it?'

'That's a fair point,' Jeremy says.

So Roz and Jeremy play cards while I just watch, chewin my nails, or what's left of em. Nel hangs around the window, waitin for this dealer to turn up. Eventually she stands up all alert, and we hear the three honks of the car down below.

'Okay, bitch, cough it up,' says Nel jokingly to Roz, holding out her hand.

Roz leans over and coughs into Nel's open palm, so Nel swipes her across the head and everyone's laughin at their antics. It's good to see em bein so playful, coz normally they're bein standoffish with each other.

Roz pulls the money outta her bra, and Nel grabs the cash and goes downstairs, whistlin a song.

Australia's goin through a heroin boom at the moment, and there's no shortage of the stuff, Roz reckons.

'Get it on any street corner,' she says. 'More or less.'

'So how come Nel's goin to all the trouble of getting it off this Brett dude?'

'Gotta trust your sources,' Roz goes, scratchin at a festy sore on her leg. 'Networking's key when you're buying dope. At the same time that it's everywhere, so are the crackdowns. Makes sense, since one feeds off the other. In a funny way, us users are helping the law enforcers stay employed.'

'In more ways than one,' sniggers Jeremy, like a child.

'So we try and stick to getting it off just a few suppliers, if we can help it.'

'What do ya mean by what ya said?' I ask Jeremy.

I actually don't like the retard. He's about my age so maybe that's somethin to do with it. Apart from Imp and James I don't get along with many people in me age group. Jeremy reminds us of all the boys from school, immature wankers that never take anythin seriously.

'Brett's an ex-cop,' Roz explains. 'But don't worry, he's cool.'

Fuckin hell! How crazy is this? Buyin heroin off an ex-cop!

Someone's boundin up the stairs of the Palace like a bat outta hell and for a heart-stopping moment I think it's a drug bust, but then Nel comes rushin through the door.

'Bretty boy's come through for us again,' Nel says all outta breath, holdin up a deflated blue water balloon.

She breaks it open and there's a liddle foil wrap inside which she carefully unfolds and there it is: a small pile of off-white powder. Me first hit of heroin.

Roz gets the needle and the tourniquet ready. Even though they're sharin a needle, she still uses an alcohol wipe on the spot where she'll inject. She says it's leftover from the disposable kits the community outreach people gave her, so she figures 'waste not, want not.'

'I don't want the needle,' I go.

I've never liked them.

Nel's not happy. 'We're all doing it,' she snaps. 'Together.'

'Fuck off, you're not the boss of us,' I go.

The thought of the needle is literally making us ill. Not coz I think any of them's got AIDS. I just don't like needles. Roz has noticed, but.

'It's her first time, stop being a pushy bitch,' she says to Nel. She waves us closer to her. 'Here. You can toot it.'

Roz gets some out onto a piece of foil and rolls a ripped up piece of cardboard into a small tube.

'Inhale it through this.'

Nel growls somethin, but Roz ignores her, heatin the foil and makin the powder bubble. It smells a bit like the pot-pourri Imp's mum puts around her house. Roz says the trick is to keep the flame away from the foil far enough that the dope doesn't burn. Under her guidance, I put the cardboard tube to me nose and follow the ball of brown sludge as it slips and slides around the foil, inhalin deeply.

The fumes literally smell like vinegar, or that slightly metallic taste when ya lick a battery.

'Ew,' I say without thinkin, sittin back and screwin me nose up.

I thought Nel would be angry at that, but she just laughs and says I shoulda injected it instead, or at least put it in me mouth, then it'd probly taste sweet.

I literally don't feel anythin, except the vinegary slightly-chemical after-taste up me nose and on the back of me tongue.

I'm about to complain about the hit when suddenly I feel it. I feel ace. Like, really fucking ace. I'm rushin, more than on anything ever, more than on molly's or xannies or any of that stupid shit. I feel warm all over, winter's over at last. It's so good. So good I start laughin uncontrollably, but after half a minute I just stop and slump down against the old armchair. Waves and waves of what feels like relief are literally comin over us, warm as the sunshine of me childhood, like bein wrapped in a blanket after swimming all day and sittin next to the window with Charlie curled up against us, his fur nice and warm from the sun. From the smack.

I had no idea that I could ever feel this way.

The other three shoot up, sharin the needle between them. Jeremy looks like he's havin an orgasm. Probly is, the dirty liddle cunt.

Roz moans, then unstraps the tourniquet and drops it to the floor.

'Love you, little sister,' she goes, kissin my forehead.

I feel like I'm home finally, that these people are me family now. Nel's got her legs spread out like she was literally king of the world, her eyes heavy lidded and her grin lop-sided.

'You're floating now, cupcake,' Nel goes.

She's fuckin right, but! I'd tried to imagine this feelin, but the more ya try to when you're straight the more ya just end up tryin to compare what the feeling might be against how ya *do* feel, which is shitty. But right now, I'm literally strugglin to remember any of the shitty problems that made us angry or sad before. None of it seems to matter much, now. There's no comparison, only how good it feels.

Me neck's startin to hurt from where my body is tryin to fold in half against the armchair, but when I try and sit up I literally just fall over onto the floor. I couldn't be fucked trying to get back up, and to be honest it's pretty fuckin good lying on the floor and lookin up at the ceiling. I can feel me whole body pressing into the floorboards like gravity has literally pinned us down hard, but me muscles aren't tense they're totally relaxed. It feels like bein at the beach and findin those shallow pools of salt-water that've been cut off from the surf, the ones that're like a tea-coloured lake. *King Kong's piss* I used to call it. They're always warm from the sun, and ya could float in them like ya were dead. That's what it feels like right now, like I'm floatin in that deliciously warm water.

I must've dozed off at some point coz I'm aware that the light's changed in the room. It looks like there's a fire out the window. The sun must be settin, which means we've been literally sittin here for hours doing fuck all.

Then me guts start twistin, and I can feel it heavin.

'I think I'm ODing,' I go.

Nel cracks up. 'Get a load of it, will ya?' she says to the others. Then she says to me: 'Don't believe everthing the media tells ya. I've never had any mates cark it from smack, let me tell you.'

Despite what she says, I'm still gonna be sick, so I sprint into the bathroom just as it comes up, unloadin my chuck all over the top of the dunny seat. It splashes back up at us, literally hittin us in the face.

Fucking hell.

I can hear them cackin themselves at my expense. I wipe me face with the only towel, hopin that it's Jeremy's but with no other towels here they probly all share. Whatever. I just need this chuck off us.

'All good?' says Roz lazily when I come back out and sit down.

'All aces, cunt,' I go. Even chuck's not gonna fuck my mood now.

'Now we just ride the high,' Roz says, floatin her hand in the air like a boat at sea. 'It's gonna be a great fucking night, girls. And boy.'

I smile at them all; Roz, Nel and even Jeremy. We're all on the floor starin at the ceiling now.

'Next time you inject with us, but,' Nel goes.

A great fuckin night.

DANCING STARS

This is definitely not the turn of events I'd been expecting when I'd stepped out tonight with Maddie.

Even as events unfolded outside the Metro I didn't think it could lead to this: incarceration into a mental ward. True validation of what a fucked up cunt I truly am.

I'd done what I could to encourage this course of action, naturally, once I'd realised the cuffs weren't coming off. Surely it's better in here than in the watch-house?

If I'd had any doubts about that, they're vanquished as soon as I see the receiving nurse's mug when she clues I've been cuffed. She's not happy at all, getting up the cops for it. I'm stymied as to what the problem is, but she's of the stern opinion that I shouldn't have been manacled in the first place. Not going to disagree with you there, lady.

So the cops uncuff me and march me straight to this office, telling me to sit and wait. I snatch the opportunity to rub my face against the coat sleeve of one of the cops, wiping the snotty strings from my face, which cling to his jacket like snail trails.

'Oh, fucking charming,' he goes, getting shitty with me.

'Dry-cleaners will sort that out,' I nod. 'Don't worry, won't come out of your pocket. Tax-payers will happily foot the bill.'

He grumbles something brutal under his breath and stands outside in case I try and do a runner, but when the on-duty psychologist turns up they take their leave. Just up and walk off, leaving me alone with the psychologist. I mean, I've been arrested for intent to kill someone, and now here I am left alone with this petite woman who looks like she could use a few nights sleep, or another stiff drink. Maybe it's not alcohol I smell on her but rather the collective stink of medication, as I'm sure she's around a shitload of pills all the time. They give off the same weird, sweet-vomit smell when they're stored en-masse.

Either way, it's a good sign. She obviously trusts me not to fly off the handle.

'You'll in for a twenty-four hour observation, Mister Halloran, and free to go after that time,' she informs me, insisting it's a far sight better than going off with the police to the watch-house, to which I'm inclined to agree.

'But how come they brought me here instead?' I ask.

'No-one wanted to press charges,' she goes, 'but the police deemed it essential that you get a proper examination. Your sister Madeleine consented for you to be admitted here.'

Sister, my arse. Onya, Maddie! Owe you a beer when I get back!

'No need to look so pleased by the outcome,' the psychologist lady says drily, sliding over a form. 'Sign your consent here.'

I'm more than curious about this place, having never been in a psych ward before, and for that reason alone I scrawl my signature on the dotted line.

She's no more pleased with my compliance than if I'd spat in her eye. In fact, I'm now getting the distinct impression she's not fond of me at all. As per usual with cunts like her – authoritarian figures who think there's a line that needs toeing – she's giving me the once over and screwing her nose up at what she sees.

'Can you explain why you're dressed like that?'

I glance down at my white button-up shirt and black coat with the pin-buttons on it. Her eyes come to a stop on my fluro green nails.

'It's just how I dress,' I say, wondering if she sees the same thing McKay first saw. The doppelganger in me. 'Can you explain yours?'

She peruses a sheet in front of her. 'The officers tell me that you think you're a vampire.'

What the fuck is this shit? I'm dressed more like Nick Cave than any fucking vampire! I actually start to laugh, but the dour expression she shoots me actually pisses me off and the chuckles die off pretty quickly. This cunt's being serious.

'I don't think I'm a vampire at all.'

'You've said it to your friends, I believe.'

Fucking Maddie. Jesus fucking Christ, can't she keep her mouth shut? She was obviously only half-listening to that conversation back in the pub about how people have the potential to psychosomatically think themselves into being anything they want to be, such as these tossers that believe they're vampires and act accordingly. It certainly has no fucking bearing upon the events of the night, so precisely why Maddie's volunteered this info to the cops is beyond me. Maybe I'll rescind that offer of a free beer.

'That's a misquote,' I smirk obnoxiously, because the dumb bitch in front of me is as absurd as her assertions, as far as I'm concerned. I recount the conversation that had taken place between Maddie and me in the pub, but I can tell by the look on her face that this woman *isn't* convinced that I don't think I'm Count fucking Dracula.

She goes through some other shit with me about how I feel and all that, digging around deeper when she's evidently not happy with my answers. I've known of cases of psychologists who've deliberately tried to provoke responses in their clients to try and fit pre-prescribed symptoms. In fact, McKay told me about a report back in the late 80s by a Drew & Holt that even went so far as to suggest that some quacks used idiomatic expressions to render sensitive topics as harmless. The report mentions one psychologist actually used idioms to deliberately make the situation worse so that they had something to analyse. I can imagine this lady doing exactly that, so I'm keeping my answers short and sweet.

Frustrated, she moves onto asking about my medical history. I keep her in the dark about that also, since I've got this massive sense of unease about her intentions. Best to let her think I've never needed medicating. She senses we've hit an impasse, and since it's getting pretty late, she decides to let me rest.

An orderly comes to get me and takes me inside a small hospital ward. I clue pretty quickly that this isn't an ordinary ward, but in fact part of the mental ward. They've done a piss poor effort at disguising it as one, if that was their intention. If it'd been a dyed-in-the-wool ordinary ward, it'd have been maintained better, for a start. I know enough about the mental health sector to know it's underfunded, and this room and its corridors reek of financial starvation.

And then we eventually come to the true hallmark of any mental institution: the lock-up ward.

There's a window on the door with what looks like small chicken wire embedded into it. The orderly buzzes us through. The other side is as unremarkable as the rest of the ward we've just passed through, save for the fact it's even more obviously financially malnourished.

A nurse greets me on the other side. She's friendly, a far fucking cry from the passionless psychologist.

I'm shown my bed for the night, and told that lights will be out in about a half hour's time but that I'm welcome to watch some telly in the meantime if I want.

I'm honestly not tired, given I was still meant to be out on the town with Maddie, so I plonk myself down on the end of a couch in the lounge area of the ward. There's several armchairs and couches here, and a heavy floor-rug, all facing a chunky TV set. Other patients are seated, too, some in pyjamas, their eyes glued to the screen where one of the characters on a rerun of *Northern Exposure* is attempting to catapult a piano across a field. It seems appropriate for the occasion.

This one cunt, though, is staring at me with absolute hatred. I'm inclined to ask the cunt what's up, but decide against it. Wouldn't want to get sedated or tied to a bed or some shit. I'm lucky that all stereotypes of a psych ward have been dashed thus far. After a bit, the staring cunt returns his baleful eyes to the screen, but when Tim Shaw from Demtel comes on to tell us all about a great deal on some knives the staring cunt goes off like a frog in a sock.

'Fuck you, Tim,' he snarls at the screen, his knuckles white as he grips the arms of his chair. 'I'll cut you up, fucker. Fuck you.'

One of the others, a woman in a pink flannel gown, shushes him, and he warns her that she'll be next. She ignores the cunt, however, and eventually one of the nurses comes over and murmurs something to him. He keeps nodding violently, his eyes rolling around the room to see if anyone's eavesdropping. I'm doing my best to but the nurse is too quiet to hear over the sound of the idiot box. Eventually she goes back to her station by the door, glancing back at the angry cunt with a look of amusement on her face.

I've decided for all his bark the dumb bastard's basically harmless. That said, I hope my bed's not next to his tonight, but I needn't have bothered hoping when providence is on my side. Turns out he's on the other side of the ward.

I get a pretty decent sleep, even though the mattress is a bit too firm for my liking.

In the morning everyone's bustling around, full of beans. The TV's on again, morning fucking television programming which I detest. No need for heavy sedatives when you've got that crap on the idiot box.

Half these fuckers are glued to it in such a state of somnambulism that no drug could hope to induce without producing harmful side-effects. The nurses flip their charts and drop pills into assorted sputum cups, placing them carefully with the paperwork and calling each patient forward to swallow them with a glass of water in full view.

When they're all done this young redhead nurse comes up to me and asks what my name is and if I've been prescribed anything.

'He just came in last night, Trace,' calls another nurse from behind their counter.

'Oh, fair enough,' she says, this Trace, then asks if I take any meds at home, since the consulting psychiatrist later on will wanna know.

I've seen *One Flew Over the Cuckoo's Nest* with Jack Nicholson, so I'm straight onto what these cunts are more than capable of. 'Nah, not on any medication, never have been.'

'All good,' she smiles, and leaves me be. I'll have to watch that one a bit more carefully than the others, she appears to have a bit of a crafty streak.

We get soggy cereal in plastic bowls, and afterwards this tall guy with hair like Ray Martin comes in and chats with the nurses. At one point I notice them looking over at me, but the guy leaves without coming over and later the nurses tell me I'm not an 'at-risk' patient, so I'll be moved to another ward. On the way over to the other ward I ask the nurse escorting me what time I'll be going home.

'Maybe Wednesday,' she goes, which comes as a fucking surprise since I signed that form that specifically agreed to a twenty-four hour holding period only. She shakes her head. 'When you sign that form it means you've handed power of attorney of yourself over to the State Government, so you're State ward then. That means if the resident psychiatrist deems it necessary for you to stay longer, then you must. Three days is pretty standard.'

Shit, I'm starting to know how Aurora D'Angelo felt!

'Pretty fucking standard for you lot, maybe,' I snap, and she looks at me sharply. I remind myself I'm now essentially their prisoner, and that I must act accordingly. 'Sorry, it's just a bloody shock, is all.'

'You'll be fine,' she says simply and stares straight ahead, ignoring me for the rest of the way.

The new ward is a lot more like a hospital compared to the lockup one, which by comparison seemed more homely, more lived-in. The beds here are paired off in rows alongside the windows, and there's the usual hospital curtains for a little extra privacy.

The head nurse asks if I've got any sharps on me, which besides my wit I don't. She explains there's soap, shampoo and a disposable razor available for my convenience, but I must ask for these at the nurses' station before I head into the showers. The bathroom is communal, and doesn't lock. She explains that this is for our safety. There's a big red button next to both the shower taps and the bog roll, which calls the nurse in if we're in trouble.

'This is an open unit,' she says, 'meaning you're free to leave the ward and attend activities in the games room or go into the garden.

For your first three days you're not to leave the vicinity of the wards, and after that time you'll be assessed for day leave.'

'What stops me from just taking off outta here?' I noticed on my way over here that the doors to the outside are wide open, and the street – and freedom – is just a hop, skip and a jump away.

'You can try, but the police will be called and when they bring you back, you'll go straight into lock-up.' She stares at me for effect, but there's no ill-will in her eyes. I nod my understanding, giving her a grin, which satisfies her that I'm clear on the boundaries being placed upon me.

One of the things I wasn't counting on was just how frustratingly boring it would be in here. There's fuck all to do, and half the poor bastards in here are incapable of small talk or simply refuse to engage. I spend the first half of the day just walking around, sitting down, watching the nurses stroll back and forth, walk around some more, sit down some more, *ad nauseam*.

The 'games room' is a bit of a joke. There's a ping-pong table but no bat or balls. There's a small upright piano in the corner that's so hideously out of tune I actually quite like the sound it produces. I run my fingers down the keys, delighting at the discordant cascade. The floor has the same puerile linoleum as the corridors, but it's older and cracked in places. Two potted plants by the doorway are in desperate need of fresh potting mix and a bit of sunlight, much like the poor cunts in the lock up ward, I imagine.

I start playing the piano, hacking out my own amateur version of Beethoven's moonlight sonata, but because I'm not musical at all it's hopelessly off the mark. I give the ivories a couple of rounds then give up, letting the sound die in the room behind me. It becomes eerily quiet. I feel lost all of a sudden, unable to even move off this stool.

I'm aware someone's just come into the room. I can hear them on the other side of the ping-pong table, circumnavigating the periphery of the room. They enter into my eyeline to my left, advancing slowly on me. I refuse to tear my eyes from the piano keys, vainly hoping the intruder will just fuck off and leave me alone.

'Needs a tune up pretty bad, ay,' goes this melancholy voice.

'Sounds fine to me,' I say through tight lips, facing the intruder.

He's dumpy, a hound-dog sort of face, all droopy and sad eyed. His shoulders hang so steeply that his arms almost disappear into the rolls of fat that bind his body. Everything about him just *droops*. I feel like I could be sucked down by the same overwhelming gravity if I spoke with him for too long.

'It was interesting, your playing style,' he goes, inching closer to me, forcing me to eventually relinquish the stool. It's simply not wide enough for both of us to share without rubbing shoulders. His pudgy fingers caress the keys, producing an actual song as opposed to the chaotic shit I'd come up with. 'It reminded me of Edgard Varese.'

'He your boyfriend?'

He ignores my jibe, continuing to wrangle a tune from the rickety piano. Whatever it is he's playing, I quite like it.

'Varese had this crazy style that purposefully flouted the principles of classical music,' he says. 'It sounded like he was making it up, but if we let our minds go, we realise it's quite a beautiful sound.'

'I dunno,' I shrug. 'Your version sounds better.'

'This is Bach,' he says, dipping his head down as his hands move like crabs along the ivories. He continues to play a little longer, his head dropping down further and further. This cunt's so into it it's like he wants to physically dive headlong into the piano. His fingers start slowing down and his head bobs a couple of times in that same way people do when they trying to resist sleep. The music gets slower until he all of sudden headbutts the fucking piano, his forehead crashing down on top of his hands, belting out a single chaotic finale.

The room falls silent, and I'm standing here staring at this fat cunt who I think has just died playing the piano!

Jesus Christ, they're gonna crucify me. Is this a fucking set-up? Have they overdosed the poor cunt and framed me for his murder?

I stalk across the room, spying the open doors to the front of the building and calculating how far I'd get if I bolted. I could race down past the park, slipping under the bridge and up over Gregory Terrace, disappearing into the city. I could hide out in the Botanic Gardens.

Too late.

This big bastard steps into the room, evaluating me with liquid eyes. He glances around and sees the body at the piano, and starts laughing his arse off.

I could still make it, even though I've been seen. This big bastard seems like a dopey cunt, and I reckon I can get past him before he lands a hand on me. Christ, those are massive hands. They swing on the ends of his arms like two wrecking balls in repose, waiting to annihilate some poor prick who's just been framed for murder.

He stomps past me, grinning, and goes over to the body. I should run now, but I'm curious to know what he's up to. Maybe he'll do something to the body that will implicate him more than me, and I can simply call for the nurses right now and have this cunt go down for the crime! They might hail me as a hero, pardon me and release me early. There might not be any need for escape, after all!

'Oi, Wazza,' the big bastard says, grabbing the dead guy's shoulder and giving it a shake. 'Wake up, stupid.'

He shakes the body until it groans into life, lifting itself off the piano keys, like Lazarus risen!

'Fuck, happened again,' moans the dumpy cunt on the piano stool, who the big bastard called Wazza. He glances around in all directions, finally seeing me beside door. 'Sorry, mate, happens sometimes. They dope me up with these meds and I can't stay awake if I exert too much energy. Psychomotor retardation, they call it. Bullshit, I call it.'

Sounds a bit like me on that fucking Zoloft I used to be on once!

I wander back across the room, and the big bastard introduces himself as Kieran, though he pronounces it as *Kirrin*. When he shakes his grip is weak, suggesting he's oblivious to just how strong he probably is.

'Warren, or Wazza,' the dumpy guy goes, and we shake. He gives the ivories a quick tickle before turning around on the stool to face the room. 'No need to tempt fate again.'

'What's it good for if not for tempting?' I say, and this elicits a little laugh from Wazza. Not from Kieran, I note, whose eyes swim with non-comprehension as he stares at me. He's obviously a bit fucking dim, this one.

I tell them how I got to be here, and Wazza's sympathetic about my arrest, telling me that he had a turn at home and was too much for his wife to handle, so she'd called an ambulance. 'But I ended up kicking their door so then they called the cops to help restrain me. Upset the wife a bit. Nurses, too.'

'Really?' I find it hard to believe from what I've seen of them.

'Yeah, not meant to cuff a mental patient. They razzed the cops for it.'

So there it is. Turns out I shouldn't have been brought here in cuffs. So the receiving nurse was pissed off for a reason.

'You had any visitors yet?' Wazza asks out of the blue.

'I don't know if anyone knows I'm in here, to be honest,' I confess, assuming everyone's figured I'd be in the watch-house instead.

Kieran starts laughing, exposing massive choppers. I'm miffed that the cunt's laughing at my misfortune, and Wazza reads my expression and quickly explains that Kieran's got an intellectual disability that means he responds to things a few minutes' after it's happened.

'What? Like a delayed reaction?'

'Something like that,' says Wazza, looking up at Kieran. 'Fucking weird, ay?'

I spend the rest of the afternoon hanging out with them, adjusting to Kieran's weird delay thing until it amuses me that he's laughing inappropriately at the tragic things we confess and looking solemn at the things that crack us up. Kieran even comes back from the nurses' station with a ping-pong set, but a half hour later we've somehow lost both the balls. A methodical search of the game's room convinces me that Kieran's swallowed them when we weren't looking.

After a while a nurse comes around and tells us to come to the station for our medications. She looks at me quizzically.

'You're new here,' she says, and I nod. 'What medication have they got you one, sweetie?'

'I'm not on any,' I confess, and she looks really surprised.

After dinner a different nurse on duty comes and finds me and tells me I've got a phone call. While I've never even seen this nurse before, somehow all the staff know our names and faces. I'd noticed that they walk around a hell of a lot doing fuck all, and had told Wazza that it'd be the kind of job I'd want, but he'd told me they were actually going around doing a head count every half an hour to make sure none of us have done a runner.

The girl at the nurse's station hands me the handset.

'Dante, it's Dad,' says the voice on the line. 'What's going on?'

'Don't fret,' I say, annoyed some cunt has told my folks where I am. 'It's no big deal.'

'No big deal? You're in a mental hospital, aren't you?' His voice betrays how frightened he is.

'Seriously,' I urge, 'I'm holing up here for a few days instead of heading to jail. The food's probably worse but the bunk buddies are a hell of a lot friendlier.'

There's a moment's silence before he returns with a reproachful tone. 'Always with the jokes.'

No point arguing with him about it; he's never gotten my sense of humour anyway.

'Does Mum know?'

'Course she knows!'

In the background she shouts out 'Oh, I know alright!' as if that means something to me.

'Listen, I'm fine. Really.'

'We'll head down tomorrow.'

'Dad, you don't have to. I'll be out soon enough.'

He can't be persuaded otherwise. Great; visitors. I've turned into a fucking exhibit.

The guy in the bed over from mine looks familiar to me, and it takes me a while before it hits me: he looks like Nel, but with glasses and an undercut! His name's Glenn, and he says he's here because his father thinks homosexuality is a treatable psychological condition.

'For real? He locked you up because you're gay?'

'What an arsehole, huh?' Glenn lays back on his bed, arms tucked under his head, staring at the ceiling. 'And it's not the first time, either. He's done it before.'

'What does your mum say?'

'Nothing,' he says quietly. 'I love her, but I wish she'd stand up to the arsehole.'

'Fuck, mate, that's rough,' I say, and we're both silent as we think about our respective upbringings. Hearing how Glenn's father treats him makes me realise I'm a bit callous towards mine. I fell out with Dad when I was younger, but in hindsight I can see that he's always cared about me, he's just not always known how to show it. To be fair to the poor cunt, I've not made that easy for him in the slightest, so I promise myself to go easy on him when they turn up tomorrow.

The nurses do the rounds of the wards shushing up every Joe Blo that's talking, reminding us that it's past ten so lights are out. I want to call out that we're not slaves to the fucking system, but I couldn't be arsed. Let the system operate as it wishes. I'll simply fly under it's radar in future. No more incarcerations, lockups, or restrictions for me. Time to get more cunning and avoid this shit in future.

Of course, come the morning they're back to being treating me like a prisoner, with only five minutes allowance to use the razor in the bathroom. I wonder if the nurses have noticed the scars on my arms from the self-harm, and what conclusions they've arrived at that lets them decide handing a razor to me is a good idea?

I do a patchy job of shaving, just letting the hot water stream down as I sit and contemplate who I am. Sabrinha reckons that Maddie once said that I was one of the most self-aware people she knows, and yet I feel like when I try and nail down who I am, my place in the scheme of things, what I mean to people, it feels like trying to hold a slab of butter that keeps melting through my fingers. It would seem easier, I reason, for my parents just to stay home and leave me to my mistakes, yet they're compelled to make the long drive down and the fucking around finding a room at a motor-inn or wherever just so they can make contact with me in a more meaningful way than over the phone. It feels just as meaningless to me, though. I can't say *why* that is, but I can certainly wonder *why bother?*

'Dante?' the nurse calls through the ajar door. 'You okay?'

'Yep.'

'Fifteen minutes is up.'

That's the maximum amount of time we can have in the shower. I want to sit under the water forever, though.

Mum and Dad arrive around about lunch time, bringing with them some Chinese takeaway. Much better than whatever the canteen was probably offering today.

'What happened?' Mum wants to know, so I tell her about Nicola and how I threatened to kill Twix outside the Metro.

'I wasn't really going to do it, though,' I say around a mouthful of battered pork. 'Just, you know, scare the cunt a bit.'

They're not here to admonish me for my actions, though. Their primary concern is when can I get out.

'The doctor in charge tells us it might be next week,' Dad goes.

'The fuck?' I say, nearly spitting my food out. 'Those cunts! First it was twenty four hours, then three days. What next, a fucking month?'

'Easy,' Dad says, glancing around nervously.

'They come past every half hour,' I tell him. 'One went past about five minutes ago. That leaves us nearly a half hour if you've got the getaway car warmed up.'

'Not happening,' says Dad. 'We'll talk with this doctor, explain the situation. You know, what this girl meant to you.'

This girl. Can't even bring himself to say her name, like perhaps she didn't mean much to me after all. To be fair, I never made any attempt to introduce them to her, but if Nicola had just given me the fucking time to I might've gotten around to it.

'I suppose Rory's lovin this,' I mumble.

Predictably, Dad defends the cunt, saying Rory's troubled by my situation.

'He got into the Police Academy, by the way,' Dad says. 'Not down here in Oxley, though. A new one, up in Townsville.'

That'd be the real reason the cunt's troubled by me being locked up in a mental hospital; he's got his rep to consider. What a fucking joke. I can just picture Rory struggling to bunker down with the other cadets, because ever since we were little the cunt's always had trouble opening his peepers first thing in the morning. He'd squint like a Chinaman when he's just woken up, and always hid in his bedroom for the first half hour or so before he'd join the rest of us at the breaky table. Dunno how he's gonna cope in Townsville.

'It just opened,' Mum gushes, about the facility, not Rory's eyes, 'so he'll be one of the first recruits in the new facilities.'

There's a kind of twisted poetry to it – albeit the shitty kind that Twix writes – that that braindead brother of mine became a copper to carry on the legacy of Joh's Pig City, given our father's shady past, but I'm gobsmacked at just how proud our folks are of the cunt.

'That must be such a disappointment to you both,' I say deadpan.

I can picture the father of my youth absolutely going mental at this news, but he's quietened down a fuck-load since those wild days, accepting my idiot brother's new career curve with grace and silence.

'I support him no matter what,' Dad goes. 'You're both my sons. I love you no matter what.'

Suddenly it's not about my brother anymore; he's very subtly referring to me as a fuckup, adamant that it doesn't change anything between us. Nicely conveyed, *pater meus.*

Glenn flies past us, power-walking like his life depends on it. I fill Mum and Dad in on Glenn's situation with his homophobic father.

'Oh, surely not?' says Mum, sceptical.

'It does happen, Mum,' I say, tired of her inability to broaden her mind to possibilities outside of her own sphere of knowledge. 'Quite a lot, Glenn reckons.' I make a mental note to check in with Nel and get some figures to throw about later on if the subject arises again. If it doesn't, then I'll shoehorn it into another conversation and brandish the facts afresh. Waste not, want not.

There's yelling down a corridor and a nurse runs past us. They've got a patient strapped down to a transport trolley who's kicking up a real stink, thrashing around so the trolley's crashing sideways into the walls. Three nurses try to constrain them. I've no idea who it is.

Mum swallows a deep intake of air, choking back tears as she watches on, horrified by the sight.

'Hey, it's okay,' I say, feeling bad about every shitty thing I've said to her or every crap thought I've had. Rollercoaster rides of regret are my speciality. 'Don't worry about it. Happens quite a lot, actually.'

This seems to upset her even more.

'You shouldn't be in here,' she sobs.

I shrug. 'Outta my hands. I'm a ward of the state now.'

'But we're your parents,' Dad insists.

'State trumps you on this one, I'm afraid. Rules are rules.'

For the first time since yonks my parents struggle with their code of ethics. They wanna defy the State Government, but they're not sure if they should.

'We'll talk with the doctor again,' Mum finally says.

Dad agrees, so we finish our Chinese food while the screaming slowly dies down and the nurses can safely transport the patient away to the lock-up ward. As it wheels past I say cheerily to the comatose lunatic: 'I'll sneak a birdbath into you later.'

Mum's horrified, embarrassed as the nurses glance down at me, but they don't say squat. Probably heard the joke a hundred times before. I'll make sure the cunts hear it a hundred more before I'm out of here.

Kieran comes in through the front doors, holding a bottle of wine. He looks so ordinary, like he's lost his way to a restaurant and is now stymied as to why he's in a hospital. He sees me and wanders over, holding up the bottle for me to see.

'Got some wine,' he goes.

'Nice. This is my parents,' I say, formulating a plan to nick a few cups from it without him being wise to it. 'This is Kirrin.'

'Pleased to meet you, Kirrin,' Mum goes, looking uncertain when she hears me snickering.

'It's white wine,' Kieran says, looking proudly at the bottle. I can see it says *non-alcoholic* on the side, fuck it. It's sparkling apple juice, basically. He's welcome to the whole fucking bottle.

'You're gonna get fucking wasted tonight, mate,' I grin.

There's no reaction from him at all, except to smile and hold the bottle out for us to inspect closer. Suddenly he laughs and goes: 'It's *Keer-run*, not Kirrin.'

Mum's confused while I smirk, waiting for Kieran to catch up still.

Along comes the psychologist who interviewed me the first night I came in, all fake-arse smiles for my parents. It occurs to me I don't even know her name. I could call her Doctor Fuckwit, I suppose, but there's no need, because she gets chatting with my folks and it turns out she's on a first name basis with them. What the fuck is this?

'And this goth thing he does, Nancy?' Mum asks her, unable to meet my eye. 'Is it part of his mental illness?'

For fuck's sake. I'd laugh if I wasn't so floored by her effrontery!

The psych looks me up and down, no less unimpressed than she was on our first encounter. 'Not really, Lauren. I'm afraid that's just what the kids are doing these days, it turns out.'

Been doing her homework, I take it. First I was a vampire, now I'm just a kid.

'Are you sure, though?' Mum insists.

I swear, she's fucking adamant that the psychologist should arrive at that very conclusion. I'm surprised Nancy's resistant to the idea.

'Oi, got a joke for you,' I smile disarmingly. Nancy humours me with a half-arsed attempt at a smile of her own. 'Three Ratbags walk into a bar to meet a skunk–'

Mum quickly butts in. 'Enough now, Dante,' she says sternly.

Enough? Enough is enough! If this is Heaven then I'm bailing out, mother dearest.

The psychologist – Nancy, Doctor Fuckwit, Bitch-Face – looks at Kieran, giving him the fake smile. 'And how're you today, Kieran?'

'Yeah, fucken wasted,' he goes, responding not to her question but in fact to what I'd said but a minute ago.

Nancy's taken aback but quickly regains her composure, because of course she's well aware of his condition. She gives me a filthy look, though, when I can't stop laughing.

BIG RED

'There's my bitch!' shouts Abi as I come through the door. 'Haven't seen you in ages, Alex!'

She's right, it has been a while since I've seen her, but I only just got back onto the dole last month. The dole office were shitty at me for, like, losing the solicitor's job so I got penalised with a two-month suspension. Mama's been forking out for my rent ever since, and I've had to take a casual position at a protein powder factory where our toilet breaks are timed and the supervisors are hypocritical about workers chatting when they themselves engage in epic conversations with each other about how wasted they got on the fucking weekend. Also, holding the bags under the chute for that stupid fucking powder mix means I get covered in the stuff and come home looking like a bloody ghost! It's wrecked my platform heel Rocs already. I should've bought some crappy shoes for work. So stupid.

'Money's been tight,' I simply say.

Not to mention my nerves have been shot to shit. There was a big funeral down in Melbourne for my ex. The newspapers reported that he'd accidentally drowned in the Brisbane River, which is kind of true. What's not getting mentioned is that his veins were full of smack, or that he'd come up here to harass me some more. Thank Gaia he never found out where I live. Even the police only had me listed as moving into my sister's place. About twenty officers burst through her front door with their guns drawn, as if expecting to find a hardened crim. They've been cool about it since, but still, it makes me nervous to think my ex's father could pull those kinds of strings.

Abi's working at a sex shop now because she lost her job at the aged care home. They found out she was supplying a resident with porn mags of all things and were going to prosecute her, because apparently he was, like, underage, but she had dirt on them about how they don't run the home to industry standards so they agreed to drop the threat of court if she packed her bags and pissed off.

Naturally that meant no glowing reference from them for the next employer but Chantelle knows the owner here at the sex shop and put in a good word for Abi. I should've also put my hand up for it, but, like, I don't really keep in contact with Chan so she wasn't to know I'm also looking for work. I'll have to stick with coming home looking like a ghost for the meantime, when the protein company can be bothered giving me more shifts.

'Besides,' Abi says, 'they didn't like me having black nail-polish on, whereas the owners of this place actually encourage it.'

'And it's a nice place, too,' I say facetiously, 'especially what looks like cum stains on the front window.'

'Fuck,' she says, slapping her forehead. 'I fucking forgot about those.'

'Just jokes, Abi. It's just, like, gobs of spit or something.'

'Nah, Alex, you were spot on the money first time around.'

I screw my nose up. 'Seriously?'

Abi nods and sighs. 'I'm afraid so. Fucking marvellous, eh?' She ducks out back and reappears with a sponge and a small bucket of water. 'One of the perks of the job is that I clean up bodily fluids. Not too far removed from my old job, at the end of the day.'

I'm like: 'How the hell did it get on there?' as we stride out front and inspect it. 'I mean, I know *how* it got on there, but like, *why?*'

'Some dirty old sod having a wank after closing time,' she says. 'Apparently the arresting sight of a barely exposed arse on a video cover several feet behind glass on a relatively busy road is too much for some people. Gotta whip it loose on the spot and rub one out.'

'That's fucking disgusting.'

There's an old woman at the bus stop behind us, glancing over her shoulder at Abi as she squeezes water over the dried flakes of spunk on the window.

I'm like: 'Things ya gotta do to hold down a job these days, huh?' shrugging for comic effect.

'What is it?' the woman asks bitterly.

'Secret men's stuff, you know,' and I make a wanking motion in front of my crotch, expecting her to smile and wish us well, but she looks horrified instead.

She's like: 'That's why these shops should be banned. It obviously brings out all the degenerates. It's just not safe out anymore.'

Abi throws the sponge down on the ground and swivels around. 'Brings them out of where, lady? They're already everywhere, selling you your petrol or your groceries, building your homes and roads, teaching your kids at school. There's not some dungeon somewhere that contains all of society's perverts who're released nightly to go around cumming on sex shop windows before being herded back to their dungeon.'

The woman refuses to acknowledge Abi's lecture, just turns away and stares stubbornly up the road for her bus.

'Fuck it,' says Abi, kicking the bucket over and, like, spilling the water across the footpath. It flows perilously close to the old woman's feet. 'Let the elements take care of the rest.'

After we head back inside we can, like, see the woman trying to discreetly inspect the window and what remains of the cum stains. Even to the prudish their curiosity for the depraved gets the better of them. The need to *know* is just too powerful. That's the selling power of porn, period.

Abi's like: 'She's right, though, in a way.'

'About what?'

'Check this out,' and she takes me over to a wire stand and rotates it around until a video cover of a man dressed like a dog, complete with a crazy rubber canine costume and all, begs in front of a woman dressed as dog-catcher. She holds a leash like it's a whip. The title is called POUND A PUPPY. It reminds me of Mister X in his pink bunny suit at Ryley's house.

'*If he sniffs your butt, growl him out,*' Abi reads from the back.

'Imagine if we'd seen this at Inferno that time,' I laugh.

'I'd have chucked a stick for it, made it play fetch,' chuckles Abi. 'But this is the section over here. Take a squiz at this stuff.'

There's a small shelf tucked beside the service counter, stacked full of scat and water sports stuff. I'd heard of this kind of porn, but never seen it with my own eyes.

'Holy shit!'

Abi hands me a couple of videos, titles like WHEN THE SHIT HITS THE FRAN where a woman done up like The Nanny from TV stands covered in what could actually be excrement while Piles the Butler holds a heaped tray up of steaming doo-doo.

'Blessed be! People get off to this shit? No pun intended.'

'They sell better than you'd expect,' Abi says with a curled lip.

I'm like: 'Cop a gander at the size of *that* thing!'

In the gay section is a video titled BIG RED'S REVENGE where one guy is about to, like, gleefully violate another guy with a massive red dildo twice the length of his forearm. The intended recipient of this assault weapon is pretending to look terrified. Gotta laugh.

'That's gonna hurt!' I laugh. 'I'm guessing Big Red is how his anus is gonna feel afterwards, never mind the name of the dildo.'

Abi's mouth twitches in a lame attempt at a smile. It's one of those smiles abuse victims get when some arsewipe tells a horrid kiddie joke. I've, like, touched on something bad here, I can tell. I've got a sinking feeling she was raped, maybe.

'I'm sorry, Abi,' I automatically say, frantically shoving the video back onto the shelf.

'What for?' she asks, keen to hide her unease.

'Tasteless joke,' I confess. 'I didn't mean it.'

She seems to weigh something up, then starts telling me a story.

'I was about seven, yeah? In grade two at school. There was a teacher whose name was Mister Easson.'

I fucking hate where this is going already, but I can't stop her now, that'd be just as cruel.

'He was pretty passionate about music and was getting our class to sing in the School Christmas Concert. He wanted us to sing *All I Want for Christmas* by some old guy called Donald Gardner. It was an old song, but it was originally written specifically for a class of small kids because Gardner, who himself had been a teacher yonks ago, noticed little kids were usually missing their front teeth.

'But my class weren't that young and we all had our adult teeth by now. Even me, except mine were covered by my gums, like literally. It was a bit gross, but the thing was that my gums were really strong, and so they just stretched down over my teeth as my front chompers grew down. They stretched so much they became translucent and you could see my teeth behind them. I fucking hated it. I wouldn't smile for photos or anything. My parents went crazy trying to find out what was wrong with me. They took me to heaps of dentists and GP's who thought I had something called Gingival Hyperplasia, but because my gums weren't sore or didn't bleed, they realised it must be something else. Eventually this doctor at the Dental School in the city found out that I had something called Isolated Idiopathic Gingival Fibromatosis. Which was pretty rare.'

'Bloody hell!'

Abi smirks. 'I know right?'

I can't help but take a peek at her teeth when they show. Hard to imagine them covered by her gums. That's, like, some next level shit!

'So Mister Easson gets all excited for the Christmas Concert and that fucking song. Because of my gingival fibromatosis, I'd wished the song had been an absolute failure and never found success, because as an apparently cute gimmick Mister Easson thought it'd be fun to black out the two front teeth of all the kids in keeping with the line *all I want for Christmas is two front teeth*. Naturally he didn't put any greasepaint over my gums so I was the odd one out, a small girl with big, shiny red front teeth on a stage full of kids with apparently none.'

'Fucking hell,' I groan in sympathy. 'I'm sorry, but your teacher sounds like a moron.'

'At the end of the day he was pretty cool,' Abi says, 'but he just wasn't using his freaking brains when it came to the concert. A lot of the parents complained that my big red teeth were a distraction, that I should've been put behind the other kids so I couldn't be seen. When he found out the other kids had told me this, Mister Easson was sad about his role in my humiliation, I could tell. But the damage had been done: the kids gave me the stupid nickname Big Red, like the Heinz soups.'

Now it made sense. Thank fuck this wasn't a kiddie-fiddling story, though! That'd be the last thing I needed to hear.

'Bloody demon spawn,' I commiserate. She catches me looking at her mouth again.

'I spose you're wondering why my gums are normal now?'

'Of course,' I admit.

'They had to cut the gum away from my teeth and cauterise the edges. A wad of gauze behind my teeth was meant to catch all the blood, but I swear I could taste some down the back of my throat. More than that, I could smell and taste the burning. I couldn't shake that smell for years, probably not until I hit puberty. After they cauterised the edges, they sewed in some subpapillary sling surtures,' – she struggles with the words, like they're a tongue twister – 'to pull the gum flaps up around my teeth and shape them into the lovely gums I have today.'

She flashes me a big, chessy grin for effect.

'Then they packed what looked like putty all over my gums, which they called a periodontal dressing, basically a zinc oxide paste that hardened and protected my surgery from infection. It looked like a lump of white dog shit after it's been bleached in the sun for a month. I wore that for a week, and it made my mouth bulge like a cartoon monkey. The whole thing was a fucking traumatic experience for a small girl, no matter how professional they were about it.'

Even though it happened when she was a kid, I can, like, tell by her voice that the whole thing's made a lasting impact on her.

'I'm so sorry to hear that, Abi.'

She shrugs her shoulders up to her ears and smiles in a goofy way.

'Never did get my revenge,' she smiles, looking at the video cover of *Big Red's Revenge.*

'Come here, you buttmunch,' I say, holding my arms out for a hug. Finally I feel like we're proper best friends, even though we haven't seen each other for a while.

I can hear sneakers squeaking on the lino and we look around to see this guy, like, staring at us with a big fucking grin on his face.

He's like: 'Cool, free floor show.'

'Fuck off, idiot,' I snap, relinquishing Abi who savagely asks the guy what he fucking well wants.

He's a bit stunned by her outburst, stammering: 'J-just some head cleaner.'

Abi sells him an unmarked 20mil bottle from under the counter. He slinks away but steals a couple of glances at us as he goes out the door, like he's trying to picture us making out with each other.

'You sell them video head cleaner for their machines, too?' I almost laugh. 'What next? VCR's themselves?'

'It's not head cleaner,' she reveals, setting me straight. 'It's amyl nitrite. Poppers. It's the ant's pants, trust me. But it's illegal to sell it so we pretend we're selling head cleaner fluid. The customer's know what to ask for, but we have some legit VHS head cleaner down here in case an undercover cop comes in asking, which they've done.'

'How do you know when they're an undercover cop?'

'If they're suss, I ask them to show me the palms of their hands,' she explains. 'If they're real customers, they'll ask the fuck why, and if they're cops they'll do it no questions asked.'

I don't get the significance of this, but Abi smirks like it's obvious so I figure I'll work it out on my own later.

'And it's not a gay drug, either,' she says defensively. 'Everyone thinks that, especially because in the Eighties it got blamed for all the gay guys not keeping their cocks in their pants and copping AIDS as a result.'

I'm like: 'Dumb question, but I guess you've taken it?'

She smiles sheepishly. 'Regular subscriber when they're within such easy reach.'

'Typical Abi,' I laugh affectionately.

'Anyway, it helps me to better inform the customer on the pros and cons of their purchasing decisions.'

We have a good chuckle. It's good to catch up again. We need to make this more of a regular thing again.

'Hey, did you hear about Dante going into the mental hospital?' I ask her, brimming with goss.

'Oh my Gawd, yes, but only a rumour,' she says excitedly. 'What the fuck happened? I heard he strangled Twix in broad daylight!'

'Not quite as bad as that,' I begin. 'Dante was at Crash n Burn and saw Twix at that indie cinema around the corner, so he chased after him with a big knife. But then he got wrestled to the ground by this bouncer. Apparently it was bonkers!'

'Full on!'

'Twix was on a date with some Asian girl and was shitting bricks, or so I've heard,' I grin.

Abi nods and is like: 'As he would be. I know I would. Fucking hell, that Dante's a psycho. He's mad as a cut snake.'

'So apparently the girl Dante was with kicked his knife down the drain and the police didn't even see it, so he got, like, locked up in the mental ward. Needless to say, Twix has gone to ground again; won't show his face in public any more.'

'Takes all sorts,' says Abi, shaking her head. She pauses and in a low voice says: 'Like this cockwomble, for example.' She nods in the direction of a blonde bloke in the far corner, perusing one of the video shelves. He seems pretty unremarkable.

'What about him?'

This must be another of these things that's meant to be obvious.

Abi's like: 'Follow me,' and grabs a broom.

As we round the corner of the shelf he sees us, and he looks guilty as. But I can't believe it because he's, like, actually got his dick out and is having a wank to the video covers! Bloody hell, on the fucking windows at night after closing time is one thing, but right here in the fucking shop, for pity's sake?

Abi says not a word, just runs at him swinging the broom through the air, aiming for his groin. The bloke shits himself, bolting for the front door without even tucking himself back in.

Abi's dropping a string of expletives when she comes back in, then sees my expression and starts giggling.

'The look on your mug right now,' she says. 'I swear.'

'I'm just gobsmacked he had the balls to do that in broad daylight!'

'He nearly lost those same balls, if I'd been quick enough,' smirks Abi. 'You get a feel for what the customers are doing, and that one had jerkoff written all over him. Also, his shoulder was shaking; telltale sign of a guy having a wank.'

'Doesn't seem safe to be working here on your own.'

'No problem,' she says with a grin. 'Let them try anything. I'll fucking finish them.'

This is a side to Abi I've never seen, but I like it! I wonder if Chantelle's rubbing off on her?

'Now, how's about we celebrate our victory over the wankers of the world?'

She hoiks up a couple of bottles of poppers and instructs me how to, like, break the seal, the best way to inhale, how the less exposure to air the bottle's contents get the stronger it remains for later on, and the various names for it, such as *animal* in the UK and *cum* in the US.

'I never thought I'd get high from cum,' I snort, and we burst into fits of laughter just as some poor bastard comes into the shop and looks super uncomfortable.

CHARON'S TORMENTS

I'm bored now, bored of the same faces doing the same repetitive shit. The nurses, the other patients, the fucking daytime TV. It's all become banal. The only relief is Wazza, who's a lot smarter than he seems, if he can stay awake long enough, that is. The poor cunt's so doped up it takes all he's got to hold a conversation, and the effort required to withstand the effect of the medication usually trips him up anyway.

Even though it's been a week already the folks are still around, forking out more than I think they can probably afford in hotel costs. They've grown more accustomed to the atmosphere of the psych wards, and have even been bringing in snacks for Kieran who they've developed a soft spot for. I think they're treating him more like a pet, like a curiosity, but that's none of my business. He's happy with the apple pies and shit they bring him, so no harm done.

However, their next visit is a strain on the old patience.

'Rory's told us about what you and Dale get up to with the police,' Mum goes, 'leading them on wild goose chases. What's it called?'

Fucking Rory and his big mouth. It's not even remotely relatable to why I'm in here, and he fucking well knows it. It's not like he's not fucked around with his mates and gotten into shit before.

'*Piggy Run,*' Dad goes.

'Oh for fuck's sake,' I moan. 'That's just a game.'

Dad nods, disappointed. 'That's right. It's all just a game to you, isn't it Dante? Is this how we've raised you? To laugh at everything?'

'What else can I fucking well do?' I retort angrily. 'Have you not noticed we've inherited the vacuousness of your generation's excesses and we don't know what to do with it? We're desperately trying to shake it off while claiming an identity for ourselves, but there's none on sale. The bargain bin's fucking empty!'

Dad sighs and Mum fidgets nervously. They don't understand this talk. They've forgotten what it's like to be young and trying to find a place in the world, how it's difficult and confusing when everything keeps changing and not for the better, either. We're increasingly told that the world wants to be digital, that we have to find our inspiration in a cyberspace where nothing's real but everything that happens there will eventually have real-world consequences. I don't even know anyone who owns a fucking computer! Even Matty doesn't, and he's studying the bastards. Mental illness diagnoses are on the rise and, like the goth scene, are branching off into ever-increasing sub-genres, their signs and symptoms joining like a massive spiderweb whose strands have become so interconnected that the whole web is a tangled mess.

There's fucking pills to treat everything now, and no hesitation to prescribe them willy nilly. Hand-in-hand with the rise of new types of mental illness are the stigmas around them, with the Mental Health Module of the General Social Survey confirming that the notion of mentally people as violent psychopaths has actually increased in this apparently enlightened decade. I thought this newfangled wide world web that no-one's evidently using is meant to be a place of learning?

The World Psychiatric Association's released an anti-stigma plan for combating these perceptions. *Open the Doors*, they've called it, but so far all I've seen is society pushing as hard as it can to close the fucking doors again. The Australian Government launched a *National Mental Health Plan*, recognising the impact that these illnesses have upon the community. We've got the *Mental Health Act of Western Australia* to define the dos and don'ts of dealing with the problem, Queensland's *The Ten Year Mental Health Strategy* (wherein Wolston Park's now called The Park Centre for Mental Health making it sound like a fucking day centre for yuppies), the *National Standards for Mental Health Services* in Victoria, the list goes on and on. There's subsidised bodies and proposed legislations, Government strategies galore, but we're still in the fucking dark ages when it comes to dealing one-on-one with someone who has a mental illness.

Just thinking about the whole thing's enough to drive me insane. The Inferno has a good chuckle at this.

The Inferno's the nickname I've given to my Borderline Personality Disorder. In the same vein as Bernie bestowing names upon the twin entities that reside inside his noggin, I've decided to reimagine my condition also as a tangible entity, albeit only one that I can mentally visualise, one that constantly goads me into doing or saying shit that I'll later regret. The Inferno seems appropriate, given how it can make me explode with rage at the smallest things, like being stared at or disagreed with when I fucking well know I'm right.

It's a good little trick to ascribe the more hideous manifestations of my condition to an apparently external source, insofar as a mental illness can be described as external, but external from my core self at least. It's hard to know sometimes where my true actions or thoughts end and the BPD begins, if there even is such a distinction. I need some method of drawing a metaphorical line in the allegorical sand and recognising that I'm on one side and my condition's on the other, so as not to overly blame myself for the actions that my BPD causes, thusly allowing myself to learn how to minimise those destructive behaviours.

Also, coming up with this notion inside a mental hospital seems appropriate, like I'll leave a little more crazy than when I came in. The perfect footnote, I reckon, on Doctor Nancy Fuckwit's career as a clinical psychologist.

The next day proves my folks have worked overtime, because they come round for their daily visit and tell me that I'm free to go.

'Yeah, we had a chat with one of the head doctors,' Dad goes. 'We told him that there's two sides to a story and that you've been under pressure since you and Nicola broke up. He saw reason in the end.'

Funny how such a simple, petty human thing like a breakup is enough to get you out of a mental ward. Of course, coming from Mum and Dad – who the hospital staff are naturally inclined to believe are more sane than I am despite the dark shadow of a fucked Christian ideology looming large in their psyches – makes all the difference.

I say farewell to Wazza and Kieran, but can't find Glenn anywhere, the guy that looks like Nel. Probably doing laps of the wards. I'd found out later that the cunt is schizophrenic and that's why he's really in here, not because his father locked him for being a fudge-packer. Glenn's schizophrenia's why he power-walks everywhere so much that he's cracked his feel open. I hadn't noticed the first time I'd met him because he'd had his feet under his bed-covers, but a few days later Glenn had come and sat next to me and I'd noticed that his heels were split open. A couple of centimetres deep in some places. I could see the meatus of his feet inside those cracks.

It feels weird getting out. I may have only been in there for a week but it feels like three, easily. Nah, if I'm honest, it feels like longer. It feels like my history has been stripped off me and there was only the hospital time, this dreamy, shiftless block of time that was marked only by day and night, where I wasn't really accountable for anything and the world couldn't touch me so long as I was in bed by curfew and didn't stir up trouble. Didn't try and fuck with the system, in other words.

This must be what normal life feels like, a timeless blob of peace, as long as we abide by the rules and keep our place in the system. None of this dropping off the grid, sleeping in streets, eating from bins. The passing of time when you're homeless is something entirely different, where people are still inclined to spit on you, or pity you, or ignore you altogether, where the scrapes of social interaction score the hours in the days, where the change in weather keeps us focused on the movement of the Earth, of life.

But the hospital blots all that out.

It's sheltered from the elements, from people with no compassion. We're noticed constantly, observed and monitored, but with the indifference of a working shift. The nurses look forward to clock off time, to going home, to closing their souls off to the grit of the outside world as they fight their way to their flats or their houses where they expel a breath of relief before they have to set foot back into it again the next morning.

Not so in the hospital ward. We avoid all that shit, where we're only encouraged to shower because perhaps we've forgotten to or couldn't be fucked, where the food doesn't challenge the palette but fulfils our needs nonetheless, where the piano might be out of fucking tune but at least we can still get a tune out of it if we know how to play Varese.

It was easy being in there. I miss it almost immediately.

Down at Chinatown, Mum and Dad are debating what to have for lunch, or rather which restaurant to eat in. It's suddenly too fucking much for me. Too many choices on offer. There's fucking restaurants everywhere. There's traffic behind me, driving too fast, too loudly. There's no nurses suggesting what to do here. The sun's too bright. It's right in my eyes.

I'm starting to hyperventilate.

'Dante, you alright?' Mum says.

I can't answer her. I can hear her, but I can't answer her, even though there's nothing wrong with my voicebox.

All I can do is stumble into the alcove of a service doorway, out of the sun, and huddle down in the corner that smells like fish juices and stale drunkard's piss.

'Son, you gotta get up,' Dad says urgently.

I imagine he's worried about people staring. Fuck em. Fuck em all.

Ooooooh fuuuuuck, this is not good.

I'm having a turn.

Fucking Inferno my arse... I'm drowning here. There's no pit of fire. I'm being swamped by an anxiety attack or something. My eyes are letting in too much light, blinding me. My mind's reeling from over-stimulation, and it's shutting me down to primal instinct and response, which is just fear fear fear right now.

I know all this, but can't articulate a single thing for the sake of my folks, not that they'd probably understand anyway.

I don't know how much time has passed but apparently one of the shopkeepers has noticed my plight because now there's a blanket draped over me, the corners trailing in the stale piss under my shoes. When I can finally look up without wincing I notice the sky is less bright. Late afternoon. Mum's sitting on the stoop behind me, looking at me with red-rimmed eyes. She's been crying. Dad comes over from the Asian supermarket, carrying a couple of lemonades.

'I didn't know if you wanted one, son,' he goes when he sees I'm in the land of the living again.

I can only close my eyes in response. I'm tired, and feeling numb. I don't want to break the muteness I've been plunged into, but from preference only. It's like Chopper Read once said, me and my mental health don't always agree. My limbs ache, but I'm afraid if I stand up to stretch Mum and Dad will want to interact, will ask about what happened. I'm not in the mood to talk about it, so I stay crouched in the corner a little longer, watching the world go by, watching as people start to fill Chinatown in search of a place to eat.

It occurs to me that I've been bottling my feelings for a week, because like Wazza said you can't show your true emotions or else they'll administer drugs like fucking crazy. They'd have jacked me so full of fucking tablets I'd have been like poor Wazza, collapsing just from the exertion of trying to have a wank in the showers. Now it's all pouring out of me, the fear and anger and frustration of being arrested and locked up in the nuthouse. How fucking weird is it that all those nurses and doctors, that fucking spastic Doctor Nancy, thought it was perfectly normal that after what I'd been through that I'd just sit there the whole week acting like nothing had happened, when the perfectly normal human response would have been to tear a fucking table apart with my bare hands out of pure frustration?

Christ, those cunts are the ones that need their fucking heads checked, not me.

Eventually I come good. Mum wants me to go home to Stanthorpe with them. I might be emotionally damaged but I'm not that fucking desperate.

'No thanks, the Prozac'll do me just fine.' I'm aware of the irony of what I've just said.

As much as I just want to get home and be alone in my room, I'm aware of the personal sacrifices Mum and Dad have made to be here for me all week so I reluctantly agree to have dinner with them. We go back to the Prozac first so I can shower and get fresh clothes.

'There you are,' Bernie smiles when we come in. 'Heard you were living it up at funny farm.'

'Good one, dickhead,' I grin. It's good to see him.

'Good to see you again, Richard,' Bernie says when my folks follow behind, shaking Dad's hand and kissing Mum on the cheek. He's so old-school. I'd never think of kissing someone's mother on the cheek.

Bernie keeps my parents busy while I shower. On the floor of the shower cubicle are Bernie's collection of shampoos and conditioners (for some reason he has several of each), and on the other side is my single bottle of shampoo which serves as shampoo, conditioner and soap for me. I like to keep it simple. Our razors sit in a soap-grimed plastic cup in the soap holder near the taps. There's no time limit on them. I can come and shave whenever I want.

I could slit my wrists, if I really wanted to.

Bernie's explaining in great detail about the different ways that both Carl and Elizabeth, the voices in his head, like to communicate with him. Mum looks pretty confused by his explanations, so I pull my Docs on and we hit the road, driving down to the Breakfast Creek Hotel for a counter-meal.

Watching Dad up at the bar order us some drinks and thinking about how he and Mum have had to cope with the last week makes me think of the kind of life they led when I was kid, which was actually a pretty rough one compared to the one they have out at Stanthorpe.

My uncle Jonas and Dad both used to be in a local motorbike club which they called CHARON'S TORMENTS, a phrase Dad got from the famous Italian poem *Inferno*. Dad was probably one of the most well-read would-be outlaw bikers around. Charon's Torments was a bit of a shit club, though, because they didn't have much of a cash income, relying on doing odd jobs for affiliated clubs and drug gangs around the Kilsythe area in Melbourne. My uncle wasn't keen on the idea but Dad and some of the other members knew it was a quick way to raise club revenue and reputation. The latter was important to acquire because basically no-one knew who they were. They weren't even on the cops' radar. Sounds like a good thing, but when you're in a supposed outlaw club, ambitions trump forethought.

So the trio of cunts Dad started drug-running for weren't exactly low profile, and they were being watched. They called themselves The Ratbag Three, which was apparently a more than apt name. Their own aspirations were hampered by the fact that two of them were also users and the third was a fucking nutter who couldn't be trusted to not sabotage the trio's network of contacts. Dad reckons he didn't know what was in the bag that he'd ferry from the The Ratbag Three to various locales, but of course he fucking well knew. Maybe not precise amounts and shit, but with The Ratbag Three's rep and the clandestine nature of his drop-off points he would've definitely clued on quickly that he was carrying copious quantities of contraband.

One night Dad got busted and was dragged before the courts, essentially fucking humiliated in front of the judge and the arresting officers, every cunt that's in there. They wanted him to snitch on the guys he was running for, but he wouldn't do it. The judge let the cops taunt him, threaten him, pull his pants down in front of everyone. My Dad was old-school: he wouldn't tell any of those fuckers what they wanted to hear.

So that's how he ended up in the Bluestone College, that fucking Pentridge Prison in Coburg. The College of Knowledge.

Uncle Jonas was heartbroken to see his little brother go down for it, of course, but what could he do? Charon's Torments didn't have the collateral strength to strike back at the dealers, and didn't have the solidarity of the other, stronger clubs to rely on them without perhaps offering up a piece of his soul.

So he did the only thing he could think of, and that was knuckle down and become a source of support to my Mum and us kids, visit Dad as much as he could and keep everyone's spirits up. Sometimes we'd be joined by Uncle Kev, who was Jonas' youngest sibling, but Kev was already something of an alcoholic by that stage so couldn't always be relied upon to show up.

A week before Dad was to get out I'd gotten into a fight with some kids at school that had escalated into an all-out brawl. I wasn't so stupid as to get into the middle of a ruckus and lose my teeth for it, preferring instead to skirt the sidelines, taking shots as opportunity presented them, so I'd only copped a couple of blows and a bruiser above my eye.

But Uncle Jonas wasn't happy about it because he was worried Dad would think Jonas had let the family down, hadn't been keeping an eye on things well enough. He'd tried to talk to me about it, Uncle Jonas did, but something snapped inside of me when he'd sat down on the bed next to me. I'd screamed at him that he wasn't my father, that he couldn't replace Dad. I'd shouted and shouted until I could see the hurt in his eyes, and when he'd tried to take hold of me to calm me down I'd lashed out, picking up the desk lamp and swinging it around to hit him in the head. The light was whirling around us like a giant firefly until the plug came out of the socket and plunged us into darkness. Mum told me later it was at that moment that Jonas really shit himself, walking out and going out where Mum was in the kitchen, visibly shaken.

He probably thought I had the Devil in me. Who the fuck knows?

Screaming at Uncle Jonas and saying those hurtful things to him was the last I ever spoke to him. The next night he was gunned down outside his home. Years later Mum told me the suspicion was that the cops did it, but an investigation had pointed all fingers at The Ratbag Three. She suspected that the cops had hoped with Dad's parole coming up he'd have a change of heart and finally snitch The Ratbag Three in. Moreso if he had a little extra motive, like the murder of his big brother.

It didn't work, though. After eighteen months of confinement the last thing Dad was interested in was retribution. He'd missed a part of our childhoods, had stranded his wife with the duty of not only running the household but trying to manage it financially. I never saw Mum cry the whole time Dad was away, although I'm sure there must've been plenty of nights where she'd cried herself to sleep. Me and my brother Rory couldn't have made life easier, either, being the little shits we were.

Dad was a different person when he finally got out. He told me about how some guy got stabbed while he was in there, and how he'd quickly jumped a wall into another courtyard so he wouldn't be included in the interrogation when the wardens rounded all the witnesses up. As a result of Pentridge, Dad had become quieter, more careful about everything. His voice didn't boom anymore.

Mum and Grandma got the funeral home to hold Uncle Jonas's body until Dad was out on parole the week after. It was good to have him back, but weird also. Rory and me sat next to him at the funeral for Jonas; but unlike my Grandpa, Dad didn't cry. He seemed sad, though. Like the entire world's sadness had been heaped upon his shoulders, and he didn't know what to do about it. For the first time in my life I thought of my father as a failure. It made me spit chips to think like that, and even angrier when I couldn't substitute it with any other feeling.

Two weeks later we were packing for Queensland. My brother and I didn't know why. We begged them to stay in Melbourne. But we couldn't, I was told. No other reason. Just *we couldn't*. I felt like we were running away from the memory of Uncle Jonas, running away from all the good that he'd done for us. It felt like a betrayal.

But years later Mum confided in me that at the time a junkie known only as Skunk was approached by The Ratbag Three about offing some guy for a few thousand dollars. It doesn't seem like much dough for killing somebody, but Skunk had a *serious* smack habit so he was up for it. Fortunately, he was a bit of a mouthy cunt, too, so when he was at the pub later on telling a guy called Jon Goddard all about his hit, Goddard turned to him and asked if the guy Skunk had been paid to kill was Dickie Halloran.

'Sure as shit,' went Skunk. 'But how'd you know?' he'd asked.

So Goddard, who not only knew Skunk but was also a mate of my Dad's, told him that Dickie's a good bloke with a young family and all this other shit that made Dad seem like the kinda guy you don't wanna kill, so Skunk got hit hard with the guilts and told The Ratbag Three to shove their hit up their arse. Of course, he was reluctant to give the cash back and got his legs broken for his troubles, but the main thing is that Jon Goddard got word to my Dad about what The Ratbag Three were up to.

That's how we ended up in Queensland.

Dad had panicked, and with his brother still fresh in the ground and the cops still sniffing around hoping he'd drop The Ratbag Three into it, he'd decided to ship the family north and away from all the crooked cops and paranoid druggies.

Mum also said that the remainder of Charon's Torments quickly disintegrated afterwards.

That's also how we ended up in that weird Christian cult. Mum and Dad were so traumatised by the lifestyle they'd been leading that they swung one eighty and went in the other direction, embracing the Lord with all their might and falling headlong into a pit of vipers if ever there was one. They'd befriended this old couple living in the boonies out on Sugarloaf Road, and at first the whole thing had seemed innocuous enough, sharing recipes for scones and shit like that, introducing Mum and Dad to the Bible which didn't seem like a bad thing at first, but eventually their stranglehold on our household became apparent, influencing the way we lived to such a frightening extent that we'd been forced to call the friendship quits.

It was me who initiated the split.

But not before several other families in the region had become enmeshed in the close-knit circle and encouraged, by ever darkening degrees, to feel more obligated to the group than to the outside world. The old couple wielded such influence that no-one batted an eyelid when they'd recommended we all undergo an exorcism to rid us of our demons.

The stupid old cunts got pretty excited during the exorcising when I'd developed a bit of a throat cough on account of it went on for so long and no refreshments were on hand. They'd leapt around and screamed at me, insisting the small growl that escaped my parched throat was in fact the very Devil himself come to confront these two delusional fuckwits.

Armed now with evidence that the Devil was hot our heels, we'd stockpiled weapons in the nearby bushland, burying them in upright canisters with a single coin between the lid and the surface so that any Joe Blo using a metal detector in the area would assume it was a few coins in the ground. This was years ago, obviously long before Port Arthur, so there were no gun rules like now.

Convinced the Australian Army was poised to take military control of the country and start branding every cunt as property of the Great Beast, we'd made plans to run and hide, deep into the wilderness, surviving on a diet of berries, grubs and any kangaroos we could shoot dead. One of the families who'd made up our crazy group were fairly obese, stuffing junk food into their gobs every available chance. These old cunts running this cult turned to the little kid of this family – a certifiable butterball if ever there was one – and told him rather matter-of-factly that the poor little fucker was going to be taken out back, come the day, and get a bullet to the brain because he was too fat to keep up with us, thereby posing a threat to our survival. The worse bit was that they told the kid this so often that if pressed for an answer as to what would befall the little cunt come the arrival of the Apocalypse, the kid would shrug and repeat back his death sentence.

It was pretty fucked.

After we defected, or as my folks preferred to term it, 'stopped seeing our old friends', it was difficult for our parents to admit that we'd become ensnared within a crazy religious cult, even taking into account the adage that there're no atheists in a foxhole and that the old cunts steering the cult had practically fabricated said foxhole environment around us. Then a couple of years later the events of both Ruby Ridge and Waco, Texas happened in America. It was that fucking whacko David Koresh and his cult, in particular, that made my folks take a good hard look at just what we'd been involved in.

We got off lightly. The discovery of Lena Malahoff's skeleton near her old hippy commune this year should've made us all reflect on the near-miss, especially given how we'd gotten into the Sugarloaf Cult around the same time that Malahoff went missing up in Cairns.

In any case, despite everything, my folks thought some good had come from being involved, namely that they'd managed to turn their lives around with the aid of a saviour, the one that died on the cross for their sins.

Not my sins, though. I've still got a bucketload more to commit yet. The Inferno will see to that.

Dad comes back from the bar with our drinks and places them on the table just as our chicken parmi's and salads arrive.

I guess I give these poor cunts a run for their money, that's for sure, but it feels pretty good sitting down to a meal with them again, listening to the gossip from back home as I sip my wine. I definitely don't do this enough with them.

SWAG PILE PIXIE

'We told you when you moved in,' goes Jules, with her man-hands planted on her hips. 'No drugs allowed.'

She'd have been one of the ones that signed up onto that stupid *Just Say No* campaign.

I want to kick her in the cunt. She's standin there like one of me teachers from school tryin to act like she's so fuckin cool and got it all together. She's probly secretly a meth-head. It's not natural for people to be totally drug free.

'Is that all your stuff?' asks Fran.

At least this other sister, Francis, is being cool about the whole thing. She told us that it was *unfortunate*, but she didn't harp on at us like Jules fuckin did when she found the needle and me makeshift works. Luckily, she doesn't know we like to trade the smack in liddle pill capsules, so she just thinks my bottle of antibiotics is just that: antibiotics. The gelatine capsules're perfect for carefully splitting open and replacin the medicine inside with good ol' capital H. Easy way to keep it premeasured for hits, too.

'Don't worry about the three weeks rent you owe us, just go,' are Jule's partin words.

The taxi takes me and my bags straight to Mum's. The bed I was using back at the flat actually belonged to the sisters, since the room came mostly furnished. All me stuff, includin me bedding, me clothes, me bright pink vibrator, me magazines and music, all of it is literally stuffed into various plastic shoppin bags which I tied the tops of.

I didn't feel any shame when I left, but, which I think was a huge disappointment for both Jules and Fran. People expect ya to get embarrassed about doin drugs, but I think it's them that needs to feel ashamed for treatin us like a leper. I wasn't hurtin nobody and I didn't do it in front of em. I didn't steal their stuff to hock off, either, which seems to be the basic assumption about heroin users.

I told Mum that the cunts at the other flat hated gothics and that's how come they got rid of us.

'That's weird,' she says. 'What, they diddin know ya were a gothic when ya moved in?'

Charlie, our dog, is fuckin ecstatic to see us and keeps jumpin up to lick me face.

'Nah, I was wearin me work uniform,' I go, and she looks at us funny coz I'm dead sure she knows I literally haven't worked a shift for Dad in yonks. It was the quickest lie I could come up with on the spot, but. Besides, there were way too many fuckin complaints from customers who reckon they saw us putting dead bugs in their fries or spittin in their burgers. I mean, I was, but I don't think the cunts really saw us doin it. Actually, thinkin about it, I didn't really hide when I did it so they probly did! So Dad was gonna be forced to fire us, anyway, if I kept goin back. Done him a favour, in the end.

After we've dumped the plastic bags of stuff into me old room, which is still painted black, Mum sits at the old formica kitchen table draggin on a fag and lays down a few house rules.

'Rule number one,' she says with her eyes bogglin to get across the importance of the situation. 'No drugs in the house, ever. I'm serious, Prudence, it's not funny.'

'I don't think it is.'

'Then wipe the smirk off ya face.' She drags on the cigarette and nearly chokes. 'Ya don't need to tell me why them girls wanted ya gone. It's bloody obvious. Look at ya! All skin and bone, and look like ya haven't slept in a week. That's drugs. I know. If the Housing Commission found out there was drugs here they'd send me packing. And that'd be me stuffed, wouldn't it?'

So she's guessed I'm using, big fuckin deal.

Mum thinks she's clever, but the suspicion of drug use is the go-to explanation for parents these days when their sprogs have hit hard times. It's hardly fair, but it's not often that far off the mark, either.

When I was about ten years old there was this TV special that was on all the channels; Seven, Nine and Ten. They got the grey-haired Prime Minister to make an announcement before it about the dangers of drugs, then this cheesy-as-fuck cartoon movie called *Cartoon All-Stars To The Rescue* comes on where the Smurfs, Garfield, Kermit the Frog and some others go after this poor kid who's stolen his stupid sister's piggy-bank. It was kicked off by McDonald's of all things, and meant to straighten out any of us liddle cunts who were gonna be tempted to try the Devil's Lettuce as we entered into our teenage years. Mum watched the whole thing with us, an experience that was probly more discomfortin than the one I'm currently in. I'm tempted to remind her about the film so I can laugh at her when she realises that that shit doesn't stop us takin drugs when we get older. Fuckin hell, I remember the boy in the movie was so fuckin high on just a joint that he didn't even bat an eyelid when Bugs Bunny walked in and started talkin to him. I'd be fuckin stoked for some of whatever that cunt must've been on.

Mum's still going on about how thin I am, and how she blames the drugs. She doesn't have a bunch of cartoon characters to back her up now.

'I didn't eat well, that's all,' I groan, tired of her harpin on. 'Those bitches kept eating me food outta the fridge.'

Mum sniffs, narrowin her eyes at us.

I decide to try my luck, see if I can't get to open her purse-strings by tuggin at the heart-strings. 'And they took an extra two weeks rent off us, fuckin bullies. Now I'm short a hundred bucks, but.'

'That brings us to rule number two,' Mum says. 'No more lies. I'm sick to death of it, Prue. I can't take it anymore. First the Satanic stuff, then the drugs, now the lies. It's obviously something ya picked up from yer father.'

That didn't take long. For her, takin a dig at Dad is like breathing oxygen, without which she'd probly cark it. It's her own addiction. I have to tune the silly bitch out or else I'll literally go mad from her bullshit.

'Satanic? Whatever,' I go, pullin a face. 'It's gothic, not Satanic for fuck's sake.'

She looks like she's ready to cry. 'And ya swear at me now, too.'

'I'm not swearin *at* you,' I go, rollin me eyes. 'Just swearin, in general.' I smirk. 'Ya not gonna give us detention for it, but, are ya?'

Which only leads her into the third rule, which is probly the worst one so far.

'I want ya to go back to school. Finish your grades.'

I'm shakin me head. 'No way, José.'

'It's the best time, Prue, don't waste it,' she says, then pulls out what she probly thinks is her trump card. 'The Teacher's Union wants Queensland schools to add another year on top. It was on the telly the other night, I saw it. So if ya decide to finish high school later on ya gonna have to do an extra twelve months on top of it. Think of that.'

'That's hardly a reason to return to that hell-hole,' I say.

'Fine,' she goes, lookin exhausted and soundin sad. 'But just think of it, Prue. You could be the first Lang to make it all the way to the Uni. Think of that! Or else you might end up just like yer father, debt up to his bloody eyeballs from blowin his measly inheritance buyin into that burger franchise. It'll go belly up, soon. Mark me words.'

She continues to get off track from the original topic, which was me goin into Uni. As if that's ever gonna happen in this stupid family! Mum lives off sickness benefits and Dad's away with the fuckin fairies doin God's work making fuckin burgers of all things. Nan shouldna left him all that money. She should've given it straight to me. Now's it all goin overseas to those slave kids instead, I bet.

When Mum's got her back to us, standin at the kitchen sink runnin the dirty plates under the tap and goin on about Dad still, I slip out to me room and break open the plastic bag, dumpin all me stuff out onto the bed. Mum's made the bed up with my old doona and pillow so I don't hafta worry about the bags with the bedding stuff in them. I hide the vibrator in a drawer inside the wardrobe, but decide that the drugs will have to be stashed somewhere else. Mum's naive, but not as naive as Jules and Fran; she'll suss that the antibiotics aren't what they seem and probly flush the fuckin lot down the drain.

Later, when Mum's havin a lie down coz apparently I'm such a handful it stresses her out too much, I phone Roz up and ask if I can come round and keep the pills at her place. It's a risk, coz she'll probly use em herself, but she surprises us when she reveals another way for us to keep em at home.

'Hide them in the dog kennel,' she goes. 'That way it's not in the house, and if the cops come and do a search their sniffer dogs will be useless as shit.'

'How so?'

'They'll get baffled by the smell of your mutt,' she goes in a way I can hear her grinnin on the other end. 'It overwhelms them and they leave the dope alone.' Roz refers to most drugs as dope a lot of the time, no matter what they are, which gets a bit confusing.

'Sweet advice,' I say and get down to business while Mum's still asleep.

The kennel's seen better days, but Mum can't afford a new one and Charlie hardly uses it much anymore, anyways. It stinks like him, but, that's for sure. I tuck the pill bottle up into the underside of the roof, wedgin it into the corner. No cunt will ever think there's such a precious treasure hidden in such a pitiful thing as this dog kennel.

The sun is startin to go down and the trees are fillin with parakeets all chirpin their spastic faces off. It's probly the only thing I like about bein out here. I fuckin hate the suburbs, otherwise. The house has seen better days, too, actually. Mum should give those bureaucrat cunts a fuckin serve about the state of the place, make them come out and paint it for her.

The sky grows darker and darker and I sit down on the lawn and watch the stars come out. The noise of the neighbourhood changes dramatically from whooshin traffic to stillness and the sounds of TVs or kitchen pots and pans. While I'm totally familiar with this change and the accompanying sounds, I've also grown used to the noises of the Valley pretty quickly in the month I lived in that flat. The traffic noise doesn't change in the inner-city places until late at night. I guess it's kinda peaceful out here, but I miss the energy of the Valley.

The kitchen light comes on, a horrible rectangle of yellow light against the darkness of the house. Mum's in there goin through the cupboards and puttin some pasta on the stove. I'm tempted to get wasted so I can pass through me first night here no worries, but watchin Mum stirring the pot and puttin out two plates makes us think it's better to be sober tonight. I think Mum needs it.

The neighbours get into a fuckin row, yellin their faces off at each other. They used to do it when I lived here before, too.

'Shut the fuck up!' I shout, but it's no use.

'You shut the fuck up, or I'll kill you!' the mong cunt yells back.

'Pixie,' Mum's voice goes, quietly, from the windows. I get up and go inside.

The neighbours keep yellin until the sound ova wooden chair getting broken into pieces can be heard. He shouts some more about how he didn't wanna do that but she – his thick-as-a-brick girlfriend, I guess – made him do it. Then the dumb cunt slams his front door and screams off up the road in his Torana. After that, only her crying can be heard.

I don't understand bitches like that. Why stay with the cunt?

Besides that, it turns out to be an okay night, actually, and me and Mum talk shit about the old days and how we used to go with Dad on the train into South Bank for a swim and ice-cream on the weekends.

'We should do that again,' smiles Mum. 'Just you and me, but. Mother and daughter.'

Shit like that normally sounds cringe-worthy, but actually this time it sounds like a fuckin brilliant idea. Maybe things between me and Mum can finally improve? Ha! Who knows, maybe I can show her that smack isn't the demon that she thinks it is, and her and I can just be chill as fuck around the house and talk shit about Dad.

Except all that's just a pipe-dream, isn't it?

Coz the next morning Mum's in the backyard screaming bloody blue murder, which it may as well be.

She's out there in her nightie and the sun's already well and truly up. I slept in a bit.

'What the fuck's all the screamin about?' I moan, still half asleep.

Charlie's lyin on the lawn, actin dead for a laugh.

Mum's face is twisted. She's looks stupid as.

But nah, Charlie's not actin dead. More like he's literally fucking dead. His poor eyes look faraway and sunken in and his tongue is hangin out with meaty-bites vomit comin from it into the grass.

Some cunt's killed me fuckin dog in the middle of the night!

I rush out to me poor liddle doggie, this poor baby who hurt no cunt in his entire life but just wanted pats and to be loved. He's an innocent animal. The cunt that's done this is the real animal. His furry liddle body is stiff in me arms.

It'll be that bastard cunt from next door. Not enough to beat his girlfriend up, obviously! Has to come and kill me dog, too.

Mum goes over and picks somethin up and stalks back to me and poor Charlie.

'Last fuckin straw,' she growls.

The sun's behind her, so I can't read her face as she stands over us, but there's no doubt that she's havin a go at us. People always are.

'What is?'

'I told you, Prudence, diddin I?' she goes, angrily. 'No drugs in the house.'

'There's not, but,' I protest, thinkin how Roz said I could play the innocent card coz technically the drugs aren't in the house if they're in the dog kennel.

Mum drops the chewed up antibiotic bottle next to us on the grass. The chemist's label with me name on it is still visible, with Charlie's bite marks in it. The capsules full of smack are gone.

'Pack yer stuff,' Mum says, strollin back into the house.

What a cold-hearted cunt she is. The least she could do is help us bury Charlie.

I lie his body gently back on the lawn before rushin in after Mum, screamin me head off.

'IT'S NOT MY FUCKING FAULT!'

I stop in me tracks. Mum's on the floor, holdin onto the kitchen table for support, her shoulders shakin crazily as she bawls her eyes out.

It devastates us.

She looks so wrecked, so frail.

I don't know what to say, but suddenly I feel a defensive anger swellin up inside us.

'How the hell is crying about it goin to help?'

She flinches at me yellin at her. Me own mother, frightened of me.

I've done nothing to deserve this.

'I must've done some terrible things in a past life,' she sniffs, wipin snot on her sleeve, 'to deserve this family.'

'Do ya think I asked to be born into this?' I growl. 'Useless parents that can't get their own shit together but expect me to?'

She shrugs. 'Maybe ya right.'

'Maybe I am!' I shout. I stare out the window, lettin the sunshine burn into me eyes. I feel transfixed by it. There's somethin pure about light that ugly domestics can't touch even as they're happenin.

'I can't have you in the house anymore, Prue,' she says softly, her voice mong from a nose full of snot. 'I'm sorry.'

'Why be sorry about it?' I say viciously, stormin into my room.

I wish I hadn't unpacked me stuff last night. I pull the bed-sheet off and pile everythin I want to take into the middle, then tie all four corners together into a sack. It looks like a bigger version of those hankie swags ya see the bums on old cartoons carry around on the end ova stick.

Mum wants to talk to us some more, tryin to block the doorway, but I shove her aside and haul my swag over me shoulder. I run down the front steps and out the front gate, and while I don't look back I can still feel her eyes boring into us.

Fuck. That didn't last long, did it? A day and a night, and that's it. Only one month at the Valley flat with the sisters. And now I've got nowhere to go. No home. I don't know what I'm gonna do. I won't last on the streets like Dante can. I'd get raped or somethin. Besides, I definitely need a fix now, and that means goin to the only source I know: Nel and Roz. Maybe they can put us up for a bit.

It's not until I'm down the road that I remember poor lil Charlie is still out on the back lawn. FUCK! I forgot to bury him.

I burst into tears, strugglin under the weight of all me stuff. Poor Charlie.

'Are you okay, lovey?' asks this old cunt with a nose like a cock from the doorway of his house.

'Fuck off, ya dildo!'

Then I remember that I've left the vibrator that Shaz gave us back in the wardrobe at Mum's. Maybe Mum will find it and put it to good use cleanin out some of the cobwebs. Might make her less fuckin uptight in future.

DANTE AND RUPERT

'Come along with me to the tav, Dante' Bernie goes.

'Couldn't be fucked,' I tell him.

'You need to mingle again,' he points out. 'You've been cooped up in here since you got back from the hospital. Even before that, you hardly went out after you broke up with Nicola.'

I hardly broke up with her. Just saw no point in trying to contact her anymore ever since she fucked Twix on air. And neither of them bothered to come and see me in the hospital, either. Fuck both those cunts.

'Besides the Winter Solstice festival,' I retort, 'the other time I went out got me arrested and thrown in the nuthouse, remember?'

'Suit yourself,' Bernie says with a shrug, picking up his umbrella in case it rains later.

He's right though, I do need to get social again since my stint in the hospital, so I tell him to give me five minutes while I get ready.

We head on down to the Spring Hill Tavern on Boundary Street where Bernie's mates Rupert and Viv are already waiting.

A lot of people don't know that this is one of Brisbane's oldest streets, but I know because Alan told me it's called Boundary on account of how the whites used to put up fences along here at night to keep the Murris out of the city. I explain this to the others as we sit down, ordering some bruschetta and drinks.

Rupert can be a bit of an unpredictable old cunt, and even though he was raised nearly his entire life in the Land of Oz, he still puts on the old European airs and graces of his Dutch ancestors and can get a bit incendiary in his opinions, so I hold my breath for his response to this one.

'Oh, don't worry,' he says, arching his eyebrows and goggling his frosty eyes, 'the fences are still there. They're just not made of wood and wire anymore.'

I imagine Alan sitting with us and raising a glass to that. Bravo!

'There's a Boundary Street in West End,' Bernie chimes in.

'They're everywhere,' Rupert goes. 'That's the point. Demarcation lines, they were. They should be renamed.'

'Do you remember that park near the train station at South Bank where they'd all meet?' says Bernie.

Fucking here we go, delving right into Bernie's long-lost history. The silly cunt's even more nostalgic than I am. I tend to reflect on the people and places of my past because of my Borderline Personality Disorder, trying to cement myself into a timeline that turns to jelly if I don't have markers along it, but Bernie's motive is that he's just getting old.

'The Manhattan Walk,' smiles Rupert.

'That's the one, I'd forgotten the name,' says Bernie. 'Near where that tattoo shop got letter-bombed. Always was a rough area. I used to study at the old Tech and have to go through the park to get to the train station. I hated it. Always kept my head down.'

'Why didn't you just go around the Palace, then?' asks Rupert.

'Okay, I'm confused,' I pipe up. 'Did the Prozac Palace used to be somewhere else?'

'He means the Palace Hotel, where QPAC is now,' explains Bernie, then says to Rupert: 'And I didn't go around because the drunks used to give me a hard time. I was fairly effeminate in my heyday.'

'Oo-er,' goes Rupert, flipping his limp wrist at Bernie.

'Something like that, yes,' smiles Bernie smarmily.

'Welcome to the club, by the way,' Rupert says to me, and for a second I think he's implying I'm gay until he adds: 'Bernie told me how you were checking out the digs, as it were, for our most besieged and vulnerable.'

He's talking about how I was locked up in the psych ward, of course. His clever speak.

'Yeah, it wasn't bad,' I say. 'Might have to go again sometime, get myself on the meds next time around.'

Rupert grins.

Bernie met both Rupert and Vivienne at a GROW group, which are informally organised support groups for people with mental illnesses. The groups follow a charter and structure that the parent organisation prints out for the sub-chapters. I went to one once, but it wasn't for me. It was underneath a church in a rec room, and there was a spread of biscuits and cordial, but the attendees were too co-dependent and awkward for my liking. Fuck that. Rupert sort of feels the same way, even though he ended up leading a chapter for a while, but Viv loves the groups. She's in her late eighties, and is the sweetest lady you could meet. Her family all live up north, around Central Queensland, so the group's a good way for her to socialise and ask some of the younger members for help around her house, because she lives alone.

Bernie meets these two for lunch every Monday, and I've tagged along a few times now. Me and Rupert usually get into these tense debates about anything and everything, and Bernie always rolls his eyes, he and Viv shaking their heads at each other and laughing. Because we're both capable of playing the Devil's Advocate so easily we often eschew our personal stance just for the sake of the argument.

American politics tend to get brought up a lot, as Rupert reads the newspapers every day and considers it remiss of the rest of us not to be caught up on current affairs. Today he's got a beef with Clinton, the American president.

'It just makes you wonder where the man's head is at,' he says, running a hand through his thinning hair and smiling lecherously at the waitress when she brings us our drinks. The effect he's after is to be charming, but his face isn't made for that. He comes off as creepy, instead. 'It's just a damned sheep, for Christ's sake.'

'Oh, but it's not just any sheep,' quips Bernie. 'It's Dolly.'

'Yes, and you know why she's called that?' Rupert leans forward gleefully, like we're naughty schoolboys ready to whisper secret boy's stuff. That mischievous glint he gets in his eye in there.

'Of course,' says Bernie, sipping at his beer. 'Dolly Parton.'

Rupert claps his hands and sits back with a grin. 'Yes,' he says, pointing at Bernie. 'They took the DNA from a mammary gland of a sheep.' He looks at me and Viv and starts to chuckle. 'These scientists and their humour, eh?'

Viv just smiles, doubtlessly hoping that we don't cotton on to the fact she's already lost the thread of the conversation and clearly hasn't heard the news that the Scots have successfully cloned a sheep which they've called Dolly. She needn't worry; we already know she's now behind on the banter, as usual.

'Not sure what that has to do with Clinton,' says Bernie, taking the bait. I'm as stymied as he is about the connection, but I'm glad he spoke up first, so I get to sit here and cast him a reproachful stare. Judging others is exactly the sort of pick-me-up I need right now.

Rupert considers him critically, going: 'The man's sense of moral repugnance, dear man, that's what.'

'I see,' says Bernie, sipping his beer again, not seeing.

'Clinton's outraged,' I guess. A sharp jab in the dark.

'And isn't he ever,' declares Rupert, only addressing the other two, proving he's none the wiser that I'm as clueless as they are. 'He's shut down all funding in cloning science because someone, somewhere, actually managed to do what they've all been trying to do! What a twit. The Great Empire is coming to its finale.' America as the dying empire is one of Rupert's favourite subjects to harp on about.

'Well,' I counter, 'I suppose his scientists are only trying to clone cells and not the whole animal. Big difference there.'

'But that's neither here nor there,' argues Rupert. 'Is it a result? Yes. Has the result in some way manifested as grossly out of the scope of what they were hoping to achieve? Hardly.'

'Well, they've created life, and from a tit no less. Probably reminds him too much of Adam's rib and thinks the Scots are playing God. I can't remember, is he deeply religious?'

'Is God deeply religious?' Rupert's face slackens like he's thinking, then breaks into a grin when I smile appreciatively. 'Hell yes, he is. Baptist. Clinton, that is. Not sure what denomination God is.'

'I can't believe you know he's Baptist,' scoffs Bernie.

'You just need to read more,' admonishes Rupert, which is funny because Bernie actually reads a lot, it's just mostly biographies of dead people. Rupert turns his penetrating gaze on Vivienne. 'Come on, Viv, don't just sit there pretending to be part of the decorations.'

She smiles and shakes her head lightly. 'I'm happy just to hear you boys discuss it.'

'As I'm sure you are,' he says darkly, remarking that she looks like E.T. the Extraterrestrial, which she kinda does because she's got these massive eyes and a long thin neck. But Rupert's got that mean spirit happening, and starts making phoning home jokes, and in response I feel myself beginning to align with him to single out the other two as the weakest links. As incorrigible as he can be, I'm probably worse because I'm deliberately encouraging him by laughing along. Bernie sides with Viv in these moments and does his best to diffuse the cruelty.

Rupert gets severe depression, and it cripples him so badly he won't leave the house for a week or so, sometimes. One time it was so bad that Bernie was really worried about him, and got me to go around and check in on him because he wasn't even answering his phone. He was a mess, his beard and hair ungroomed and his eyes red-rimmed and looking hollow. The house stank from being shut up, and Rupert admitted to me he hadn't eaten in three days. I did what I could do, talking to him mostly, but in the end we just had to wait for him to emerge from the depression. But he told me all about how his marriage broke up years ago, how she works in the finance sector now in America and sends him a monthly stipend. She worries about him. It was obvious that he was still heartbroken about the split, but what can we do?

I don't know what illness Viv has. Couldn't even guess. She just seems so pleasant all the time. But that she's also been held in the nuthouse I do know: Rupert's mentioned it in passing before. And not until her condition flares up could I even guess at what she's got. The thing people forget is that a psych ward is still a hospital, albeit one for the mind. And just as having a broken leg's only temporary, so's having a broken mind.

'Speaking of ET and eyes,' Bernie goes to me, 'we have to tell you about our psychiatrist.'

'Yes! Yes!' goes Rupert and starts laughing so hard his face flushes red. Viv grins and nods. 'Fuck, that eye! I can't believe you've never told him before. You tell him, Bernie, I can't...' and Rupert folds his arms, pressing his fingertips into his eyes, sniggering.

'You have the same psychiatrist?' I ask. I didn't know that.

Rupert nods, still sniggering.

'Yes, and he looks a bit like Edgar Allan Poe, which I'm sure you'd appreciate,' Bernie goes, 'but he's got a fake eye, you see. It doesn't move. That is to say, Ménard – that's his name – Ménard will look out the window without turning his head, but only one eye will actually look out the window. The other one, made from glass or somesuch, just stays right where it is.'

'But the best bit is,' laughs Rupert, barely comprehensible, 'is that when he puts his head down to write his little notes, the eye keeps looking at you where you sit!' He nearly cracks up howling this time, slapping his knee.

Viv has a good chuckle, folding a napkin over and over and over.

'Yes,' grins Bernie, 'it does do that, doesn't it? I'm sure he doesn't know it does, but I have to try and keep a straight face. It's not easy.'

Rupert calms down, wiping the tears from his eyes. His mirth is infectious, and I'm having a bit of a chuckle, too, imagining this wild-haired Frenchman with a single glass eye trained on his patients at all times.

It's funny that Rupert and Bernie both see the same psychiatrist. A lot of people I know who see psychiatrists long-term have a tendency to get possessive of them, like they're the teacher's favourite pet and they don't want to share them with anyone else. I used to be friends with a girl who was also seeing my old psych Doctor Bourne, and she demanded that he stop seeing me, the fucking cheek. She went fucking nuts on him one day when he tried to reason with her and the cops were called.

Bernie is smiling away, maybe thinking about Ménard or maybe just enjoying the friendship. It strikes me that I don't see him smile that much, or at least not laugh that much. He did say to me once that his schizophrenia makes it hard for him to show emotion, but that he's almost never aware of it.

I split a slice of cheesecake with Viv, because I suspect she's a bit low on cash this week, and Rupert smiles warmly at me, like a father pleased with the courtesies of his child. Talk of eyes leads the guys onto Fred Hollows, the country's most famous eye doctor. He died a couple of years ago.

'Now, I didn't know this until recently,' says Rupert, shifting in his seat, 'but he stole from a hospital once. I don't know, maybe more than once.'

'Nonsense,' scoffs Bernie, motioning for the waitress.

'No, truly. Back when he was teaching at one of the universities in New South Wales.'

Bernie orders another beer from the waitress. She catches Rupert staring at her arse, and makes out she's retying her apron as she walks back inside so that she can cover her butt with it.

'Why would he need to steal from a university?' prompts Bernie.

Rupert folds his hands into a steeple across his belly. 'He wanted equipment and the likes for the first ever Aboriginal medical centre. *The first ever,*' he emphasises.

Bernie's eyebrows dart up like he's impressed, but otherwise he's lost interest in the conversation already.

This sounds like something I can drop on Alan next time I see him, impress the cunt with my knowledge. So I dig for more info. 'When was this? About the Twenties?'

This gets a guffaw from Rupert. 'He was born in the Twenties! He didn't do this on the way out of the womb.'

'Yeah well, not all of us sit around learning about dead people,' I grumble.

'Didn't you read that book about Vlad Tepes just last week,' muses Bernie, being a smart prick.

'Yeah yeah yeah,' I say, pulling a face at him. 'Just get on with the story, already.'

'Naw, he built it in the late Sixties,' says Rupert, looking solemn. 'Right about the time of the referendum which removed Aboriginals from the Flora and Fauna act. That was for plants and animals.'

'Yeah, I got that,' I say, cause he's addressing me as though I can't possibly know what that means.

'So essentially they were taken from status of animal and given rights as a human being. They could now vote and everything. Can you imagine that? What it was like for them?' He gets a stricken look on his face, like he's in pain or about to cry. I glance at Bernie to give him a hint he should intervene, but the cunt's too busy reading the fucking menu for the umpteenth fucking time even though he's got no intention of ordering anything.

'And the medical centre, Rupert?' asks Viv sweetly.

Rupert squints across at her, musing. 'So Hollows promised some Aboriginal protestors that they'd have their health clinic, even though they didn't think he could do it with so much red-tape in the way, but he made it happen by simply stealing the stuff. Brilliant man,' Rupert says, shaking his head like he can't believe the hide of Hollows to dare such a thing.

'That's wonderful,' chips in Vivienne.

Rupert regards her with haunted eyes and smiles wanly. 'It is, isn't it?' He looks so frail and tired, like the weight of the world is on his shoulders and in his mind and he can't cope with it anymore.

Later on I catch up with Alan and tell him about Fred Hollow's robbing the university hospital to build the first Aboriginal medical centre, but he counters with details that the university knew about it and assisted him in taking the stuff. That's burst my balloon. Then I remember the rest of Rupert's story, so I fact-check it with Alan, who says even most Aborigines today don't realise they could vote long before that referendum, and that pretty much everybody still thinks the referendum was the instigator for more than it really was.

'We could legally vote even before Federation,' he says, 'but no bastard would tell us. Why would they, when they was still puttin up fences to keep us away from the city at night, ay? There's Boundary streets all over Australia, in every city, like they were trying to keep the wild animals out.'

That puts me in mind of Rupert's other claim, the one that made him so maudlin and ashamed of Australian politics.

'What about the Flora and Fauna act thing?'

Alan gets an evil glint in his eye, like he could kill a cunt. 'Yeah, that one's true,' he growls. 'There's some people saying it's not, that the amendments were just to remove some discriminatory parts of the Constitution, but I got rellies out bush and way up North who can tell you stories about being hunted like fucking dogs and no bastard ever did anything about it. We were fucking animals to them, alright, no two ways about it.'

I wonder about Rupert's theory that America is a dying empire, and how that empire surely superseded the British one, and that gets me to thinking that perhaps Australia is simply the embodiment of Britain's death throes, and we're deluding ourselves if we think we might detach ourselves from the Great Empire and aspire to our own greatness, especially now with a monarchist as PM.

PRINCESS PIXIE

Since I was kicked out of me flat and then booted out of Mum's place, I was just about homeless. But, thankfully, Nel and Roz have literally saved me life by offerin us to stay with them. That's how ya know you've got ace mates, coz they've got ya fuckin back no matter what.

More's the point, I don't miss out now when there's a score.

Me mum's just a jealous old bitch coz she never had the same kind of fun I'm havin when she was my age. Instead, she got knocked up by a retard who decided when I was still in primary school to ditch us both and literally start over again like it's that simple. She was stuck with a fuckin kid to raise on her own. Couldn't even do that proply. She deserves to be alone and miserable, the bitch.

'Nah, go easy on her, cupcake,' says Nel. 'She's the only mum you got, after all.'

'Fuck her,' I spit. 'I have no mum anymore.'

'Well, be that as it may, Pixie,' says Nel loftily, 'but your arse is gonna get a bit fucken sore sittin on the floor all the time.'

She's right, but. I've rolled a towel under me bum but it's not that comfortable. Roz says that even between them they don't get enough from the dole to get some decent furniture in.

'We don't even have a proper bookcase for Nel's pride and joy,' she points out.

The bookcase is actually just bricks and milk-crates with planks of wood for the shelves. Nel has lovingly laid tea-towels over the timber to protect all her books, a super impressive collection of Stephen King hardbacks. Her pride and joy, as Roz puts it. Nel's not shy about tellin everyone that they cost her an arm and a leg, either.

'How come Mum's goin to help me now?'

'Because you're still her precious princess, no matter what,' says Nel snidely.

'Princess Pixie in the Palace,' sniggers Jeremy.

'It's true, though,' says Roz. 'You might have fucked up, but you're still blood. That's how it works with families. They'll forgive you anything.'

Nel glances at her and somethin passes between them.

It's probly true, but. If I ask Mum enough times she'll budge and buy us some shit to put in the flat.

'Then we can hock it off for some more H,' says Nel matter-of-factly. She sees the expression on me face and adds: 'What'd ya think, kiddo? That they hand out drugs for nix?'

'Well, can't we just hock off those books, then?' I go.

Nel immediately gets hostile. 'They stay right there. I know every single fucken one. If a single one goes missing, I'll fucken know!'

She glares round at Roz and Jeremy as well, so that no one's in any doubt as to the rules regardin her collection.

Roz suggests we all head down to the bottle-o for some supplies, something to take the sharp edge off the withdrawals. Their stash is gettin low and they've started rationing, so they wanna stretch it out far enough until they have more cash again, especially now there's an extra person to divvy it up with.

As soon as we open the door there's that stupid moggie crouched on the landin, starin at us like we're monsters. I think it belongs to Raven and's called Lunar, but I call it Lunatic coz whenever I see it it's always actin mong, runnin round like a headless chook. Nel tries to kick it but it piss-bolts down the stairs at a hundred miles a fuckin hour.

'Fucken thing, always pissing in the stairs,' spits Nel.

There's no more sign of the cat when we leave the Palace, not that we give a fuck. If the others are anthin like us, their clothes are plastered to their backs with sweat. The downside to when we can't afford a hit.

On the way up the road Nel comes up with a plan to get some easy money.

'It's no biggie,' she says to us, suckin on her ciggie and blowin out a big cloud of blue smoke that breaks apart when she walks through it. 'You just snap a pic of yerself in the buff and send it into Piccie mag. They'll pay five hundred bucks like *that*,' she snaps her fingers, 'for a full frontal shot. No good me or Roz doing it, we're past our prime. No-one needs to be subjected to that sort of trauma.'

I could be wrong, but I think Dante suggested the same thing, once. Dunno, I was pretty wasted at the time. And what Nel says about bein past her prime is also literally what me cousin Shaz was sayin about prostitution, too, about how there's a point where they're too old for it.

'Cash for yer gash,' jokes Jeremy, which actually turns out is the name of the feature in the magazine.

'I dunno,' I say slowly, thinkin it sounds a bit dodgy. What if like what happened to me cousin Shaz happens to us, and some of me family members see it?

The other thing is, is that I know I'm not fat but I still don't think I've got a good body. Normally I just wear jeans and a t-shirt to hide it. The only time I've felt good with even me legs exposed was when me cousin bought us a beautiful dress last month, until some foreign cunt pissed blood all over it and ruined the fuckin thing.

'If she doesn't wanna do it, she doesn't have to,' says Roz, walking ahead.

'I'm not saying she *has* to do it,' Nel protests. 'I'm just saying it's easy money.'

'I'd fucking do it,' sniffs Jeremy, jutting his chin out.

'Bloke's get fuck all cash for it, but,' says Nel. 'Or follow Chan's lead and do some porno fillums. Bit a cash in those.'

'What?' Jeremy's head snaps around at Nel and his mouth hangs open. 'Is that Chantelle that used to live with you? She did pornos?'

Nel nods like she knows everythin, and Jermy-germs the liddle sleaze literally starts droolin.

I remember one time Imp took a pic of himself naked at the end ova roll of family photos his brother KK had taken at a family weddin. Afterwards he was super fucking paranoid about KK or his father gettin the film developed that he stole it and paid for it himself. For a laugh, the processors at the Big W put a GET THIS ONE ENLARGED sticker right over his bits. He cut that piece out of the negatives and left the envelope of photos, without his nudie one obviously, on the kitchen counter. His mum was pretty confused about how keen he was to get the photos developed since he'd hated being made to go to the weddin in the first place.

Inside the bottle-o Roz rushes straight for the cask wine, clutchin a cheap lambrusco. It's too fuckin heady for us, and I'd rather we got a fruity-lexia but we've only got enough dosh for one cask and some tallies for Nel and Jeremy. Bein the new flatmate means I don't get much ova say in it.

Then Nel notices this older dude who reeks of old soap steppin around the display stands and stacked cartons a bit unco, like the old cunt's pissed already. He's got a slab of Fosters under one arm and's fumbling with his wallet with the other hand.

'Oi, got a live one,' she whispers to us, keen for some Jack Daniels instead of wine.

She strolls up to the old dude as confident as can be while Roz hovers around behind him waitin for any opportunity to come up.

'How you doin there tonight, buddy,' says Nel, soundin like she works here. 'Anything in particular you're after?'

'Aw, gidday mate,' the dude says, lookin straight at Nel but with unfocused eyes. 'You a new bloke?'

Cunt's blind as a fucking bat! Needs a fucking walkin cane and all, except he doesn't have one. It's like he doesn't want anyone to know he's lost his sight. That's how come he's back here out of sight of the counter, strugglin to open his wallet: he doesn't want to do it in front of the cashier and reveal his disability.

'Yeah, man,' says Nel, droppin her voice an octave or so to sound more manly. 'Saw you were having a bit of trouble there.'

The old cunt looks stricken, caught out in his deception.

'Yep, not seeing too well these days, mate, I gotta admit.'

'No worries, I'll grab the dough here and save you the walk up to the front counter,' she goes in that cheery kind of helpfulness some retail staff use that makes ya feel like ya can't say no.

The old cunt seems relieved at the offer, but.

He slides a twenny from his wallet, feelin it between his fingers so's he doesn't pull the rest of his cash out. It's a Wednesday night, so the amount of cash in his wallet and failin eyesight means he's on a disability pension. Wednesday's when they always get paid.

'Nah, that's just a fiver, man,' says Nel.

The old cunt looks doubtful, but Nel gets pushy and tells him to speed it up coz she's got customers waitin over at the counter. The poor bastard pulls out a few other notes and before he's had a chance to try and work out what they are Nel's whisked them away into her back pocket. She must've grabbed nearly fifty bucks just then.

'No worries, old boy,' she goes, slapping him on the shoulder and leadin him toward the door. 'That's you all settled.'

'Okay, thanks, mate,' the old dude says, shufflin out with his slab tucked under his arm, takin with him the stink of his old soap.

The big cunt behind the front counter notices our victim leavin with the beer and yells out for him to stop. When the blind dude keeps goin, but, old mate gets the shits and runs out after him.

Nel wants to go up and grab from the open till, but I can't let her risk it with two other customers standin there. They're watchin the drama outside the store but they'll notice Nel straight away if she tries to swoop on that cash drawer.

The old dude's debatin with the guy outside, who peers back into the store suspiciously. We start actin like we're still lookin around for somethin to buy, glancin at the goins-on outside with barely any interest. Old mate forces the old blind dude to fork over more cash, and inside me stomach a liddle knot forms. I guess the blind cunt was a pretty nice guy, really, and it sorta sucks that he's had to get stung twice like that.

Old mate storms back into the store.

'Unbelievable,' he says to the other customers, shakin his head. 'Silly old prick tried to tell me there's another bloke working here, that he already paid him for the grog. Fucking cheek.'

The customer's suitably indignant. 'It's shocking what the world is coming to.'

We're last in the line and Jeremy's over by the fridges pickin his nose like his mong life depends on it.

'Oi, give us half that money back,' I say to Nel.

'Shut the fuck up,' she hisses.

'Nah, seriously,' I whisper. 'Just half of it.'

'What for?'

Tell her or don't tell her, she's not goin to give it to us either way. Roz sees the look on me face, a kind of sadness I imagine.

'Just give it to her, Nel.'

Nel glares at Roz but shoves the notes into me hands.

'Thanks,' I say.

'For nothing,' sulks Nel all narky.

Out on the street the blind old dude's slowly makin his way along with the heavy case of Fosters beer under his arms. It's easy to catch up with the poor old bastard.

'Oi, dude, wait up,' I shout when I'm closer to him.

He turns around with a grimace. This is the same smile that really old people give us on trains or in shoppin centres, like they're scared of us coz I'm a gothic. It makes us feel even more sorry for the cunt, coz he's probly shittin himself thinkin I'm ready to pinch his booze or somethin. As if I'd touch Fosters! Yuck!

'Hey, sorry about what happened back there,' I say. 'Me friend was tryin to help and got mixed up about which carton costs which.'

Of course he's not buyin this bullshit. He might be blind, but he knows he got tricked into payin for the beer twice. In our case alone, he paid about three times as much for it.

'Here's ya change,' I go, grabbin his free hand, pressin the notes into it. I notice it's not even half of what Nel fleeced him of, but it's somethin at least. He clamps his wrinkled hand over mine, and at first I think the cunt's gonna fuckin attack us, but then I see his mong eyes are fillin up with tears. Stupid old cunt, he's gonna make me cry if he starts sookin.

'Thanks,' he says. 'Name's Kevin, by the way.'

Fuck. I didn't wanna know his name. They reckon when a serial killer abducts ya, always make the cunts learn ya name so they can empathise with ya more. That's the last thing I need right now.

'No problem, Kevin,' I say, tryin to sound as friendly as. 'You have a lovely night, okay.'

'Yep,' he says, and shuffles off again.

When the others catch up, Nel scolds us as if she's me dad.

'Use yer fucken brain, Pixie,' she says. 'Your little stunt right there could've totally blown us wide open. What if the prick called the cops on us?'

'Duh, how's he gonna do that when he can barely see?' I retort.

'Not him, princess,' snaps Nel. 'The bloke in the shop. He started to suss what we'd been up to when you wanted to return that cunt's money.'

'Whatever, Sir,' I say, scowling.

'You've got too many morals to be a junky,' laughs Roz, passin us the lambrusco. 'Here, have a swig.'

Even though it's not my preferred alcohol I happily hold the cask above me face and suck from the nozzle like a baby on a tit. Anythin to blot out Nel's voice. If it's not Mum goin off at us for doin the wrong thing, it's Nel goin off at us for doin the right thing. Can't fuckin win.

And now me hands smell like old soap.

THE BLEDISLOE

I forgot the footy was on today out at Lang Park, and the city is teeming with cunts from both sides of the match all revved up and looking for action of any kind, be it by fist or gentialia. There's a sea of black and yellow jerseys in the Queen Street Mall, all red necks from the collar up. Matty remembered the game was on, however, because of course the stupid bastard is a Rugby fan from way back when he used to watch it with his dad as a kid. I'll never understand the fascination for the sport.

'Yeah, it's the Tri Nations match, Dante,' he says excitedly.

'Fuck off,' I go. 'Try hard more like.'

'It's Australia verses New Zealand, but,' he dribbles, getting up in my face and risking a smack in the gob. 'Go the Aussies!'

'Fuck the Aussies. Look at them, Matty, they've got facepaint on – and poorly done I might add – all dressed up in their footy costumes like a bunch of sheep and they've got the hide to laugh at us when we're dressed in black with goth makeup on!'

He rubs his nose and shrugs, humouring me as I rant.

Remembering that he and Angele had come by the flat earlier to ask if we had a tent they could borrow (Bernie had one) so they could camp out overnight at Indooroopilly to meet someone off the X-Files TV show, I add caustically: 'What d'ya think they'd say if they knew you were sleeping at a fucking shopping centre just to meet a TV star, you nerd?'

Some guys with yellow paint on their angry faces stroll past us, shaking their fists and shouting 'Go the Aussies!' Matty, the stupid cunt, reciprocates and for a moment he looks to me like nothing more than one of these bogan clowns. He's far more Matto than Malik, right now.

Cunt wanted to hang out in the city, reminding me that I owe him one because he came to the Winter Solstice Festival last month. I'm pretty much fresh outta the mental hospital so this is the last fucking thing that I need, being caught up in this circus. Matty's too dense to realise it, and continues to try and revel in what he's calling 'a ripper atmosphere'. There's some other guys with Kiwi accents at Jimmy's on the Mall who raise their beers to us and start whooping. I guess because we're both dressed head to toe in black they probably think we're All-Blacks supporters, the New Zealand team.

'There's no-one's laughing at us, but,' Matty points out, which strictly speaking is true.

'Maybe not right now,' I counter, 'but Matty, every other fucking day these arseholes treat us like shit for dressing the way we do, for the music we listen to, for wearing eyeliner and black lipstick, and then one or two days a year they do the very same thing, scarves and facepaint and shit with cockroaches and cane-toads on them – both of which are, tellingly, introduced pests – and we're expected to join in on the celebrations?'

'Okay, no need to spit the dummy, I get what you're saying,' he says, losing his enthusiasm, 'but tonight's a way for two nations to come together, to put aside differences and have a good time. And the roaches and toads is State of Origin, by the way, not the Tri-Nations.'

'Same fucking diff.'

I can see my attitude's getting him down, but I've never made any fucking secret about how I feel about football and its idiot fanbase. I've had enough cunts in Rugby jerseys treat me or my friends like shit on buses, trains, supermarkets, on the streets... the list is fucking endless. It mightn't be fair to draw parallels between footy fans en masse and the cunts that dish out the hassle, but it's not fucking hard to, either. I've never had another footy supporter try and nullify the behaviour of the cuntish ones.

I cave in just to keep him happy because the last thing I need after the bullshit of the mental hospital saga is mopey cunts bringing me down. We duck downstairs into Her Majesty's and into the fire, so to speak. If I thought the Mall was choked with footy fans, I can barely move down here let alone find the bar. It's packed to the rafters with all manner of cunts in football jerseys, although of the New Zealand supporters just about all of those are males. Straight away there's all sorts of hostile vibes directed our way, but Matty's oblivious to it and squeezes through the crushing crowd in the direction of the alcohol.

I keep my eyes down, ignoring the sneers as best I can, while keenly observing where every unmanned glass or ashtray sits. If the circumstance arises where I need to avail myself of a weapon, I like to be informed of my choices. As it is, all I've got is The Inferno rattling inside my noggin.

'There's fucking buckley's chance of a drink,' says Matty when we're a couple of people deep from the bar. 'It's way too packed.'

'Fuck, I think we're stuck here,' I groan.

This big bastard wearing deck shoes and a Canterbury jersey in front of us looks over his shoulder and frowns deeply, like he's just seen the most unfathomable thing he's ever encountered. I swear half these footy cunts never come into the city until it's game day, so they're rarely exposed to a good dose of subcultural contact.

I'm about to ask what the fuck he's staring at when he goes: 'Youse over for the Bledisloe?'

I stare at him blankly, wondering what in hell a *bledisloe* is, when Matty steps in.

'Nah, mate,' he goes, affecting a slight Aussie twang, 'we're locals, ay. Go the fucking Aussies!' He pumps his fist up in a hook like he's trying to get his arm all the way up a cow's anus.

'So why youse wearin fucken black, then?' the guy sneers.

'Just back from a funeral,' I swiftly offer before Matty can come up with some half-arsed explanation of his own. He frowns at me, shaking his head imperceptibly. The cost of being my friend, cunt. 'My grandmother passed away from Witzelsucht disease.'

'Sorry to hear it,' the big bastard says, offering to buy us both a beer out of sympathy, though Matty tries to refuse the offer.

'My mate thinks it'd be rude to accept on account of Grandma,' I explain, trying to counteract Matty's fucking around. At least Twix would have had the good sense to play along.

'Bullshit!' barks the big bastard. 'It's to honour her memory.'

Try and argue with that, dear Malik. His eyes tell me he's not impressed I've wheedled some free drinks, but it's probably the only way we're actually gonna slake our thirsts in this horde.

The big bastard calls over to the barmaid for a couple more pints, but she gives him a dirty look since she's in over her head serving the crowd at the other end of the bar. They look like they're giving her a hard time of it, too. He tries again, getting agitated, but she flat out ignores him this time.

'No worries, mate,' I say, holding up a pint I just swiped from the counter. 'We're all sorted.'

The big bastard does a little double-take at me and Matty holding our drinks.

'Catch ya around,' I say, and steer Matty away, careful not to spill too much from our glasses as we try and navigate through the crowd. I can hear the burly cunts standing next to the big bastard at the bar demanding to know who stole their drinks, and it sounds like a bit of a biffo is about to ensue. I wish I could stay and watch, but I've got no doubts the big bastard would drop us in it and then we'd be made mince meat of.

'Don't do that shit,' Malik goes, annoyed.

'Drink up, cunt, and stop your whinging.'

'You're gonna get us killed,' he persists.

'It was your idea to come in here,' I point out, 'so it's your fault if we get murdered. At least you like beer. Fucking rancid stuff.'

We wedge ourselves into a corner by the payphone. It's too noisy in here for anyone to make any calls anyway so this should be a relatively safe spot to stand in.

A group next to us is comprised of couples, and one of the women, a scrawny hag even at thirty or whatever age she's trying to dress as, gives us the once over, pulling a face like she's sucked on a lemon, and goes: 'What are you two supposed to be?'

'What d'ya mean?' says Matty, dumb as fuck. Never engage.

'It's not Halloween?' she whines like a mozzie, speaking in that high-rising terminal of the bogan, or *upspeak* as it's being termed these days. Apparently young people in Britain are starting to talk like this now, making the ends of statements into questions, and the press have rightly blamed it on a steady diet of shitty TV shows like *Neighbours*. The English have dubbed the phenomena as AQI, or Australian Question Intonation.

The rest of her entourage clock us and are as unappreciative of our dress standards as the hag in their midst is.

Malik gets into a debate with them about street styles and young people, and thank fuck they remain jovial about the whole thing even if they're still critical of how we choose to dress. I just sip my beer and listen quietly to the inane natter, variations of which I've heard and participated in a hundred fucking times over the years. The hag's intonations are starting to get on my nerves, however, so I turn to a couple of big Maori fuckers behind me.

'Gay chief,' I go, and their heads snap around to take me in, in all my gutter-goth glory.

'Tssss, go on, ow,' they hiss.

'Just sayin g'day, chief,' I smile disarmingly, so the cunts relax up. 'Good night for a game, ay?'

I'm starting to get the hang of this shitty banter.

'Yeah, true, ay,' one of the Maori guys goes, looking round the room idly. 'Could go a root later, but.'

The other one readily agrees, but notes there's not many mouldy chicks in the house.

'If you guys want mouldy girls you could always try Toowong Cemetery,' I go. 'But you'll need a shovel.'

One of the Maori fuckers stares at me, then bursts into raucous laughter. 'This cunt,' he nearly cries, pointing at me.

Then the other one goes: 'I'm talkin bout *MAO*-REE chicks, bruh.'

'Oh, Maori girls? Why'd you say mouldy then?'

He shakes his big head, grinning. 'Youse Aussie cunts are always saying it wrong, ay,' he goes, following with a lesson on the proper pronunciation for *Maori*, and again I swear he says *mouldy*.

Despite the elocution tutorial being somewhat interesting, I've grown bored of their provisional company already, so it's actually a fucking relief when the game finally starts. Matty's obviously feeling the same way, cause he breaks away from arguing with the lady that sounds like a drunk galah and rolls his eyes. Everyone's attentions are now glued to the idiot boxes mounted on the walls. I could probably strip naked and do a little jig and no cunt would even notice.

It's raining outside, evidently, because the players on the telly are running around on a muddy field.

'Aw yeah, it's a master-class in wet weather footy,' booms the hag's husband, a guy whose head sits on a cushion of blubbery red neck rolls.

The whole stadium's built on the site of an old cemetery, and even though most of the graves were moved to Toowong Cemetery, rumour has it that there're a lot of Aboriginals still buried under the stadium because their gravesites were unmarked. I half-imagine their spirits getting mightily pissed off by the ruckus above and rising from their forgotten graves to reclaim some peace and quiet, tackling the players to the ground and scoring themselves a few points in the process.

Matty's mistaken my daydreaming for genuine interest and tries to give me a running commentary on the action, but I'm content with trying to ridicule it instead.

'This is like a religion to these people,' he warns. 'Don't insult it.'

His painful commentary resumes unabated. On the screen one of the Wallabies players, a Michael Brial, gets stuck into a Frank Bunce from the All-Blacks, holding onto him and swinging a few punches into him. The crowd around us goes mental, calling for the refs to send Brial off the field, which they don't.

'Fuck off, Fleming, ya hori cunt!' screams this guy with a bull-neck next to us. His eyes are bloodshot from alcohol and bulging from his head with rage.

Even the commentator on TV is calling for it: 'He must be sent off. Brial *must* be sent off.'

The players break the two apart and the stadium crowd are booing, but nothing compared to the atmosphere in here. I'm fucking clueless as to what's actually going on!

'The bloody fuck?' says a guy in a yellow jersey. 'They reversed the penalty!'

'Chur, so they fucking should, ay,' says one of bull-neck's buddies to yellow jersey in a Kiwi accent so thick it makes his words sound short and sharp, like gunshots. Yellow jersey and his mates bristle at this, and the two groups start arguing about the game, the veins on their foreheads and necks swelling.

'Why don't youse fuck off back to New Zealand, ya cunts?' shouts an Aussie supporter.

'Can't, ya charlie,' says the bull-necked Kiwi, 'gotta go round your place later and bone your missus. She's like a bit a dark meat, aye?'

The guys in the black jerseys all roar with laughter at this, and to their discredit the guys in the yellow jerseys actually look remarkably offended by this simple insult. Degrading each other's partners is one of the top tiers in footy-fan humour, I've noticed. Since most insults are generally intended to tap into the fear of the recipient I can only conclude that in their opinion the worst thing that could ever happen for these fuckheads is to be cuckolded. Fuck knows why, though, because their girlfriends are hardly model material. Then again, these guys aren't exemplary specimens of appeal and personality, either.

Bernie's got this theory – which he reckons is actual fact born from personal experience on the beats – that half the pro-footy players are closet gays, marrying these dowdy women for the public security a marriage offers, enabling them to continue to play around with balls off the field and affording their wives such lavish lifestyles that they'll keep their mouths shut if they know what's good for them. He reckons he's polished a few of their heads in the glory holes beneath the pubs along St Paul's Terrace back in the day, the dirty old bastard.

The two sides inside Her Majesty's Bar start shoving at each other, and one of them takes a swing at the other. I'm not sure who throws the first punch, only that fists start flying.

'Fucking hell, Matt.'

'Yeah,' he drawls. 'Might be time to go.'

'Of course it is. The last thing I need is to get locked up in the mental hospital again for trying to kill a cunt.'

'I might join you if I miss out on seeing Gillian Anderson!'

We're trying to squeeze our way through to the stairs, but the crowd's too gee'd up to notice, and we keep getting pushed back or elbowed. It's like they've formed scrums of their own and are about to commence a game right here in Her Majesty's. Horrible thoughts pass through my mind such as this is a version of Hell and I've been condemned to live in it forever, or like we're trapped in that vampire bar in *From Dusk Till Dawn*. The visions spur me on even harder and in a fit of inspiration I drop to the floor and crawl between everyone's legs.

In no time I've reached the stairs, albeit with a couple of crushed fingers, and I wait as Matty tries the same trick. His head pokes out from the melee, and the relief on his face is testament to the horrors he must have encountered in there, too.

'Up! Up! Up!' he orders, like there's any need to. I'm up those stairs faster than he is.

The festive atmosphere in the Mall has turned sour. There's groups everywhere from both sides of the rugby camp squaring off against one another. One group starts punching on. Poor bastards just out for a night on the town who aren't even interested in football are getting caught in the crosshairs, trying to duck for cover. From Edward Street I can see the flashing lights of the red and blue, as a paddy-wagon starts inching its way up the Mall.

Some cunts in yellow jerseys turn on us, calling us Kiwi scum.

I can feel The Inferno urging me to kick off.

'Let's G-O-G-G-O,' says Matty in that voice from the Yellow Pages ad on telly as we duck down the stairs under the Wintergarden building and scoot through the dimly-lit arcade to Elizabeth Street where it's a relatively normal night, punter-wise.

'That was a close call.'

'Central's this way,' he goes, and we head up around the long way via Creek Street just to be sure we're out of the danger zone, but have to double back because more of these footy cunts are spilling that way from City Rowers down at Eagle Street Pier. It's starting to feel like a survivalist movie.

'Fucking hell, Matty, just take me back to the nuthouse now. It felt a hundred fucking times safer in there.'

'Stop being over-dramatic,' he says, as we finally get clear of all the celebrations or brawling. It's hard to distinguish which is which as we watch from the footbridge over Adelaide Street.

X MARKS THE SPOT FOR MALIK

Gillian Anderson, star of the one and only X-Files, is appearing at Indooroopilly Shopping Town tomorrow, and because me and Angele are fans we've come along to see her. A day early, but, because we caught wind that people were going to camp out overnight to see her. So after I got back from town with Dante (what a fucking disaster *that* turned out to be) I borrowed a tent from Bernie, who said he only had it as a joke (something about being camp), and got there at ten o'clock just as a small crowd of people were setting up as well.

Not our usual Saturday night, ha!

Security were shitty about everyone being here so early (a whole day!), and organised with management that we could all camp out on the top carpark roof like a bunch of derros. It's a bit fucking rich in the middle of winter, but if we wanna be first in to see Gillian that's just how it goes.

Angele, light of my light, has had the foresight to bring a thermos of hot coffee, because as soon as that sun sets behind Mount Cooth-tha the temps fucking plummet! Everyone starts freezing. Doesn't stop more and more people turning up, but. By about midnight there must be about a hundred people in sleeping bags and tents.

Looks like street-scummers central.

Me and Angele have one of the best spots, right up next to the door that the security are going to use as the beginning of the line-up for people to get a ticket, that will allow us to then get an autograph. Thousands of people are expected to turn up to see her, big star and all, and it's not reasonable to expect her to sign that many video covers or books or whatever, so they're limiting the numbers.

First in first served!

Turns out the tent's useless, but. There's nowhere to stomp the tent pegs into the ground cause it's all concrete. In the end we settle for using it as an extra covering over our blankets.

'You guys got a good possie, ay,' this guy a few spots up goes.

'X marks the spot,' I grin, trying to stop my teeth from chattering.

'Clive,' old mate goes, shuffling over to shake my hand.

'Malik and Angele,' I say.

Angele's noticed the guy is chewing hard on a chuppa-chup stick even though the lolly's long gone.

'You got anything to pass the time?' she asks, a twinkle in her eye.

'Yeah, ov corse,' he grins, flicking the chewed stick between his teeth.

He brings his sleeping bag over to where we are, which makes the people camped between us bitch and moan about fairness.

'He's a mate,' I snap.

'Bullshit,' this woggy prick goes. 'You just met him.'

'WE KNOW HIM FROM WAY BACK,' screams Angele, making everyone look over our way. 'HAPPY?'

She gets pretty toey with tossers like this guy.

'Yeah, fuck off,' the woggy prick mumbles, going back to rubbing his hands together under his blanket, the wanker.

Clive chuckles. 'Fiery as, love it,' he smirks.

Turns out Clive's dropped acid and is having a fucking ball of it, says the cold's not affecting him that much.

'Like, I can feel it but I'm more like one with it, ay, y'know?' he says. 'It feels fresh. Not like these other dumb cunts shiverin their arses off.'

I'm actually shivering my arse off here, but Clive's point is that we're his mates now so it's share and share alike. Of course, I know he's just doing it to get in front of line with us, but so what? Good luck to him, I say.

Angele's keen as for a drop, and since there's no sleep to be had on this hard concrete we accept a tab of blotter paper each from our new friend in opportunity. Besides, after the evening I had with Dante trying to avoid getting my head punched in at Her Majesty's, I deserve some time out of my head. The acid tabs're tiny, and shiny like wax paper.

'These are just Flying Keys, ay,' Clive explains. 'Not bad, but not the best. Strawberries back in the day were bloody ace. Double dipped, the fuckers. Here,' he says. 'Down the fuckin hatch, then.'

It turns out to be nothing like I'd thought it'd be. Movies always paint acid trips to be like a psychedelic cartoon experience, when in fact it's more like everyday life with tweaks here and there and a full on fit of the giggles. Holy shit, but Angele, Clive and me are laughing at everything like a bunch of scalliwags!

The woggy prick next to us is getting real toey cause he's trying to sleep.

'You're a bleepin dead alien if I ever saw one,' I tease him, which makes Angele and Clive cackle so hard they almost choke.

The lamps at the corners of the carpark and directly above us swell up and down like glowing jellyfish, but if I concentrate hard enough they turn back into normal lights. The fur on Angele's jacket collar moves as if in a gentle breeze, when the night air is as still as.

'Sometimes I can taste colour and smell sound, ay,' Clive goes, which sounds like stereotypical drug talk to me but he insists it can actually happen. 'Like if I was to look at that light up there I might hear a piano playing. That sort of shit, ay. Synesthesia it's called.'

'I wanna experience that,' coos Angele.

'Not on these FF's, you won't, ay,' says Clive, glancing around the carpark and noticing for the first time how still and quiet it is. 'Looks like everyone up and died.'

We burst into a fit of giggles that wakes the woggy prick, who grumbles about calling the cops. He just tries to go back to sleep, but. Where's he gonna get cops at this time of night? Sure, there's a cop-shop across Moggill Road but it means walking all the way down to the street in the freezing cold.

I wonder if Gillian's hair will be the same as Scully's or if like a lot of actors she'll look completely different in real life. You see it in the magazines where some celeb gets caught going out for fish and chips or whatever and they look no better than the derros begging for change in the Queen Street Mall.

Perhaps I've been dwelling on these thoughts a while, or perhaps the conversations between Clive and Angele is going in leaps and bounds, because when I try and focus on what they're waffling on about all I hear is Clive's impassioned voice: 'Humans make those laws, and no god inspires anyone cause God doesn't exist, ay. What *does* exist, but, is the human tendency to be the one owning the mystical supremacy.'

Fucking religion. Of all the things to talk about when you're high.

My teeth ache, like really fucking ache.

Clive's still yattering away, chomping down on the chuppa-chup stick the whole time. 'So God becomes the flunky to project it onto, ay, to put responsibility for choice on something besides themselves.'

I'm feeling fucked, as well I should be cause I've been awake all fucking night. I curl up and try and get some shut-eye, but try as I might sleep eludes me. It's not even like there's thoughts running through my head, more like my mind is desperate to try and find something to think about.

After about an hour of this shit I sit up and moan: 'Oi, Clive, ya scalliwag, does this shit keep you awake, man? I've been trying to doze off here for the past hour and can't.'

'Don't exaggerate, babe,' Angele goes. 'You were lying down for about ten minutes.'

Ten minutes? I swear it felt like an hour or more.

'Shit, felt longer,' I groan.

'Yeah, time's a bit of a shitter on LSD,' Clive goes, sounding really subdued.

Sleeping bags start flipping open as some of the crowd get up and start seeking out a coffee. Most of em head off in search of an all-night McDonald's, which is a bit of a hike down the road.

'Thank fuck, must be nearly time,' I go, rubbing my hands together and trying to decide which video I'll ask Gillian to sign. I've got only got three of em since Fox just started releasing the episodes on VHS this year, so it's a toss up between *Pilot*, *Conduit*, or *Fallen Angel*. Maybe she'll sign all three for me?

'Mate, it's only six in the morning,' Clive says. 'Shopping centre doesn't open until ten.'

I nearly scream into my blanket. I'm really fucking tired! I just wanna get my tapes signed and get the fuck home for a decent sleep!

The sun breaks over Taringa's apartment towers and hits us full force. We're set up behind a concrete wall but the brightness is the same as when trying to deal with daylight after a night out clubbing. It's the last thing your eyes, or whole system, wants to deal with.

The woggy prick stands up and stretches, giving us a surly look.

I curl under my blanket again, my ears tuned in to every tiny sound the outside world makes, my jaw muscles starting to seize up from being clenched so hard. Eventually Angele crawls under with me, also moaning about a lack of sleep.

'I fucking hate acid,' she whimpers.

'Thought you loved it.'

'Normally,' she groans. 'Not at the moment, though.'

I can hear her teeth grinding together.

'You need a chuppa-chup stick,' I go.

'Should borrow Clive's,' she jokes, and we start giggling again, but not from the acid this time.

Next thing I'm aware of is sweet darkness, and a heaviness lifting off me. No, it's not heaviness, it's consciousness, actually. I'm coming into consciousness.

Someone's tapping my foot.

'Up an at em, you two,' a voice says, a guy's. Not Clive's, but.

I fling the blanket back, instantly regretting it as the high noon sun punches me fair in the face. I block it with my arms.

'Clive?'

'No-one here, matey, just you two losers,' the guy says again.

I blink, squinting around, noticing that the carpark is full of cars. The campers have all gone. We must've fallen asleep finally!

'Angele, wake up, quick!'

She shoots up, her haired messed up on one side like an imitation of Robert Smith, dribble trailing down her chin.

'What's the fucking time?' she gasps.

'Midday,' this guy standing over us, a security guard, says. 'X-Files is over.'

No. No, this can't be happening.

I'm on my feet and running to the door. Down in the middle of the shopping mall is a stage set up in front of the entrance to Myer, but it's empty. Gillian Anderson has left the building.

'You two look ratshit as,' laughs the guard obnoxiously. 'Fucken derros.'

There's a scar running down the left side of his face from top to bottom. I imagine some prick probably glassed him at a bar once, and can imagine why.

Me and Angele pack our stuff, basically bundling it all up inside Bernie's tent and slinging it over my back like Santa's sack, and head off. The security guard follows us, giving us the bum's rush.

Down at the bus station we park the carcass on a seat and Angele moans about just wanting to sleep forever.

Clive comes out of the shopping centre looking stone cold sober, and boards the Kenmore bus, smiling at a video case in his grubby hands. I'm guessing he got Gillian Anderson's autograph, the prick. Fair play to him, but.

'Fuck it, let's get a taxi home,' I go, much to Angele's relief.

PIXIE GOES SHOPPING

Roz has this friend, as much as junkies can have friends, who likes to smoke meth pretty regularly. Her name's Christina, or Chrissy.

'She's a cunt, though,' says Roz, even as we're on our way to catch up with her.

This isn't a social call. It's business. It's just another scam in Roz's ever-increasin logbook of scams to source cold, hard cash. It's almost exhausting tryin to mentally catalogue all the shit she gets up to, and all the different lies, personas and networkin needed for each one. When drugs become a constant part of ya life, networkin is fuckin key to survival. If she wasn't a full-time junkie, Roz'd probly make a successful business entrepreneur with her strong mental talents.

She's brought me along coz today's activities require numbers. We're gonna go on a five-finger discount spree and confuse the fuck out of store managers along the way.

'It sounds like a caveman approach,' says Roz when we're on the train, 'just barging our way through it, but it's bloody effective. You'll see.'

Chrissy's already waitin for us at Strathpine station, wearin dirty pink uggies and an ugly, oversized pink jumper with a cartoon koala on it and the words MORE THAN A KOALA CAN BEAR.

'Yew must be Pixie,' Chrissy says before I'm even clear of the train doors. She leans in to shake my hand, her arm jerkin around like she's got no control over it. Like she has cerebral palsy or some shit. 'Name's Chrissy. These're the sprogs.' She's got three kids, one in a big-ass pram. The other two're about three years old, maybe older. A boy and a girl, chasin each other around the platform. Chrissy screams at em: 'Stop runnin near the fucken edge, yew liddle cunts!'

I've never been to Strathpine before. Turns out it's pretty shit. Full of retirees and people tryin to start families, but like poor families. There's no money here.

'Not here there's not,' Roz agrees. 'But further out there is. Rich housing estates starting to pop up all around the Pine Rivers Shire. They flock to these centres for their needs, who in turn are pumping out the goods. We'll hit it and get the fuck out of here, pronto.'

'Then after a few fucken monfs they'll forget all about us,' adds Chrissy, who I'm learnin always wears an expression like she's just got a whiff of dog shit. 'That's when we hit the cunts again.'

I notice Chrissy's got this oozy lookin sore on her shoulder, pokin out from her singlet. It looks fuckin gross as! I think she needs to go and see a doctor bout that.

Predictably, the shopping centre's also shit. We make straight for the big department stores, but Chrissy's liddle boy, Brayden, is bustin for a piss so we make a detour for the dunnies first.

'Oi, Nelly Jelly, yew stay wiv your aunty Roz, yew hear me?' says Chrissy to her liddle girl, who just nods like a retard. The kid literally smells like vinegar, which makes me wanna eat some salt and vinnie chips.

Chrissy and her kid disappear down the corridor to the toilets.

'Is her name Nelly?' I ask Roz, noddin at the liddle girl who's dancing round us.

'Yep,' she beams. 'Named after Nel. Cool, ay?'

'I guess,' I shrug. I'd fuckin hate to have a brat named after me, but. Especially with a mong name like Prudence. Who'd do that to their kid on purpose? 'I noticed that sore on Chrissy's shoulder.'

'Stupid bitch,' Roz scoffs. 'That's what meth does to you, Pix. She's been rubbing away at the skin until it's broken open. Notice how her face looks all puffed up? Meth bloat. But don't say anything about it, okay hun?'

'Sure, no problem. Her kid's aren't on it, too, are they?'

'Fuck no,' says Roz, a bit agro by the suggestion. 'Chrissy's a cunt, but she loves her kids.'

'Sorry, it's just I noticed the liddle girl sorta moves like her and thought it might've been from the meth, too.'

Roz glances down at Nelly, and for the first time notices the kid's got unco jerky movements, like she's dancin to a song in her head.

'Fucking hell,' says Roz slowly, her eyes goin wide.

'What is it?'

'You're right,' she goes, and I feel pretty bad for pointin it out now, coz it's probly like the last thing Roz wants to have to think about.

'Are ya okay, Roz? I'm sorry if I've done somethin wrong.'

She glares at me. 'It's okay. It's nothing for you to worry about.'

When Chrissy gets back Roz pulls her over next to a service door for a serious discussion. I keep one eye on the kids while still tryin to eavesdrop as much as possible. They're not makin it easy for me, but.

I hear Chrissy whine: 'Yeah, nah, she's awright, but.'

'Are you fucking kidding me?' spits Roz.

'I just didn fink, that's all, Roz. Fuck! C'mon, yew know me, cunt! Yew know me! I wouldn do it on purpose. Her jumpers and shit was in the wash basket when I lit up and I just didn fink about it, that's all. Fuck!'

'Jesus,' whispers Roz hoarsely. 'It was on her clothes? Babe, it's on her fucking skin.'

'I know, I know, I fucked up big time,' says Chrissy, eyes dartin round, catchin me watchin. I quickly look away. 'The tweaken will fuck off when it's gone from er system. Don worry bout it.'

Roz crosses her arms. 'You know they've tested monkeys with it and their brains are still rooted two years later?'

'Don say that, c'mon, Rozzie,' pleads Chrissy. 'Fuck's sake, tha's just fucken cruel.'

It strikes me as strange that a meth-addict and a junkie are debatin the wrongs of substance abuse, but it's clear that Chrissy must've smoked crack round her liddle girl's laundered clothin and now the poor brat's absorbed the meth through her skin. Her nervous twitchin is the result ova methamphetamine high.

Roz has Chrissy by the shoulders now, starin deep into her eyes and getting up her more. She's whisperin real quietly now, but, so I can't hear what's bein said, but Chrissy casts her eyes to the floor and nods sadly. Then they wander back over to us.

'Ready for some shopping kids?' Roz asks excitedly, and the liddle cunts cheer in response.

Chrissy won't make eye contact with me, now; just roughly grabs the pram off us and leads everyone to the closest store.

Once we're inside, the two brats start runnin round like spazzos, gettin more outta control by the minute. The store speakers are playin some shit local radio station, and I imagine the kids runnin in time to the music like I'm watchin Rage at one o'clock in the mornin wasted off my nut.

'Did I do the wrong thing before?' I ask Roz.

'No, why do you think that, sweetie?'

'Your friend doesn't seem to like me much.'

Roz smiles. 'Don't worry about her. She doesn't like anybody. Probably not even me, to be honest. She's just embarrassed, that's all. The last thing an addict wants is to be exposed in any form.'

'So what are we doin here?' I need to ask, coz all we've done so far is wander round lookin at shit on the shelves while the kids get more and more insane.

Roz laughs. 'Open your eyes, Pix. Don't you see it?'

I see sweet fuck all, is what I see. We're just walkin round while Chrissy randomly picks stuff up to look at before shovin it roughly back onto the shelf.

'I can see this area's not in your skill set,' tuts Roz.

'Of course it is,' I say defensively. 'Just how d'ya think I got this Manson shirt I'm wearing? I ripped off this bitch at me Dad's work.'

'You bought it?'

'I stole the money first, but,' I point out.

'Not the same,' Roz goes. 'Money's easy to grab. I'd be impressed if you'd managed to filch the shirt itself, instead.'

I didn't come here for a fuckin lecture. I thought we were all gonna hang out, have a laugh, steal some shit. Instead it's been borin as fuck and the only one who seems to be high and havin a great time is the fuckin kid. Maybe I should lick her clothes?

And then I literally see it, and Roz catches on that I've seen it by the look on me face. She looks a liddle bit proud of us.

Chrissy doesn't always pick up one item off the shelf, but two. Except, only one item goes back onto the shelf. She slams it down in fact, like she's disgusted with it. The other item, in this case a bottle of Tommy Girl perfume, stays on top of the pram. A bit more browsin and Chrissy briefly fusses over the baby below. When she's done, the perfume's gone.

Roz nods slowly at me.

'And the bald cunt behind us several aisles back,' she says quietly. 'Don't look back. The cunt that's been following us, that's undercover security. Dumbest of the fucking dumb.'

I start gettin nervous. We've been made. It's one thing to stir the security cunts out on the street, but this is their territory. We're gonna get fuckin arrested before we can even leave.

'Calm down,' Roz says firmly. 'Everything's fine.'

The two brats tear down past us, knockin stuff off the shelves. As they round the corner behind us, I can hear a nerve-wrackin crashing sound as a whole display stand goes down.

Roz chuckles, quickly tuckin some bottles of makeup foundation under her shirt.

I get it now.

'The kids are a distraction,' I go.

'Yep,' nods Roz. 'Although for Chrissy I think it's also a way to get back at the world. She could control them more but chooses not to.'

I feel emboldened that Roz has done this before, that she knows what she's doin. Then the store sound system starts playin a Primus song, *On The Tweek Again*, and I feel like we're the rulers now. I used to fuckin love Primus, or more like I did when I used to hang around with Imp after school. Everythin's going our way.

Except, when we all get to the exit and try and leave, the bald cunt that's been followin us suddenly walks up next to us. 'Ladies, do you mind if I check your bags?'

'What for?' demands Roz, in what seems like a role reversal for her and Chrissy.

'It's fine, babe,' says Chrissy calmly, unclippin her bag to show the dude that there's not much to see. As she's clippin it back up, I notice there's loose tampons scattered inside. I know for a fact that they'd probly normally be in a pocket, even in a meth-addicts handbag. She deliberately left the tampons loose so the security cunt would be too embarrassed to check in her bag proply. Guys've got such a hang-up about that shit.

Roz pretends to be pissed off but reluctantly lets him look inside her bag, too. When he asks to check the pram, Chrissy fuckin loses it.

'HOW FUCKEN DARE YEW TOUCH MY BABY!' she screams, so loudly that everyone at the cash registers stare at us.

The security dude immediately goes pale.

'Who the hell do you think you are?' demands Roz loudly, jabbing a finger at him. 'You've got no right to touch our baby!'

'CALL THE POLICE!' yells Chrissy to no-one in particular. 'This guy's a fucken paedophile!'

Now the security dude is literally shittin himself.

'Ladies, please be calm,' he says, uselessly. 'Please.'

'You're going to fuckin prison,' I quietly snarl at him, enjoyin his discomfort. How many fuckin times have these security assholes gone through me bags or ask us to open me hoodie so they can see if I stole something and then I've caught them starin at my boobs? Too many times, that's what.

Fuckin squirm, ya piece of shit.

'Un-fucking-believable,' Roz is sayin loudly as she helps Chrissy from the store, who's actin like she's crushed by the accusations. The kids are over at one of the service counters snatchin at chocolate bars, runnin back to us with fistfuls of em. No-one's game to say anythin about their blatant theft.

Shoppers outside the store are literally starin at us as we pass, but we're feelin fairly confident that we caused enough ova scene that the security dude won't bother followin us. Confident we're in the clear, we hit a jewellery store next with the excuse that Chrissy's old man is feelin guilty about havin knocked her up with the baby in the pram outside of wedlock. Roz pretends that the other two brats are hers. I'm not assigned a role, just told to keep my trap shut and stand close.

We ask to see an assortment of rings which the dude behind the counter dutifully places before us. We make out we're inspectin each one, debatin the qualities of each and tryin to figure out which one we should demand Chrissy's fictional boyfriend to purchase.

Roz and Chrissy can't seem to agree on one, so ask to see more. The counter's already full of selections at this stage, and as soon as the poor cunt turns round to grab some more for us to check out, Chrissy whips her hand out lightnin fast and snatches one of the rings. It's gone by the time the dude stands up and turns round again.

He puts the new rings on the counter, lookin over them. I'm waitin for him to realise one's missing, but there's so much stock on the glass it'd take a genius to remember it all, I reckon.

'Don't touch that!' yells Chrissy at Brayden, who hasn't actually done anythin wrong.

The dude behind the counter gets paranoid, but, and strains to see over the counter at the kid. Roz swipes another ring from the counter.

'Sorry bout that,' says Chrissy sweetly to the sales dude. 'I fought he was goin to break the glass on your beautiful display case.'

It'd be hard to think that it could break such thick glass just coz a stupid liddle kid touches it, but the dude smiles at Chrissy, relieved that the kid isn't about to destroy somethin.

This time he does notice that somethin's missin, and he's lookin at us all in turn like he's pretty sure we took it, but coz we're all actin like nuthin's happened he's obviously not sure. He checks the floor underneath him, then looks over all the rings. Ya can almost hear him tryin to count them all and estimate if anythin's really missin.

'What about you, hun?' Roz asks him, distractin him from his task. 'Which one, as a man, would you buy for yer girlfriend?'

'Not sure,' he stammers. 'I don't have a girlfriend, so I guess–'

'No way!' shouts Chrissy, makin the dude jump from fright. 'Yew don have a girlfriend? Girl's don't know what they're missin out on with yew, I reckon.'

He smiles bashfully, still glancing nervously down at the rings.

'Probly hung like a horse, too,' Chrissy adds, fairly fuckin drooling as she stares at the dude's crotch. He goes bright fuckin red, which cracks me up something shockin.

'Don't flirt with him, Jackie,' says Roz to Chrissy, usin the name they'd agreed to use outside the shop. 'You've got a fella already.'

'I wasn't flirting,' says Chrissy icily. 'I was just complimentin the gentleman.'

'Gentleman?' snorts Roz. 'Oh, listen to miss high and mighty here.'

'Fuck off, bitch,' snaps Chrissy.

Her aggression's literally so convincin in her hostility that I'm actually worried a real fight has broken out between these two.

Roz rips into Chrissy who gives it back just as good. Liddle Nelly starts bawlin her eyes out while Brayden's mesmerised by the fight, blockin the path of several other customers who've decided that they don't want to stick around and are tryin to leave. I'm lookin at the guy apologetically, and his face is startin to go from shock to annoyance.

'I think we better go,' I say to Roz and Chrissy, but still lookin at the sales dude.

Roz snaps her head round as she confronts him. 'Oh, I'm sorry, am I embarrassing you, Sir?'

'Well...' the dude goes.

'Oh don't worry, I'm fucking going,' declares Roz, grabbin Nelly and Brayden by their tiny wrists and stormin out.

'Yew've got some fucken nerve, cunt,' snarls Chrissy to the dude, steerin the pram out of the store.

'Sorry,' I say meekly to him and rush out as well.

Outside the shopping centre Chrissy and Roz burst into giggles, and when we're back on the train platform we check out the haul. It's such a random assortment of items it's hard to imagine any of it is worth anythin, except for the two rings which the guy promised were real gold.

'Don't worry, we'll be able to trade well with this stuff,' says Roz of the rest of the haul. 'Check out the prices on em.'

Sure enough, everythin has a pretty steep price attached. Top of the line makeup, a couple of electronics like the new Sony Discman, some CD's. Probly a couple of hundred dollars worth all up. A bit more, maybe. Another couple of hundred with the rings.

'Let's see what yew got,' Chrissy says to me.

From me waistband I pull out the few items I managed to squirrel away. It's not much. Mostly low-range cosmetics, a packet of black hair dye and, for some fuckin reason, a stainless steel kitchen spatula. I've no idea how come I grabbed that last thing; it was shiny, and just caught me attention, is all. The rest is stuff I'd personally use, but. It becomes shamefully obvious I was out of me element.

'Is that it?' says Chrissy, curlin her lip up in a sneer and exposin her ruined teeth.

'Go easy,' snaps Roz.

Chrissy snorts and looks away, mutterin as she sorts through the haul, intentionally shovin my items aside as unworthy of inclusion. I feel me cheeks blushin. Fuckin cunt meth bitch.

Roz squeezes me hand, givin us a tender look. She's like Mother Teresa to me, making sure I'm okay even when I've fucked up. If it wasn't for her, I'd probly start cryin which would be the worst thing to do in front of Chrissy. I've got a feelin she'd lap that up, and her fuckin brat kids, too.

I start willin for one of those liddle cunts to trip and fall off the edge of the platform and get stuck in the tracks, but the train comes and we all board without incident.

On the way back into the city Chrissy makes plans to catch up with Roz next week for another blitz, this time at Coles in the city.

'But it's closing down, isn't it?' Roz goes.

'Nah, not anymore, not until January I fink, at least,' she smirks. 'Failed at auction. Hit it one last time, I reckon.'

'Yay! Pudding!' cheers the liddle kid, Nelly, as she jerks around on her seat like a fuckin spazzo on an ant's nest.

'They fucken love that cafeteria upstairs,' grins Chrissy, scratching at a weepy sore on her neck. Some pus comes off onto her fingernail, but she doesn't notice and next thing she's chewin on the same nail.

'They're as bad as the old grannies that flock up there on pension day,' laughs Roz, stroking the brat's hair.

There's no mention of me taggin along, but, which suits me just fine actually coz anyone who wears as much pink as Chrissy does is obviously a retard anyway.

HAPPY HOUSE

My sister Lisa runs, like, a nifty boutique store in Paddington, on La Trobe Terrace amongst all the other trendy joints.

Her speciality is kid's clothing, designer stuff. She's tapping into a niche market that has yet to be suitably exploited, so she says, and exploit it she certainly will. All her stock is sourced locally, some from interstate, but her one rule is that it's not factory-made like the stuff from the bigger stores, who make an ugly profit on garments brought in from places like China and India where they use slave-labour. Lisa's whole ethos is that people will, like, pay heaps more for conscience-clothing, as she calls it.

Once she got set up and got herself profiled in some of the local magazines that are delivered to the inner-city suburbs, specifically targeting well-off neighbourhoods, business started booming for her.

Since I lost the job at the law-firm, she and Mama have colluded to make sure I don't rest on my laurels, as they put it, even though I've been getting shifts at this fricken awful factory over in Cannon Hill thanks to the job agency I signed up to. I thought they'd, like, try and get me somewhere more suitable, but they didn't give a toss. Nabbed that subsidy from the Government and dusted their hands of me.

I hate it there, but it has its moments.

Like, last week when I was chewing on my sandwich quietly in the corner at smoko time, the other workers – who're mostly blokes because it's basically laborious work – were having a gander through a *Picture* magazine. One of them, this young guy called Corey, got real excited by the centre spread. 'Phwoar, go the tits on that one,' he'd said, then grabbed a fistful of protein powder from one of the sacks we'd been filling. He'd stood there with fist at groin, sprinkling the powder on the ground, making moaning sounds and announcing how he'd 'give the slut some protein awright.' The other blokes had shifted uncomfortably in their seats and nodded their heads in my direction. Poor Corey nearly died when he'd seen me sitting over in the corner, blending in with the shelves behind because they both covered in the same powder I was. 'Aw, shit, sorry Alexandra,' he'd stammered.

It was all good, though. I didn't mind, and it was pretty funny to be able to, like, eavesdrop in on a boys' conversation.

Gotta laugh.

I don't know, though... like, I haven't heard from the shift manager about when they need me in next. I'm worried the other blokes have said it's basically not the same atmosphere having a girl around. I could be out of yet another bloody job!

A while back Papa had given me his old SLR camera, because I'd, like, talked about enrolling in a photography course out at Ipswich. I never did the course, but I played around with the camera and learnt some nifty tricks, like how to compose a proper shot and stuff. I take a pretty decent picture, even if I do say so myself.

So Lisa's got me around to her boutique on a cash-in-hand basis to take some pictures of her inventory. She wants to use them in a new catalogue. The money will tide me over while I, like, wait for the dole to clear me for payments again. Bit of a wait for that since I got kicked out of the solicitor's firm.

It's a fantastic shop, Lisa's is. I really love it. It's a tiny cottage with, like, slatted walls and a peaked, iron roof. There are four rooms and a balcony, with a modern built-in space downstairs. The land slopes on this part of the Latrobe Terrace, and the cottage stands on stilts, so she has her office down under it and the rooms of the cottage itself are all sales space. Lisa's done really well with it, and even though she mostly sells, like, children's clothes and some arty-farty knick-knacks like recycled paper diaries with pressed flower covers and whatnot, she gets a decent stream of people through the doors.

'Sorry, Alex,' she says, making me a cup of tea when it gets quiet, 'we can't shoot today. The new stock didn't arrive.'

She can see I'm dejected by the news. I was really looking forward to showing off what I can do with the camera, not that we wouldn't see the prints for, like, a couple of days anyway. Not until I could get them processed. But the truth is I could have saved that bus fare now that I'm jobless.

I'm like: 'S'okay,' pressing my hands around the warmth of the mug. 'It's always nice to, like, come visit. I love this place, actually.'

She smiles warmly, looking around the shop like she's seeing it for the first time. She's real proud of this place.

She's like: 'You know what? Let me get onto the supplier and see what's up,' and crosses to the phone. 'They're just across in West End. Don't want to waste your time.'

She calls him up and after a bit of back and forth, Lisa tells me that some of the stock is ready, just, like, not the whole order.

She nods discreetly at a young couple in the next room and is like: 'When these two are gone, I'll close up for a half hour and we'll go over and grab what's ready. Get you started. Might even drop in to The Three Monkeys for a coffee. You'll like it there.'

I smile and nod, and we chat about Papa's latest operation on his knee. The young couple don't buy anything, thank Lisa and leave. Lisa locks the door and writes a note for the door: BACK IN 30.

In the car on the way over, though, the sisterly bond slips away when the conversation turns to my recent unemployment.

'Mama was hoping you'd stick at that job this time,' she says matter-of-factly, like my disappointments have become so routine they don't elicit any emotion anymore.

'They were arseholes. Period.'

Lisa gives me a wide-eyed look, like she's already tired of my back-talking. 'A job's a job, Alex,' she says. 'You think I got to where I am without arseholes along the way? It's par for the course.'

I grit my teeth and stare out the windscreen, reaching forward to tap my fingertips against the rego sticker to distract myself from her whining.

For as long as I can remember, Lisa's had this mental game of one-upmanship going on with me, even if I'm not inclined to participate, just because she's my *mikrí adelfí*, my little sister. She's done it since we were kids, when she used to boast about being able to ride a bike first or, like, swimming first. She's only eighteen months younger than I am, so we've both pretty much had the same opportunities at the same time, but even as a small girl she took to them ferociously, determined to master each new challenge of childhood and rub my nose in it at the same time, like she had to make up for being born second. The rents don't realise, of course, because they think it's a natural thing for a kid to do, and maybe it is, but Lisa's always used her accomplishments to set herself well above my station in life and claim some satisfaction in proving that I was never going to amount to much. And as a kid, for frick's sake! Rather than rise to her challenge and try and knock the snooty bitch from her pedestal, I was always inclined to, like, defer and let her have her little victories, allow her to think they were hard won in the hopes it would shut her up faster and leave me alone.

As the years went by, I was more disposed to take a different path, often out of resentment I suppose, so I was only ever half-heartedly devoted to my interests. In fact, I would've loved to have, like, taken up swimming as a sport when I was a kid and maybe pursued it as something in high school, but after Lisa won the Junior division of the 1987 Bayswater Swimming Jubilee and brandished that pathetic looking medallion around like a talisman of triumph (even wearing it every day for the next couple of weeks so I'd have no chance of forgetting her conquest), I'd decided to help Mrs Mears run the Book Club at the school library. By then I'd already grown sick and tired of everyone's bullshit and, like, basically started wearing more and more black. Mrs Mears confided in me that she used to be a punk when she was a teenager in the late Seventies. That was, like, so cool. So she understood.

I was put in charge of writing the posters for each week's library theme, and Mrs Mears arranged with Mister Herron for me to use the art room at lunchtimes and have free reign of the glues and glitter and paints in there. There was no way Lisa would want to try and conquer this territory, especially as she'd now become captivated by having an audience cheer her on in her achievements. Even the boys I used to hang around were into Lisa. I fucking hated them by then, anyway.

The art room at lunch times was always empty, and became my solace away from the noisy playground where I was always going to be second-best to my sister. *Alex? Oh, Lisa's big sis, yeah?* Basically, that's how people began to relate to me, as just the older and more useless sister of someone so much better.

'It's not like you can afford a bad rep,' Lisa continues, steering the car around past the Museum and swinging right, towards West End. The under her breath she mutters: 'Although seems you've already got that.'

She's referring to how the cops stormed her house after Zak died.

It was hardly my fault, and no-one in my family's listened to me before that he was stalking me back in Melbourne, so what do they expect? Anyway, after a big family discussion Lisa's been told she can't keep rubbing my face in it, so, like, now I basically get snide remarks and muttering instead.

Of course, she's only just getting started. 'You've got like what? Five or six jobs behind you? No solid skill set. You're gonna do what? Walk into the next job with no references except for the Red Rooster one from a few years ago?'

The lights ahead turn red, the car in front braking suddenly. Lisa almost doesn't notice so we screech to a halt, the car lurching forward as we brake hard. It feels like I'm about to be propelled out through the windscreen. I press my hands against the dashboard for support, my fingers repeatedly flicking the rego sticker like it's a swollen clit.

'*Mia zoí malákas!*' Lisa yells, cursing the idiot driver, although I suspect it's partly directed at me. 'Geezus, did you see that?' then she gives the car in front a blast of the horn, but, like, the bloke gives us the middle finger out his window.

Lisa scoffs, shaking her head, then gets back into giving me a hard time. Like, not even a near-miss breaks her stride, can believe?

'You don't even have any certificates or any education to back you up. Darren's seeing to that for himself–'

'Oh, here we go.' Ever since her idiot husband enrolled in that business development course, he's been another yardstick I've failed to measure up to. Her boutique and marrying Darren have replaced the swimming medallion as tokens with which to humiliate me.

'Seriously, Alex! What do you have?'

'I'll be alright. I can get some regular work on, like, Scene or Time-Off doing some gig photography–'

'Oh, come on, Alexandra. Honestly.'

The lights turn red and the guy in front turns left as we go straight ahead, up Boundary Street. He flips his finger in the air one last time, but, like, Lisa doesn't see it, thankfully. The rego sticker looks like it's coming loose again, so I tap it back into place.

Lisa's like: 'You pick up Papa's old camera and now you're sitting flush? It takes a hell of a lot more than that. You gotta do what Darren is doing, back yourself up with some knowledge and have something to show for it.'

'He's doing a TAFE course,' I smirk. 'You make it sound like he's coming out with a Uni degree or something grouse.'

'Okay, for a start, stop saying *grouse* up here or they'll think you're a spasmo,' she says, 'and secondly, at least he's doing something. Not just fucking around wasting his life. And can you leave the fucking rego sticker alone!'

We both go quiet.

To be honest, I'm pretty fucking cranky and close to telling her to, like, pull the car over. But as much as I hate to admit it, she's right. This camera's not paying the bills anytime soon. And I can't keep losing jobs and references at this rate. I need something stable. So I sit and say nothing, aware that Lisa could afford a proper photographer but extending the offer to me on Mama's insistence. Maybe I'm being naive about the street press and photography, but I don't know where else to start unless I go back to serving in a food court or something, and I hated that enough the first time around at the Bayswater shops.

We finally pull up outside the house on Thomas Street.

'Let's just get this done,' Lisa says simply, reaching back for her business diary and handbag.

There's no answer at the door, but we hear some, like, weird high-pitched string music coming from under the house. There's a bottom level that is all besser brick underneath the raised cottage, so we head down the driveway around to the back of the house.

The back lawn is overgrown and there's sheets strung up on the line. A few little Chinese kids are playing over by the fence, running a stick along the wooden slats and laughing delightfully at the sound it makes.

We find a door that leads under the house to a room full of Asian women with toddlers and babies sitting on the floor on cushions or folded towels nearly shoulder-to-shoulder with a sewing machine each. They glance briefly up at us, then get back to sewing. The kids are all fidgety, grinning at us.

A short Chinese guy over on the far side of the room is holding up a garment, looking closely at the hemming. The woman beside his feet taps her sewing machine, saying something in rapid-fire Chinese.

'What the hell is this?' says Lisa, a bit shocked.

The guy jerks his head up, equally shocked. He sees me and Lisa, and absentmindedly drops the garment back onto the woman's lap, stepping around the other women and, like, coming toward us. He's all like: 'Who you are? What you want?' his voice punched by his accent. He waves his arms to shoo us out the door.

'I think this is a sweat shop,' I murmur to Lisa, dumbfounded.

'Get out!' the man screams, and we back away as he, like, waves us into the backyard.

Lisa gets cranky by this treatment.

'How fucking *dare* you,' she snaps. I'm not surprised that she's more outraged by his treatment of herself than of the women inside. 'What the hell kind of operation is this?'

He tells us to leave, trying to take my arm to push me back around the side of the building. I shake him loose and tell him not to touch me again. Lisa snaps her fingers in front of his face and is like: 'Hey, over here buddy. Is this how you make my stuff, is it?'

'No, no, this different,' he says both confidently and angrily. 'You go away. You trespass!'

I'm like: 'That's a freaking sweat shop, mate!', pointing inside.

There's eyes burning bright in the gloom beyond the doorway. The sight makes me feel ill, knowing they're cramped together, working on the floor.

He ignores me and continues to argue with Lisa, going on about calling the police which Lisa welcomes him to do. They're at each other's throats, neither willing to budge. My mind spins as I watch this fiasco. The kids by the fence have stopped playing and are staring at us, the stick discarded in the grass. I'm, like, desperately trying to avoid glancing back towards that doorway, but I can feel their eyes on me. Before I go mad, I decide to leave. I basically start walking back up the driveway to the street, relieved as the yelling gets fainter.

But out on the street I feel worse, like I've abandoned Lisa.

Thomas Street is quiet; only a few cars come and go on it. Vulture Street ahead is busier, and I feel like I've stepped from a nightmare and am drifting towards the waking world, the sane world, the hustle and bustle of a typical Brisbane day.

I turn past the Vietnamese bakery on the corner, unable to make eye contact with the owners, a hand against the wall for support, and get across the road to the bus stop.

Before I know it, there's a bus in front of me. I let everyone else get on first, feeling reluctant to leave, knowing that just around the corner there's a sweatshop operation full of women who I assume have, like, no say; have no other option. The thought begins distressing me. But Lisa's there, she'll sort it all out. She'll fill me in later on what the real gist is. She'll make it all better.

The bus-driver is glaring down at me because I'm fumbling with my purse. When I pass him the coins for the fare to the Museum stop so I can jump on the southbound train home, my hand's, like, shaking so badly that some of the coins tip out and clatter onto the floor. I see a twenty cent coin roll out the door into the gutter.

'Sorry, sorry,' I stammer, trying to find a replacement. A young guy gets out of his seat and picks up the coins from the floor for me, and I barely manage a thank-you for him.

The bus driver turns back to the windscreen and, like, refuses to look at me, just stubs a finger onto coin tray and waits for me to drop the money there. I can feel the hostility coming from him, and meekly take my ticket. Inexplicably, I bang my hand against the ticket dispenser and then the coin tray, shuffling down the aisle to a seat, using the backrests for support along the way.

The driver slaps the door shut and lurches the bus into the lane, swinging it around onto Boundary all in one motion. I fall forward fast, reaching for the yellow hand pole. I miss, my shoulder and the side of my face crunching into the metal pole. It really fucking hurts, and I basically fall into a seat beside it, next to this old Greek or Italian man who openly glowers at me before staring out his window. I'm, like, super embarrassed, and not just feeling hurt by the pole but by the driver also, who's frowning at me in the rear-vision mirror.

Why do people do this to us? Who cares if I wear so much fucking black? Or that my hair's dyed black? Or that my eyeliner wings curl up into curlicues?

I feel like crying. My whole face feels hot. I can feel people staring at me.

'Hey, don't worry about it,' says the young guy who picked the coins up for me. He leans over, speaking in hushed tones. 'There was a junkie on a couple stops back who gave the driver a hard time about the fare. He's just shitty about that, is all.'

The guy smiles sympathetically.

The driver probably thinks I'm a junkie, too. Heaps of mundanes have thought that, just because, like, I'm a goth. They don't have a freaking clue. But, like, it doesn't make me feel any better. They just shit on us and shit on us and shit on us, making themselves feel better in the process. Like Lisa does.

Lisa thinks she's adaptable. She believes that's her strength, that whatever there is in life to achieve, she can reach out, give it a go, and succeed. She has done it with every available opportunity in life: she excelled at school, became dux in her final year, went from sporting achievement to sporting achievement, got herself a steady boyfriend who she later married, moved to Brisbane and developed a niche-market enterprise as a self-employed business operator, blah blah blah. She attributes these successes to some misguided notion that she's got an adaptable personality, can see fluctuations of opportunity and ride their waves.

But it's not true. My sister's a stubborn, pig-headed bitch who was too afraid to date after high-school and is too committed to a life with her ridiculous boyfriend who she probably secretly hates. And as for her booming entrepreneurial clothing store, I happen to remember a friend of hers called Sarah Duxhill from Bayswater High who used to chat with her about starting up a niche market business. She didn't call it that, but I remember the two of them making plans in Lisa's bedroom after school lots of arvos, coming up with fanciful ideas that they thought they'd turn into pots of gold. When she graduated the following year, Lisa moved up here and Papa took out a loan to co-invest in Lisa's grand idea for a clothing store, and no mention was ever made of Sarah Duxhill in our household ever again. For all I know, poor Sarah's still sitting down in Melbourne with a head full of dreams that my sister stole for herself. Everyone praises Lisa for her ambition and her vision, but secretly we all know she couldn't scratch out an original idea if her life depended upon it.

There's one arena that I know Lisa never excelled at, despite her popularity, one that she positively feared.

Sex was a bland and tasteless dish for her, and she was more than content to be bullied into losing her cherry to that dipshit Darren Stevenson. I caught them feeling each other up in her room one day when Papa was out in the backyard, and she made Darren threaten me if I told, as if I fucking would. Getting laid was exactly what she'd needed, in my opinion. Just a shame it was fumbling around with that idiot, paranoid Papa would walk in at any moment. I imagine Darren finished in record time and gave my sis so little satisfaction beyond being able to boast at school that she'd *done it*. I can just picture that stupid phrase coming out of her mouth, along with the cringe-worthy *he put it in me.*

I remember when Lisa got her period first. I was already jealous as fuck of everything else she'd excelled at, but she still made a song and dance in front of me about going with Mama to Woolies to get her own tampons. I felt, like, excluded by this union between mother and daughter, watching them with a sinking heart as they walked to the car together and drove off. I'd wanted to tear apart her most prized possessions, Mama's too, so they could regret erecting this partition that excluded me. It drove me toward Papa and his fatherly affections with a vigour that I think he'd found a bit disturbing, because, like, while at first he seemed happy about spending time with me he started looking at me all funny and finding reasons to keep me at a distance, like mowing the lawn and stuff. It stung me, and more than that, I became aware that more and more I was behaving towards him in a flirtatious way, the way that adolescents can sometimes be with older people. The knowledge he was aware of it and sorta rejected me was humiliating, though.

I was crushed... Mama and Lisa had their newfound sisterhood and Papa had the fucking lawn to see to.

The upshot of it all was that the next time the boys at school were teasing me about my boobs, which were embarrassingly substantial on a thirteen year old, I led them on with furtive smiles and let my skirt ride up whenever I was, like, sitting down around them. It took no time for them to start dropping the hard word, laughing like they weren't serious. But I could see that dark look in their eyes, how their mouths twitched when they laughed. One of them, Nate Harrington, had really nice legs and arm muscles. I'd always liked the look of him. I took his jibes and scolded him, tried to belittle him a bit. He took it on the chin and dished it back, and that just got me humming more. So I hooked up with him behind the Milk Bar on Canterbury Road near the old steel-mill factories and had probably, like, the most unfulfilling sex I've ever had, but it didn't matter.

It wasn't long after that that I realised that I was, like, the butt of the boys' jokes, anyway. From there I launched myself into being alternative, and eventually found goth, secretly admiring some of the year eleven girls who'd gone against the school rules and, like, started dying their hair black and wearing more than just sleepers in their ear lobes.

I didn't tell Lisa that my first time hurt like fuck. She was still a virgin, more or less, and it would be several years before her and Darren became an item and, like, did the nasty in her bedroom, and I wasn't gonna let her in on any of the secrets of sex. That became my power over her: I was first over that finishing line. She could never, like, take it back for herself.

I don't know why I didn't see it coming, but she'd gone and told the rents what I'd done. I didn't bother denying it. I was still cranky with them that they'd favoured Lisa once again over me, and had let me wither in her shadow. But they were fricken angry.

Mama was all like: 'Your father's even too angry to say anything,', her mouth turned down with, like, bitter disappointment probably.

'Or he's just jealous,' I'd retorted, instantly regretting my cruelty.

Mama had flown into such a rage that she'd grabbed me by the hair, screaming that I should apologise to my Papa, which of course I did. But I still wondered if maybe that's why he'd pushed me away, that he felt something for me, for his own daughter whose tits were bigger than his wife's. I'd caught him idly staring at them sometimes when he thought I was focused on reading or watching TV.

I got grounded for two weeks, probably more for what I'd said about Papa than what I'd done with Nate Harrington.

The bus pulls up outside the Town Hall, and as everyone starts ambling off I, like, consider telling the bus driver to take his notions about me being a drug-addict and shove them far up his retentive arse, but there's a deep-set trembling in my bones and I just get the hell off the bus and hide behind the Town Hall from the city crowds, shaking like I'm cold. I don't know why, but I have a desperate urge to get home and basically lock myself away for awhile.

The next day Lisa calls me and tells me not to tell anyone about what happened because it'll ruin her reputation.

'He's done for,' she says down the line with dramatic finality. 'It's going to take a bit of work for me to get back on my feet again, but I'll get you around for a new photo session soon, hun, I promise.'

Then she starts crying, and I don't know what to say.

I feel bad for her, having to deal with this, and an overwhelming sense of guilt comes over me that I've been resentful towards her of late. She's my little sister and, like, just trying to get by. Then along comes muggins here fucking my life up and she tries to take me on, too. I feel like shit, now, and want to call her back and apologise and all that, but I don't want to burst into tears, either. And I know I will. I can, like, feel it brimming up inside me.

All I can think about is how, like, something bad's gonna happen to Lisa, or to Mum or Dad. I keep having these thoughts that they'll, like, get hurt or killed, and I can't shake the thoughts or the feeling.

Abi's worried about me, about these obsessions I've developed, so come the weekend she takes me out on the pretext that I've been cooped up too much lately, which to be fair is true. We head into the Valley to look around the markets and, like, basically soak up the atmosphere.

It feels good to be out with her again, even though I was reluctant to leave the apartment. There're heaps of people in the Brunswick Mall, and a cute guy is on guitar strumming out some songs, a bit of everything, some Offspring even. There's a nice vibe going on, and the sun's not too strong either; just right, in fact. It feels good to have it warming my hair and back, easing out the tension. I'm careful to make sure the sun's not hitting my arms or face, though: last thing I need's a tan! Period!

We pass a stall that's selling some kid's clothing, and they look kinda familiar, like if I haven't seen them before then I know the brand or something. I stop for a gander, tapping my hand across the various items, and then suddenly this feeling of, like, dread washes over me, and I feel my cheeks and arms pinprick. Without meaning to I quickly glance up at the stall-holder, this old Chinese guy, who's looking at us earnestly and moving some samples of his wares around so we can see more options.

My heart starts beating furiously.

'It's you, isn't it?'

The guy just smiles briefly and tells me he can do a deal if I buy three. I can't tell if it's the same guy with the sweat-shop from West End. I'm afraid to admit that I probably couldn't pick him from a line-up. They all sort of look the same to me.

'Alex?' says Abi, looking concerned.

'Are you the same guy?' I demand loudly, angrily, but the old guy just shrugs and continues to flop more samples of the clothing down in front of me, listing their attributes. *This one is nice cut, this one is good texture, you feel.*

I flip some of the clothes on the table at the guy, shocking him.

'Alex, you okay?' Abi rests her hand on my arm, but I shake it off.

'ARE YOU THE SAME FUCKING *TON POUSTH*?' I'm screaming now, and the guy, like, steps back, clams up, waves his hands like he wants us to go away.

Abi starts hoiking me away. She's like: 'Alex! What's wrong with you?'

I let her drag me away, because I'm really confused right now. It's why I'm so angry. If I just knew it was him or not I'd know what to do, right? Well, not exactly, but I'd probably go straight over to the police beat on the other side of the mall and get him arrested.

But, like, I don't know if it's the same bloke or not. That's what's really bugging me.

My chest is starting to hurt, like I can't breathe. I wonder if, like, I'm having a heart attack?

The stall-holders next to the old Chinese guy check on him, casting me wary looks, like as if I'm a dangerous person or something. They console the guy, who shakes his head and shrugs.

So I don't think it was him that ran the sweat-shop, just a massive coincidence. It's been playing on my mind so much lately that I've jumped the gun and started taking it out on people. I'm bloody lucky it's not *me* that's getting arrested!

We walk past people who are staring and whispering about me.

Abi leads me down to the corner of the mall and Wickham Terrace. I mustn't have much balance at this point, because, like, my hand keeps going to bins and lamp-posts as if I need support. Abi notices this, and wraps her arm around me, leading me by the hand.

Just as we're going around the corner, I glance back one final time at the kid's clothes stall and see the old Chinese guy standing with his arms crossed, watching me with a big grin on his face.

DANTE WINS SOME, LOSES SOME

'Donger, it's been a tops afternoon as usual, but I must depart.'

I climb down off my stool, testing my sobriety, or lack thereof. It's enough that I can make it home in one piece, I reckon.

'Piker,' he jeers. 'You run out of dough?'

It's alright for him cause he's got more of a cash-flow now that his flatmate Lachie's back home from the slammer and paying rent again. The stupid cunt spat in a copper's face outside a gig in West End a few months ago and got sent down for it, which meant Dale and Spaz have had to prop up the Indro house with their own meagre dole checks. It's been a laugh watching them moan about how it ate into their drinking funds, but now the laugh's back on me it seems. If only I could convince Bernie to rent out the couch for people to crash on, I wouldn't be so broke all the time.

'Nah, got a psych appointment this arvo, ay,' I wink at Donger, although in reality I've only just enough cash for the bus or train back to the Prozac. 'Never done it half pissed, before.'

It's weird, because when I was homeless I used to stay at Twix and Raven's flat all the time, so I was practically a stone's throw from McKay's office. Now that I'm actually living at the Palace I always seem to be a million fucking miles away from it whenever I'm booked in to see McKay. Weird how that goes.

'Oi, Dante, know what you should do?' Donger goes, big shit-eating grin on him. 'Film yourself killing your family and show it to him, but try and tell him that he killed them.'

Fuck this cunt comes out with some random stuff sometimes, but it gets a good laugh outta me.

'Catch up next pay day, then,' he goes.

'It's a date.'

From here he'll probably head down to the Bananalounge in the tin shed behind the Gabba Hotel to get pissed some more, play some pool and dance his little heart out to the likes of The Fred Band or maybe The Onyas. Whoever's playing, he's not too fussed.

Outside the Railway Hotel I've got a choice to make. Do I walk up past Clarence Corner and the Mater around to Vulture Street Station and get the train to Central, which means short walk over to Bowen Street, or do I walk down to the bus stop on the corner of Main and Stanley – which is closer – and get off in the Valley, which means a longer walk up to Bowen Street? The train seems easiest, because at least I don't have to deal with a stroppy driver that way.

If it wasn't for the fact that a lot of my punk mates are all spread out over the place, it'd be so much fucking easier to drink at a local watering-hole such as the Oriental rather than traipsing half way across town to the Gabba all the time. But besides 501 Queen Street and the pub at Chardon's Corner in Annerley, this is the punk hub what with the Railway Hotel, Van Gogh's Earlobe, the Bananalounge,

Sally's Coffee Shop. Just to name a few. So it's just as easy for everyone to catch up here, even for casual drinks, until the dole check runs low, which I've been doing more of recently. And lately Matty's been a bit funny about hanging out with me as much, always coming up with excuses for not catching up. I don't know if Angele's been in his ear or not. She doesn't seem that fond of me.

Funnily enough, Alan's told me in the past that the Gabba used to be known as a place of water holes by the local Aborigines (and a Bora ring behind the Railway Hotel itself!), so it seems only fitting that there's a shit load of pubs and bars to choose from now.

As I'm passing this tiny bar called the One Mile a few doors down on the corner – I've never been inside it because it's as about as pokey and dingy as the bar under the grandstand at the Ekka that should by all rights be condemned – the door swings open and this fat cunt in a faded green polo steps out and pulls a face like he's just sucked on a lemon, raising his hand to shield his eyes against the sun. As he does so, the cunt's foot misses the step and he just kind of falls like a tree, like one of those cartoon characters that stay stiff and fall like a plank for comedic effect. Except, I'm not laughing because the stupid prick falls straight into me and we both go down. I curse out loud, trying to shuffle out from under him as he rolls like a fucking tortoise onto his back with his hands and feet up.

Someone calls out to him from inside, *oi, Bill!* His foot's jammed under the door as it was swinging closed, so through the gap there's faces staring out looking all concerned. Some guys get up from their stools along the bar to come and assist. Stupid drunk cunt.

I push him off sharply, keeping my eyes trained on the cunts inside lest they see the hostility of my actions. I jump to my feet, still half bent over as though I'm ready to reach down and help the cunt up, but in fact delaying for as long as I can so his barfly mates can get out here and do it for me. Yep, even now they're holding the door open and getting around him to lift him like the sack of potatoes he is.

'You awright, Bill, ya old fool?' says this old bastard with a bushy white beard and greasy yellowed locks tucked behind his ears. 'You fucken duffer, ay?'

'Yeah, thanks, Donny,' says Bill.

I do my bit and hold the door for them as they steer him in onto a chair. They're fussing over him and making jokes about too much to drink and all that, but I've sort of tuned out because I've spotted the barmaid, who's topless. And not only are they a fine pair of tits, but I also recognise their owner!

She clocks me, too, and her face goes red because she knows me as well. It's Karen, Twix's ex from last year, or earlier this year. I can't remember precisely when they broke up; it was of little interest to me in the long-run. She turns away from me and covers her chest with her arms. I skip on in, heading to the bar with haste, in case she has a mind to head out back and avoid me.

Karen checks to see if I'm still here and is very fucking alarmed to see I'm but a few feet away. Another barmaid, much older – the nape of her neck red from baking in the sun – clocks how awkward Karen's acting.

'Everything alright, Kaz?' she goes, and poor Karen spins around as if she's been caught red-handed doing something she shouldn't; and maybe she shouldn't be, after all?

'Yeah, sure,' Karen says, unconvincingly.

So I give the woman a big smile, a kind of cheeky grin, really, and inform her that Karen and I run in the same circles. The old barmaid gets it, then, her mouth forming an O. 'Always a shock, first time,' she shrugs, going over to join the others in checking on Bill's welfare. Her flat tits slap against her chest as she walks.

I shudder at the sight. They remind me of those canvas water-bags strapped to the sides of camels in the movies. Except without the potential for sustenance.

'How about that, ay?' My eyes rove up and down Karen's torso, a far less sorry sight than the water-bags, pausing at her crossed arms as though I had x-ray vision and her attempts to cover her boobs were futile. Just letting the message drive home, as if it needed any further driving.

'Listen, Dante,' she says, her voice trembling slightly. 'Can you not say anything? You know... about this.'

Grabbing the bull by the horns, eh? Leading the charge, as it were. Admirable, Karen, but no dice.

'Does nobody know, then? That you work here?'

'Nah,' she says, trying for a casualness she can't possibly muster. Not here, undressed like this.

And what of it, so what? They're just tits, right? But I hold grudges easily. That's my thing.

'It's a bit hot out there.' I lift my arse up onto a stool, resting my elbows on the counter. Karen looks stricken. 'Can I get a Coke?

I'll have to jump the train without a ticket and bolt through the gates at Central and hope they don't give chase. I'm a bit too pissed for that, though, unless I get some water in me to sober a bit.

'With ice?'

Her expression goes kind of hard; maybe it's pleading, maybe it's just shitty. Either way, she complies, trying to scoop the ice up into the glass and tap some Coke into it without revealing herself too much. I just smile the whole time, staring at her chest. I truly don't have any problem with Karen at all, but it's guilty by association, I'm afraid. Who knows how many times she obliged Twix by chuckling at his jibes about me? Willing fucking participant, I bet. Regrets it now, too, I'm certain.

The cunt with the greasy yellow hair, Donny, falls against the bar beside me, huffing as if he's just done a days' work in an hour. His belly's so huge it stops him from getting too close to the bar, but not enough that he reaches out for Karen, beseeching her to come closer. She seems to realise whatever he's up to and looks mortified, but I suspect it's more to do with me as witness than anything else.

'C'mere, sweets,' he coos. 'I'll show yer friend ere a lil trick.'

'Not now, Donny,' says Karen.

'I like tricks,' I beam hopefully, like a kid ready for a magic show.

'It's a good one,' Donny says, then starts coughing like he's about to keel over. Hold it together long enough, man.

'See, you've gone and over-exerted yourself again,' chides Karen, but without any feeling.

'I'll be right,' wheezes Donny, his eyes watering as he struggles to regain his composure.

'Pity they're not lactating still,' I go, and Karen's eyes go wide with horror. 'I've heard that's a real niche market for some punters.'

Her mouth gapes like a fish out of water, and finally she splutters: 'Twix blabbed about the baby, then? Typical.'

Her eyes glass over like she's going to cry.

Actually, he didn't, I'd suspected one night when we were drunk as skunks and I'd coaxed it outta him. As far as I know, to this day he has no recollection of the confession. But it doesn't matter, anyway, because Alex told me that he's already spilled the beans to her when they were clubbing. He's lucky the news hasn't spread throughout the scene like wildfire.

The old barmaid passes behind me and venomously goes: 'Finish your drink and get out.'

I consider spitting something caustic back, but figure it wouldn't take much from her to rally the bar against me and it'd be worse than having some drunk geezer fall on me out the door. I can tell some of these tradies are itching to have a fucking go at me. Instead, I quickly down my drink, which has the effect of feeling like someone's punched me in the back of my throat (though I don't let it show on my face), giving Karen's boobs one final appraisal then spin off my stool and stroll out the door, big smile in defiance to everyone I pass.

When I get home Bernie's outside on his chair having a smoke.

'You had a couple of visitors today,' he goes.

'Did these visitors have names or are you gonna make me milk it out of you?'

He grins at me luridly.

'I mean milk it out of you with extreme violence, smart arse,' I say.

'A couple of police officers,' he goes.

'That bitch must have called them as soon as I left the bar,' I say, thumping my fist into my palm. She wasted no fucking time, I'll grant her that.

'What bar?' Bernie goes. 'They said something about a girl from a festival you went to.'

It takes me a moment to work out he's talking about Rosie.

'Girl called Rosie? Did something happen to her?'

'Yeah, that's the one,' he nods. 'The cops just wanted to know if you live here. They're not going to do anything.'

'Anything? What the fuck are you on about.'

'Statutory rape,' he says.

I feel the blood drain from my face as the pieces slot together. That cunt of a father must've forced himself on her when she got over to

America! I feel fucking sick.

'Fuck, I need to sit down.'

'This is my chair,' the cunt goes, refusing the courtesy of giving a wounded man a seat.

'What the fuck happened?'

On the one hand I don't want to hear it, but on the other hand my curiosity will get the better of me in time, so I should get the details now before they evaporate from Bernie's head.

'What, you don't remember?' he says, rolling his eyes at me. 'And I thought I was the one with memory issues.'

'Wait a minute...' Now I really *do* feel sick. 'Are the rape charges against me?'

'Apparently,' shrugs Bernie. 'Something about a May-December romance?' He looks so fucking relaxed about it all, like he's simply telling me about what happened on one of those stupid fucking TV shows he watches during the day. All day.

'What the fuck does that even mean? What the fuck, Bernie?'

'Don't shoot me, I'm just the messenger.'

I'll kick the cunt's head off if I want to, messenger or not.

'He's pressed charges against you, Dante. The father has. But the police said they're not going to do anything about it even though the Yanks are pushing for you to be arrested. That's what they get for trying to strong-arm our local boys, I guess.'

'I don't believe this,' I say, pacing back and forth, feeling the blood return to my face. 'I mean, I knew she was young, but this is fucking ridiculous.'

'She was fourteen, they reckon,' says Bernie, wincing for dramatic effect, the prick.

Fucking hell, I'm almost as bad as Twix with his ephebophilic tendencies. I'd thought Rosie might've finished school at least on account of heading over to see what work was available in the States. If schoolkids would stop being so fucking ambitious about returning to the days of child labour then I probably would've sussed the situation out earlier and not fallen into this fucking mess.

'So what do I do now?'

'Nothing,' shrugs Bernie. 'They just said they had to make contact with you, and that's it. I probably wouldn't take a holiday to America anytime soon, though.'

'Oh yeah, I'll just pool my meagre dole offerings for a trip across the world, huh? Fuck!'

'The good news is there's some left over pasta on the stove if you want some.'

I glare at the cunt as if he's just made a really inappropriate joke, but he sits there idly watching the traffic whiz past as if nothing of significance has happened.

'Yeah, thanks for that,' I mumble and head inside, though I'm definitely not in the mood for anything to eat anymore.

A few days later Rosie's mother rings me. She got my number off Dad, for fuck's sake, by sleuthing through the White Pages and ringing all my rellies.

She's fucking livid, by the way. So pissed she can't speak beyond identifying herself, so her boyfriend Tom gets on.

We slowly get to the details of what's happening, how Rosie's biological father went through her diary and got the cops to drag her out of school to a doctor's where she was inspected to see if her virginity was still intact. I'm guessing I wasn't her first by a long shot, so can fairly imagine the disappointment on the father's face. The doctor, on the other hand, must've been thanking his lucky stars he got to poke around in some young pussy, the old perve.

'They didn't even ask her,' Tom's strangled voice goes, choking with emotion.

The cunts. And I'm the one being accused of statutory rape?

'Bill – that's Rosie's dad – is turning it into a custody battle,' Tom explains sadly. 'It's starting to get ugly.'

There's a long pause, wherein I imagine Tom summoning some gumption from deep inside his gut to continue. Finally, he decides to get down to brass tacks.

'Did you fuck her?' he goes, voice wobbly with barely suppressed rage.

I'm sure it's all in her diary, every miniscule detail, but the poor cunt sounds anguished enough so it only seems appropriate to go easy on him. By which, I mean easy on the truth. Spare him the sordid details, in other words. A gentleman never tells, after all.

'Naw, mate, no penetration,' I lie. 'She was way too tight, ay.'

I can practically hear the cunt wince over the phone. He needs to just relax a bit, I think. There's a sharp intake of breath before he goes: 'There's more at stake here than whether you go to jail or not, Dante. You need to seriously consider how this is affecting Barb, how it's affecting me. How it's affecting Rosie, for crying out loud!'

Fuck, but he's really laying it on thick. Next he'll be trying to sell me the steak knives, too. Move over Tim Shaw, this cunt's got his game play on.

'Look, Tom, I appreciate where you're coming from with all this fatherly-like concern, but you've got to recognise that it was perfectly consensual sex. It wasn't fucking rape, for Christ's sake.'

'SHE WAS UNDERAGE, YOU FUCKING DROPKICK!' he yells down the receiver, nearly deafening me. Then in more measured tones he hisses: 'That makes you a monster, *mate.*'

'I've got fuck all interest in your moral standing,' I snap back. 'What you think is right or wrong is of little concern to me.'

Bernie starts snickering, and I know it's not because he's watching the idiot box. *Step By Step*'s on.

Tom roars: 'YOU SELF-RIGHTEOUS LITTLE–'

I hang up the phone.

No-one's got time for that shit.

Bernie smiles smugly, rubbing a finger in his ear as if Tom had yelled right into it, and goes: 'Sounds like that went swimmingly, then.'

ALL PIXIE EVER WANTED

We're waitin for Brett to get his ass round to the Palace so's we can score a fix, but he arrives an hour late, typically. Probly standin out in the fuckin dark watchin the place for signs of police activity. I guess ya can't be too careful dealin drugs with shady cunts like us.

He's a pretty decent dealer, actually, but. Nel reckons she's had some that just act like outright pricks all the time, even kickin doors down if they think you've tried connin them or some shit. They always know where we, the customer, lives, coz there's no fuckin way they're gonna hand out their address to bottom feeders like us.

Brett's an ex-cop who did some undercover work and literally got addicted to heroin in the process. True to form, the coppers treated him like shit for it. He reckons the uniform pigs just looked down on him like he was the same as us junkies, like he was no better even though he only used so could infiltrate the gangs and drug hierarchy as part of his job. They've got no fuckin love or gratitude for their own in a position like that, but.

First time Roz told me about Brett's past I was fuckin skitzy about gettin stuff off the dude. She said she used to use this other dealer called Black Ronnie, and his bastards, but she avoids him these days for whatever reasons.

I like Brett for a couple of reasons. One, he usually comes to us. Two, he doesn't treat me like a piece of meat, in a sexual way. Three, he's not a cunt. I think maybe being treated like shit by the police force for his own addiction and driven from the job has made him sympathetic to us. He says the shrink he was made to see every few months as part of the job definitely wasn't compassionate, either.

Funnily enough, we've actually got the TV turned to SBS when he comes in, on a doco called *The Heroin Wars*. It's about the trade of illicit drugs in Burma and how the revolutionaries are usin opium to fund their fight. The narrator reckons that literally two-thirds of the world's heroin comes from Burma, so I feel some solidarity with those fighters. We turn the volume down and Brett gets straight to it, layin his wares on the coffee table. He tumbles some brown stones out ova ciggie pack. Cunt's obviously tryin to have a laugh.

'What's this?' scoffs Nel, outraged. 'Rock? No China White?'

Brett's unapologetic. 'That's all there is. Heroin doesn't just spring from the fucking ground, you know.'

'Pretty sure it does,' I go, thinkin of that doco and how they were getting it from the plants, but Roz shushes us.

'What's the issue, guys?' Brett asks. 'You know rocky gear means it's probably more pure, anyway. Less likely to have been cut down. You should be fucking grateful.'

'You're dressing up lazy production line values as our benefit, but still charging us a premium,' Roz says.

'Rock's always been shit for me,' whines Nel.

Brett goes on about how Melbourne's the OD capital of the whole world right now coz of all the grade four white smack down there. 'And let me tell you something, it's rock. So just dissolve it with some lemon juice.'

I suspect that's meant to be a dig at them bein lesos.

'This is hardly a four, but,' Roz goes, nudgin the liddle nuggets.

'Because it's brown? Colour means fuck all on the streets, Roz. You of all people should know that.'

'Now now, no need to get personal,' Nel tuts.

Brett's gettin frustrated.

'Sorry, guys, rock's all I can get since the bust. Take it or leave it.'

Mention ova bust puts us all on edge. He is, after all, an ex-cop.

'What fucken bust?' growls Nel, sensin a set-up.

'Calm your fucking tits, woman,' Brett goes, irritably. 'Don't you guys ever watch the news?'

I look at Nel, who shrugs. *The Heroin Wars* is still on silent behind us. That's a lot like news of the world, isn't it?

'My suppliers got busted on the way up from the Gold Coast last Tuesday,' Brett explains. 'The CPO made contact with his controller on the way up and snaffled the lot. That's Chrissie and Westie out of the fucking game.'

It's highly fuckin unusual for a dealer to actually name their sources the way Brett just did.

'What the hell's a CPO?' wonders Roz aloud.

'Covert police operative,' says Brett without expression.

'Of course,' mumbles Roz.

Me and Nel trade smarmy smiles as though we knew what the hell a CPO was already, though Nel probly does know, but.

'Any risk of you being named?' asks Nel. 'Being followed?'

Brett gets angry. 'You think I'm a fucking snitch?'

'No, man, no,' says Nel quickly. 'Just gotta look after *numero uno*, you know?'

'Course you do,' he snaps. 'All I can say is to watch yourselves in future. They've combined a lot of individual surveillances into one big operation they're calling *Operation Shield*. It'll help them to start connecting the dots more. While the funding allows for it, anyway.'

'Fuck,' whispers Roz, echoing my sentiments.

While we're probly safe from police suspicion, in our current state of paranoid it literally feels like a noose is tightenin round our necks.

'So you want the rock or not?'

'We do, naturally,' says Nel, fishin into her pocket for the cash.

Brett shakes his head. 'Always with the fucking drama first, eh?'

Nel always hangs onto the money, never hides it round the flat. She wouldn't trust the rest of us, and rightly so, but to be fair it's mostly the cash that Roz gets from prostitution, so it's technically not Nel's anyway. She always gets the lion's share, but, coz she's become somethin ova dealer now. Or so she keeps sayin, even though we're still relyin on the likes of Brett.

One of the GP's that we were regularly seein (not Doctor Death) in order to score prescriptions for a variety of pills – a Dr Jimmy Farrell – well, his ex-wife hung herself after tryin to deal with the shame of his sexual deeds. That's all I've heard of it, but it must've been bad if she did herself in coz of it. Farrell was at an all-time low, apparently, ready to also top himself, when he outright asked Nel one day about drugs when she'd gone in to trick the cunt into prescribing some Valium. He must've clued that she was a substance abuser, askin outright if she knew anyone who could get 'stronger' drugs. So right there and then Nel turned dealer, gettin less profit than Brett of course, who in turn gets less profit than his now imprisoned 'Chrissie and Westie'. In return, Nel has blatantly put the squeeze on Doctor Farrell for as many prescription drugs as possible, for both personal use and for on-selling as a means to raise cash for yet more heroin. In this way, Nel has become the lynch-pin in our liddle circle of users, coz networking is absolutely necessary in this game.

That Farrell cunt's gonna be pissed when he finds out Nel can't score proper smack anymore, but.

When Brett's finally gone, Nel resumes her usual arrogance.

'Bright side is, bitches, this here's more potent than what we're normally used to,' she says, grinning down at the dirty beige-coloured chunks.

Makes me literally wonder how come we were arguin with Brett in the first place, then.

'So how do we inject *that?*' I ask.

'Never fear when Nel is here,' she goes.

She snatches a lighter off the makeshift bookshelf behind her, next to my old cheapo stereo that has everything: radio, CD player, a tape player. The CD part's useless, but, coz we don't own any CD's. Before we hocked em all (mine included), Roz made sure we copied a lot of em onto cassette. So, on one side of the stereo are Nel's Stephen King books, lined up in order of publication, and on the other side is the stack of cassette tapes. Some of the recordings are pretty crap, though, where we literally stopped the CD mid-way and whatever coz of how wasted we were.

Roz comes outta the kitchen with a spoon and some ciggie filters.

'Rock needs to be cooked and filtered,' Roz says as she destroys the filters, pulling them apart until they're all fluffy. 'It's not like the dope we're used to. It's better for smoking, too.'

'Which we're not gonna do,' Nel says sternly as she pulverises a Vitmain C tablet into the spoon. They say it'll make the smack safer if it's not number three, which is a grade of heroin.

The flame highlights Nel's face as she applies it under the spoon, making her look cruel. She gently pushes on the brown rocks with the blunt end of the lighter when it's hot, crushin it down to a soup. She dabs Roz's home-made cotton balls in to strain the impurities out.

We all take a hit, sharing the needle round. I still haven't budged on shootin up, so I rub it in me mouth instead. And by fuck Nel was not fuckin wrong, but! This is definitely more potent than what I've had before. Or at least faster actin, I give it that.

'Goooood shit,' moans Nel.

Before Roz gets any ideas about playin some Nirvana like she normally would, I crawl across to the stereo and put in my Bauhaus tape that I copied off Imp. I fast-forward, lookin for a particular track.

'Not Manson again,' whines Nel. 'Can't stand him.'

I bite me tongue, coz hearin anyone diss the great MM is fuckin hard to stomach. It'd be like sayin Jordan Catalano's an ugly cunt.

'This is Bauhaus,' I go.

'C'mon, Pixie, not that depressing shit again,' Nel goes, rollin her eyes.

She's never happy with whatever I play. We'd only ever listen to John Denver if she had her way.

'Shut the fuck up,' I go. 'I'm trying to find it.'

Eventually I get to the beginnin of the song *All We Ever Wanted Was Everything*, then lie back in utter bliss as the gentle plunkin of Daniel Ash's guitar pulls at my soul. There's the perfect amount of silence between each strum of the strings, as it builds slowly up. Then Murphy's voice claims the song title so gracefully and painfully that, despite Nel's earlier protests, she sits back and slowly closes her eyes.

The TV continues showin liddle Burmese cunts at war with each other in the jungles, lyin on stretchers with blood tricklin down their foreheads or literally shellin each other from dirt trenches. We're all just layin here while the smack melts our muscles, and Bauhaus lulls our minds to jelly, every week of our lives being squashed not into a day but into this moment. A soldier with a rifle strapped across his body looks bored as he studies the jungle from a cliff, the camera panning across to show the dense rainforest literally rollin away into the hazy horizon.

Oh, to be... the cream...

PIXIE GETS TO WORK

The madam of Roxanne's Door is like a stereotype of the small, angry Asian madam ya see in the movies. Literally! As soon as I went inside she was checkin out what I was wearin and cluckin her fuckin her tongue like a stupid teacher. Like, what the fuck?

The massage rooms have doors on em, not curtains. One of em is open and empty, and inside there really is a massage table and a liddle shelf with towels on it and everything. I guess they literally do actual massages, too. One of the workin girls strolls past and checks me shoes out, givin us a warm smile.

'Hi, sweetie,' she goes and I just smile back.

Me and the madam take a seat each in one of the dimly-lit massage rooms. Her name's Julie Wang, and she has a small mouth that I'm bettin literally never smiles. Despite what I thought, she's not actually that angry.

'I'm firm, Prudence,' she goes. 'Roxanne's Door has house rules. Easy to follow, but some girls seem to struggle with that.'

'Okay.'

'First, your arm,' she goes, motionin for us to stretch me arm over to her. She snatches at me wrist and yanks me arm forward, inspectin it for needle tracks. Then she does the same for the other arm. Of course, my arms are clean thanks to Roz's forethought. 'Good. Junkies are too unreliable.'

'I see.'

'You can make a lot of money here, Prudence. I have good clients and they know how to behave. It is strictly no sex. Prostitution is still illegal in Queensland, so we don't allow it here. But anything else that you and the clients arrange is between yourselves.'

'Okay.' I'm not sure what the fuck she means, but I can just find out later.

'You'll be employed as an independent contractor. So no vicarious liability on my part, you understand?'

I nod, completely not understandin, but. Whatever.

'You work straight away, on your first shift. Up to you what you do, but basics are simple: do what the customer wants, don't let them touch you, don't let them pull their penis out. They do the last one, you let me know and I'll throw the jerk out. That goes for ejaculating in their pants, too. Understood?'

'Yup.'

'The other girls can give you some pointers about dressing and dancing.'

'Okay. Um, how many shifts will I get?'

'I'll start you off on three a week,' she goes. 'If you behave, and the customers want to see more of you, I'll bump it up. You okay to start tonight?'

On Friday the 13th? Fuck yeah, the perfect date for me new career!

'Sure.'

She shakes me hand like we're literally concludin a business deal, and gives us a liddle tour of the place, which isn't really that big. The carpets are old, but other than that everythin looks decent. Unless I just can't tell, coz the lightin in here's literally fucked. It's so dark in some places. I guess that makes us look better, makes the guys use their imaginations more.

Ms Wang introduces us to the girl who liked me shoes.

'Prudence, this is Sindi with an S,' she says. 'Sindi, Prudence.'

'Real name's Brigette,' says Sindi, strokin me arm. Real touchy-feely, this one. 'What name do you go by, honey?'

'Oh,' I say formin an O with me mouth and looking to the madam for a hint. Then I just think *fuck it*. 'Pixie, I guess.'

'Yes, cute,' beams Sindi.

'Stick around a bit and chat to Sindi,' Wang suggests; sounds more like a direct order, but.

'If it's okay with Sindi?'

'Sure thing. I'm in early to do the laundry,' says Sindi. 'So hang with me.'

The madam shuffles off and Sindi takes us out back, through a door that leads to a half-rotted wooden stairwell behind the building. It leads down to a besser-brick walled space beneath road level where there's a commercial-strength washin machine and a clothes dryer.

'Friday's are the big laundry days, so I gotta get the towels on the line,' she goes.

I help her hang em while we chat.

'I've never done this work before,' I admit, meanin the strippin.

'I figured as much,' she goes. 'But don't stress it. Once you get into the swing of it, you'll have a ball. It's actually a lot of fun.'

'Me cousin is a prostitute in Canberra.'

'Yeah, there's a bit of that goes on here, too, but you don't need to worry about getting into that side of the game. You're young, so capitalise on that to its fullest before you start resorting to whoring.'

'I thought Ms Wang said there's no sex allowed.'

Sindi laughs, a beautiful sound. She actually looks amazing when she laughs, like a fuckin model. 'There's sex, trust me. There's a few places around Spring Hill and the Valley that do massage or stripping that don't also do sex.'

'What will I need to wear tonight?'

She considers what I'm wearin now: NIN shirt, black skirt, ripped tights, thick-soled pinstripe creepers.

'You can wear whatever you like, but because you look young you should play that up,' she advises. 'Lose the goth look, though, because that'll probably scare some Johns off.' She runs her fingers through me hair and punches them into two tufts. 'Definitely pigtails. White blouse tied up to show off your belly button. Tartan skirt if you can find it. Slutty schoolgirl never fails to impress.'

After chatting to Sindi, I hit the op-shops in the Valley to see what I can find like what she suggested, but we're literally on the tail-end of winter so there's not a lot of options for short skirts.

I bump into Dante, who's always in op-shops like he fuckin lives in em or somethin and I swear he just tucked a CD from the shelf into his coat pocket, the sneaky cunt. I tell him how I need to find this skirt.

'You finally took my advice and gonna be on the cover of Hustler, eh?'

'Somethin like that,' I go. 'Do ya know anyone who owns a school uniform or somethin?'

'What do I look like? A pedo?'

'Fuck off, I've seen posters for clubs doin *Back to School* themes. Ya must know someone with one.'

'Yeah, true, but mind, all they've got are pleated sports skirts,' he goes. 'Or pinafores.'

'Fuck.'

'Didja try over there?' he goes, pointin at the kids section.

'Thought ya said you weren't a pedo?' I smirk.

'Oh ye of little faith,' he says, waggin his face in mine before going over to the racks with the children's stuff on them. 'Seriously, this is where you wanna look. You've got such small hips, after all.'

'It's all the drugs,' I moan. 'I literally can't put on any weight.'

'Most girls would kill for that,' he mutters, flippin through the hangers.

'It'd probly kill most girls first, but,' I reply, and he laughs.

'Here you go,' he says brightly. 'There's heaps of skirts here.'

He's right, but. The ladies section didn't have anythin decent, but the kid's section is a fuckin treasure trove of short skirts for some reason. I guess people can just chuck one of these over some woollen tights on their toddlers and with their liddle legs it means the skirt is literally like a dress. Dante pulls out a tartan skirt made of wool. A cotton one would be better, but beggars can't be choosers and it's hardly gonna stay on long.

I test the skirt against me body, doubtful it'll work. The waistband looks tiny.

'Trust me,' goes Dante. 'Try it on, at least.'

I grab a shirt from the ladies section as well, just so the old woman behind the counter doesn't get too weirded out when I say I wanna use the changing rooms while only holdin kid's clothin. True enough, Dante's right, the skirt *does* fit, although it literally shows me butt cheeks. I wouldn't be able to bend over without revealin what I had for lunch! On second thought, that's probly exactly what I need.

'Well?' goes Dante.

'It fuckin fits alright.'

'Come on then, show us.'

'Fuck off, ya perve!'

He starts laughin loudly, and I grin when one of the old volunteer mongs tells Dante to keep the language down.

The rest of the day's a bundle of nerves, so I decide a quick shot of smack should help, heading home to the Palace. I haven't injected in ages, not since after I moved into the Prozac and Mum told me on the phone that she'd noticed the sores on me arms the night I stayed at hers, so I've been rubbing it under me tongue instead. Nel hates us doin it and says I'm wastin it, but Roz reckons there's not a lot of difference in the highs ya get between doin it intravenous and doin it sublin... sublingule... by the mouth.

'It's a quicker hit,' she reckons, of IV. 'For some people, a deeper hit. All the other ways are just prolonged. But if you really want the best result without the track marks, you should plug it.'

'What's that way?'

'Up yer bum,' she goes, hookin her thumb up in the air.

It cracks us up. 'Oh my God! For real?'

'Yep,' she nods. 'Inject it in the anus and you get a slow, sustained hit without any wastage. That way instead of flaking out now, you'll get the effects and still be able to work tonight.'

'Fuck, that's a bit risky with the needle, isn't it?' I go, imagining it poking a hole in my asshole. I'd be bleedin all over the place like the backbacker with Cousin Shaz that time.

'Naw,' Roz goes, 'you just cut the top off the pin, or just use a needleless one from the chemist. The kind they use for giving babies medicine.'

'Shit, alright,' I go, tryin to picture how it's done. 'I'll try it.'

Roz grabs a syringe and removes the cap. She has these cute liddle chinaware soy sauce dishes from some place in the Valley that she likes to dissolve her smack in. She dissolves some rock down with water and pulls it up into the syringe.

'About a mil and a half is all you need,' she says sagely, 'otherwise you'll flood your arse. You'll end up leaking a trail of dope for the cops to follow!'

We snigger like liddle schoolgirls.

'The blood-vessels in your anus are delivered directly from your heart, so this'll spread it through your system easily.'

'Won't it leak, but? It's the last thing I need, givin some dude a lap-dance and squirtin drugs into his lap.'

'Nah,' she smiles, holdin up the syringe. 'The internal sphincter is watertight seal. It'll hold this bad boy in forever. Now, bend over.'

I've never actually gotten naked in front of Roz before, but how come I should be worried about it now? In a few hours time I'll be doing it for a living. So I hike me skirt up and drop me undies, gettin onto all fours. Roz kneels behind us and uses one hand to pull me cheeks apart.

'Nice bum,' she coos. 'Okay, I'm guessing you're not a regular for Greek-style so we're gonna have to lube you up, otherwise it might hurt a bit.'

'Okay.'

She squeezes some KY onto her fingertip and rubs it on me anus, and damn it actually feels good. But then she starts to push it in and it's not so good.

'Wait, wait, wait,' I gasp. 'I think I'm about to shit meself.'

'Naw, hun,' she goes, 'you're just not stimulated is all. It's natural. The only way around it is to get turned on.'

'Yeah, I'll pass thanks,' I say, realisin she's gettin horny from seein me ass and of course me pussy, too. 'I'll just suck it up.'

'Literally,' she sniggers, removin her finger to insert the syringe.

The finger felt better than a piece of plastic with hard edges, but the lube's helpin. She gets it in and there's a liddle rush up me ass, like I've got the runs but in reverse.

'Done,' she goes, slidin the syringe out.

I'm expectin to literally feel the water slidin down me thighs, but they're dry to the touch.

'Can I move?'

'Of course,' she says, unable to resist slappin me ass like cowboys do to the horses in movies. It pisses us off that she did that, but she isn't askin any money for the smack so I guess I just gotta suck that up, too. If Ms Wang saw her do that, she'd literally boot Roz out the fuckin door. Me too, actually, for usin drugs.

'Thanks, Roz,' I go. 'I don't know what I'd do without ya.'

'Anytime, hun,' she smiles all motherly like. 'Ooh, so excited for your big night!'

'Me, too,' I go, feeling the nerves melt away from the heroin.

Turns out Sindi's not workin tonight, but all the other girls at Roxanne's Door are real welcomin. We all get changed in the same area, swappin the massage rooms for the open space of the communal area. There's no dance floor or stripper poles here, coz it's not a club, but there's no chairs either, so I sit on the floor to get changed.

'There's no chairs because we won't do any lap-dancing out here in case the cops turn up,' explains Annie, who introduces herself to us straight up. She's pretty, but not beautiful.

I get into me slutty schoolgirl outfit, the liddle kid's tartan skirt barely coverin me bits at all. I stole one of Nel's black G-strings from her drawer when Roz was in the toilet, and it feels a bit funny goin up the crack of me ass but I get used to it pretty quickly and decide with me first pay I'll head out to Bargain Briefs or Paddy's Market or somewhere and get a whole heap of em.

I was expectin everybody to have amazin bodies, literally pumped up titties and big hair and incredible makeup. But a few of these girls have saggy bums or cellulite, and the hair and makeup leave liddle to be desired. Not that I can talk, all I can do is Spookykid makeup, so I carefully watch one of the other girls who at least as some clue, and try and match her makeup. I totally fuck it up, but, endin up lookin like a mong version of Edward Scissorhands.

'Don't try and look more pale,' says this older brunette girl called Heidi. Not sure if that's her real name or her stage name, but. 'It doesn't make you look younger, just stranger,' she goes.

She tosses us a makeup remover to rub it all off. I feel frustrated. I haven't even started the real part of the job yet, and already it seems too hard.

'Here,' goes Heidi, grabbin us gently by the chin. She starts runnin a lipstick along me bottom lip, then the top one, and moves onto me cheeks with a powder. When she's done, she stands back and we both look at me face in the mirror. It's amazin, actually, coz I look like me still but just so much prettier. Heidi's like a miracle-worker.

'You've got nice skin, Pixie, so just leave off the foundations,' she advises. 'It's pale enough without makeup. And when you do your eyes, a little bit of black eyeliner on top and the bottom corner, but for the schoolgirl look you want to keep it away from your bottom lids. A bit of mascara and no eye-shadow, or stick with warm browns.'

'Thank you,' I gush. 'That's so helpful!'

'Look at you,' laughs one of the girls to Heidi. 'Wonder Woman.'

Heidi smirks at her in the mirror. 'If I was a superhero, Colleen, you think I'd still be here?'

'Don't ya like it here?' I ask her.

She laughs. 'It's okay. But I'm over it. The money's good, though, and I'm starting my own business, so I'm still here for now.'

'Oh! Are you startin a strip club, too?' I'm already picturin myself runnin off from Wang's cold-front and goin to work for Heidi.

'Nope,' she goes, clickin her lipstick shut and placin a finger inside her mouth, closin her lips round it then yankin her finger out. Fuckin bizarre! 'That stops the lipstick from going on my teeth,' she explains when she sees us starin. 'But to answer your question, I'm not starting a strip club, no. I'm opening a mental health clinic for women.'

'Really?'

She's takin the piss, right?

'See? Wonder Woman,' goes Colleen, slappin Heidi's ass.

'Really,' grins Heidi. 'My sister has anorexia. She's in and out of hospital all the time, poor thing. Anyway, she was going to a clinic but it gets too full-on there with some of the men, you know? They just won't respect boundaries. She said if it wasn't for the men seeing her as an easy target, she'd keep going there.'

'Shit,' I mutter. What to fuckin say to that?

'Anyway, the clinic would be mental-health specific, but it'd be an all-purpose clinic as well. I want a safe space for women to address all sorts of medical needs, from mental health to sexual treatments and basic general practice care.'

'Sounds ace,' I go.

'I've got a business plan all laid out, and have spoken to financiers, too, to help with initial costs. I might earn a lot here, but there's bills and shit, you know?'

I nod like a dumb cunt. Bills are hardly an issue for us, but.

'My earnings from here go toward the trial clinic. There *was* an independent counselling space for women called Children by Choice that was also a pro-choice abortion clinic,' she goes on, 'then little Johnny Howard got in and the funds soon dried up. But The Annual Mental Health Services Conference is on at the Convention Centre next week and I'm going to present my idea to a panel and try and float something more sustainable, as soon as possible. I mean, it's not like it's an entirely novel idea, but it's not always easy to get services for women up and running.'

She's lost us. I'm here to make money to buy drugs and get fucked up. That's *my* plan. It's seems fuckin pathetic compared to hers, but. Perhaps the rest of the girls are here for the same reason I am, and it's Heidi that's the odd bitch out.

I've decided to ignore Heidi for the rest of the night, and dedicate me free time to chattin to Annie instead. The smack is doin its job, not as hardcore as an intravenous shot, but I can feel it still. It's like I've shed all the nervousness, and now I just couldn't give a fuck about bein the newbie here. Normally heroin would make us just want to lay around and do fuck all, be lazy, but I'm here for a reason so it's good that the hit is coming on slowly.

Ms Wang bustles about doing her thing, and we put the finishing touches to our outfits before she opens up shop and the Johns – as the girls call the guys – come up and start picking out girls.

It's slow goin at first, and the guys that rock up early are regulars who've come to see a specific girl. One of em looks us up and down longer than is normal, and I smirk thinkin about how easy it could be to steal that cunt away in future from his regular girl.

We don't hafta wait long for the less discernin customers to trickle in, but.

'It's good if they're spaced out,' Sindi says of the Johns. 'You get too many in here at once, and we can't cater for them straight away. They can get a bit shitty about it.'

'That's how come we have those two, right?' I ask, noddin at the muscle-bound dudes that came up before the doors were opened.

'Yup, that's Gavino and Dominic, our bodyguards.'

Fuckin bodyguards! I've got bodyguards. It means there's danger here, and that more than anythin turns us on. Fuck all the Johns and the slutty outfits. There's danger here!

'Almost nothing ever happens, though,' adds Sindi. 'They're for just in case.'

Still. It's considered necessary for them to be here, right? That's all I need to know.

When I catch Dominic lookin at me legs, I turn and flick me skirt up at him to literally flash me ass off, but he just goes back to chattin to the other dude and pretendin as if he hadn't seen. I giggle for real at that.

Now it's time. This old guy's come up and's keen on us.

He hands over his cash to Ms Wang, who'll take her cut and give us the rest at the end of me shift. She motions for us to take the client through to a room.

'She's new here, first night,' she says to the old fuck, but says it in a way that insinuates all this other virgin-type shit. She winks at us when he's not lookin, so I catch her drift. He's probly another regular, and she knows what he's into.

'A yearling,' the old cunt says smugly, nearly droolin on himself.

'Oh, I hope yer gentle,' I go, formin an O with me mouth and tryin to look as scared as the smack will actually allow us to. He narrows his eyes like maybe he thinks I'm taking the piss. Was I? Maybe, I dunno.

Inside the room he sits in a padded chair. It's got no armrests. And there's no massage table in here, either. Seems not all the rooms have em, or Ms Wang had em taken out before I got here. Just the chair and a small, empty bookcase with a tiny portable CD player on it.

My John's name is Marcus, and he says he's turnin sixty soon, the old fuck. He delights in tellin us this, apparently turned on by the yawnin gulf between our ages. I told him I was eighteen. I'd told Ms Wang that at the interview, too, and she didn't bother to check any ID coz she probly knew I was lyin.

Marcus' got a suit on, and while I don't know much about suits I'm guessin this isn't an expensive one. It's dark brown, for a start. And baggy. From a pocket he takes out a CD of the Teen Queens that came out at the end of me last year at primary school! We used to listen to that awful shit coz everyone was into *E Street* back then.

Roz had showed us a couple of moves to do when I'm dancin, so I pretty much just wing it. I'm pretty shit at it, to be honest, but the old cunt is right into it, tellin us how cute and beautiful I am and rollin his eyes like he's can't choose which to stare at: me face or me ass pokin out from under the skirt.

I'd forgotten just how bad this music is, but Marcus is right into it, bobbin his stupid lookin head.

'*Be myyyy, beee my liddle bay-bee,*' he sings, the fuckin perve.

At least the heroin up me ass is workin like magic. Probly the only thing stoppin us from snappin his precious CD in half.

Despite Marcus' music, I've got me god Manson growlin in me head, tellin us I'm the angel with the scabbed wings, which makes this horny old fuck in the chair the cunt who wants to deflower the freshest crop. I gyrate this liddle ass right up near his face. If that's what the cunt wants, that's what I'll fuckin well give him. I hope he has a fuckin heart attack imagin himself tryin to get at me body.

Fuck his music. It's kicked into the second track so now he's started calling us 'sugarpie' and 'honeybunch'. It's pullin us from the fuckin moment, ruinin me dance. All I can do now is try and get this old cunt off, the same way Cousin Shaz was tellin us about how she makes the young guys cum too soon so she doesn't have to keep performin. Services rendered.

I start flickin me skirt up, showin off me undies (or Nel's, more like), pullin me top open so's he can cop an eyeful of me tits before coverin em up in mock indignation just as quickly. At one point I'm slidin me ass up and down his body, brushin his nose with me ass cheeks. I slide me underwear down as sexily as I can, wigglin me ass in front of his face then squattin down over his crotch to gently rub myself across the boner in his pants.

In horror I feel dampness against me ass cheeks and the awful cold touch against me bare vagina.

Oh fuck no! The heroin plug Roz injected into us has squirted out!

I jump up and spin around, starin wide-eyed at Marcus's pants, and sure enough there's a big wet patch there.

Shit shit shit!

I start babblin me apologies to Marcus, ready to beg the cunt not to tell Julie about this, when I notice he's got his head lolling back and his face is slack, like he's literally had a heart attack!

This is not fuckin happenin.

'MARCUS!' I scream, grabbin his shoulders, yankin him forward.

His eyes snap open and he looks petrified.

'What? What?' he goes.

'I thought you were fuckin dyin,' I gasp.

'Oh, no, sorry,' he says quietly, puttin a hand over the tent in his pants where the wet patch has made the fabric darker by several shades.

Only then does it dawn on us that me plug didn't leak all over me client, but that the cunt literally went and cummed in his pants and I rubbed myself on it.

'Ew, ya fucking perve!'

He tries to hush us, lookin panicked, probly worried that Dominic or Gavino might come chargin in at any moment.

'Ya know you're not meant to fuckin cum on us,' I snap, sensin a power-shift here.

'I know, I know,' he babbles. 'I'm so sorry. I didn't mean to.'

At least the old cunt kept it in his pants. But I rubbed me vagina on that! What if I get preggers?

Fuck, the thought makes us feel sick. Or maybe it's just the smack. I dunno.

'I'm so sorry,' he keeps goin, reachin into his coat for his wallet and pullin some cash out. 'Let me make it up to you. Here.'

We're not supposed to get tips in here, even though Julie said whatever we arrange to do with the clients is our business. But two strict rules were the clients couldn't cum while we're dancin, and the other is we don't get paid directly. All cash goes through Ms Wang, so she can get her cut.

'Here's two hundred dollars,' Marcus says, thrustin the money at us. 'Think of it as an advance, of sorts. Get yourself a good wig, white panties, some thigh-high boots.'

Un-fuckin-believable. The cash isn't strictly hush money. The old cunt actually thinks he still has power to mould us into his perfect doll. Old people are like this, walkin all over young kids like we don't fuckin matter and don't have a say. I could go dob this fucker in and the evidence is right there in his lap, wet and dark for all to see. He'd be right out of here on his ass. But Julie would still be pissed with us probly, the old cow, and more's the point what's this old fuck gonna say or do if I just take his money and blow the whole fuckin lot on drugs?

Fuck all, is what.

Although I should probly tell him to keep some for himself so he can go buy some decent fuckin music.

I snatch the cash out of his meaty hand.

'Say sorry again,' I demand, 'and mean it.'

He does, but it doesn't sound like he means it. It sounds like he's horny, and literally enjoys apologisin.

Whatever. I have the money. I'm the fuckin breadwinner now. Nel and Roz are gonna think I'm the fuckin ace one. Jeremy can suck it.

'Right. Dance is over. See ya next time.'

He bitches and moans but knows he's gotta leave. I'm a fuckin natural at this!

'Don't forget ya mong CD,' I call out as he's headin out the door, yankin the Teen Queens from the CD player and throwin it at im.

He tries to catch it but literally drops it, fuckin butterfingers.

As he struggles to bend down and pick it up, somethin about him suddenly seems so ridiculous and pathetic that I actually feel a bit sorry for him. It's like he reminds me of me grandpa wastin away in the old people's home. I assume grandpa's still alive, coz if he wasn't Mum would've told me.

When Marcus is gone, I get ready in case there's another customer that wants us to dance for them, which of course there is. I'm not only fresh meat, but I'm obviously fresh *young* meat, and that counts for somethin here at Roxanne's Door.

ARRESTED

I'm not sure why I took it, since I didn't initially intend to, but I'm standing out on the bridge that connects McWhirter's with the Plaza and the shopkeeper's going off her nut at me. Despite that, I'm more interested by the view. I can see right down (or up, depending which window I look out of) Wickham Street. I'm more familiar with the street level view, since I've never paid too much attention from up here when crossing over the bridge. But now that I've been stopped on it mid-way, I'm rather distracted by this new perspective on an otherwise familiar stretch of road.

The shop lady's frustrated by my attitude, even though I've already made a half-arsed apology for stealing the book, which I also handed back to her. *Popcorn*, by Ben Elton. I like his work on the *Young Ones* so I'd thought I might give this a read.

'I don't run a business just so thieves can rob me blind,' she's saying, among other shit about how long she's run her business and how she started it to support her husband after his redundancy from Telecom, blah blah blah.

Un-fucking-believable. Some people will take any opportunity to give you their life story, relishing in details about how hard they've had it and how cunts like me make it even harder for them. Her voice is echoing through the corridors until it catches this insecurity guard's attention. Thank fuck it's not Twix. I couldn't stand another stint in the fucking psych ward for attempted murder.

The guard wanders up to us, debating with himself whether he should get involved since I'm looking a bit bored by all this, but I guess it's the ranting and raving of the lady that finally convinces him to ask what's up.

'Thank god *you're* here,' she says to him, but a little patronising like she's accusing the cunt of being lazy. 'He's stolen from me and 's just treating it like a joke.'

'I'm really not,' I tell the guard.

He glances from me to her, like he's wondering if he's on the tail end of some private joke. Not only am I acting like none of this has got anything to with me, but I can feel that The Inferno's practically gone on annual leave. I'm as a cool as a cucumber.

'Don't listen to him,' says the lady. She holds the book up, the all-incriminating piece of evidence. 'He just walked off with this and acts like it doesn't matter.'

'I honestly think it doesn't,' I say to her, convinced that this simple explanation will calm her the fuck down. 'I didn't exactly want to read *that* book, necessarily. I just thought that I might if I had it.'

'Wait, so let me get this straight,' the guard butts in, still confused. 'You stole the book, yeah?'

'He did,' snaps the lady, frustrated by the lack of action being taken over the matter. I nod to concur.

'Okay,' says the guard, stymied as to what to do next. He grabs his walkie talkie off his hip and calls centre management, telling them to phone the cops and let them know he's taking me over.

The lady looks satisfied at last, smirking up at me. 'I hope they throw the fucking book at you,' she hisses, and I'm about to make a crack about the book she's holding but couldn't be bothered.

'Follow me,' says the guard, walking ahead.

I'm highly fucking amused as I follow behind this cunt, out into the mall. At any point I could simply walk off. I wouldn't even need to run since he has his back turned to me the whole time. I could simply slip behind and of these pillars in McWhirters and be off. He'd be none the fucking wiser!

We cross over the Brunswick Mall to where the cop station is.

'Head in and let em know what you're in for,' the guard goes.

I thank him for the escort, and head into the beat on my own. I glance back through the window and can tell that the insecurity cunt must've turned away before I'd even opened the door because he's almost back inside McWhirter's already.

'How can we help ya?' says this cheery kind of cop behind the front counter. He's stapling some paper together, and I'm struck by how tall the cunt is. Either that or their desk is improbably small. There's a bunch of cops further back dealing with something.

'Yeah, was just brought in by the guard over there,' I say, jerking my thumb in the direction of McWhirter's. 'For a book.'

The cop looks puzzled.

'Stole it,' I add.

'Ah yes!' he grins, like I've revealed the obvious answer to a riddle he's been struggling ages with. 'No worries. Come through.'

He leads me around behind the counter and into the cramped, and short, corridor beyond.

'Got the 124 here,' he says to the others, who're joking around with each other. Everyone's acting as casual as fuck, more or less like that dipshit insecurity guard. Is everyone in the Valley fucking stoned today, or what? No one's taken responsibility.

There's a guy in cuffs sitting on a bench at the back of the station, glaring at me like he wants to kill me, though I've never seen the cunt before. Maybe he just hates goths?

'Righto; name?' says this cop with a severe expression, probably the only one here not under the influence as per my stoner theory. She pulls out a notepad from her breast pocket.

'Dante Halloran.'

'Righto, Dante, what's your story?'

I tell her about the book, which she wants to know the name of because I've curtailed that bit deliberately.

'*Popcorn*,' I go, and the cunt in the cuffs sniggers.

'No worries,' she says, scribbling away in her pad.

The others are discussing the details of the guy on the bench, who apparently has been caught walking down the Brunswick Mall with a loaded gun. The fucking tosser. Gotta wonder how he's got it since

Howard ordered all guns to be handed over after Port Arthur.

'Mate, any weapons or similar devices on your person?' asks this older cop with a beer belly. Considering they've just arrested a guy with a gun, the cunt seems pretty friendly in his approach. I gotta give this lot credit for their handling of my situation. I've been treated far worse for far less.

'Yep.'

'Watcha got?' he goes, with the kind of indifference the cashiers at Woolies do when asking how my day is.

'Knife, about yea long.' I hold my hands up to indicate the length of a school ruler. 'In my waistband.'

'Can you take it out?' he says, his hands on his cocked hip. The rest of them are looking as bored as this guy.

I pull the knife out of my pants, careful to hold it by the end of the handle with thumb and forefinger like it was a diseased thing. It's a calculated gesture, given that they've already dealt with a gun-toting wanker. Last thing I need is them going apeshit on me.

Which is precisely what they do.

'DROP THE KNIFE! DROP THE KNIFE!' several of them scream, while a couple of them actually unholster their guns and point them at me. In such a small space as this I wonder about the wisdom of doing that, but clearly they haven't.

I drop the knife, and it rams into the carpet point first, then topples over. The beer-bellied cunt shoves me against the closed door next to me.

'Arms up. Spread your legs. Any more weapons?'

'No,' I say, feeling humiliated, especially in front of the cunt on the bench sneering at me. I turn my head to face the street instead.

They pat me down and satisfied there's no more weapons, order me into the interview room. They even insist on opening the door for me. It's a complete fucking turnabout from the relaxed atmosphere I'd walked into only a few minutes ago.

One of them, a guy about my age – with hideous tufts of black hair growing out his shirt front and out his ears – comes in with a small torch. He tells me to face the wall and drop my dacks. Sounds a bit fucking suspect to me, but he's adamant. I do as I'm told.

'Squat,' he goes.

'Please,' I chastise, but with no response forthcoming I consider it best to do as he commands.

'Now spread your cheeks.'

What the fuck is this? I sigh, and grab my arse cheeks, spreading them as far as I can. The torchlight flashes through my legs onto the wall in front of me, making shadow puppets from my dangling bits.

'Lift your sack,' the cunt goes.

How far's this shit going to carry on?

'Thanks,' he says simply. 'Take a seat.'

I hear him shuffle outta the room, and yank my dacks back up. This is it, I'm finally being done for stealing after all these years of getting away with it. It's the first time I've ever been caught, and to be fair I've made it really fucking easy for the cunts, but it's not the first time I've been in serious trouble with the law. There's that time the cops came around checking where I lived because of that statutory rape charge in America. If that comes up on their computer systems I could be well and truly fucked here. The cunts might extradite me to the US of A yet, where I'll be drawn and quartered as an example of America's might over us backwater convicts.

After some wait the lady from before and this new guy comes in. Straight away I've clocked him as pretty laid-back. I guess the threat of me and my knife has passed, ay. They introduce themselves as Constable Grenier (her) and Senior Constable Ballow (him).

They put a small tape recorder on the table. Grenier has upgraded her small notepad for a clipboard and some forms, which she starts filling out with a pencil. My knife's on the table, too, in a sealed clear ziplock bag. It's weird seeing something of mine, something that brings me relative comfort, sitting in an evidence bag. Untouchable.

Grenier asks about the book, or more specifically what I did, so I tell her the facts as they stand. That's all pretty simple, really. I took the book, the storekeeper chased after me. The thought comes to me to defend my proud track record of shoplifting by explaining that I had initially intended to pay for the book and was standing in the line before I suddenly decided to simply walk out the doors, all right in front of the shopkeeper herself. It was certainly a perplexing theft, both for myself and the shopkeeper. I don't think she's seen anything so brazen before. But you know, she was hardly a sleuth about it.

For me, there's so much mystery to that very fact that I'm a bit disappointed when the cops are more interested in moving on to the knife. That seems the least complicated part of these proceedings.

'So why did you have the knife on you?'

I shrug. 'There's a lot of crazy people out there. For example, guys just wandering around the mall with guns, I hear.'

This elicits a smile from Senior Constable Ballow, but none from Grenier. I don't mean to blow my own trumpet, but I know how to time my quips and I thought that one was fucking spot on.

'And what were you planning to do with the knife?' Ballow says, giving his partner a breather.

'Nothing. It's just a security blanket,' I go, thinking of Linus in the *Peanut* strips. 'Knowing I have the upper hand because of the knife means I can actually remain calm; talk my way out of a confrontation. That's all.'

'You've never used it on anyone?'

'Never needed to,' I admit, though Twix could affirm that's not strictly true. 'It's not easy out there being a goth. I don't get to carry around a gun and lay down the law to some arsehole who wants to beat my brains out because he doesn't like the way I'm dressed.'

'But what if you get into a fight and the knife falls out?' suggests Constable Grenier. 'They could pick it up and use it on you.'

'Irrelevant,' I say quickly, enjoying this parry of wits. 'I could pick up the nearest object on the ground and use that, too. Everything is a weapon. That tape recorder's a weapon,' I go, pointing at the machine sitting between us. 'That pencil's a weapon. I could grab it off you and poke you in the fucking eye with it, then where would you be? On the ground, blind, while I use the chair you're sitting on to finish the job. Or my knife that you've dropped after you've been blinded.'

She looks like she's ready to spit chips from this, but to his great credit Ballow actually manages a laugh. I may have gotten a bit loud there for a moment, and a bit graphic, but the cunt has the good sense to see the humour in my logic. Life's a stage and if I can't perform on it, what am I on it?

'Besides,' I add, hoping to mellow her out a bit, 'the kinfie's not even sharp. Check it out, the point's been broken off.'

She remains unimpressed, so Ballow tells her it's okay and they'll wrap it up. They leave me alone in the room for a few minutes, with the door closed, and when Ballow finally opens it again he tells me I'm good to go.

I've done it. Once again I've talked my way out of an impossible situation. I thank the officers on my way out, noting that the cunt in the cuffs is gone. Good riddance to bad rubbish.

'Here's your receipt for court,' says the tall cop at the front desk, stapling a white and a yellow sheet of paper together, handing them over.

'For court?' I'm a bit confused.

'Yeah, just turn up next Wednesday and give the court clerk the back sheet,' he says. 'The other one's your copy.'

Fuck it. Court?

I skim the form and see that I'm being charged with shoplifting and possession of a concealed weapon in public. Cunts!

'Rightio,' I go, trying to appear cool. I notice he's got my knife in the ziplock bag. 'Do I get my knife back?'

He laughs, a genuine and easy chuckle that suits him. In spite of myself, I like the cunt.

'Nah mate, C&D. This gets melted down after the court case.'

'That's a shame,' I say sadly. 'It has really good balance.'

He tests it on his extended finger. Even in the plastic bag, the knife balances across the fulcrum of his digit rather beautifully. 'Ha! Does, too,' he grins.

I wish him a good day and he likewise wishes me one, and I push the door open, stepping out into the mall where I now know people are wont to walk around with loaded guns. Classic Valley.

JUST A TWIST, MALIK

I've been a bit tired of Dante's antics lately, like the ruckus at Her Majesty's during the Bledisloe, and then he goes and gets arrested for shoplifting yesterday. I swear he's just addicted to drama. It's like Angele says, if we wanna succeed in our goals we've gotta surround ourselves with successful people. Although I've come to like Dante, he'll hold me back.

In a funny twist of fate, I got a call from Twix yesterday and we're gonna catch up for drinks because I haven't seen the little bugger since he went to ground months ago. He's got a steady job, a steady girlfriend, and he's working on getting his own place, too. Fair play to him, he might have fucked up at the radio station but everyone's holding that against him way too much. It's been tough going on him.

'You off to the shops?' asks Raven when pass by her door.

'Nah, going to meet Twix over in the Gabba,' I reply. 'If you want something from the shops I can bring it back for you, but.'

'Yeah, I need some eggs for a cake,' she says.

'Then you'll owe me a slice,' I smirk.

'Fine,' she sighs. 'I'll make you a separate one. A small one.'

Dante pokes his head out of his flat.

'Oi, Matty,' he goes. 'Say hi to Twix for me. No hard feelings for trying to kill him and all that.'

'Are you taking the piss?'

He looks insulted. 'Dead serious, cunt.'

It's fucking ridiculous that he wants me to play messenger, but I'm not Australia Post so he can fucking well tell Twix himself. But just to keep the peace I lie and say: 'Will do, mate, if I remember to.'

'You can remember to bring back some eggs for Raven but can't remember to pass a message onto Twix for me?'

He's been a pushy bastard of late. Always questioning everything, trying to find the flaws in people. I'm a bit sick of it.

'Yeah, if I remember,' I say.

'No problem, all good,' he says, then comes out and looks me in the eye with intense seriousness: 'And consider going to a different bar. The Railway's a rough crowd and Twix prefers a more congenial setting. Like that smaller bar a few doors down. It's called the One Mile. Much more intimate. More his thing.'

'Right, thanks for the tip,' I say warily, wondering if he's angling for an invite. If he is, he can forget it. The last place I want to be stuck is between him and Twix and their domestics.

'The One Mile, don't forget it,' he goes as I head outta the Palace.

I get the bus around to the Gabba, something I haven't done in ages. If I do come over for the odd gig it's usually with Raven in her car. I've started getting more and more into experimental music, and there's a couple of events run by a small crowd normally in the city, but. Always in basements, like under the Metro, places like that.

The pub's chocka-block full of AFL fans from the Brisbane Bears game at the Gabba, where Twix also did a shift. He's still got his security uniform on, too, and he tries to score us a round of free drinks by flashing it off, but the publican's not having it.

His girlfriend Amai-li is here, too. If I'd known I'd have brought Angele and made it a double-date. I vaguely remember Amai from the party that Twix and Raven threw at the Prozac earlier in the year. If I recall correctly, I caught her getting humped by her then-boyfriend in the dunny, like a couple of derros. Not frigid at all, this one.

'Sometimes it works, sometimes it doesn't,' Twix says, about his uniform. 'Got Amai a free ticket into the game with it, though.'

'A bit of an AFL fan?' I ask her.

'Not really,' she says with reservation. 'But it seemed important to Travis that I go.'

Showing off is why he'd have wanted her there, but. See him in his uniform, doing his thing. So transparent, but so Twix. Fair play to him, but, even though he's not much into the game himself, being in amongst it has managed to gee him up for it.

'Stand out had to be Alastair Lynch, hands down,' he says when we find a spot to park our butts and our drinks. 'He collected seven goals, and when he got that last one on a free kick I yelled out – from where I was standing guard on the sidelines – I went HOW BIG'S YER DICK? The umpire held up his fingers, about thirty centimetres apart, so then I shouted BULLSHIT!'

His story gets a laugh out of us, but I've heard similar things from way back about the AFL crowds, so it's doubtful that Twix's story even happened. More of an urban legend. Not that it matters much.

There's a couple of other familiar faces in this crowd who start making their way towards us. The neo-Nazi's, Sean Fenny and Linsey Howison. I know Sean only by reputation through my brother Marty, but I knew Linsey in highschool by his nickname Pez. He got it from dispensing pills like lollies, selling them dirt cheap because he used to steal them from his grandmother. Took enough of em, but, and other stuff besides. Fried his brain, what little of it he had to begin with. Made him a simpleton, all before his eighteenth birthday. This other scummer with the number 1488 hand-painted onto his black t-shirt, Pez's mate Sean, he's a different kettle of fish, but. You can tell from his eyes that he's not dumb, that he knows exactly what the fucking score is. Makes him being a skinhead all the more sinister, you know?

'Fellas,' I nod when they come right up to us.

'Matty Tadlow, yeah?' Sean says, scowling at me not because he's rank with me but because that seems to be his whole thing. 'Marty's younger brother?'

'The one and only,' I say. 'Heya Pez, how's things?'

'Yeah, awright,' he says, shrugging his shoulders up to his ears.

Sean's eyes swivel onto Twix and Amai, and his teeth bare like an animal's when it's angry. He leans over and in a low voice murmurs to Twix: 'You fucken race traitor.'

'Oi, enough of that shit,' I bark.

Sean tells Pez they need to get a couple of drinks in and some chicken schnitzels, so they head to the bar, telling me they'll be back in the shake of a lamb's tail.

Poor Twix is feeling really uncomfortable, you can see it on his face and in his body language. Everyone's got the right to free speech, of course, but if the bastard tries so much as to lay one finger on either Twix or his girl, I'll kick seven shades of shit out of the motherfucker. Simple.

'They your friends?' Amai asks me. She seems worried.

'Not a fucking chance.'

Fair play to Twix, I think he could take one of them in a scrap, but he'd have buckley's chance with both at once, so naturally I'll stand by him. Thing is, I know from experience that girls hate it when guys get into fights, so while the neo-Nazi's are up at the bar I suggest to Twix we get a move on to somewhere else, which he's keen for. We haven't even finished our beers, leaving the glasses half full. Amai drops her ciggie in hers.

We choof it down the street and there's a sign hanging above a door that reads OLD MILE. Dante did say it was a friendly bar, so it's probably perfect for a quiet drink after the bullshit at the last place.

'Oi, let's duck in here,' I say. 'I've heard good things about it.'

Well, it certainly is small. It's a very narrow bar that goes up the side of the building, and it's full of blue-collar types and not many from the footy match, either. Locals mostly, it seems. We're the odd ones out, but, and all eyes have turned on us as we approach the bar. Thankfully, after a cursory glance over us, the punters return to their conversations and drinking.

The first thing I notice about the dogger behind the bar is she's naked. Or at least she's got no top on. It's not a pretty sight, either. Her titties sit flat against her torso all wrinkly at the top, and there's a scarlet bib under her neck and across the top of her chest where she's been sunburnt whilst wearing a low-cut t-shirt. The contrast is almost as nauseating as those crinkled flaps.

'What'll it be, hun?' she goes, and I realise I've been staring at her breasts.

'Three lagers, thanks.'

'A titty bar?' Twix says sardonically with a cocked eyebrow.

'A good choice, Matty,' beams Amai, looking around the room brazenly. Keen as, this one. 'And check out these characters!'

'Someone's happy, but,' I smirk at Twix, who laughs.

And then suddenly the laughter cuts dead as we both notice who comes from out back and walks in behind the bar. Suddenly I feel stone cold sober, lost for words. But not Twix.

'Karen?'

Fuck me... he hasn't seen her in yonks, as far as I know. None of us has. She sorta disappeared off the scene after they broke up. Here she is, but. And her baps, too, out on show for all to see.

'What the hell's going on?' Twix stammers as Karen freezes at the sight of him. The blood drains from her face. 'Where's your clothes?'

Her hands clap closed over her tits and she looks like she's been punched in the guts. But then something defiant comes over her. Her face gets sorta cranky looking, and she drops her arms and stomps down the length of the bar to where we're standing, her tits bouncing delightfully the whole way. Amai's staring from Karen to Twix and back to Karen again, not sure what's happening.

'I fucking work here,' snaps Karen viciously, like she's taunting him with the obvious. 'Tops aren't compulsory, unless you haven't noticed.'

'These aren't mates of that scruff with the pigtails, are they?' the old barmaid wants to know.

'Pigtails?' says Twix, screwing his face up with the effort to try and work out what's happening. 'Dante?'

'Your friend Dante, the one that attacked us outside the movies?' says Amai, looking very confused. 'How's he got anything to do with this?'

Twix is too busy banging the heel of his hand into his forehead, arguing with Karen, to notice his current girlfriend's distress.

'Don't worry about it,' I tell her. 'Dante's just a shit-stirrer.'

She grits her teeth and says: 'Well, shit-stirrers should be made to lick the spoon, isn't it?'

This old bastard with a massive belly and lank, greasy yellow hair comes out of the dunnies and waddles over to us, sitting his fat arse onto the stool beside me. I'd noticed his pint sitting there untouched but had just assumed it's owner had gone home. He stinks of stale sweat, and his hair's that colour from smoking too much. His stubby fingertips are stained a dirty orange colour from nicotine.

'Yeah, I suppose Dante put you up to this?' Karen goes, planting her hands on her hips and making no effort now to hide her boobs. The only one of us looking at them, I notice, is Amai.

'No, no,' babbles Twix, looking at me. 'It was Malik.'

'I didn't know, okay,' I say, my hands up in surrender.

'I'll show you a trick,' says the fat bastard next to me.

'Is this your ex?' Amai asks Twix carefully, but gets no answer.

'I bet you a dollar I can make your nipples hard without even touching them,' the fat bastard says to Karen.

'Donny,' Karen says in a warning tone. 'Not now.'

'Look, we can go, it's no problem,' I say, backing away from the bar. The old woman with the wrinkled flaps waves her hand sharply in the air, wishing us gone.

'So this is it, huh?' says Twix, his voice escalating. He's becoming irate. 'You get rid of our fucking baby and just start getting your tits out for everyone, yeah?'

Whoa! Baby? What baby?

'It wasn't yours, idiot!' she yells back at him.

It's like a slap in the face. He visibly jolts, blinking repeatedly.

The old barmaid's down the end now talking with a couple of guys that look more than willing to rough us up if need be.

'Twix, let's head off, man.'

'Donny, why don't you show my friends your trick?' Karen goes, staring straight at Twix.

The fat bastard, Donny, wobbles on his stool with excitement. 'It's a helluva trick, fellas,' he says to us with a stupid grin. 'I bet you a dollar, Kaz, that I can make your nipples hard without even touching them.'

'Go on, then,' she dares him, turning to point her knockers at him.

He flicks his greasy locks behind his ears and cracks his knuckles for effect.

'Karen...' whines Twix pathetically.

She ignores him, bending slightly at the hips so that her tits swing out closer to the manky old fuck beside me. Donny reaches across the bar with both hands, pinching Karen's nipples between his hideous fingertips. He squeezes and rolls them a couple of times and sits back with a satisfied smile. Karen's nipples pop out on high beam.

'Damn it,' Donny pretends to curse. 'Owe you a dollar now.'

'Wouldn't be the first time,' sneers Karen, the evil fucking minx, smirking at Twix.

The poor bastard is shaking visibly.

'YOU FUCKING SLUT!' he suddenly screams, shocking everyone. Me and Amai jump, and Karen takes a step back. She laughs at his him, mocking him. 'FUCK YOU, BITCH! SLUT!'

He's fucking lost it!

Two guys at the end of the bar stand up and storm towards us. I grab Twix in a bear hug and drag him towards the doors, shouting for Amai to follow. But the thugs won't be denied their sport, and I'm no sooner out the door and onto the footpath than they catch us up.

'Fellas, we don't want any trouble,' I go, but one of them swings a punch at me.

I let go of Twix and stumble, falling onto the concrete. They grab hold of Twix and start belting into him. I'm off the deck quick as and tackling the guy that took a swing at me. I try and pick him up but he's too heavy, dropping out of my grip, clutching at me as he falls. We're stuck in an awkward position with him half on the ground and half in the air, hanging onto me as I hang onto him. In the moment it takes me to realise I could just let him go and stomp on him his mate launches into me from the side with a fist straight at my jaw. My head whips back from the punch while I see double vision, then I drop the cunt I'm hanging onto and face this other motherfucker.

'Let's go, Matty!' yells Amai, who's holding Twix up for support.

Me and this other guy stare at each other, and then I see in his eyes he's willing to let me go, so we inch around one another. He tends to his mate on the ground while I take the weight of Twix off Amai.

'You alright, man?' I ask.

'Yeah...' Twix says with a cracked voice.

I don't know if it's the fight that's made him emotional or the confrontation with Karen, but he starts crying.

'There, there, mate,' I go, not sure what else to say. 'Fuck em all.'

'Fuck em all,' he repeats.

We get down to the Mater Hospital and check out our injuries. Apart from a twisted ankle and the blow to his right ear, Twix is okay physically. I've got an egg forming on my jaw. Amai's A-okay. They had the decency, at least, not to touch her.

'Now it all makes sense,' Twix moans, sitting down on the park bench at the bus-stop. 'It wasn't my baby.'

'Oi, what fucking baby, Twix?' I ask. 'I didn't even know Karen was pregnant!'

'No-one did,' he says, 'except Alex.'

I've been friends with the bastard ever since he moved into the Prozac, but he chooses to confide his biggest secret with the new girl in town. Sometimes you're left wondering what mateship's even for.

'That's why we broke up,' Twix says quietly. 'She had an abortion, but I didn't want that. I thought I was gonna be a dad.'

Amai looks like she's over all this drama. She's so far out of the loop, and is meant to be his girlfriend. She's standing with her arms crossed behind the bench he's sitting on so he can't see how she's reacting to all this, but I can. She's fucking pissed off. Which makes it harder to say what I need to.

'Listen, man,' I go, getting down on one knee, putting a reassuring hand on his shoulder, 'you gotta talk to her. Not back in that shit-hole bar, but at home. You guys have gotta get your heads sorted about all this stuff, otherwise it'll eat you up.'

He wants to go home.

I'd prefer to go with him, but he only wants Amai for company. She looks like she'd prefer it was me, too. I wave down a cab for them and when they're gone I wait for another one for me. Fuck trying to bus it from here. I just want to get home and get an ice-pack on this jaw, unwind all the shit that's going through my head right now.

As I'm going up the stairs of the Prozac, Dante's reading on a chair just inside his doorway, like he's waiting for me to come past. He puts his book down and goes: 'How'd it go?'

I stop in the stairwell.

'You used me,' I say simply.

He cackles. 'Nothing personal,' he says. 'Jesus. Get over it. Just a fucking joke.'

I feel like punching the living shit out of him right now.

'It was a fucking cheap shot, you cunt,' I growl, charging up the stairs for that ice-pack.

'Did you remember my eggs?' Raven says as I pass her doorway.

SLOW TO LOAD: PEZ'S TALE

'I've asked ya to do the dishes twice now, Linsey,' muh Ma goes. 'Ya can play your video games later.'

'I'm goin out wif Sean later, ta the Railway in the Gabba,' I shout back, yankin the controller this way and that way as if it makes any difference ta movin the characters. I dunno why I do it, it just happens. Sean does it sometimes, too, I've noticed.

Ultimate Mortal Kombat 3 is not bad, a bit slow loadin, but it's taken until now ta get muh hands on it.

Muh Pop was good wif his hands. That's why he was a handyman. If ya needed somefing fixed in the neighbourhood, people would say 'just call for Les, the handyman.' He could fix anyfing. 'Any job, big or small,' he used ta say.

When he wasn't around no more, I got bullied a lot by the other kids at school for bein a dumbarse, so I dropped out as soon as I turned fifteen, part way frough year ten. The teachers tried ta get Ma ta change muh mind, but she's just a liddle Dutch lady tryin ta raise her son on her own, and she got confused by us sayin I wozzen goin back and them sayin it was better that I go back. In the end she gave up and let us stay home, playin video games on muh SNES all day.

That's how I met Sean. I was pickin out a game ta rent at the Civic Video down the road when he came over and told us which was the best ones. I was holdin a new one called *Wolfenstein 3D* and wanted ta play it really bad, but Sean said it was shit.

'They've edited out all mention of the Nazi's, but,' he'd said, angry. 'All the fucken flags, the German language, even Hitler's moustache. It's a fucken outrage. Heads should roll for it.'

He reckoned the Sega games were better coz they still had the blood and guts in them, but I only owned a Nintendo. So he got us ta distract the shop-keeper by 'accidentally' knockin over a shelf of videos while he pinched a Sega console behind the counter. Except we forgot ta pinch the game as well and knew we couldn't go back and hire it in case the shop-keeper had noticed the game console was gone. I begged Mum ta drive us ta anudder Civic, which she only did so that Sean would keep bein muh friend.

Sean's really smart, which is why I always listen ta what he's got ta say. When I was still at school I hated it so much I useta get high by pinchin me Gran's tablets, all the different medicines she had. She still had all of Grandad's tablets, too, even though he'd been dead for years. I pinched them all, and used ta sell them ta the kids at school, which made us a bit popular for a while. They useta call us Pez, then, like the little PEZ lolly fingos, and I was feeling better about meself until one day I asked if I could kiss Melanie Leventis and her boyfriend Jonesy decided ta punch muh head in. After that I started ta get bullied again, mostly by Jonesy's mates and then their mates and so on.

I dunno if it was all the tablets or all the punches I used ta get, but somefing made us like that *Ultimate Mortal Kombat 3*: slow ta load.

I wish I'd knowed Sean back in them days. He would've sorted the motherfuckers right out for us.

He might've sorted muh Pop out, too. He sorta needed it.

Pop went ta the prison after that Mister Chaudhary who owns the dry-cleaners accused Pop of touching his tiny kids. They got muh Pop ta do some handyman stuff around the daycare, coz he was good wif his hands, but Ma says it was a set-up. That's all she's said about it ta this day. 'It's a set-up,' she said ta us one day durin the court trial. She doesn't talk about it no more, and gets the shits if anyone tries, even us.

Afterwards whenever Mister Chaudhary'd see us in the street he'd smile and wave, but like in that sad way like he pitied us. I'd ignore him, or walk the udder way. I diddin want ta look at him. He made us sick, what he did ta muh Pop.

When I got inta muh first year of high-school, Pop took us ta the pub ta celebrate. We got counter-meals and he bought muh first beer for us. 'He's fucken old enough,' he told the bloke behind the bar. Because I'd never had it before I wasn't sure about the taste of beer, but Pop just laughed and said it'd put hair on muh chest. I wasn't so sure about that, either, until I found out that some of the girls in muh class really liked the bits of hair that came out the top of the shirts of the boys in Year Eleven and Twelve.

'Sean's here, Ma,' I yell as he bangs on our screen door.

I know he doesn't like hangin around our flat so I jump up and head out straight away wif him. It's not until we're down the road that I remember I forgot ta turn the Sega off. Ma can do it.

Me and Sean like ta get counter-meals some days after his work, like we are now. We sit around wif a cold one and order chicken schnitzels wif chips and he tells us how the unions are doin fuck all about savin his job from the migrants that are comin over in fucken droves. I dunno much about the world and politics and workin, so I always agree wif him. It's usually better ta agree wif Sean anyway, or else he gets a bit upset wif ya.

Today we was gonna sit wif that Matthew Tadlow and his mates, the one wif the bat tattoos on the side of his head and the little slope girl, but they left before we got back ta the table. They musta got bored waitin for me and Sean ta get our chicken schnitzels.

I remember Matty from school. He was awright. And his brother. The older one, not that poofy little one. Fuckin hell, that bloke could fight, even as a teenager. Tadpole they used ta call him, behind his back, but. Not me, but. If ya sayin it behind the person's back, then that means they probably won't like it, so I never called him that. I wonder what they used ta say about us behind muh back? The stuff they useta say ta muh face was bad enough.

'That Maffhew Tadlow and his friends are gone,' I go, puttin the plate of food and the beer down. Sometimes we get milk instead of beer, coz Sean says milk is what made the white man superior. He says it changed our DNA, which is the stuff I fink is made up from our spunk.

'Don't waste your tears over those cunts, Pez,' says Sean. 'They're exactly the kind we don't need clogging up our work queues and hospitals and stuff.'

See, that's somethin I'd never have fought of, but Sean just *knows* this stuff.

Even though I've been a skin for nearly free and a half years now, I've never really understood it the way Sean does. He says it's good for us ta have something ta believe in, ta help us grow stronger so that I'm better than muh old man. Sean reckons he's a piece of shit, and if he could, he'd kick his head in. I dunno how ta feel about that, but I guess Sean's never touched us the way muh Pop used ta touch us, which is the way I hated, and Sean knows all this stuff about politics and beliefs. Ya have ta give him that.

'Trust me, Pez,' he goes, shovellin the schnitzel into his mouf like he's been starvin for weeks, 'the likes of those gothic cunts and their chinky pet are gonna learn the hard way to bow to the likes of us one day. Mark my fucken words.'

And I will mark em, Sean's words, because I've never had anyone bow ta us and I reckon it'd be great ta have the boot on the other foot for a change, so ta speak.

JIGSAW FEELING

The doctor says I've got anxiety. It's the last thing I needed to hear.

I tell him I think I might be having a series of strokes and how it's sometimes hard to breathe, but he just smiles knowingly: 'You've got anxiety, Alexandra.'

Just like that. Doesn't check anything. No x-rays or cavity searches. But I guess he'd know because it's, like, what he does day in day out, right? So mote it be.

It sucks, because I couldn't hold onto that crappy protein powder job. As shit as it was, I really needed the money, but trying to leave the house most days has become a full-time job in itself, period. I, like, get the shakes bad.

The doctor says he's going to give me some Valium for my nerves, that I have to be careful not to overtake them.

'No worries there, I'm not suicidal,' I try and joke, but he doesn't laugh. Poor bloke probably has to deal with families who've actually experienced a suicide, I guess.

He enquires about my lifestyle, like what I do for fun, and when he hears about my gothy way of life, the clubbing and heavy drinking and stuff, he, like, clucks his tongue.

'You have two major stress factors right now. The first is obviously being unemployed. It plays on your mind all the time. But you have become unwell, Alexandra, so some time off everything is exactly what you *do* need. You will be able to find work when your health returns, I promise you. It won't be a problem for you.'

'And the second?'

'Vitamin D,' he says simply. 'The sun.'

I start laughing, right, because clearly I'm sitting here dressed head to toe in black with dyed black hair and a spiked collar. Like, what is it about me that says I like the sun?

'I'm serious,' he smiles, superficially. 'When we don't get enough sun, it's easy for depression to set in.'

'Without my social life I definitely would be depressed, though!'

'I'm not talking about your lifestyle, as such,' he says, 'but where you live. You said that your flat is surrounded by trees and that it's very dark inside? If you can, find another place to live that has good light, lots of windows that face the sun.'

'That's going to be easy without a job,' I say snidely.

'When you can, do it, but if it's not possible just yet, it can wait,' he suggests, ignoring my sarcasm. 'But you cannot live in a gloomy place. You're like a fungus, when you should be more like a flower.'

For a crazy moment I'm utterly embarrassed that he's somehow miraculously guessed that I've recently developed an infection in my nether-region, making walking painful. It's blown up into a red-raw rash. But when the doctor sees me going bright red in the face he, like, misunderstands and chuckles bashfully, trying to set the record straight by explaining he didn't mean to flirt with me by comparing me to a flower.

As if that's what I was thinking! Puh-leeze.

Could've been worse, though: he really could've guessed about my heat rash. Then he'd need to take a gander at it. Being Indian, not sure he'd be game for it, though. Aren't they shy about muffies? But talk about laugh. I'm such a bloody dingbat, sometimes!

When I'm outside and feel the sun on my face, heating my hair, I suddenly regret my bad attitude with the doctor, realising that the sun *does* actually feel good. Out here in the light and warmth I feel more relaxed than maybe I do at home, where it's dark and cold. Funnily enough, the darkness and cold is exactly what I liked most about the Gillingham Street flat when I'd first moved in.

I grab a bottle of Valium at the chemist, the pharmacist blatantly scrutinising the script in case it's a fake. I was going to wait until I get home to pop one but figure now's as good a time as any and find a dim stairwell across the road, because, like, I don't need anyone (the pharmacist) copping a gander at me popping Vallies on the street.

Mama arranged yesterday (by phone all the way from Melbourne, no less!) for me to head over to Lisa's and resume my photography for her catalogues. Lisa's not interested in me shooting for her anymore (the feeling's mutual) but between her regular photographer falling crook and pressure from Mama, Lisa relents. Because I'm, like, still strapped for cash, I grab my camera and jump on the train to Roma Street. I'll save myself the bus fare to Paddington by walking from the train station. I've, like, developed this style of walk where I if I waddle and keep my feet apart like they're in a spreader bar, the infection doesn't get rubbed raw as much.

Part of me doesn't want to, like, go and do it though, because I don't want to remember the faces peering from the dark at Thomas Street or that smug grin at the Valley markets. Because it's a great day out, a deep blue sky and a warm sun, I reckon the flowers at New Farm Park would all be in full bloom right now. That would be a better way to spend the day. I could shoot a few rolls there and maybe get a portfolio together of flower photography. Pipe dreams, Alex! Who the hell would want photos of flowers?

Turns out Lisa's being standoffish, and it's, like, not helping that I'm so reluctant to be here, either. The Valium is settling in and I feel much calmer, even a little bit sleepy.

I cop a gander at a stack of boxes in the other room. The delivery label on it that says it's from Thomas Street in West End. My blood runs cold, and the dreaded quiver in my bones flares up. My heart hammers hard, my breath coming in short gasps. I have to get this anxiety under submission, but weirdly the words THOMAS STREET trigger a full-on attack, even though I'm blocking any mental pictures of abused women being taken advantage of.

Well, I was. Now they're suddenly in my fucking head.

Lisa notices my hands are shaking and asks what's wrong. Her eyes look small, the way they do when she feels confronted. She's probably guessed I've seen the boxes. I just want to leave, run home, sit in my bedroom with the blinds down. But since Lisa already, like, suspects that I know, I just blurt it out.

'Are you buying from that slave guy again?'

She's silent, but straightens so she's taller, and her knuckles, like, go white as she clasps her hands together in front.

'Fuck,' I gasp.

'It's not like that, Alex.'

'Isn't it?' My voice is small, incredibly calm. Maybe it just seems that way because, like, my heart sounds so loud in my head? BOOM BOOM BOOM.

'I was going to dob him in, honestly,' she says, her voice reedy and forceful, staring at my hands. She looks me in the eye. 'But you don't know the full story. You have to get all the facts first, Alex.'

I can't listen to this shit. She's making excuses for herself now, not for him. She's buying from a sweat shop where women and children are working in shitty conditions so that she can sell overpriced kiddie clothes to yuppies with more money than sense.

She's still, like, harping on, but I can't even hear her any longer.

The blood's whooshing through my ears, my breath has become ragged. Lisa looks worried, puts a hand on my shoulder, bends down to look me eye to eye because I've doubled over. She implores me to wait while she runs to the phone. As soon as she's facing the other way I stagger to my feet and, like, right out the door, basically power-walking down the street as much as my lungs will allow.

I feel like I'm going to have a heart attack, but I know that's just the anxiety. I have to get home, now. Like, *right now*.

Fuck the expense. I hail a taxi.

Half way home I reach for my bag to take another Vallie and, like, realise neither my bag nor my camera is with me. Shit shit shit. I must have left them at Lisa's. My purse is in my bag so, like, I can't pay for this taxi. Suddenly I'm crying, deep racking sobs that shake my shoulders. I can hear myself howling in despair.

When we get to the Gillingham Street flat, the tears are still there but not out of control like before.

'I left my purse at the other place,' I explain to the taxi driver, and rather than be sympathetic he gets cranky. He's probably guessed that's why I was crying and now he's, like, pissed off I didn't ask him to turn around when we still had the chance. 'But there's some change inside the flat,' I blubber.

'Righto,' he says gruffly, facing the front. What else can he do?

So I run inside, and immediately the cold and gloom hits me. It's a massive difference to the warm sunshine outside, and, like, I don't know why I've never figured it out before. I always liked how dark my place could get, convinced it helped me stay pale and added to the goth ambience. But now it feels like a self-imposed punishment.

After I've managed to find some change to pay the driver, who drives off shaking his head, I turn and face my little unit.

I've had some good times here, and feel settled, and the last thing I could face right now between my anxiety and being unemployed is moving house again. But suddenly it seems like the right thing to do. The doctor's right: I need sunshine.

That's something I thought I'd never say. *I need sunshine.*

I repeat the words over and over inside my head and it, like, just makes sense. I can't grow in the shade. I can't be happy here. It's like I'm Moorhen Flats and I need a Jai all of my own to, like, help me renovate my life. As if that's going to happen. I hesitated with Jai and now he's gone, just like every other good opportunity that comes my way.

Since I'm stuck here for now I'll have to content myself with this place as best I can. Not all of us are free to make the choice to move somewhere better so easily. I'll need money, first. I'll need to go back with my tail between my legs and do those shoots for Lisa, if she'll even have me back.

But it also means permitting her to continue supporting that sweat shop business. And I can't allow that. I might, like, have the choice to move on from this cold and depressing unit – when I get the means to, that is – but those women at that sweat shop are basically held to ransom by my sister. And that's something I can do something about. If my sister won't cut herself off from that evil little bastard's slave labour business, then I'll see to it myself. And in doing this, maybe it'll, like, give me the resolve I need to move on, find myself a flat with good airflow and even a little sunshine. I could grow some herbs and start cooking fresh meals. Herbs here have no chance, in the cold shade. There's, like, a massive forest of black wattles and bamboo surrounding the units. Literally no sunshine gets through those.

I head back inside, playing that child's game where you step on every crack in the footpath to avoid bad-luck, and flip through the white pages, tracing my finger across name after name until I settle on a couple of numbers to call, things like the ACCC. It was formed last year to deal with stuff like this, so I give them a call and drop that slave trader straight into the shit.

Thomas Street, West End, is about to get a visit it won't forget.

It feels good, final even, to have made that phone call. Like I've finally got an emotional handle on the issue I have with Lisa and the Chinese guy and those women and children. Just to be sure, I knock on wood, tapping my fingers on anything within reach that's made from timber.

The front doorway is aglow with the day, framed by the perpetual gloom of my lounge. I feel like I'm inside a cage, an unproductive sweat-shop of my own making.

If it's sunshine I need, maybe it's time to call it quits to pale skin, too. I don't mean hit the beaches or anything, but at least I could, like, stop trying to actively avoid my skin browning a little bit. Add some colour to it; put a little life back into it.

And just like that, I suddenly feel like I'm basically done with the whole scene, period. Time to hand in the goth card. How's that joke go when we stop being goth? We turn into ravers, right?

THE WEDNESDAY DRESS

The day of the court case has come around, and Amara wants to join me. I'm reluctant to have anyone with me as I don't wanna lose face but she's adamant that she wants to support me. We meet outside the magistrates on Roma Street, and she's wearing a gorgeous slinky black dress that reaches down to her Roc platform boots with the buckles on them. With it's white Peter Pan collar, the dress looks like what Wednesday Addams would wear if she were a sultry woman. The sun's casting strong shadows today, so it becomes immediately obvious that Amara's not wearing a bra. The dress cups her breasts and outlines her puffy nipples, which look like the rubber nubs on the ends of pencils, so that the shadows highlight she's on high-beam. I don't know about Amara, but suddenly I feel exposed. There's a lot of scum smoking in groups outside the courts, whinging about their cases. I quickly usher us both inside, through the security screening.

Dale Donger advised me to get myself a duty solicitor when I got in here, so I go over to this counter at the far end of a seating area and ask the lady behind the screen for one. She jots down my details and tells me to take a seat by her window and that a solicitor will see me soon. A few other people sign on for the duty solicitor, too.

Amara's boot buckles rattle as she throws one of her long legs over the other. I'd told her to dress down for the occasion, try and keep it low-profile on the dark stuff, but she's teased her hair up into a messy stack and wings of black eyeliner lick from the sides of her eyes. She's drawing a bit of attention from pretty much every cunt in the waiting room, as if these losers have never seen a goth before. I wore the simplest things I could find, but now I realise even my efforts weren't the best. I probably should have ditched my black coat, or at least taken the pin-badges off it.

This Asian guy with a clip board is going around to a couple of the other court attendees, asking them a couple of questions and writing something down. He gets to me and introduces himself as David, the duty solicitor. He confirms my name, writes down the offence I'm being charged with and asks if I'll be pleading guilty, which I am. He tells me there's a bit of a wait but he'll eventually be able to talk with me.

'My office is through that door there,' and he points at this plain wooden door next to the glass sliding doors of the courtroom.

'Yeah, he's gay,' says Amara when he's gone.

'Camp as a row of tents,' I agree. Though he wasn't actually camp.

'I've never been in a courtroom before,' she confesses.

'Me neither,' I go, and she gives me a little look of surprise. 'What? You shocked to hear that?'

'Yes, frankly,' she laughs.

'In a way, me too,' I admit. 'My psych says despite appearances I'm pretty good at judging when to draw the line, so I'm also good at avoiding facing the law.'

'Like a sixth-sense,' she smiles.

'My dad's been in one, though.'

'What happened?'

I check to make sure no-one's eavesdropping. It's the last thing I need in a courthouse full of cops. 'He was busted for drugs when I was kid. Drug running. Reckons he didn't know what was in the bag. As if. He went to this one house where there was a sting, but the cops didn't want my dad, The Ratbag Three.'

'The what?'

'The guys he was running for,' I clarify. 'But he wouldn't dob them in. So the cops made an example of him instead.'

This derro looking cunt a few seats away is staring at us, and I give him the eye to try and make him look away, but he's not even aware of me. He's staring at Amara's tits.

'Did time for it at Bluestone College. Eighteen months.'

Amara screws her nose up, which is like one of those cute button noses some girls have. 'They sent him to a college?'

'Nah. Pentridge. The prison. They just call it that in Melbourne.'

'Shit,' she says, 'I hope it doesn't go that bad for you.'

'I'll be right,' I smile, winking at her. I check my crappy little two-dollar watch. 'Fuck, we've been here for an hour already, and I still haven't seen the solicitor yet. It's not even open yet,' I say, waving a hand at the glass doors to the courtroom.

'Should've brought a book,' yawns Amara, pulling a bored face which gets a chuckle from me.

Finally, David calls me into his poky office. There's thick, leather-bound books of law on a shelf behind him, crammed in next to less-impressive vinyl ring-binders. David's got a woollen vest pulled over a crisp business shirt. He looks very much the part, which is more effort than I've put into playing mine. I really regret now not ditching this ludicrous coat.

He explains that he's funded by the Legal Services Agency to assist people like me who're pleading guilty, and that he can help represent me inside the courtroom, if I'd like him to. He's dressed for the part, and knows his way around all this stuff far better than I ever will, so I tell him I'm more than happy for him to go ahead and do his thing. He seems chuffed by that phrase.

'Do you have a copy of the QP9 form?' he asks.

I shrug. 'I don't know what that is.'

'Don't worry,' he goes, rapidly reading the arrest report. 'Huh!'

'What is it?'

'Oh, nothing to worry about,' he laughs, and I'm thinking that's okay for you to say cunt, you're not in my position! 'I just noticed that one of the officers that interviewed you has the surname Ballow. There's a building called Ballow Chambers in Spring Hill where a couple of doctors were shot dead by a crazy German man carrying bombs and stuff back in the fifties. My grandfather was involved in the ensuing court case.'

'Yeah, I know that building,' I go, because I have a fondness for looking at the old structures around the city and it's only a couple of streets away from The Prozac Palace. It's got the name in big concrete letters on front of the building: BALLOW CHAMBERS. 'It's up the road from where I live.'

'Small world!' David squeals. 'How crazy is that?'

I shake my head in mock disbelief at the apparent impossibility of such a coincidence while David keeps grinning at me. The moment stretches a little too long and abruptly turns awkward.

'Okay, um, tell me what were the events that led up to your arrest, then,' he coughs nervously.

I tell him everything, including what McKay said about me being 'fey', when I'd told him what had happened. I disclose it in the hopes of convincing David that on my own psychiatrist's admission I'm somehow inculpable, but he's not swallowing the bait. Just like that bastard McKay, who refused to write a note to the courts stating such. What's a guy gotta do around here to be considered mentally unstable enough to be exonerated?

Out of the blue, David goes: 'We'd keep similar company, I think.'

'Eh? Is that a pick-up line?'

He looks completely embarrassed, even blushing a bit.

'No, no, I just meant that I know where you're coming from.'

Ah, so it's not a come-on line. He's empathising or something.

'You're like a sponge,' he goes. 'You soak up everything around you, the good and the bad. Every time you go into the city, you absorb it and become like it. Take on the negative associations.'

It sounds a bit metaphysical, some New Age type spacey shit, but the thing is, that is exactly how I *have* been feeling! I'd never have made the comparison to a sponge before, of course, but now that he's articulated it aloud, it really resonates with me. It must show on my face, because he is undeterred from continuing.

'You need to get away from the city, actually, even for a little bit.'

'It's funny you say that,' I tell him. 'I do get out sometimes, up into the countryside, and when I come back I actually go into the city and just sit and people-watch. Just sit there and soak in the atmosphere. It's funny you've picked up on that.'

'We're both sensitive people,' he says, which floors me, because I always thought I was actually a bit of a cunt. 'We feel all the energies around us, and we respond to it.'

It's beginning to sound like he thinks I'm innocent of my crimes, which I definitely know I'm not. But when I think about how McKay said I was being fey which confused the security guard and the cops, I start to think David's onto something. Maybe I was a bit compelled by the city, maybe I am absorbing it and simply throwing it back at itself, and it doesn't like what it sees? What the fuck am I thinking?

'So, we can try and get me off the hook here with a not-guilty plea or something?'

'Oh no,' he says with dead certainty. 'You're definitely guilty.'

This prick's wound me up. How can a sponge be wholly culpable?

'But I'll try and see the magistrate's not too harsh,' he promises.

Back out in the waiting room I tell Amara what happened with David, expecting her to laugh her head off, but she agrees with him instead.

'We attract all this energy toward ourselves,' she says, seemingly picking up where David has left off. 'When you get treated badly by people, it's because you're drawing that attention to yourself.'

'Are you saying I deserve it?' I say, irritably.

'Of course not,' she says. 'But if you think you *do*, then you will attract blame to yourself.'

I didn't know she was into that kind of thinking, but with a name like Amara I should've probably expected it. It's short for something, can't remember what, something about eternity or everlasting, and when you think about it anyone who names their kid that is going to raise them with a New Agey ideology. I've faced this nonsense before, with Simone.

I'm grateful for the courtroom doors opening, as I'm getting pretty annoyed now. Everybody shuffles inside past the magistrate guards and we all take seats in the gallery. The judge and court personnel come in after a wait, taking their places up at the bench and whatnot. To my dismay, I notice a couple of loners in the crowd with notepads and pens; must be reporters for the newspapers. I've read the little side columns in the papers where they give a paragraph or two on the court cases and name the people involved. I could do without being mentioned in one of those.

The court clerk tells us all to stand for the judge, who strolls in like he's emperor and takes his time sitting down. He's wearing a long black gown like you see judges wear in movies. I wonder about the importance of it, or rather the necessity, and can't really think that it has one beyond being symbolic or sentimental of the entire judicial process. I wonder if people laugh at him outside of the courthouse the same way they'd laugh at one of us for wearing a cape?

First up is some scruffy looking guy probably in his forties, I'd guess. The cunt hasn't even bothered to make himself presentable. His hair's all over the place and he has an unkempt beard. He's dressed like he's been digging potatoes outta the ground. Accused of driving drunk, on a suspended licence, and in an unregistered vehicle. The cop reading out the report also goes on to say the potato picker gave a fake name and insisted on it even when they knew who he was, because he'd been done for drink driving before, which is how he lost his licence in the first place. He's shameless standing up there, telling the judge that he did these things. The judge orders that his licence suspension be increased and gives the cheeky fucker a fine for three hundred bucks. The guy walks out of the courtroom with a smile on his face, like it's all old hat to him.

Then this petite girl gets called up to the front, while we all watch from the gallery. I don't know why, but I thought we'd get called in one by one and face the judge without a room full of spectators. Naive on my part. The judge listens to her crimes, which is stealing some disposable razors from Woolies which the girl claims is so she can look presentable for work. The judge hassles her about her income, which the girl confesses isn't much on account of her boss has lapsed on giving out wages to his employees. The judge gives her a critical look, like he thinks she's full of shit, but the girl's shaking with fear where she stands. She's hunched over, holding her hands together like she's facing a firing squad, which is probably how she feels. The judge rips into her, like he's got the taste of blood and can't stop, and the girl gets confused because the stupid cunt keeps using legalese terminology. I don't even know what any of it means, much less her. She's crying now, and the judge is losing his patience, repeating his absurd questions. It's pissing me off, and I'm beginning to get the temptation to stand up and call the cunt out on his bullying. But then this big bastard across the aisle with a Salvos logo on his shirt-pocket half-stands, whispering assistance to the girl. It confuses her even, but the judge decides to drop the torture act and just end the whole drama by fining the girl a couple of hundred bucks. I'm sure I'm not the only one here thinking how the fuck's she gonna pay that since she had to steal in the first place.

The girl leaves the courtroom bawling her eyes out. In a way, I guess the judge's job is done, because I doubt the girl will ever be in here again. That's the justice system in action for you.

Then I get called up. Fuck. Here we go.

First off the bat, everyone seems to be shitting themselves in front of this judge. My duty solicitor, the cops, the court clerk. I hadn't noticed that back in the gallery, but up here it's as plain as day. I can't work out why, though. I mean, sure, he's the big cunt in the big chair, but honestly, he still shits and pisses and bleeds like the rest of us.

They get things underway, no hesitation. I acknowledge that I am indeed one Dante Halloran, and the cops read out the charge, which is sparse on details except for those that prejudice me. When he reads out my explanation for carrying a knife, the cunt simply goes: 'the accused says he's afraid of being bashed.' A murmur of objection escapes me, and David frowns at me to shut me up.

'But that's bullshit,' I whisper back. 'I'd never use the word *bash*.'

It sounds so fucking primary school level. I'll have to rectify that with Amara when we get out of here. The judge peers over his glasses at me, same way the teachers at school would when we'd be talking in class, so I pipe up and sit back.

David gives such a paltry defence that I should've just represented myself. Having him means I can't squeak a fucking word, though. I feel so frustrated having to sit here and listen to the horseshit these fuckers are feeding each other. But before it's even begun, it's ended. David tells the judge that I plead guilty, and the cops sit back down and flip close their manila folder.

'The defendant is hereby requested to pay the court a restitution of four hundred and fifty dollars, with no conviction recorded.'

And that's that. Case fucking closed. Except, four hundred and fifty fucking dollars later!

I'm half inclined to stand and tell the fuckhead what I think of the system, but I know that will just end even worse for me, so I satisfy myself with leaning in to the microphone and in my best Nick Cave imitation declaring 'thank yuh very much', the way I've seen him do when the audience cheers after a song, which is him imitating Elvis Presley anyway. But no cunt notices over the murmuring through the room as cops change places and the court clerks confer. The judge doesn't even scowl in my direction, even though I can clearly hear myself through the speaker system. I needed more sarcasm for these dipshits to register the joke, obviously.

Back in the court's corridors I get my fine given to me on a slip of paper, but for whatever reason the cops don't have the finger-printing available here, and tell me I need to present myself to a cop shop in thirty days from now to get them done. *Present myself,* they actually said that, like this was all some well-to-do affair where I wasn't just fleeced a fortnight's dole money.

When me and Amara get outside there's a group of seedy looking cunts gathered around smoking, wearing those hideous Adidas pants that button up the whole length of the leg and slinky baseball singlets that do nothing to hide their emaciated frames. Their faces are spotted with zits from all the junk food they doubtless thrive on, and there's gross tufts of hair on their chins and top lips. They look like fucking sewer rats, and their beady hateful eyes take everything in, especially Amara's breasts bouncing around without a bra.

'Oi, fucken check those ones,' I hear them say.

'Fuck yeah, I'd do it,' says another and starts making smooching noises while the others laugh.

I swap sides with Amara, using the pretext of showing her what's written on the documents the cops gave me because I don't need these seedy cunts to know I've heard them. It only encourages them further.

'Oi, gothic cunt!'

They wolf-whistle Amara and call out how they're going to punch the living shit outta me. My heart's hammering and I'm doing my level best not to turn and say or do anything, especially in lieu of the court case. I don't even have a fucking knife anymore, for fuck's sake. Stupid fucking pigs. They're all inside upholding the fucking law with guns holstered to their sides, and we're outside putting up with the scum of the fucking earth.

There's a car parked across the street, and when we get kerbside I check the reflection in its windows to make sure we're not being followed by these pricks, but they're all still huddled over by the garden bed, strutting around like they own the fucking place.

Amara's stealing glances at me and it's pissing me off. I feel at any moment she's going to try this *share how you feel* shit and this really is the wrong fucking place and time for it. How's this for attracting energy to ourselves?

Thankfully, we round the corner of the towering and windowless edifice of the police headquarters on Roma Street, out of sight of the scum rats. But my head feels hot with rage, and I can't look at Amara.

I mean, there's a part of me that feels I've failed her, that I should be able to stand up to them and have the cunts apologise or at least shut the fuck up. But it wouldn't happen. They don't feel shame, or think we're worthy of respect. Those cunts probably face the courts all the time, are probably familiar faces to the system.

It's better we're on our way now. Past the Transcontinental and down along George Street. I think if Amara wasn't with me, there's a good chance I'd have turned and told them to go fuck themselves, or made some clever remark about how they like to fuck each other, something to appeal to the almost certain presence of a homophobic streak in every single one of the cunts. That said, there was almost a dozen of the fuckers; it would've kicked off and that would've been me done for, then.

Girls are good at putting that shit behind them. I guess they deal with it on a daily basis, and they don't have the escalating levels of testosterone blinding them to the possible reality of having the shit kicked out of them, so they process confrontations differently. More expediently. Amara talks gently with me, avoiding all mention of the the courthouse, suggesting we catch a movie. Cronenberg's *Crash* is playing at the Dendy in an hour, so we grab a couple of tickets and wander the streets until it opens.

But I'm still feeling sensitive about being around people, and can feel my paranoia and agitation starting to feed one another, so I veer us into the Town Hall where the corridors and wide stairwells are relatively quiet. You can hear your own footfalls in here, and I feel the frenetic drive of my brain start to calm down a bit. It's also poorly lit inside these corridors, which curve around a central hall so that the shadows are always deep and unforgiving. It's perfect for me to try and relax in. I come in here quite a bit when I'm in the city, actually.

Now that I've got stock of my mind again, I'm giving Amara a bit of a tour of the inside of the Town Hall, showing her different rooms and pretty much guessing at what they're probably used for, but she seems impressed at least. I take her hand and jog her up the marble staircases that lead to the next level up, watching as her tits bounce wildly. If she's caught onto my game, she hasn't protested.

'We'll catch the elevator for the next one,' I say, and deliberately hit the down button. 'Damn it, slip of the finger. We'll need to get the stairs back up again.'

'Or we could just use the elevator to–'

'Nope!' I cut her off with a swish of my hand. 'They don't allow it! Stairs again it is.'

She gives me a sly smile, and we run up the stairs again, laughing. She knows I'm watching her tits for sure this time, and keeps her hands balled up beside her head like an anime character to best show them off.

I steer us straight for the rear of the Hall this time, down the stairs again for some more jiggling action, remarking to her how fucking good her boobs look. She actually jumps up and down on the spot a couple of times for me. It's all I can do not to reach out and play with them. I'm fucking dying to.

'I should've worn a bra,' she says, smirking at her own body.

'No way! I love em just how they are.'

'You're not the only one,' she giggles, almost spoiling my mood by bringing up those cunts back at the courthouse.

I lead her through to the green room behind the main auditorium. Testing the handle proves the door's unlocked. There's a window at the top, through which I can see the room's empty. We go inside, locking the door behind us. There's some chairs, a waste basket, a toilet with lockable door, and several mirrors with lights above them.

'What are we going to do in here?' She's acting coquettish, and it's driving me crazy. I can feel my cock stirring in anticipation.

'This is where the performers come before a show,' I say, dropping my voice, leaning into her, pressing her back towards the mirror.

'They come here, huh?'

'Before a show,' I repeat, breathlessly. 'The warm up, so to speak.'

Our faces are close now, our breathing irregular. Her breath smells sweet, the way that some girls get when they're horny. I wonder why that is? I hope mine doesn't smell rancid, trying to recall if I brushed them today. I've no idea.

She has the cheekiest little smile, and our lips touch, once, twice, then press together more earnestly on the third. I feel her tongue poke at my lips and respond in kind. We're making out now, pressed against each other. She scoots back, lifting her arse up onto the bench-top. I pull back, staring at her tits, unable to fight the urge to touch them. Her nipples are poking through the fabric so much it's difficult to believe she hasn't slipped a couple of pencil erasers under her dress to fool me, but as soon as I get my hands on them I'm left in no doubt. Her breasts are paradoxically soft and firm at the same time.

I run my hands along her thighs, pushing her dress up towards her panties. I don't know if it's the angle or not, but her legs seem really long. The envy of other girls I imagine, which is maybe why she's always wearing dresses that reach around her ankles. Girls can be vicious when they're jealous.

'I wanna eat you,' I whisper.

Her eyes sparkle, and she pushes me away a couple of steps. I've blown it. Some girls when they're young don't like getting eaten out. Not sure why, but they're embarrassed by it and insist on avoiding it. I used to think maybe I just wasn't doing it right, but Twix said it's happened to him as well. Not many time, but it has. I wonder if he tried it with Nikki?

Amara pulls her dress back down over her legs, sliding off the shelf. Then she faces the mirror and pulls her dress back up again, up over her arse this time, leaning over the bench-top, hands splayed against the mirror. It's a fucking beautiful sight: long legs with white socks and black platform-boots, white panties contrasting against her bunched up dress. It's like if Wednesday Addams did porn.

Hesitation's for lost cunts. I kneel down behind her arse, running my hands up her legs, tugging her panties off. A little waft of pungent heat greets me, and I spread her arse-cheeks to get a closer look at her hairy little pussy before I nuzzle in.

'What're you waiting for?' she says testily.

'Righto, just enjoying the view first.' I slip my fingers into her to test the waters, and holy fuck is she tight!

'Eat the pussy already!' she growls.

I don't know why, but I suddenly recall Rosie from the Winter Solstice Festival and how after we'd done it she'd straddled my face and demanded that I eat her out. Like Amara, Rosie had been quite demanding for it, too, despite the fact I'd just had my dick in there her vagina smelled really good so I'd been more than happy to oblige at the time.

After a bit of tongue-action on Amara I start priming myself in anticipation of some doggy-style. Christ, I'm ready to burst already.

A tickle begins at the back of my throat which I can't ignore. It escalates into an itch, right at the back of my throat. Maybe I've swallowed something? I start coughing, still trying to keep the pussy-licking up, but the coughing becomes too persistent, and Amara gets worried.

'What's wrong?'

'I don't know,' I wheeze. 'Something's caught in my throat.'

I cough and hack until I spit up a pube into my hand. The scratchy sensation goes away immediately.

'I swallowed a pube.'

'Eww,' she says.

'What? It's one of yours, you know!'

'Still eww,' she laughs. She's fucking beautiful when she laughs.

'I gotta pee,' she confesses, yanking down her dress and nipping in to the toilet, closing the door. Weird how I can lick her most private parts, but she hides when she needs to piss.

'I'm glad it was just a pube I swallowed, then!'

I've still got a mongrel despite the near choking I had. Normally my dick's kinda small when it's not in use, which my ex Jillian said was a blessing because I can tuck it easily into my dacks. Looking at it now, it looks huge poking out of my fly half-engorged.

Someone taps on the glass of the green room's door, and I nearly sprain my neck spinning around to look, freezing in shock at the same time.

There's an insecurity guard peering through the window at me, and not just any insecurity guard either: it's old flinty eyes that I swiped the money from at the ATM yonks ago, the one with the crappy toupee. Turns out he's security here! He's glares through the grimy glass, his enraged eyes flicking from me down to my exposed dick and back again. The door starts to rattle fiercely as he pummels it. Then I hear the jingle of a set of keys while the cunt tries to find the one for the green room door. I've only got a few seconds before he's in here and dragging me out for a thrashing, an arrest, or a bit of both.

There's a couple of windows on the far wall with latches on them.

I climb onto the bench-tops next to the mirrors with my dick bobbing around like it's full of curiosity for the world, and get one of the windows unlatched just as I hear the door behind me unlock. A push on the glass swings the window out, revealing a garden in a central well surrounded by high concrete walls. This must be some kind of ventilation area for all the air conditioners in this side of the building. I get out through the window, scraping my elbows and knees on the sill and nearly giving myself a second circumcision, and drop down to the ground just as I hear the insecurity guard get to the window. The cunt's too slow to catch the likes of me, because I'm the Gingerbread Man! I see his silhouette disappear from the glass. I better hightail it out of here fast. That cunt'll know this place better than I do, and he'll be bound to reach this alcove maybe faster than I can reach the street.

I start climbing a rusty drain pipe toward another window on the opposite wall.

Then I suddenly remember that Amara's still inside, in the dunny. I've got precious seconds to decide her fate, but I figure even if the guard realises she's there, she'll be able to talk her way out of it. She's a girl, after all. She's got the charms. As long as she doesn't drop my name, though.

I get the fuck out of there as quickly as I can, hoping that by the time I reach the street my dick's softened enough to stuff back into my dacks.

THE LAST BEAT OF MY HEART

There's, like, thousands of people in the streets, swarming *en masse* towards the Botanical Gardens, the same direction as Abi and me are headed.

She's getting frustrated with me because I'm, like, touching all sorts of shit on the way down, basically anything that stands out such as signs on shop windows or cracks in the wall. I'm going to exhaust myself by the time we get to the River Stage, never mind probably make my fungal infection flare up again.

The rash in my groin has been getting worse, accompanied by a crazy stinging pain that's, like, relieved by basically only cold water or lying naked on my bed with my legs open. If only I could say the same thing after a date, right? Eventually I'd had no choice but to go see the GP about it (the rash, not a date), and being an old bloke (I thought I'd spare the Indian one by trying someone else) he seemed more than happy to get a gander up my skirts. He said that with the onset of the Spring weather I've developed a common fungal infection – which I'd already figured it was because I had something similar in high-school during one of Melbourne's infamous heat-waves – and he told me to grab a tinnitus cream from the chemist for it. The cream's helped a lot already, but I need to put it on a couple of times a day for, like, the next couple of weeks at least. Bizarrely, he also told me to, basically, find a spot near a window at home and sit with no knickers on so that the air and sun help it out. More of that healing Vitamin D!

'I'm not interested in washed-up musos like Braithewaite, mind,' says Abi, who's been nattering on and on ever since we got off the train. 'Who the hell wants to turn up for that, besides the sheeple around us? Stuff that. It's those *Home & Away* stars I'm pretty keen for. They're the real prize.'

'I don't even watch that show,' I admit.

'Oh my Gawd, Alex, you fucking hafta,' she grins. 'It's sooo banal. I hope they rip each other new arseholes onstage, too, right in front of everybody, like they do on the show. That'd be the fuckin ants pants, wicked as.'

I'm like: 'Oh, puh-leeze. You know they're actors, right? They probably, like, have a great working relationship together and lead wonderful lives.'

Abi thrusts her palm at my face. 'Talk to the hand, because I ain't listening. But you gotta see em, Alex: the perfect representation of normals tearing each other apart in their apparently perfect and idyllic suburbia. It makes me sick to see.'

'Yet you watch it all the time.'

'Have to,' she says, stopping to check that the goon bladder hidden deep in her oversized bucket bag isn't leaking. Sneaking grog into events is the only reason she owns that bag. 'They might bring Shane Parrish back from the dead. I hope he's here today. I'll totally give him a kiss if he is, no buts about it.'

'Kissing an actor from *Home & Away*?' I jeer as we continue on, pressed on either side by, like, families of mundanes and their demon spawn. 'You sound pissed already, ya dingbat.'

'In time, my lovely, in time,' she grins, patting her bag.

Talk about laugh!

At least once we're inside the Botanical Gardens the families, like, fan out a bit, some chasing their sprogs over to the ponds or the playgrounds, so we've basically got a bit of room to ourselves at last. I feel like I can breathe a bit better. Abi wisely steers us onto the grass where there's a lot less things for me to tap. We follow alongside the paths towards the back of the gardens.

Abi's like: 'You know, you should get that checked out. It's not normal. It's a bit OCD of you, actually.'

What's remarkable about this is that Mama actually called me the other day and said she's coming up to see me soon because apparently Lisa mentioned something similar, the stupid skank. So freaking petty to, like, drop me in it. Spiteful *kargiola*. So Mama wants to take me to, like, a specialist for a second opinion on the development of my anxiety, which is the last thing I want to hear. I'm determined not to be labelled with any more diagnoses, period.

I guess coming to things like this bloody picnic in the park doesn't help. I normally try and avoid crowds as much as possible now, but it's difficult because, like, I'm not familiar with when all the major events are on up here, and it doesn't help that the council renames them so it's harder to find out. Like, for example, the Warana festival – which used to be a bit like Moomba down in Melbourne – just got split into a biennial event and is now called the River Festival. One part's already been on, which I managed to avoid like the plague, but I'm not sure about the other part. If it hasn't already happened then knowing my luck I'll, like, walk straight into the middle of it one day and get stuck with the crowds. Shit, even the locals seem confused by the name changing and when stuff's on.

Thinking about Moomba makes me kinda wish I was a kid again, without all the stress and issues of being an adult. The kids are laughing and throwing stones and twigs into the ponds for the ducks to chase, their parents looking haggard as fuck. It's like the demon spawn are sucking all the life outta the adults. I don't think it was like that with our parents, though, as all I can remember are happy memories of Papa taking us on the train to go watch the Yarra River water skiers before watching the Moomba parade. When it got dark he'd buy us ice-creams – even Mama would have one, peppermint – and we'd watch the city lights slide past the train on the way home, always looking for the massive neon Allen's lolly sign and Little Audrey skipping up in the night sky. Papa would play a game with us to see who could see the signs first, and if I beat Lisa to it then she'd sook the rest of the train trip home.

Great memories; Papa always seemed more excited for the festival than us. Maybe it's just a generation thing?

The other thing I like about Moomba compared to the festival up here is the name. Apparently 'Moomba' is an Aboriginal word that basically translates as 'up your bum'. Classic Melbourne humour. Beats boring old 'River Festival' hands down any day.

Finally we get to the River Stage at the back of the Gardens, where the words BRISBANE DAY FAMILY PICNIC IN THE PARK are emblazoned on a banner above the gates. Could they make the title any longer?

It turns out that the *Home & Away* stars aren't on until much later, so first we gotta, like, sit through four guys in coloured shirts singing and dancing for the little kiddies, who go fucking mental for them. It's like watching a pint-sized rock concert, like you'd see at Festival Hall. Thankfully, Abi gets our drinks poured, being less than discreet about it and causing a few parents to, like, glare at us. It's completely shit wine, but beggars can't be choosers.

One of the things I start to notice is just how many happy couples are here. Like, they're not even trying to fake it. They genuinely look pleased with their lot in life. Abi and I were pretty convinced that everyone would, like, be miserable having to look after their demon spawn and come to crap family events like this. But turns out it's actually not the case.

And oh for pity's sake, the amount of girls my age preggers with big overripe bellies, leaning against their boyfriends who look, like, super fucking supportive! I want to throw up, not from disgust but from jealousy. Why the hell don't I have that kind of relationship yet?

It's all those skinny, immature and effeminate goth boys with their pasty, pimply skin and their commitment phobia. That's the problem. What the fuck have I been doing with them all this time?

'What's the matter?' says Abi casually, noticing how I'm staring weirdly at the happy couples. 'Do you know em?'

'I've fucked everything,' I say pitifully. She raises her plastic cup in toast. 'It's been about skinny goth boys all along when, like, I should've been chasing after a real man.'

'Like Shane Parrish,' she says dreamily.

'Fuck Parrish or whatever his real name is,' I spit.

'I would if I could,' she grins seedily.

'Fuck Twix and all those other guys,' I continue unabated. 'I get more support and less grief from an underwire bra than any of those dickheads. I'm over the whole goth scene, and the scene boys. You know? I need a proper man, someone with, like, a broad chest and no torn fishnets on his arms. Someone serious about love, who knows what they want without all the drama and the games.'

'Someone who knows how to boil a fucking egg, too,' nods Abi, referring to the time she told me when Twix had to be taught how to do just that.

I'm like: 'Amen, sister,' which makes us laugh because we'd both sworn never to use that stupid phrase.

After security kick us out of the picnic because Abi got way too sloshed and started, like, screaming at the top of her lungs for Shane

Parrish to come fuck her brains out right there on the grassy knoll, I grab a newspaper from the newsagency and for kicks we scan the personals. There's a decent amount of em, basically older blokes past their prime, but there's a few that seem promising.

We're having a right laugh reading them out to each other and nitpicking the details, reimagining the realities behind the personals into the typical letdowns guys usually manage to exhibit, the poor things.

Quietly, I notice one that reads:

> **FUN GUY** 32 years young, employed with own car, looking for genuine lady to start a life with. John. Northside. **Phone: 285-6554**

Abi snorts with derision. 'Employed with own car,' she cackles. 'He's a pizza delivery boy.'

I pretend to laugh along with her, but there's something so austere about this ad that it hooks in my mind. Like, it reminds me somewhat of Jai, the guy I met ages ago on the train that was fixing up the natural corridors at Moorhen Flats. I really liked him but never had the guts to ask him out, and then I lost my job and haven't seen him since.

At home Abi's crashed in my bed, snoring lightly, hugging the nearly empty goon bladder.

I telephone the bloke from the ad, but a woman answers and she doesn't sound that old. My hopes begin to fade, thinking, like, this might be his missus and he's made the advert on the sly. I ask for John, trying to think of a lie I can offer if she asks why, but she begins to explain that John is a client of theirs, a really wonderful man with a great sense of humour.

Something's amiss here.

'Sorry, what do you mean by client?'

The woman's laugh is tiny, like glitter falling through the air. There's no mockery in it, just a quiet joy. 'We're a dating agency that John has joined with,' she explains. 'John's looking for the right lady and has trusted us to help narrow down his search. He's serious about love and doesn't want to waste his time on clubs and pubs.'

Even as I'm trying to process the fact that I've called a dating agency, my mind latches onto the guts of her pitch about how serious John is and how he's basically sick of being jerked around. That's exactly how I feel!

She's like: 'Does John sound like someone you'd be interested in meeting?' I confirm it's indeed why I've called. 'That's great, I'm sure he'd like to meet with you and get to know you a little better.'

She asks about me, so I tell her I'm between jobs at the moment but do photography normally, that I have my own place (I infer that I own it without saying as such, so it's not exactly a lie), and that I'm looking to, like, spend quality one-on-one time on the weekends with a funny, down-to-earth guy. Sounds like a lot, but it's pretty vague, and in the end I'm divulging more about what I'm looking for in a man rather than my personal traits. Obviously, I omit my involvement in the goth scene. I'm done with that anyway, right?

'John sounds perfect for you, Alex,' the lady gushes, getting my hopes up.

'I can't believe it,' I quietly gasp, almost bursting into tears. Isn't it magical how the universe can provide just when you're ready to give up altogether. Blessed be!

'You can come down and see us on Monday,' she says. 'My name is Crystal, so just ask for me.'

I can't believe it. Just like that, after complaining this morning about not finding Mister Right, I've already got a date with someone not in the scene! A real man! Cool beans!

I decide not to jinx it by telling Abi about the phone call when she wakes later, though it's bloody hard to keep mum about, that's for sure! She senses something's up, and tries to prise the news from me, but I'm tight as a frog's arsehole with my secret. She's not too happy about being kept in the dark, but I promise her I'll tell her what's happening soon. I start fantasising about arranging a catchup with her and turning up with John on my arm, a hunky, ordinary bloke with a killer smile, Abi swooning over him and declaring me the luckiest girl in Australia.

Monday morning sees muggins here all jittery and, like, nervous as I don my least-gothy dress and head into the Valley where Crystal said their office was. She's a lovely girl, much younger than she sounded on the phone, but also much taller than I am. That said, I estimate she'd be about my weight, only that it's spread out more over her towering frame. She's got an amazing smile that sucks me straight in.

John's photo is a bit dodgy, taken on a Polaroid here in the office. It's got the same plant and painting in the background. Besides that, he looks like the kind of bloke I could get to know. I'd never really considered dating his type before: blue jeans with polo shirt tucked in and short hair parted on one side. He's solid of build with slightly muscular arms and a shy, lopsided smile. Crystal tells me he was nervous about getting his picture taken and seemed reluctant to admit he was good looking. I feel myself soften to him upon hearing this, and can imagine myself bolstering his self-esteem at gatherings when a group photo's taken. My mind starts to spiral with the possibilities, picturing us, like, driving up the Sunshine Coast in his car with the windows down and Coil blasting on the tape player.

'Now, we only allow signed up members to access one another for their safety, you understand,' says Crystal sympathetically, adding that personally she thinks John and I would be a perfect match. 'Our membership is two hundred and thirty dollars and that gets you up to five dates a week with all our clients of your choosing for the first month.'

Why would I need five dates with anybody else? I already feel that John and I are meant to be, period. I imagine his voice, low and stuttery like Pete Murphy's, echoing my sentiments.

I head out down the street to the bank and withdraw the cash, aware that I've overdrawn on my savings and that I'll be, like, short on rent and groceries for the next fortnight. When Mama gets here I'll spot her for the cash, no worries. I'm sure when she meets John she'll agree it was worth doing and cover my rent no dramas.

Crystal takes my photo on her Polaroid camera and completes my profile, taking the cash and telling me she'll get in contact with John straight away and let him know all about me. I'm grinning like an idiot the whole time because I'm so bonkers happy.

On the way home I'm not even tapping. Completely cured! The Beatles were bloody right all those years ago! All the world needs is a little love.

It's a different story, though, when I catch myself in the closet mirror. I've hated my body ever since the onset of puberty. It wasn't kind to me. But there's no need beating myself up about it, not when there's things I can do about it. I change into my sneakers and some loose clothes, as best I can find anyway, and go for a jog.

Exercise isn't normally something I'd do, and not a snowball's chance in hell I'd normally do it in public, either, but at least it's night-time so there's, like, not many people on the streets. That'd be way too embarrassing, period! To make it even more private, I veer off Logan Road, weaving through the industrialised areas where all the mechanics shops are, mercifully closed up at this time of night, and head towards Moorhen Flats.

I've never been down in this part of my suburb, so now's as good a time as any to see what it's like, especially since I've heard so much about it from Jai back when we'd ride the same train. I've thought sometimes about dressing up in work clothes as if I'm still employed and catching the same train again, just so I could bump into him. But the fares are more expenditure than I can afford. At least, that's what I've been telling myself, anyway.

It turns out to be really quiet in this part of Woolloongabba. Or is it Coorparoo now? I'm clueless. In any case I find the much lauded Moorhen Flats, which is just a big flat piece of land behind some warehouses with a creek running through the middle of it. Even by the light of the moon I can see that there's been concentrated efforts to landscape the area, with a turtle pond and a gazebo in place.

But otherwise it's not much to look at. I suppose it's more than when Jai and his friends first started, though.

My groin's stinging from the running, but I didn't bring any cream with me like a total dingbat. Hoiking my skirt up, I sit down on one of the seats in the gazebo and yank my knickers down to my ankles, basically reclining enough to spread my legs and expose the infection to the cool night air. The inside of my thighs are so inflamed it looks like I've got a massive pash-rash going on. I probably look like a total skank sitting like this but it's like an instant relief, so much so that I could almost cry from joy.

Suddenly a bright light shines on me, from the front, straight onto my exposed muffy, giving whoever's behind the light the full gander of my red raw groin. In a mad panic I swing off the seat and shove my skirt down, grimacing with embarrassment and more than a little fear.

'Alex?' a voice says behind the torchlight, followed by the sound of a shovel falling on the ground.

I know that voice straight away.

'Jai?'

'Alex, what on Earth are you doing?'

I hold my hand up to shield my eyes from the bright light, but he continues to keep it trained on me. I don't know whether to be more relieved that it's only Jai or even more embarrassed *because* it's him!

'Are you prostituting yourself?' he says, disbelieving.

I'm dumbstruck. And insulted. I'd like to tell him to fuck off, but I'm just too dumbstruck to.

As I stand I realise my knickers are still around my ankles, and I nearly fall flat on my face hoiking them back up.

'This isn't what the Moorhen Flats are for,' Jai says, a bit peeved.

That's it. I can't take this anymore.

I run blindly, any direction will do as long as it's away from him, desperately hoping I don't, like, fall into the turtle pond and make more of an arse of myself. Palm fronds are whipping my face as I sprint along a path and out into another clearing, finding a road and running down it, huffing and puffing the whole time. The mechanics' shops whizz past, so I know I'm headed in the right direction, at least, tears streaming down my face from the burning agony of my heat rash being rubbed raw by my thighs. But I can't stop until I've gotten all the way home, safe in the Gillingham Street flat.

THE BLACK DOG

Sometimes life's all about going through the motions, because the alternative is to stop, which is a terminal kind of alternative. At least by mindlessly going through the motions I'm still propelling myself toward a moment when the depression will break and I will emerge somewhat my old self again.

That said, it doesn't actually feel like this will ever end. It never does feel like it will. But I know from both experience and on an intellectual level that naturally it must.

So I stay the course, persevering with my theory of going through the motions.

In the meantime, I bow to its pressure, of The Inferno and its step-brother Depression, feel my blood turning to shit and my thoughts spoiling like rotten food. Every fucking memory I've ever had is now tainted; the good with the bad thrown into one stinking cesspit and not a single rose among them. They're all tainted, all the good made into shit because I can either see a fresh, skewed perspective to it or I cannot imagine ever having a positive or happy experience again.

And why would anyone want to try and create happy memories with a worthless cunt like me?

If I really think about it, I can't even come up with a logical reason as to why any of the people I know even hang out with me. I run through a mental list of candidates, weighing up their commitment or level of interaction with me, and the quantitative measure of both, and decide that my friends are probably as desperately useless as I am and like the proverbial birds-of-a-feather we've merely unconsciously flocked together. Not out of genuine friendship, mind, but as a sort of last resort, a grasp at normalcy, attempting to fit in as much as us losers possibly can.

Which says a fucking lot about me, really.

Even at the arrival of this stunning conclusion, I'm aware that it's a falsehood, that The Inferno has skilfully conjured a crippled reasoning to once again convince me of my own worthlessness, and that this will now be a constant and revolving thought-cycle for the next few days – maybe even weeks – while I sink deeper and deeper into this depression. It's hideous that I'm able to comprehend the process and yet be utterly powerless to thwart it, to divert myself down a better path. I can't do that because no matter how hard I look, all the paths are strewn with rotten fruit. Even if at a glance one might appear to yield some hope, it's not long before my eagle-eyes spy the deceit and the rot is again revealed.

Over and over and over again my thoughts revolve on questions of my own worth, and over and over again the answer is unsatisfying, at least to both self-esteem and ego, so that I'm forced to confront the terrible truth about myself: that I'm freak and a fuckhead and simply wasting my life away.

This is what Depression does to me.

This is what my Borderline Personality Disorder does to me.

They've done it to me for so long it feels kinda familiar, like an old jumper I look forward to slipping on. Because while the depression might convince me that everyone hates me, and that I in turn hate them, conversely it knows me so well that it remains my only friend. It's easy to slip into, like slowly sinking under water but unaware that the surface of reason is too far away until it's too late, at which point I relax into this state of being, drifting on its turgid currents, letting it carry me wherever it wishes to.

But where it takes me is to deeper, darker waters.

Darker waters, indeed. My recurring vision of the country being swallowed by a flood of Biblical proportions springs to mind. I first had this vision, if it can be called that, back when I was part of that crazy Sugarloaf Road cult. We were fed too much end-of-the-world bullshit – mostly of being over-run by a military mad on power, the Devil's power to be precise – but it resonated with me at the time, and ever since I've had this one, persistent vision where I'm standing on a mountain-top, watching the entire eastern coast of Oz being swamped by a monstrous flood that rolls from inland, from where it's already submerged the rest of the country west of the Great Dividing Range.

Deep, dark waters.

They swirl and block out the light, pulling strange desires and self-loathing from their depths.

That's how I ended up here, polishing off a fucking bottle of wine after having emptied every pill bottle or blister-pack in the flat I could get my hand on, such as my old venlafaxine that I stopped taking a while ago, and even including Bernie's assorted medications for his Schizophrenia, like his olanzapine. The cunt'll just hafta get over the fact and haul his flabby arse up to the chemist to fuckin well purchase some more, won't he? I think it was his wine, too, so he'll have to get a fresh bottle of that, too.

I thought about cutting my wrists, using a razor blade to draw an opening from wrist to the crook of my elbow, but a painless solution seemed more optimal given I'm already in enough emotional pain as it fucking well is. Also, there's something about a smooth blade edge slicing open flesh that just really disturbs me, how it just sluices into the layers of skin down to the meat in a single, soundless glide. Give me serrated knives any day, where you can feel and kinda hear the teeth clawing at your skin and tugging it open.

But that'd be a rough way to achieve the task, so pills it is. And alcohol, because all these medications come with warnings about not mixing them with alcohol. Seems like a ripper way to go.

This isn't a spur-of-the-moment attempt, either. I might be reckless and spontaneous, but my decisions are still carefully considered. How well considered is open for debate. All manner of cunts have all sorts of rationale as to why we shouldn't kill ourselves, and the cunts aren't shy when it comes to sharing their opinions, either, including such tried-and-tested methods of prevention such as 'phone a friend'. Well,

I did that. I called three, in fact. There was no answer on Alex's number, Raven was heading out shopping and asked if she could call back to which I cheerily informed her she was most welcome to, and the last was James Swift. Radio James. The same James whose radio programme that fucking untrustworthy cunt Twix sabotaged in the very act of sabotaging our friendship.

I don't actually know James all that well, and despite having his phone number (Megan wrote it down one night for me with a whole heap of other numbers I'll never use) in my list of contacts, I really only make small-talk with him at the clubs, and even then only because he seems fairly likeable and easy-going. In fact, I know him so little that he didn't even know that the girl Twix brought into the radio station was my girlfriend until someone told him she was.

James seemed as surprised as I'd expected him to be when I'd first called, and we'd ended up having a pretty in-depth conversation for almost an hour about all manner of topics that didn't include death and depression. Top guy, Radio James. But by the end of my chat with him, I was feeling no better about the world or myself and so the time was nigh, as we like to say.

It was time to die.

Except, it's taking fucking forever.

My guts are starting to twist up, like it wants to cramp, so that's a good sign. It means I might be getting somewhere, after all. It'd be preferable if I didn't end up in excruciating pain for any extended period of time, though, as that's precisely the fucking thing I was hoping to avoid by going the pill route. Then it occurs to me that this might be a reaction between the wine and all the drugs, and that I may have been better off forgoing the booze after all.

I wonder if I should call my folks, let em know their son is nearly done with the world once and for all. Then I decide it's too dramatic, and too cruel. Let them hear about it through the proper channels, via police and the likes.

But it triggers a dialogue in my head about how people might react to my suicide. What would they say about it, and about me, and would they pass their judgements? Any Joe Blo who knows me well enough knows I'd tell them to get fucked for it, but it never seems to prevent people from airing their opinion all the same. Would they pull out the tired and outrageously inept 'suicide is not the answer' line? Hearing that shit again would actually be enough to make me commit suicide! It goes hand in hand with the morality argument, suggesting that's it's not just immoral to take one's own life but that it practically verges on the sinful, although the crazy Christians'll have you believe it's a one-way ticket to Hell. Which would suit me fine for the absence of Christians there, by their own admission only.

I've never been one to wholly hang my value system on a pre-decried structure of morality. By whose yardstick do we measure our own morality against? I'd rather decide for myself what works for me or not, and insisting that suicide isn't an answer simply because it might upset those around me is negating my own suffering. That in itself fucking outrages me, because then I'm at the mercy of others' opinions who should only be speaking for themselves to begin with. I can say that with some certainty!

The self-pity of earlier has finally passed; I'm now pissed enough from the wine to find myself in a more relaxed and contemplative state, where I'm neither inclined to live nor die but fairly uncertain of having a preference between the two. What a fucking quandary. The Inferno is as confused as I am. But given that I *am* actually still alive, I suppose I must face the fact that this is the default state to be in, and that until as such times that I can earnestly commit to one or the other then alive I should probably remain. That thought alone – that my self-doubt must dictate a default condition upon where I might reflect further on my choice to die – is depressing in itself. I wish I had more wine.

Bernie gets home, isn't amused at the state of me but tries his best not to show it, and goes through into the kitchen with a shopping bag of groceries. I ask him, hopefully, if he got any wine, and he notices with extreme annoyance that I've drunk all his red. This prompts me to confess my other crimes, namely that I've depleted his medications in an attempt to kill myself.

He remains unsympathetic to my situation.

'Great, now I have to go back up to the shops and get more,' he grumbles, doubtlessly thinking about the hole it'll burn in his wallet.

Naturally, I don't offer to reimburse him for his loss.

'You need to shower, too,' he says rather testily. 'There's yellow crust stuck to your underarm hairs.'

Cunt's getting a bit personal.

After much fucking around in the kitchen, banging cupboard doors in an effort to frustrate me because he knows I hate sudden loud noises, Bernie fucks off back up to the shops. I call out a request for more wine, and am certain I hear him to tell me to get fucked.

Righto, chap.

My stomach continues to do little backflips as a result of the pills, but I've lost all faith that they're gonna do their job and cease my existence. More's the shame, I suppose. It's back to deliberating the pros and cons of continuing my life.

There's a knock at the door.

'Don't be a funny cunt,' I moan.

The knock comes again, and I remember Bernie's mood when he left, realising it can't be him playing funny buggers. I haul myself up off the floor where I've been lying since Bernie arrived home, opening the door to see Raven standing there with Xanthe, who I actually don't really know that well. Her hair's a fucking mess, but there's no wind outside. They've both got complimentary Uni tote bags chockers full of thick textbooks.

'Hey, can we come in?'

'What is this, grand central fucking station?' I grumble, leaving the door wide for them as I shuffle back inside.

'Geez,' says Xanthe, rolling her eyes at Raven, going tight-lipped when she realises I've caught her in the act.

'Sorry, Dante,' goes Raven, 'but we passed Bernie down the street who said things aren't going well for you. Is everything okay?'

For fuck's sake, can't a guy get some peace around here?

'It's not actually,' I go. 'Can't even seem to commit suicide right.'

Raven pokes her head close to mine, looking closely at my eyes. 'Holy shit, your pupils are huge.'

'All the better to see you with.'

'It's scarcely a laughing matter,' scoffs Xanthe with about the same amount of conviction she's evidently applied to teasing up her hair, plopping herself down in Bernie's chair and dropping her textbooks to the floor with a heavy thud. She glances around the room like she's in a museum.

'Tough crowd,' I snarl, but she pretends not to hear.

'Honey, why are you doing this,' says Raven softly, squeezing my arm.

I have this sudden urge to try and blame everything on her, to try and wrangle some perspective that allows me to dump it all square on her fucking shoulders and cause her pain, just for the crime of being compassionate. There's no angle to make it happen, so instead I shrug and say: 'Why the fuck do you care?'

'But I do,' she goes.

Xanthe mumbles something, and I creak my head slowly around to glare at her.

'Sweetie, you should have–' Raven starts.

'What the fuck did you say?' I growl menacingly at Xanthe.

She snaps her head around startled, her eyes wide like a deer in the headlights. 'It was just a joke.'

'What was?' asks Raven.

'I said *Suicide Chump*. But I was only joking.'

I'm about to rip her a new arsehole when suddenly the reference dawns on me: it's a Frank Zappa song about a failed suicide attempt.

Raven sees me smirking – because let's face it, it *is* funny – and she gets even more confused.

'Dante, you should have said something to me. I don't want to hear you tried to do this, sweetie.'

Although I can't express it at the moment, I'm actually touched by Raven's concern. There's not enough people like her in the world. Too many cunts like me and Xanthe, who're always fucking over people like Raven. The downfall of having a good heart is that she's always looking for the angel inside a demon. I find myself torn between loving her for it, and resenting her for it.

'Would you like a cup of tea?' I go.

Raven looks like she wants to cry, but she manages to nod.

I put the kettle on and tell her about how Amara phoned but I instructed Bernie to tell her I'm not home. I don't let her know that I abandoned Amara at the Town Hall, but at least I imply that I stood her up which is kind of the same thing at least.

'Slow down, Dante,' says Raven. 'You're talking a million miles an hour.'

This is news to me. Nothing feels any different for me, until I look down at my hand holding the mug and see that it's trembling. Fuck, all those pills must have me wired and I didn't even realise it!

'Don't worry about Amara,' Raven says gently. 'She'll call back. She obviously cares about you.'

Raven's treading into dangerous territory here with her soft voice and talk of people caring for me. In this mood I've got little tolerance for all that airy-fairy talk about how I'm loved and I'll be missed, especially since Bernie said Amara sounded pretty pissed off with me. Zero fucking patience for it. It sounds trite, like a cheap psychological trick.

'Okay,' Raven says simply, reading my mood, and glances away.

It occurs to me that I've been death-glaring her just now, and feel a wash of remorse come over me. My hormones are all over the fucking place. I have to keep my back to the kitchen window because the light from outside is overwhelming, boring into my fucking eyes like it hates me. The teaspoon stirring around Xanthe's mug is magnified, grating on my nerves. It's all I can do not to storm over and swat the fucking thing out of her hand. Finally she stops, putting the spoon on the coffee table.

After our cuppas, Raven says she doesn't want to leave me on my own; the words are like a balm. I could never ask for her company in a time like this, but it's suddenly all I want. Or need. So she stays, mostly chatting with Xanthe about stuff but making the gesture to try and include me. I'm quite content to just sit here, listening to the drone of their voices while I wander my thoughts, dwelling mostly on how alone I feel in the world and how cunts like Twix will always be around to betray me.

I don't know how much time passes, but eventually the girls say cheerio, Raven kissing me on the forehead before heading upstairs. Although I swear, she hesitates like she wants to kiss me on the lips, or maybe it's me that looks like I want to kiss *her* on the lips and she's confused. Fucked if I know.

Bernie's back, watching TV, not talking to me naturally. It never lasts, though, because his memory's like a sieve and in no time flat he's usually forgotten he's got the shits with me. All this thought of death reminds me of something David the duty solicitor told me when I had to face the music for shoplifting.

'Hey, Bernie, have you heard of the Ballow murders?'

'Sure, I have,' he says happily enough, confirming my theory about his short-term memory being shot to shit. 'Why?'

'This guy at the courts was telling me about it, but didn't say what the cunt's motive was for killing those doctors.'

Bernie rubs at his chin, doubtlessly consulting with Elizabeth or Carl, the gatekeepers to his mind. They're like librarians, searching for info on Bernie's behalf.

Finally he goes: 'He was a migrant, the guy that did it, who had apparently fled from the rise of the Third Reich, as I recall. He was angry that the doctors wouldn't put him on a pension after hurting himself up north, near Cairns somewhere. They said he was faking his injuries, so he tried to kill them.'

It seems kinda funny that someone trying to get away from Hitler's influence would then bomb and shoot people here, and conversely we have in this day and age dumb cunts doing exactly that *because* of Hitler's influence. But maybe the cunt truly thought he was injured, and wasn't faking it at all? That'd piss him right off, for sure.

Bernie looks curiously at me. 'Was he a relation, or somesuch?'

'Nah, not a bit,' I say. 'Just noticed some patterns emerging, that's all. To do with Ballow Chambers.'

'Synchronicity, as Jung would say,' he goes.

I watch the windows grow darker with the onset of night-time, thinking everything over and over again. David the duty solicitor's words at the court tumble through my mind, how he said I was like a sponge soaking up all the shitty things this city has to offer, unable to process them properly. Then there's Raven, patiently waiting for me despite all the horrible shit I've done or said to her, waiting for me to see reason where there's none and devote myself to her. I already know I'm not the world's best friend, and hardly need more evidence piling up to prove it. And the more I ruminate, the more I realise that I've been pretty shitty towards Amara most of all.

One thing I keep going back to is how she told me at the courts that we attract psychic energy to ourselves. At the time it sounded like horseshit to me, because I was pissed off that David wouldn't try and plea temporarily insanity on my behalf. But actually, when I think about it, what Amara's saying is not far off what I tried to tell that psychologist in the hospital: that if someone *thinks* they're a vampire, then for all intents and purposes they *are* a vampire, solely because they'll try to do the things they think a vampire would do. It seems to me that Amara and I are on similar wavelengths with our theories, which is essentially that the mind has the ability to trick itself, and potentially others too.

When the phone rings and Bernie says it's Amara, I'm willing to take the call and face the music like the suicide chump that I am.

TWIX IN DEFICIT

The lunchtime crowds have gone their merry ways and left a pigsty behind. I'd hate to be the cleaners in this pit. There's no way ol Twixxie here would stoop to clean this shit up. And it's not a far-cry to call the food-court of the Broadway a pit because it actually *is* a whole basement-level floor of eateries accessed at either end by a set of escalators and an elevator in the middle. No other way in or out, and every table piled with plates of scraps because the dirty sods don't think they have to use the bins provided. In the event of a catastrophe, everyone would bottle-neck those escape routes and be fucked.

At least the loos are decent, although maybe not the ladies'. Amai's taken to leaving the loo unflushed when she stays over and is on her rags, so that the blood splashed around inside the bowl is like a warning not to try it on. Raven used to do that sometimes, too. Not that her and I ever were on together, though. As for me, pissing lately has been a fucking task, I'll say, since it feels more like fire coming out. At least my balls have healed over nicely. Shaking the droplets of urine loose I make a resolution to cut down on my fluids so I don't have to go through this trial of fire again.

Amai's still not here yet and there's a newspaper left on one of the food-court tables, so I snatch it up and get to reading while I wait. She should've been here ages ago, and I used the payphone over next to the chemists to call her house and check if she was still coming. Sally had answered and said Amai was on her way, and hung up on me before I could thank her. Runs hot and cold, that bitch.

The news isn't improving my mood any, either, ay. The Deputy Prime Minister is criticising the Government about the budget when it was Beazley and Keating who stuffed it up in the first place. When they were in power, they kept saying the budget was in surplus when it was actually in deficit. And not in deficit by a little bit, either. But a fucking lot. Deep in the fucking deficit, you might say.

I flick a few more pages over and there's an article about an Asian woman who got brutally raped last year under a bridge by a serial rapist who bashed her head in with a bloody rock! The legal system fucked it all up and allowed the prick to walk free while further traumatising the poor woman and her husband. Reading the article makes me feel sick, and I wonder how Amai can fantasise about this stuff when it's really fucking horrible in real life.

Coming down the escalator is Michael Carlyon and some chick. I quickly pull the newspaper up in front of me so the joker won't see me, but then I hear his voice close by.

'Fancy seeing you around.'

The smirk in his tone is more than evident. I could potentially kick the opposite chair out from under the table and hope to hit him with it, but maybe I'd hit the chick or worse, some little old lady.

'Yeah, fancy,' I return, lowering the paper to meet his eyes.

I fucking regret that. It's like we immediately lock into a staring contest.

'You heard any of my sets on air, man?' he has the nerve to ask.

'Haven't been listening to the radio much. Too busy.'

'You used to say it was one of the perks of being a security guard, the radio. Used to boast that you'd get paid to sit around listening to it while the rest of us worked our arses off. Guess they've bumped you off the cushy jobs, eh?'

The bastard walks off smirking while his stupid girlfriend or whatever she is looks around dumbly at me, then catches him up.

My blood's boiling. I wanna go up and smash the prick.

'You look like you're big time constipated,' says Amai, coming up next to me.

'Shit, I didn't even see you come down,' I say.

'I know,' she smiles, 'because you were staring at that girl.'

'Nah, I was staring at the bloke.'

'Should I be worried?'

'I'm not a poof, if that's what you mean,' I retort.

'You know, you shouldn't use that word. It's offensive. I've got gay friends.'

'Sorry. It's just that bloke fucking bugs me so much,' I go, glancing at Carlyon as he and the chick exit the Broadway on the Mall, making for Adelaide Street.

'Not a friend then, by the sounds of it,' Amai says, sitting down beside me. 'Listen, so we can't go yet because I'm meeting Ma here.'

Bugger me, this is all I need. The mother-in-law! I'd prefer to get Carlyon back here even if he's rubbing it in my face that he's got the radio spot now.

'Don't roll your eyes.'

'I didn't,' I protest.

'You did, dammit,' she insists, looking peeved. 'And you still look constipated.'

'Sorry, it's not cause of your mum, honestly. I'm just worried we'll be late.'

'She's actually headed to an art function just upstairs,' says Amai. 'Paintings by some local artist called Nathanael Hunter. I just have to grab some flyers off her, so I mean it's hardly going to take long.'

'Fair enough.'

A silence settles between us, but not the good kind. She's irritated with me, or *by* me maybe. The relationship has definitely been feeling more strained of late.

That new song called *Wannabe* by this group calling themselves The Spice Girls comes over the mall radio, and Amai's nodding her head along to it. Ever since it came out last week or so, people have gone crazy for it. I just don't get it. It's kind of annoying me that she's into it. She reckons it empowers young girls. Sure it does.

There's a woman coming down the escalators looking at us, who could be Amai's mum.

'That her?' I nudge Amai, nodding in the woman's direction.

Amai looks up. 'Yup.' Thankfully, she's stopped nodding along to the stupid song.

Mrs Nyan comes over and at first totally ignores me, giving Amai a bundle of flyers for the art show, but when Amai introduces me her mum becomes quite cordial. Naturally, I wonder if this is a front. The old woman probably hates me.

'How do you do, Mrs Nyan?' I say.

Amai's mother pulls her head back in slight surprise, and when she shoots Amai a quick sidelong glance Amai rattles something off to her in Chinese and they both have a little giggle.

Maybe Rudd's Report was correct: I could have taken one of his Asian languages and cultures programs that he set up years ago and I'd know what these two are saying about me. I'm beginning to think that Pauline Hanson is on the money about the Asians coming here and taking over. It's like she says, we're putting up with it because of noisy minority groups that are funded by us taxpayers, groups that get moral support from the likes of do-gooders such as Raven and her sodding Uni mates who want the world to follow this PC craze.

'I'm well, thank you, Travis,' says Amai's mother, nodding at me. 'Nice to meet you, at last.'

'And you, too, Mrs Nyan,' I go, but again I see the corner's of her eyes crinkle like this time she's amused by something.

'See you later, Zyu-Zyu,' she says, jutting her chin out for Amai to kiss.

I presume *Zyu-Zyu* must be Amai's nickname.

When her mum goes upstairs in the elevator, I ask Amai what they were giggling at.

'You're so paranoid,' says Amai dismissively.

'Paranoid is another word for well informed,' I go, trying to sound clever but even to me it comes off as smarmy. I heard another security guard say it once, the week before he thought there was a break-in at the influent pump house at the Oxley Creek Sewage Plant and in his rush drove the security vehicle straight into the grit pit where the raw sewage flows through. They had to tow the car out and decommission it because there was too much shit seeped into the trims that the smell stayed no matter what they tried. We all called him True Grit after that, and eventually he took the name on with pride. And it turned there was no break-in at the pump house: he was just super paranoid all the time.

'So, you pronounced her name as *nian*,' chides Amai, crossing her arms and staring stonily at me. 'It's the name of a monster, isn't it?'

'Shit, I didn't mean that.'

I actually do feel bad about it, especially because I was honestly hoping to make a decent impression on Amai's mum.

The stony expression on Amai's face softens, and she manages to crack a smile for me. Which prompts me to be a bit cheeky.

'Sorry, Zyu-Zyu,' I say, caressing her arm.

The stoniness immediately returns.

'Don't call me that,' she says coldly.

Fuck it, I've done it again. Can't win!

'But I heard your mum call you that.'

'She did that to remind me that I'm her baby and not to run away with boys. That's just how it is, isn't it.'

Some parents just can't stand to see their kids turn into adults.

'Isn't Zyu-Zyu a nickname?'

'Never mind,' Amai says, annoyed.

'Okay, I was only asking.'

We get to the top of the escalators and head out onto the street.

'Don't get defensive,' she goes. 'It's not your problem.'

'It's a problem, then?'

'No.'

'So why did you–'

'Zyu-Zyu is my milk-name, okay?' she snaps, cutting me off. 'Like a nickname. But *you* cannot repeat it. So just drop it, okay?'

'Yeah, rightio,' I laugh. 'I don't even know what a sodding milk-name is, anyways.'

She narrows her eyes at me.

'You're really fucking annoying, you know that?'

'Not my problem,' I retort, kinda smugly.

'Okay, Twix, be like that.'

She turns and storms off down the street without warning, so I'm not sure if I'm meant to follow or not. At the traffic lights she sneaks a glance back at me, then stares at the walk signal until it goes green. I half expect her to come running back and apologise, or try and make up in some way, but she crosses the intersection and heads into the Anzac Square building where she'll probably cut through under Ann Street for Central Station.

Fucking *milk-name*. Of all the things to fight about, and I'm still clueless as to what it was about.

It felt like the whole time that there was something between us, and I don't mean her mother. There was some other kind of distance between us, like I couldn't connect with her.

Later on she calls me at home and says we need to talk, and that I should come round to her flat. I hate that expression: *we need to talk*. It always means disaster, but more than that, it means emotional disaster. Besides that, I can barely walk at the moment anyway with my balls the way they are. I've already reached my tolerance quota for the day.

'I couldn't really give a toss for a *talk*,' I say sarcastically, which sets Amai off.

'You can be a real asshole sometimes, Travis.'

'And you're a real bitch.'

This makes her go crazy. She's yelling all sorts of names down the phone at me, so I just hang up. Immediately she calls back and picks up where she left off. This time I hold the phone out at arm's length, and even Greg in the kitchen can hear her screaming. She's trying to make the distinction that she said I was only an arsehole sometimes but that I inferred she's a bitch all the time.

'I said no such thing,' I say calmly.

'You smug fucking asshole!' she yells.

Eventually the line goes dead, which is good because she could've made me deaf with all that screeching.

'Sodding women, mate, I tell ya,' I go, shaking my head at Greg, who doesn't look too impressed with me. 'Nah, fuck her shit. I don't need that, at the end of the day. It's over.'

First Karen shouting at me at that topless bar, trying to get me to believe the baby wasn't mine, yeah right, the spiteful cow; and now I've got Amai going bananas.

'You need your head read, buddy,' Greg says, straining his kefir curds. 'She was fine as.'

'Fine for a while,' I laugh, scratching my groin. There's been more than just a burning sensation when I piss lately. 'Hey, Greg, take a look at this for me, will ya?'

I amble painfully into the kitchen, feeling like someone's scouring my nether-regions with steel wool, and unzip my fly.

'For fuck's sake, Trav.'

Not the first time I've had to show my junk to a flatmate, but I won't tell Greg that. Let him have his kefir in ignorance, ay.

'I'm serious, Greg. There's something growing next to my tockley.'

He takes a quick peek and recoils.

'Fucking hell,' he goes, holding his nose. 'It's all red and blistered. Looks like Freddy Krueger's face down there. And it fucking stinks.'

'What the hell am I going to do?'

He can obviously see the desperation and fear on my face, hear it in my voice.

'You really need to go check in with the sexual health clinic, my friend,' he says, and when he passes me to head back to his bedroom he gives me as wide a berth as our little kitchen will allow. 'You've got the gift that keeps on giving.'

'And what's that supposed to mean?'

He pokes his head out his bedroom door and goes: 'All I'm saying is you shouldn't've eaten your girlfriend's peas. Coz they're herpes.'

He chuckles, ducking back into his bedroom.

Herpes.

The only person I can think of who has had it is Amai's flatmate Sally. Bugger me, she didn't rub her slit all over my face when I was sleeping over at their place, did she? Nah, that's ridiculous. What's not ridiculous, though, is the idea of Amai sleeping with the stripper who threw his jocks at Sally and gave her herpes in the eye. I remember Sally telling some random about the incident when we were out clubbing one night, and if it was on his underwear then it was on his tockley, too, and that must have been where Amai got it before she gave it to me. I only hope she's got it worse than me.

I let my fingers do the walking and find the number for the sexual health clinic in the White Pages. The lady on the end of the line says it's walk-in appointments only and it's all anonymous, except for my first name and suburb for their filing system. The clinic's down in what used to be an old wharf area between the Valley and the City, a stone's throw from the Prozac Palace. My bus swings right past the street it's in so there's not too much walking involved.

There's a folded piece of paper with the words SEXUAL HEALTH CLINIC typed on it taped to the inside of the glass door, but other than that there's nothing here to reveal it's a clinic for STD's. It's a quiet area of mostly run down, abandoned buildings. Rent must be cheap, which means not a lot of State funding goes into the clinic. I take the steps two at a time up to the first floor.

'What's your name, sweetie?' goes a middle-aged woman behind the counter.

There's some jokers slouched along a bench seat against the wall, camp as fuck. I swear they're checking my arse out, which makes me uncomfortable.

'Travis,' I say as quietly as I can.

'First time here?'

I nod. 'I'm not gay or anything.'

She freezes, narrowing her eyes at me. 'No-one asked,' she goes.

She gets me to fill out a form that asks about my sexual history and prior STD contractions. I keep it short and simple; obviously blank for the sexually transmitted diseases bit.

'Take a seat, Travis, and Terry'll be with you shortly.'

I cringe when she says my name out loud. What if there's someone hear who knows me, or one of those poonces behind me tries to get into a conversation. Let them and the next thing you know they're trying to get into yer strides. Then I notice a corridor down the side wall with more chairs at the end. I'll take my chances down there.

On the wall next to a water cooler's a rack of pamphlets on various STD's. I wanna grab the one about herpes since I know fuck all about it, but there's a gorgeous chick with a head full of tight curls sitting at the end of the room, and I don't want her to know what I've got.

Then it makes me wonder: what's she got? I mean, no-one's here for any other reason than to be treated for a venereal disease, so that must be this total hottie has the clap or something. It's weird trying to imagine her fanny crawling with lice or angry boils. She's dressed in an expensive looking blazer and trousers, with a gold watch on her wrist. She looks pretty upper class, but here she is in the same room with the likes of me, presumably as infected as I am. Obviously a real goer in the sack, ay?

She clocks me gawking at her so I tip my head and smile, but she looks away, crossing her arms over her chest, like she's assumed I'm trying to pick her up. Yeah, right! The sheer arrogance of her!

Eventually I'm called into one of the consultation rooms, and to my dismay it's a woman who's seeing to me.

'I'm Doctor Terri,' she says. 'First name basis.'

Sod it, I thought I was getting a bloke. With her short hair, I doubt this chick knows her way around a tockley.

The consultation room's as surprising as the doctor is: it looks like an ordinary doctor's office. There's a computer monitor on the desk and jars and tubes and stuff on a counter top, and a bed with a curtain around it in the corner. No weird sexual stuff at all.

'What can I do for you today, Travis?'

'Well, it's a bit embarrassing, actually,' I laugh nervously. 'I think I may have gotten something off a friend, who maybe got it off a stripper. I don't know, maybe.'

I'm stammering, and the doctor's noticed.

'It's on your genitals, yes?'

I nod, and she asks if she can take a look. Fuck me, but what if I get a boner?

'It's okay, I've seen literally hundreds of penises in here,' she says, sensing my reluctance. 'Don't worry about it, nothing can shock me. Just drop your dacks and hop up onto the bed.'

I whip em down, jocks and all, lifting myself backwards onto the bed. It's a proper hospital one that can be tilted up so that the patient sits up, which is what Terri does. She pulls some rubber gloves on and a headband with a light on front, and leans over my groin like she's about to give me a blowie. To my absolute relief, my tockley stays completely flaccid. It's funny how I had no problem flopping it out in front of the lads back at the flat.

'So you have a rough infestation of herpes,' she says. 'You feel tingling pains, yeah?'

'Yeah.'

'And painful urinary discharge?'

'That, too.'

Terri stands up straight and snaps the gloves off, telling me I can get dressed again.

'It looks a lot worse than it is, trust me,' she says.

'I've got herpes,' I say loudly, my voice thin and reedy with stress. 'It can't get any worse.'

Terri smiles knowingly. 'Every fella who comes here with herpes thinks that. Would you believe me if I told you practically everyone in the world already has herpes in their system?'

'That doesn't make any sense.'

'Travis, it's true. There're all sorts of strains and we carry them for our whole lifetime. You just need to look after yourself and treat any inflammations that occur. And use protection when you have sex in future. Prevention is better than a cure.'

'Look, *Wild Mood Swings* might not be their best effort of late, but it's not their worst album.'

At first she just looks at me, then a small smile creeps onto her face as she actually gets the reference I'm making.

'Funny man,' she goes, looking more impressed now.

As I'm carefully tugging my jocks back on I take a last look at the red, angry mess that's become of my groin. I have to give Terri one thing: it certainly does look a lot worse than it feels. If I'd seen this for the first time I'd have expected to be rolling around on the ground in agony.

'So what am I gonna do about it?'

'There's not a lot we can do to actively treat herpes, I'm afraid,' she says with a pityingly look. 'It'll clear up in a few weeks' time.'

A few weeks!

'Whoa, sorry, but I need this gone a.s.a.p. Part of my job involves walking a lot.'

She just shrugs and apologises. 'I can give you some free packs of ibuprofen to help ease the pain and some cream for the burning, but unfortunately it heals of its own accord. You need to let it run its course.'

Oh, fer fuck's sake!

She hands me a tube of Valaciclovir and a box of pain killers.

'One other thing, have you been sexually active of late?'

'Not really,' I shrug.

'You know you need to tell your partners about this, right? They need to get checked out, too.'

'Not necessary. I'm single, footloose and fancy free.'

'Be that as it may,' she says sternly, 'that doesn't prevent you from engaging in sexual activity with anyone.'

I wasn't aware I'd cop a lecture when I came here.

'There *was* someone, but she's old news now. She doesn't want to see me anymore.'

'You still need to let her know so she can get herself checked,' Terri insists.

'But she's the one who gave it to me, after her rompy pompy with that stripper,' I say. 'So she already knows! Her friend already got herpes from the stripper's jocks when it hit her in the eye.'

'Travis, the thing about herpes is that it might stay dormant in a person's system for some time. There's still the chance she doesn't know. And as for her friend, I doubt very much she got it from a pair of underwear. It's contracted from skin-to-skin contact.'

It feels like Doctor Terri is kind of defending Amai. What did Pauline say in that letter to the Queensland Times? Something about how the powers-that-be are always listening to noisy minority groups at the expense of the rest of us. How sodding true that seems to be right now.

'Oh, she'd know alright,' I nod sagely. 'She slept with the stripper, no doubt about it. And anyways, she yelled at me last time we spoke.'

Terri sighs and types on her computer. 'Okay, well, you seem to have made your mind up despite facts, but please keep in mind what I've said. And again, you've got to keep your immune system up and get regular exercise.'

'I could if I worked regular hours,' I moan. 'I'm a shift worker. I just need to get a decent job and a car and all that stuff first. I don't have any direction in life at the moment.'

Fuck, if even Malik and Angele can reach that goal soon then surely I can, too? Shacking up in a flat with two other blokes isn't good enough. At the end of the day I still need my own place, a car, the whole fucking lot!

Terri turns around and faces me, placing her hands on her knees. 'Travis, listen to me. I'm a thirty-five year old doctor who rides to work on a bicycle because she doesn't own a car, and every night I go home to my shared flat with another nurse and two cats, and I've been single and perfectly happy for two years now. You don't need to buy into this so-called dream that society puts forward. Just be your own man, and be it well. That's all that you need to do. Anything other than that and you know you've strayed.'

I'm not following her one bit. It sounds to me like she's suggesting I should be happy being poor and tired all the time.

'I'll give that some thought,' I say, pretending to think about it.

'Okay,' she laughs, standing up, 'but maybe think about it on your way home.'

Yeah right, as if that's what I'm going to be thinking about. I'm more interested in just how Amai got herpes to begin with. There's a phone-box up on the corner, so I drop some coins in and dial Amai's number. It rings out so I try again, and eventually she answers it.

'I got a question for you.'

The line is quiet for a moment, and then she says: 'Travis?'

'I just wanna know: did you root that stripper?'

'WHAT THE FUCK ARE YOU ON ABOUT, TRAVIS?'

I jerk my head away from the earpiece so fast my head bounces off the glass window behind me. Fucking hell she's got a pair of lungs on her.

'Did you get herpes from the stripper?' I demand, raising my voice. I'd yell back, but there's people walking past and they don't need to hear I'm infected.

'Fuck you, asshole,' Amai snaps, then adds: 'What herpes? Have you got herpes?'

Denial was on the cards, of course.

'From that stripper you fucked, you whore!'

'No-one fucked any strippers, you paranoid loser!'

The line goes dead just as I draw breath to yell back. Shit.

I cradle the receiver on its hook and hobble into town, heading left down past Eagle Street Pier, cutting across the Gardens to meet Raven after class. Besides Malik, she's the only person I've kept in contact with after what happened at the radio station.

After an uneventful wait, a mass of students pour out of a corridor and amongst them's Raven, gossiping with one of her classmates, a fat chick who smiles way too much.

'Can we talk?' I ask, and Raven looks gravely at the fat chick who smiles at us and apologises before hurrying off.

'And stop apologising for everything!' Raven yells out to her, then turns to me and grimaces. 'What have I done?'

'Nothing,' I say, realising I've used a variation of the dreaded *we need to talk* line on her. 'No, nothing like that. I've just come from the sexual health clinic.'

Raven's face drains of colour. Being pale really suits her, as she has naturally dark hair and thick eyebrows. I think she's about to cry.

'I'm not dying,' I add, and then she does start crying. 'Jesus, what the hell, Raven?'

'I thought you were about to say you've got AIDS,' she sobs.

Fuck me, I'll never understand how chicks think.

'Sorry, sweetie, we've been doing case studies all day long on how AIDS is still affecting the youth sectors in Australia,' she explains.

'It's herpes,' I whisper, glaring at a couple of blokes walking past who're watching us carefully. Raven gives them a little wave and they wave back. Classmates. 'Let's go down here,' I suggest, walking her down into the park where there's fewer nosy pricks to eavesdrop us.

'How've you got herpes, but?' she goes.

'Well, I thought it was from Amai-li, but she swears it's not her. Whadda you think?'

Raven breathes deeply from her nose, making a whistling noise. 'I don't know, Twix. Are you sure it's not just because you feel guilty about Dante?'

'I feel guilty about Dante so now I've got a venereal disease?'

She frowns at me. 'I honestly don't know how you got that out of what I just said. What I'm saying is, maybe you're jeopardising your relationship with Amai because you feel guilty about being part and parcel to ruining Dante's relationship?'

Sodding hell, Raven, dig the fucking boot in why don'tcha?

'Stiff shit. Dante was over Nicola anyway,' I scoff. 'He told me so himself, more or less. So it's hardly as bad as everyone's making out it was. It's more like I rooted his ex. Or nearly ex.'

'I honestly don't know how your thought processes compute, sometimes,' she says, looking at me incredulously.

I shrug dramatically. 'Well, Raven, that's the difference between love and herpes. One of them's for life, so it turns out.'

She looks really disappointed.

'You had sex with his girlfriend. I'm not joshing around about this, Twix. It was wrong.'

Thing is, I kinda know it was wrong, otherwise I wouldn't be avoiding everybody from the scene. Can't she understand that? I've been trying to steer clear of dwelling on it, but I've had this recurring thought that if Dante had've fucked Amai at some point, I'd have wanted to punch the shit out of him. I'd probably not speak to him ever again. Maybe I've been in denial about Dante's feelings. The more I think about it, the more it *was* wrong, even if I didn't exactly know it was the same Nicola.

Then it suddenly hits me!

'Nicola!'

Raven jerks her head around, checking the park for signs of the dirty punk bitch.

'I must've got it off her!' I nearly shout. 'Not Amai at all!'

'Are you sure it could be from her?' says Raven.

'Without a fucking doubt!'

Raven tips her head to one side and opens her mouth. She looks like a dead fish.

'Oh no,' she says quietly, looking shocked. 'That's not good.'

'Of course it's fucking well not,' I go, but she's staring into the distance, not listening. Always got sodding Uni stuff on the brain, this one. 'In a funny way, this is like Dante's revenge on me. Like it's a trap: root his girlfriend, get herpes for it.'

'It's not funny at all,' whispers Raven.

'Except for that prick, I bet,' I say, now certain it's from Nicola that I got it from. 'I bet he'd be laughing his arse off.'

'Where'd you say this clinic was?' asks Raven.

DANTE THE ADDICT

I've rubbed my cock so raw I've got no choice but to give it a rest for a while.

Actually, a while isn't going to cut it. I need to go cold turkey on the masturbation front for a few days at least, and let the broken skin properly heal. It won't be easy with this bastard depression hanging over me, because I tend to wank a lot when I'm in this long, drawn-out state as the depression wallows gently inside my head.

And right when I get a few nudie pictures in the mail, too!

For the last few months I've been writing to a girl called Effia from the Gold Coast. The place in Africa, not just down the road. I saw her personal ad in the back of *Penthouse* sometime after I stopped seeing Nicola and thought why the fuck not? At first we just wrote about things we liked in general, and where we lived. I asked her shitloads about life in Ghana, but she didn't seem too interested in what was going on here in Brisbane. She moved the conversation onto marriage pretty quickly, actually, and with nothing much better to do with life I kinda let her know it was possible. It wasn't like I was looking to get married, per se, but it'd have been good for a laugh at least.

But then she'd needed cash to come and visit me, and wrote asking me to send her a cheque. I don't even own a wallet let alone a cheque book, and I couldn't see the dole office approving a loan for a couple of grand. So I'd had to let her down gently, saying it was a wonderful dream but I probably wasn't the guy she was looking for. Imagine if she could see me, this scruffy swampie boy in a shared apartment in a building that should probably be condemned, living day to day on the dole.

Then something between Amara and I started to develop, so I'd pretty much lost any residual interest in this dark-skinned beauty in a faraway land.

But now she's sent another letter, which arrived this morning, and inside are three photos of her in the nuddy. The supposed salt on the bread. Except instead of entice me, as I'm sure was the intention, it's made me suspicious.

Bernie wanders past and sees the pics on the arm of my chair.

'Helloooo,' he sings, tilting his head for a better look. 'Who's your friend?'

'That girl I've been writing to in Africa.'

Bernie squints closely at one of the photos. 'It looks like a photo of a photo.'

'I know, right?' I agree. 'Has to be a scam. Whoever I'm writing to has simply taken a couple of photos of a magazine.'

'I've never even seen African porn mags at the shops,' says Bernie, still eyeing the photo hungrily.

'Well, I'm sure in Ghana it's pretty normal,' I say sarcastically. 'But it's hard to imagine they could get these pics processed down at the chemist or their local Big W. They must have their own set-up for developing them, the sneaky fucks.'

Bernie turns the photo over and notes there're no markings on the back like we get on our photos, like Kodak or Fuji or whatever.

'Depends on their laws, of course,' he says. 'In Queensland you can't photograph a penis more than three quarters erect before it's classified as pornography, which of course is illegal to make here. Might be different over there.'

'How the hell do you know that about erect cocks in Queensland?'

Bernie shrugs, grinning. 'I learnt the hard way in my youth.'

Bernie's bisexual, and apparently back before the antipsychotics and other drugs to keep his schizophrenia in check dampened his sex drive, he was quite the lad, as Twix might say. Who the fuck knows what shenanigans he got up to?

'Can I keep this?' he says, holding up the photo.

'Fuck off and find your own African scam artist,' I go, snatching it back.

'You've got enough porn already,' he complains. 'I've never seen anyone amass so much so quickly before, and I've known a few sex hounds in my time, trust me, including an old dung-puncher who blew significant amounts of his inheritance on blue movies and rent boys.'

'Go put the kettle on already,' I suggest, ignoring his whining. 'I'm going to need a cuppa to help me plan my next move to outwit this scammer.'

'So I'm your maid now, eh?' he says, but nonetheless goes through to the kitchen and flicks the kettle on. 'You know, being possessive over one measly picture proves you've got a porn addiction.'

'Shut the fuck up, trying to think here,' I say loudly, scanning the letter from 'Effia'.

Fucking *porn addiction*, stupid cunt.

The thing is, a lot of people with depression – or mental illness in general – often do develop addictions to a variety of things such as alcohol, drugs, smoking, swearing, self-harm or even gambling. The usual stuff. There's sex addicts, too, but I've never heard them referred to as having a mental illness, per se. Perhaps they do?

Thinking about it, though, I know Bernie's right: I do, after all, have a significant collection of skin mags. It might seem I'm addicted to porn, but I prefer to think it's the wanking that I'm addicted to. Because the thing about masturbating is that it releases endorphins and serotonin which in turn relieve stress. Of course, relieving stress probably isn't the reason why I'm at it four or five times a day, but the excuse will do in a pinch. Mostly, I think, I just get bored so a wank fills the time.

As a society we've got all these terminologies inspired by the very act itself that we use negatively against one another, such as 'wanker' or telling someone to 'go fuck themselves'. I wonder if we stopped vilifying the act of self-pleasure whether we'd all be much happier?

But perhaps one of the true indicators that I might be addicted to porn is the irrepressible urge to get more and more of the stuff. Especially since half of it's procured without the exchange of cash. I like to employ a system called buy-one-get-one-free, purely for its effectiveness. Essentially, I've found that purchasing an item tends to stave off suspicion from the proprietor to any further shoplifting, and so paying for something while there's all sorts of other items stuffed into my backpack or inside my coat is a brilliant smoke-screen. One particular trick I've employed at a fine establishment in the Valley – where they've got a five dollar cheapo-bin next to the counter – is to grab what I really want from the shelves and drop it into the bin as I do a couple of casual laps of the store. Then I select something at full price, something costing no more than ten bucks at least (usually the newsstand variety of porn mag needs to tone down the explicit nature of its content because they're dependent on advertising revenue, but not so in the sex shop so the harder stuff like *Barely Legal* can sell for considerably less than its softer companions from the newsstand) and as it's getting rung up at the register, I craft a last-minute ostentatious show of selecting a few items from the cheapo-bin. Even though these fresh items are marked at around twenty bucks each, the proprietor accepts that they came from the heavily discounted bin by the counter and hey presto I've expanded my wanking stockpile without carving too hefty a chunk from my meagre dole benefits. Technically, I guess, it's not strictly theft, so no harm done.

But fuck all people know about my porn collection. My opinion is simply that we all know we do it – sex that is – but we don't need to hear about it. Like religion: keep it behind closed doors, I reckon.

Actually, it's most likely religion that's made me reticent about disclosing the full measure of my collection. The Sugarloaf Road cult really did a fucking number on me. One time we held an exorcism and were made to confess our sins, which of course masturbation was right up there and for which I had plenty of blood on my hands for. It was a humiliating experience for a young fella to have to put himself through.

Some mediaeval theologians even considered masturbation worse than raping nuns and schoolgirls and insisted that Penitents confess to having had a toss.

It puts me in mind of something. 'Oi, Bernie!'

He wanders down from the bathroom, his flat feet slapping on the linoleum of the hallway. *Slap slap slap*. Like a wet wank.

'That cunt Jesus must have masturbated fairly regularly, huh?' I go. 'Otherwise he'd have had prostate cancer. I mean, they reckon he didn't sleep with anyone or anything, so he must've been prone to the odd Jackin the Beanstalk.'

'Maybe that's what really killed him,' counters Bernie. 'Prostate cancer. But then again, I don't think he had all his bits and pieces. You know, like a Ken Doll or Bowie in that film.'

'*The Man Who Fell to Earth*?'

'Probably,' shrugs Bernie, plonking himself down in his chair. 'Sounds appropriate. Jesus was a starman, too.'

Bernie has this theory that all figures in history who had abilities to heal or do miraculous things were, in fact, alien beings. I wish I'd known Bernie when I was in that cult; it would've been fun watching him ridicule all our rules and beliefs, exonerating me on accusations of sinful self-pleasure.

But quite often, depression can kill my sex drive dead. I can even go a week or two without a wank. Quite the feat, I reckon. Other times, like now when I'm in the aftermath of its onset, masturbation is a cold comfort. Both it and the borderline personality disorder (an illness also conducive to developing addictions) heighten my need for that serotonin, so Bernie can go get fucked with his accusations of addiction because porn's my medication.

Besides, having a wank when depressed is like having a canary in a coal mine: the day I can't get it up for a quick tug is the day I know my depression has hit rock bottom.

Bernie's staring dull-eyed at some mindless shit on the TV. Talk about addictions! He'll be glued to the fucking idiot box for the rest of the day now.

McKay told me about one of his other clients who started a porn distribution line once. Said there's fucking big money in it. But he reckons this guy, who was manic-depressive, began as an accountant here in Brisbane and just fucking lost it one day, slipping into a manic state so ludicrous that without telling anyone he hopped a plane over to America and started up this label that sourced and redistributed porn from all over the world. He was fucking rolling in it, McKay reckoned. Went from zero to a hundred like that, click of the fingers. But when the mania receded it was replaced by a deep depression, and this cunt's millions couldn't save him from what happened next. His company spiralled out of control without the driver at the wheel, with crazy new deals made against common sense. Within a couple of weeks he was bankrupt. Every single employee made redundant. The company's assets and the poor bastard's house and car were absolved to pay creditors, and the government booted his broke arse back to the Land of Oz where the house he'd owned here had been sold and his wife and kids had returned to her parents' and she wanted fuck all to do with him. Wouldn't even let him see the kids. Said she'd thought he'd found another woman or died or something, and that the banks said his accounts hadn't even been touched since his disappearance. His old boss and co-workers gave him the cold shoulder, too, and he came to McKay saying he'd hit rock bottom.

But McKay's a clever cunt.

He told the guy that suicide was actually rock-bottom, and hey presto the guy began to turn his life around.

See, McKay reckons the guy's mania made him addicted to the thrill of success and even in his depressed state the poor bastard was addicted to the notion of it. But all McKay had to do was let him know that he hadn't entirely reached the lowest of lows yet, because being dead was the lowest point. This gave the guy some measure of accomplishment, in that at least he had managed to outwit even that final outcome.

But McKay told me that the guy didn't have suicide ideation, so the gamble was relatively risk free. There was more chance that the guy would realise he had more to live for than not. Apparently he was back on a six figure salary within a week and had a down payment on a new place within a month.

Addicted to success, imagine that. The antithesis of me, McKay reckons. He says I sabotage my potential successes, but I reckon if he got an eyeful of my porn collection he'd reconsider that position. It's an impressive pile of tits and arse, the sort that that porn star Ona Zee could have waved in the faces of those pollie cunts down in Canberra when she gave them a mouthful back in April about how Australia's becoming a bunch of wowsers, God bless her raven locks.

Even Amara hasn't copped a peep at the collection, although she's asked to have a look. But the thing is, so much porn is just full of old cunts with sagging skin and crows-feet that the makeup artists have failed to conceal, amplifying them by reducing all other blemishes. At least with the *Barely Legal* stuff the models are in their early twenties, even if they do have their hair yanked up into pigtails. Twix has already slyly tried to insinuate the pedo angle on that one, the cunt, so I hardly need Amara voicing it, too.

I haven't seen her since my fuck-up at the Town Hall when I stranded her in the green room, and she's meant to be coming around later on so we can talk it over in person instead of on the phone. I hope to Christ it's her time of the month and makeup sex isn't on the agenda, otherwise with my dick in its current condition my orgasm face might be too much like pain and not pleasure.

Fuck it, I can't think of a single witty thing to write back to this scam artist in Ghana. I'll settle for just drawing a big diseased looking dick on a piece of foolscap and post that instead. I might give it a smiley face, too.

BALLS IN PIXIE'S COURT

All the cunts in the carpark are starin at us.

'What the fuck are they all starin at?' I go.

'Ignore em,' Roz says. 'They know we're not here for the match.'

'We could be, but.'

She smiles like I'm stupid. 'Nah, these people probably go to every match. They know we're not regulars.'

'Fucking Brett and his dumb ideas,' Jeremy whinges.

He's right, but. It *is* a dumb fuckin idea.

'He's just playing games,' Nel tells us all. 'We just gotta go along with it and get what we're after. No fuckin rock this time, either,' she says bitterly. 'That cunt's gonna give us what we're prepared to pay for.'

And what we're prepared to pay for is a few shots, which can fill a syringe. They go for fifty bucks, but we've also got the option ova hundred bucks' worth straight up. The smack comes in pill capsules that can literally be split apart so we can tap out only what we want to use and save the rest for later. The capsules are dropped inside a water balloon that can be hidden inside our mouth, and dependin on whether ya get the fifty or the hundred depends on the colour of the balloon. Blue is fifty bucks' worth and red is a hundred bucks' worth. Today we're after one of each.

The football oval's not big, and there's only one tiny grandstand where every cunt's packing into, includin us. We're down the front, but, leanin on the rails so we can get closer to the game and spot Brett comin from any direction.

We know he's come into a new supply since the Gold Coast bust coz Forks told Nel that he's been scorin lately from him. Cunt never told us. Brett's normally more reliable than that, Roz reckons. Forks reckons we just gotta keep an eye out for the light on the Hairdresser's Needle. Always comes on when a new shipment gets smuggled into the country, he reckons, mostly by comin in through remote beaches coz the smugglers can keep an eye out for the coastguard who fly past like clockwork.

'How the fuck would Forks know all that, the lyin cunt?' Nel said afterwards when Forks had fucked off. 'Wouldn't even know what a beach looks like.'

We must look a right fuckin sight, but, the four of us, down next to the field on our own when every other knob's up on the grandstand seats dressed for a nice spring day. Coz the smack has been fuckin with our immune systems we've been strugglin to regulate our body temperatures, or we've been gettin sick, so we're all dressed like it's winter, except for Nel who's only wearin a denim vest over a dirty white singlet tucked into her denim jeans. Me and Jermy are decked out in black, of course, and Roz has a duffle coat draped over her with big round black glasses hidin half her face. I wish I'd thought to bring some sunnies.

'Oi, I know that one,' Roz goes, pointing at one of the young guys joggin onto the oval. The one with the number 8 on his back.

'Who's he?' Nel sniffs, lookin absently around for Brett.

'Customer one time,' Roz says. 'I remember his forehead and ears. Looks like a troll.'

He does, too, now she mentions it.

'He hurt me,' she suddenly goes.

'The fuck ya mean he hurt you?' Jermy goes.

'He was rough,' Roz says, not able to look at the guy or any of the other players on the field. 'More rough than most. And he didn't pay.'

Well, this sets Nel off, alright.

'He didn't pay?' she snaps, spinnin on Roz and glaring at her. Roz doesn't even flinch. Nel points out at the players. 'You sayin that cunt never coughed up for services rendered?'

Roz doesn't say anythin, just looks at her nails where she pulls a strip of skin off her cuticles and tries to dab at the blood to stop it from oozing.

Nel's grindin her jaw, lookin out at the Number Eight cunt.

'I'm gonna fuck him up,' I growl.

Roz's like a mum to me, like the mum I never had but fuckin well deserve. How dare that yuppie cunt touch her! How dare he rip her – *us* – off!

'Calm yer tits, Pixie,' Nel mumbles.

As the team runs around the oval's perimeter to the applause of the crowd, Nel singles that one cunt out.

'OI LADIES!' she yells. 'CHECK OUT THE FUCKIN BALLS ON NUMBER EIGHT!'

The cunt goes red as he jogs past us.

'LET EM HANG, MATE!'

It's embarrassin the shit out of the cunt, so I decide it's my turn.

'SHOW US YER BALLS, NUMBER EIGHT!' I scream.

Roz starts chucklin, hidin her face.

Jermy climbs up onto the rail, holdin the light post for support, and thrusts his groin repeatedly at the players. Some cunts in the grandstand literally start booing us, tellin us to go home.

'NUMBER EIGHT! NUMBER EIGHT! WE THINK YOUR BALLS ARE GREAT!' me, Nel and Jermy start chantin as the players come back around again to start gettin ready for the match.

'Fuck off, you whores,' shouts one of the players as the team coach wanders over to us with a pissed off look on his stupid mong face. We've stopped yellin out now but literally can't hide our sniggerin as the he comes up and tells us to piss off or he'll call the cops.

'Yeah, righto cunt, just having a bit of fun, hold yer horses,' Nel goes.

We wander round to the side of the grandstand coz we'll be fucked if we're leavin without our smack. I'm seriously proud of how we all banded together to defend Roz's honour back there, but. It makes us feel proud to know these guys. Fuckin family!

'There's Brett,' Jermy goes.

Back at the oval Brett's chattin with the team and the coach. Seems he wasn't wrong about callin the cops, but joke's on him when he finds out Brett's our mate.

'Looking well, Bretto,' Nel says cheerfully when he strolls round the corner. 'Ready for business, mate?'

'I don't think so,' he says flatly.

'Everything alright?' Nel asks.

'The boys tell me youse were picking on my son before,' he goes.

'Number Eight?' Jermy goes, and me and Nel glance at him like we could literally kill the cunt.

'Just a bit of a misunderstanding,' Nel laughs lightly. 'We're just gee-in em all up for the big match, ay.'

'That's not how they tell it,' Brett goes, still unamused. 'Coach says he wants you lot outta here or the cops'll be called. That's the last fucking thing I need.'

'C'mon Brett,' Nel wheedles. 'We'll just grab the dope and head off. Won't take a minute.'

'Are you fucking junkies even listening?' Brett growls. 'Number Eight,' and he jerks his thumb over his shoulder in the direction of the players, 'that's my son. He's not happy, so I'm not happy. You're horrible people, the fucking lot of youse. So you lot need to fuck off right now and never call me again, or you'll regret it.'

What the fuck's that supposed to mean, regret it? And who cares if we're horrible people or not? Lifes not a fuckin popularity contest. The only thing that matters is scorin a hit, which I think isn't gonna happen now.

'No worries,' Nel says quietly.

Just as we're turnin away Brett goes: 'And think about havin a group shower. Youse're all on the fucking nose!'

We take it on the chin, but as we're walkin off Jermy turns and tells Brett he's a fuckhead, so Nel clips him around the ear so hard his head'll be ringin for a fuckin week!

We literally came all this way for nuthin. Four fucking return train tickets to Wynnum wasted, as if we can afford to be doin that. We only paid for the tickets coz we thought we'd be headin back with a score and didn't need any hassle from the ticketies or cops, otherwise we'd have just jumped it.

At the train station Nel goes and sits on her own. There's two riot-girls sittin in the tree growing in the middle of the platform and some fuckin derro cunts under it threatenin to punch their heads in. The bloke behind the ticket window ignores everythin, readin his *Picture* magazine. Dante likes to call this area 'Wynnum World, Queensland's weirdest theme park'. Free entry, he always says, but ya pay with a piece of ya dignity.

'Don't worry about Brett,' Roz says to me and Jeremy. 'He'll come round again, when he's settled down and wants our money. Until then I guess we gotta start goin to another dealer.'

On the way back into town we get off at Vulture Street Station and head into the Gabba to score some pills off Doctor Death. We all take turns goin in to see him and gettin bulk prescriptions. It's easy as, but, coz the cunt knows we're literally there just to score so he doesn't fuck us around and gets straight to it, literally givin us whatever we ask for. The chemist next door must be fuckin rollin in it, as a result.

'This is why networking is a fuckin necessity,' Nel goes, poppin some Adderall. She likes to try out the new drugs on the market, and considers herself something of an expert on the subject.

We follow Nel over to the phonebooth where she pulls out her wallet to read the numbers she's written all over it in biro, turning the dial then blowin snot from her nose. I can't hear what she's sayin coz she's mumblin like fuck, but when she hangs up she's lookin happy as.

'You're up, Pixie.'

'For what?' I sound understandably wary. I could be up for fuckin anything knowin Nel.

'You're doin the next score, on your own. Time to earn your keep, cupcake.'

'Yeah righto, whatever,' I shrug.

But it's a big deal. She makes another call and Jimmy Farrell picks us up. I've only met him a couple of times, when I used to go into his doctor's office to bullshit him about bein depressed or insomniac and so he'd give us some pills. He worked in a practice near Chermside and was known to be pretty easy-going about dishin out whatever we wanted – a bit like Doctor Death in that regard – right up until Nel took over as his exclusive dealer. She'd get small quantities of smack for him from Brett, in exchange for an endless supply of pills she could sell on the streets. But that's all fuckin kaput now that Brett wants nuthin to do with us, the cunt, and the animal desperation is startin to show in Farrell's eyes when he pulls up.

Roz quietly reminds us to fuckin watch this cunt coz he got busted last year with two schoolgirls that he'd literally drugged before raping them.

'They pulled their testimonies from the courts after he hassled their families,' she whispers. 'So he got off, naturally. But it finished his marriage.'

I remember now. Apparently the girl killed herself coz the media, *Today Tonight* and all that, kept houndin her for her side of the story, sayin she must've known about his activities and kept silent. Nel told us about it a while ago like it was literally the funniest shit she'd ever heard. Which it pretty much was.

The car's a fuckin pigsty, but, with junk food wrappers and shit on the floor and piles of musty clothin on the back seat. We've gotta push it up on the parcel shelf behind our heads.

Farrell goes across the Story Bridge into the Valley, where I'm to score from a cunt Nel just calls The Morlock. She won't tell us his real name, coz knowledge is power and she literally wants all the fuckin power for herself.

Farrell stops (illegally) at the top of the Brunswick Mall on Ann

Street, where Nel shoves us outta the car, reiterating the importance of stayin calm and makin the score.

'Yes, Sir,' I snap. 'I got it.'

'You got a mouth on you, girl,' she grumbles as she pulls the door shut and Farrell guns the car up the road.

It's good to be on me own again, but. I even think about maybe just headin off somewhere and spendin the rest of the day to meself, but I can feel the lure of the score like a siren's call, literally pullin us down the Mall to where the cunt I'm to meet – The Morlock – stands outside the cop shop with his dirty yellow baseball cap, just like Nel said he'd have. Nel reckon's the last place the coppers would suspect a drug deal to take place is right outside their own fuckin premises, which sounds pretty right to us. Can't argue with that logic!

I go up to this Morlock dude, the Percocet I got from Doctor Death keepin us steady like I'm inside a dream. This Morlock cunt doesn't intimidate us one bit, but I think he's tryin by starin at us and flashin his yellow teeth. His skin's really pale, and so's his hair. It makes his eyes look really fuckin small. I can't be sure, but maybe he's got pink contact lens' in, coz there's deffo a pink colour to em.

'Got a smoke, cunt?' I go.

'Yeah,' he drawls, and hands us a pack of PJ's. Inside I can see the shot, a liddle foil bound in cling-wrap, tied to a cigarette by a rubber-band. I pluck the ciggie out, deftly droppin a rolled up fifty note in its place. Like a fuckin pro.

'Thanks, mate,' I go, handin the pack back.

'No worries,' he goes. 'Just mind yer manners next time.'

The fuck?

Whatever. I ignore the pale cunt and stroll the few metres down to the traffic lights. Comin down the road is Jimmy Farrell's car, and he swerves into the loadin zone right before the lights.

'You get it?' Nel says before I've even got in the back.

'Like a fuckin pro,' I brag. 'Cunt could use some sun, but.'

'Give it here,' she says, holdin out her hand.

'Wait til I've pulled away first, fuckin coppers just there,' barks Farrell, pullin the car out into the traffic and accidently runnin the red light. At least I think it was by accident.

When we're down past the Wickham I give Nel the dope, keepin the ciggie for myself.

'Now we're fuckin set,' she grins.

'At least until it runs out,' Jeremy points out.

'No worries,' Nel says, distracted with unwindin the rubber-band. 'In the meantime, I'll sort something out with Black Ronnie and his Bastards.'

I don't like how Roz looks worried by this. She keeps her mouth shut, but.

SUICIDE CHUMP

This cunt's in the mall waving around a tin for donations. Seems there's always someone doing that these days. Gets a bit monotonous.

'Spare some change,' he goes, less request and more expectation like he's said it a thousand times and it's lost its polish.

'What's it for?' I ask suspiciously.

'Suicide prevention,' he goes. 'We're collecting as part of National Mental Health Week.'

He rattles the tin at me.

A lot of these industry workers are replacing the word *illness* with *health* these days, subtly shifting the focus away from affliction and onto recuperation.

'Sorry, mate,' I chirp. 'I'm broke as shit. But did my bit for suicide prevention this week already.'

'Oh, you're a volunteer, too?'

'Nah, saved a life.'

He's impressed as fuck, as well he should be.

'I hope they're doing okay now,' he says ever so gently, almost reverentially, the way people tend to do around sensitive topics like death or race.

'I'm doing A-okay, thanks,' I grin.

He looks a bit put off, like I'm winding him up.

'You seem pretty happy for someone who's tried to commit suicide recently,' the cheeky cunt goes.

'Of course I am,' I shoot back, cheerful as ever just to confuse him. 'I'm alive, aren't I? My sort-of girlfriend's talking to me again and I've got a great place to live at last. What's not to be happy about?'

He still looks sceptical, and it occurs to me I've got someone so green behind the ears you could mow back there. This poor cunt's probably never even been suicidal in his life. Volunteered to a cause, is all. Make a difference. Pick one out of the hat. *What's this week's flavour? Suicide? Okay, sign me up.* Fucking shit for brains. It gives me an idea.

'Listen, mate, there's nothing to worry about with me.'

That's more true than he could possibly realise; I saw a GP the day after my so-called suicide attempt, mostly at Megs' insistence because she was worried sick about me, and the doctor divulged that the gutful of tablets I dropped wouldn't actually kill me, that the bastards are manufactured to make a fatal overdose unlikely. At most, they'd make me high as fuck and set my liver back a few steps.

'I've got myself relatively sorted out, for now,' I confess, 'as long as The Inferno keeps quiet. It's others you need to be concerned about, like those poor homeless bastards down in the Square.'

He's intrigued, asking to know more.

'Come, I'll show you,' and I lead him over to King George Square where Micko clocks me coming with the panhandler in tow.

I introduce the guy as collecting for suicide prevention, and he's got the sticker on the tin and the print on his shirt to verify it. Then I launch into a spiel about how Micko is on regular suicide watch by the street missionaries who make sure they check in on him when they're doing the rounds.

'Even the police have instructions to come over from time to time and check on him,' I inform this guy in sincere tones.

Micko and the others take up the mantle, laying it on so thick the poor cunt's heart must be bleeding. Suddenly every bastard in earshot has become suicidal, with various stories about either having recently attempted it or feeling an inclination to attempt it soon. The poor cunt looks overwhelmed by all this, and despite the stories now beginning to conflict or sound too outrageous, the guy succumbs to his anxiety and promises everyone that he'll share the contents of the tin with them.

I'm remembering the time earlier in the year when the wildlife couple were here dressed like koalas, and how the street kids had basically robbed them on the spot. We're legitimately doing the same thing without the guy any wiser to the fact!

He prises the lid of his tin with the assistance of a twenty cent coin, which Old Graham tenderly pinches away from him when he's done. The guy's about to resist, as though it were only the contents of the tin that these bums are welcome too, but thinks better of it. Old Graham spirits the coin away amongst the grease-shined rags he calls his suit.

I stand back, considering the panorama before me. The suicide prevention guy looks like a missionary as he tips the tin up, shaking the coins loose into the hands of the homeless guys all around him.

Of course, once he's been relieved of his funds, everyone shuffles back to their perches and has nothing more to do with the dense cunt.

He still looks a bit shocked by everything, probably turning over in his mind if he's done the right thing and if there's a chance to get the money returned. Before he comes to that conclusion, if that be where his thoughts are currently wandering to, I go up and slap him on the back to congratulate him.

'Mate, I've seen some real charity in my time, but that was divine intervention if I've ever seen it.'

He scratches his ear nervously. 'How does this help them, though? I mean, it's not much.'

Oh, bless his heart! The stupid cunt's still caught up in the scam when it's well and truly revealed itself already.

'I can come back with people,' he stammers. 'To help, I mean.'

So sincere is he that I actually feel a pang of remorse for setting him up. But at the same time, it had to be done, so there's no point beating myself up about it.

'These guys here,' I go, feeling inspiration come to me via Malik's fucktard younger brother Beau, 'these guys now have cash for a coffee, something to warm their bellies. But more than that, you've given them hope in mankind. You've demonstrated here today that people haven't forgotten them. That suicide isn't the only option.'

My words, as Hallmark as they are, bolster the cunt up somewhat. I don't go so far as to deter him from coming back here with more aid, however, as it'd be cruel to deny my compadres a second chance to fleece Mister Suicide Prevention and his community worker mates.

'Forget about this now,' I suggest, throwing an arm round him and leading him away. 'Let's go grab a bite to eat and talk about what infrastructures we can put in place that can continue your good work here.'

He agrees to lunch, citing he feels pretty peckish, and tells me his name's Barry. I take my new buddy Barry up to the pizza buffet next to JoJo's. It's pay up front, then eat all you want.

'I'll grab us a table by the window,' I say, wandering in, leaving him at the cash register with no option but to pay for the meals.

I've got us a couple of plates full of pizza slices before he's even managed to get over to the table.

'Dig in, Baz,' I go, stuffing a whole slice into my gob.

The poor cunt still looks pretty depressed, probably still thinking about how he lost all that money back in the Square.

'Seriously, don't beat yourself up about the cash,' I go. 'People're really sympathetic to causes. You'll make that twice over again before the day is out.'

'It's not that,' he confesses glumly, but says no more.

Fuck's sake, I feel like he's the money tin and I've got to prise him open to get to the goodies inside.

'Problems at home?' I mumble around the second slice.

'Sorta. It's my brother.'

'He didn't commit suicide, did he?' I ask, quaffing a big mouthful of creaming soda from my cup. Imagine the poetry in that! When I put the drink back down on the table, I notice Barry's frowning at me.

'What's wrong with you?' he says, shaking his head.

'Too frank?' I enquire. 'You'll get used to it. I've got a condition called BPD. Hey, you should collect for that!'

My avowal is enough to mollify the cunt. He leans on the table, poking at his pizza, and goes: 'My brother's in hospital with brain damage.'

I realise he's not going to eat his food, so reach across and snatch a slice for myself. He barely notices.

'He OD'ed on drugs on Sunday night at a Gold Coast rave. GBH and Super K, they called it, the police did.' He screws his nose up in disgust, but whether it's because of the drugs or the way I'm chewing with my mouth open, I can't say.

'And it gave him brain damage?'

'Yeah. Apparently he stopped breathing. Nine other people, too. Airlifted him up to the RBH and he's on life support, but the doctor's said he's got brain damage from the lack of oxygen.'

'Fuck, that's pretty intense,' I go.

'Sure is.'

'Is that why you're doing this fundraising stuff, Barry?'

He sits back and sighs.

'You think it's bullshit, don't you?'

He doesn't sound angry with me. He just looks tired.

'Mate, if you're soul-searching, that's great. But you're not gonna find it pinching pennies from the people who couldn't give a flying fuck about people who top themselves. You've got to get out and really mingle. That lot back at the Square took you for a ride, and can you blame them? They're not alone, mate. Everyone's out to take everyone for a ride.'

'You set me up.'

I start laughing. 'Well, sure I did. What'd you fucking expect? But Barry, you're going about it all the wrong way. The problem with these agencies that you've signed up to is that they have admin fees. All those coins you collected weren't going into research for youth suicide or wherever the fuck they say it's going. If you wanna make any kind of change, you've gotta get grass roots about it. Hang out with the real deal people out there making changes, from the ones fighting legislations in the political arena to the ones serving soup out of vans in the parks.'

He thinks about what I'm saying, nodding along.

'I just didn't know where to start. I can't think straight with what's going on with my brother. I'm meant to be studying but I've just been hanging out in the mall with the collection tin.'

'Jesus Christ, Barry. Get back into the fucking study, mate. You're not doing your brother any fucking favours at all by fucking your own life up. You think he wants you moping around a Pizza Hut with a shameless cunt like me just because he's a vegetable now?'

Barry's eyes go wide and fierce, but I just stare the cunt down. I'm deadly fucking serious.

'Tell you what, I'll strike you a deal: you help me to feed those bastards back in the Square with pizza, and I'll absolve you of your sins, just like one of your precious priests.'

He looks at me inquisitively, and starts on about how he's getting low on funds.

'Give me a break, Barry. You've got Catholic guilt written all over you. Just follow my lead and pile as much pizza onto your plate as possible.'

He does as I instruct, following me over to the smorgasboard of lukewarm offerings, from whence the pile of pizza we ferry back to the table's so ridiculous it teeters in our arms, threatening to tip onto the carpet.

'They're not going to let us take all this away with us, are they?'

'Not at all,' I wink, 'which is why we gotta get cunning about it. Now sit to the side here and block the view of our haul. I'll be back in a minute.'

I waltz up to the front counter and tell the girl behind the register that my mate's gorged himself and is about to be sick.

'Do you have a bucket or something? Quick!'

She glances around, taking her sweet fucking time about it. The fucking service industry, seriously.

'Hurry, he's about to chuck all over your carpet,' I go, which makes the simpleton get her slack arse into gear, extending her search out back, obviously horrified at the prospect of having to clean vomit out of this plush flooring.

She returns with a cleaning bucket, and I give it a quick whiff to make sure it doesn't reek of chemicals.

'This'll do the trick,' I smile, leaving her puzzled as I race back to the table.

I thrust the bucket at Barry.

'Here, pretend you're being sick into this.'

'What?'

'Fucking do it, quick!' I snap. 'We're being watched. Just put your face into it and make chundering noises.'

Barry hesitantly lowers his face into the bucket, tenderly sniffing at it in case I'm trying to pull a trick on him. With his face inside the bucket he starts moaning like a B-grade movie zombie. I have to hide my face so the cashier doesn't see me crack up.

'That's done the trick,' I tell Barry when I see the cashier walk out back for the manager. 'Get your stupid mug outta there and shove the pizza in.'

We slide the pizza slices off our plates so they plop into the bucket. Altogether they're a hefty weight. The rest we stuff into Barry's empty money collection tin.

'Now let's get the fuck out of here, pronto.'

I scoot out from the table with the collection tin as Barry snatches up the bucket. As we're heading out the door the cashier appears with the manager, an angry looking cunt about my age with parted hair and a tan.

'Oi, where the hell do you think you're going?' he says.

'Run!' I yell to Barry, making a mad dash for the escalators, taking it down two steps at a time with Barry hot on my heels.

The manager yells for us to stop, but I instruct Barry to ignore the cunt. At the bottom I clear the end of the escalator but Barry missteps as the tread levels out and goes arse up on the concrete, tipping the bucket underneath him.

'Shit, up ya get, ya duffer,' I tell him. 'Quick!'

The manager bounds down the escalators, looking pissed off.

Barry climbs to his feet, moaning about the pizza slices squashed on the ground.

'No worries,' I go, scooping them back into the bucket.

The manager reaches us so I swing the collection tin at his head, which makes him jerk back. He steps back and the rubber handrail of the escalator catches him in the small of the back, yanking him down. In an effort to resist falling, the stupid cunt twists an ankle and cries out like a pansy as he hits the concrete.

I'm standing there laughing at him when Barry pulls me away.

'Let's go,' he says urgently, glancing nervously at the people who have stopped to stare at the fiasco. He's yet to learn that the world is a spectator and won't intervene while there's sport to be had.

We hit the pavement and by the time we get up the steps at King George Square, we're both out of breath. I check to see if the cops are after us, or that manager cunt, but we're in the clear.

I pass the collection tin full of pizza over to Barry, whose hands are grazed from the fall off the escalator.

'The honour's all yours, Baz.'

He looks down into the bucket, disappointed. 'But they fell on the ground.'

'Those bastards over there aren't going to care,' I laugh, licking the pizza sauce off my fingers from when I had to scoop them back into the bucket. 'They eat outta garbage bins, for Christ's sake.'

He takes my point. We head across the Square, where Micko sees us coming. He jabs one of the others in the ribs and they burst into hysterics at the sight of Barry carrying the bucket, which they assume is empty.

'At least it'll fit more coins now,' cackles Old Graham.

'Shut the fuck up, you ungrateful cunts,' I snarl. 'He's brought you food, out of the goodness of his heart.'

This gets them curious, and they wander over for a sticky-beak.

'Pizza!' exclaims Old Graham when Barry peels the lid off the tin.

The others join us, and soon everyone's huddled around Barry as he hands out slices of pizza like Jesus handing out bread and fish. The guys are slapping him on the back and telling him what a good sort he is, and I can see Barry's changing. The mopey cunt from earlier has been transformed, smiling and joking with my homeless mates.

When the bucket's finally empty, he can't thank me enough.

'I mean it, Dante,' he says with serious conviction. 'This has been more therapeutic than the last few days put together. Thanks, man, I really needed this.'

I shrug. 'Go back to your studies, Barry. This lot get along alright without you. But if you're ever in the city, think about shouting them lunch. They won't forget you now, so you'll always be welcome here.'

He nods and grins shyly.

'I will do, brother,' he says, shaking my hand.

He strolls across the Square, waving goodbye to the others who whistle after him and wave back.

He seems like a top guy, that Barry. Like, a decent brother to have. I wander back over to the others, who sit around like fat frogs full of flies. Old Graham kicks the empty collection tin away, and it scrapes along the concrete.

'You should show that tin more respect,' I tell him.

'What the fuck for?' he growls.

'That's your ticket to free cash every day,' I grin, picking up the tin and shaking it in front of his face. 'Spare a dollar to help suicide prevention, sir?'

Old Graham grins wickedly as Micko roars with laughter.

'You cunning fuck, Dante!'

THE LONELY ONE

The call takes ages to get picked up but it's not Crystal who answers. This woman sounds distracted, and, like, basically a bit terse for it.

'Listen, I saw Crystal over a week ago and she was, like, going to introduce me to John, but I've not heard anything. Period.'

My fungal infection rash thingy has finally cleared up, blessed be, thanks to that tinnitus cream, otherwise I wouldn't even be bothering to follow up on this useless dating agency. It's not like I'm asking to be introduced to, like, Mister Right here. Mister You'll Do would work just as well.

'John who?' the woman on the line says exasperated, as though, like, this is suddenly all too difficult to deal with.

'I'm not really sure,' I admit, trying to remember if Crystal had mentioned his surname. But of course she didn't;, it's against policy she'd said. 'Crystal said she was going to get in touch with him.'

I give the woman my name and hear her shuffling some papers.

She's like: 'Aw, I'm sorry, Alexandra, but John's found someone,' but in this overly-sympathetic way, like she's taking the piss.

I'm starting to feel ripped off, and more than a bit embarrassed. I deliberately didn't tell anyone about going to the dating agency, not even Abi, because of the, like, stigma attached to it, like as if muggings here's too inadequate to find herself a boyfriend. Which is basically true, in the sense that I can't find one that will take me to the next level in life. I mean, like, I could get a goth boy easily, but I'm over that, right?

Hearing that John isn't available deflates me, but I've paid my bloody money so I should have been told about this and, like, offered someone else to meet. It's what Crystal said would basically happen, so I remind the woman on the line of this and she says that they've actually got a new person who fits my criteria perfectly and they were actually going to, like, call me later today and arrange a time to meet him.

I'm not sure I should trust that info, but I've got no choice, really, and agree to meet up with him. She says she'll pass my number onto him – Gavan, his name is – and he'll be in contact soon.

I spend the rest of the day feeling like shit for being conned, but as I'm prepping my tea I get a phonecall and it's a guy's voice.

He's like: 'Is this Alex? I'm Gav. Do you fancy catching up for dinner tomorrow night?'

Cool beans! Gav it is! Feels relaxed and casual already, thankfully!

We arrange to meet at a Chinese restaurant in the city tomorrow night, and after the call I'm feeling some relief that the dating agency finally came through. Like, I guess some people need a little shove to get things done.

The next twenty four hours is spent fluctuating between elation and anxiety. I don't even know what Gav looks like! I have only his name and voice, and even forgot to get his phone number in case I need – or want – to cancel.

Naturally I wear black for the date, because it's both slimming and because there's, like, not a lot of colour in my wardrobe. If Gav turns out to be the one, that'll all change. The restaurant's on Elizabeth Street and just the walk to there alone from Central chaffs my thighs together so that by the time I've arrived my hideous potato body has conspired to make me feel uncomfortable. I hope this cream holds up. It's difficult to stay positive when my brain is starting to betray me by focusing on all my flaws.

Gav's waiting for me outside, wearing the blue shirt with the flowers on it he said he'd don so that I'd recognise him. It's basically a Hawaiian-print mumu, as far as I can tell. The bloke is huge! Like, obese. Not at all what I was expecting. For all I know I'm not what he was expecting, either, but at least I'm sure he's getting the better deal here.

We exchange pleasantries, him admiring my dress and me replying lamely that there's definitely flowers on his shirt. I fall short of saying they look nice. There's just nothing I can think to compliment him on. He's got a small, choppy handlebar moustache that extends down into a close-cropped goatee, and his hair is thin and lanky and nearly reaches to his shoulders. He's as far removed from John's photo as can be, and it's a shame that I couldn't have, like, seen his profile before agreeing to the date.

He holds the door open for me, at least, proving chivalry's not entirely dead, and I walk ahead so I don't have to, like, witness him struggling between the tables. If I hear any of them crash over onto the floor I'm just going to turn around and and call it a night. To my surprise, he manages to sit down on the small chair, though I'm sure he can't be comfortable. Watching him being entirely gracious about it makes me feel bad that I'm not giving him even half a chance, so I, like, endeavour to lighten up.

'You dye your hair black,' he observes, more than a little curious about it.

The dress I wore definitely isn't darkwave, just black, but even when goths try and dress down there's always something off about us that will basically give away that we're part of a subculture. Gav's obviously picking up on this, but unsure how to process the clues.

'Needed a bit of a change,' I lie, then follow up with a fact I hadn't actually consciously dwelt on but now hits me as something I must do: 'I'll be growing it out, though, and going natural again.'

'Me, too,' he jokes, rubbing strands of his stringy hair between sausage-like fingers.

We laugh uneasily together, and when he holds my eyes a fraction too long I flip the menu open and start perusing the list. He orders the lemon chicken, possibly the most inane selection, while I settle for a chow mein.

While we wait for our food, Gav tells me he's from Ipswich but works for a firm that is currently helping out with renovations on the

Wintergarden Building, work that he says will extend into next year.

He's like: 'It's a big project. I work in the book-keeping side of it. They asked if I did double entry and I told them not without buying me a drink first.'

Boom-tish. I carry on laughing graciously at his efforts to be funny, which loosens him up enough to admit he doesn't go on many dates.

'Actually, you're the second one and I've been with the agency for four months now,' he confesses.

I realise he's probably being used by them to palm off onto clients who get pushy about services not rendered, which is what I did. It makes me feel a little sorry for him, and for myself. How dare they treat us this way because we don't fit their agenda of attractiveness! But despite that, their plan's effective: there's zero chemistry between us, and I'm sure Gavan knows it, too.

The dinner and the conversation both prove as equally lacklustre as each other, and afterwards Gavan offers to give me a lift home in his car. I only accept it because, like, I figure it'll actually be less awkward than being on a train carriage full of total strangers and dealing with their bullshit. However, Gavan's parked way over on the other side of Roma Street, saying it's all he could, like, find without paying for something closer. The long walk to his car grinds my thighs red raw, and by the time we get there I'm nearly limping from the agony of the chaffing. Gavan basically broke into a heavy sweat as soon as we'd started walking.

The drive home is no less strained than the rest of the evening, so I decide to lay my cards out on the table.

'Listen, Gavan, about tonight, right? I'm sure you're a wonderful guy but you gotta admit, like, we're basically not clicking, are we?'

The air whistles out of his nostrils and he slumps his shoulders. Please Gaia, don't tell me he thinks otherwise!

'I know,' he sighs.

I'm like: 'Cheer up. I'm sure the right girl's just around the corner.'

'Well, you'd think after three dating agencies I'd have had more luck,' he says, clenching his jaw.

I hope he doesn't go postal on me, decide to drive the car straight at a wall and take us both out in a fit of despair.

Now that it's out in the open that we won't bother seeing each other again, Gavan seems more relaxed, and the conversation actually improves somewhat. Even his jokes, which still aren't that funny, are, like, much better than before. Less strained.

He pulls up outside my flat and switches the engine off. I was basically just going to wish him luck for the future and go straight inside. I hope he's not, like, going to burst into tears and tell me his life story.

He's like: 'I'll give you a hug for luck,' and although I'm not keen on it I figure anything to expedite my exit. He reaches over as best he can but I'm the one who has to put all the effort in, and I feel my lower back twinge as my body twists awkwardly into the embrace. Without thinking, I wrap my arms as far around his body as I can, my hands planting directly onto a wet patch of sweat-soaked mumu.

So gross!

He leans back in his seat, looking me directly in the eyes, and is like: 'Hey, since this'll be our last date, how about a blowjob?'

Is he fucking serious? I lock eyes with him, unable to, like, think of a reply, and to my horror I realise he's actually serious! The fucking audacity.

'I've got a fungal infection in my groin,' I stammer, thanking Gaia that I'm able to dredge up my recent complications to put him off altogether, but the *ton pousth* just shrugs and says it was worth a try.

Worth a try? For pity's sake, is that what I've been reduced to, basically the girl you try and get a blowjob from when all else fails?

I sulk back to my flat, feeling worse than ever, playing the whole evening over and over in my mind. I can barely sleep, so the in the morning I give the agency another call to let them know I'm basically less than impressed with their 'professional services'.

It's the same woman on the line who set up the date with Gavan. I wonder what happened to Crystal? Perhaps she's just the front-piece, the point of contact, and once they've, like, reeled us in they use one of those call-identifier phones to screen the clients, reserving Crystal for the newbies.

'Yeah, hi, I spoke with you the other day about a date but, like, didn't catch your name,' I start, determined to try and take the upper hand this time.

'Who is this?' she demands, but my name means squat to her.

I'm like: 'Remember, you set me up on the date with the big bloke in the mumu from Ipswich?'

'I hope it went well,' she says, her voice twisting enough to tell me the *kargiola* is smirking.

'Well, we had a good laugh about your company, so it was worth it for that alone,' I say, my heart thumping madly in my chest and my palms becoming uncomfortably damp. 'Did you even take a look at my profile to see what I'm basically looking for?'

'Well, the good-looking men are popular, as you can understand,' she says, and I can hear her rifling through some paperwork. 'Hard to get a date with them. Okay, I'm looking at your profile. Alexandra. Nice name. Pretty. Huh, says your religion is...'

She trails off as if unable to read my handwriting.

'Pagan,' I offer. It's not really, not strictly so, but it's the closest thing I can think to, like, identify with.

'Why pagan?' she snaps.

I actually shrug instead of answering, because I find her tone too confrontational. Unrelenting, she continues without waiting for me to respond.

'Why don't you believe in God?'

'I don't know,' I reply. 'Maybe I do.'

'If maybe you do, then you should put that on your profile,' she proposes. 'Not *pagan*. Men don't want *pagan*.'

They don't? When I think about all the guys that I know, a lot of them would be suitably impressed with it, but then of course they're mostly goth or metal guys. The crowd I'm trying *not* to attract.

'I don't know, maybe you're right.'

'Of course I'm right,' she says in a way that really bloody annoys me.

'But, like, isn't being a Pagan just worshipping the things God made anyway?' I say, gasping from lack of breath, trying to reclaim some footing in the conversation. 'I'd prefer to do that than worship something intangible.'

'God is everywhere, not invisible,' the woman replies. 'I'll change it now.'

I can hear a pen scribbling on paper, and I want to tell the woman to stop, that I don't want my profile changed. But I feel forced into this, I feel violated by the changes being made. But no words come out of me in defence. Only that rising panic in my brain, my heart hammering away like it's basically about to explode.

The woman continues to berate me down the phone, presumably about God and religion, but I, like, can't hear any of it, only that I know the woman's still speaking at a hundred miles an hour. The blood's rushing through my ears, deafening me to the world.

The phone slams into the cradle and I'm hyperventilating.

I don't know if the phone call was over yet, only that I know I needed it to stop.

How ridiculous is it that you can't even buy a decent date these days, let alone some fucking courtesy? I need to face the fact that the agency is a scam, and that I've basically wasted my rent and grocery money on nothing. Fuck, I even paid for my half of the meal last night! I'll have to, like, think of some lie for Mama about why I don't have the funds for this week when I ask her to help me out. She'd be livid if she knew what I really spent my dwindling bank balance on.

The day's made way for night and the torrential downpour's put an end to the music, with half the crowds pouring out of Musgrave Park and down under the Cultural Centre towards the train station. No matter, we've got the lights of the beer tent and the mighty rainbow phallus over yonder to light up the night sky for the rest of us! The storm's mostly passed over but there's still lingering heavy rain and lightning. The bolts of electricity streak across the heavens as the needlepoint's searchlight scans the city across the river.

Some guys have got a mudslide going on outside and all manner of punks and ferals are sloshing around trying to outdo each other on how far they can slide. Dale wants to have a go, too, but I think he's too pissed for it. Or perhaps he's tanked just the right amount for it, who knows? The coppers on the other side of the fence along Russell Street are getting edgy, and some have donned oversized yellow rain coats for their best Paddington Bear impersonations.

There were still a few more bands to go on, and Dale's shitty that he didn't get to see them. I got to see Dogmachine live finally, so I'm stoked at least.

Alan's band Sodomy Finger was meant to play but he couldn't pull himself together for it so got dropped from the lineup. I don't see him much these days, since his stillborn baby. I've kind of distanced myself from the emotional maelstrom that buzzes around him. As a result of that emotional turmoil he rarely plays these days, but it's so funny when he does because there's two songs where he sings the chorus in his native tongue and we all try and sing along with him and balls it up. Alan pisses himself with laughter when we mangle it and everyone gets a good chuckle from it, too. I guess I miss the silly bastard.

'Good line-up this year, but,' enthuses Dale. 'The Invisible Empire. Love bands with more than one drummer. What else? Dregs of Humanity! Fuck yeah, local stuff!' He thumps his fist down on the table in triumph.

'I missed Ostia. I wasn't paying attention because of those girls we were chattin up.'

'You and your fucking goth bands, dude,' he goes.

'Fuck off! Ostia are alright. You should give em a go sometime, or afraid you'll end up liking em, eh?'

'*You* fuck off,' he says, frowning at his can of VB like he's unsure how it got there. 'Fuckin Cure, fuckin... who else? Oh yeah, fuckin Marilyn Manson.'

'They're not goth.'

'Bull-*shit*, Dante! All you uptight wankers in your lacy shirts say that.'

'It's true,' I insist, laughing because he goes to point threateningly at me and knocks his can over, cursing as he stands it up again. 'Nah, seriously. You're just naming the mainstream stuff.'

This guy across from us has heard some of our convo, and he leans across and shouts: 'Alien Sex Fiend! Fucking top band!'

I hold my hand palm out toward the guy and pull a *there-you-go* face at Dale, who just shakes his head.

'More punk than fuckin goth,' he argues.

'So, so,' goes this other guy, wobbling his hand in the air in a gesture of uncertainty. 'They're pretty dark, still.'

'Fuck off, cunt,' Dale fires back. I suspect these two already know each other; everyone here seems to know or know of Dale Donger. 'They're a mess, that's all. Don't know where they fuckin stand.'

Dale's grinning, his eyes hooded. A crack of lightning captures his features in stark black and whites, making him look like a comic book villain. He's pretty drunk now, and getting argumentative. I'm wary because he might decide to lash out, convinced his violence is playful. I can read him pretty well, and we sort of just bounce off each other that way.

One time back in film college me and Dale got into an argument about music licensing for video production, and it'd got so heated that we were trading insults at each other, but he was parrying like a master fencer thrusting his blade in, getting jabs at me until I'd become increasingly incensed. In the end it got so personal that he'd gone: 'Better make sure your doors are locked tonight.' I'd bared my teeth and snarled: 'they'll be wide fucking open, cunt, ready to cut you into pieces with my knife.' The argument had stopped there, not because either of us were worried about the imminent threat of the other, but simply because the argument had nowhere else to go. So we'd stopped and simmered, and everyone else in the room just sat there shitting themselves. Not even the tutor had known what to do, resuming the class tutorial as if naught untoward had taken place. To everyone's confusion, me and Dale were fine with one another by lunchtime, sitting together at the communal table as per usual with no animosity at all. That had really stumped the others!

Through the crowd I spy Nicola. She's with this tall guy and Tim, who still looks like a shifty lil prick. I saw them earlier when Blitz Babies were tearing it up onstage, where Nicola and I'd made eye contact. I don't wish her any ill-will anymore, so we'd nodded at each other across the audience. The taller guy seemed to be going out with her now, but there'd been no sign of Darcey anywhere. Anyway, I'm with Amara now and couldn't be happier. Or so I tell myself.

Looks like some of the Paddington Pigs are leaving, heading to their cop cars. Guess the rain is just too much for some.

'Oi, Tess,' goes this girl with dreadlocks who looks vaguely familiar, nudging Donger aside and taking a seat, addressing another girl across the table. 'News just in: the Hague Conference got America to sign up to the Convention.'

'Fucking result,' grins the other girl, Tess.

'You go, girls,' whoops Dale, raising his can. 'We should toast.'

Tess shakes her head at him. 'You don't even know what we're on about, Donger.'

'Sure I fuckin do,' he replies. 'It's all you two've been goin on about lately.' He turns to me, winks, and says: 'You know me, Dante, always keep my eye on the prize. These two lovely activists have some refugees holed up at home.'

'Yeah, because the Government's stopped the Asylum Seekers Assistance Scheme,' says Tess, her big brown eyes fixing on me in the fervent manner of the good shepherd who will not be denied their flock. 'So the refugees that're waitin for the RRT to grant them refugee status aren't even allowed to work. How're they supposed to survive?'

She shrugs, shaking her head at the state of things.

'What's that got to do with The Hague?' I bite. 'Isn't that all the way over in France?'

'The Netherlands,' Jane corrects me, her dreadlocks dipping into her beer without her realising.

This Tess girl's all fired up, the light in her eyes almost as bright as the lightning earlier. 'The Hague Convention determines international laws for the protection of children. And Australia's a party to that. It's brilliant timing, actually. We're hoping to try and use these laws to leverage some protection for refugee families here while they wait for the Refugee Review Tribunal to get their shit together.'

'And in the meantime you girls are looking after these families?'

'Someone's gotta,' says Jane. She still looks excited by the news. She's clued on that her dreadlocks have been dangling in her cup and are soaked, so she tips the beer out.

'Fuck, don't waste it,' Dale protests, staring sullenly as Jane's split beer soaks into the mud beside him.

Jane snuggles against Donger, trying for a sip from his can.

'So, you're Dante?' she asks, and I nod. 'You're Maddie's mate?'

'Yep. You know her?'

'Yeah, real well. In fact, I went to a party at the Prozac Palace with her once that you apparently invited her to.'

'Oh yeah!' I laugh, remembering how Raven and Twix spat chips about that. 'You girls sold everyone fake acid trips, yeah?'

'It was a fucking riot,' grins Jane like a seasoned stoner.

Tess nearly cries with hysterics as Jane recounts the events to her.

I'm impressed by Tess. She's dedicated and knows her stuff, is willing to take on the big guns armed with their own laws, their own rules. And her eyes are fucking amazing. I'm pretty much broke as fuck, but I want to impress her by giving her some cash to help out with the family that she's looking after, so I discreetly try and fish a twenty dollar note from the vinyl bank card holder that serves as my wallet because I couldn't be bothered buying an actual wallet.

I'm about to strike up a convo with her about my mate Maddie, who also looks after refugees sometimes, figuring she might even know her if they're all part of the same underground group, when I notice the cops've begun removing sections of the fence. The mounted police ride on through, parting the punters leaving the park.

'What the fuck are they up to?' Jane says with suspicion.

'They want to come and join in on the fun,' sneers Tess, looking around toward the front gates.

'They wanna be like pigs in mud,' I quietly quip; the others laugh.

But I'm not laughing. Even from where I'm sitting I can see the cops hassling the volunteers who're trying to pack up the tills at the front gate. I slip the money back into my pocket, and promise myself to try and get it to Tess before the night's out.

The horse mounts trot to the end of the mud-slide and are trying to say something to the muddy fuckers tumbling around. Behind them the rest of the pigs have filed in through the gates dressed in riot gear. Jane's spot on: what the fuck are they up to?

The mud-covered punks and the cops get into an argument, and it looks like the latter aren't into it because one of them rushes forward and swings his baton around, and the punters rear back. I can't tell if any of them got hit, but the fucking pig hasn't finished. He keeps charging at them, and now some of the others join in. I see a feral, head to toe in muck, slip over and go under one of the horses.

The rest of the cops have formed a line with their shields up and are beating their batons against them, chanting: 'Move. Move. Move.' They start advancing on the beer tent, so a whole heap of us pick up empty cans and throw them at the cops. I make sure I throw at least one that's nearly full, but it misses the mark. The rain of cans clatter against the shields and helmets, and obviously unable to endure the restraint any longer a couple of the pigs rush forward and challenge the punks, who in turn pelt the coppers with more cans. Batons come down and I can see that Angela Thorogood, a local activist for civil rights, is kneeling on the ground, holding her head. The formation of cops continues moving forward with their chanting.

'Shit!' yells Tess, and her and Jane run after Angela and try and get her back to the merchandising tent.

By now the mood has really spoiled. People start screaming bloody murder, and the cops break from their formation and get stuck into everybody. The beer cans are no match for the batons and shields as people get clubbed. I can see blood flowing freely.

Enraged, Donger launches himself into the affray, roaring. I'm off after him but slip in the mud, finding myself trying to ward off boots as I get trampled by a group being herded back. I've lost sight of Dale, and can feel the mud seeping into my clothes and down into my Docs.

'Move!' screams this copper, his visor up. Someone pegs a full can at his face and he reels back, wincing.

Toward the western corner of the park there's hordes of punters fleeing, pushing the cyclone fencing down. Over at the corner of Russell and Cordelia Streets, from behind the boarding house on the corner, emerges a new threat: what looks like guys in army fatigues, and a fucking APC unit behind them! Might just be a bulky looking van, but looks more than that to me.

I can't fucking believe it.

'Dale!' I scream. 'Dale, we gotta get the fuck outta here, man!'

'Donger's down, mate,' yells this guy with a red mohawk, pointing back into the mass of people struggling with the cops. I can just make out Dale sitting in the mud amongst them. I goosestep over to him, careful not to fall over again, using the crowd to balance myself.

Donger's got a fractured eye socket by the looks of it, and it's swelling up real bad. He can't see well and's standing lopsided. He's still drunk, too, so he's not feeling any pain yet, insisting on walking.

'Dale, seriously!' I scold. 'Hold onto me. I'll get you out of here.'

It's a fucking madhouse. Cops are walking around smashing into people, who are trying to retaliate but to no avail. Some punters are demanding to know the names of the officers, but are either getting ignored or whacked across the skull for their efforts. It's a bad scene.

'They've fucked it,' Donger says to me.

I see Tim amongst some others yelling at the cops, pushing against their shields and demanding to know what the fuck's going down. I consider trying to lob a can at the cunt's head, but Donger needs me to get him out of here. The cops've started cuffing people, and I've got no intention on being one of them.

The fences start falling left right and centre, so I shuffle us toward Edmonstone Street, out of the park. There's people streaming through with us, talking about how it's all fucked up and giving the forks to cops standing watch up this end. Some people are still in good spirits, though, and are laughing about the whole thing.

Scab's here, his mohawk flattened to his head from the rain.

'Oi Donger,' he goes, 'you alright, mate?'

'Who's that? Is that you, Scabbie?'

'Yeah, mate,' he says, putting his arm on Donger's shoulder and getting a good look at the wounds. Donger's eye has closed over now. 'You got a fucking whalloping, eh?'

'Always too close to the action,' Donger says drolly.

Scab helps me to carry Donger the rest of the way into West End where we wait out the rain under the shop awnings on Boundary Street, soaked to the skin in our drenched clothing. Some Murri kids are playing on the concrete goanna, soaked to the skin. They love this weather. Storm kids.

Donger's swollen eye is getting bigger and darker.

'This is fucked,' I tell Scab. 'He needs to get to the hospital.'

Scab agrees, so we drag Dale across the road to the cab rank and get up to the Mater where the triage nurses in emergency get us to wait. A lot of the nurses are petite little Asian girls, probably fresh outta Uni, and they look a bit worried about the amount of muddied punks in here sporting all sorts of injuries.

This big woman with a cut in her hairline that dribbles blood and muck down her face leans over to us. 'You guys at Musgrave, too, eh?'

'Yeah,' moans Dale. 'Fuckers...'

'You know what we need?' I say to the woman, loud enough for everyone in the room to hear. 'We need The Hague Convention to write punks into their jurisdiction.'

The big woman nods sagely, though I doubt she has a fucking clue what I'm on about.

KK THE COWBOY

All sorts of people come to Roxanne's Door for a night of fun and big spendin, but I never expected to see someone I knew!

Imp's brother KK's here with his construction mates, and they're literally droppin cash like there's no tomorrow.

'Holy fuck! Is that you, Prude?' he goes when he sees us, using the nickname the cunts at school gave us. I've given a couple of em black eyes for it, too. 'Not livin up to your name no more, ay?'

'Shut the fuck up,' I hiss, glancin around.

'What for?' he goes, laughin.

'Name's Pixie,' I say sternly. 'Ya don't know us outside of here, okay?'

'Yeah, no worries, babe,' he goes, checkin us out, 'I'm just another punter, ay.' He looks us up and down again. 'Fuck me, my brother's a dumb cunt if he's not banging that.'

'Thanks, I think,' I go sarcastically. 'But this isn't for you. No way.'

'Ease up, girl,' he goes, 'it's cool. But hey, you should come to my birthday bash this weekend. I reckon you'll fucken love it, ay.'

'I dunno.'

'Nah, for real, but,' he goes. 'I didn't know you were a pretty cool chick. I'm gunna be the big two-one. You gotta come. It's at the Nash in town. Free piss all night on tab, strippers, jelly wrestlin, the fucken lot!'

Sounds ace, actually. I'll just tell Nel I'm workin again. She always wants to know where I am these days, fuckin controlling cunt.

'Maybe...'

'Don't worry, Imp's not invited. Too young,' KK goes, which is a bit weird coz I'm literally the same age as Imp.

'In that case, ace! I'll come, but promise not to tell Imp about it.'

KK runs his fingers along his lips as if he's zippin em shut.

'Right, go have some fun and let us get back to work,' I go, wavin him off.

'Yeah, righto,' he chuckles, lookin us up and down as he staggers away, pursin his lips in admiration.

At the end of the night the other girls tell us that KK and his boys spent up big time in a massive fuckin way. The girls are more than impressed with the cash flow, so that's melted any doubts I have about goin to KK's birthday bash. I just hafta hope he's not bullshittin about Imp not bein there, coz I could do without that judgmental cunt tellin us how or how not to live me life.

Come the night I get ready but Nel's literally in me face about what I'm up to, where I'm goin and all that.

'You don't have any shifts tonight,' she says.

'How would *you* know?'

'Don't backchat me, Pixie, I'm not in the mood.'

'Yer not the boss of us,' I snarl.

'If you walk out that fucken door, I swear...' she goes, raisin her hand like she's gonna slap us.

How fuckin dare she! I race out the door anyways, and she literally punches a hole in the wall next to it. What a fuckin psycho bitch!

I head over to the National Hotel and get ushered to the party room out back, which is full of the roughest crowd of cunts I've ever mixed it up with. The gothic clubs are fuckin unco as compared to this shit. There's such a weird vibe here I'm startin to wonder if this is such a good idea after all, but then KK pops his head up in the crowd and waves us over to his table where his boss, Bazza, is holdin court over a table full of beer. He's an old cunt, skin dark and wrinkled from workin in the sun all his life.

'This is my mate Pixie,' says KK, going with me nick thankfully instead of Prude, which he usually prefers.

'Your date, eh?' leers Bazza.

'Fuck off,' I go, wrinklin me nose up and glancin sideways at KK.

'I said *mate*, you deaf cunt,' says KK to his boss, laughin lightly.

'Sure, ya did. Big fucken do tonight, but, KK,' Bazza goes, lookin round the joint. It's packed as. 'Four twenny first's on tonight!'

'Fark me,' goes KK, 'must be a good age then, ay?'

His workmate, Grubber, smirks at us. 'So why're you dressed for a funeral instead ova birthday?'

'Yeah, ha ha, never heard that one before,' I go, spitefully. 'I'm a fuckin Spooky Kid, ya mong.'

'Not fucken wrong there,' Grubber goes (and I'm sure Bazza goes 'especially about the kid bit'), then adds: 'Givin me the spooks just looken at ya.'

'Whatever,' I go, and Grubber grins at us like he's won.

'Pixie's alright,' KK goes, and grabs us round the shoulder, kissin me on top of me head.

His boss's got a lil foil of cocaine that they're all dippin into and rubbin on their gums. I've never done coke but I'm more than game, especially coz for some mong reason I literally ate some rat poison before I left home. Like, *literally*. Fuck knows how come. It was just there, on the stairs inside the Prozac. I think someone's tryin to kill that stupid moggie Lunatic. They looked like liddle pills sittin there and so for some reason I popped a couple down the hatch, and now I can feel em wormin inside me tummy, makin us crook in the guts. I reckon the coke'll fix that, easy as, but. It pops and fizzles from me saliva and me gums are shrinkin. I feel fuckin great, like I've had too much coffee, and immediately dip in for more.

'Whoa, ease up there, cupcake,' Bazza goes, pullin the foil away so I can't go back for thirds.

Me vision starts to blur for a moment, but then me adrenalin's on fire. Lookin round the room I realise there was nuthin to be worried about with this crowd, who're really just a bunch of thick-as-bricks tools and retards.

The girl collectin empty glasses off the tables comes up and goes: 'Better put that shit away, Bazza. Last thing we need is getting even more tied up with The Joke.'

'No worries, hen,' Bazza says, foldin the foil and pocketing it.

Who's this bitch think she is, tellin us what to do?

'What's *The Joke?*' I go.

'Police corruption,' Grubber smirks.

'But how come it's called The Joke?'

'Cause everyone's in on it, darl,' Bazza goes, reaching past us to hand the girl his empty glass.

'Oi, Jenny,' KK says to her, sittin back and openin his arms wide. 'It's me twenny first, love! Fucken celebration, ay? Gotta celebrate!'

'Yeah, I bet you do,' she says, obviously charmed by his infectious grin. 'You'll get yours one of these days, KK.'

'Not if I give it to you first,' he goes, grabbin his crotch and flickin his tongue at her.

Jenny just laughs and goes: 'Yeah, we'll see.'

'Fucken hot to trot, that one, but,' KK says to the table when she's walked off.

Bazza turns to us. 'And what about you, darl? Gotta boyfriend?'

'Oi, she's dating me lil bro,' says KK, pointin at us.

'No, I'm not. He's a retard.'

'Spot on there,' agrees KK, sippin his beer. He grins lazily at us, enjoyin himself massively.

'Another round!' shouts Bazza, although I'm thinkin another go on the white powder would be better.

'I'm glad you came, ay,' KK goes, raisin his glass to us. 'You're one cool fucken chick, man.'

'A cool chick-man, yep, that's me ya dumb cunt,' I go, while the other cunts cack themselves.

'Got some balls on this one,' grins Bazza.

'Is that what ya like in a chick?' I go, tryin to be a smartass.

But he's quicker, or more fuckin sober, and goes: 'I like to get more than just me balls into em!' Then he heads up to the bar for another round.

Good fuckin crowd, but. Good dudes all round for a bunch of normals, except maybe for that Grubber cunt. Haven't worked him out yet. We scull our drinks and bang the glasses down just as Bazza comes back with more.

'FARK YEAAAAH,' roars KK, doin the devil's horns in the air on both hands.

He's a crazy cunt, alright.

The beer's makin us drowsy but the coke's got us fuckin wired. It's a weird feelin, like havin insomnia. The dudes at the table are makin sure me glass is never empty, but, the hopeful cunts. I'm not fuckin stupid. Chicks can spot a horny dude a mile off, they're so fuckin obvious. Bazza and KK are the only one's not tryin any moves on us. These others could learn from them.

A guy with dreadlocks pokes his head out from next to the bar and hands a floppy old baseball cap to one of the punters. It gets passed round the whole bar, and everyone drops some cash into it.

'I don't hafta,' says KK when it comes round to him. 'I'm one of the birfday boys.'

'Me, too,' goes Grubber, rubbin his nose and sniffin loudly.

The hat continues round the table.

'I'm literally broke,' I go, before it can reach us.

'Oi, she's alright,' says KK, urgin them to let the hat skip over us.

'What's it for?' I ask.

Grubber, goes: 'We're chippin in for da strippers. Local sheilas dat gotta earn a few more quid.'

'Helps em raise their kids right, ay,' says KK with a wink.

'Too right,' agrees Grubber, passin the hat onto the next table.

The guy with the dreadlocks walks out in front of the bar, holdin a microphone.

The crowd chants: 'Ryley! Ryley! Ryley!' then ends with a group hoot, like a forest full of monkeys. That's all these cunts are: fuckin monkeys.

'What's so funny?' goes KK.

'Nuthin,' I sneer, chucklin to myself.

'Glad to see so many turned up,' says Ryley into his microphone, and the crowd cheers. 'Four big birthday bashes tonight. Four twenty firsts! We got Krazy Kenny, Johnno Mackie who youse all know as Grubber, Stevie Harris and Big Brucie.' Each dude's mates all roar out when his name gets mentioned. 'So drinks're on the house tonight!'

The sound of everyone in the place cheerin is deafening.

'Oi, he got it wrong,' moans KK to the rest of us. 'It's KK for Krazy Kunt.'

'Bullshit it is!' goes Bazza, his face red from cackin up.

Before long there's another round of pots on the table, and we're throwin em back like no tomorrow.

A blow up kiddie pool gets dragged out into the middle of the floor and filled with tubs of jelly from the pub's cold-room.

Ryley's back on the microphone: 'And now ladies and gentlemen, tonight's entertainment! I present to you the loveliest ladies this side of the Great Dividing Range: Chasely, Marie and Janie!'

The strippers – one who's got a lollipop in her gob and who all definitely look like a bunch of ordinary girls – get into the kiddie pool dressed only in bikinis. They do what's probly their best at lookin sexy and shit, but it's not a patch on the girls at Roxanne's Door. I reckon even Roz could outperform these skanks.

The crowd goes apeshit as the girls start to circle each other, but, slappin at each others faces and sizing their opponents up.

The coke's gone to me fuckin head, spinnin us right round baby right round. I'm on me feet, feelin the urge to fuckin hit somebody, screamin at the girls to kill each other.

'DON'T JUST FUCKIN STAND THERE, YA DUMB SLUT CUNTS,' I scream with all the power in me lungs.

'Holy shit, KK, she's a lil firecracker,' laughs Bazza, impressed as, which he fuckin well should be.

'A right lil banger, I reckon,' adds Grubber with a leer.

I could kick that cunt in the fuckin chops right now, no problem.

The crowd roars as a bikini top is snatched away and flung into the jelly pit. It gets mashed underfoot.

'Grab er tits!' yells KK to the one of the girls.

'You fuckin grab em,' I snarl at him.

'Eh?' he smiles, wary of the vicious edge in me voice.

I gotta calm the fuck down, but I just want more of that coke. It's no heroin, not even a patch on it, but I feel like I could take on the fuckin world right now. I *want* to take on the world right now.

I shove KK towards the edge of the blowup pool.

'Get in there, ya pussy,' I go.

'Looks like we have another contendeeerrr,' goes Ryley into the microphone, and two of the girls notice KK by the edge so they start beckonin him in.

'Stop being a cheeky prick and put your money where your mouth is,' goes the one with the lollipop, called Chasely.

'Go for it, son,' dares Bazza, slappin KK on the back.

'Righto,' KK goes, startin to strip off his shirt, but when he's only got it over his head I give him a shove into the jelly pit. The poor cunt trips over the edge and goes down hard, belly-floppin onto the jelly. It flies up everywhere and some of it hits us on the leg. I scoop it off and pop it in me mouth. Lime.

KK tries to get to his feet but the girls start yankin at his boardies, to the absolute frenzy of the crowd. The sight of his skinny body sets a lot of the dudes off, hootin at him and wolf-whistlin. He turns and gives them both fingers, a cocky grin on his face. The girls take his moment of distraction and fully dack him, undies and all. His dick's nested in a bush of dark pubes, dead from too much alcohol.

'No fair,' he whines, 'I had me fucken back turned, but.'

Marie, the dark haired girl, twirls KK's boardies in the air and flings the fuckin things at us. I try and duck but they graze me cheek, leavin a fuckin gross as wet jelly-patch on us.

'Oh yeah?' goes KK, and returns the favour, wrestlin her to get her bikini bottoms off. He gets a smack across the head for it, but still gets em off, sendin the crowd into another frenzy.

Janie, the red-headed girl, grabs the lollipop off Chasely and tries to penetrate her with it, but Chasely fends her off by kickin her legs wildly, so Janie settles for poppin it in an out of Chasely's mouth like it's a cock.

They get another birthday boy into the pool and do the same to him. Fuck, he's pretty hot, but. Got a good body on him. At first he's shy about bein naked, holdin his hands over his bits, but the girls grab him by the wrists and hold his arms up like he's a champion, exposin his cock for all to see. Hung like a fuckin horse, that one.

It doesn't take long for KK to wrestle Chasely onto all fours and start doin her doggy style in front of everyone, coz he finally gets it up. I can't believe me eyes! He reaches round and takes the lollipop off her and sticks it in his gob.

'Gettin a bit dry down there, love,' KK goes, and scoops up some mooshed jelly, lettin it slide down the crack of her ass. 'Much better,' he grins, pumpin away harder than ever.

I once masturbated with one of those long, twirly lollipops when I was younger. Never again. Got a yeast infection from the sugar and had to beg Mum to do somethin about it. Ended up with a vaginal cream that the chemist lady said to only use before I go to bed as it can cause leakage. I was young, and itchin, and put it on in the car straight away so that by the time we got to me uncle and aunt's house for lunch me pussy was leakin like a tap. Can imagine sugary jelly up in there havin the same effect.

Watchin KK and the hot guy fuckin the girls in the jelly pit in this crowded pub has got us horny as, but. The hot guy's ass cheeks are squeezin together as he thrusts, and me lust must be noticeable coz Bazza comes up next to us and reaches between me legs with his thick fingers, feelin us through me jeans. Me pussy feels electric from his rough handlin.

'Uh uh,' I say, wagglin me finger at him.

'Aw, c'mon, cupcake,' he pleads softly.

He seems to get the picture, but, coz he pulls out his foil and taps some onto his fingertip. This time he makes us snort it.

FUCKIN HEADRUSH.

I growl at him like an animal, which makes him grin like fuckin Ronald McDonald, ear to fuckin ear, the cunt.

His hand goes to me crotch again.

I check to see if anyone's givin us the evil eye, but everyone's either watchin the boys do the strippers or they've started on each other. There's a couple already bangin each other against the bar, and a girl blowin two dudes at once a couple of tables away.

It's turnin into a fuckin orgy. I feel like such a whore with Bazza's hand shovin down the front of me jeans, and his other hand now gropin at me breasts.

'More coke,' I demand.

'In a min,' he growls, his voice dark with lust. I hear it rumblin next to me ear, deep and dangerous. Such a turn on.

'I said more coke, cunt.'

'You're gonna make your brain bleed, you silly bitch,' he says, but pulls the foil out again at my insistence. Me hands are shakin as I lick me finger and dab it into the diminishin pile, then rub it across me gums. It feels like me teeth are gonna fall out if me gums recede any more.

Bazza tugs me fly open and shoves at me jeans. A liddle wiggle of the hips and they slide straight down me thighs. Straight away the dirty old cunt's hands are on me ass.

'Fucking hell, baby,' he moans. 'An old man's dream come true.'

As long as the cunt doesn't put the Teen Queens on he'll be right.

Roz would have a fuckin fit if she knew I was just givin it away. Ha! I'd love to see the look on her face. Or on Imp's. Imagine that judgemental liddle cunt seeing this? He'd be fuckin crazy mad at both me and KK.

The girls in the jelly pit are makin out with each other now, the guys still ridin them doggy. KK's lookin over at us with that stupid, drunken grin on his face and all.

'YEEEEEE-HAWWWW!' he yells, wavin his hand in the air like he's a cowboy on a buckin bull.

Bazza's pulled me undies down now.

'Bend over, baby,' he coos, pushin on me head.

I hope the old cunt blows his load quickly and we can get stuck into some more coke again.

The bar's turned into a full-blown orgy now, with cunts suckin or fuckin in every direction. Anyone not doin any rootin's either wankin off or sittin there with big grins on their faces, includin the old dude behind the bar.

This is too fuckin crazy, but it's too late to stop now.

Bazza's got us over the table, pressin me face into the spilt piss, gruntin like a fuckin walrus, goin on about how sweet and liddle I am and callin us his liddle slut. Yuck. Sounds like a fucking pedo. How come they're always fucking pedos?

'Hurry up and fuckin cum,' I go, imaginin Marilyn Manson behind us instead of this old, fat cunt. 'Then it's more coke, okay?'

BAD GOTH POETRY

There's a terrible row happening upstairs between Pixie and Nel. Seems those two are always at each other's throats' these days.

That's why it was so good to get out tonight and have tea over at Amara's place. Got to meet her parents for the first time, and her mum even cooked roast lamb! Haven't had that in years! So fucking good. Amara was pretty nervous about introducing me to them, especially since her old uppity school chums have given me a pretty frosty reception so far (I expect she'll slough them off when those halcyon schoolgirl days begin to recede with the onset of adulthood), but I was at my most behaved except when I yelled out to her mum in the kitchen: 'Bring out the food, woman!' It made everyone laugh in the end so that was alright. Her dad was the kind of man that made you feel good about yourself when you had his undivided attention. He's got the presence of a man in complete control, like those chess-players on the idiot box who've considered every move and aren't surprised by anything. But I know that they considered me as an amusement rather than as a serious relationship for Amara. It's because we're subcultural, they see how we live as a phase that we grow out of eventually, and naturally with it the very relationships that we form within that context. But not me; I'm gonna be with Amara forever. She's the one for me.

'Should we call the police or something?' Amara goes, wide-eyed as she stares up the gloomy stairwell, the shouting match bouncing off the walls. Pixie's going hoarse with rage.

'Let em just finish each other off,' I say dismissively, locking the door behind me cause Bernie's checkin out some beats tonight. 'Might get some fucking peace and quiet around here, at last, then.'

Raven's door's open and there's already a small crowd here for pre-club drinks. There's Megs and her new boyfriend Shadow – so-called because he follows her everywhere and doesn't say a word – Xanthe's here, flipping through an old *JTHM* comic I must've left behind yonks ago back when Twix was still living here, and Raven's mate Taime with her little ankle-biter whose name I think is Willow or something. Alex's also already arrived with a fascinating new friend in tow, whom she introduces as Phoenix.

I notice Alex's hands tremble, always fidgeting with the hemline of her Batman shirt. I know she got her sister accidentally arrested and all, but there's something else going on deep down with this one. Takes a fellow loony tune to recognise it.

While Megs and Shadow fog up the bathroom with hairspray, teasing their locks up into Robert Smith do's and fixing their makeup with a few short bursts of the same spray, I take Amara through to the kitchen and pour us a couple of wines. There's a half dozen East Coast Coolers in the fridge, Raven's fave drink (and a half dozen empties next to the bin), and a bottle each of vodka and passion pop. Just the sight of the latter makes me want to chuck up everywhere.

There's something about this new friend of Alex's that I can't seem to put my finger on, until Amara whispers: 'Is that a boy or a girl?' Then it hits me, I haven't a clue, although I'm leaning towards the female of the species, despite the flat chest.

Of course, I've got no inhibitions about raising the question, which Phoenix takes in her stride and answers with the grace of an angel, which is what she makes me think of, like one of those ones my parents still secretly harbour hopes of being visited by, I'm sure.

'When I think of myself, my *real* self, I don't see male or female but a more complex inner self,' Phoenix explains. 'Growing up I was always aware of a pit inside me, something painful, you know? And as soon as I started seeing myself as being xenogender-specific, that pit started to feel less empty. It hurt a lot less.'

Alex is nodding emphatically, and Amara's narrowed her eyes in serious contemplation of Phoenix's confession. The rest are up a gum tree, confused as fuck but trying not to show it out of respect, except Raven, who's had a few too many East Coasties.

'I don't get it,' she goes. 'So you hate being a girl?'

'No, I just wasn't one,' says Phoenix.

'But you've got a vagina, yeah?'

Alex and Phoenix exchange knowing smiles, like they've heard this a hundred times before.

'I'm sorry, no offence,' continues Raven, urged on by Taime's enthusiastic nodding, 'but it just seems like a slap in the face to womanhood. You didn't even reject it to become a guy, you just flat out rejected it. Seems devoid of any meaning.'

Now Phoenix doesn't look so smug, and I feel kind of bad because I think I get where she's coming from. She's rejected several gender identities available to her in favour of a wholly new one that society – or part thereof such as dear old Raven there – is at odds with. It reminds me of that Clive Barker sketch *Nine Genital Forms* where he supposes we're not just stuck with being only male or only female, but can broaden the horizons a little more, even to perhaps none at all! Whereas I struggle to maintain a consistent identity by absorbing traits and influences from people around me, from films and books even, in order to formulate a tangible and relatable individuality, Phoenix has seen the futility of that and simply ceased all definition of what we think she is. Well, not she, but however Phoenix chooses to be defined, at least.

A thought suddenly pops into my head. I wonder if Amara would be open to a threesome with Phoenix, and if she wasn't would it be so bad then if I had an affair with Phoenix myself? It can't be that bad, surely, otherwise people wouldn't always be informing me that my anger towards Twix is unreasonable.

There's an uneasy vibe in the room now, thanks to Raven, but it's her flat so no-one says anything about it. Fortunately Amara breaks the tension by complimenting Phoenix's buzzcut.

'I love the feeling of it,' Phoenix goes, rubbing a hand over it.

'Ooh, soft,' Amara coos, encouraged by Phoenix to feel it.

I'm fucking all for that. I can feel the beginnings of a boner stirring in my dacks just from witnessing my girlfriend paw at this fascinating creature. I'm keen to touch her head myself, but Phoenix pulls away.

'Guys don't know how to do it very well. Only girls have the right touch.'

Fucking hell, okay.

Obviously sensing more drama, Alex changes the topic entirely to a new darkwave zine that she saw upstairs at Rocking Horse, which is the zine that Erina's put out, compiling most of it herself. Of course Alex would've noticed it: there's a big fucking cutesy anime-style bat drawing plastered across the cover. Got way too many bats in the flat, that girl. Her place is smothered in them.

'This one?' Xanthe says, rummaging under the coffee table, pulling out a copy.

Unsurprising an example can be found so quickly, really. We're a desert for locally-relevant subcultural content that we tend to suck it up like we're dehydrated for it when it's available, myself included. I got a copy of Erina's zine on pension day. I now expect to find one in practically every goth home in the city.

'What's in it?' Alex goes, her hand resting on Phoenix's knee for reassurance.

Xanthe hands it to Megs so she can keep reading the comic book.

'The usual shit,' Megs scoffs, flipping through the pages as black eyeliner streams down her cheeks. Whereas most girls try and avoid makeup running, there's a trend amongst us to spill liquid eyeliner into just under our bottom eyelid so that the resulting tears run it dramatically down our faces. 'There's crosswords, word-finders, out-of-date album releases, that sort of thing.'

Her and Raven skim through an article about the apparent current pros and cons of the local scene, counting how many times the word *goth* appears, and Xanthe and even Shadow, petty cunts that they are, laugh along with the ridicule.

I bear Erina no ill-will (why would I?) so find myself defending her against these cretins. 'Lay off her, you fiends. Fuck.'

With some little suspicion, Amara asks: 'Who's Erina?'

'Oh, some would-be journalist we all know,' I confess casually, as though to infer she's old news to all present, but Amara continues to eye me with that sly judgement girls get when they sense there's more to the story.

'Nearly forty times!' Raven announces, chuckling. 'Dead-set, she uses the word *goth* nearly forty times.'

She's having as much fun as Megs is, tearing into Erina's work. I already knew Megs hates Erina – she's never made any secret of that – but for some reason Raven's acting like she doesn't either. Her jealousy knows no bounds, I guess, but where was it back when me and Erina were casually seeing each other? And I wonder what she says about Amara behind my back?

'What else is there?' I ask Megs, keen to divert Amara's attention from the topic of Erina while careful at the same time not to defend her overly much. Megs pretty much likes to sardonically lump those of us who get along with Erina into one group that she calls 'Erina's Fan Club'.

'There's some photos taken at Midian,' Megs goes, holding up the zine to show us the cut and paste montage of faces.

I didn't go to that club, but evidently Xanthe did because she suddenly hisses: 'She stole my soul!'

That old nutshell, where some cunt pretends to be aligned with the beliefs of pre-modern cultures in order to appear more mysterious. Besides which, the poor photocopying job has rendered each face as unreadable as the next. Stole her fucking identity, more like.

Taime's little one starts reading from the zine over Megs' shoulder.

'*Eternal... darkness... has...*' she reads carefully, struggling to finish the sentence.

'*Spun*,' Megs says. 'Well done, Willow! You're a good reader!'

The little girl beams broadly.

'She learnt to read from the tombstones over the road at Toowong,' admits Taime proudly.

'Aww, so clever,' gushes Megs.

'Hopefully Blobby's just as smart,' Taime goes, patting her belly.

'Blobby?' I enquire.

'Name of the new baby for now,' says Taime. 'It's still in the first trimester, so the foetus looks like a blob on the ultrasound. So gross,' she laughs.

'Blobby's going to be a girl,' says Willow.

'You hope,' Taime smiles at her kid.

'You're such a good mum, Taime,' Xanthe says, but with that air of insincerity I've always hated about her.

'I just love being up the duff,' Taime grins. 'I could spend my whole life preggers. It's a great feeling.'

'So's what comes before it,' Raven goes, making a circle with the fingers of one hand and thrusting her index finger from the other through the gap, which gets a cackle out of the girls but makes Shadow blush. Poor cunt's not used to how dirty girls can be behind closed doors.

'You don't know what you're missing out on, girls,' smirks Taime playfully.

'And what precisely, pray tell, has this so-called Eternal Darkness spun, Willow?' wonders Raven, stroking the girl's hair.

'It's a poem,' Megs says when Willow shrugs. 'There's a whole bunch of em in the back.'

'Poems! Yes!' says Xanthe, clapping her hands like a little kid, instantly dropping her apparent displeasure at having had her photo taken. She'd have been too fucking wasted at the time to have even realised it was being taken, I bet. 'Read some poems,' she says excitedly.

The last thing we all need is bad goth poetry bringing the evening down, but Xanthe's childish glee cannot be suppressed. I find this deliberate insistence on appearing infantile tiring in my goth peers. But it's not just them, it's the fucking re-enactors, too, those fat, bearded cunts who seem to have latched onto our subculture and are starting to turn up to the clubs in droves. Child-men, the fucking lot of them, parodying themselves.

'The *Eternal Darkness* one's by Twix,' Megs reveals.

'Read the whole thing out,' I blurt rather too enthusiastically, which gets a grin out of Alex. 'I bet it's written in French.'

So Megs reads it out for us:

> *'When eternal darkness has spun*
> *An eternal web of lies*
> *I seek for solace but find none*
> *I seek for redemption*
> *But it evades me like a bat in the night skies.*
> *We all have our burdens to bear,*
> *Ye verily I do, too*
> *But when the eternal darkness has spun*
> *And my body has dried up every single –'*

She pauses. 'Um, the next word is *tear*, as in tear-drop, but he's tried rhyming it with *bear*.'

You fucking twat, Twix.

'Such a dork,' Raven goes, managing the impossible by shaking her head in disbelief while still drawing cobwebs at the corners of her eyes with a stubby eyeliner pencil.

'So how's it end?' asks Xanthe. 'It's really good so far.'

To her shameful discredit, Amara's of the same mind as Xanthe on the apparent worthiness of this drivel.

'It's fucking horrid, is what it is,' I laugh.

'It's art,' Xanthe spits, as if I wouldn't know what art is.

'Fucking bad goth poetry,' I mutter, but let Megs finish all the same.

> *'But when the eternal darkness has spun*
> *And my body has tried up every single tear*
> *Then I know I am finally...'*

Megs pauses for dramatic effect, then adds: '...*done.*'

'And thank fuck for that,' I go, which gets a chuckle out of both Megs and Raven.

'If you think you can do better,' challenges Xanthe, colder than a witch's titty in a brass bra, 'then let's hear it.'

'I wouldn't stoop to honour such a pathetic litmus test,' I retort. 'All bad goth poetry should be put to rest.'

I don't think the silly bitch has clued that I've just delivered exactly what she asked for. These cunts are as clueless as that fuckin Martin Bryant who now reckons he's not guilty of killing all those people down in Port Arthur. There's just no helping some people.

'You think you know everything, dontcha Dante?' Xanthe angrily counters.

'I think we both know that I know a lot more than you do, you know?'

She glowers at me like a furnace. 'Still trying to be super clever, huh?'

Alex jumps in the middle of this little spat: 'Like, what's the deal with people who answer rhetorical questions?'

'I know, right?' I go.

Megs has a chuckle but everyone else looks ill at ease. 'It's just a poem, everyone,' Megs goes. 'Take a chill pill, jeez.'

'Gotta laugh, though, hey?' says Alex nervously, digging her finger into her shoe to scratch at her foot.

Begrudgingly I concur. 'I suppose we do.'

It's funny, because though I'd never admit it out loud to this lot, deep down there's a part of me that misses the silly prick. We had some fun times, me and Twix, until he fucked it up. I wonder if that's what his poem's about?

Xanthe grumbles some shit about being sick of hearing me picking on Twix. 'He's paid for his crimes, so just move on already,' she says quietly, shaking her head and getting up to go to the shitter.

'Why's he called Twix?' says Phoenix so plainly that it's charming.

Alex snickers and goes: 'He does this thing with girls,' – and she holds up her thumb and pinkie in the classic surf grommet *hang loose* gesture – 'one for the pink and one for the stink. Talk about laugh, right?'

Her naivety cracks me up.

'Is that what he told you?' Raven chuckles.

Alex blushes. 'Yeah...'

'That's not it at all,' I snort, shaking my head, imagining Twix spinning his unique brand of bullshit to Alex.

'It's from when he got so shit-faced at Morticia's one night–' ('that used to be a club here,' Megs interjects) '–that he passed out on the floor of the toilets with his dacks down and did a turd that was so long and straight someone compared it to a Twix chocolate bar.'

'Two turds,' Megs corrects. 'There was a second one, don't forget.'

'And the name stuck?' Phoenix giggles.

Me and Raven nod. 'Like shit to a blanket,' I go.

'Remember T-Rex Tony got a photo of that?' Megs goes.

'Yeah, didn't Twix eventually get a hold of it and the negatives and burn em?' says Raven.

'Uh huh,' Megs nods slowly. 'But he doesn't know Tony gave me a copy. It's on the wall at home.'

Megs has a whole wall in her loungeroom of pics taken at clubs or picnics or whatever, all blu-tacked up in a massive montage. It's quite impressive. I stood back once and stared at the centre to see if it'd turn into one those Magic Eye piccies, but nearly gave myself a headache instead.

Xanthe's got a mug on her like someone's wiped shit under her nose. 'He's such a fucking closet misogynist,' she goes.

'Who, Jess? Tony?' asks Raven.

'Him, too,' Xanthe goes. 'A lot of blokes are,' she adds, flicking a look in my direction for a fraction of a second. She can fuck off with those snide insinuations for a start.

We finish getting ready and down the last of the pre-club drinks and head out, leaving Taime and her kid at Raven's flat, stampeding down the stairwells of the Prozac like a herd of elephants, making a ruckus as we go that's enough to wake the dead. Someone yells at us from upstairs – maybe it's Nel – but no-one gives a flying fuck.

The club's under the Alliance just up the road, who love hosting goth events on account of the owners are gay and understand the prejudices we face, so we're there in no time even with humouring Alex while she steps on every crack in the footpath, passing a small gang of skinheads on the way. They were further up the street but stopped to look at us as we trudged through Cathedral Square, probably put off saying anything to us due to Shadow's sheer size trailing after. He's a big fucker, that's for sure!

Once inside the club we grab more drinks and lose ourselves in the crowd. Xanthe can get fucked if she thinks I'm gonna mingle with her for the rest of the night, though she seems to feel the same way as she melds in with another group in the far corner of the room.

Megs and Shadow go join T-Rex Tony and some older goths at the pool tables. Megs clued me in on the way over that she finds all the fuss over Phoenix pretty silly. 'What's so special about being asexual anyway?' she'd asked me, whereupon I'd had to point out that Phoenix is androgynous. 'Whatevs,' she'd shrugged, screwing her nose up. Megs has always been dismissive of new experiences, having always essentially exhibited a fear of the big wide world. It's why she keeps a close-knit inner circle of friends whom she turns over like a farmer tilling earth as they wear their welcome thin, only to pick them up again a year or so later like they're besties and have never stopped being such. There's only so much to harvest from sowing old seeds. Why anyone would deliberately limit their capacity to learn from the experiences of others I'll never understand.

'My first time at a goth club,' Phoenix reveals.

'True shit?' I raise my eyebrows. I order up a drink for her on the house, but notice I've spent the last of my cash, so I ask Amara if she can get this one. She's unimpressed but gets the drink for Phoenix all the same, and one for her also. Leaves me out, though, as if to make a fucking point.

'What attracts you to this scene?' Phoenix asks.

'It's natural to be subcultural,' I reply, but of course a clever answer isn't what she's after. 'In truth, if I went somewhere else, like the Dome or City Rowers, there's a fair chance I'm gonna get my teeth kicked in. But here, no cunt cares how I'm dressed. And the music's a hundred fucking times better.'

'You swear a lot,' she remarks, the cheeky fuck.

'A lot of people with a mental illness do,' I go, but she's sceptical.

'I've got a friend who's got depression, moving into Alex's place,' she reveals. 'She never swears.'

'You swear on that?' I crack, getting annoyed by our convo. I like Phoenix, and I want to continue to like her, so this tete-a-tete needs to finish now. I turn to Alex. 'Gettin a new boarder, ay?'

'No, I've gotta move somewhere cheaper,' she goes. 'I basically can't afford the rent there anymore without a job. Phoenix's friends are, like, taking over my lease. It sucks big time.'

'Why don't you move in with Raven?' I suggest, spreading my hands as if I've just solved everything. 'She's got a room empty. Cheap. With all your mates at the Prozac.'

'I thought of it, actually,' says Alex. 'But that building is too chaotic. Like, the whole vibe of it. It'd exacerbate my OCD.'

I shrug. 'Just seems like it'd solve a whole lot of problems, is all.'

'I know, and it would in a way, but you know...'

The Prozac definitely has its own energy, true enough, but no I don't know. I suspect Alex is more messed up than she realises. I need to investigate this further.

'How about we catch up for lunch next week?' I offer. 'After my pay-day. I'll take you to Govinda's, next to the Elizabeth Arcade. You'll like it, as long as you don't mind vegetarian.'

She smiles. 'Sounds good.'

'You're welcome to come, too, Phoenix,' I go.

'What about me?' Amara sniffs.

Fucking hell, forgot about her.

'You're invited by default,' I go, trying to sound put out that she'd suggest otherwise. 'Goes without saying.'

The girls exchange meaningful looks. Nothing gets by them.

THE SLOW DECLINE

I found out that Lisa's gone to Melbourne to stay with the rents until her next court appearance comes up. She's already had one, the week after the bust, and she pleaded not guilty, so now it's been adjourned until November.

Long story short, the sweat-shop in West End basically got busted not because it was a sweat-shop but because the bloke wasn't a registered business or, like, paying his taxes or anything like that. He was shonky as, apparently. He'd been flying under the radar for ages, and the worst bit is that Lisa the stupid bitch was in cahoots with him after she went and, like, bought into his business not long after we'd first gone there. So the police nabbed her, too. While that's not exactly worthy of a prison sentence, she's, like, made herself culpable and apparently word is that the judge might want to make an example of Lisa given similar crimes recently by others.

I feel sick to my stomach thinking about it.

I'm meant to be checking out new places to live, somewhere much cheaper, but between the mundane family drama and being jobless I'm neither motivated nor cashed up enough to move house. The latter predicament is, like, mostly my fault, though. The shops are starting to stock up on pre-Halloween decorations and there's a shit-tonne of stuff with bats on them. I've noticed the Gillingham Street flat's basically starting to look a bit like a batcave with, like, all the bat prints or stuff with bat wings on them. Still, I couldn't resist once again draining my bank account to stock up on more stuff. Made me feel good at the time, and to be honest I like being surrounded by it all. There's something about having it that makes me feel safe, period.

As for breaking my lease to get out and find somewhere cheaper, I spoke to the landlord about it and he turned out to be a right so and so, but Phoenix wants to take over my lease as soon as I'm ready to move out, thank Gaia.

I hadn't seen Phoenix much since we met on the train after my I lost my job at the solicitor's (technically, it was after I got kicked out of the barbecue, but it amounts to the same thing), but Phoenix has been checking in on me lately and making sure I'm okay. Abi's been a bit unreliable as a friend. I think she's taking too many poppers, like she's just swapped it for opiates. I worry about her but I'm in no condition to start looking out for others.

Right now I'm just waiting for Dante to swing round and pick me up. We're gonna head out for lunch, a sort of pick-me-up treat. I really just want to, like, stay in bed and hide under the sheets, to be honest, but Dante insists on getting me out of the house to, like, break my stagnant routine. And in order to make me even more compelled to do it, he's coming all the way over from Spring Hill to get me before heading back into town with me. He wanted to change it to a place in West End, but I can't face that suburb again, so he's agreed to take me to Govinda's in the city instead.

The phone rings again, and again the caller ID tells me it's Mama. I went and got it after I'd realised that's what the dating agency people were using to screen clients. Mama's been leaving messages on my machine for the last two days and it's starting to fill up. I guess I should answer it at last.

'Alex? Oh, Alexandra, at last. Why haven't you returned my calls?'

'I'm depressed, Mama. You know that.'

'Piffle,' she scoffs down the line, and I can just imagine the disdain in her expression. 'You just need to pull your socks–'

'For the love of Gaia, Mama!' I snap. 'Please don't say it. Geez.'

When Dante gets here I tell him about the phone call, and how even my own mother likes to stigmatise mental illness.

'Welcome to my world,' he crows. 'They can't see your illness, so they're dismissive of it.'

Of course, I'm preaching to the converted here. It totally slipped my mind that Dante's, like, been to a mental hospital recently!

I'm like: 'That's so true! If I had a bandage around my head, maybe that'd make a bloody difference.'

I was trying to make just jokes, but it comes out really full on.

'Hey, hey, silly,' Dante coos tenderly. 'Don't beat yourself up over it. It's not you; it's them.'

It's good to hear it... more often than not I'm used to hearing that I'm to blame for all the crap that happens around me.

'On the other hand,' he says, 'it's also up to you to make sure you don't hug the condition.'

'What's that supposed to mean, then?'

'Don't allow your illness free reign,' he says. 'Don't pass your own failings off as the work of your condition. That's all.'

It's something to think about, I suppose. Like, where do I end and the illness starts?

'Oi, that little friend of yours the other day, the androgynous one,' he says with a small grin.

'Phoenix?'

'That's the one,' he says. 'Does he or she have a significant other?'

'It's not he or she, it's they,' I say flatly. 'And more's the point, *you* have a significant other. Period.'

I like Amara, she's basically done no wrong by me, so I find this line of inquiry highly fucking offensive.

'Doing yourself some damage there, my dear,' he says, indicating that I'm picking repetitively at the skin on my foot, which has now become, like, an open wound. 'Saw something similar in the mental hospital, except he got his from walking too much.'

I'm ashamed that he's noticed, but then again he's got scars up and down his arms from self-harm. Maybe he of all people gets it.

'I can't help it,' I admit. 'And no, I'm not *hugging my condition*, as you put it. It's, like, my OCD.'

When I'd first started picking at my foot, I'd thought it must have been an allergy, especially because I'd, like, do it without realising. I could be watching TV or eating my tea and basically my hand would unconsciously stray to my foot and start picking at the skin until it bled. Now it's a cavern of a wound, but I can't seem to leave it alone. The worse it gets the more I need to run my fingers across it and try and even out the rough edges by picking at it.

Between my anxiety and this I've developed depression, and all combined together it convinced my GP to refer me to a specialist who in turn thought I should, like, be on special welfare for it.

'They're looking into whether or not I'm eligible for the Disability Support Pension,' I confess to Dante.

'You might have to go on it, at this rate,' he says.

'I don't want to. Period.'

'You may have no choice,' he insists.

That's what scares me most, is that I'll have no say in my own health, and be, like, forced to accept my fragility and go onto DSP. That I might need it, I can accept, but only on my own terms. I've always advocated free choice – not in that ridiculous and adolescent way that Dante insists on, where he basically does whatever he wants and fuck the consequences. I advocate free will through responsible and measured decision making. We're all free to be informed and act on that for the betterment of society as a whole. But lately I'm feeling robbed of my choice, my decision for my own welfare. Apparently I'm, like, no longer capable to choose wisely for myself and act on it.

Dante says I'm being silly.

'You're looking at it all wrong,' he says. 'You've still got choice. Right now, it's follow what those cunts think you need, or find your own path. Don't want the disability pension? Tell them to go fuck themselves. It's simple. But if you choose to govern independently, which let's face it, you have been, then whatever happens to you financially is on you. Free choice: not necessarily the wisest one.'

'I'm just sick of being sick,' I complain, burying my head in my arms on the table.

'All the DSP is, Alex, is a way for you to take the time out you obviously need. You push against the grain on this one, and you risk a full on breakdown.'

He's talking sense, but I hear a slightly smarmy tone in his voice, like he's lecturing me on the ways of the world. In some ways, he's a lot like my sister, and I'm sick of that, too. In a way I envy how he, like, doesn't seem to care about the consequences of anything, but I don't know how he can be like that.

'You know how I wear these old suits?'

I nod, not even remotely interested in this tangent. Especially since it once again, surprise surprise, centres solely on him.

'Most people think it's because I'm into Nick Cave in a big way, but that's not actually why. Years ago the DSS ran a skills course through an employment agency to get the terminally unemployable of Stanthorpe up to scratch for job interviews. Mostly resumé building and job interview preparations and role-playing. That sort of crap. None of us were particularly interested in it, but having been told it was the course or suspension of payments we all dutifully turned up for our four days a week over a two week period at the local motor inn where they held the course in the crappy restaurant area.

'There was this one cunt called Rick, or fucking Slick Rick as I came to call dumb the cunt. He was a bad egg, in the most half-arsed ways possible, but he still made an impression on the rest of us. He was impolite to the dickhead running the course, always turned up late, wouldn't get involved in the group activities, proclaimed to be a write off job-wise. Fuck, he even wore denim jeans and a plain white t-shirt, and had scruffy hair that was slightly too long on top which he'd slick back. He looked like Johnny Depp in that movie *Cry Baby*. It did seem odd to be styling oneself after the greaser look when no-one else was doing it, but who was I to judge the cunt's style? Well, we all thought this guy was gonna be the first to get kicked off the course'

At the mention of Johnny Depp I start paying more attention to his long-winded tale. I want to hear more about this guy he knew on the course, if only to momentarily distract me from the harsh realities of life.

'Was he? The first to get kicked off?'

Dante shakes his head. 'Nah, on the last day of the first week, the guy running the course started really getting the shits with Slick Rick and told him to wait behind after class for a fucking talking to. My suggestion to Rick was to tell the cunt to go fuck himself, but Rick was a bit worried they'd cut his dole money off, so he stayed back. First day back the following week this new guy walks into the room, except he's not new at all. It's Slick Rick. Gone is the greaser look, ludicrously replaced by a suit and haircut and a fucking briefcase of all things! What the fuck was he going to do with a briefcase on that stupid course? Every day we got a pencil and a sheet of paper to take notes, and every day those sheets got handed back empty. A briefcase was about as useful as tits on a bull.'

'Sounds like it was a set up.'

Dante slaps his hands together and points at me, like an imitation of an arvo game-show host. 'Bingo! The cunt was a fucking plant. An actor paid for by the Government to sit in with us and be the rebel, just so's they could turn the cunt around as a shining example of what they wanted us to be. It was so fucking obvious Blind Freddie could have seen it, but do you think any of those other dipshits on the course could see it? I called the cunt out straight away, asking him how much he was getting paid for the charade. Even his reaction to me was the complete opposite of what it would've been the week prior. In his new, prissy voice, he went *it's best to follow the standards set to us by those who have the skills and information to secure work.* Such textbook horseshit, but no-one else recognised it for what it was.'

Knowing Dante, I can basically already imagine his response to all this. 'So you went and got a suit too, huh?'

'You betcha. Fucking raced down to the op-shop after the course and grabbed one off the shelf. The old biddies were fussing over me because to them those dusty old suits were the fashion in their day. I turned up to the course the next day looking like a poor man's Slick Rick in my shitty threads, but instead of seeing the funny side to it everyone just got confused and thought that I was in on the deception, another Government stooge. Overnight the cunts had finally come around to my way of thinking, but because they were clearly a few fucking bricks short of a barbecue it was going to take them another day and a night to realise that I was now only taking the piss. The dickhead running the course got it, though, and was pissed off with me. But what could he do?'

'You're lucky.'

'Not really,' he says, having paused to allow me to think that was the end of the story. Loves a grand finale, this one. 'The employment agency cunt went back to Social Security and made up all this bullshit about me stealing wine from the place we were doing the course in, and threatening the other attendees. That last bit was mostly true, of course, since I got the shits with them not realising the suit was a joke and I threatened to kill Slick Rick on our lunchbreak up the street. I thought if we were out for lunch it didn't constitute as being part of the course and therefore not punishable, but turns out I was wrong about that. Got cut off the dole for about three months before I could reapply. They were lean times, but at least I had the suit.'

'Sooo, what's the moral of the story?' I ask.

He looks at me like I'm speaking an alien language. 'You serious? Those cunts wanted me to toe the line, but I went my own way instead. That's what I'm saying. Don't be like those other wankers and believe the bullshit.'

Now he's completely contradicting his own advice, for pity's sake. On the one hand he's telling me to go along with being put on a disability pension, on the other he's telling me to, like, do whatever I want even if that means I don't want to go on the disability pension.

'So what happened to those other wankers?'

Dante shrugs. 'Turned into sheep. Made the papers holding their certificates of completion, and two of them were pictured grinning from ear to ear like complete cocks because they'd landed shit jobs at the local supermarket.'

'So they got work and you got cut off the dole?'

'That's not the point,' he says irritably. 'I was at least happy with my lot in life, not moping around like a fucking loser because I had a crappy job or because the DSS were forcing me to do shit I didn't want to do.'

'Like go on DSP?' I retort.

It takes him aback, and he loses some of his fire. 'I didn't mean that. I just mean you gotta be happy.'

Now I'm starting to understand that not giving a damn about the consequences isn't a path to happiness. Turns out there's nothing to envy about how Dante approaches life. He's a kind of train wreck, when I really think about it, except he, like, keeps walking away from the crash and basically won't take responsibility for the damage.

'You know what?' I say, pretty much feeling over his company. 'I'm not in the mood for going out anymore, period.'

He looks amused; clearly knows I'm annoyed. Who cares?

'You want me to go?' he says.

It's a puerile challenge, like he gets off on being forthright and watching others squirm with societal niceties. It's a button I didn't need pushing.

'Yes. I fucking well do need you to go.'

He doesn't say another word, just gets up and goes.

My hands are, like, shaking and the tightness in my chest makes it hard to breathe again. I rush to the door, leaving a small trail of blood droplets from my foot, and throw the deadbolt, hoiking the curtains closed over the windows.

I picture my old friends, my Melbourne friends, their faces painted luridly on the walls, basically taunting me and laughing, saying I've fucked up by moving up here. They flicker like projections, their faces distorted by the corners and the door jamb, stretching over the curve of my couch. It's a hideous manifestation, and I feel myself shrinking before it, feeling crushed by the knowledge that I've, like, become a joke to my so-called mates, and not just the ones down south either. I can imagine Dante running out to snigger and gossip about how I'm a wreck and will be 'pensioned off', as he prefers to call it.

I DON'T CARE

Bernie's friend Rupert died the other day.

Actually, he committed suicide. Dante said that Rupert had severe depression and was going through a pretty bad bout of it recently after he got news that his ex-wife was remarrying. Apparently she supported him financially as well as being on a disability pension, but she was going to have to stop doing that at the request of the new husband.

I saw Bernie cry. So did Dante, and it really upset him to see Bernie like that. Bernie went up to Dante and cried on his shoulder.

I was so proud of Dante at that moment. He's been really trying lately to improve himself. Dead-set.

Nel was around to see it, too. Her toilet wouldn't flush so she came down to see if Bernie could come and take a look at it for her, which he said he would do once him and Dante got back from the funeral for Rupert.

When they were gone, Nel turned to me and said: 'Use yer fucken brain, Raven. He's got a girlfriend now.'

MCKAY PART 3

On my way down to my psych appointment I run into Megs coming up the street and convince her to delay her visit to the Prozac and come with me instead.

'Is it okay, though?' she's keen to know. 'I mean, wouldn't your psychiatrist get angry?'

'Nah, it's alright,' I go. 'I'm the one paying for the session, after all.'

That's not true, of course. The fucking taxpayer's footing the bill for this. Fuck the cunts, too. Always regarding me with such disdain from their lofty heights. Serves the cunts right.

McKay's surprised I've brought a friend with me but composes himself quickly enough, rather pleased by Megs' presence. Turns out he thinks she's Amara.

'Finally, I can put a face to the name,' he goes, which gives Megs the impression that she comes up a lot in my therapy sessions.

After I've clued McKay into who Megs really is, the cheeky cunt gets a bit flirty with her, if I'm not mistaken. It occurs to me to jokingly remind him that he's a married man with kids and all, but he might take it the wrong way and get stroppy.

'And how's the Divine Comedy of Dante?' he starts off, with more enthusiasm than usual. Yep, he's definitely showing off in front of Megs.

I remember one time me and Nicola were making out on a grave at Toowong Cemetery and that dumb cunt Tim yelled out: 'I didn't know you were so famous, Dante! Or funny!' He'd found a plaque in front of the biggest monument on the hill where it lorded over all the other graves. According to the writing on it some cunt called Griffith was the first guy buried at Toowong, buried right under our feet, but more than that he'd also translated *The Divine Comedy* nearly a hundred years ago and got it published by UQ, no less! Darcey, Tim's girlfriend, had been impressed as fuck by that.

'Well, it's definitely pretty funny,' I begin with little trace of irony, explaining how I'm going through my phase of hating humanity on a really base level, something I seem to do at least once a year. 'Present company excluded of course,' I quickly add.

'Good to hear,' goes Megs, mock-offended, which gets a flirtatious chuckle out of McKay.

'The thing is, and this is probably the worst bit,' I continue, 'is that I can smell the cunts. Really, literally, smell them. Like it's their body-odour and unwashed clothes, but I know it's not. It's actually their essence, their fucking souls, oozing out of them into the air. Like a rotting pit of souls.'

Fucking melodramatic, I know, but it's how I feel. More than that, it's what I can actually smell: an awful pong clinging to everything – to buildings, buses, sunshine – that I attribute to coming off humanity itself.

'It's like a pheromone thing or something, being exuded so as to repel me,' I conclude, and McKay misunderstands, thinking this time I'm specifically talking about romantic attraction and my lack of interest in it.

'Well, it's normal not to always be *on* as it were, looking for a mate,' he goes. 'Sometimes other needs, such as the need for shelter, or sustenance, will over-ride the urge to seek out a mate, especially if we're not well. Our brain will prioritise our needs and create the illusion that some needs are less desirable so that we don't go after those first and neglect the most pressing ones.'

'I'm not talking about fucking sex,' I snap. 'The great stinking cesspool of humanity is what I'm on about!'

He's annoyed by my irritability, I can tell, but tries not to show it. He's got this face he pulls when he's trying to be more professional than professional, where he squints his eyes and smiles tightly. With Megs present I'm sure he's even more determined than usual to retain this facade.

'Oh, okay,' he nods. 'We've talked about this before, haven't we?'

'Yeah, last year,' I go, and he almost goes to roll his eyes as if to say that's a long fucking way back to hafta recall.

'Yep, yep, okay,' he nods some more. 'Maybe this is a good time to hermatise, refocus your energies.'

'Normally I'd try and hermatise when my libido's going crazy,' I remind him, as sometimes happens to me. Can't walk down the street without falling in love with every second girl I see. 'Now I just look around and see walking bags of meaningless pus and shit, toxins oozing from their pores and stinking up the air.'

'Jesus,' giggles Megs. 'Tell us what you really think.'

It puts McKay in mind of a joke. 'How do you make two kilos of fat attractive?'

I shrug.

'Put a nipple on it.'

I smile. 'Okay, I'll pay that.'

Megs goes: 'Pain in the neck, literally,' and shakes her voluminous boobs from side to side, which definitely grabs McKay's attention.

'I bet,' he says, struggling to tear his eyes away from her chest.

'I've been getting that vision again,' I go, ignoring whatever the fuck is happening between these two.

'The flood one?' he asks.

'The very one,' I confirm, describing again how I'm standing on top of a mountain while a great flood slowly rolls across the earth and drowns the Land of Oz. 'I don't know, but I've got this heavy feeling in my chest. Like it's all about to go bad soon.'

Megs is uncomfortable, and stares at the bookshelf to her right. As goths we're used to flowery, purple-prose inspired musings, but I've come to realise that this end-of-the-world talk is a bit too dark for some. There's nothing visceral or anything about what I say, it's more the quiet certainty I have when I say these things. It's The Inferno stewing away silently in the background, like the hiss of radio static in my ear.

Outside McKay's office Megs wonders aloud why I didn't bring up Rupert's suicide and funeral. 'It seems to me like those are things you might talk to a psychiatrist about.'

She's got a point, I suppose, and she goes on about how she thinks that Rupert's suicide is probably affecting my mood. As much as that might sound like a reasonable assumption, the truth is that his suicide sort of excites me. It's like a confirmation of how shit this world really is, like maybe he could smell it too and knew that death was the only way to avoid the smell. I see his death less as a tragic failing on his emotional state and more like he woke up and smelt the truth.

Megs is worried. She's got that look on her face people around me get when they think I'm losing my grip on reality. It's like a mixture of fear *for* me and fear *of* me. It's a look I don't understand, because whatever it is that she's feeling in this moment I don't think I've ever felt myself. McKay says that because of my Borderline Personality Disorder I live in a very black and white world, a strict mentality where I quickly judge and divide according to a set of core principles that don't require an emotional objective. Thus I don't ever use that look that Megs' currently got going on. I know whether I feel sorry for someone or not. I know whether I fear them or not. I don't flit between the two like a schizophrenic hummingbird.

Outside on the street Megs goes: 'That was random and quite interesting, though! The way you talked in there made me think you should study psychology.'

For fuck's sake. Psychology: the new Art History for Uni cunts unsure what they want to major in. Easy to get into, easy to swap for something later.

'Can't afford it,' I offer instead, not really wanting to offend poor Megs who doesn't know any better.

'I was impressed that your psychiatrist said *nipple*, by the way,' Megs laughs.

I notice that her boobs, which are about an E cup, are stuffed into her dress. They jiggle as we run across the road.

'Occasionally he even says *fuck*,' I reveal, much to her amusement. Old hat to me.

Twix has always liked Megs' tits. The bigger the better, he always reckoned, even when I'd tried telling him that he's like a kid picking a lucky dip at the school fete, automatically going for the biggest parcel on the assumption that it'd contain more value than its smaller counterparts.

The other day Abi confided in me that Alex's new bestie, Phoenix, had her tits cut off for no real reason except because she refuses to be defined by a society she doesn't fit into anymore. Of course, I know she's an androgyne, that was made clear the other night at Raven's place, but I hadn't considered that it was an act of defiance, that it could strip oneself of their *actual* identity, their gender identity notwithstanding. I'd understood clearly enough that we were alike by definition of identity fluidity. But by declaring no gender, Phoenix has sidestepped every conceivable expectation society could have. No need to get married: no gender. No need to buy a house: not getting married, because no gender. No need to have kids: no gender. No need to ever conform again to any preconceived notion of humanity as it currently stands.

I wonder if Phoenix ever smells the collective rot of souls?

'Whatcha thinkin?' Megs goes as we head into the Prozac.

'That fucking flood,' I reply. 'Taking it's sweet fucking time getting here, isn't it?'

TWIX AND THE DOGMEN

In order to move ol Twixxie on from shitty security work, I've come to my old stomping ground in the Valley to meet a bloke called Dave Ross at the Osbourne Hotel, home of the old Painter and Dockers, the infamous union and not the band that named themselves after it.

Dave runs a Dogmen course. Essentially, Doggers are responsible for slings on loads and directing cranes on construction sites, and it pays a fuck of a lot better than security, that's for sure.

I ran into some trouble with NiteWorks recently when I got a bit jack of the way they were treating us guards out on the field, jerking us around on timetables and payslips. I wasn't the only one getting jack of it, but ol Twixxie here's the only one with the guts to speak up about it. Turns out that's not such a great idea, though.

NiteWorks manager Gary started cutting my shifts after I had a whinge to one of the duty guards from Cubby Security, sending me out to sites in the middle of woop woop, Beaudesert and places like that, only to find out another guard was scheduled for that shift. So of course when I finally got jack of that shit I got onto the union about it, and they were more than interested because NiteWorks has been flying under their radar all this time. So I spilled the beans on how we didn't get paid super, how our pay didn't match the description of either a subcontractor or a wage. Told em the fucking lot! The union lady, Rhonda, was over the bloody moon, going on about how she not only hates NiteWorks but Gary especially.

Next thing I know, though, I'm hearing from Daryl – this other guard from NiteWorks – that Gary's got wind of everything I've told the union. Basically, the blokes at Cubby and Rhonda at the union must've checked in with him and divulged everything I'd told them, because Gary was fuming apparently. He kept a lid on it when he confronted me, though, calmly informing me that my hours are going to get cut back pretty harshly for a while because there's hardly any work going around.

Yeah, right! Such bullshit!

Later on I scored a shift with some of the other boys, Daryl and Pieter and that, and when I told them what was going on Pieter had a right fucking laugh at my expense.

'Didn't it click that if Gary's been off the union's radar then the bitch at the union couldn't hate him?' Pieter he'd said. 'Dude, Rhonda more than knows about him: they used to fuck. She's just never had any dirt on him until now.'

Daryl had nearly laughed his arse off. 'Served up on a silver platter by one Travis Haynes.'

So as soon as I saw the ad in the paper for this Dogman course, all expenses paid, I was straight onto it.

This Dave Ross seems pretty decent, and there's seven other lads of different ages come to the Osbourne to meet him as well. He hands each of us a fifty buck note and tells us to head to the bar and grab a beer. Keep the change. I'm thrown for a bit, because that's a lot of sodding money to just throw around. Some of the other blokes are grinning their heads off. I know what they're thinking: if this Dave Ross joker's throwing it around like it was nothing, then this is a good game to be in. You little beauty!

We all get back to the table, some of us with two glasses each, and Dave puts another two hundred dollars on the centre of the table and tells us that's for more drinks as the day goes on. Fark, we're gonna be plastered before the end!

'This is the raddest interview I've ever been to,' laughs a lad.

'That's how we want it,' grins Dave. He looks at us each in turn. 'If you're here, I'm guessing you've all got dead-end jobs or maybe don't even have one yet. But we're going to fix that up tonight, boys.'

There's a round of *whoops* and *hell-yeahs*. I opt for the latter.

Dave spreads some paperwork out on the table, separating them into piles. He slides his drink out of the way. He's got the photocopies of our driver's licences or 18+ cards that we had to mail into him last week. They start soaking up the condensation left behind by his beer glass.

'I hope I've learnt you all by name now,' he jibes, flashing one of the photocopied ID's.

Not mine, thank Christ. I look like I fell out of the ugly tree and smashed my nose against every branch on the way down. Every photo ID I've ever had always makes me look bloated.

'Right. Rigging and dogging. Good money there,' goes Dave, and believe us, Dave, there's not a one of us that doubts it. I pocketed the change from my beer, and hope to score my next round from the cash on the table. Feels pretty good having forty bucks in my pocket. 'So, we offer a course that goes for eleven days, and by the end of it you'll get five licences that you need to start in the industry, including your High Risk card. It's all in there, boys, and won't cost you a cent.'

That's why we're all here, really. We're getting this for nix. I know I certainly couldn't afford this course.

'Queensland's economy is outstripping the rest of Australia right now,' explains Dave, 'and if you hear otherwise, take it from me, it's straight up bullshit. Right now,' and he jabs a finger onto the tabletop for emphasis, 'we're poised for a construction boom. And you fellas are gettin in at the right time. A few years from now you're going to have so much work you won't know what to do with it.'

I've got a warm feeling, and it ain't the beer. I can see my future getting a little brighter. If Brisbane's gonna shake off its winter coat and stretch in the sun, then dammit I want in on that.

Dave hands us some paperwork, and we're all gabbing on about who's best to work for and what sites we can try and get onto. Dave explains that we're pretty lucky the course is Government subsidised, otherwise we'd be shelling out about five grand each for all these licenses. I know I'm grateful: I don't have that kind of money. Not working as a frigging security guard, that's for sure.

There's a bit in the forms where we need three signatures from people we've known for more than five years.

'Right, for that bit, just write three as best you can,' says Dave, draining his glass dry. 'Don't make them look like each other, either. Here, use a different colour pen, too.' He tosses his pen across to us.

Some of the other lads seem hesitant about forging signatures, and the bloke next to me has written down his three signatures but they all look exactly the same. He's just changed the names. I suggest to a couple of the other lads that we swap forms to do the signatures, so the handwriting looks way different. That'd be what Dante would do if he was in my shoes. Clearly his shifty ways have rubbed off on me.

'That's the spirit,' winks Dave, going to the bar for another round.

'This is a bit fucking dodge, but,' one of the others whispers. His blonde goatee dips into the head of his beer when he stoops his head down to hide how hinky he's being.

'Yeah, but it's free, so,' I shrug.

'Mate,' goes the first guy with the goatee, jabbing a thumb towards the bar. 'This bloke is getting five grand a pop for each of us from the government. He doesn't give a fuck. He's rolling in it.'

'Ten grand? Holy shit.'

Blonde Goatee nods wisely at us all. A small, dark-skinned bloke to my left gets real jittery, and starts murmuring about how he's not so sure about all this.

'Fuck man, if the ACCC or some shit got onto this,' chuckles this skinny lad with a stupid looking Celtic tattoo on his neck, which has become all the rage now.

'Yeah well, they fucking won't, will they?' growls Goatee at Celtic. His eyes blaze with challenge.

'Chill, dude,' says the tattooed spaz. 'Just havin a laugh, you cunt.'

'This isn't good,' the little dark-skinned bloke is saying, shaking his head.

'Shut the fuck up and just enjoy your beer, mate,' hisses one of the other blokes.

'It'll be fine,' I say to the little joker. 'Dave's done this a hundred times, I'm sure. He knows what he's doing.'

But we can't squash his growing paranoia, and when Dave gets back to the table with another pint each for all of us, the little joker pipes up and tells Dave he's had a change of heart. Thank fuck he doesn't spill that what we've been whispering about.

Dave looks well disappointed, and why wouldn't he? That's ten grand down the drain for him, and he probably could've easily had some other geezer fill this bloke's place instead. The little joker makes some lame excuse about an old injury and that he's a hundred percent sure that construction isn't his field. Dave tries reasoning with him, but the little joker says he already got an offer to go work with his brother and leaves, waving hooroo to the rest of us, though none of us reciprocate. The whole time this was going on the lad with the blonde goatee was death-staring the little bastard to make him keep his trap shut about our private conversation.

Despite the loss, Dave keeps the spirits up. When the barmaid brings out a basket of steaming hot garlic bread for us to share, Dave picks out some parsley from it and holds it up.

'What's the difference between a nice, juicy pussy and parsley? No-one eats the parsley.' We all have a laugh as he throws the little tuft of green over his shoulder, but it lands on the chest of this bloke walking by with his mates, who stops and gets agro with us.

'Throw your fucking shit at me, mate?'

'Sorry, matey,' says Dave sincerely 'Didn't see ya there, ay. My mistake.'

Bugger me, the bloke's not having it, though.

'Nah mate, no fucking mistake,' he snarls at Dave, his eyes like embers boring into him. 'You're a fucking smart cunt showing off to your pussy mates, aren't ya?'

Blonde Goatee goes to him: 'Pull ya fucking head in, mate. Man said he was sorry, what more do you want?'

The other bloke's buddies start to circle around, so a few of us get up from our table to square up against them, including me. It was a sodding mistake, as Dave says. He didn't know they were gonna be walking behind him.

'Youse lot wanna fuckin go?' demands this skinny little prick with crazy eyes.

'Oi, oi, oi!' calls the barwench. 'Take it outside, you lot!' No-one pays her any attention.

The Celtic Tattoo lad and Blonde Goatee inch around the table. Goatee's eyes blazing like hell. 'C'mon cunts, right fucking here,' sneers the Celtic lad to our aggressors. He and Goatee have set aside their differences in the face of a common enemy, as blokes are wont to do in a pub brawl.

'I'm gonna smash your fucken heads in,' the skinny lad with the crazy eyes goes.

Just then this new bloke comes through the door, huffing a bit like he's been running, and sees what's happening. He runs over to join his mates against us, but he sees Dave and starts laughing.

'Davo, ya mad bastard! Long time, man,' and he pushes past his hinky mates and gets Dave into a powerful handshake, slapping each other hard on the shoulder like they were packing stolen meat into a truck.

'Fuck, Bazza, I thought you went north, Cairns way?' says Dave, grinning at this Bazza bloke and dismissing the entire rumble that was about to go down. The rest of us stand around confused as shit, still looking at one another with hostility but now wondering what we're meant to do.

'Yeah mate, I did, made a fucking mint, too,' enthuses Bazza. 'Back now, but. Brisbane's gonna boom soon, mate.' He turns to the other blokes across from us. 'It's awright, fellas. This is Davo, old mate ov mine. He got me inta the game.'

The skinny prick with the crazy eyes in his crew is still steamin though, so Bazza has to tell him again.

'Oi, KK, cool yer fuckin jets. Davo's awright. And if he's awright, so's his crew.'

They all ease off, including this KK prick, so we shake the tension from our shoulders. Turns out Bazza and Dave started construction together a few years ago, and that's how they got into rigging. Dave had found a scheme the government were trialling and he dragged a whole heap of mates into it, setting them up with jobs and getting the idea to pursue this agency racket he now has going on.

To settle the earlier conflict once and for all, Dave snatches the two hundred bucks from our table that he had set aside for us, and shouts the other lads a round.

'Oi, Suzy!' he calls over to the barmaid. 'A round on these blokes over here,' he says, pointing to where the other lads sit themselves. 'Top blokes, this lot.'

We don't mind, actually. Dave seems like a top bloke himself, and the other lads are chuffed when he shouts them. We even get chatting with some of them and it turns out they all work with Bazza on another construction gig. They've sussed we're getting our licences for nix through Dave, but they don't seem to care. Maybe Bazza has a similar scheme going and they got into the industry that way, too?

We're throwing back the piss and my head starts to get groggy. I'm in need of a piss badly, so I go through to the loo and point the old fella at the porcelain. I'm thinking about this scam that Dave's got going on with the subsidies, and start doing the math, calculating that if the little joker hadn't run off scared then Dave would be pulling in forty grand just for tonight's session alone. One of Bazza's blokes told me that Dave goes around the whole of Brisbane recruiting, and that he can only go to the same area once a month. I don't know where else he goes, but if does about ten different suburbs on average, from Beenleigh to Caboolture, Ipswich to Cleveland, he could easily pull in four hundred thousand bucks monthly off this hinky scam. And if the industry's about to boom, as Bazza reckons, more and more men are going to be needed. Dave's sitting on a sodding gold mine here!

Back at the tables everyone's in full convo mode. Business has concluded, and Dave's got all the papers tucked away in his satchel, trying to get a signal over by the door for his mobile phone. Now he's just doling out the dosh; the piss flows freely. Everyone's having a blast; even Blonde Goatee and Celtic Tattoo are getting along like old mates and having a laugh with KK. I'm going along with it all, too, but I'm watching Dave and thinking about his scam. I have an idea forming, and I'm feeling a bit sick about getting the ball rolling on it. At one point Dave catches me watching him, and leans over.

'You alright, Trav? You look a bit green around the gills, mate.'

'Oh yeah, no worries,' I go, affecting a smile. 'Booze just going to my head, I think.'

He laughs heartily. 'Fuckin lightweight.' He gives me a slap on the knee and resumes his convo with Bazza.

The arvo wears on. We're all right royally pissed now, and start heading home. Dave tells us that once the security checks have been done on us and cleared, he'll let us know that we're officially accepted into the course. Unfortunately, he says, the checks are Government run so he has no control over them. I've got no worries there, as I'm a security guard, so my checks are all good.

Dave seems to want to stick around in the Osbourne with Bazza, so I ask him if there's any time he and I can catch up privately in the next day or so and talk. He gets pretty curious about this.

'Yeah, sure, buddy,' he says. 'What's on your mind?'

'Not here,' I tell him, shifting my eyes slightly to indicate I didn't want to talk in front of his mates.

He frowns and smacks his lips, straightening up a bit. He drops his voice.

'Everything all okay, Travis?'

'Yeah, Dave.' I swallow hard. I crack my knuckles just so I can try and hide the shaking in my hands. 'I think I might have a bit of a business opportunity, is all.'

He actually smiles slyly, almost like he can read my mind.

I shake my head to try and throw him off the scent. 'No big deal or anything,' I say. My palms are clammy now.

'Sure, buddy, we can talk now if you want?'

I nod.

'Oi, Baz,' he says. Bazza turns to him, too sloshed to focus without effort. 'Baz, mate. I'm off. Gonna run the young fella home.'

Bazza leans to one side, squinting suspiciously at me through beer goggles. 'Oh yeah, no probs, Davo. Catcha later, mate.'

They slap each other's backs, then Dave steers me outside to where his ute's parked. He's in good spirits, telling me about this one time he and Bazza worked on a house, remodelling the bathroom.

'After it was done,' says Dave, chuckling and searching his jacket pockets for the car keys, 'our boss gets a call from the owner of the house who wants us to go back out and inspect a problem with the bathroom. So me and Baz go back and this guy goes *look at that* and points at the dunny. Yeah? What are we supposed to be lookin at, I go. The guy goes: the water in the toilet's too high and every time I sit down my cock dips in the water and gets shit on it.' Dave cacks himself, his face going red. 'Get the tip snipped off ya dick then, goes Baz. The guy put in a complaint to the boss-man who couldn't stop laughing on the phone.'

The inside of his ute is comfy as, with plush bucket seats that hiss as you sink into them. The leg room is amazing. And he's got a second mobile phone, too! I'd frigging love a mobile phone. The ultimate status symbol these days. He's got money coming out of his ears. The engine rumbles into life beautifully, and he veers out onto Ann Street and guns it westwards.

'So, what's on your mind?' he says to me.

Time to give it the best whirl I've got.

It's easier to talk with him while he's busy watching the road. He can't read my eyes or stare me down or anything, so I start going on about how I worked out that he's on a good wicket and earning a bucket-load, and how I don't really think working on a construction site's for me. He's twigged where I'm going with this, of course, but he's forcing me to say it out loud by pretending to be clueless. My heart's hammering in my chest, and though I just wanna ask him to stop the car so I can get out, I figure my plan's half out there already and he knows what I'm driving at here, so I push on.

'I reckon I could help you out,' I suggest.

'I already have help,' he counters. 'There's two of us who run the course. Another bloke called Jody.'

I didn't figure on that.

'I know loads of young people,' I offer. 'I go clubbing all the time, and heaps of friends have friends of friends all coming out of school. I'd be a good contact point for the boom that's coming.'

He glances sharply a few times at me, a half-smirk wavering on his lips like he's trying to figure me out maybe.

'I can streamline the whole recruitment, too,' I continue. 'The fake signatures, the lot. I can get some of the club kids set up to write them out so they don't all look the same.'

'You reckon that's a problem?'

'Yeah, probably,' I go. I'm warming up now. He feels less resistant to the idea than I thought he would. 'It's only a matter of time before someone on the Government end catches on, I reckon. One of those lads back there wrote the names all in the same handwriting. I think I can help to really tighten up those aspects of the business.'

I'm feeling pretty bloody good right about now. Dave's nodding thoughtfully, pursing his lips like he sees my point. I think he and this other bloke, this Jody geezer, have got the whole scam worked out pretty good, but it's the little details that they've gotten sloppy on. The small stuff. Someone like me can come along and just clean it all up and none will be the frigging wiser.

'Yeah,' he says slowly. 'I see what you mean.'

Yes! The sinking feeling in my chest surges into a full flight of elation. The feeling is as overwhelming as the dread I felt before, and my heart's hammering anew in my chest. I'm trying not to think about the possibilities that lay ahead of me, I don't want to jinx it, especially because nothing's set in stone yet. But Dave's thinking it over. Those stupid bastards back at the pub just had their eyes on the small prize: five poxy licences for a job in the sun and concrete dust. But that's no good for me. I can see better things working alongside Dave, looking for young lads to sign up. I could be Dave's street man, working the field so he can sit back and reap the rewards without any effort at all.

I'm blabbing all this to him, letting these ideas roll out off my tongue as fast as I can think them. He looks impressed with the speed with which I leap from idea to idea, laying out the foundations for a business deal that cuts only a little more into his profit margin while freeing him up entirely from the time-consuming recruitment process.

'Okay, okay, slow down, matey,' he laughs. 'You're working it out, and I gotta admit it's not a bad deal from where I'm sitting. But we gotta still run this past Jody. He's in it fifty-fifty with me, so it's up to him now.'

I break into a big sodding grin. I can't help it. I've a good feeling about this. I don't know this Jody bloke, but with Dave on board I'm already half way there.

You fucking beauty!

Dave drives me to a little office block behind the McDonald's in Milton. I'm nervous as hell as he takes me up the unpainted wooden stairs and introduces me to Jody, who's a big beast of a bloke with massive hairy arms and a sloping bald head. Dave tells Jody about the conversation we had on the way over.

Jody looks me up and down. He's not the friendliest of people, and he takes the news of my ideas with some reluctance.

'I get it,' I go, my hands up in mock-surrender. 'You blokes've got a good thing and it's not broke, but I can fine-tune the smaller details for you guys.'

I give him some quick examples based on my observations back at the pub, all the stuff I told Dave about already. He sniffs, considering Dave for a moment, who grins back at him. I'm trusting Dave to help push the big man over the line on this.

'Where do ya work at the moment?' asks Jody.

'I work security,' I say. 'Weekends, I look after all the offices and contractors that come and go at the meatworks out Ipswich way. The rest of the time I do the rounds of the plazas in the Valley. It's a sucky gig, man.'

'I bet it is,' laughs Jody. The first positive response I've had from him. 'Which company is it does that, then?'

'It's NiteWork Security Management,' I tell him, and he nods as if he knows them. 'Yeah, they're mongrels to us. Shit wages, and right now they're stuffing me around with my shifts all cause I raised some issues with the union.'

'Got a flair for sniffing out the deals under the table, eh?' says Dave, giving me a wink. I just laugh, and hope I haven't turned red. That'd be a fucking disaster.

'Mate, I know exactly what you mean,' says Jody. 'I was in your place not even ten years ago. Cunts shafting me all the way into next week. There's no feeling like tellin em to go stick it.'

My heart almost skips. If I'm not mistaken, it sounds like I've just been tentatively ushered into this big-buck operation. Two years of shitty security work and low pay has led to what feels like this karmic moment, like finally I'm getting repaid for all the wrong turns. The look on that prick Gary's face when he finds out he's just lost one of his best guards will be the cherry on top.

'Whatta ya thinkin right now?' asks Jody.

'Telling those assholes at NiteWork to go shove it.'

He laughs and goes: 'I thought as much. Mate, how much notice do you have to give?'

'Who knows?' I go, shrugging. 'I don't get holiday or sick pay, just a flat rate no matter if it's Monday, Sunday or Christmas sodding

Day.'

Dave shifts his weight against the banister. 'Trav, mate, why don't you just leave them in the lurch a-sap?'

It's a dream a lot of us on NiteWork's payroll has, and we talk about it pretty regularly: finding a position in life whereby we can make those sods scramble like chooks to fill our shifts at a moment's notice. Swapping all their guards around according to their aptitude to fill the vacancies. They'd have a tough time of it, too. They've built up a base of semi-literate morons, a shallow gene pool as Dante once called it, and most of their guards are barely responsible enough to handle the sites I was usually rostered to, including the meatworks gig. The thought of leaving them in the lurch is too exciting to resist. I'll become a hero amongst the remaining guards. They'll tell the story of Twix shafting the company to each other during the shift changes.

'There's the phone,' nods Jody.

I pull a folded piece of paper from my wallet that has my contacts carefully listed in waterproof ink. I run my finger down the list until I find Gary's phone number registered as NITEWORKS. While it rings I'm aware I'm holding my breath, so I exhale nice and slow. Steel my nerves. Finally Robert Heeley answers the phone.

'Didn't wake you, did I?' I ask, dripping sarcasm.

'No,' he says sourly.

'Gary there? It's Travis.'

Heeley turns from the receiver, yelling out: 'Hey, Gazza. It's that Haynes arsehole.'

Gary jumps on the phone and gruffly goes: 'Yeah?' Like as if I've interrupted his sodding dinner or something. No respect from these mongrels.

'Hey, Gary, it's Travis here.'

'Mate, you didn't turn up for your shift today,' he growls. 'Daryl had to pull a double.'

'Not my problem,' I go, surprising myself with both my bravado and with how much I sound like Amai-li right now. 'I had to rush off to an important appointment.'

I glance round at Dave and Jody who're laughing at some joke, but they stop and give me the thumbs up when they clock me watching. I point at the phone and give em a wicked grin, which pleases them.

Gary mutters something then goes: 'No worries, Trav. By the way, we've had to cut your next three shifts.'

Yeah, right! Stupid prick thinks he's got one over me, punishing me for my insubordination. Have I got news for him.

'Care factor zero, mate, because I fucking quit anyways.'

The line goes quiet.

'Do you hear me, Gazza, lad?' My voice commands admiration. For ages I've wanted this bastard right where I've got him now, so I want to hear him squirm.

'I heard you fine, you little fuckhead,' he snaps irritably. 'You won't get paid for the last fortnight, by the way. And don't bother getting your union mates to sort it, coz your name's mud with them.'

I'd forgotten that we get paid fortnightly and that payday's still a couple of days off, but no matter. I'll be well off, soon enough, thanks to Dave and Jody. But I'm still disappointed by Gary's tone. He isn't squirming like I'd hoped. Arrogant to the end. Wanker.

'No bother,' I tell him. 'Where I'm going makes what you pay look like peanuts, you prick.'

The line goes dead, and for a second I'm feeling gutted, because I'd wanted to be the one that hung up first. I slowly lower the receiver to the cradle and turn to Dave and Jody with an expression of *holy shit, I did it, lads!*

'Sounds like you told that cunt what the fucking score was,' says Dave, smiling.

'Shit yeah,' I burst out laughing. Jody has a chuckle, too.

'Free to move on!' whoops Dave.

You little beauty! What an amazing feeling. I feel like I've won the fucking lotto!

Jody's big meaty arm whips out and his knuckles crack into my jaw so hard that for a split second I actually black out.

I'm on the floor when I finally come to, with Jody's hulking frame standing above me, blocking the light to the doorway.

'You think you can blackmail us, you little cunt?' His voice booms at me, even though he barely speaks above a conversational tone. A feeling of menace drips from him. I can't help but hold up a hand as if to ward him off. A useless gesture.

He grabs me by an arm and a leg, and I hear myself yelp like a dog as the room spins, daylight flaring, blinding me momentarily. The timber stairwell digs into my ribs as I land and spin over the ledge. The world whirls around and around as I tumble down the steps. I can hear the sound of thunder as the figure of Jody flies down after me, looming large. I try and get up to descend the last few steps and get away, but I'm shoved from behind, flying through the air and landing on the concrete footpath, cracking my wrist beneath me. The metallic taste of blood swells in my mouth, stinging my nose.

Jody flips me over and glares down at me as though I'm just dog-shit. Dave comes down the stairs casually with a contented smile. He has a piece of paper in his hand.

'We offered you a great fucking start in construction, mate,' says Jody. 'Wouldna cost you a fucking cent; what more didja want?'

'Everything, apparently,' says Dave drolly, passing Jody the sheet of paper.

Jody starts reading it aloud. 'Travis Haynes, of unit five, 90 Bowen Street, Spring Hill.'

Huh? That's my old address, at the Prozac Palace.

Fuck a duck! I haven't changed over my driver's licence to the new address at St Lucia, and this bastard's holding the photocopy of it! I could almost laugh at his error, if I wasn't in so much pain.

'Next of kin is mother, one Angela Haynes of Caboolture,' Jody continues, and suddenly the mood for hilarity passes. 'Well, Travis Haynes of 90 Bowen Street, we don't take kindly to people trying to muscle in on our legitimate business, so if anyone comes questioning us about it, you're a fucking dead cunt. *A fucking dead cunt.* Hear me?'

I let out a wheeze by way of response and try to nod my head, but my neck is twinging with pain.

Dave drives a boot into my gut that makes me double over into a foetal position, spewing a stream of blood out of my mouth in place of a scream. A jarring ache spreads across my shoulders and down my back. My guts churn with nausea.

Jody and Dave head back upstairs, telling me I'd better not be here in ten minutes time or I'm really going to regret it, before closing the door.

It hurts all over, and blood's dribbling down my chin, under my cheek. Lying as still as possible on the cool concrete is preferable, but I really need to get outta here. I get onto my hands and knees and crawl across to the carpark behind the McDonald's, and with great effort manage to get around to the petrol station where I call on the taxi payphone for my flatmate Billy to come and get me.

Next I call Raven, but it goes to her message service.

'Hey, Raven, it's Twix here,' I gasp, as pain blooms right across my jaw from talking. 'Long time, no hear. Listen, spot of bother I'm in. Some blokes've got the Prozac address and they're not the nicest of jokers. So don't open the door to any strangers anytime soon, okay?'

The bloke behind the counter of the petrol station gapes out at me in shock, and jumps on his phone. I just hope Billy can get here first before the ambulance or police or whoever it is that the attendant has called turns up instead.

PART FOUR

A COCK OR TWO

I'm traipsing up Moggill Road on a lovely day with the sun warming my back. The cars are rushing by, all fucking noise and mayhem. But on the upside, it's the time of year for the star-jasmine flowers to be out in bloom, and there's a whole bush of them in place of a fence for one of the homes that I pass. Their scent makes me giddy and fills me with a kind of nostalgic delight, like they're dredging up everything good about the past without bringing forth any particular memory. Ahead there's a pattern of squashed dog turds on the footpath, and instantly the awful pong evaporates the charm of the jasmine flowers. But I guess that's life, isn't it? It's all ups and downs, roses and shit.

'*I walk the line between good and eviiiiiil,*' I sing at the top of my lungs, making a dog across the road bark crazily inside his backyard prison. 'Hang in there, my friend, your revolution is coming!'

Donger's front door's open and there's a removal truck next door at the shops, blocking the driveway down to the shop's carpark. There's no driveway for Donger's place so here's as good as any to park, I guess. Old mate from the convenience store's having a row with one of the removalist's about how inconvenient it is to block the carpark off.

I nip inside the house, narrowly avoiding being knocked over by a cunt carrying a box of stuff.

'What's going on, Donger?'

He's in the kitchen chatting with Lachie. 'Oi, Dante,' he says with a big smile. 'Spazza's movin out. Wanna grab his room while it's still available?'

'Nah, I'm good at the Palace,' I go.

'Wait, is that the Prozac Palace in Spring Hill?' Lachie asks. 'Dya know a goth chick who calls herself Raven?'

'Yeah, why?'

'No reason,' he grins lasciviously, the seedy cunt. I'm pretty sure he's not Raven's type, but then you never know. She's been known to indulge indiscriminately in a cock or two, if Twix is to be believed, which is maybe not much in all honesty.

'Where *is* Spazza, anyway?' I go.

Donger rolls his eyes. 'Probably out getting plastered. Left us to deal with the removalists on his behalf, but. His dad's coughed up the dough for it in advance, thankfully.'

'Dropped it around last night in an envelope and told us to keep it out of sight from Spaz,' smirks Lachie.

'On the plus side,' I note, aware the removalists' are nearly done and they only started when I arrived, 'being an alcoholic means fuck all stuff to have to move.'

'Fucken oath,' goes Lachie. 'The bastard's got more stuff than me!'

'It's all his parents' stuff, but,' says Dale. 'When he first moved in all he had was the clothes on his back. He's a privileged lil shit.'

Donger's parents died years ago when he was still little so he was raised by his uncle and aunt. He doesn't talk about them much, but I inferred once from his ramblings that his uncle was pretty abusive. Maybe even sexually, who knows? I think the cunt resented having to raise a kid when he'd already done his duty in that department. None of Dale's cousins, who're older than him by at least ten or fifteen years, want anything to do with him.

'So, how's your head?'

Donger bows so that his forehead swings down in front of me. The cut is still visible, but it's healing over and the stitches are dissolving. The skin has a shiny, robust shine to it.

'Good enough to head out for an arvo to Chardon's Corner for Splurt, by the looks of it,' Lachie goes. 'Soon as these mugs shove off.'

The removalist guy gives us a sour expression, which makes me, Donger and Lachie start sniggering.

'You and Dante go,' says Donger. 'I'm gonna stay home for a bit.'

Lachie shrugs. 'Don't forget to square em up.'

Donger pulls an envelope down off the top of the fridge and heads outside.

Lachie checks to see he's out of earshot, then says to me: 'Don't say anything, coz he's a mate, y'know, but I'm probably gonna head off soon, as well.'

'He already knows that, ya twit,' I say, then immediately realise Lachie's talking about moving out of the house, not heading to Club Splurt. 'Wait, you serious? What's goin on?'

'I don't know,' says Lachie. 'I don't want to rag on the bloke, but he's become a bit fucken unbearable of late. He's gotten some funny ideas.'

Geezus. Donger's a bit of a wild child at heart, but he's a fucking top guy. I'm pretty taken aback that Lachie would suggest otherwise. To be honest, I don't actually know this Lachlan cunt all that well, so maybe he's the problem. I wouldn't put it past Donger to tell the cunt where to go if he was out of line. Some cunts don't like being told to toe the line.

'Yeah, sure thing,' I nod, tapping my nose. 'Mum's the word.'

'Cheers, Dante,' he says, patting my arm as Donger comes back into the house.

'Done and dusted,' says Donger. 'Cuppa?'

'Nah, mate, I'm offski,' says Lachie and snatches up his wallet and house key. He gives me a sympathetic look, as if to secure my secrecy.

When he's gone, I tell Donger all about Lachie's plans to move on.

'I'm not surprised,' says Dale sadly, putting the kettle on. 'He's been a bit out of order lately. Spazza couldn't handle it anymore. I should've made him move on sooner, but it's not my style, ya know?'

That's always been Dale's problem: he's too forgiving and lets the trash pile up. But it's a bit suss that he's trying to shift the blame onto Lachie.

'Well, what's done is done,' I go. 'No use dwelling on it.'

'I'm not, really,' replies Donger. 'Some things are just meant to be.'

It feels like my Providence argument after a fashion, but when I put it to him Donger reckons it's something more.

'When I was under those horses in the park, Dante, getting kicked in the fucking head and tasting mud down my gob, I had something of a revelation. I didn't exactly know it then. It was later when the nurse was stitchin me up.'

'What revelation?'

He shrugs, and passes me a mug. 'Nothing precise, just that I was doing things all wrong. Like I'd put myself under that horse's feet and I could've just stood back and not participated.' He snaps his head around. 'Oi, go put some music on. It's too quiet in here.'

On top of the tape player's a pile of cassettes, one of them marked *Spill Compilation #1*. I put it in and the first song that comes on is *Def Whitlam* by Volvox. If memory serves, one of the band members – who all go by the name of Reg Egg – came from Brisbane.

We head out the back door with our mugs of tea and sit on the old wooden steps of the improbably long staircase. The land steeps so sharply from the main road to the back fence that the front of the house looks like it sits on level earth, but from the back yard it towers on wooden stumps. Could easily fit another two storeys underneath.

'Isn't participation what it's all about, though?' I say, continuing the discussion. I'm not arguing with the cunt, because even on the night I thought it was madness to throw himself into the riot the way he did. I was the one trying to get him out of it.

'Time and a place, but,' he says sagely, blowing on his tea.

'Shit, Donger, it's like you've seen the error of your ways.'

'Yeah, yeah, laugh all you want, mate,' he says. 'But I'm serious. I could've lost an eye.'

I nearly start laughing, because it's the old joke, isn't it? The one we're told when we're kids, about calming down before someone loses an eye? Donger never had those lessons, though, at least not from his parents. I don't know if his aunt and uncle drummed it into him as a kid or not.

'Let me get this straight: you could've lost an eye, so now your housemates are abandoning you? It doesn't make any fucking sense, Donger. Sorry.'

I know that, personally, when things are going really well, I'm an optimist. When they're shit, I'm a pessimist. I go from one extreme to the other, without finding a middle ground. Donger's rationale seems to be the opposite: our night last week turned shit, so he's reaching out and finding the positive. I suppose that's a pretty normal thing to do, ordinarily, but I'm highly fucking doubtful that alienating your friends is meant to be part of the process.

'But I'm not doing that,' he insists. 'I'm just seeing things from another perspective. If my mates are alienated by that then they're a bunch of soft cocks. I'm still Dale Donger, aren't I? I'm still punk, aren't I?'

These things are irrefutable. He definitely still is Donger the punk, there's no doubts there. 'Dale, I'm struggling to understand precisely what's happened that's made the others move out.'

'Like I said,' he goes, 'there's a shift in consciousness and what happens is it pushes outwards. They're feeling it and not responding, is all. At least, they're not welcoming it. So they're interpreting it as a sign to move away.'

Amara would know what this is all about, I bet. It sounds like her language. But if I'm understanding correctly, then Donger's simply getting his shit together at last and the others can't handle that and it's lead to some domestics.

'I need to change, Dante,' Donger says, almost imploring me to understand. 'I can't keep living like this. I'm gonna fucking burn out, mate. You know me, how it is. Like a shooting star. Burning bright and all that.'

'Yeah, I get it,' I shrug. That Lachie seems like a bit of a tosser, and if Donger doesn't wanna live like that anymore, then good for him. Maybe he can be the example that I need myself? Or maybe I'm the example that he needs. After all, me and Bernie live a pretty quiet life in our flat, even with all the madness of the Prozac Palace around us. But then I fucking well insist on the peace and quiet, don't I? It seems that's all Donger's doing here.

The convenience store owner's taking some rubbish bags out to the bins at the back of his carpark, and when he scowls up at us on Donger's back steps, Donger gives him the finger until the cunt sulks back up the driveway and into his shop. Donger hasn't changed that much, really.

Just then this cockatoo lands in the palm tree just over the fence, and it must be an escaped pet because it starts chattering away and I swear it says: 'Get farked ya cahnts.'

Me and Donger glance at each other in surprise and then nearly piss ourselves with laughter.

A FEELING

The times are getting a lil rough. I can feel it.

I can sense it, as if I can smell it's fragrance on the air.

The Inferno can feel it, vibrating through the ground and up the walls as if to destabilise our monuments to greatness.

Bernie just shrugs whenever I talk like this, as if he couldn't be bothered. He's tuned out to it, turned his focus inward and is lost in the layers of his psych, talking to imaginary people. But I'm looking outwards, and I don't like what I see.

The news is full of hints, of course: blizzards in North America, the Lijiang earthquake, Hurricane Fran, the Amarnath Yatra pilgrims in India. People are dying everywhere. If it's not the May storm on Mount Everest killing a half dozen then it's thousands of Hutu slaughtered by Rwandan soldiers in the Congo. We've got Mad Cow disease, the Centennial Olympic Park bombing, human avalanches at a Guatemalan stadium. Fuck, even apple juice isn't safe, with some in America contaminated with E. Coli. They've got school shootings in Washington and San Diego and planes falling apart or crashing in Indonesia and Florida. The Netherlands has the Hercules Disaster and there's even more shootings in America, as always; this time at Fort Lauderdale.

Locally we've got crazy shit like the Hillcrest Murders and Port Arthur (he's pleading not guilty, so the papers reckon). Blackhawks colliding in the sky in WA because of strict safety laws, if you can believe it. The Attorney General wants to wind-back a High-Court decision that would mean no freedom of political speech, despite the Government banging on recently that free speech is what we need.

The Prime Minister publicly admitted he thinks many Australians share the views of that halfwit Hanson, but at least he added that she's wrong about Aboriginals not being disadvantaged. If that wasn't enough, then the deputy Prime Minister had to clue up the Asia Pacific Cities Summit that Hanson's opinions on Asian migration were fucking up our trade potential with Asia. A Taiwanese delegate at the same conference went on record saying that Hanson was now a synonymous name with racial intolerance back in Taiwan. Stupid bitch can't see beyond her own back-fence.

It doesn't end, it never does.

Then there's Rupert's suicide.

I'm no stranger to the idea of killing oneself. Christ knows I've half-heartedly tried it myself a couple of times, and thought about it heaps. The Inferno's adamant on that score. But it's different when someone you know, someone you quite liked, actually manages to get the job done.

Bernie's been feeling numb about it, and won't meet up with Viv anymore. I feel sorry for her, and probably should try and catch up with her myself at some point. See how she's doing. Let her know that life goes on. For now. Make sure she isn't feeling the same sense of dread that I am. I can introduce her to Amara. I think she'd like that, Old Viv. I suspect she's a romantic at heart.

It's funny, but while on one hand I'm eager to make sure Viv is okay, on the other I've been avoiding my closest friends who're really in need. I'd seen Alan the other day down in the Valley, and he's a fucking wreck. He's hit the bottle so hard he said the band won't perform with anymore. You know you've got issues when a crap punk band thinks you're not fit to front them. Obviously Alan's more affected by the stillbirth of his firstborn than he's always let on. The poor cunt was looking at me with such longing that I'd started feeling bad for not having kept in contact with him, but then he blew it by coming out with some shit about how he'd needed me in his darkest hours and I wasn't around for him. I left the cunt to it after that, left him sitting in his own stale piss in the Valley mall, screamin at me about how everything's coming to an end for us.

But I open my eyes in the mornings and I can feel it, the sense that the world is getting more destructive, that something big is coming, something that won't just be on the news happening across the world, but happening right here in Brisbane. Maybe that's what's made Donger calm the fuck down. It's not that the riots at Musgrave Park necessarily knocked his brain loose, but that deep down he felt the symbolism of it and doesn't know how to interpret the information. It's knocked him for a sixer, maybe?

The poor cunt's been going on so long about humans evolving into a greater species or some shit, when in fact I simply think we'll be faced with something so enormous we'll have no choice but to decide what kind of people we want humanity to become. Whatever it is, I envision a disaster on a massive scale.

PRIVATE AND CONFIDENTIAL
NOT TO BE CIRCULATED

Australian Prime Minister has ~~has~~ contacted by telephone the Queensland Premier and advised of situation involving Russian spacecraft trajectory.

Have been advised by contacts in Washington that object is from failed Russian launch and expected to impact ~~Queens~~ the region of South East Queensland.

Advised object is probe from RUSSIAN MARS 96 ORBITER and loaded with 200 GRAMS OF PLUTONIUM.

US GOVT tracking object.

Will update as details emerge. Keep lines of communication open.

ETA NOT YET KNOWN.

Emergency services are notified and readying for potential major catastrophe.

NOTE: MEDIA AND PUBLIC NOT BE NOTIFIED AT THIS STAGE.

Details of potential impact zone not yet known.
    a) Ground response requirements not yet known.
    b) Casualty expectation not yet known.
    ~~c) Clean up~~

FOR PRIVATE EYES ONLY

HIGHWAY ROBBERY

A fire-engine roars down Breakfast Creek Road, sirens and lights splitting the night.

Pixie, Nel and Roz watch it tear past as they lean against the cold shell of a burnt out car in the middle of a paddock.

'Can't we wait out on the road?' whines Roz, sniffing a trail of runny snot back into her nose. 'There's probably snakes in this grass.'

'Use your brain, bitch. Snakes don't come out at night,' snaps Nel. 'The cunt said to meet im here, so here is where we wait.'

The fire-engine disappears down the road, sirens growing fainter as it goes.

'Maybe we should apologise to Brett again?' Roz suggests, but no-one answers her.

Pixie thinks about how Roz is starting to get on everyone's tits lately. All she ever does is moan and complain about her job, how she's tired of the men who rough her up, of the ones who refuse to pay, of the cops who constantly move her on from the laundromat. Nel's been pushing Pixie into the game herself, but after the orgy at the Nash she wants no part of that scene. It was fun at the time, but afterwards the way all the men had looked at her made her feel disgusted with herself. She'd actually wanted to feel more disgusted at them, but it just hadn't worked out that way. The power of the patriarchy, eh?

Headlights cut across the wasteland, and Pixie's about to voice that it's time for business when Nel grabs her by the sleeve and pulls her forcefully to the ground, ripping her shirt.

'Cunt!' bellows Pixie.

'Shut the fuck up,' hisses Nel, her beady eyes trained on the police car as it sweeps past.

'That was close,' Roz says. She'd ducked down at the same time as Nel.

'No need to rip me clothes, but,' Pixie complains.

'Maybe you want a fucken smack in the mouth instead?' warns Nel, and Pixie takes the hint and says no more.

Another car comes past, goes down the road further, then doubles back. It parks kerbside of the old gasworks ring and two men exit, coming across the field towards the girls. They're at least an hour late, but that's routine for an unfamiliar dealer. They like to fuck around deadbeats like Nel, Roz and Pixie.

'Heya fellas,' Nel says in a cheery voice, wiping her clammy palms on her jeans.

The men approach, standing just a couple of metres way.

'Nelly fucking Beeston,' sniggers one of them, a man called Black Ronnie. His skin's almost as white as The Morlock's. 'Nelly the Beast! Self-proclaimed terror of West End.'

'Those days are behind me,' Nel mumbles, keen to forget them as much as the moniker she's tried for years to shake loose.

'Course they are,' rumbles Black Ronnie. 'You kick about in Spring Hill these days, ay?'

Nel and Roz blanch at this revelation, that Black Ronnie's kept his ear to the ground enough to have tracked their movements over the years. It proves that knowledge really is power, especially to someone in Ronnie's line of work.

'Thought you'd be dead by now, to be honest,' he confesses.

Nel laughs nervously. 'What can I say? I've got too much to live for.'

'Yeah, sure you have,' Black Ronnie scoffs. 'You lot normally deal through Brett, dontcha?'

Nel's not comfortable with this being common knowledge, least of all because Brett is ex-police. Regardless of how the force has treated the man, he'll always have that in his past and it makes dealers like Black Ronnie wary.

'He's a cunt,' Nel says. 'Old news, mate.'

'Maybe this is a set-up?'

Cunt sure asks a lot of questions, thinks Pixie. She also thinks this all feels really wrong, but Roz squeezes her hand to remind her to stay calm. They'd told Pixie before getting here that Black Ronnie was going to try and frighten them, that it was on the cards.

'Maybe I should stuff your fucking bodies in that burnt out car for the fucking crows to find in the morning?'

'Nah, mate, it's all good,' Nel says, shuffling from foot to foot.

'Is it really?' snarls Black Ronnie, nodding to his accomplice who pulls a gun from his Carharrt jacket and advances on Nel.

'Yeah mate, it is, I swear,' Nel begs, her voice shrill with fear. She won't back away because she knows the rules of this game, that it's a test of wills, but she's starting to wonder if this is going south in a bad way.

The man with the gun grabs her by the shoulder and forces her to her knees.

'Saw that cop car earlier,' Black Ronnie says, seizing on the chance routine of the patrol car as leverage for further intimidation tactics. 'One of your mates? You turned snitch, Beeston?'

'No, man, I swear,' says Nel. The gun presses against the top of her head, ready to blow her brains through her anus. 'I swear, I fucking swear!'

'This is bullshit,' mutters Pixie, who feels Roz's nails claw into the skin on her hand as a reminder to hold her tongue.

Everyone goes stock still, Black Ronnie slowly turning his head in Pixie's direction.

'Oh, I'm sorry,' he says smarmily, 'am I holding you up, dear?'

'We just want some smack,' Pixie says sullenly.

Black Ronnie stares at her steadily, then roars: 'AND WHAT THE FUCK AM I, THEN? A FUCKING POPPY TREE JUST GIVING THE FUCKING SHIT OUT FOR FREE?'

His voice echoes across the field to the river, where it is seemingly amplified by the water. It bounces clear across to Bulimba.

Pixie recalls a documentary wherein she'd learnt that opium comes from flowers, not trees, but she decides she's said enough already and keeps her mouth shut.

'Christ,' Black Ronnie spits, 'now every motherfucker within coo-ee's heard me. Finish it, Dingo.'

The man with the gun – Dingo – grunts in response.

'Wait wait wait,' begs Nel, tears and snot streaming down her pimply face. 'Don't kill me! Please!'

'Fucking simpletons,' sneers Black Ronnie to Dingo, as the other man pockets the gun and walks back to the car, shaking his head.

Nel peers up and stops her snivelling when she realises that she's not going to die, after all.

'What ya think I'm gonna do?' Black Ronnie says. 'Start offing my customer base? You girls really are fucking stupid, you know that? Including you, missy.'

He points a bejewelled finger at Pixie.

'You think you're brave?' he sneers. 'You're not. You're an idiot. You pull that fucking shit with someone else you might just get your teeth punched in. But I've got a daughter, in her teens. I know what you brats are like. Think yourself fucking lucky I'm a dad.'

Pixie just scowls at Black Ronnie.

Dingo returns with a deflated balloon in his hands.

Roz exchanges the money with Dingo, who gives her the balloon. She immediately lifts her skirt and stuffs it inside her vagina. Dingo tries to cop a free look, but Roz has done this plenty of times and it disappears without so much as even her thigh being exposed.

'You girls take care,' Black Ronnie says. He cocks his head at Nel still sitting on the scorched earth. 'Don't hesitate to call when you need more. As, surely, you will.'

Dingo winks at Pixie. 'Give us a call,' he says. 'Pretty piece like you could work for yer hit.'

'Fuck off,' Pixie says, and Roz slaps her on the back of the head, which makes Dingo laugh.

'Lookin forward to doin that myself,' he says of the slap, an evil smile on his face, and follows Black Ronnie back to the car.

'Fucken cunts,' snarls Nel when Black Ronnie's driven off, well out of earshot. 'I thought everyone was meant to have given their fucken guns over to the Government. Port Arthur means nothing to you cunts?' Then to Roz and Pixie she says: 'Let's go.'

Both Roz and Pixie know better than to say anything about how events have unfolded. They're just happy to have the heroin in their possession. It'll tide them over for a few days more. While the drug might be plentiful, the cash to purchase said drug isn't, and the girls have had to struggle to increase their resources lately. As the months have passed so too have their appetites grown, their bodies craving the opiate more and more with every passing week until they've found that their need has outstripped their collective income.

The atmosphere at the Prozac Palace has grown increasingly tenser with this increased need, too, as the other residents have noticed the callous way that the girls scan the other apartments for stuff to steal. They may have honed their skills for theft and lying but the desperate junkie need in their eyes cannot be masked.

Pixie has even considered robbing her father's burger store at Kangaroo Point, relishing the idea of putting The Fear into him and into that stupid stuck-up bitch Olivia. Fortunately, she didn't mention the idea to Nel or Roz at the time she'd had it, mostly because she was too fucking wasted to, because the following week she'd seen Dougie down the road and he'd told her that the store had been robbed last month. Some guys with stockings over their heads and baseball bats had come into the store, smashed some stuff up, and stolen the day's takings. He said the cops believed the robbers had gotten away by simply vanishing up Ipswich Road. Still on the run.

The news had caught Pixie by surprise. As much as she'd relished the idea of doing it herself and seeing the terrified look on her dad's face, the thought that someone, some stranger, had actually terrorised him and that he might've died had shaken her up. She couldn't remember the last time she'd spoken to her father. It felt like years, even though it has only been months.

'Don't worry,' Nel crows, as they pick their way across the field. 'I've got a plan. I'm gonna start dealing. Time to smarten up, ay.'

'I thought you already do, but,' Pixie sniffs.

'Nah, Farrell's just one customer,' Nel says. 'I mean deal properly. Heaps of clients. Get up to my eyeballs in fucken cash, ay.'

'How're you gonna do that?' says Roz. 'We've been begging and stealing to get this far as it is.'

'I just need to rip some stupid cunt off big time, don't I?'

'Nel,' Roz says meaningfully, rubbing a scar on her arm, thinking of an incident where she'd done a similar thing years ago.

She'd shafted what she'd thought was a small-time dealer, some backyard hack, but the guy was well connected as it'd turned out and Roz had been visited by the next rung on the ladder, who'd insisted with brute force that she not only cough up the cash as quickly as possible but with interest added. He'd wanted thirty percent on top, and if she hadn't got it all by the deadline then she was going to be dead meat.

The arsehole had kept shifting the deadline closer, however, and all the stealing and whoring wasn't going to get her the money in time. Fearing for her life, she'd poured her heart out to Nel, who she knew from the Sporties and who had a bit of a rep as someone not to be messed with. Nel, who was still only a recreational user in those days, had launched into action, rounding up as many people as she could to hock off their unwanted goods and raise the money for Roz. The story Nel gave everyone was that Roz's real estate agent had been siphoning her rent money and now the landlord was threatening to boot her out.

That was when Roz had sworn a lifelong allegiance to Nel, and their friendship had become unrivalled. Or so it had seemed.

'Won't be like that,' Nel says, squaring her jaw. 'I'll be crafty as a cat about it. You'll see. Give that prick Brett a run for his money. I'll start small, build up slowly. Be good to try and rip off Black Ronnie and his lapdog Drongo eventually.'

'His name's Dingo,' Roz says.

'Fucken Drongo in my books, but,' Nel says with a wry grin, satisfied with what she considers is her razor-sharp wit.

'What if he shoots us, but?' Pixie wants to know.

'It's just a replica,' Roz says, so Nel turns on them both, eager to stamp out any suggestion she'd been made to piss herself in fear from a fake gun.

'Listen you idiots,' she says sternly. 'You don't fuck around with Black Ronnie lightly. That's no fucking replica, trust me. I'm lucky to be alive. But you'll see; they'll get theirs.'

When they're finally back on the street they see a figure leaning in the shadows against a wall, merrily drunk and high on life. At first they assume it's another of Ronnie's bastards, until the figure steps out of the shadows with a wolf's grin on him.

'Fucking hell, it's Dante,' mumbles Nel to the girls, immediately turning her back on him.

Roz and Pixie peer around to confirm his presence, so Nel curses them for making eye contact.

'Well, hello there, girls,' Dante chirrups as he approaches. 'Fancy seeing you homebodies out here of all places!'

'Yeah, and fancy seeing you out here, too,' Pixie retorts.

'Been at the Waterloo for the Love at First Bite Ball,' he smiles, jerking his thumb over his shoulder.

'Love at First Bite Ball,' Nel sneers, resuming her old self now that the humiliation of Black Ronnie has passed. 'Fuck, you gothic cunts have some stupid fucking names for your clubs.'

'Hell of an entertaining show you lot put on over there,' he retorts. 'I loved every minute of it, especially the bit where those gangsters were going to shoot you dead, Nel. Nice touch.'

'They weren't gangsters, you wanker,' Nel snaps.

'Certainly behaved like gangsters.'

'It's none of your fucking business, okay mate?' Nel's eyes bulge threateningly.

'Is it not?' he asks evenly, his hand straying to the waistband of his trousers.

Pixie knows what that gesture means, knows that since his second arrest Dante's gotten another knife (maybe one of those Demtel ones off the telly?), and she's keen to see how this plays out. An armed drunk against a desperate junkie? Sounds about even odds.

Roz has other ideas, though.

'Come on you two,' she says, hoping to avoid the worst. 'Knock it off.'

'Yeah, calm down kids,' laughs Pixie, secretly disappointed that a potential fight has been thwarted.

Dante backs down with a laugh, saying it's the booze talking. No-one believes it for a moment.

'You're such a shit-stirrer, Dante,' chides Roz playfully, hoping to further nullify any residual confrontation left in him.

He simply grins. 'Well, Roz, someone's gotta give it a stir once in a while, or it'll harden like a fist of constipation in your guts.'

Nel sees red; it's obvious to her that Dante's taking a poke at the fact heroin makes one constipated. She can't recall the last time she had a satisfying dump, and the reminder makes her cranky.

For her part, Pixie reflects on how their desperation for opiates is misunderstood by the likes of Dante, and the rest of them, how they can't understand that it's a real sickness that's in her, Nel and Roz, and that it needs to be treated as such. Not constantly thrown in their faces, taunted for their lack of moral will to resist temptation. But she figures that'll never happen as long as people keep judging them with as having a criminal mindset. It's like how Roz has to go to Binkinba for her methadone treatments, reasons Pixie, how it's like a proper program to fix her addiction. Proof is in the pudding!

'What would you know anyway?' Nel barks at Dante.

'I know you cunts wanna start thinkin about your actions,' Dante warns. 'The rest of the Prozac is getting a bit fed up with you lot.'

'Pot calling the kettle black,' Nel says stalking away, muttering something about his blood not being worth bottling.

There's no need for her to motion Roz and Pixie to follow: she's the one holding the heroin. They'll follow her to the ends of the Earth if they have to.

HIS HOLINESS

I saw Jane with the dreadlocks in the Valley the other night – after I'd left the Waterloo and my little run-in with the lesbians from upstairs – and Jane had said that the last time she seen Donger he'd lost the plot and turned into a bible-basher. At first I'd thought it was a joke, the bit about him becoming a Christian that is, and just reacted as such with a sneer.

'I shit you not, Dante,' she'd sworn. 'He's now a weary, white, word-wasting wowser. It's really sad to see.'

Jane doesn't seem the type to make bullshit up or cast aspersions on a friend's character, so since I've got fuck all on today I decide to see this apparent transformation for myself. I jump a train out to Indro and leg it up Station Road and past that shitheap they call Westfield to where Donger lives next door to the shops on Moggill Road.

The little girl from next door isn't out playing hopscotch, but evidence of a recent game lies scrawled upon the concrete. In the grass beside the path is a jumble of coloured chalks. I can't help but idly wonder if she finally lost her balance and went sprawling under one of these speed freaks that fly up over the crest here. The way some of these fucking morons drive along here the little girl wouldn't stand a chance if she *had* fallen onto the road. But the tarmac looks blessedly free of blood stains, so there's that.

I bang my fist on the front door of Donger's house, and I can hear his feet thump onto the floorboards and then pad through the whole house, shaking it with every step. I'm anticipating a hopeless case to answer the door based on Jane's observations, but Donger is still the crazy-looking punk we all know and love. He's even still got a semblance of a ratty mohawk whereas I was expecting a parted comb-over. The cut above his eye from the riots at Market Day is nearly healed.

'It's the Dante dude,' he drawls, making me grit my teeth at the choice of nickname.

'Donger,' I nod. 'I was in the neighbourhood.'

'Of course you were,' he says, gesturing me in. One of the first things I notice is that there's a decidedly noticeable lack of furniture. I sneak a peek at Lachie's room and notice it's empty. There's not even a mattress on the floor anymore.

'By your lonesome now, huh?'

'Yeah, first Spaz and now Lachie,' he says soberly, pushing open the door further as if to reveal the obvious.

He sounds wasted, but I can't smell any weed or booze on him.

'You straight?' I can't help but ask.

He's not offended.

'Yup, clean as a fucking whistle,' he beams.

Often people who've been taking something like pot on a daily basis will eventually appear quite lucid, but as soon as they go off it their brains scramble and it's only then that they'll appear stoned.

'You haven't found God, have you?' I smirk, ostentatiously baiting him.

'I suspect you've already heard, but,' he says reproachfully.

'Unbelievable,' I say. I'm still convinced it's one of his stunts.

'No it's not,' he says with a glint in his eye. 'It's a miracle.'

We both crack up, which is a fucking relief. Jane can get a bit weird in her intensity sometimes, so I'll just put her analysis the other day of Donger's conversion down to that.

'I was right all along, wasn't I,' I tease, 'about the angels and shit? You know, how you're always goin on about that *Celestine Prophecy* book?'

'Well, that's different,' he says, not at all defensively. 'You start opening your mind to different possibilities when you look around for them. That's all I was doing. And then I found the Word of God.'

I want to suggest that turning to the Bible seems like a backward step, but figure it's best to keep my opinion to myself. The tension of the last week has slipped off my shoulders, and I no longer feel as if the world is coming to an end, if indeed that's how I did feel about it. Whatever was going on – the planets misaligned as Megs might say – has passed, at least for me. Maybe this is Donger's knee-jerk reaction to that gut feeling I'd had?

'How about that, ay?' I glance around the room expecting to see Jesus posters or crucifixes hanging up. None. Only his PiL poster that he'd pilfered from Skinny's on a dare and a few gig flyers like the Big Bongin Baby one from when we went to watch The Madmen play at St Paul's Tavern that time. And, of course, his real pride and joy, that rancid piece of carpet nailed to the wall that he calls the *Dutchman of History*. 'You going to church now, then?'

'Nah, fuck that, dude,' he snorts, plonking himself down in his battered vinyl armrest. Next to him, on a stack of milk crates that serve as a side-table, is brand new copy of the Holy Bible with the lettering in shiny gold. 'There's no way they represent the Good Book, the cunts.'

'Glad to hear it,' I smile. 'They're all a bunch of pedos, anyway. Only because the Courier Fail recently started exposing what those cunts are up to and how they protect their own has the church decided, *ohh, you know what, better get a PR team onto this.*'

Donger's not too enthusiastic about this topic, it seems, but he does go so far as to acknowledge that there needs to be Federal inquiries into all the churches rather than relying on them to conduct their own biased internal investigations. His stalwart mistrust of the establishment is hardly diminished, at least. He's just upgraded one absurd book for another.

I grant him this: he's much calmer than the Dale Donger I'm used to. I can only guess that this is the effect of his newfound religion. He was always a bit predisposed to crossing over, I guess, what with wanting to earnestly join the Hare Krishna's once upon a time but for the rule of abstaining from alcohol. Maybe this'll be an improvement on the wild and devilish Donger that rears its ugly head when he gets drunk?

'You still drinking?' I ask.

He shakes his head and turns his bottom lip down. 'Nope. Givin it all up.'

'Even pot?'

'Even,' he says, raising his chin proudly.

'That's some resolve, Donger. I have to hand it to ya.'

'Speaking of drink,' he says, shoving himself out of his chair and strolling into the kitchen. 'Want a cuppa?'

'Sure. Weak. Milk.'

'You seen Scabbie, lately?' he says over the sound of the water boiling in the saucepan. I guess the kettle belonged to Lachie.

'Nah,' I shake my head.

Despite our solidarity last month in getting Donger patched up in the hospital, Scab and I have hardly turned into the best of buddies. Some rifts just take longer to mend, if at all. But it puts me in mind of a probable instigator for all this God-bothering nonsense.

'Fuck me, Donger, is that all it takes?'

'What do you mean?'

'The whack on the head you got from the pigs at Market Day. That's about when you probably turned to religion, yeah?'

'Yeah, after then, so fucking what?' he growls, concentrating on making the cups of tea.

'Just asking,' I go, holding my hands up in surrender. I came and visited him after that day and there was no sign then that he'd found God. Perhaps I needed to be around more to see it, like Spazza probably had by then.

'You know something, Dante?' he says, turning and pointing a dripping teaspoon at me. 'You go on about religion all the time like you know it all. Like you've got all the fucking answers.'

'I was in a cult, remember?'

'Oh boo-fucking-hoo, mate,' he snaps, tossing the teaspoon into the sink with a loud clatter. The noise grates on my nerves. Between that and his attitude I can feel The Inferno beginning to rise from its slumber. 'Instead of maybe wasting our tax dollars on chasing down pedos in the church we can get little Johnnie Howard to finally commit one way or another on his stance towards immigration and foreign aid. Eh?'

What the fuck is this cunt on about?

'You don't pay tax, you dumb bastard,' I point out.

'And neither do you!' he nearly yells, then eases back and cradles his tea between his hands as if to soothe his temper. My cup of tea remains forgotten on the bench behind him.

'No shit, Sherlock.' My voice has that distinctive edge to it. I need to remain calm. Donger is, after all, a mate. 'Listen, all I know is that I've come round here to find everything is a bit fucking topsy-turvy and I'm just trying to get a handle on it.'

'You're as clueless as the rest of them,' he scorns. 'That hospital was fullo fucking Asians. Mate. Did you not notice when you and Scab took me in or were you too busy tryna be a smart cunt as usual going on about the Hague Convention to impress that boong lady in there?'

'Whoa! Out of fucking order there, Dale,' I warn him. 'I'm a crass cunt, yeah, but I draw the line at pricks being racist.'

'I'm not being racist,' he says sincerely, 'just facing facts. Even Blind Freddy can see that. We're just dishing out money left right and centre to the Aborigines, welcoming Asians in with open arms. Over a hundred million dollars in aid to Indonesia, who're still just a country of pirates at heart, just so they can build an army to invade Australia! Where does it fucking stop?'

'Who's *we*, Dale? You're on the fucking dole, you stupid cunt! Same as me, same as whoever the fuck you're going on about. Same boat, you...'

I breathe deep, feeling the familiar shake starting in my bones. What's happened to my friend? I'm starting to see why Spazza and Lachie haven't bothered staying here any longer.

Same boat.

There's only one witless deadshit that I can think of that Donger would be hanging around with that shares this fucked up rhetoric I'm hearing right now, and that useless bald cunt's always going on about 'boat people'.

'You've been hanging around that fascist cunt Sean again.'

No question. Just a straight up accusation.

Donger's a bit surprised I've made the connection, but it all makes sense now. Only a thick-skulled boot-boy could draw all these threads together and unite them under a faith that has spent an eon crushing darker-skinned nations under its heel. Dale has now joined the ranks of the rabid far-right. Probably has a framed photograph of Pauline Hanson around here somewhere that he wanks off to.

I'm more than disappointed by this, of course. I'm fucking gutted.

And the realisation leaves me without fuel for rage. Instead, I feel my mind itself shutting down to all stimuli, hoping to block out the ridiculous rhetoric still spewing from Donger's hateful mouth. Only moments ago I was building up to the kind of anger that might have seen me maybe try and bash my mate's brains out with his tea cup, and now all I can feel is a deep despondency.

Jane was right: Donger's lost the plot. It's only a matter of time before he shaves his head and dons a pair of headkicking boots.

I stand up, my eyelids heavy as I stare at Dale rabbiting on and on. His face looks ugly.

'Shut the fuck up, Dale,' I go, my voice steady and emotionless.

'How about you wake the fuck up, instead?' he retorts as I make my way for the front door.

Out on the front steps I pause for thought, trying to think of something to say to him that might salvage our friendship, or this moment at least, but the door slams behind me and actually startles me. I feel the hairs on my neck prick up and a low growl come out of my chest, cause loud noise makes me aggressive. But the door's well and truly closed now. There's no threat of violence here.

Out on the footpath I catch a glimpse of something pale in the grass next to the road.

The chalk.

I snatch a piece up, stalking back to Donger's front door, and against the dark panel I scrawl a huge pentagram. Under it in letters large enough to be read from the street I write: THE DEVIL LIVES HERE.

I toss the chalk away and rub the dust off my fingers, walking at a fast pace past the Moggill Road shops and back down to the train station, recalling a chauvinistic joke Twix once told that essentially posited that God created the yeast infection so that women knew what it was like to live with an annoying cunt. I wish I could have twisted that to suit my purposes somehow and fling at Donger, but I'm too angry to have articulated something anyway.

As I'm about to round the corner, I glance back and notice a cop car roll to a stop in the driveway to the underground carpark of the shops. Two officers climb out and head for Donger's front door.

I remember now that he told me a while ago that the cops have been regularly bugging him about the body of that old woman found in the construction site he was working on at the beginning of the year, asking him the same questions over and over. He said he gives the same answers over and over, but confessed that it felt like they suspected he either had something to do with the lady's death or knew someone who had.

'I know fucking squat, Dante,' he'd insisted, which of course was the truth. Donger's a bit of a dipshit at times, but he's no liar.

Whatever's going on inside that head of his, he's on his own now.

SLOWDIVE

The courts are intimidating as hell, period.

There's basically police everywhere, there's lawyers and crims or, like, what I think are crims, at least. It's a bit hard to tell who is who, but at least some of the defendants are easy to spot because they look like right dingbats in their cheap, ill-fitted suits and clashing ties. I bet they can't wait to get back into their crap Mambo shirts and deck shoes or suede rollers.

Lisa's nerves are shot. She's in a shitty mood, basically snapping at everything her husband Darren says. He looks haggard, like he's not been sleeping, and I can easily guess he's bearing the brunt of her all her frustrations at home. That's Lisa's way: blame everyone else, play the victim card out to its fullest. The poor guy hasn't got a hope against that when he's in the eye of the storm.

She hasn't said one word to me, not at her place, not in the taxi on the way in, nor out in the corridors when we arrived. I could have offered her a Valium if I'd known she was so strung out, but I didn't bring any because I was too scared that the police might think I was a drug dealer or something. So I left them at home, but not before popping one myself. There's no way I could, like, get through today without it, although I wish now I'd popped two.

The rents are fussing over everything as usual. Papa reads every sign in the building, even just the basic emergency evacuation ones, like they were crucial documents handed to us by the court itself. I have this niggling fear that the evacuation signs won't be enough in the case of an emergency, that something will happen where not even those signs cannot help us.

Lisa's getting annoyed by my constant need to tap everything, but she won't break her silence with me to tell me to knock it off. I can see her watching me from the corner of her eye, clenching her teeth. As if I could stop anyway. May as well tell a man with, like, no legs to get up and walk.

Instead, she snaps at Darren, like: 'Can you not swallow so loudly, please?'

He almost goes to shake his head, I can see him begin the motion, but then wisely reconsiders and just hangs it instead, basically staring at the floor between his feet.

Inside the court room we take our places and Lisa goes up with her solicitor, Scott Mannington, who specialises in Tax and Revenue Law. He's been helping Lisa through all this stuff ever since the arrest, and Papa has spared no expense on him. It's Papa's number one priority that Lisa gets off the charges scott-free. No pun intended.

The Commonwealth Director of Public Prosecutions, or CDPP, are basically the ones bringing the charges against Lisa, and they've set up shop on a table across from Lisa and Scott.

Where the hell's Dante? He said he was going to be here when we arrived and, like, hang out with me for the duration of the trial. I didn't want to face this alone, which is how I've felt the last few days despite Mama and Papa being up here. It's like the family unit has banded together but because I'm the traitor, the Judas in their midst, I'm cold-shouldered aside but still expected to, like, follow them around and participate in the family affairs just because I'm blood. It's fucked.

My legs are jittery, bouncing my foot off the ground.

'Control yourself, *kóri*,' Mama hisses.

I half expect her to threaten to lock me up in an Epeirot dungeon and make me grind barley corn all day and night.

'I can't,' I whine.

'This is about your sister,' grumbles Papa as low as he can so he doesn't disturb the court, 'not about you.'

I feel like bursting into tears. As if being OCD isn't hard enough, now I've got the rents treating muggings here like I'm basically doing it to get attention. So mote it be.

'I need the toilet,' I whisper.

Mama rolls her eyes and is like: 'Hurry up, then.'

I excuse myself as I slide past the people next to me and into the aisle. As I leave the court-room, I can hear my sister swearing on the Bible. Her small voice in that room of hushed judgement gives me the chills.

I don't need the toilet at all. I need out. Outside, away from the constriction of the system, of being held responsible, of a family who harbours an unspoken resentment of me. The police stare at me with suspicion as I power-walk through the security doors and outside.

I run around the corner and burst into tears, covering my face and, like, gulping in lungfuls of air as I sob. It hurts my chest, but the pain feels good.

'You alright, chicken?'

It's an old guy, even older than Papa. He's having a smoke on the other side of the garden bed, peering past the palm fronds at me. There's, like, snot running down my top lip into my mouth, salting my tongue. I wipe it across my arm.

The old guy's like: 'No, no, wait up,' and comes around to me, hoiking a hanky from his pocket. 'It's clean, I promise.'

'Thanks,' I sniffle, wiping my face then my arm.

He's like: 'Keep it. You may need it again. Did you get done for something or get off?'

I shake my head. 'Not me. My sister. The case just started.'

He gives me a pitying look. 'Sorry to hear to that, chicken. It can be tough.'

'Are you on trial, too?'

'Nah, not me,' he says, dragging on his cigarette and offering me one, which I accept even though I don't ordinarily smoke. He's like: 'I'm a contracted cleaner. Fredrik's the name. Someone's gotta keep those windows clean and the bins empty, don't they?'

The cigarette burns my throat and the smoke fills my lungs, nearly suffocating me. It's precisely what I need, though.

'So who's the magistrate she's got?' says Fredrik.

'Justice Delahunty.'

He sucks air in through his teeth.

I start freaking out, and I'm like: 'What? Isn't he any good?'

'It's not a matter of any good,' Fredrik explains. 'A judge is above it all. They can be fully shit at their job and still avoid consequence. The problem is that Leighton Delahunty is a bit of a prick. It's nothing for him to go from whoa to go and turn into an utter mongrel.'

My heart sinks. That was the last thing I needed to hear.

'What would happen to someone, for example, if they were, like, part of a tax fraud situation?'

Fredrik screws his nose up. 'What do you mean *part of?*'

'Well, Lisa isn't the one who lied to the tax department,' I explain. 'Not initially, anyway. She was working with this other bloke, right, who was, like, dodgy as, and so anyway he invested in her business and she gave him these, like, kinda business loans.'

'Holy shit,' says Fredrik, shaking his head. 'That's not simple tax evasion, chicken. That's money laundering.'

I know the term, of course, from the movies, but beyond that it means little to me. Period. Fredrik can tell by my expression that I'm clueless.

'That's a pretty big deal,' he adds.

I feel the blood drain from my face.

Frederick's like: 'Don't worry about it too much. That fuckstick Martin Bryant got thirty-five consecutive life sentences yesterday in Hobart. It was a good day for the justice system. It might've put Delahunty in a good mood, if you're in luck.'

'Luck's not what we're hoping to rely on,' I mutter, not meaning for it to sound as whimsical as it probably does.

Dante crosses the road, beads of sweat dripping down his face.

'Alex! So sorry I'm late! I really am.'

I instantly take my fear and frustration out on him without even thinking.

'You knew this day was important to me, Dante! How could you?'

I sound like my mother, I realise, but I can't stop. I keep scolding Dante until I'm crying again. Fredrik, ever the gentleman, quietly takes his leave and heads back inside via a back door. I notice he's left a couple of cigarettes on the garden ledge next to me.

Dante hugs me and he's like: 'Alex, I'm sorry. Is it over already?'

'Nah,' I sniffle, finally calm again. 'They just started not long ago. I can't go back in, Dante. It's awful.'

'So just stay out here, then,' he suggests, sitting down on the edge of the garden bed with me. I notice the cigarettes are now gone. He's fucking quick, I give him that.

'So I've got some news,' I say. 'My parents came up last week to prepare for Lisa's court-case, obviously. But, like, they also took me to see a specialist who says I'm basically OCD.'

He nods. 'Yeah, that was kinda obvious.'

'But not like in that stupid scene way,' I say, thinking of all the people I know who claim to have it, as if it's something to be proud of. 'I'm, like, properly diagnosed with it, and it's fucking up my life. I can't go anywhere without doing this fucking tapping shit. I hate it, Dante...'

I'm crying again. I'll be fucking dehydrated before the day is up at this rate.

'If I don't tap something, if I don't touch it with my fingers at least, I feel like something bad's gonna happen. To my family, I mean.'

'Well, one of them is currently on trial,' jokes Dante.

'That's a bit insensitive,' I say. 'But it's true, isn't it? See, bad stuff *is* happening.'

He looks at me blankly.

'But the specialist said it's manageable, didn't they? This OCD stuff?'

I shrug. I honestly don't recall. My mind grew progressively more numb during the session, but Mama did tell me afterwards that the specialist said there are behavioural modification therapies available, but, like, at this stage they'd be looking at medication.

'Go onto a pension if I can't pull myself together,' I add.

'Okay, first off,' says Dante sternly, sitting up straight. 'There's no pulling yourself together. That's the kind of bullshit people like your family are going to quickly insist you do. But you don't have to listen to that shit. You know that.'

'True,' I nod, sighing deeply.

'Secondly,' he says, continuing his lecture, 'the DSP is there for people who need it, and if you need it then that's fine. It's no crime to be unwell, Alex. And if later on you feel like you don't need the pension, then you just come off it. It's up to you. You're not locked into against your will.'

We've had this convo before, it occurs to me.

'It sort of feels like that's what's happening,' I confess.

'You know, that's probably where a lot of your problems are stemming from. You feel like you've lost control of your life. You lost your job, became unwell, etcetera etcetera.'

'Yeah, etcetera's not the best way to sum up that I dobbed my sister in and now she's being charged with tax fraud. You dilute it to a minor misdemeanour when you put it like that.'

'Fine,' he says, throwing his hands in the air. 'Not a problem. It's a major catastrophe, then. But the thing is, it was still a situation that you felt was beyond control until you gave it a go. Now it's only gotten worse. That illustrates my point even more, is all.'

'Okay, you've got a point,' I concede. 'But so what? What am I meant to do now?'

'Go on the pension, take the medication, whatever it is you need to do to recover. If it means hiding away from the world for some time, then do it.'

Curiously, his advice makes me feel much better. Up until now, everyone's been telling me to pull my socks up, get my shit together, all that sort of talk. No-one's said to just, like, let it go or run from it. And while Dante's not strictly saying that, because he's also telling me to address my problem medicinally, what he's doing is saying there's no pressure. And so far, pressure is all I've had from people. Especially from my family.

I'm like: 'On that note, then, maybe I should stay in Brisbane.'

The news surprises him, which isn't easy to do.

'Oh? You were going to leave?'

'Mama and Papa have already spoken with my landlord about breaking the lease,' I inform him, 'but Phoenix said they'll take it over since they want to, like, move closer to the Valley anyway. So it's all arranged. Mama and Papa helped me pack the other day, and Phoenix is moving in this weekend. Basically, Lisa's trial should be over today and afterwards I'll head back to Melbourne with the rents.'

'Fuck,' says Dante, sliding his palm down the side of his face. 'It'll be sad to see you go. Just make sure you remember what I told you, though. Don't let any ol Joe Blo, not even *them*,' – he points towards the courts, but I know he means my parents – 'don't let them tell you that you've got to get better any faster than you need to.'

'Thanks, Dante,' I smile, and hug him.

He's like: 'Look after yourself, you duffer.'

The look in his eyes is so tender and raw, that when he leans in and kisses me on the forehead for some reason – maybe because I'm overwhelmed by gratitude, who knows? – but for some reason I plant my lips fair on his for a pash session.

He's shocked, and pulling away he's all like: 'Whoa up, girl!'

I'm fucking mortified! I don't know what came over me. All I can do is stare at him agape, hoping he'll come up with an excuse on my behalf.

Just then I hear my father's voice and turn to see him talking with Scott Mannington outside the court. Scott's got his hand on my Papa's shoulder, and Papa's, like, staring at the ground in a solemn way.

I'm like: 'Where's Lisa?' as I approach them, a rising panic in my voice and in my step. 'Where's Lisa, Papa?'

Papa just shakes his head and apologises to me. His eyes are red and wet.

'I'll leave you with your family,' says Scott to Papa respectfully. He turns to me. 'We did our best, Alexandra.' He comes over to me and, like, squeezes my hand, leaning in to kiss me goodbye on the cheek, but instead he whispers in my ear: 'Mister Calthorpe sends you his condolences.'

As he's pulling away from me, I catch the smallest of smirks on Scott's face before it disappears. He nods curtly to Papa, then walks back inside the courts.

I'm fucking gobsmacked.

Papa goes to put his arm around me but I shove him off, and the look of hurt in his eyes is unbearable. But I can't do this right now. Like, I don't know what the fuck is going on.

Calthorpe? *Calthorpe?*

What the fuck does that *ton pousth* have to do with any of this?

'Alex, what's wrong with you?' My Papa's voice is strained.

Dante was right. It's not me that's in the wrong. The whole system is fucked. One massive boy's club, the fucking patriarch shitting all over us. I can't know Papa's not in on it, too, but why would he be? It's his own daughter, after all?

'Papa, I'm sorry,' I say, but without feeling. My heart's gone cold. My whole body has.

Papa's like: 'You look like you've seen a ghost.'

Dante's behind me, and he's like: 'What'd he say to you? I saw the cunt smirking.'

'Who's this?' demands Papa, looking Dante up and down.

Scott Mannington. The name rings a bell. Then it hits me. One of Calthorpe's associates, of course. I remember him briefly from when I worked for Calthorpe.

'Where'd you get that solicitor from, Papa?'

'Who're you?' Papa's glaring at Dante. Did he see us kiss?

'PAPA!' I scream.

He jolts and looks at me in horror, his face going red as a beetroot.

'Where did you get that solicitor from? Did you speak to a Lyndon Calthorpe?'

'*Ai sihtir,*' he whispers quietly in Greek, grimacing.

Suddenly, Papa staggers and, like, slowly falls to the ground. It's weird watching him doing it, like he's taking the piss out of me by basically pretending to have a panic attack. Dante rushes past me and grabs hold of my Papa.

'Fuck, I think he's having a heart attack,' says Dante.

'Oh, shit!'

Mama appears at the doors to the court. 'Steve?'

'Call an ambulance, Mama!'

'Steve, what's wrong?' says Mama, still at the doors and frowning at Papa.

'Mama!' She snaps her head up at me. 'Call an ambulance!'

She nods dumbly, glancing down one more time at Papa as she disappears inside the courts.

'It'll be okay, Papa,' I say, kneeling down next to him. 'Mama's getting help.'

Some police officers run out the doors and ask what happened. Dante, who's cradling my Papa's head so it doesn't fall on the ground, remains tight-lipped.

'He's having a heart attack,' I announce, my voice loud even to my own ears, like I'm shouting inside my head and not outside of it.

Papa's staring past me at the sky, clenching his jaw. It occurs to me I never got to ask him what happened to Lisa.

PIXIE AND THE PRUDENTIAL

I've been beggin for change all day like a loser. Me feet are literally fuckin killin us.

Nel never ended up rippin off Black Ronnie and becomin a big-time dealer like she'd said she would. We're still as broke as ever. She did take me spare pair of Doc Martens, but, and throw em over the powerlines out front of the Palace so everyone'd know she's started dealin. Didn't ask us if she could take me Docs, but. Just fuckin did it.

We've been gettin sicker and more desperate as our need for more and more heroin grows each week. We sold the last of what we could from the flat, then started stealin from the other flats. Everyone started gettin suss and locking up even when they're home, so we hit the neighbourhood, pinchin anythin that wasn't nailed down and hockin it off at Cash Converter's or the Valley pawn shops. We broke into the yuppie's place across the road one night and took off with a Nintendo and a plastic bag full of games and CD's just as the cunt got home. Nearly got busted!

But it's not been enough. Our needs aren't bein properly met.

We've now literally taken to beggin, which is fuckin stupid. Nel says we gotta do it, but.

So basically we get dropped off outside King George Square in the mornin, and then we just spend the whole day goin round the city centre in circles askin people for money. We tell em all sorts of shit, but mostly I just stick to one story which is that I need money for the bus home. I suspect a lot of the time I get the money just coz they want to get rid of us. They see us comin, look sideways at us, but when I get to em they either don't make eye-contact or they look scared when they do. Especially the women. I target them the most.

Today it was me, Nel and Jeremy. Since livin with Nel and Roz, Jeremy's slowly started usin, and is now permanently a junkie. The other week Raven and Nel were arguin about it out in the hallway and now Raven's not speakin to any of us. She won't even look at us if we see her round, but we don't give a shit. Raven does, but. Her eyes get watery when she has to walk past us.

Some days Roz comes out with us, too, but she gets lazy and can't be fucked walkin around. So her modus operandi then becomes to simply ask anyone who sits next to her at the bus-stop she parks her fat ass on. It works, half the time, and then the victims get confused when she doesn't board the next bus with em. She was meant to come out with us today, but her and Nel had a massive row last night like they were a married couple, and Roz stormed out. Haven't seen her since.

I think Roz is gettin really sick of turnin tricks. She's covered in junkie sores now, so it's hard to imagine she'd get many clients. The cops've let up on hassling the streetwalkers down at the Laundromat on Brunswick Street, so she's been hangin out there again.

I feel sorry for Roz, but. She's past her prime.

Nel's been so intense lately. She doesn't go clubbin anymore or see any of her old fetish-scene friends, like Chantelle. Her days have become centred on heroin, acquiring it and tryin to make sure the rest of us are as addicted as she is. I suppose she'd feel miserable doin it on her own all the time. Coz of this, I've tried to keep me distance from her a bit, which is pretty fuckin hard since I live with her. A lot of times I use the excuse of goin out to see Imp and James, even though I literally haven't seen those cunts in yonks. I think Nel's aware of that, but. I dunno. I've stopped tryin to keep up with the lies I've come up with.

I heard about this girl in America that killed her parents. She was part ova group of teenagers that had formed a vampire cult. There was about thirty of em. I don't know what made em vampiric, but. They didn't drink blood or nuthin. But this girl, Heather Wendorf, bashed her own mum and dad's brains in with the help of her boyfriend.

Wendorf's school principal said Wendorf was 'new wave', and that she couldn't be faulted for it.

Reminds us of the Wiggington woman here a few years ago. She thought she was a vampire, too, and killed that taxi dude. Wendorf. Wiggington. Shame me last name's Lang, and not Wang or some shit. We could've been a vampire trio. I could just kill any cunt that pisses us off. I wouldn't hafta be beggin on the streets.

But there's work to be done.

I go up to this complete normie cunt at the phone box and ask him for some change. He tries to ignore us coz he's on the phone, so I tap his elbow. He scowls at us, as if that would make us piss off. So I tap his elbow again and hold up me palm, giving him the courtesy of continuin his phone call but helpin us out at the same time.

'I gotta go, see you tonight anyhow,' he says quickly to the cunt on the line, then slams the handset into the cradle. As he storms away he barks at us: 'If I give you my money then what do I have?'

'I gotta eat,' I snarl at him.

'And so do I!' he shouts, literally bulgin his eyes at us. 'I'm on the fucking dole, too! Same amount of money, girlie.'

He charges off and crosses the road.

'Go fuck yaself!' I scream.

Nel comes up beside us, itchin for a fight.

'What'd that fuckhead say to you?'

'Fuck im,' I snap, annoyed by how protective she's actin. I think that's what her and Roz were fightin about last night, about how Nel always has to try and be there for everyone lookin after them when we don't even want it. Which is ironic, coz we all consider Roz to be a kind of mother figure. It's almost like Nel's doin it to control us.

'I'll kill the fuckin cunt,' she says, askin a random dude for change in the same hate-filled breath. The dude apologises, literally picking up his pace. 'No worries! God bless!' Nel calls after the dude in a friendly, matter-of-fact tone.

'I wanna go home,' whines Jeremy sookily, his eyes sunken into blackened pits.

His nose runs all the time now. I'm sick of his whining. I've never liked him since I first laid eyes on him at the Palace. He creeps us out with his droopy, wet eyes and his slack mouth that literally won't shut. It gives him the appearance of always being sick. His face looks like an open wound. No wonder his idiot girlfriend dumped him.

'Right, time to call it quits,' Nel decides, goin into the phone booth to call Jimmy Farrell, even though it's only a cheap taxi fare back to the Palace. None of us would dare think of spendin our donations when we can get a free ride, but, even if it is from that fuckin pedo creep Farrell.

Jeremy sits on the garden wall next to the entrance to the Red Cross cafe, literally huggin himself like he's fuckin cold. It makes us realise I'm cold, too, even though the sun's literally out. Yet another reason to hate this fuckin kid.

Nel pulls her cap off and orders us to drop the day's takings into it. The coins spill from our pockets like a beautiful waterfall into her greasy cap. It's a relief to get the fuckin weight off, even if it is hard to part with all that cash. Nel's cap strains under the burden of the load.

'All of it,' she insists, lookin at us meaningfully.

'That's all of it.'

'Bullshit,' she goes.

People are starin at us as and at the bulgin hat of coins.

'It's all there, Sir,' I argue.

'Shut yer flaps with that *Sir* shit,' she growls. Roz has told us I gotta stop callin Nel *sir* coz it's really pissin her off, but it's like I told Roz, I can't help it, it's just a reflex to Nel bein so bossy all the fuckin time. 'Your fucken pockets are still heavy, I can see. Turn em out.'

'Whatever... lyin cunt.'

'You're the lying cunt,' she growls, puttin her face up to mine.

'You're not the boss of me,' I go and push her face away, but it just makes her angrier.

She literally throws a swing at us, but holdin the hat full of money makes her miss. It cracks me up somethin shockin until half the coins tip out of her hat. I reckon it's about sixty bucks worth, some of it rollin down into the gutter.

'Fuck fuck fuck,' she's sayin desperately.

While she's trying to scoop the ones from the gutter I'm snatchin the ones off the footpath and stuffin em into me pockets. Jeremy's tryin to get some too, so I stomp on his fuckin thieving cunt hands.

'What'd you do that for?' he says angrily.

'Fuck off, prick, or I'll cut ya,' I hiss at him, and take off up the street before Nel can get a hold of us.

She's yellin something at us, probly threats, but I don't fuckin care. She's worse than me dad. Everyone in the street stares at us like they've never fought with their friends before.

The sun starts to set behind Mount Coot-tha. The whole of Brissie literally gets painted by this amazin orange sunset which hits the front of the Treasury building. It makes it look like somethin from a

Hollywood film about Greek Gods or whatever. Then the picture's destroyed by a council bus disappearin into the bus tunnel in front, just across the street. I'm standin in the awning of the Prudential Building, this massive abandoned art-deco building that goes six stories up. It's totally empty and ready for demolition, but here on the street in it's boarded up alcoves and doorways are heaps of homeless bums sittin about pissed or passed out. Across the street yuppie cunts are headin into the brightly lit interior of the casino, the orange sunset makin them into Gods and Goddesses.

I wish I had that kind of money.

I'm fucked, too fucked to walk anymore. Me body's beginnin to crave some smack, dammit. I sit down near some of the bums, old guys that look like they've been doin this for fuckin donkey's years. The concrete is cold. It never really sees the sun here.

I count the coins out. It's not much. Not enough for a shot of anythin, and the smoke shop behind us closed down ages ago, is as empty as now. There's enough cash for a movie ticket, but. The new *Crow* movie's playing, *City of Angels*. I could pass the time with that for a coupla hours. It'd be ace to be in a city of angels, where they cared for ya and gave ya everything ya need. Like, all the free smack ya could take. Pure shit, but, not that crap cut with God knows fuckin what in it.

I don't know how long I'm here for, but the sun has set and I notice a yuppie dude hangin around. Not too close, he's walkin up and down the street, comin up onto the footpath when the cars drive through to George Street. He's dressed pretty decent, like clean and shit. A total normal. He's dressed the way Dad would approve: in *slacks*.

The dude's actually watchin us, I realise. What the fuck?

He gets closer when he notices us watchin him back, and tries on a few weak greetings which I ignore, starin hard at the cunt like he's a literally ghost or somethin.

Eventually he pulls his wallet out and starts lookin through it.

Okay, now the cunt has me attention, but.

'Hey, don't know if you're interested or not,' he says.

I think, interested or not in what, cunt? I notice his voice is shakin.

He pulls out some notes, a couple of twenny's. I'm tryin not to look too keen, but I feel me neck crane to inspect the cash.

'What do you want?' Me voice sounds hollow.

He doesn't say anythin, just moves over to the side of the building, tryin to shield himself in an alcove where no-one has set up in. I know how come no-one's sleepin in that one, but; it's coz they've all been pissin in there since I got here. The young dude literally unzips his fly and waits for us to respond.

I use the wall for support to stand up, coz I'm not crawlin over to this cheeky cunt like a fuckin dog.

'Money,' I demand.

He gives us the cash, which I stuff down into me undies.

Encouraged by the transaction, he takes charge, pushin down on me shoulder until I'm kneelin, then pulls his dick out. It's starting to get hard, but that's about all I can tell of it in this gloom. I don't even know if it smells or not, coz the overpowering stench of urine on the ground blocks out all other odours.

'Put it in, bitch.'

A part of us is about to resist, tell him to fuck himself if he's going to call us names. But I'm too fucked to react, and he forces his member against me face until it's literally in me mouth. Again, I'm too fucked to do anythin but I try. But the muscles in me jaw are protestin about havin to work at all, let alone perform oral sex.

The thing is, it's not called a blow job for nuthin. It's hard fuckin work, sometimes. That's what dudes don't appreciate. Stick ya finger up ya ass then get a whiff of it. Then imagine doin that with a dick in ya mouth, while literally tryin not to spew. Hard fuckin work, alright.

The dude gets angry, tellin us to get to work coz I've been paid. His dick's down me throat and makin us choke, so I push the cunt back and start dry-heaving, leanin on the piss-stained concrete.

'Don't back out now, you lil gothic bitch.'

Where the fuck's all this anger in him comin from? He looked like a docile cunt stalkin up and down the street before.

'Can't,' I manage to gasp between my heavin.

'Fuck,' he spits, then demands his money back.

'Get fucked,' I nearly crack up. 'You're not the boss of me.'

He reaches down and tries to pull us up, tries to reach into me jeans for the money.

'Fuck off,' I yell, tryin to fight him off. I'm not up to it, but.

'Give me the fucking money back,' he says in a strangled voice, his arms holdin us in a rough bear-hug.

'What's goin on?' one of the drunks further down goes.

'This cunt's tryin to rape me,' I go. 'Call the police!'

The drunk cunts just shuffle away, like they can't be fucked gettin involved. Unless it's the mention of *police* that bugs them, as if sayin it aloud magically makes the useless cunts appear on the spot. If only.

Eventually the prick lets go and tells us he hopes I get raped and die of AIDS.

'You stupid slut,' he sneers as he quickly walks away.

Stupid slut. That's literally what KK's boss called us at the Nash after he'd finished with us, and everyone includin KK had laughed, except me. Fuckin typical. I thought KK was gonna be different from everyone else, but he's just like this rapist cunt here. Just another part of the problem.

I'm too shaken for an insulting come back. Instead I collapse on the concrete and start bawlin me eyes out, sobbin like a baby as I wish over and over again that Mum would turn up and take us home, her home, where it's warm and safe and just holds us like she used to when I was liddle.

The cars comin across the Victoria Bridge roll by, their headlights flashin bright and then glancin off the dividin wall for the bus tunnel. I can hear the sound of people laughin, makin jokes, comin across from the Treasury. Everyone sounds so happy over there. They've got friends, or family, and money, and no addictions. At least none that leave them cryin at night in someone else's piss puddles.

Finally I get up and shuffle like a zombie past all the drunks that turned away when I needed them, callin each one a cunt in turn.

'You, you're a cunt. You; cunt. You, a cunt. Cunt...'

There's a fat woman who looks old, lyin amongst them. I call her a cunt and then realise I know her face. It's Roz. My heart actually feels happy at the sight of someone familiar, someone who's never turned away from helpin us, someone who's a friend.

'Fuck, sorry Roz, didn't mean to call you a cunt.'

The bum next to her glances at her as if to say 'shit, ya know that little gothic bitch?' Then he shifts his ass to the side to give us room.

I kneel down next to her, sittin against her legs, glad of the touch.

'Fuckin arsehole tried to rape us,' I confess, feelin the tears in me eyes again.

But Roz just ignores us.

'Are ya still pissed about Nel from last night? Fuck, yer not angry with *me*, are ya?'

No reply. I didn't do nuthin wrong. I should just leave her to all these homeless pissheads and fuck off back to the Palace. Nel's probly forgotten what happened earlier by now, anyway.

'Roz?'

She hasn't blinked, I realise.

My heart lurches. All the hairs on me arms stand on end.

Her skin feels deathly cold.

I don't know what to do. I just sit there, unable to think what I should do. If I should call someone.

I don't know.

But now I'm cryin again.

I can't believe me friend has died on the footpath out front of this abandoned building right in the middle of the fuckin city and no cunt's even noticed, not even these stupid fuckin homeless fucks that are sittin all round her.

There's a needle on the ground beside her, and a plastic spoon. Anythin else has probly been taken by these fuckin greedy drunks.

'FUCK YOU FUCKING CUNTS!!' I scream at the top of me lungs, directing all me fury at the casino across the road. 'FUCK YOU ALL!!'

Through the blurred vision of me tears I can see their pale faces turn to look, the lights behind them like diamonds sparklin.

Roz...

Her face looks purple, frozen like she's in shock.

My beautiful Roz.

My cold and lifeless friend, Roz.

I will miss you.

TWIX IS A LIABILITY

Well, I've managed to really fuck everything up.

My wrist is slowly on the mend but my back still has issues. I should've been going to a physio, but I need to reserve my financial expenditure now I've got no job.

There was no way ol Twixxie of all people was going grovelling back to Gary for the old NiteWorks position. Even if by some miracle he took me back there's no way I'd get it easy. He'd cancel shifts left and right, make me travel extreme distances for jobs that are only a few hours long, and probably let it slip from his mind to pay me for several others. That's if he didn't just laugh in my face and tell me to fark off.

Fact is, I'm pretty dispensable, at the end of the day. They could snap their fingers and get a hundred young lads signing up tomorrow looking for easy work. A letter in the newspaper questioned the training young security guards are getting these days after some shit the author witnessed at an AC/DC concert in Toowoomba. I know the answer to that: sweet fuck all. A basic course that's paint-by-numbers, a couple of hundred for the licence and you're in. We're becoming a dime a dozen, and the bosses hold all the power now. Best bit though was the name of the guy who wrote the letter: *Devil*. The Courier Mail even wrote a disclaimer beneath saying: 'The writer changed his name to Devil by deed poll.'

Fark, but it hurts to laugh. Ribs are sore as.

I tried getting some work with Cubby Security, who I'd done a little subcontracting for, even though it was through NiteWorks. They said I couldn't legally switch over to them because of their contract with NiteWorks. I told the guy, Will his name was, that I'd thought that'd be on the cards but that I wasn't switching over because I'd already quit NiteWorks. Of course, I know it's not how it works in this industry, and that I'd hafta wait several weeks before he could legally consider me, but I was hoping he'd look the other way on that and sign me up straight off the bat. Not so.

So I'd waited, because I really wanted to work with Will. I knew the guards in his companies from the changeover shifts, so I knew he paid really well compared to the lousy wages Gary doled out. Over the weeks, though, my savings started dwindling down and all the normal places (warehouses, supermarkets, the Council) I'd dropped my resume off to didn't even call back, so I'd been forced to bug Will again about work. He ended up admitting to me that it wasn't going to happen, that Gary would stir shit up with the unions and make waves for Cubby.

The fucking union.

Frustrated, I'd bitten the bullet, trying a few other security places but it turned out Gary had already rung around and told them that I'd been fired for stealing a shitload of stuff over time from one of the clients, so now my name was mud.

I couldn't believe it! I'm no fucking thief!

I was so fucking wild I'd ended up accidently knocking the telly off its stand off some steam at home, and the sodding thing had fallen against the wall, putting a huge arse crack in the glass screen. Billy and Greg got the major shits with me, demanding that I pay for a new one, which of course I couldn't do because I still had to cough up for rent and groceries.

Those shit-stains hadn't been sympathetic at all. Go figure, right?

'Just spot me until I get another job,' I'd said, but Billy'd called me an arrogant fuckhead.

'Don't fucking well tell us what to do,' he'd said.

'I'm not,' I'd barked back. 'But you're loaded, Billy. Why're you getting your knickers in such a twist over this?'

'That's not the point,' Greg had said, looking at me like he was so fucking righteous.

'I'm always buying your fucking milk for you, you hinky tosser!' I'd yelled at him.

Greg then called me a cocky upstart and a massive argument broke out. At the end of the day, they'd told me to pack my bags and to piss off pronto.

My old man came down with his workmate's ute and we piled all my stuff in. Currently, everything I own sits stacked in the old man's garage. Thank Christ neither of those jokers have my parents' phone number, so they can't call and hassle me about getting them a new telly.

So now I'm back living again with the parentals – in Caboolture of all fucking places – with no job, no references and no girlfriend. I had about a hundred bucks on me, which would've been this weeks' rent and groceries but'll tide me over now until I can figure out what to do next.

Mum's happy as Larry to have me home again, recommending I stay for as long as I like, with the implication being that I can stay indefinitely. Dad's far less subtle about it, telling me he could hook me up with work locally if I stick around.

Thing is, I fucking hate Caboolture. I didn't when I was younger. I thought it had everything. But it's not easy having shoulder-length black hair and little bat tattoos in your shaved hairline. Locals don't seem to respond well to it. And there's no way I'm dressing down for these normals, either. My kick-arse boots with buckles stay. There's no fucking way I'm swapping them for fucking deck shoes, which now seem to be all the rage for the middle-income suburban wankers that look down their noses at me in Coles or Woolies.

My options are pretty limited for work, though. Lots of goths I know are getting into IT, or already in it. Even that puny kindergoth kid, Craig, the one that was mates with Ursula, is studying it. He's probably graduated by now and earning more than I ever did. Malik's just finished his course, too. He's hoping it'll lead on to much bigger things. He always reckoned IT is the future for job opportunities. He reckons the internet will be in everyone's home in future, and that businesses will be dependent on it. I can't see it myself, but Malik swears that's where future fortunes will be made. Who am I to crush his pipe- dreams?

And I don't care what that doctor at the sexual health clinic reckons, either. Fact is, if you wanna get by in this world you need money. Capitol. Assets. Collateral. A sodding advantage.

I finally got desperate and gave the old man a few copies of my resumes for him to drop off with his mates next time he saw them. I'd finally resigned myself that I'd be stuck working in Caboolture, after all, if any of them bothered to get back in contact with me.

Which of course they didn't.

Since passing out my resume has done fuck all for me, Mum's decided to give it the once over and see how it can be improved. The benefits of moving back home, I guess: mum's will do anything for their kids.

I'm not the only one who had to move recently, either, it turns out.

Because my old man works on the trains I get free travel anywhere I want. It's pretty helpful since I'm now staying all the way out at frigging woop woop and have no job to boot. So I'd jumped aboard the citybound the other day to go and see Alex, who I hadn't seen in ages, but her flat had been empty. One of the neighbours, a skanky little chick, thought I looked a bit suss and had started watching me carefully, asking shit like if I was also into witchcraft, so I'd ignored the question and had asked where Alex had gone.

'Dunno,' the skanky chick had said, hugging a broken coffee mug with Boris the Black Knight printed on the side, that weirdo from the TV when we were kids. I always thought he was a bit hinky. 'One moment she was here; next, gone! Still, left all her Satanic shit on the nature-strip, didn't she?'

On the grass beside the road had been a pile of crap like lamps and cushions and a plastic chair, and some other stuff. Everything had one thing in common: bat prints. It was on everything. And a lot of it was Batman related, even though I know Alex has said before she's not interested in comics or superheroes.

There'd been something really odd about it.

'She had a few bats in er belfry, no doubt,' the skanky chick had mumbled with the tactical nous of a dead blowfly, spitting a mouthful of coffee at a top-knot pigeon sunning itself in the dirt close under the stairs, smirking as it flew off with that gatling gun noise they're known for. 'I hate those birds,' she'd grinned at me.

'What do you mean?' I'd asked.

'Their lil red eyes, just staring straight inta ya soul,' the skank had replied, boggling her own bloodshot orbs for crazy effect.

'I mean about Alex.'

'Oh yeah, her,' the skank had coughed. 'Silly cow couldn't check the letterbox in the end without steppin on every crack in the concrete on the way down. Then had to check it five times and touch it on top. Like she was patting it, ya know?'

I hadn't known. I'd been too busy lying low after the incident at the radio station with Dante's girlfriend that I'd thought I could just catch up with Alex again after it'd blown over. I hadn't expected her to just up and go like that.

It's funny, because Alex always seemed to have her head screwed on, but it'd looked anything but normal that day. We've all got stuff with skulls or bats on it, but there'd been something too frigging overwhelming about that collection of junk on the footpath. Like there was just way too many bat prints and patterns.

When I got back to Caboolture I asked the lady at the library to email Alex's old man for me. I went back a couple of days later but they said there was still no answer.

Eventually Malik told me that Alex's father had had a heart attack when he was up here and after he got released from the hospital Alex returned to Melbourne with her parents. Then he told me she'd been diagnosed with OCD and some other stuff. So weird.

But I heard through Celia (who heard it from someone who knows Abi) that Alex got her sister sent to prison for a couple of months for rorting the Tax system! They thought she'd get off with just a fine, apparently, but the judge had decided to make an example of her.

'You should give Karen a call,' Mum goes, casually going over the section that lists my job history.

Yeah, right! Ever since we broke up after the abortion, Karen and I have only spoken to each other once: at that seedy topless bar she was working at. If I recall rightly (and I do), I'd called her a slut in front of everybody.

'Probably a wind up,' I murmur, idly watching the cricket on TV.

'Nonsense,' says Mum. 'I saw her and Carol the other day. She asked after you. I always liked Karen.'

Carol is Karen's mother. It's weird, because they look very much alike, but in some strange way Karen actually looks older. I used to sometimes imagine her mum's face instead when we had sex. But not until after ol Twixxie'd gotten bored with her, that is. You know, the 'honeymoon' period.

Matthew Elliott collects the ball and sends it spinning across the grounds of the Gabba. The TV cameras can barely keep up.

'What'd she say?'

'She said you don't go out much anymore,' Mum says. 'To The clubs, I mean. It seemed to me like Karen's been hoping to bump into you at one of them.'

Huh. Well, time *does* heal, I guess. For some. I didn't think Karen would ever go clubbing again. Not after what happened.

Frig! Elliott and this other joker, Mark Waugh, run smack into each other on the cricket pitch, spinning through the air. 'Excellent running,' the commentator drawls without any hint of irony. Looks like Elliott's snapped his leg in two, but the funny thing is the joker's out in the field can't even get him out. He clears his bat over the line before the stumps are knocked.

'I think I see your problem, Trav,' Mum goes.

'What problem?'

'On your resume,' she goes, holding it up for me to see. 'You've got your name at the top, but no contact details.'

I can't believe it. I've been handing that useless farking thing out for months now. No wonder no-one's called me back about any jobs!

Mum thinks it's hysterical, of course, and tells the old man as soon as he comes inside, who just raises his eyebrows as if he's got a poonce for a son. It's a pretty simple mistake to make, though, at the end of the day.

ABI AT THE FUNERAL

Mum and Dad have gone to a lot of trouble trying to get people to come along to Rosyln's funeral. She managed to piss a lot of people off in her time, but for Mum and Dad's sake most of the people they troubled to ask make an appearance. That's what my folks mean to people.

My folks. No longer *ours*, dear sister. You've abandoned me for the final time.

There's a group of her junkie friends turned up, as well. As much as I have the urge to ask them to leave, I figure they were as much her friends as anyone was, and perhaps in the end they were more family to her than even I was. God knows, I was always ashamed to admit to anybody the connection I shared with her. But these people had no qualms about associating with her. But they're a fucked up family if that's what they were to her.

There's Nel, looking gaunt and snide, like she's the ants pants, surveying all present with an air of distaste. Long sleeve button-up shirt to hide her fucking junkie sores. Beside her is Chantelle, who I used to kind of be mates with but she's also mates with Nel since she used to live with her, so I don't see her much nowadays. Some snotty-nosed teenage boy is with them. And then there's the little goth girl, who I've seen around. Her name's Prudence Lang, so I'm told. Apparently she was the one who called triple zero. Like Nel, she's got that junkie's arrogance about her. Or is it indifference? It's the same thing in the end, as far as I'm concerned.

None of the family knows that Nel's the one that got Roslyn onto heroin in the first place, but I know. More than that, as far as I can tell Nel isn't even aware that I know. Roslyn told me about it once on one of the numerous times we tried to repair our relationship, back when she was still turning up to family dinners at Christmas. She implied that Nel was a control freak and that the bitch is the one who initially encouraged Roz to become a prostitute so that they could afford more smack. I don't think I could ever find any forgiveness in my heart for that cruel and remorseless cunt.

The funeral director – Ken his name is – approaches the lectern, so everyone takes a seat. The junkies are on the other side of the chapel from me and the family. There's others over there, too, from the Prozac Palace, including Dante and Bernie, and Raven. It's nice to see them, at least.

After a prolonged, dramatic moment wherein Ken looks us over, affecting what is presumably both warmth and heartfelt sympathy in one expression (perhaps to save time expressing them each on their own?), he addresses the congregation in an impressively deep voice befitting the solemn service. Shit, even Nick Cave himself might have struggled to match this guy's portentousness!

'Many of you knew Roslyn as a happy and intelligent little girl, playing in her parents' backyard with her favourite dog, Gummie,' Ken intones.

A photo appears on the wall behind him, projected by a machine that makes a *thunking* noise as the picture slides into view. It shows Roslyn at about age seven, maybe? She's with an ugly and scruffy little dog, which I'm told she'd named after a cartoon show. *Gummie Bears* or something. I was either not born yet, or just a baby. I've got no memory of that dog, or of my sister being so small.

Ken continues waffling on about the keystones of Roslyn's life, touching on her scholastic achievements, her brief stint as president of the book club in Year 7, her excitement at making high-school. More photos flash up. More redundant history to mask the awful truth of what became of my sister. *Thunk. Thunk.*

Thunk.

Ken pauses for dramatic effect, to let all that we have heard and seen sink in. It's poor timing, however, because he launches into the next phase of her life, opening with 'Roslyn's difficult teenage years'. The crowd titters uneasily as it's no secret to anyone present, with the exception of Ken himself obviously, that Roslyn was a right fucking bitch in her teens. She went from perfect little daddy's girl to a carbon copy of Courtney Love. This is an unintentional faux-par on Ken's behalf, and reading the room he smiles and tries out a little joke that falls flat on its face.

'They can be hard to live with, I'm sure,' he says, referring to the age bracket and not the fact she's now dead. He realises his mistake a couple of seconds later, making his apologies before he stumbles awkwardly through the rest of the service.

When he's done – I suspect he had more to say but he's wrapped it up prematurely – Ken issues an open invitation to anyone who wants to share their own memories of Roslyn. There's an uncomfortable silence as people shuffle and glance furtively around the room. Uncles and aunts glance my way, so I keep my eyes downcast on the bible I'm fidgeting with. Then, to my horror, that bitch Nel stands up and strolls as confident as ever to the front. Dad doesn't see her coming, and he stands to go up, but as Nel bounds past and up the steps to the lectern Dad just sits back down again without a word. He looks like he's trying to hold in an explosion of anger, though. He takes my hand in his; firm and strong like when I was little. I wish I could wind back time to when we were happy, and all together still.

Let it out, Dad.

I'm seeing red, too. I feel like shouting her off the podium, but for Mum and Dad's sake I can't do it. Roslyn caused so much drama and grief in our lives that the last thing they'd want is for their remaining daughter to take up the mantle.

'Roz was a friend, a lover, and a mother to all those who were with her to the end,' Nel says into the microphone, suggesting she's the one who stood by my sister when no-one else would.

How fucking dare she use my sister's funeral to grandstand and cast judgement on my family! I'm going to kill that fucking slag when

I get a chance, mark my fucking words. Dad grumbles something under his breath, and Uncle Joe squeezes his shoulder.

I want to shut my ears to Nel's words, block them out in case I commit them to memory, they and her smug face haunt me forever, but I can't help but hang on her every word, seething inside.

'What can I say about Roz that we don't already know? I was probably closest to Roz in the end, and we shared–'

'BOO! GET OFF THE FUCKEN STAGE!' roars Uncle Joe, standing up and balling his fists. He points accusingly at her. 'You! You're the reason my niece is gone!'

'It's okay, Joe,' says Dad, getting up and holding onto my uncle to placate him.

Dad seems so calm. It's like all Dad's rage from before's somehow channelled into my uncle and poured out of him like a dam bursting. Everyone's stunned into silence, their eyes going from Uncle Joe to Nel and back again, waiting for one of them to make their next move. But Dad gets Joe seated again, who's muttering apologies to Mum and Auntie Crystal but defending his actions at the same time.

'No worries, Joseph,' my mother says to him. 'You're a good bloke. You're totally in the right.'

Nel, to her credit, decides to forgo the rest of her speech and return to her seat. She's fucking lucky someone doesn't kick her out. I can picture Uncle Joe grabbing her wasted body and dragging it to the chapel doors, tossing it to the footpath like a bag of rubbish.

My eyes bore into the disrespectful bitch, and I feel the little goth girl looking my way so I turn my anger on her too, and she faces the floor with shame. As she fucking should. They're all to blame, all of them, even Chantelle. Not a single one of these arseholes tried to turn my sister's life around. They kept her in the game, feeding off the profits of her prostitution like vultures.

I hate them all.

Ken the funeral director wraps up proceedings and finishes with a live version of Nirvana's *All Apologies,* from their MTV Unplugged performance, blasting through the speakers while we're encouraged to reflect on Roslyn's life, for what it was worth. In some way, this seems like the perfect song for her, even though I know it was only chosen because it's her favourite band and my folks would've flicked through the track list until they'd heard the simple instrumentation and sleepy vocals of this song.

I can't help but wonder if Roslyn's spirit hovers nearby, watching the proceedings and realising how torturous she's made life for Mum and Dad. Or maybe the Grim Reaper has snatched her away already, like that one in the ads from when I was a kid? It may not have been AIDS that she died from, but it's the same Grim Reaper that came for her all the same. When you think about it, the reaper gets a bad rep because he's not the one making people cark it. He's just the one trying to help them out afterwards, like a customer service attendant showing you how to find what you need in the shop. Yet, we all heap shit on him like he's the killer. He's the innocent party, if anything.

It's things like heroin that's the killer.

Because she's older than me, Roslyn remembered the impact those ads had on the youth. She reckoned it helped boost support for the local AIDS council here in Brisbane at the time, saying that there were so many calls from people scared shitless that the AIDS Council had to open up its first twenty-four hour phone counselling service. So I guess a lot of good has come from the Grim Reaper, when you think about it.

I can't help but sneak another peek at Roslyn's friends.

Nel reminds me of the Grim Reaper, actually, the one of the skull face and black robes. But something about the girl that found Roz – Prudence – makes me wonder. The police told my folks that ever since they busted a couple shipping a load of heroin from the Gold Coast in August, many users had been relying on a source the police have had more difficulty in busting, and that the grade of the drug was inferior. Basically, they told us that Roslyn had died from a shitty batch of smack. But if that little goth girl over there had been shooting up with my sister at the time, wouldn't she have died as well? The cops didn't elaborate on this Prudences' exact involvement at the scene of death.

This is why I'd never get serious with a drug like heroin; it takes you into dark areas and you've got no way of judging how it appears looking from the outside in. Junkies will tell you they know, but that they just don't care. I know I'm no fucking saint, and that I've had my own addiction to oxy, but it's hardly the soul-destroying shit that Roslyn got into. She fucked her brain.

The song comes to a close, Cobain's voice droning in repetition on the last part before my dad, uncles and male cousins carry her casket to the funeral car out front. Everyone gets up and follows it out, and to my satisfaction I note that my cousin Benny, who's grown to be quite physically imposing, has deliberately stood at the entrance to the pew that Nel's in and he's pretending not to hear her quiet pleas for him to move so she can be first to follow my sister's casket.

I'm going to have to shout Benny a coupla pints when the family catches up afterwards at the pub down the road.

The funeral car drives away and Mum bursts into tears. I follow suit. Dad's furiously wiping away the tears, too, and my Uncle Joe gives me and Mum a big bear hug. I want the hug to last forever.

'Look at me, I'm a mess,' Mum says, wiping the running mascara off her cheeks.

'Naw,' smiles Joe warmly, 'you're doing just fine.'

Dad comes over and him and Joe shake hands and start chatting about gathering everyone to head to the pub, working out the car pool arrangements.

'Those junkies can fuck right off, though,' growls Joe.

'Don't worry,' says Dad, 'it's just family and friends.' He wraps his arm around my shoulders. 'How're you doing, chicken?' That's his pet name for us, for both me and Roslyn, especially when we were just little girls.

'Holding up,' I smile, though it's forced.

I'm feeling gutted that my big sister's gone. She may not have been a part of our lives all these years, but I always knew where she was, and just how she was even if it was just via the gossip grapevine. But now there's a void there. Not an emotional vacuum or anything, but I can still feel it inside me, this dull ache.

'That's my girl, strong as ever,' Dad says, kissing my hair.

Him and Joe wander away to sort out the car-pooling, and I stand away from all the rellies to catch a breather.

Prudence approaches, alone and timid, and comes right up to me. Gone is the air of arrogance. I death glare the horrid little shit, willing her to fuck off and go home and never be seen near my family again. I've got fuck all I want to say to her, let alone hear from her.

'I'm sorry about Roz,' she says lamely. 'I just wanted to say that she meant a lot to us.'

She hesitates, like there's more on her mind but she can't find the words. I glance around for Nel or Chantelle, but can't see them.

My throat feels dry, constricted. I want to punch this little junky in her stupid face.

'Is it true you found her?' My voice sounds thin.

The girl's brow creases up, but whether it's because she's confused or at pains to confess I can't decide.

'Listen,' I say, trying to master my anger, 'I loved my sister, no matter what you think. If you're here because you did, too, then that's some small comfort. I suppose. But I can't condone how you lot live. Take a hard fucking look at yourself, at what it's done to my sister... sort yourself out.'

'Yes,' she almost whispers, before turning and hurriedly passing through the crowd and disappearing around the corner of the chapel.

'Righto, love,' Mum says to me, 'let's get off, then. You okay, Abi?'

'Yeah, why?'

She looks concerned.

'You look like you've seen a ghost.'

'It's the whole funeral,' I lie, wiping my hand across my face to appear tired.

'Let's head down the pub and put it all behind us, finally,' she says, tugging me along with her to the car.

I have to vow to stay clear of the drugs from now on. For this woman's sake. For my mother's sake, who loves me unconditionally. It's time to clean my act up.

PIXIE LEARNS A TRUTH

Roz's funeral is a fuckin disaster. When we enter, we cop dirty looks from the family, like they know we're literally scum of the fuckin earth, which maybe we are. They cold-shoulder us and make me mood and self-loathin even worse than it already is. I wasn't expectin a red carpet to be rolled out for us, but I wasn't expectin to be singled out from the crowd and treated like a fuckin leper either. Dante and Raven are here, but, and they chat with us before takin their seats, which is good.

Roz's parents and sister sit up front, and her sister keeps lookin back and death-starin us the whole time.

'Look at Big Red looking round with nothing but contempt,' Nel mutters. 'Ignore the silly bitch.'

I don't want to ignore her, but, and I don't think she's a silly bitch.

Nel's been agro all mornin, combin her thinnin hair to within an inch of its life over and over again and snortin at dabs of speed. When we grabbed a taxi to come here she'd kept dissin the driver, insistin he floor it, until he'd literally had enough and asked if she wanted to drive. She'd said she'd be more than fuckin willing if it meant we could keep the fare for havin done his job for the stupid cunt. When he'd pulled over and ordered us out I'd broken down in tears and begged him to take us the rest of the way. Nel was weirded out by me crying, and sat back and let the driver do whatever speed he fuckin well wanted to.

When we'd got to the funeral, Nel had ducked into the dunnies to do some more speed, so now she's sittin here buzzin and tappin her knee repeatedly like there's no tomorrow, barely able to sit still.

The funeral priest dude takes the stand and plays some photos on the projector of Roz from when she was a small kid, playin with her dog and shit, and more photos of her in her high school uniform on the first day and dressed for her first job at a book store. But it blows us away to think she was once a kid! I mean, I know it sounds fuckin stupid, coz of course she was, but I never thought of her like that. She was always just Roz, older more mature Roz who knew lots of stuff about drugs and who was like a mother to us all and always there if ya needed a shoulder to cry on.

Then the funeral dude offers for people to go up and say somethin, so Nel shoots to her feet and shoves past us.

'Nel, no,' I whisper, but she ignores us.

When she gets near the front Roz's father rises, like he's goin to tell her to sit back down or somethin, but he hasn't seen her and actually starts approachin the same stairs until he sees Nel. Me heart sinks. I can't watch this. Nel just ignores the poor guy and keeps goin up the steps to where the liddle desk thing is with the microphone. Me heart literally melts as Roz's father sits back down. But the whole family is lookin super pissed at Nel.

The priest adjusts the microphone for her.

'Thank you, your Lordship,' Nel goes in her best respectful voice, then looks proudly at the audience and says into the microphone: 'Roz was a friend, a lover, and a mother to all those who were with her to the end,' then goes on about how she was probly closest to Roz more than anyone else here.

What is this? How come she's sayin this?

'I first met her in West End when we were both in our teens,' she continues, 'where Roz and some others from the gay community had a graffiti war goin on with the council at the Dornoch Terrace bridge, or what came to be known for a time as Dykes Bridge.'

It's obvious this kind of talk isn't appreciated by Roz's family. A short muscly cunt over in the family side flies to his feet, shoutin at Nel. 'Get off the fucken stage,' he screams, accusin Nel of Roz's death.

Nel's stunned, starin at the cunt, literally unable to move. It's like she's seen past the bravado of the speed and realised what a mockery she's made of herself. When Roz's father calms the other cunt down, Nel slinks away from the microphone without another word. She slips back into her seat, and me and every other person is lookin at her like she's nuthin but dog shit.

From the pew in front I hear Dante mutter: 'Good one, fuckhead.'

I glance over to Roz's family and her sister's lookin at us with such hatred I can almost read her thoughts. Her intentions, at least. She'd probly strangle us to death, me and Nel, if she could get away with it. Nel's fucked the funeral, and we're all to blame, us sorry band of misfits sittin here in crappy clothes and fucked hair, smellin like we literally haven't showered in a while, which we haven't.

It's hard to deal with all this: Nel's behaviour and the family's hate and just bein inside a church. I've literally been swingin between feelins of anger and sadness over Roz's death. A part of us just can't believe she's gone.

How come you left us, Roz?

How come you left me?

When the service is over they play a Nirvana song on the speakers.

Nel leans in close, whisperin hoarsely: 'Wasn't even her favourite song. Dumb cunts didn't know her like I did.'

'Whatever. Like it matters,' I whisper, really fuckin annoyed, but.

'What?' she says, her eyes drillin into us.

'Nuthin,' I mumble. People are startin to stare at us again.

Then everyone stands up after the song, and the coffin's brought down the middle of the hall with different dudes carryin it, includin Roz's dad and the cunt that yelled at Nel. Everyone starts piling out of the pews to follow the coffin.

'Shove on, Pixie,' Nel goes, pushin me shoulder roughly. 'Let's get up front near the coffin.'

'I can't,' I go. 'There's a dude blockin the way.'

'Hey, man,' Nel whispers hoarsely over me head, tryin to catch the attention of this broad-shouldered dude, 'let us pass, ay.'

The stupid tool doesn't hear us, but. He just stands there blockin the way while everyone gets out of their pews and starts leavin the chapel. We're the last left.

'Oh, sorry,' he goes, turnin round and seein us finally.

'Nice one, idiot,' spits Nel angrily.

The tool smirks, but his neck muscles are tensin up. It's obvious he must be related to the family, so how come Nel's stirrin the cunt up like she is? She can't fuckin help herself, that's why, not even at the funeral of her best friend.

When we get outside, the funeral car's already left and people are also startin to leave. There's no sign of Dante or Raven anywhere, but Roz's sister's still here with her family.

'Fuck, we missed it,' growls Nel. 'Oh well, mumsie and daddy must be over the fucken moon. The last fuck-up of Roz's they'll ever have to foot the bill for.'

Some normals glance back at us, lookin Nel up and down and scowlin. She doesn't even notice them or their disapproval, but.

'Right, everyone back to the Palace,' she goes to us in a way that suggests there'll be no arguin with her plans. 'We'll toast Roz there.'

'I'll catch up.'

She glares at us. 'You fucken be there, girl.'

'Righto, Sir,' I go, pissed off with this all curfew shit. She's worse than workin for me dad.

She points her finger in me face and sucks her lips into a thin line, like a warnin.

'I'll be there,' I say sourly.

She jerks her head at Jeremy and Chantelle to make em follow her across the lawns like good lil puppies. Fuck, am I glad to see the back of her. She's just too intense today, and I don't think it's the speed. She's lost the fuckin plot, literally!

Roz's sister's standing on her own over by the corner of the chapel. As I approach her me heart's hammerin in me chest. I don't think I've been this nervous in ages. Maybe I'm too used to the smack takin the edge off everythin, makin any problem simply vanish into thin air.

When I'm within reach of her I pause. She's glarin at us with pure hatred, which makes it hard to try and say anythin. I'm the one who found her sister dead, but, literally cold and stiff on a piss-stained footpath outside of an abandoned building where only drunks and junkies congregated. I sat with her sister's body and screamed until someone called the cops and finally help arrived. Not for Roz, but for me. I was as frozen to the spot as Roz was that night, broken and wrecked and in need of revival.

I hadn't got it, of course. I'd got the third degree. Grilled about substance abuse and what I might have coursing in me veins, which was fuck all coz Nel had had us out walkin the fuckin streets all day pan-handling for change. But the cops didn't believe it, and despite my friend dead in me arms the heartless cunts were going to have us arrested.

How do I say any of this to the young woman in front of us? Why the fuck would she care? I wouldn't be tellin her about Roz's final hours, I'd be tellin her about mine, this fucked up liddle girl who's crashed her sister's funeral and made a joke of it.

Finally, I reach deep down into meself to find the words, however simple they are. They're raw, and honest, and it's all I need to say.

'I'm sorry about Roz. I just wanted to say that she meant a lot to us.'

She stares at us in disbelief, squinting her eyes. She looks around at the others, maybe lookin for that muscled tool that blocked the pew so he can throw us out. I'm not sure what more I can say, to make her understand how I'm feeling, that I'm truly sorry.

Finally she turns to us, and says she loved her sister despite her flaws, then says bitterly: 'Take a hard fucking look at yourself, at what it's done to my sister... sort yourself out.'

Her words strike us fair in the fuckin chest, hittin home where me heart should be, causin us so much pain that it's all I can do not to double-over from it.

'Yes,' I gasp, knowin she's a hundred percent right.

I need time to think, but, to work out what exactly I'm goin to do about it.

What I can't do right now is face Roz's sister a moment longer. I spin round and barrel through the last of the funeral attendees, runnin the circumference of the chapel and up onto the road, just gettin as far from there as possible. In me mind I can still see Roz as I last saw her, pale skin that looked wet but felt dry with her eyes looking lifeless. Her eyes scared the shit out of us, and still do. I couldn't handle how there was no focus in them, no movement. Roz might have been many things to some people, but she didn't deserve to die like that. I found out later that she'd been lyin there dead all day and not one single fuckin cunt had thought to check on her. She'd died durin the night before, after she'd run out of the Palace from fightin with Nel.

Eventually I catch a train back to the city and walk home to the Palace just as the sun's startin to set.

Everyone in the flat is fucked. Nel, Chantelle, Jeremy, Malik and the two dudes from flat number six are sittin around the evidence ova group hit. There's needles and broken pill capsules and all sorts of shit on the coffee table.

'Really, guys?' I ask sarcastically, coppin an eyeful of the mess. 'Ya couldn't wait for us?'

'Celebratory hit,' goes Nel. 'Our farewell to Roz. You missed out.'

How come she's still bein such a cunt? The smack's obviously done fuck all to take that edge off her.

Malik's lookin like a guilty dog. Whatever.

Thing is, I'm fuckin tempted but.

'Too fucken bad, cupcake,' Nel goes. 'It's all gone. Like everything. Like Roz.'

'How come ya sayin this?' I demand.

'Oh, you don't like it?' she says with such venom that the others pretend to look away. Anythin, so long as they don't get sucked into the fightin. Nel pushes a piece of paper at us with the word SORRY on it.

'Fuck off, ya cunt,' I croak. I'm not interested in stupid half-assed apologies from the bitch.

'It's from Roz,' she says simply, all the fight in her gone.

'What do ya mean?'

'I came home that day and realised Roz had been here while we were scrounging in the city. And I found that on my pillow. It's her hand-writing.'

'Holy shit,' murmurs Chantelle.

I don't understand, but I do. I just don't wanna face it.

Suddenly rage fills us and I fly at Nel, tryin to kick her face.

'Get the fuck off me,' she screeches, tryin to whack us.

Jeremy the fuckin mong cunt grabs us from behind and pulls us across the room.

'Stop it,' he goes.

'Everybody calm down,' pleads Chantelle.

'Don't touch us, cunt,' I growl, so Jeremy finally lets go of us.

Nel's on her feet. 'You're a fucken psycho, Pixie. You need yer fucking head read!'

'Do the cops know about this?' I yell, holdin the note up.

'Course not. Use yer fucking brain, retard.'

I don't get it. I don't understand how come she'd keep somethin like this a secret and let everyone think Roz died a junkie when she was usin it as the final means of escape. She was fuckin escapin this psycho heartless cunt in front of us, that's what!

I storm outta the flat.

'Pixie!' Nel shouts.

I bound down the stairs, shakin the banister so much that Raven pokes her head out the door to see what's up. I call her a cunt, too, and run from the Palace past old Bernie sittin in his chair out front. Twilight's set in and the fruit bats are makin their lazy way across the sky, headin toward the orange glow of the sunset. I head in the opposite direction down Bowen Street. There's a phone booth down near the corner, so I call Mum reverse-charge.

She sounds worried, coz it's been ages since she last heard from us.

'Prue, is everything okay?'

'Not really.'

'Are you safe?' It's her number one concern with us these days, that's how much she trusts the people I hang with. Thinkin about it, I realise she's got every right to be concerned about that, but.

'Yeah. It's just been shit lately. One of me friends died recently.'

'Oh,' she says quietly, and that's all. I can imagine her runnin through all sorts of scenarios in her mind like AIDS or murder. Probly OD, too, of course.

'I'm okay, but,' I go.

'That's good to hear.'

How come I've called her? The silence on the line gives us time to think about it. When she next speaks, I've got the answer ready.

'Prue?'

'I want to come home, Mum.'

Silence again, followed by a tentative: 'Are you using?'

'No...'

Then the tears come. Forceful sobbin tears that hurts me chest and makes it hard to swallow any air. Me throat feels sore and me nose dribbles snot all over me chin.

'What's meant to be so funny, Prue?' Mum goes, mistakin me cryin for laughter. I guess that's how it must sound over the phone.

'I'm so unhappy, Mum,' I bawl.

'Oh, Prue,' she says sadly. She sounds heartbroken.

So Mum and I talk for a bit more and she tells us to come home. I'm going to go tonight. Go back to the Palace and grab me things and get a taxi to Mum's place, where she'll pay the driver.

When I finish the call I can feel a massive fuckin burden has been lifted from us. I dry me eyes, holdin me hand across me chest where it still hurts. But it feels good to have made some steps in healin the rift between Mum and me. I'm lookin forward to a warm, home-cooked meal and a clean bed.

Outside the Palace the yuppie dude across the road says somethin to us which I don't proply catch. Probly askin how come I'm cryin. Old men always fuckin zero in on young girls who're upset, like they can take advantage of us.

'I'm okay, thanks,' I go.

'I couldn't give a flying fuck about you,' he goes. 'I said I'm onto you pricks over there. Breaking into people's homes, eh? Steal my kid's Nintendo, eh?'

This is the last thing I need, some random cunt blamin us for more shit. I just feel so low right now.

'Makes you feel like a big man, eh?' yells Dante from the doorway of the Palace. He's leanin against the doorjamb beside Bernie, half a bottle of red wine in his hand. 'Hey, Leechie? Big fuckin man, picking on a little girl!'

The random dude – Leechie is what Dante called him – slaps his work satchel on top of his fence and starts comin across the street. I quickly back up towards the Palace.

'Or maybe it was you, you little prick?' he snarls at Dante. 'Don't think I've forgotten about all those CD's bought in *my* name.'

Dante starts crackin up somethin shockin.

'I thought you had those scummy two from down the street pegged for that, Leechie boy?' Dante goes, swiggin from wine bottle.

Bernie gets up from his chair and ambles inside.

'Turns out it wasn't,' Leechie goes, reachin the footpath outside the Palace. 'But *you* seem to know my name, you fucking thief.'

I'm not hangin around when that cunt decides to go off, and inch me way over to the front door of the Palace, ready to make like Bernie and get the fuck inside.

'Why don't ya go fuck yaself?' I snap at the stupid yuppie.

He jabs a finger at us. 'I know where you fuckers live.'

'And I know where *you* live, cunt,' retorts Dante, steppin from the doorway towards Leechie. 'Maybe I'll burn your fucking house down in the middle of the night while you and your family are asleep.'

Then Dante suddenly flings the wine bottle at the cunt. I watch it spin through the air like it was in slow-motion, the wine splashin out in liddle spurts. The bottle literally misses Leechie by at least a foot, thankfully, and smashes across the road, but he acts like he's been hit, holdin his arm.

'I'm calling the police,' says Leechie, stormin back across the street and disappearin through his garage door.

'Fuck, he needs a chill-pill,' I go. 'Thanks, but.'

'No worries,' says Dante.

'I don't get how come normals always hafta call the cops to sort out all their problems.'

'They lack the emotional fortitude to stand face to face with their insecurities,' says Dante. 'They hide behind this constant need to be appeased. That's what having the law come sniffing around does for them. Tells them they're right and we're wrong, the dumb cunts.'

'Sounds like someone I know,' I moan. 'She'd never call the cops, but. Just takes it out on the rest of us.'

He's curious, so I tell Dante about Roz's note and how it sounds more like it was a suicide than an accidental overdose, and how Nel hid it from the cops and is acting irrational and crazy now.

'Shit, poor Roz,' Dante sighs. 'Come inside before Leecham comes back out with his piggy mates.'

His and Bernie's flat is the funniest thing, but. There's lots of really old time stuff around, like their kitchen appliances. Some things it's obvious what they're used for, but other things just look weird and alien.

'Hi, Pixie,' says Bernie with a big smile from his armchair in front of the TV. He's got a toasted cheese sandwich on a plastic plate in his lap. 'It was a nice send off today.'

'Yeah, kinda.'

'Everything okay?' Bernie goes to Dante, who tells him one of the neighbours is whining like a baby as usual.

Then Dante says to us: 'Bernie's mate Rupert committed suicide not long ago, actually.'

Bernie doesn't seem fazed about the info just being thrown around like this. Maybe Dante does it all the time and Bernie's gotten used to it?

'I'm sorry to hear that,' I go, wonderin if I already knew about this. It's hard to keep track of the shit that happens in everyone's lives when you're on smack. Mostly, you just don't give a fuck. I vaguely remember Roz sayin somethin about it once, but, I think.

'Thanks,' smiles Bernie.

It's a bit fuckin odd how he reacts a lot of the time. He's a schizo, apparently, so maybe that has somethin to do with it.

'And then Roz, and now Nel's acting funny,' continues Dante. 'It's like that thing...' He pauses, tryin to remember somethin, then looks at Bernie and snaps his fingers over and over again. 'What's that thing called, Bernie?'

'What thing?'

'The domino effect thing when people kill themselves.'

Bernie tries to talk around a mouthful of his toastie, nearly burnin his tongue. 'Werther Fever?'

'Werther Fever,' Dante grins at us triumphantly. 'That's what the cunt's called.'

'What is it, but?'

'It's contagious,' says Dante, raisin his eyebrows lecherously.

I take a step back, lookin concerned. The cunt cracks up somethin shockin. Honestly, between Bernie and Dante, I'd go fuckin insane tryin to live in this flat.

'It's a social phenomenon,' goes Dante. 'Kinda like a copycat thing. When one person sees someone do something, others in their close circle feel influenced by it. Like when a long-term couple breaks up, and then not long after their friends start breaking up, and so do *their* friends and so on.'

'I've never heard of it,' I admit.

'It does exist,' insists Dante, turnin to Bernie for backup.

'Yep, and it's called that from Goethe's story *The Sorrows of Young Werther*,' confirms Bernie, who everyone knows is a walkin fucking encyclopaedia.

'Sounds like a Tim Burton book, eh?' winks Dante. 'I've only read his *Faust*, so I wouldn't know. Goethe, that is, not Burton.'

'And only the English version,' sniggers Bernie, dissin Dante.

'I can't read German, can I?' says Dante.

I have to interrupt them or get nowhere fast. 'I don't get what all that has to do with anythin?'

'Sorry, my dear, I do digress,' goes Bernie, who'd probly also bow if he'd been standin. 'The central character, Werther, commits suicide, and after it was published there was a crazy reaction to it where lots of people committed suicide all across Europe all because the fictional character did.'

'That's insane.'

'It is,' admits Bernie. 'The book got banned for years because of it. But we now recognise that as Behavioural Contagion, where people will copycat their friends for absolutely no reason at all.'

'But how are they connected?'

'Not very well,' laughs Bernie. 'But Roz did meet Rupert once when he came to visit, and I told her about his suicide at the time.'

All I can think is how Dee Dee, the guy from King George Square, literally threw himself off a bridge. Then this Rupert dude, followed by Roz. Is there really a pattern?

'And now Nel's goin all weird,' says Dante, leanin on the kitchen counter and tryin to clean under his nails with a butter knife.

'Fuck.'

This is so messed up. What if Nel does commit suicide? What if the cops decide shit's goin down and bust us wide open, maybe find evidence of heroin use? What if I go to fuckin prison for it?

'I feel a bit sick,' I tell the guys, headin back upstairs to me flat. To be honest, it pisses us off how calmly they both talk about suicide, but, like they're fuckin Uni academics with no feelings.

I inform Nel that I'm leavin, that I'm headin back to Mum's. I start to pack me stuff, wonderin if I can get me spare Doc's down off the powerlines somehow. Good thing about smack is that I hardly own anythin anymore, so it's literally quick and easy to pack. The mattress on the floor isn't mine, neither are the blood stains on the corner of it or that big yellow sweat patch in the middle. Most of what I own sits on the floor round it or piled into the open suitcase in the corner.

'Why? Just stay, Pixie.'

'I can't, Nel.'

'I've already lost Roz. I need you.'

'I can't stay, Nel. I'm sorry.'

'So that's it? Just up and walk away from everything when it gets too tough? Run back to mummy?'

I can hear Jeremy snortin with amusement out in the lounge, the fuckin cunt.

'Yes, Nel, I'm sure that's it.'

'Fine! Go. Fuck off, then! I'll just stay here and fucking kill myself too, then!'

There it is. In less than ten minutes Nel herself has proven Bernie and Dante's theory about copycat suicide.

She storms outta the room.

'That's a fucked thing to say, Nel, under the circumstances.'

'WELL, WHAT ELSE CAN I SAY?' Nel screams from the lounge. I can hear her preppin a hit.

What else? There's literally a hundred things she could probly say, but I can see there's only one path she's hell-bent on goin down, and I don't want to be along for that ride.

On the floor beside the mattress is Nel's hardcover copy of *The Shining*, and it suddenly occurs to us that Nel probly has all these books from when Roz used to work in a book store when she was younger. I can just picture Roz sneakin em out of the store to give to Nel. I realise that Roz worshipped the ground that Nel walked on, and got fuck all in return. In a way, I probly did too, but. When I think about it, it's not really heroin that killed Roz, but all of Nel's bullying. Years of it was finally too much for her, I reckon.

After checking Nel's not watchin, I pack the Stephen King book as well, just out of spite.

I haul me suitcase out onto the stairwell landing. I've got a bit more stuff left in the flat, but I'm willin to leave it behind just so I can get the fuck out of here and back home without any more drama tonight. Normally I'm the one startin the drama, or encouragin it. I feel sober and cold in the harsh reality of the last few days. Roz's baby sis Abi really jolted us with what she said to us after the funeral.

'Last chance,' says Nel in a steely voice, backlit in the doorframe. 'Stay.'

I don't answer her; just drag me suitcase down the stairs. A couple of people call out farewells from open doors, where they've doubtless been listenin in to the argument upstairs. Bernie tries to give us a bottle of red as a parting gift, and as tempted as I am to use it to take the edge off me creepin withdrawal, I tell him to keep it. I can't turn up to Mum's with either drugs or alcohol if I want her to trust us again.

Somethin Roz once said to us comes to mind: 'You've got too many morals to be a junkie.'

Thankfully the Leechie dude's not out the front when I take me suitcase down the road to the phone booth to call for a taxi, but a cop car passes us and slowly cruises up to the Palace, stopping outside Leechie's house.

Dante'll talk his way out of it. He always does.

I can see Nel framed in a top window of the Prozac Palace, watchin us make the call to Mum.

MIXED TAPE FOR PIXIE

It's been weird bein back at Mum's place again and spillin me guts about what I've been up to, tellin her all about the heroin and the stripping and stuff. She cried, of course; we both did, coz as she put it I'm still her baby. No matter how old I get, I will always be her baby she reckons.

She showed us where Charlie's buried. The drought means that the grass hasn't completely grown over the spot but there's meant to be a thunderstorm later so maybe that'll help. Meantime, I've started taking a bucket of water down to him and tippin it across the thirsty earth.

I feel like crap still, but when I don't anymore Mum's promised we can give Charlie a proper goin away. Like a funeral, sayin the stuff ya'd say at a funeral and all that. Like at Roz's funeral.

Mum doesn't completely trust us just yet, but I'm doin me best to gain it back. It's not easy, but. I feel the temptation all the time, literally makin us batshit crazy, and already Mum and I have had some nasty rows. But like I said, we're both workin on gettin through this together. Fortunately I wasn't such a hardcore user that I needed to go on a methadone program or anything, but. It never did Roz any good, goin to that Binkinba centre for those wafers. If anythin, they literally made it worse, especially coz it only handled the withdrawals but it was always the hit she was after. She only used the methadone if there was no smack.

Out of everyone from the Palace, Roz is the only one I miss.

Me old room's still the way I left it from the first time I left home. Me Marilyn Manson and Cypress Hill posters are still up, and the walls are still painted black. I remember when I first did that, which was last November durin a fuckin heat-spell. Mum had said no to it, so I'd stolen all these tubes of *chromacryl* paint from the newsagents down the road and slowly covered the walls and ceiling. I was fuckin wrecked by the end of it, but it was worth it, especially when Mum went absolutely fuckin mental over it. She'd told us to wash it off, but I never did. It's funny now, lookin around the room and thinkin how much ova shit I was. Still am.

There's a mixed tape on me old bookshelf that Roz gave us back when their stereo could still record, the one they said Dante literally threw out Jeremy's window. After that they'd lived without music until I'd turned up with one. But I left the fuckin thing behind! Now I think about it, I used to own a lot more stuff that Mum either dropped off at the flat or bought us when I'd asked for it, but we sold it all to keep our habits goin. Before I'd come along, Roz once told us, Nel was always hockin their stereos off so Roz started buying the cheapest ones she could find that were worthless, so that even if Nel tried hocking it off no-one would want it.

Pretty smart, ay?

The tape on me shelf's got Roz's chicken-scratch handwritin on it: MIXED TAPE FOR PIXIE.

I'd tried to listen to the tape at home after Roz had given it to us, but about a quarter way through I'd given up coz the songs were all choppy. Some of em had no sooner started than they'd suddenly stopped to be literally replaced by a different song, as though Roz had changed her mind about it bein on the tape and instead of rewindin and recordin over it she'd just continued from where she'd stopped it. It was literally torture to listen to, coz ya'd get into the vibe of the song and it'd get killed by the choppy recording.

I feel like playin it again, but, even if it's for the last time. Roz had made it especially for me, and it feels like betrayal or somethin if I don't play it all the way through at least once.

Since I've left me stereo at the Palace, I hunt around for me old Walkman. It's under me Paul Jennings books in a box at the back of me closet. It's pretty embarrassin, coz it's got these puffy stickers of unicorns and shit on it. Admittedly, it's literally from when I was about twelve and wasn't into Marilyn Manson yet.

I slip the tape in, pressin play.

There's silence for about the first minute, then a clunkin sound and the music starts. Nirvana. Always Nirvana with Roz. I smile as I recall how crazy for Cobain she was, even though she was a lesbian. She used to tell us how his sister was also a lesbian, as if that meant there was some connection between her and her idol.

I sit through the tape again, listenin to the mess that Roz makes of it. Twice I hear snippets of her voice or just of her laboured breathin when she accidently clicks the record button for the mic instead of the second cassette. It's obvious she's wasted. Every second song, at least, is a Nirvana one, if not more.

After a song about a cornflake girl (of all things!) finishes, there's a long pause, then a clunking sound, which is the stop button, but I can still hear a small voice. It's Nel's. Roz must've accidently pressed the record mic button again. Nel sounds like she's in the kitchen.

I'm tryin to make out what's being said, but I can tell that Roz is upset. She's raisin her voice and tellin Nel she's sick. Sick from the heroin?

'I just told you why...' whines Roz on the tape. Nel says somethin I can't catch, and then Roz's voice goes: 'No, I really am sick of it, baby.'

Not sick from heroin, but sick of somethin. And she called Nel 'baby'! The whole time I knew em, I'd never heard Roz call anyone that, let alone Nel. I used to wonder, at first, if they were lovers, but Nel used to be on with Chantelle, or so I'd heard, and was never lovey-dovey with Roz at all. I'd even started to wonder if Roz wasn't really a lesbian at all. She only ever seemed to sleep with guys, even though that was for money, but.

'Do it... for me,' I hear Nel sayin, closer to the recording now.

I drop the Walkman onto the bed, as if Nel can sense my presence through it. It's fucked up, really, that she puts that kind of fear in us.

Fuck.

I never thought of it like that before, but that's what it is. Fear. I was afraid of Nel. All the times I would talk back to her or disobey, I wasn't doin it coz I was brave but coz I was scared of her and so I was lashin out.

Even though she's dead, I feel protective of the recorded version of Roz. I literally want to shout into me headphones for her to get away from Nel.

'Not for me,' corrects Nel's voice. 'For us.'

She's doin that cajoling thing she does with her voice, where it's half plea and half command. Manipulatin.

Roz protests some more, but Nel's shootin all her arguments down.

Finally Nel goes: 'Go now, or you'll get a fucken smack in the chops. He's waiting. Make em wait too long and they knock the price down.'

I realise she's talkin about prostitution. Roz was a junkie, and not a slim woman. She wasn't exactly at the high-end of the market, not even in the same league with the girl's I knew at Ms Wang's massage parlour. Maybe more like Two-Buck Mary over on Caxton Street.

'Don't be long,' says Nel on the tape. The rest of side A plays out to sounds of Nel shufflin round the flat and gettin wasted in silence. I can hear the *click click* ova bico lighter, so she must be blazin up a joint.

I just sit here the tape's finished, listenin to the faraway sound ova lawnmower.

Roz used to tell us it was her decision to be a pro, and hers alone. But that was all a lie. She lied to protect Nel, who insisted Roz turn tricks so they could afford to get smacked out. More than that, even though I never saw it, it seems like Nel used to hit her if she didn't do it. No wonder Roz's sister Abi fuckin hated us.

I throw the Walkman at the wall and start kickin me bed and cupboards. I want to break something so fuckin bad.

Mum comes halfway down the hallway.

'Prue?'

I stop kickin shit.

She retreats back to the kitchen. She knows withdrawal's difficult. The hardest part, actually, is the depression that follows it, that just swims into ya head like it owns the fuckin place and tells ya you're not worth shit.

I'll tell ya who's not worth shit, but. Nel's not worth shit.

I hate her so much I could literally kill her.

I just want to get through this and come out the other end like a normal human being, hang out with me old friends again and do normal teenage delinquent stuff while I'm still a teenager.

'I have some lunch ready if you want it,' Mum calls out.

I feel me heart swell at those words. I wonder if Mum could ever understand the power of lunch prepared by her hands. I've missed that so much I could almost cry.

PROZAC GOES DOWN

The first thing I hear is my name being screamed.

'RAAAAAVEN!'

It scares the shit out of me, because it sounds loud but also far away, like as if I'm still dreaming.

The next thing I'm aware of is the smoke, because it's everywhere. All through my room, in the lounge, dead set everywhere! I jump out of bed and stumble through to the lounge, choking from the smoke. My first thought is that I've left the stove on and a saucepan's melted.

'RAAAVEN!'

'In here!' I shout, not sure who's calling me.

It's Malik. He comes running through the smoke, crouched over, trying to cover his face with the lapels of his duffle coat.

'What's going on?' I shout, because there's a rushing noise like a truck passing by, but the sound just keeps going on and on.

'Fucking house is on fire!'

Shit shit shit.

I start panicking, wondering if I should try and save something or just run. Malik, thankfully, grabs hold of my arm and starts pulling me to the door.

'I have to put something on,' I tell him, resisting slightly because I'm still in my singlet and undies.

But Malik keeps pulling me through the door, into the hallway. Above us is a massive blaze. The next floor up is filled with fire, and the heat's so bad that I instinctively pull back into my flat to get away from it.

'COME ON!' Malik tugs on me harder, hurting my arm, leading me down the hall to the stairs.

'Lunar!' I suddenly yell. 'Where's Lunar?'

Malik pauses. He has a love-hate relationship with Lunar, but all in all he mostly likes the little kitty. He's got a good heart behind his hard exterior, Malik does.

There's other people moving through the smoke, too, but visibility is so poor there's fat chance of telling who they are. It's like when you see those sandstorms in the movies and there's figures moving around but it could be anyone. Angele appears next to me.

'I told you to get out!' Malik yells at her, but she ignores him and takes my other arm.

'Where's Lunar?' I gasp.

'There's buckley's chance anything's surviving in that,' he says, glancing back at the flames.

'Don't worry, she'll have got out before any of us,' Angele says. 'Focus now: first step,' she adds, leading me carefully down the stairs with Malik. The closer we get to the front door, the less intense the heat is at our backs, but it's still so hot that I feel like I'm getting burnt from it, and I'm worried that I might suddenly combust.

Outside the night air is like cold water thrown in our faces. Malik and Angele lead me across the road into Mein Street, and I start gulping down fresh air until I feel my chest seize and I double over, coughing and hacking. I can taste the smoke in the back of my throat. Someone's patting my back, encouraging me to cough up the shit on my lungs. Angele's kneeling on all fours, hacking up her lungs, too.

'How many more?' someone asks Malik.

'Not sure,' he replies. 'Upstairs maybe.'

'Fuck,' the other person goes. I look up and see it's the bogan guys from next door. 'It's too late, mate. That fire's ripped through already.'

'Fuck fuck fuck,' Malik curses, stamping his feet and running his hands over his face. 'FUUUUUCK!!'

I'm trying to get my voice back so I can ask him about Dante, but all that comes out is a small croak.

There's a siren headed our way, but it sounds so far away and the whole top part of the Palace is burning. It's actually quite beautiful, this massive bonfire lighting up the whole neighbourhood, reaching up into the night sky. The flames are getting longer even as I watch, dancing with each other and stretching higher and higher. Somehow, I can't quite equate that this is my home that's burning down.

'Deano, grab some blankets,' one of the bogan guys instructs his housemate, who runs inside their house even though it sits perilously close to the Prozac. He shields his face from the heat with his arms.

'Here's some water,' this old timer says, and the bogan guy thanks him, squatting down beside me. 'Here ya go, get a bitta this inta ya,' he says, pressing an old cordial bottle of water into my hands, helping me to tip it up so I can swallow a mouthful or two. I start violently coughing again, spitting a lot of it back out. He passes the bottle over to Angele, who gulps it down without any problem.

'Ambulance is on its way,' the guy says, leaving me in Malik's care, who thanks him on my behalf.

'Malik,' I choke out. 'What happened?'

'Dunno,' he says sadly, watching the flames drop to the second floor and spread. 'Started at the top somewhere. This is so fucked.'

'Where's Dante?' I go, but Malik doesn't answer.

For the first time I realise how many people have come out to watch our home burn down. The whole street's full, standing well back because the heat from the fire comes at us in waves, reaching easily across the narrow street, making it unbearable to get any closer.

'Malik,' I ask again. 'Where's Dante.'

I think this time he just didn't hear me, because he's chatting with the bogan neighbour, pointing out parts of the Prozac's interior he recognises that's being exposed by the disintegrating walls.

Deano's back with some blankets and a flannelette bathrobe for me. I notice he hesitates when he puts it on me, checking me out in my undies. Right now, I couldn't care less.

'Is everyone out, Malik?'

He doesn't answer, just grinds his jaw.

'Malik?' I say again, angrily, my voice raw from the smoke.

'I don't know,' he snaps. 'Look at it, Raven! Who knows?'

All the windows are alive with the frenetic energy of the flames now. They speed by incredibly fast, shooting up through the building and out the top. The roof has started to cave in, I notice. Anyone still up there is basically dead.

The fire department's here, their truck climbing slowly up Bowen towards the inferno. It stops short, and the fireys jump down and start running about. A couple of them stroll casually towards the Palace, as though the heat doesn't affect them at all, and then they stride across to where we're all standing at the entrance to Mein and ask who lives there. Malik raises his hand and they start asking him how many people live there and their whereabouts. Angele gets up and joins in on the discussion.

I'm feeling a bit numb. All I can do is sit and watch the Palace light up the night. No-one's telling me if Dante got out or not. He rarely goes out these days, so I know he would've been home.

To my left, sitting on top of his garage roof with his kids, is David Leecham, the neighbour from across the road. They're watching it like it's the New Year's fireworks display. To my right, the old verandah of the squat is so loaded up with the junkies and the bums that live there that I swear it's going to give way soon and collapse. Everyone's too mesmerised by the fire to notice.

Over in a hedge I spy Lunar peeking out from the branches. Thank God she's safe! Her eyes look huge and glossy. She'll be too skittish to try and catch at the moment. Her fur's soaked through with sweat from fretting.

Malik comes back over to me and says the ambos are on their way and will take a look at me.

'I just want to know if Dante's okay,' I say, on the verge of tears.

'Yeah, he got out,' snaps Malik. 'Seriously, Raven, you gotta get over that idiot. Start thinking of *numero uno*.'

Angele puts her hand on his arm. 'Time and a place,' she says.

Malik takes a deep breath and looks at me sadly, then falls down next to me and puts his arm around my shoulders.

'Sorry, crow-girl,' he says quietly, his old nickname for me that he hasn't used in a long time. 'Don't worry. He's safe.'

'Thanks, Malik,' I say softly.

He kisses my forehead and I lean against him, grateful to be able to snuggle and feel safe. Angele's arguing with a firey about something, who shakes his head and walks away when she's in mid-sentence. When she turns around and sees me snuggling against Malik, but, her face goes expressionless.

I sit up and stare at the fire, unconcerned with whatever bullshit she's thinking. Malik's a friend, that's all. The past is the past.

Bernie shuffles by, looking lost. I want to call out to him, offer him some comfort, but I can't. I've got no voice anymore, and not from the smoke. From shock, I think. The poor guy has a stricken expression, like his whole foundation has been torn away and his schizophrenia is having a field day. My heart would break for him, but I'm just too numb to feel anything.

'Jeremy!' Malik's spotted the boy, motioning for him to come over.

'This is fucking insane,' Jerm says. He's hyped up with excitement for it all: the fire, the crowds, the fire engine, the destruction.

'What about Nel?' Malik wants to know.

Jeremy looks around, searching the crowd. 'Dunno.'

'Was she inside?'

The boy's too amped. He keeps searching the crowd, but his eyes are sweeping too fast to be genuinely looking.

'Nah, she's not in there, ay,' he goes.

'Jeremy!' Malik's voice is fierce. 'Where's Nel? Where was she, last you saw her?'

Jeremy looks at Malik like he's hurt him. 'I don't know. She hasn't been home all day.'

The kid is fucking wired on something, but it's not smack.

'Just leave him,' Angele says to Malik.

Malik waves a dismissive hand at Jerm and begins to slowly walk in circles, chewing his bottom lip as he looks around, scrutinising the Palais and its flames for any sign of movement.

I finally see Dante standing over on the gutter's edge on the other side of the old squat. He's not looking at the Palace like everyone else, but. He's carefully scanning the crowd, his face hateful and his eyes sucking in the light of the flames. I will him not to look my way. I don't want to lock eyes with that kind of energy right now.

'Here's the ambos, Raven,' says Malik, trying to lift me up.

'Leave her,' says Angele tersely. 'They're coming over, Mal. Just leave her.'

Malik lets me go and I slump down, hunched over.

The ambulance people are carrying around a small kit, and an oxygen tank. They ask me some questions which I don't really hear, but which Malik answers, so they put a mask over my face. It smells like clean rubber, which is strangely a comfort. Perhaps I associate the smell with hospital visits as a child, and feel like the adults are taking care of me, making everything better. Cold air swirls against my lips and nostrils, driving out the stench of burning timber from my nose.

I sit like that for ages, my oxygen mask distancing me from the scene, allowing me to view the whole thing like I was looking at a single moment captured inside a snow-dome, but instead of swirling white flakes of confetti the centre piece is an impressive torch of flame. There are jets of fine spray directed at this torch... futile efforts by the fire department to dampen its life, to negate its only purpose. As the oxygen cleans my lungs, so too does the fire cleanse the Prozac Palace. All congestion will be burned away until every passage is renewed again, clean of our physical clutter and our spiritual muck.

Eventually the mask is taken away from me, and I feel like a life-cord has been denied me. I feel vulnerable again.

The sky's brightened. It's a lovely pink in the east, over New Farm, that bleeds up to a soft blue. It looks like it's going to be a good day, a bright sunny one. The kind that Queensland's famous for. Good beach weather. The kind that makes goths want to stay indoors. If we could.

I notice Bernie is sitting next to me. Every now and then he tries to get up and wander away, but Malik orders him to sit down again.

The crowd is still here, but has diminished. Leecham's garage roof is empty, and the junkies on the old verandah have either retired inside or sit in small groups, chatting languidly amongst themselves. I can't see Dante anywhere. A small part of me feels crushed by his absence.

Angele is chatting with one of the bogan boys from next door, and every now and then they point at some part of the charred remains of The Palace. One of them has caught Lunar for me, and brings her over. Her fur's still saturated from sweat, and she's trembling but otherwise she seems okay. I hope she's not in shock. She lets me hug her close; I can feel her tiny heartbeat through her skinny body.

The fire's gone now. Or rather, it nearly is. There are small parts of the building that still burn, and while the fireys linger they no longer hose water on the flames.

'There's no water pressure left,' explains Malik. 'They're letting the rest burn itself out. I checked your car out back, but. It's safe. Not a scratch on it, luckily.'

That's good to know. At least I'll have somewhere to sleep tonight.

The Palais looks pitiful by the light of the day. It's still our Prozac Palace, but it already looks abandoned. The roof is gone, and so is the far wall. It collapsed sometime before dawn, sending up a show of sparks and embers that drifted across the rooftops of the neighbouring homes, all of which had been evacuated already. None caught fire, though. Only the Palais stands charred and half collapsed. I can still see parts of the stairwell standing in the middle, but it looks black and skeletal with bits missing. As for the floors, they're practically gone. Where there was once three storeys is now just one gaping great room inside the frail shell of the whole.

'What happens now?' My voice is hoarse, like Tom Waits after a heavy bender.

'They'll knock it down,' says Malik. 'It's fucked now. And full of asbestos.'

'I only just put up the Christmas tree yesterday,' is all I can say.

All my stuff. My clothes, my music, my fridge, my bed, my photos, my books. My course material. All fucking gone. Just like that. In one night I've lost everything. But not just me. My friends, too. I know Malik's been studying hard; that he had a mountain of paperwork, or *coding* as he called it, in his bedroom. Without it, he won't be able to finish his course next year. He only had another six months to go and then him and Angele had plans to move on from here. London, they'd been hoping for.

'Where's Jeremy?'

Malik shrugs, staring at the fireys as they pack up their trucks.

The sun breaks across the sky, clearing the cliffs on the other side of the Story Bridge, and glancing off the scorched stucco wall on the front of the Palais. It catches the lettering on the front of the building, making them golden in colour. The glorious PALAIS, gutted and destroyed.

It really hits me that I'm now truly homeless.

I don't know where to go, except home to *ana* and *ata's*. Back to the parental nest. Up north in Gympie, no less. Fuck that.

'Hey, hey, don't cry,' says Malik gently, scooting down to reassure me, patting down Lunar's fur on her back where it's stuck up like bed-hair.

'Fuck off!' I snarl.

How dare he tell me not to cry when everything's fucked.

Malik looks stunned, but backs off and walks over to where Angele's laughing at something the bogan guy's said.

I feel hollow.

And then, I fucking swear it, beside me Bernie mutters aloud: 'I feel hollow.'

NOT DINKI-DI LIKE US

'What do you mean the baby wasn't mine?'

I can't believe Karen's telling me this again. Since she revealed it the first time, I've managed to put it down to her just being a spiteful bitch, looking for some way to get back at me for walking in on her at the topless bar. With Amai on my arm, no less.

The phone goes silent, and Mum glances up from her coffee, knitting her brows.

It would have been a year old this week. Our baby. Mine and Karen's. A little Sagittarian.

'Karen?'

'Just that, Twix,' she finally goes. 'It wasn't yours. That's why I got rid of it. I told you this before.'

Fuck a duck. She really *did* cheat on me! I can't believe it. Just as fucking well, then, that I'd been seeing Abi on the side that whole time. But still, the fucking nerve of her.

'Who was he?'

She may as well spit it out now. I was pretty fucking ropeable the first time she told me, but the idea's got traction this time, I guess. It's less of a shock.

'I don't know,' she says, which tells me straight away that's it someone I must know because Karen's not the type to make out with a complete stranger. Then again, I didn't think she was the type to have an affair, either.

'What's goin on?' Mum says, pursuing her mouth like a cat's bum as she bobs her head around trying to catch my eye. I shoo her to be quiet.

'I can't have this conversation on the phone,' I go.

Karen's a terrible liar and it shows on her face straight away, so if we're face-to-face I can start listing names of potential suspects and I'd know exactly who it was as soon as she heard his name. Then I'd have the prick!

'No,' she says quietly. 'I don't want to meet. I just thought you should know.'

'After all this fucking time?' I snarl into the receiver. 'You put me through hell, Karen.'

'It's been hell for me, too, Travis,' she goes, sounding pretty put out. The fucking cheek!

'It wasn't Dante, wasn't it? Oooh, fuck, if it was that prick I'm–'

'It's no-one you know,' she says over the top of me, then starts crying.

Admittedly, hearing her cry always stops me in my tracks no matter how angry I am with her. It's the one thing that fucking breaks me, is hearing her upset.

She continues to bawl for a bit then finally sniffs and blows her nose.

'Do you remember when I went to Melbourne for a week to visit my auntie in hospital?' she says.

I do.

'Well, I went out to a club. Abyss.'

'And let me guess,' I interject derisively, 'it was love at first sight?'

'I was raped,' she spits back.

I'm too stunned to say anything, so Karen continues her narrative.

'I went to the 7-11 afterwards, and he was there. His girlfriend had just dumped him because he wouldn't keep spending money on her. He studied medicine and all his income went to that, he said. So I felt sorry for him, telling him it'd be alright, and we got chatting.'

I feel sick listening to this. I want her to stop, but it'd be cruel to say so.

'He bought me a hot chocolate and gave me a lift back to the hotel in his car, even though it wasn't far, just over in South Yarra.' Her voice is strong and sober as she recounts the events, but otherwise without emotion. She rushes the words together, like she just wants them out before she can't go on anymore. 'He seemed nice, so I took him up on his offer, except by the time we got to my hotel I was feeling really bad. He helped me up to my room and asked if we could catch up again before I headed back to Brisbane. But that's the last thing I remember, because I woke up two days later in a soiled bed with vomit in my hair and no clothes on. I didn't know if anything had happened, or if I was just sick, so I didn't say anything to anybody.'

'I remember you had to buy another ticket because you missed your flight,' I go, my voice choking. I also remember being furious with her, telling her she was stupid if she couldn't even remember what day her plane flight was. My vision's blurring up with tears as I remember. My poor Karen. I yelled at her at the airport, and she just let me. She even apologised to me afterwards.

Fuck.

'Yeah, I was in such a panic I forgot to see Auntie Joan one last time at the hospital.'

Her Auntie Joan died two months later. Cancer. It happened very fast, no warning. The cancer reacted to the medical treatments with a vengeance. I booked Karen a ticket to go down for the funeral, even though we'd broken up because of the abortion. She didn't want to go, and I'd thought she was being petty and ungrateful, refusing to take the ticket because it came from me. Refusing to attend her aunt's funeral just to spite me. I'd called her immature.

'Travis? Are you still there?'

'Yeah, still here,' I say, then go quiet again.

A couple of months ago, beginning of October some time, there were a couple of cases in America, in Texas, of teenage girls getting roofied by gangs of men then left for dead in hotel rooms.

'You're lucky to be alive,' I go into the phone, not sure what else to say.

'I don't feel lucky,' she replies, devoid of all emotion.

'Are you free tomorrow?' I suddenly say.

I need to see her. I need to hug her. I need to beg her forgiveness. Suddenly I'm crying.

'Yes,' she says simply. 'It'd be good to see you again, Travis. I've missed you.'

I arrange to meet her for lunch, and slowly hang the phone up, reluctant to break contact with her. All I can think of is her face, and a mental image of the old days when we were happy, walking arm in arm to the clubs or to the movies. Good times.

'Was that Karen?' Mum goes, being snoopy.

'You know full well it was,' I reply, prudently wiping the water from my eyes.

'I like Karen,' she goes, swishing the dregs of her coffee in the mug. 'Nice girl. Easy on the eyes. Not like your last one, what was her name? Something foreign sounding.'

This is getting old. Even though Amai's name is perfectly easy to remember, Mum's always making out she can't get her tongue around it. She's got the tactical nous of a dead blowfly.

'Amai's alright,' I go, wondering if, like Karen, I've wronged her in some way, too.

'Huh, if you say so,' Mum snorts. 'I just think if boat people can afford a boat trip, then it just goes to show you, donnit? I mean, what about me? You think I can go on a bloody cruise holiday? Not on your life. Too expensive. Shows they're not hard done by at all, donnit?'

'Amai came here by plane, for starters,' I go. 'With her family, when she was a kid. It's not the same thing.'

'Either way, though,' Mum continues, really starting to bug the shit out of me now, 'they bring their fucked-up foods and stuff here, pardon my French.'

'*Mon Dieu*, mother,' I scoff, shaking my head.

'And then there's that,' she says, waving her spent cigarette my way, ash flying all over the table cover and burning tiny holes in it. 'Your poofy vampire quotes.'

'Lestat's not a poof,' I retort, but then when I think about it there were actually lots of homo moments between him and Louis in all the books. 'It's just different for vampires,' I decide, but Mum just snorts with derision.

I can't even bothered arguing with her anymore, but it's stupid because when she does the groceries every Friday up at Caboolture Square, she treats herself to a plate of sweet and sour pork and special fried rice from the Chinese takeaway next to Safeways.

'I'm not trying to be racist, love,' she persists, noting my tired expression, 'but they're not like us, are they? Not dinki-di like us. Take that preggo priest for example.'

The baby got aborted because it wasn't mine. Karen was roofied, was raped. The baby wasn't mine.

'That one from Thailand,' Mum carries on. 'She was a bloody migrant, and look what's happened! Even the church ways aren't safe. Case closed.'

Mum shakes her head and taps another cigarette out of her pack, lighting it up.

'I'm pretty sure the papers said she was from Taiwan,' I correct her. I've been paying more attention to the news lately. Dante would be proud.

'You say *potater*, I say *potatoe*.'

There's nothing I can say, or want to say. I just want to be alone for a while, think about what Karen's told me. Mum hasn't even asked again what the call was all about. She's so fixated on rubbishing Amai-li instead.

'My Doc's are starting to fall apart,' I say, showing Mum the loose flap where my toes stick out on the right boot. 'I'll have to get some new ones off that lad in the Valley store.'

'Well, don't look at me,' Mum goes, 'I haven't got any money for em. If I did I'd be on that bloody cruise, wouldn't I?'

I slump my shoulders with resignation. I've got to get back into meaningful employment again. It's driving me mad living with Mum, and I hate Caboolture, and I hate having no money for new Doc's.

'I gotta go hand in my dole form,' I tell her, heading straight out the door before she can ask me to bring back supplies with money I don't have. The sixty bucks I've got left needs to last me ages.

Only one car yells out 'freak' on my way up to the shops, which is something of a record. It doesn't even bother me. My head's a mess from Karen's news.

When I'm in line at the dole office watching the cricket on the telly I hear a bloke behind me go: 'Trav Haynes, how they hangin, matey?'

It's Ian Jackson, although after his termination from NiteWorks we started referring to him as Wacko Jacko. He'd been sprung having a quick wank in the change rooms at The Big Block when he was meant to be standing watch and counting how many items customers took in. It was one of my old shifts until the incident with Dick Fuckhorn got it cancelled on me. Looks like Wacko Jacko's likewise struggled with the job market since.

'How's it, Ian,' I nod.

'Not bad, matey,' he sniffs. 'Gettin by. You?'

'Bit fucked for a job,' I go. 'Got the boot not long after you. For the best, probably, the pricks.'

'Yeah, reckon,' he goes, shifting from foot to foot and bumping into the bloke behind him.

'You right?' the bloke behind him goes, all annoyed, but Wacko Jacko just ignores him.

Wacko reeks of alcohol, I notice. The fumes waft out onto my face every time he opens his mouth.

'Check this shit out,' he goes, laughing and pointing at the telly up in the corner.

It's cut from the cricket to a news update showing a massive house fire.

'Fucking hell, that looks bad,' I go.

The roof of the building has collapsed, and they show a shot of

Brisbane from a distance with a huge pillar of black smoke billowing up into the sky. It's huge, dwarfing Mount Coot-tha even.

'Wouldn't wanna be those bastards right now,' Wacho Jacko says, alcohol fumes creeping over my shoulder.

The telly shows a couple of shots of the crowd in their pj's as they watch the house burning down, and I recognise Malik and Raven and Angele! Suddenly it cuts to a close up of Malik with black smudges all over his face.

'Like that,' he says on the telly, clicking his fingers. 'It went up so fast we barely had time to get out. Thankfully nearly everyone's accounted for, but.'

HOLY SHIT.

The Prozac Palace burnt down.

Wacko Jacko's still talking but I can't make out what he's saying.

'You can have my spot in line, mate,' I go, racing out the door and stuffing my dole form into my pocket. The pricks'll just have to accept it a day late.

I get up to the train station and grab a ticket, further reducing my dwindling cash reserves on it.

The sun's beating down on the platforms, but there's a bunch of bogan fuckheads hanging around under the shade of the station-house so I settle for cooking down the end of the platform. I'm gonna burn up under this sun.

I can't believe the Prozac's burnt down. Never in a million years did I ever think it could disappear from the Brisbane landscape.

Looming behind me is a billboard, but it's angled the wrong way to cast any shade over me. The poster on it is an advert for Nando's showing three chickens – one white, one brown and one black – and the line WE'RE ALL THE SAME ON THE INSIDE, PAULINE.

Finally the train turns up and it's a fucking relief to get out of the sun. I'm sure the parts of my scalp that are shaved are now burnt red.

The train trip into Central is uneventful, except for the turmoil inside my head. I've got a rotating train of thought, like chickens cooking on a rotisserie, of Karen before and after the abortion, the weird change in her that sickened me when I realised she'd been happy to get rid of what I thought was our baby, and the other of the Prozac Palace engulfed in destructive flames and Malik's charcoaled face mouthing those words: *nearly everyone's accounted for.*

...nearly everyone...

I bolt from Central straight down Turbot, all the way to Bowen Street. There's no more smoke in the sky, but the whole way I feel a dread just thinking about how it'll look now. Sure enough, as soon I hook around the phone box down on the corner I can see straight up to where the Palais used to stand.

It's gone.

It's all gone.

Just a pile of blackened timbers being pulled down by a backhoe.

I'm out of breath, my lungs ready to burst, and have to stagger slowly up the street. There's a small crowd watching the final stages of the Palais' deconstruction, and amongst them is Malik and Angele.

'Twix!' Malik shouts when he sees me, breaking away from the crowd.

He runs over and we embrace. His eyes are sad.

'Fucking all gone, brother,' he says with equal sadness.

'Is everyone accounted for?' I blurt.

'Everyone except Nel.'

I burst into tears.

I'd thought Dante was dead. I don't know why. Maybe it's because of how he was always on about how the world was going to come to an end, but I just had this niggling suspicion in the back of my brain that he'd died in the fire.

'Where's Dante?'

'I don't know,' Malik goes, shaking his head. 'He took off earlier. Just like that alcho uncle of his, always running from his problems. But it's sheer chaos, man. No-one knows anything. Everything's gone. Everyone's just scattered to the winds.'

Fuck. It's just so fucking weird.

'How's Angele?'

Malik glances back where she stands with his lil brother Beau, staring at the backhoe with her arms crossed defiantly. The little Mongolian lady from a few doors up has made a tray of steamed dumplings and is passing them around. She recognises me and waves her arm around with a big smile. I wave back, feeling guilty that she's happy to see me when it's meant to be a time of grief.

'Not sure yet,' Malik admits. 'We're still trying to process all this. It's a lot to take in, but. Can't bum rush the process, ay. We've lost everything, you know? Well, nearly everything.'

He manages a grim little laugh and holds up a half-burnt issue of *Dark Angel* magazine. The one with Sade on the cover.

'My whole collection up in smoke. All my study books. Every-fucking-thing.'

'Fucking oath, I'll say,' I mutter. 'You know if you need anything at all – *anything* – it's yours.'

'Thanks, buddy,' Malik says with a small smile. 'You're a good friend. I guess all we need right now is a place to stay. On top of that, maybe some funds to help replace our essentials. We've got buckley's now.'

Shit. Neither of which I can help with. Coming here means I'm not getting paid this week until I sort out why I didn't hand my jobsearch form in, and there's no way Mum can fit more people into her little home. The return train ticket means I'm now down to fifty bucks.

'Yeah, no worries mate, we'll sort you out,' I go, because the last thing I want to do now is give him more bad news.

We go up to the crowd and I give Angele a hug, while we watch the demolition crew do their thing, trampling all over our history and for some, our home. And while my heart feels bruised by the sight, it's the thought of Karen that really makes it bleed.

DANTE PICKS A SIDE

Dad found out about the Palais burning down and rang around the few numbers for my friends' that he had on his fridge until he'd found me at Maddie's last night. It took him a few days at least to track me down. He'd sounded scared, like maybe he'd thought I was dead or in hospital on life-support. He'd been relentless about me moving back to Stanthorpe with them until I get myself sorted again and it was starting to piss me off so I'd cut the call short.

There's no fucking way I'm going back to that shithole. I'll crash here at Maddie's for a bit then probably hit the streets again. Find myself a good spot to camp out and get away from everybody. The house is full of refugees, mostly from Indonesia, Thailand, places like that. The Government's got fuck all idea where they are. That kind of anonymity suddenly appeals to me.

But Dad's not the only one that's been asking around for me, as it turns out.

'Dante, someone's at the door for you,' Maddie says, poking her head around the doorframe to what serves as my temporary bedroom. It actually looks like it might've been a kitchen back in its heyday, before the cottage was refurbished. It's a tiny space, with a sloping ceiling and a hole where a flue might go. There's a mangled dream-catcher stuffed into it; the feathers have all but disintegrated. Maddie pokes her head back in, grinning like a shot fox. 'And *Fish n Chip Bitch From Ipswich* is number one on 4ZZZ's Hottest 100,' she goes.

It's Twix at the door.

I'm taken aback, unsure how to react to his presence. I did, after all, try and kill the cunt but a few months ago. Or threaten to, at least.

'Thank Christ you're alright,' he says with genuine emotion.

Maddie's hanging around in the background on some bullshit pretext so she can eavesdrop.

'Yeah, I'm lucky to get out.'

It's funny, cause I feel absolutely no hatred for him all of a sudden. Maybe something simmering below the surface, but it's like seeing him again, seeing his concern, has made all my hate just magically melt away.

'I wasn't sure if you went back to your folks or not,' he says. 'I just wanted to check on you. See if you needed anything. I guess you probably lost everything, huh?'

There wasn't much to lose, to be honest. One of the benefits of being piss-poor.

'Yeah, heaps of stuff. Gonna cost a fair bit to replace.'

'Here,' he goes, rummaging into his wallet and pulling out a fifty. 'For starters. Sorry it's not more. I'm kinda unemployed now.'

I take his money without thanks. It's the least the cunt can do.

'Do you want a cuppa, Travis?' calls Maddie.

'Yeah, love one,' he says brightly, then glances at me. 'If it's okay with you?'

I shrug and move to let him through, but as he passes he hesitates, then suddenly lunges at me and grabs me in a bear hug. He's more distraught by the Palais burning down than I am, I reckon.

'Yeah, righto,' I go, gently pushing him off.

'Sorry, it's been rough not knowing where everyone is.'

I guess he's talking about Nel. Raven, who's a fucking emotional wreck and shacked up with her Uni mates, told me Nel's still not been accounted for, even though the authorities say they've found no bodies in the wreckage of the Palais.

I wonder what it says about me that I'm barely concerned about Nelly the Beast being missing? I mean, it's certain she's not dead, at least not in the house fire. Forensics sorting through the wreckage confirmed that. But I feel no connection with her absence at all, like she's now just a distant memory, whereas Twix here is behaving like he's just been dumped by the silly bitch and he's worried as hell about her.

'So I heard you're not an insecurity guard anymore,' I go.

'Nah, threw in the towel,' he shrugs, but he's grinding his jaw. He always hated me calling it that. 'On Social Security benefits in the meantime. Figured I'm owed that much at the end of the day, right?'

For as long as I've known him, Twix has always felt like the world owes him, like he's been hard done by. He's whined on about it enough times. He's always gone on about dole bludgers sucking his tax returns dry, whatever the fuck that means. It must be a savage blow to his ego to be on the other side of that argument for a change.

Maddie gets a brew going and we all sit around the kitchen table with our mugs of tea, Twix trying to hide his revulsion at just how messy the place is. He's not used to punks much, or whatever the fuck Maddie doesn't want to be 'labelled' as these days.

Maddie pushes across a tin of gingerbread men.

'Help yourselves,' she goes.

I had one last night and found they've gone stale, which is not surprising since she's had em since at least a week before Christmas.

Twix plucks one out and examines the crude icing face. 'This one looks like Dante,' he goes. 'Run, run, run, as fast as you can...'

'Looks nothing like him,' says Maddie, deadpan, God love her.

'Private joke,' I say.

If the cunt thinks I've forgiven and forgotten enough for him to start getting smart at my expense, he's got another think coming. He starts going on about the Palais fire and how he'd seen it on the news, and true to form can't help but take it too far by boasting he might know a gun-for-hire in forensics who'd investigate it, which doesn't make any sense for a start.

'Seriously?' says Maddie, unimpressed.

'Yeah, for sure,' he crows pompously, unable to read her revulsion. 'I've still got a few friendly contacts in the biz. Networking's key when you're in security. Always gotta know who's got what fingers in what pie.'

This is typical Twix bullshit. He wouldn't know any of Brisbane's crime syndicate if he passed them on the street. He was a static guard for shopping malls. And yet it's oddly comforting having him around again, going on and on with his brand of bullshit. I lend him only half an ear and let the rest become a long, monosyllabic drone.

In response to my silence Twix decides that he's overstayed his welcome, and makes to go. I walk him out onto the front balcony.

'Sorry for trying to kill you that time,' I say gently, enjoying this moment of bonding, not really wanting him to go but unable to find the drive to ask him to stay.

'Nah, it's all good,' he smiles. He looks kind of sad. I notice both his fangs have now snapped off. 'I know you were only trying to scare me, for what I did at the radio station. That's why I didn't want to press charges, even though one of the officers wanted me to.'

We shake our heads. 'Copper cunts,' I murmur.

'So what's the plan now the Prozac's all over, red rover?' he goes.

I honestly don't know myself, beyond simply laying low and mixing it with Micko and the guys at King George Square for a while.

'I might head up north,' I lie. 'Travel a bit.'

He looks surprised. 'That's very random.'

I shrug.

'You look like you need it, though,' he says. 'You look like shit.'

'I haven't been sleeping that well.'

That's an understatement. I've been sleeping fucking terribly, and the pre-New Years fireworks last night were definitely of no help (loves itself some fireworks, Brisbane does – any excuse'll do). I keep thinking I can smell smoke during the nights, besides just last night of course, and come to in a complete panic. I can't get back to sleep after that, either. I have to go around the house and check out the windows for evidence of a fire in the neighbourhood. I wish I could say it's a relief that there's never one, but I can't.

Tragically, the refugees watch me do the rounds, sympathetic to my distress, given they've fled situations much worse. I wonder, if like me, they're prepared to fuck everything up for a return to that chaos?

I live in such a black and white world. The Inferno's world. It's either plain and calm, or its chaos and turmoil. More often than not it seems I'll favour seeking out the chaos and turmoil, upending my inter-personal relationships to cause desolation and strife, reducing my financial and living arrangements to mere rubble, testing my endurance. It's like I'm always trying to break myself in half. And as much as it makes me content, it doesn't make me happy. Not a whit. I yearn for a simple life, the kind that Bernie leads, the uncomplicated routine of the everyday. To paraphrase Twix quoting a chocolate bar commercial, I've tried both and now I need to pick a side.

But how do I do that when my brain wants to trip me at every turn?

'Anyways, a Happy New Year to ya and hooroo, Dante,' says Twix, hugging me goodbye. 'Let me know what you plan on doing next. I'm staying at Mum's nowadays since I lost my job. And me and Karen are talking again. Might get back together. Lots has changed. We should all catch up again, like old times.'

He squeezes my shoulder, looking at me with what I assume is pity, but I realise as he trundles down the steps it's actually genuine concern.

He pauses at the letterbox then turns and out of the blue asks: 'Oi, you don't have herpes, do you?'

'I don't, but thanks for asking.'

'Huh,' he snorts, more to himself. 'I knew it. Amai all along.'

On that rather mysterious note he waves goodbye. Only when he's gone it occurs to me that he didn't leave his Mum's phone-number. My note book with everyone's addresses and phone numbers went up in flames with the rest of my stuff.

I'd never admit it aloud, but I guess I love Twix. Like a brother, maybe. It says a lot that he's hunted me down to check on my well-being after what I've done to him, yet my own girlfriend hasn't bothered to come around and see me in person yet because she says she can't afford the bus fare. So, yeah, there's that.

'That went well,' says Maddie when I go back inside, but I'm not in the mood to reflect on how I feel about reuniting with Twix. What's done is done, leave it at that.

'I'm gonna head out and get this voucher done,' I go, referring to a slip of paper for the Salvo's a cop gave me back at the ruins of the Palais.

I'd gone back later in the day and he was there off-duty, and said he'd felt so sorry for us all that he'd swung around some of the community aid agencies and got us all vouchers to get some free clothes and stuff. I was really blown away by his gesture, and moreso that it'd come from a copper. I have to admit I'm more than guilty of judging one by the merits of the majority. That's always been my perspective of them, anyway.

'Apparently, it's redeemable at the sorting warehouse. Might even drop by the Palais, see if Nel's turned up.'

Maddie nods as I head out the door into the sunshine. I couldn't give a flying fuck about Nel, in truth. Just another dead junkie, probably. Needs to happen to a lot more of the cunts, in my opinion. Couldn't give a flying fuck about the Palais, either, at this stage. All I know is that I can't be indoors anymore, so the op-shop warehouse it is.

I cut across the guts of New Farm, noting how decidedly upmarket the area's starting to look. It's still shabby as fuck, thankfully, but there's pockets of yuppiedom encroaching on it in all directions. McKay does volunteer work here at the Binkinba Drop-In Centre for the mentally fucked and recovering addicts and he's said a lot of the clients are feeling the pressure as the Merthyr Village Community Association – a local committee made up of cunt landlords and small business owners hell-bent on urban development – is trying to reform the area and have started by jacking up rental prices to force the economically disadvantaged out of the area. One of their first steps was to raise funds to have blue anti-junkie lights installed in the public dunnies. So far all their efforts have failed: the boarding houses are thriving as usual, as evidenced here along Merthyr Road, and the old tramways powerhouse where the homeless bunker down.

The rich cunts in business tell the corrupt fuckers in politics that the rest of us too greedy and that we should be reigned in with higher fucking taxes and lower living conditions. Welcome to the Australian nightmare.

I shoot down the Hastings Street stairs onto Macquarie Street, Teneriffe, where the mostly abandoned wool-stores line the riverfront like mighty sentinels. Massive fires gutted a couple of them just before I first moved up to Brisbane, but there's now an ambitious redevelopment project happening by the council. I can't see it being too successful, to be honest. Who wants to live here of all places? Apart from the Sunday trash and treasure markets there's not a lot else to draw people down here: a secondhand furniture store, Paddy's Markets in the corner building where loads of goths go for cheap fabrics to make capes and shit, and of course the ever-present el-cheapo store, the hallmark of any suburb in the vice-like grip of crime and high unemployment. Lots of fucking sunlight, too, that's for sure. I'm fairly fucking cooking by the time I reach the sorting warehouse. Cunts could do with a few fucking trees down here.

In the distance I can see the old gasworks ring where I saw Pixie and the lesbians doing their dodgy drug deal at that burnt out car the night of the Love at First Bite Ball. Fuck, that feels like a lifetime ago.

The woolstores are no less ominous during the day than they are at night. Maybe I could find a hidey-hole in one and call it home for a while?

The op-shop's sorting house is on the bottom floor of the Elders Woolstore building, and the ladies inside obviously aren't used to the public wandering in off the street because they take my presence the same way as I would stepping into a runny pile of dog shit.

Regardless, I carry on with my endeavour cause I honestly couldn't give a fuck what a couple of old grannies think at this stage. I show them the voucher the cop gave me, and get a grilling over it.

'Who gave you this?' chirrups one of the old cunts. 'Can we even accept this?' goes the other.

I'm about to tell them to stick it up their arse and leave when they finally relent, telling me I can get a few bits and bobs, even though the voucher expressly states I can collect up to fifty bucks' worth. But with these two old battleaxes going on like I'm a fucking thief, trying to rort them, I couldn't even be bothered going through the piles and piles of clothes they've got on the tables.

'You know what, ladies, fuck it.'

They nod knowingly at each other as I leave, loudly confirming their suspicion that I was indeed just a druggie cunt trying to exploit a loophole in their system. Typical of these cunts, to be honest. I've heard they're hard-line when it comes to helping out gay people, even if the poor cunts are as homeless as the best of us.

I'm not in the mood to head back to Maddie's, where the rest of the household have probably started to rise. Maddie's taken in a lot more than just me, with whole families of refugees filling her spare rooms to capacity. Roshan and her have been in touch with each other a lot ever since I introduced em, and Roshi's since put Maddie in touch with some families in need of sanctuary after the sweat shop in West End they were working in got shut down by the cops. They've been here ever since while Maddie, Roshi and their network tries to raise enough money to set the refugees up with bond and a months' rent. I believe Dreadlock Jane and her mate Tess have taken some families on, too.

Without people like Maddie and Roshi in my life, I'd be as fucked as those refugees were. Whether I like it or not, I really do rely on my friends more than I could ever realise. These stuck up ladies could learn a few things from my mates.

Without intending to, I've followed the old tram tracks, eventually finding myself making the long trek all the way up to the Valley train station. Being amongst strangers who've no idea who I am or what I've been through feels good. They're treating me no differently than strangers have always treated me. I'm scorned, ignored, gawked at. They shield their small children from me.

I'm just another gutter goth, a jobless leech who could afford to wash more often and eat better, who should call his parents more and treat his friends better and be nicer to his girlfriend. I'm just another fuck up on the train, another fucked up kid with fuck all destination in life.

Maybe I'll go to Buranda, check to see if Alex really has moved back to Melbourne. Again, I'd call first but alas, no note book full of phone numbers. I haven't seen her since the day her dad had a fucking heart attack on us outside the courts, where her sister got sentenced to two months inside the BWCC at Wacol for tax fraud. Alex blames herself for that mess, but she shouldn't beat herself up so much. Shit happens.

Then the fucking ticket inspectors get on at Roma Street.

Cunts.

'Ticket?' one says to me.

I ignore the cunt, but the other one goes: 'I recognise you.'

'Like fuck you do,' I snap.

'Nah, I do,' the weasely prick says, not to me, but to his mate. I can imagine the cunt sucking him off in the fucking dunnies back at the Valley station. 'I remember him from earlier in the year. Didn't have a ticket then, neither.'

'Fuck off,' I scoff.

Thing is, I think the cunt's right. I'm not saying he's familiar to me as well, because there's fuck all that's remarkable about him, but it's true that I was on a train without a ticket and had feigned sleep to make the ticketie give up and walk away. I guess the cunt's held a grudge ever since, because he's not ready to let it go this time.

'Yeah, repeat offender this one.'

This gets the response he's after from his big mate, who glowers at me with hostility as if I've personally slighted the cunt. 'Call it in, Mike,' he goes, and the weasely prick grins widely as he reaches for his walkie-talkie.

These arseholes can't touch me, can't do jack shit to me, but they can call the cops and arrange for them to meet the train at a station further up the line.

'Come on, guys, give me a break? I've got no money. My house burnt down last week.'

'Must've been karma,' the weasel says.

My head's feeling hot, like I'm over-tired. I can feel my eyelids pulling back, giving me that hateful stare that normally registers alarm in others. It seems to excite these two who think there's gonna be a fucking show put on when the cops get on board.

Fuck these cunts. The train's pulling up at South Bank station, which isn't enough time for any pigs to arrive for a meet and greet, so they'll probably try and intercept the train at Park Road.

'Your fly's undone, you fucking paedophile,' I say to the weasel, pulling the doors open when the train's stopped.

'Yeah, fuck off, you scum,' says the big bastard.

The little cunt wants to check his fly, but he's reluctant to do it while I'm eyeballing him. I jump onto the platform, spinning to face them. The weasel's eyes twitch and his hands surreptitiously hover in front of his crotch to hide any potential embarrassment. People have got such a fucking hang-up about correcting themselves in public. I like ostentatiously picking my nose in public as a subtle civic reminder to others of this hideous quality they harbour.

'When you blow that little cunt there, do you spit or swallow?' I ask the big one.

It's obvious he's thinking about getting off the train and having a proper go at me, but at the rate we're stirring each other up it couldn't end well. Especially for him, since he has to maintain a front of professional conduct befitting his role. Me, I'm just fucking scum. I'm expected to do whatever the fuck I want, however antisocial it is.

The doors close and I flip the finger at them. As the train departs the big cunt grins evilly and points his finger at me as if to say we'll cross paths again one day and then I'll be sorry.

Fuck it.

I can't do plain and calm. It'll always be chaos and turmoil for me. It just seems to happen naturally. The more I think about it the more my lie to Twix about heading north sounds like a good idea. Just disappear for a while. Go way, way north. Like maybe Darwin or something, someplace where goths can't be found, where the cunts can't complicate things, where I can start anew and be the kind of person who is calm all the time.

There's a snap inside my head, like an electrical jolt with a sound and everything. I actually feel it ricochet around inside my skull. Fuck, that's scary. I've never had that before. But instantly I feel a lot less stressed out. Not totally fucking blissed out like a meditating hippie, mind, but a lot less frenetic than when I got off the train.

I know that my neuroreceptors that fly all the serotonin around can't actually be felt, but it's what I picture when I think of that jolt. I imagine one of them has just misfired or has overloaded on built up serotonin and has let a motherload through. I'm sure I've got how neuroreceptors work and their distribution of serotonin all wrong, but who gives a fuck?

Actually, it felt more like a snapping sensation than a jolt. Like a taut cable stretched too far and simply snapping in two. A gunshot crack as it tears apart. Two halves loosed from one another. Like both hemispheres of the brain are no longer moored in the same berth, but suddenly now floating away from each other, destroying the self and inviting chaos.

Always chaos. Always The Inferno.

That never goes away. Wherever I go, whoever I try to be, there's always the chaos. As long as I'm breathing, the chaos is with me. It's built into me. Hardwired to my chemistry. Only some William Gibson pneumonic type shit could probably unlock that part of me. That's the fucking future. This is 1996 for fuck's sake. I've got fuck all hope of disengaging The Inferno stuck here in this timeframe.

'Fucking hell, I gotta get my shit sorted, gotta get away from it all,' I hear myself saying aloud.

At first I thought it might've been someone else, glancing around to see this guy sitting on the bench. He's watching me without trying to be obvious about it.

'Oh, you fucking like that, cunt?'

I'm louder now.

'Well fuck you, mate. FUCK EVERY JUDGEMENTAL CUNT WHO THINKS THEY KNOW BETTER.'

If I died right now, who would care? Would Amara? Like fuck she would. If I did die, there'd only be a fucking queue of self-righteous pricks ready to deliver their judgements. All sorts of tripe would spew from them about how life is fucking precious or some such shit.

Fuck your preciousness and your train tickets and your stupid pointing fingers.

POINT AT ME, THE CUNT! WHO THE FUCK DOES HE THINK HE IS?

Pick a side? You pick a fucking side, Twix, you dumb prick.

Fuck, my head feels ready to burst...

PIXIE AS WITNESS

I haven't seen Imp in ages, but he's agreed to catch up at South Bank station, and he's bringin James as well. It feels really weird gettin back in contact with em, especially since I wasn't nice to em much before we lost contact. I thought I was above em and didn't need em anymore.

It feels good, too, but. The old gang, together again.

They'll see the changes in us, of course. I haven't got me health back a hundred per cent yet, but a day in the sun hangin round the South Bank swimming lagoon, lookin at the birds and lizards in the Gondwanaland Centre, will be just what I need. Maybe even go into the butterfly house! Haven't been there in yonks! We'll ride the mini canal boats from one end of the parklands to the other. It'll be ace!

Mum's been amazing. She's forgiven us completely, says she just wants her daughter back. If I'm going to do this for anyone, clean myself up completely and get me education straightened out, it'll be for her. She keeps tellin us I gotta do it for myself, but, and for no-one else. She tells us I'm the most important person in the world for me. I've never heard her talk like this before. I guess addiction changes the people around us, as well.

It reminds us of somethin someone said once, Brett who used to deal for us, the cunt that used to be a copper. He yelled at me and Roz and Nel and that liddle cunt Jeremy at a football match, and said we were horrible people. We'd laughed about it later on, makin fun of him, but the thing is I realise now he was right. We were complete cunts to literally everyone around us, even to each other. We didn't care about ourselves, about how we affected our families or friends.

That's how come I've gotta make it up to the boys, show em I'm still the same Pixie I used to be only better. A proper friend again.

Imp and James' train is still on its way, and there's barely anyone at the station yet. It'll get fuckin packed later on, but, when everyone comes in for the New Year's fireworks.

Dante Halloran's on the other platform, across the tracks, but he hasn't seen us yet.

I was thinking about yellin out to him, but I'll just sit here and watch him instead, coz it's so fuckin amusin. He's pacin up and down talkin to himself. But not just talkin, like I've seen him do in the city; he's literally arguin with himself this time. Throwin his hands up in frustration and stuff like that. It's a fuckin cack, somethin shockin!

There's another guy on his platform, sittin on a park bench behind Dante, and he's watchin Dante closely. Probly shittin it that the crazy gothic boy's gonna snap and try and kill him. Hilarious!

Unfortunately, a train's comin in from Vulture Street so the show's gonna be over soon. I think about yellin across to Dante and chuckin him the finger or something, stir him up some more, but he's pretty agitated as it is, so I'll just tease him about it next time I see him. The announcement reckons his train's comin anyway, so he'll probly stop rantin when it gets here.

The train from Vulture Street pulls up in front of us, but Imp and James don't get off it. This must've been the Cleveland one, so they'll be on the next one, the Beenleigh line one. The doors of the train hiss shut, but it sits here waitin for the Platform 1 train to come in from Roma Street direction.

It rumbles in, slowin right down, blockin the view of the other platform, hidin Dante from view.

Suddenly the air splits in half with a terrible screechin sound that makes everyone on the train cover their ears. Bein outside, I'm coppin most of the noise. There's sparks and shit literally flyin up against all the windows and this fat liddle lady starts to scream and run away from them, whackin her leg on the edge of the seats and fallin over near the open doors.

What the fuck's goin on?

The other train finally stops and the sparks disappear. So does, thank fuck, that deafenin screeching noise.

Then this man forces the doors open on the carriage, and comes out lookin really scared.

'Did you see it? Did you see it?' He's goin.

'The sparks? Fuck yeah,' I go, but I can already tell by his face that's not what he means.

He vomits onto the ground. Now there's the smell of that as well as the burnin brakes of the train. Fuckin great.

Somethin's wrong here, but. I run inside the train and there's a group of other passengers, mostly old women wearin pastel-coloured cardigans, starin out through the windows. But there's nuthin to see except the other train carriage, where there's also people lookin scared and starin back at us. This is turnin into an episode of *Amazin Stories*, I swear.

One of the women in the cardigans who's holdin her hand over her heart keeps sayin it's horrible over and over again, and the rest are all bobbin their fuckin heads around like pigeons to get a good look at what's happened.

'Oi, dude,' I say to the guy outside, wipin the vomit on his pants. 'What the fuck happened?'

'He jumped,' he goes, starin wide-eyed at us, and then back at the other women when they gasp and start formin O's with their mouths. He's about to be sick again.

'Oh my! No!' the women gasp.

Some more people come in from the other carriage and everyone starts conferrin like it's a fuckin meetin.

'What the fuck do ya mean he jumped?' I shout. Me voice is shaky.

This lady who came in from the other carriage turns to us and looks pale as shit. 'There was a guy over there, and he jumped.'

'Someone said he was acting weird,' goes this other woman with her.

What the fuck? Like seriously. What the fuck?

I go over to the window to see for myself, shovin one of the pastel fucks aside.

'Excuse *me!*' she goes, but shouldn't have bothered coz I couldn't give a shit.

I can't see anythin, just the train next to us. The people on it are now bein evacuated, herded away from the train and down one end of the platform, near where I'd last seen Dante.

Where I'd last seen Dante.

I can't see him anywhere through the windows of the next train.

Fuck.

Too much death. Too much death. Charlie. Roz. Dante. What did he call it? Behavioural Contagion. Of course!

I suddenly start to feel crook in me guts.

The announcer comes over the train speakers. 'Sorry, folks, for the delay. Can you please exit the train in an orderly manner and wait on the platform. There's been an incident, and we'd appreciate it if you could follow any directions given to you by train staff.'

I just wanna go home right now. I can feel the urge for smack. It's desperate, wormin in me brain, tellin us I can't cope with this level of shit. It says heroin will wipe it all away, make us not care.

But I *do* care. I think that's meant to be the fuckin point, isn't it?

How come I shouldn't care about the death of someone I know?

'It was a suicide,' someone's sayin to the faces pressed to the glass, scannin the tracks for details.

'Well, he's going to Hell for sure, then,' a lady says, no compassion in her voice at all.

I feel sick. I wanna go over and kick the bitch.

'Off the train, please,' one of the train workers is sayin as he walks down the length of the platform, openin the doors that are still shut. 'Please, wait out here on the platforms, if you will. Thankyou very much.'

He's fieldin a dozen questions from people as they pile out on the platform. The other train workers are runnin round the ends of the train and jumpin onto the tracks.

I should go and call Mum, reverse the charges, ask her if she can pay for a taxi if I just take one home right now.

KNOWING WHEN TO JUMP

A train travelling at just under fifty kilometres an hour will usually knock a person sideways onto the tracks or into the platform. If they're fortunate, the person will only sustain non-life-threatening injuries as a result of both the impact and the fall. Unless they're lying across the tracks: then they're mince-meat.

When a train travels at greater speeds than fifty kilometres an hour – wherein it needs approximately a hundred and thirty metres to stop safely – a person is likely to explode like a bug against a windscreen. The person will be rendered unrecognisable, and in so many chunks that police officers and first responders are not often even able to determine the sex of the deceased. They pick up the pieces and dump it in plastic bags or pillow cases until the identifying organ is located.

Pretty much in every train driver's career there's a fatality driven like a railway spike through their records. It's the rare driver who gets through forty odd years without anyone acting upon suicide ideation under their train.

The pay's not too shabby, but, especially on weekends, and the maternity/paternity leave is more than admirable. Once you're in the job, you're set. There's no dealing with shitty customers or snooty managers peering over your shoulder as you work. But the shift work is soul-destroying. Three AM starts to warm the engines, pissing in an empty Coke bottle while thundering along between stations with a heavy lunchbox planted on the deadman's pedal. Fifteen months of training, seven of which is vigorous study. Then some cunt throws themselves in front of you.

It happens. Cars stall, tiny faces peering up as you slam into them and crush the lives from their little bodies. You turn away, block your ears, duck your head down under the control panel... anything to avoid having their final moments seared into your brain for constant recall. A mother's attention is averted and the baby's pram rolls down the platform and off the edge. You can't stop. You can drop the brake but even at twenty kilometres an hour there's no way to avoid rolling over that pram. The handbrake or the big red button to cut power will cause mayhem to a moving train, endangering entire carriages full of passengers. It's a no-win situation.

Great pay, though.

Therapy, a course of antidepressants, reuptake inhibitors to keep you functioning, shutting out the world as you retreat to your fortress, the home that no longer accepts visits from friends, the one where your marriage quickly dissolved and the heavy drinking flourished.

Of all the suicides by people undergoing psychiatric care, data shows that less than fifteen percent is done by throwing themselves under a train, but the impact on a driver is a hundred per cent. Some even confess that they have seen the spirits of the people they have killed riding with them or standing trackside when they pass by the impact zones.

Even though there have been roughly only five collisions between a car and a train at railway level crossings in Queensland during 1996 alone – instantly killing everyone in the vehicles and causing millions of dollars in repair and infrastructure to the crossings – the deaths are recorded by the Bureau of Statistics as a road accident. Similarly, when someone commits suicide under a train, it isn't considered as suicide because both the ABS and the National Coronial Information Service identify it simply as 'other specified' in their reports. Rail safety regulators and the Bureau of Transport Safety push for recognition of *suicide* by rail, but even the driver's aren't convinced that the problem is entirely appreciated by anyone above their own station.

There's the story of one driver who drove over the legs of a cunt sitting across the tracks, and the driver managed to get to the victim and save him, although he credits the train's wheels sealing shut the fool's denim jeans over his amputated legs to prevent him from bleeding to death. In some ways, it's like the train and their operator work in unison when tragedy strikes.

KICK AGAINST THE PRICKS

The Inferno's in full fucking swing by now.

The train on platform two has already boarded but it's still sitting there with the doors open. It won't go until our train arrives from Roma Street, even though there's clearly enough fucking track ahead for both trains to pass by comfortably.

Pick a fucking side, already!

There must be a reason why both trains can't share the tracks but I'll be fucked if I can see it. Ergo, why I'm not a train driver, I suppose. There's rules and procedures that need to be adhered to, and there's people who understand that and then there's those of us who fucking well can't. Quite simply I'm not cut from the kind of cloth that allows for that kind of understanding. I'd be the train that says *fuck it, there's two sets of tracks there, so I see no reason why I can't go now.*

But I'd take off and fuck everything up. It'd be a train wreck.

Amara is someone who follows the rules. She wouldn't question why both trains can't go when there's two sets of tracks. We're so different in our thinking, she and I. It'll be our undoing, eventually.

I miss her so fucking much it hurts. I already feel like we've separated. I've got that heartache that only the unexpectedly dumped get, that raw wound deep in the chest that fucking kills.

Well, fuck her and fuck every other cunt. I'm not going to be goaded into following the path, cajoled into a direction in life that feels fucking unnatural to me. In the Bible there was this poor bastard who tried doing the same, but there's Jesus moaning to fuck about how the cunt won't play by the rules. *It is hard for thee to kick against the pricks*, Jesus said to the guy. He was talking about the stick with the metal point that farmers used to steer their cows around the field with, meaning the cows should just do as they're fucking well told to because it's easier for them. I like to imagine this cunt stood up to Jesus and told him to go fuck himself.

Point at me through the fucking window, will he? Why didn't that ticketie cunt grow a pair and face off with me out on the platform?

'Are you alright, mate?'

It's the guy sitting on the bench behind me. He approaches me.

'Of course.'

There, I've given you your answer, cunt, now fuck off.

'You seem a bit agitated. You're swearing and yelling an awful lot.'

Who is this cunt? My psychiatrist now?

'I'm fine.'

'Sometimes you just need someone to talk to.'

'I said I'm fine, cunt.'

He just laughs lightly, like we're mates sharing a private joke.

'Okay, just take it easy,' he says.

That's akin to telling me to be calm when provoked, probably the cardinal sin with me. I'm ready to fly off the fucking handle.

KILL THE CUNT, The Inferno roars inside my skull.

'I just thought I'd check on ya, that's all,' he continues, oblivious to me death-glaring him. 'Sometimes all we need is someone to hear what's going on in our lives. We've all got something. Take me, for instance: I found out a few months ago that my wife was having an affair with her boss. It was fucking hell to find out, but after I laid down the law I thought everything was okay again.'

This cunt doesn't take a fucking hint too well, that's for sure. I've accidently gotten into plenty of conversations with fuckers like this, cunts who're unable to absorb their own issues so they hang around in public looking to offload their shit onto somebody else. They're as bad as the repressed boofheads who hassle me about the way I dress, except this cunt wants me to enjoin him in his misery and confusion.

'Then last week I found out Jenny's been seeing him still.' He shrugs, scratching at his scalp. 'What am I supposed to do with that?'

'Kill the cunt. What else?'

He looks a bit shocked by my response.

'But he's a solicitor.'

I sneer nastily. 'What's he gonna do, sue you from the grave?'

A loud toot from down the line signals the arrival of our train. I can hear the hiss of the doors closing on the other train across the tracks, on Platform 2. The guy motions for me to come towards him.

'How about stepping away from the tracks, eh? You're making me nervous.'

What's this fucker's game? Does he think I'm about to commit suicide or something?

'Don't tell me what to do,' I snarl. 'I'm not your fucking wife.'

'No worries,' he replies. He's got a syrupy voice that I fucking detest. Like a fucking wannabe therapist.

Our train starts to get close, barrelling in toward us. The tracks below shake, rattling the stones. I'm wary of this cunt who's now come up next to me. He might try and grab me in a bear hug or something, some vain and noble effort to thwart a would-be suicide attempt. This cunt's got more front than fucking Myers assuming the worst from me.

The train starts to slow as it reaches the platform.

'If you fucking touch me,' I warn, bugging my eyes and baring my teeth.

Suddenly the cunt breaks into a run, sprinting away from me and up the fucking platform. This isn't what I was expecting, and quickly try and analyse the manoeuvre for some sort of reverse-psychology effect until I realise he's trying to outrun the train pulling up. He's doing a good job of it, gaining distance as it decelerates.

Then he swings to the side and throws himself off the platform.

Straight under the train.

I bolt up the platform as the train hits the brakes. There's sparks flying up from under it, spewing from the gap between the carriages and the platform, raining down on me. By the time I reach the cab the entire train has ground to a halt. There's a splash of blood up the front, but other than that the tracks look fairly clean. On the other side of the train, between it and the train waiting at Platform 2, I can see the cunt's legs wedged between. It's obvious that the top half of him is missing. He's been ripped in half.

The driver's door swings open and this poor bastard who looks like he's seen a ghost hobbles out on a gummy leg and stares at me.

It's Twix's dad.

I've got nothing I can say to him, no words that can pull him back from the brink of this. Except perhaps to point out the fucking obvious, and that's that the fight is fixed.

He's no choice but to face this on his own.

'Happy New Year,' I go, then race down the stairs of the station and onto Grey Street, belting along the footpath up past the museum, trying to put as much distance as possible between me and death.

Fuck the pricks.

They can run, run, run, but they'll never catch me cause I'm the Gingerbread Man.

ABOUT THE AUTHOR

Brian Craddock was born in Melbourne and now resides in Brisbane.

In the 1990s, under the pseudonym Dakanavar, he self-published several underground comics centred on Brisbane's goth subculture, notably *Crimson: Riot Goth*, and co-directed three video reviews of the scene titled *Everyday Devils & Angels*.

He has worked as a puppeteer throughout Australia's Outback and in Pakistan; his webseries *The Hobble & Snitch Show* can be viewed online. In addition to special effects makeup work for independent film, he was a makeup artist for *The Lion King* stage musical in 2015.

Brian Craddock is previously published in *Midian Unmade: Tales of Clive Barker's Nightbreed* (Tor Books) and *The Refuge Collection* (Oz Horror Con), *Between the Tracks* (Things in the Well), *The Body Horror Book* (Oscillate Wildly Press), Below the Stairs (Things in the Well), Behind the Mask (Things in the Well), Beneath the Waves (Things in the Well), and *Petrified Punks* (Oscillate Wildly Press).